The following is inspired by true events. However, some characters, places and events have been fictionalized for dramatic purposes and to protect the victims and the innocent.

To my Boys,
You're my light and the keys to my heart.
You're the reason I am so determined to be a better person.
To my Best Friends,
Thank you for your never-ending encouragement,
being my sounding boards when needed, and
always giving it to me straight.
To those who lived this story with me,
There are too many of you to name by name, but know this,
I THANK YOU ALL.

DEADLY PEACE

*Sometimes finding peace
can be deadlier than you expect*

K. ROCHELLE

Delta Four Publishing

INTRODUCTION

There's an old saying: Dead men tell no tales. Well in my line of work, dead men, women, and children have a lot to say. That is, if you know where to look. And lately there were lots of stories being told, and I needed a mental break. So when the suggestion was made that I extend my 2 days off a little while longer to attend Homecoming back at A&M, I decided that maybe the open road would do me some good. I never dreamed that my peaceful road trip, would turn into a "true confessions" convention, and I would be the keynote speaker.

I had just put the twins on a flight to see their dad for 2 weeks, so I decided to take a couple of days off and drive down to Atlanta to relax. Maybe the fresh air and change of scenery would clear my head. Besides, I'm dying to drop the top on my new toy. I just bought my first brand new car in 20 years.

I don't mean to brag, but it is gorgeous. It's all shiny, and it has that new car smell. The real new car smell, not the new car smell that comes from a bottle. I waited to pick it up until after I dropped the boys off at the airport. I really would have hated to have to kill a child before their vacation began because one of them dripped, dropped, or spilled something, or God forbid put their big feet up on my soft, beautiful, clean leather on accident. Let's just say it wouldn't have been pretty and probably would have ruined all of our time off.

I gave the dealer such a fit about what he felt were little picky things. I know he is glad to see me drive away finally. My baby is an E550 Convertible Mercedes-Benz, special order of course. The dealership didn't have a Silver Mercedes Convertible to my specifications on the lot, so they had to order one. Then the one they ordered came in with a black top and black seats. I didn't mean to be picky, but for what I'm paying, I deserve to get exactly what I asked for. 3 weeks later my baby arrived. Mercedes Silver, gray upholstery throughout, wood grain, chromed out 22-inch wheels, and last but not least, a grey soft top.

It has taken me nearly an hour to compose myself and drive off this lot.

After all of that would it surprise you to know that I've just been pulled over for speeding? And for the first time in years, I might add, and I'm not even 5 miles from the dealership, Damn! And you thought I'd be driving like a little old lady, huh? That's not my style, but you'll catch on.

"I can't believe this!" All I could do is lay my head back on the headrest and wait for the inevitable. Well, my secret is definitely out now. No one knew about this car. I even swore the dealership to secrecy. I watched the officer approaching in my side-view mirror thinking, *'Now the shits really gonna hit the fan.'* I'll explain in a minute.

"License and registration ma'am," he said, glancing down at me without really seeing me.

"Sure officer, may I ask what I did wrong?" as if I don't already know. I tried to subliminally get him to look up from his ticket book to see exactly who he'd just pulled over once I'd gathered my license and other documents together thinking... *'Look up. Look up!'*

Still looking down at his ticket book already writing, "You were doing 50 in a 35 zone, ma'am."

I sat quietly thinking, *'Stop writing and look up, you knucklehead,'* as I hold my license and paperwork out the window. "Here you go officer. I just got so excited about my new car. I guess I wasn't paying attention as closely as I should've been," I say finally able to read his name tag. Sadly, I didn't recognize his face until I saw his name tag. CPL. D. JONES.

Corporal Jones finally looking up from that silly pad, completely surprised to see me sitting behind the wheel, "Dr. Morgan? I didn't realize it was you! Now if anybody knows better, it should be you." He was doing a poor job of trying to hold in his laughter and disbelief. "We heard you were taking a couple of days off, but this is an even bigger surprise then that," as he looks up and down my car like he can't believe what his eyes are seeing.

"I know, I just couldn't help it," as I caress my steering wheel, with an innocent bat of my eyes. *'And why is he leaning on the side of my, Brand, New, Car...?'* is all I can think when I glance back over to see him half in, half out of my car. *'I swear if he scratches my paint or dents my door, I will get out of this car and beat him down in the middle of the street with his own nightstick.'* I continue to smile, trying to maintain my composure.

"Does Brian know you bought this? I can't believe he wouldn't talk you out of this! He hates European cars but, not as much as he despises convertibles," he says as he stands up straight, scratching his head, really looking my car over now. "You know better than anyone these things are death traps Doc," he continues.

I'm speechless and dumbfounded at the moment. And I still can't believe

I'm sitting here on the side of the road receiving a vehicle safety rating lecture. There's no telling who could be seeing this and tell Brian before I do and that would be beyond a disaster. "I know, I know!" as I waved him off. "You forget. I've worked many of those accidents right alongside you and Brian. Motorcycles and convertibles are two of the deadliest machines out there," as I remove my sunglasses to make better eye contact with him so that he can see how annoyed I am with this entire situation. And he's really got his nerve. Like I need him to tell me what Brian does and does not like. "But it's so cute, and I've always wanted to feel the wind in my hair, so I bought it. And don't you dare tell Brian," as I poked him in his chest when he leaned back in the window, looking around again. "I want it to be a surprise when he gets back from that conference," I explain.

You could tell I surprised him. He bumped his head as he jerked back trying to pull his head back out of the window. "OH NO! I'M NOT TELLING!" still rubbing his head. "The Chief would demote me just for being the messenger. I think you're on your own with this one," he snickers.

'Really?' as I check my door frame to make sure he didn't scratch it when he jerked away from me. Now the fact that Officer Jones is laughing at me so uncontrollably should be bothering me, but it's not. What's bothering me is the fact that he's holding onto the side of my, BRAND NEW CAR, to maintain his balance and to stay out of traffic. That's what's Killing Me! As he starts to regain his composure, "Well Doc, I'm gonna give you a verbal warning because I think you've got enough to worry about," as he looks up and down my car again. "Your wedding may be off when the Chief sees you in this," he snickers again.

By the way, he's still holding onto my car while he's laughing at me. I just keep looking annoyed as I stare at his hand thinking about how I would love to pry his grubby paws off my car so badly! But that would only compound my problems, and besides, he is soooo right. Officer Jones finally composes himself enough to let go of my car and give me back my paperwork and license.

"I can't wait to radio this one in. Everyone is going to bust a gut on this one," as he starts to giggle again. "Have a nice day Doc. And be careful out there," patting the roof as he turns and walks away.

'He just patted my roof... Is he crazy?!' All I could do is sit there with my mouth hanging open in sheer disbelief, as I watched him walk away in my side mirror. I could hear the little weasel on his walkie talkie as he walked back to his patrol car. Hell, I might as well drop the top now, as I push a button and my roof automatically retracts and disappears. Everybody is going to know anyway, who cares who sees me now. My secret is out, and

Brian is going to be so pissed. I glanced back again as I pulled back out into traffic and damn if Officer Jones isn't still sitting in his patrol car laughing. I know he's on his radio telling everyone what he just saw... how on God's green earth do I keep this from getting back to Brian for 2 whole weeks? *'I'm a dead woman...'* That's all I can think. Well, there's nothing I can do about it right now. So I'm going to enjoy my car and drive it till the wheels fall off. If I only had realized then, how dealing with my car choice decision was actually going to be an easy conversation compared to what I had yet to come.

CHAPTER 1

Maybe I didn't tell you before... I'm Dr. D.J. Morgan, MD and I live in Murfreesboro, Tennessee, a small town outside of Nashville, Tennessee. I'm the Chief Medical Examiner for the Eastern Region of Tennessee. Brian is my fiancé and the Chief of Police here in Murfreesboro, nothing that unusual actually. Well, maybe nothing that unusual except for the fact that I'm not white and well... he is. We really turned some heads when we first went public with our relationship, nearly a year after we started dating. I must admit it wasn't that easy at first, but we survived it. I honestly feel it has made us both wiser and stronger.

Don't get me wrong. Brian is a sweetheart, but he is very set in his ways about certain things. For example, how he feels about, oh say, cars. He'd prefer you to buy American, but he will tolerate you buying Japanese. He calls Mercedes, Audi, Porsche, etc., European trash. And absolutely no motorcycles or sports cars, especially for teenagers, and yes you guessed it, no one needs a convertible. He tried to go out car shopping with me, but I insisted on doing it by myself. We discussed what to look for and what questions to ask, but I guarantee you he never dreamed of this. Brian wasn't happy that I wasn't trading my SUV in on my new car, but he understood. My SUV is paid off, and the twins can use it when they get their licenses in a few weeks. He is so understanding but this, I'm not sure what to do about this. I guess I didn't think this through well enough. But on a good note, Brian is better about racial profiling since we've been together and much more minority friendly. Who am I kidding? I'm so screwed... he loves me, but I'm pushing him to his limits with this one.

Now here we are, 2 years later, planning our wedding. Or should I say, I'm planning our wedding? He basically nods, grunts, and writes the checks. I suggested eloping, and he wanted nothing to do with that. He just keeps telling me that *'the sky's the limit and you are more than worth it. I want everyone in the world to know how much I love you!'* You would think that simple was against the law. I want small, intimate, and private. He wants grand, meaning half the state of Tennessee, and all the lights and cameras.

I'm telling you, between the twins' activities, church activities, working death investigations, and planning this wedding, I truly need a mental break. So a couple of days in Atlanta, away from everything, will do me some good. If only I could shut this phone off, it would be a great break. Strangely enough, it's been pretty quiet today. It's giving me the time I needed to check my personal emails, finish tidying up the house, and finishing up my packing.

Let me call Cyn now while I'm thinking about it. I grab my cell phone and hit the voice command button. "Call Cyn..." Oh no, I can already tell by how long the phone is ringing, I'm gonna get her voicemail. I really hate answering machines, but if I don't leave a message, she will bug me the rest of the day... *'Hello, this is Cynthia Dubois. I can't accept your call at this time. Please leave your name, number, and a brief message, and I'll return your call as soon as possible.'* beeeeep... "Hey Cyn, it's D.J., I'll be on my way as soon as I finish packing and make a couple of calls. I'll definitely be there by dinner time at the latest. I'll talk to you later. Bye," I explain. Now back to what I was doing, going to pack.

Alrighty then, I think my bags are officially packed, as I look around at what used to be my neat and tidy bedroom. It's hard to tell with all of this stuff lying around that didn't make it into my bags. After surveying the damages for a couple of minutes, it hits me. *'I guess it's up to me to get my bags down to the car... there's nobody left here but me.'* After I finish cleaning up my mess, I struggle to get my luggage downstairs, and I can't help but wonder, *'why do we always pack so much to go away for 2 days?'* I sure hope these wheels don't scratch my new hardwood floors in the kitchen. As I make my way down the stairs and head off towards the garage door, it hits me... *'This really makes no sense, a hanging bag, a large suitcase, and an overnight bag.'* Okay back upstairs to re-pack. As I bumped the walls and doorways with the bags slung over my shoulder, I turned to go back up the stairs to re-pack, and all I could think is, *'What was I thinking?'*

This is not a tropical beach getaway, it's just Atlanta. Okay, this is better as I unpacked and laid multiple outfits out across my bed. I picked out 2 dressy outfits and a few casual ones. I can mix any of these outfits, and I will look great. Now, this makes much more sense, a hanging bag, a small bag for shoes, and my personal items in a small overnight bag. After I moved my bags over to the door, I turned around and couldn't believe my eyes. It's hard to believe how much stuff is lying all over my bed, again. But this time it's going to have to stay until I get back. As I gather up my bags and head back downstairs, I realize how much easier it is to manage them without all those big bulky suitcases. So far so good, I've made it through the kitchen and out the garage door and without bumping or scraping a wall or my new floors.

Okay now, gently in the trunk without scratching my car. "Nice job Doc! if I do say so myself," as I closed the trunk without having to adjust anything around. As I stand gazing at my beautiful car sitting in the driveway, I'm pulled away by the sound of my cell phone ringing inside the house. I know it's one of the twins by the ringtone. I turn to run back into the house nearly tripping up the step back into the kitchen, how sad. Luckily the phone is on the counter right inside the back door. I caught it just in time...

"Hey baby how was your flight?" I say slightly out of breath.

"It was fine. We just landed. Are you doing okay there by yourself?" it's E.J. my youngest. He's definitely the most protective of his Mama between the two of them, and yes, I kept the initial tradition alive.

"Yes dear. I'm doing just fine. What, you don't think I can survive without you?" unable to control my giggling at him.

"Hi mamma! You okay?" now J.T. chimes in.

"Yes baby, I'm fine..." still laughing; now realizing they have me on speakerphone. "You two acted like you had just a little bit of home training on that plane, right?" as I sit down at the kitchen table with a bottle of water.

In unison..."Yes, mom..." I hear the phone beeping. Must be theirs because it isn't mine. "We gotta go mom, it's dad on the other line," I'm not quite sure who said that.

"Okay. Love you guys. Have a wonderful time and be careful."

"We love you too. Gotta go!" E.J. said

"Bye mom! Love you!" J.T. followed.

And just like that, they were gone. I couldn't help it as I closed my eyes and whisper a quick prayer out loud... "Lord. Please take care of my babies. I know they are young men now, but they are still my babies, so can you keep an extra eye on them for me, please? Amen."

I just sat still for a few minutes staring out the window into the backyard, watching the birds chase off a squirrel sneaking food out of their bird feeder. I'm not sure why, but I always get nervous when they go stay with their dad. I guess time does heal all wounds but forgetting is something totally different. "Slow deep breaths, slow deep breaths, in your nose and out your mouth." I could hear myself talking me through it, as I came out of my trance. *Now get up and believe they will be home in 2 weeks, none the worse for wear.*

As I finished gathering the rest of the papers on my desk it hit me, *'I'm ready to go.'* I locked the drawer to my desk and shut down my computer.

As I glanced around the room to make sure everything was in its place, I decided that all I had left to do is check-in with the office one last time and then I can get on the highway. I hit Speed dial #5 on the house phone and by the second ring as always...

"Medical Examiner's Office. How may I direct your call?" Mrs. Melody answered.

"Hi Mrs. Melody, its D.J., I'm just checking in. Anything pressing I need to know about before I take off?"

"Well hi, my baby! Melvin from the District Attorney's Office in Manchester is looking for the results on your findings on that poor baby boy that died last week. I looked in your office, but I didn't see the file," she said in that motherly tone.

"I'm sorry you wouldn't. I brought it home to dictate some additional notes. I'll bring it by in a few minutes," I replied as I unlocked the desk drawer to find what she was asking for.

"Are you sure? I bet it could wait a couple more days. You know if you come in here, you'll never get away."

"No, it's fine. I'll come in the back door, no one will see me. I'll see you soon," I replied.

"Okay, then baby. Bye-Bye." And just like that, she was gone.

As you can tell, we are rather informal amongst ourselves. Mrs. Melody could run the whole place in her sleep. She's been with this office since it was created, but she worked as the receptionist for the police/morgue for nearly 35 years. You would think Mrs. Melody was our mother instead of the receptionist. She's like a mom to all of us that no longer have a living mother, like me, and a second mom to all those who work here who still have their mothers. She never forgets a birthday, anniversary, or one of our children's graduations. You've just got to love her. She took me under her wing when I first came to town about 4 years ago, and I've been her daughter ever since. See the deal is she had 6 sons, no daughters, or daughter-in-law's for that matter, so I guess she kind of adopted me before I had anything to say about it.

As strange as it might sound, I was hired by a panel of politicians and physicians out of Nashville and Memphis, for a newly created position to cover Eastern Tennessee, but headquartered here in Murfreesboro. So the surprise on everyone's face here in Murfreesboro when I walked through the door was pretty much expected, at least by me anyway. They were expecting Dr. D.J. Morgan, MD, the "man," not Dr. D.J. Morgan, MD, the "woman." More specifically, the "Black" woman. So, when I showed up to the office boxes in hand and introduced myself as the new Chief Medical

Examinar, everyone was pretty much stunned. I guess you couldn't blame them really. Not only did a woman show up, a "Black" woman showed up.

But Mrs. Melody didn't skip a beat. She gave me a warm smile and the world's biggest hug. She apologized for the "Neanderthals," as she called them, and then showed me to my new office like nothing was out of the ordinary. We walked down a long hallway back to a corner office with a very nice size street-facing window and a glass inside wall and door. It was actually pretty modern on the inside despite the solid red brick exterior you see when you pull up to the building. She sent a couple of officers out to my SUV to get the rest of my things and proceeded to unpack my office for me. I was a little taken back, but I had no choice but to join in with the unpacking, as she then arranged things how she saw fit.

While we unpacked, she answered all my questions about the staff, and in the process, she questioned me as well, in her gentle southern drawl. When she was satisfied with our unpacking job, and to all my answers to all of her questions, I guarantee one thing was true... She knew the answers to every question the menfolk would want answers to. She then called an officer in to give me a guided tour and be my chaperone for the rest of the day. When she turned to walk out of my office, there was no doubt in my mind that no matter what I or anyone outside of this building believed, she was the one who is actually in charge of this office.

Officer Anderson walked me over to personnel so that I could finish up my paperwork, get my passcodes, and then get my ID badge made. Next, we went in and out of the different divisions causing jaws to drop left and right and any work being done, to come to a complete stand-still. Finally, I was able to look over the labs and begin getting ideas as to what equipment I had and what equipment I needed to get. I called a meeting after lunch, to introduce myself to the medical staff and begin getting a feel for them and allow them to get a feel for who I am. Before I could get out of that meeting good, I was summoned to the Chief of Police's Office for what I call "my inspection meeting." An inspection of me by the heads of each Police Department and DA's office that could make it on such short notice, that fell under my jurisdiction. Basically, they had to see me for themselves to believe that I was there. And that I wasn't a joke, a really bad joke.

By the end of the day, all I wanted was a hot bath, a stiff drink, and a few dozen aspirins. I'm still not sure what was more surprising, the fact that I was a woman or that I was a Black woman. I can only imagine the phone calls that the board who hired me received the rest of that week. Needless to say, we had a little bit of a rough start. But once they realized that they weren't going to intimidate me or run me off, nor was the governing board going to replace me, eventually everything calmed down. But I will admit that it did take more time than even I figured that it would for them to understand that A: they had no choice but to get used to me being there, B: that I was the one in charge of my department and that the people in my department had to do things my way, not theirs, and finally C: and most importantly, that I was a Black woman who was more than capable of handling them and the job I'd been hired to do. Believe it or not, it's ended up being kind of like having dozens of big brothers. As the only girl in my family with 4 younger brothers, it wasn't really that much of a change for me. I'm just one of the boys, but occasionally I'm in a skirt.

Okay, that's it. My bags are in the trunk, the files I need to drop-off at the office are complete and ready to go, and the house is all locked up. It's a beautiful day today, but just in case, I'll keep the top up until I'm on the highway headed to the ATL. I guess I'll drive the speed limit too, no need to attract any more unwanted attention. Listen to how my baby purrs. And it's so smooth around these curves and over the hills. My excitement was written all over my face until I got closer to the office that is.

I slowly pulled into a visitor spot so as not to draw any attention to myself before I leave, which would be impossible if I park in my reserved spot. As I sat in my car, I realized how quiet it was around the building. It was actually too quiet, as I looked around for some sign of life. Now that should have been the first indication of what was yet to come. There's usually a lot more traffic in and out of here on a Friday afternoon. I think maybe I need to check-in again, something's up.

I touched a button on the steering wheel, "Call Office."

"Medical Examiner's Office. How may I direct your call?" Mrs. Melody answered.

"Hello Mrs. Melody, it's me again," I replied.

"Hi baby. How are you? Where are you? It's awful quiet," she asked in her motherly tone again.

"I'm fine, there's no need to worry. I'm sitting in my car, in the parking lot, because it's awful quiet out here, too quiet. Is everything okay?" as I looked around the unnaturally still parking lot.

"The coast is clear baby. Come on in," she said with a bright smile on her face even on the phone.

"Okay. I'll see you in a few seconds. Bye."

"Bye-Bye baby. See you soon."

As I quickly gathered my things and gently closed the door to my baby, it hit me. I haven't named her yet. I'll have to work on that. I tickled myself with that one as I made my way into the building, through the back door.

"Hi Mrs. Melody. Here is the file you were asking about and a couple of others you may need before I get back," I said as I entered the reception office.

"Hi baby! Thank you so much. You all ready to go?" she asked as she left her desk to hug me. As always, I'm greeted with a big hug.

"Yes ma'am. I just need to check my messages and make sure who's covering me, and then I can go." I glanced over to my message slot and see that there aren't any written notes, but I can't help but notice that there aren't many people around the office either.

"No worries baby. Sammy's going to cover for you so turn off that silly phone and get you some rest," she said as she took the files and went back to her seat. "If you ask me you need to take off for more than a couple of days," she says as she looked over the top of her glasses at me.

There's no point in me answering her or trying to talk until she's finished with the lecture I'm about to hear. So I sat down next to her desk and waited for what I knew was coming.

"You haven't taken any real time off since you came to work here, what 5 years ago?" she asks, still staring at me.

"Yes ma'am, I've been here almost 5 years. And no ma'am, I've never taken off any extra days," I answered quickly, trying not to roll my eyes. WOW! It just hit me...we really do act like mother and daughter.

"That makes no sense. Why haven't you gone home for the holidays? The twins have. And I bet your father and your brothers would love to see you for more than a day. When's the last time you saw your nieces and nephew?" she snapped as she reshuffled the papers on her desk, obviously ignoring my squirming.

"I'm not sure... I love my brothers, but they know where I live too, you know. Why do I have to go to them? Why can't they come see me? I work just as hard as they do if not harder," I said as I stood up and started walking towards my office, fighting to hold back my tears.

"Wait baby! I didn't mean to upset you," she says as she gets up and follows me out of the lobby. "I just mean you work so hard and such long hours sometimes. You deserve a break just like everyone else around here, that's all," as she hands me a tissue and then gives me another big hug. Still patting me on the back, she wraps her hand around my chin, pulling my face up with her free hand and gives me one of her award-winning smiles, before returning to the reception area.

Like I said before, she acts just like my mother. You just have to love her. And after she chastises you like a child, she always finishes it off with what else, but a big hug and smile. By the way, did I mention she's my fiancé's mother? But that's another story for another time.

When I finished with what I needed to do, we walked out the building laughing, just as if nothing had ever happened, arm in arm. She walked with me, all the way down the sidewalk into the parking lot, still talking about taking more time off and how family is more important than any job — the usual mother-daughter stuff we both missed so much, me being motherless and her being daughterless. As we cleared the side of the building, I was totally taken back by the scene that was unfolding before my very eyes. Remember how I made it into the building unseen? Well, I definitely didn't make it out the same way. It looked like a ghost town when I arrived, but when I go to leave, it was the complete opposite. I swear they must have made an all call that I somehow didn't hear. I'm telling you everybody was outside milling around, MY NEW CAR....TOUCHING IT AND EVERYTHING! You'd think they had never seen a Mercedes or a convertible before. As we got closer, the snickering got louder, and people were backing away, shaking their heads as they stared at me.

I guess no one else was brave enough to say anything to me, so of course, Mrs. Melody, in her gentle way, spoke up. As she patted my hand, she cleared her throat, like a signal, to get everyone to quiet down. All at once, the crowd went silent, and she began to speak just loud enough and clear enough for everyone to hear, "Baby it's a beautiful car. But you must be a glutton for punishment." That's all it took for the entire crowd to erupt into uncontrollable laughter. Then even Mrs. Melody started rubbing my baby like it was a cat or something as I stiffened up with her still holding onto my arm as she walked me to the door.

I somehow maintained my composure, gave her a peck on the cheek, and without a word, I disarmed the alarm, opened the door with my head held high, and slipped ever so gently onto my beautiful gray leather seat. I started up my elegant, silver baby. Pushed a button and dropped the top and then gracefully slid my sunglasses on. I pulled the seatbelt down and clicked it into place, then cleared my throat and they all grew quiet again. I pulled my sunglasses down onto my nose to see over the top of them, then loudly stated for all to hear, "If anyone of you breathes a word of this to Brian before I tell him, I will make your life miserable! So God help me, I will!" as I continued to glare at all of them over the top of my sunglasses then slowly pushed them back up my nose to their proper place.

On some silent queue, everyone in the crowd, including sweet old Mrs. Melody fell out laughing as I backed out of the parking space and drove out of the lot. I quickly shuffled through my CDs and found Indie Arie and 'Voyaged Back to Indie' as I made my way onto I-24 East to Chattanooga, with the wind in my hair and the feeling of utter joy and relaxation coming over me. I've known for a while how a new outfit or even a hairdo could make you feel better about yourself, but it's amazing to me how a new car can make you feel so invincible. It's like you're on top of the world, and nothing or no one can affect you. I truly love my new car and damn it, no one's going to spoil that for me today! Hell, I will deal with Brian when he gets back from DC.

CHAPTER 2

I couldn't believe how smooth this car really was. I drove all the way to Atlanta with the top down. The only bad part, other than the obvious windblown hair, is that I arrived in the ATL as rush hour traffic was in full effect. I might as well start making those, *'I made it safely calls.'* First up is Mrs. Melody of course. As always, she picked up by the 2nd ring.

"Hello."

"Hi Mama M, its D.J. I just wanted to let you know that I arrived okay. I'll have my cell on so if you need me, call me."

"Okay baby. Have fun and at least try to get some rest, okay?"

"Yes ma'am, I will."

"And D.J...."

"Yes ma'am?"

"It really is a pretty car." I could hear her snickering as the phone went click. I'm surprised I don't have a mouth full of bugs the way my mouth fell open and just hung there. I just don't know what else to say.

I made it through calls to the boys and their dad. Come to find out he didn't even pick them up from the airport. He left his backup car there for them to drive themselves out to his house. Apparently, he had pressing business to take care of and couldn't pick them up himself. Some shit never changes. He knows they only have their learners permits and I don't care how you slice it, 2 learners permits don't equal a legal license, even if they are 16. Well, at least they made it there in one piece, no thanks to him.

"D.J. just sit back and relax. Enjoy the ride," I said out loud to myself to try and calm me down.

As I played with the buttons on the steering wheel, I just smiled and thought to myself... *'Lord I Love my car.'* I can dial a number and hold a conversation, all with the touch of a button, without taking my hands off the steering wheel. Right on time, Cyn is calling.

"Hey Lady! What's up?" I asked.

"Where is your tired ass at? I'm getting hungry!" she replied in true Cynthia fashion.

"Yo tiny ass is always hungry. I'm sitting in this parking lot you call a highway," I replied, starting to laugh.

"What highway?"

"I'm still on I-75, but I'm almost to 285. Which way do I go? I never remember," as I tried to politely merge over to the right, which is not always so easy to do in this city.

"Take 285 East and get off on Roswell Road to the right. My complex is directly on the left with the security gate and the fountain in front."

"Okay cool," I replied, finally getting over to where I needed to be safely in all this traffic.

"And hurry yo butt up. I'm almost home so when you get here we can go meet some friends for drinks."

"Damn girl! Can a sista relax and freshen up first? I need to check-in at the hotel before we do all that anyway."

In her outraged, ghetto girl, over the top voice, "Hotel!? Hotel!? What's with the hotel? You know you can stay with me. My couch is your couch!" she said.

"Calm down. I know, but I don't want to be any trouble, and I really do want to get some REST. And we both know that ain't gonna happen at Cynthia's playhouse," as I started laughing.

"Oh see...you ain't right! You know you ain't right!" now both of us are laughing uncontrollably.

The joke is that Cynthia is a bona fide workaholic. Literally, everywhere she goes, ends up being about work. And work is always spread out everywhere in her apartment. On the floor, on the couches, chairs, cabinets, and even in her car. Cyn is a reporter for Fox 5 News, here in Atlanta, but she also moonlights as a co-host on a Gospel radio show, every Sunday afternoon. You basically have to clear a path and stick to it in her house. There are beta cassettes and papers everywhere. And let's not forget the hysterical tirade you will cause if anything is moved. It's unreal. Yes, the hotel is my best option.

"Well at least stop by first and pick me up. Then you can go check-in at that old, stank hotel. Which dive you staying at anyway?"

"The Ritz-Carlton on Peachtree," I said.

"Oooooh! Nice digs. Guess playing around with dead men pays pretty well."

"It definitely pays the bills. Oh, gotta go. Brian's on the other line. I'll see you in 20," I tell her as I see his name flash across the caller ID on the radio.

"Ok girl. Tell Mr. Officer I said, 'What's Suuup!?!?'" all you can hear is her giggling on the line.

"Bye girl, you are too silly for words," as I click over just in time.

"Hi Sweetie! How's it going up there in big, bad DC?" I ask in my playful, sexy voice.

"Okay honey. I'm definitely ready to come home. I really miss the slower pace and calmness of a small town. I don't know how these big city folks do it every day," he sounds disgusted and frustrated. That can't be good.

"Ohhhh, poor baby. It will be over soon," I say trying to sound empathetic.

"What's all that noise in the background? It sounds like your outside."

"Uhhh, the windows are down... *and the top*," but we'll have that conversation later. "So is the small town all you miss?" I quickly respond, trying to change the subject as I pull onto the side of the road and close the top.

"Well there is this beautiful, mocha, goddess that I have a thing for, but hey, I'm in what do you call it? Oh yeah, Chocolate City, that's right. So I can pretty much satisfy my sweet tooth anytime I please up here." All I hear is his laughter as I merge back onto the highway annoyed, *'that comment really wasn't called for.'*

"Is that right? Well, don't forget you are talking to someone who knows how to hide your body parts if I have to so no one can find them, so don't test me. Don't make me come all the way up to our Nation's Capital to handle that sweet tooth in person. And it won't be a pleasant experience either Mr....."

"Ha, Ha, Ha! Calm down there Little Lady. You're the only sweet thang I crave. Besides, none of the women up here can hold a candle to you baby."

"Now that's more like it," I say as we share a light-hearted laugh together. "But seriously, how is it going up there? Are you getting anything accomplished?" I asked as I merged over again to get back in the right lane to get off on Roswell Road.

"Good question Doc. I'm between meetings as we speak. Looks like tonight's going to be another all-nighter. This drug epidemic is killing everybody across the country and eating up precious resources. I'm not sure what to say or do to get through to these boneheaded bureaucrats up here. It's like the lights are on, but nobody's home."

"Sweetie, it'll be okay. Treat them with kid gloves until you've got them in the palm of your hand, then turn on that Drill Sergeant demeanor that we all know and love so much. That's how you tricked me into marrying you," as I try to comfort him and lighten up the conversation.

"Is that right?" he chuckled.

"Yes that's right. You acted all sweet and chivalrous, and then when you knew you had me, you pounced. And before I knew what hit me, I was engaged to a mad man!" cracking up laughing again.

"Very funny. Very funny. You know that's the furthest thing from the truth," he said.

"Oh yeah? How's that?" I asked with a smirk on my face like he could see it through the phone.

"I think you have the roles reversed. I was the deer caught in your headlights. I'll admit I was skeptical about you working here, but then I really started getting to know you. You were all sweet and soft-spoken the first few days then out of the blue this tiger lady showed up, cracking the whip. All I could do is come to attention and say, 'Yes Ma'am!' like everybody else. Then those big ole brown eyes started melting my heart. You know you had me sniffing behind you like a hound dog in heat. And then before I knew it, you had wormed your way into my heart. And when I just couldn't take being apart from you, I asked you out, and to my utter delight you said 'Yes!' But when you showed up to the Mayor's dinner party with another man... that was the final straw. You knew exactly what that would do to me, so I had to do whatever it took to make you mine!" as he finally took in a deep breath.

Very calmly I said, "So basically what you're saying is you stalked me," knowing that would set him off again.

"No! No! No! That's not it, and you know it!"

Now I'm giggling again, and I can't control it. I have to keep picking at him, it's too funny, and I just can't stop now. "That's what it sounds like to me. You stalked me, on and off the job. Which by-the-way is also considered sexual harassment since we work together. Then, on top of all that, as if that wasn't enough, you misrepresented yourself when you had your 'friend' show me the rental property that I now reside in, that just so happens to belong to you... I bet you have the place wired for sound and video, don't you?"

"WOW! You really missed your calling. Sure you're not a lawyer in disguise?" he calmly asked as we both start laughing again.

"Very funny mister. Well, whoever lured whom; you're stuck with me now," I said, smiling again.

"10-4 Roger that! Well, people are starting to show up, so I guess I better let you go hon."

"I love you Sir. Keep your head up, it will be over soon, and you will be back home, in the safety of my arms," I say still smiling.

"I love you too Doc. Bye the way how's the new car? Mom told me you and it were made for each other. But she wouldn't give me any details other than that or explain exactly what that's supposed to mean. What gives?"

"Oh, that's nothing for you to worry about right now baby. We'll talk about it later. Don't worry about it. You just concentrate on those Senators and other lawmen that are now waiting on you. I love you Sweetie. Talk to you later," I quickly say, not so subtly, trying to get off the phone before I had to explain exactly what she meant.

"Well okay, but what's the big deal? Why's everyone so hush, hush?"

"Got to go sweetie, I'm pulling up to Cyn's now. Bye the way, she told me to give you a message..." as I start giggling again. Mainly because I know they don't really care for each other.

"Oh boy.... I can't wait," he answers sarcastically as I expected.

"She said, 'What's Suuuup!!!?'" as I crack up laughing. Brian still can't get into talking in slang, or as he puts it, 'ghetto-talking.' Which is quite funny to me since he and the good ole' boys, pretty much do the same thing, only in a country, redneck kinda way.

"On that note, I'll talk to you later Doc. Have a nice time and call me when you're headed back home," he says in his stern policeman voice.

"Will do Chief. Now back to work," I instruct with a loving flair.

"I Love you. Bye Doc."

"Bye-bye baby, I love you more." And with that, he was gone.

CHAPTER 3

Why on earth do people live on the top floor of a 5-story building with no elevator? I know she didn't think that I was going to drag my suitcases all the way up here. 4 flights...she really is losing her mind. As I made my way upstairs, I had to admit that this is a much nicer place than the last one she stayed in before. And the new brass door knockers aren't too shabby either. When I finally reached her door, I just had to pound on it extra hard for effect...CLANK! CLANK! CLANK!

"Who's there?" came from inside the apartment.

"The tooth fairy. Now open the door nut!" I say laughing.

"Hey girl!" Cyn said as she opened the door, with a huge grin. "Glad you made it," she continued as she stood there looking me up and down holding the door open with one hand and the other hand on her hip. "What do you mean, you need to freshen up? You're dressed to the 9's now."

"If you say so. Can I at least go to the bathroom and get a drink of water? Damn!" as I pushed past her and step inside her apartment.

"Right this way," she replied as she curtsied and pointed in the direction of the bathroom.

I couldn't help noticing the cleanliness of the room as she closed the door behind me. "WOW! A real walkway. I can even see the furniture," I said as I surveyed the area and quickly made my way down the hall to the bathroom.

"Well I figured it was a special occasion, so I tried to tidy up a bit for your visit. I told you, you could stay here. My office has a daybed in it with your name written all over it."

"Whew...now I feel like I can breathe," I said as I came out of the bathroom noticing how clean her bedroom was too. "Good job with the clean-up. I'm impressed. Nice office too," as I peak in the door. "But I think I'm a little too big for a daybed. Thanks for the offer though," I smiled as I noticed what she's doing.

"Water my dear. Just as you like it, light on the crushed ice," bowing as she passed me the glass.

K. Rochelle

"Well thank you," as I took the glass giggling. "Girl, you are too silly for words," reaching out to hug her. Hugging and rocking as we always do, now both of us are laughing. "Who are we going to meet and better yet, where are we going to eat?" I ask while sipping on my glass of water.

"You know me..." she shrugs and walks away giggling.

"That's what I'm afraid of." I'm amazed at how fast she zips around this place picking up her things, as she's getting ready to go.

"Be afraid. Be very afraid," she moans as she scurries about the room collecting her things and then sliding into some bad red heels. That's bad in a good way.

"You know if you wore a real woman's size shoe, those would be going back to Tennessee with me." She wears a size 6 ½ shoe. Only kids have feet that small. Hell, I wear anything from a size 8 to a 9 ½ , depending on how wide it is. She picks up yet another bag and then grabs my arm and drags me out the door.

We'll have just enough time to check you in and make our reservation. I'll follow you to the hotel, then you can ride with me," as she spins around to lock the door.

"Sounds like a plan. But you still didn't answer my questions."

"I'm not one of your suspects. I'll answer when I'm good and damn ready. So just relax and trust me. I have a big surprise for you," she says as she whirls back around and starts pushing me down the stairs.

"And what on God's green earth made you move onto the 5th floor of a building with no elevator? You must have bumped your head," I asked with her hand still on my back.

"Oh quit complaining. It's good exercise. Which I can tell you've been getting plenty of," she replies while she's still pushing me down the stairs.

I'm trying to slow us down, and she's pushing even harder. "I'm wearing a 4-inch heel. Do you mind?" as I try to slow us down again. "I choose not to fall and break my neck," as I grip the handrails for dear life.

"Yeah, yeah. Girl, you've lost a lot of weight, and in all the right places, I might add," she says still pushing me but feeling my sides at the same time.

"You are so crass. I am getting married, remember? I had to tone it up to get the dress I liked to look and fit the way it should. Having rolls and things poking out where they have no business is not a good look," I explain.

"Are you sure you want to marry this man? He's nothing like anything I've ever seen you with before. And he's so dry," she says over-exaggerating the word dry.

"Whatever and yes I am. He's a real sweetheart when you get to know him," I said as I glanced back looking over my shoulder but still paying

16

attention to my footing. Whew...we finally made it to the bottom floor safely and in one piece. I felt like I was running on a treadmill, downhill, in a 6-inch heel.

"Please D.J., he ran my license plate for warrants when I came to visit you. Tell it to someone else," she said obviously still pissed at his actions. We never lost our stride as we walked arm in arm into the parking lot, still catching up.

"Come on. Don't take it personally. He's just very cautious, and besides, that is what the man does for a living. He just takes a little time getting used to is all. The boys love him, and he's great with them. Cyn, I love him more than I ever dreamed I could love another man," I said.

"Yeah, but he's 'White.' And I bet him, and his redneck friends call you a nigger behind your back," Cyn said so matter-of-factly.

Well, that stopped me dead in my tracks. I turned to look her in her eyes, with a stone face... "That is not his style, and you really don't know him. Besides, you know my philosophy... Every White man's fantasy is to get with a 'Black' woman. And this 'White' man treats me like a queen, I want for nothing," I said, still making eye contact. You could tell I startled her, but she quickly recovered and started pulling my arm to start me walking again.

"Yeah, yeah, but can he put a hump in your back?" she replies as she begins giggling and doing a little funky dance.

"Wipe that silly smirk off your face. He does everything just right. He does it the way I like, and he's shown me some things I never dreamed I would like. You should try it, you may just like it. But you have to find your own," I finish as we both start laughing just before she starts making a regurgitating sound.

"I'll leave the whole jungle fever thing to you if that's okay?" she finally replied as we reached her car. She starts looking around and finally asks, "Where's your truck?"

"Oh, I bought a new car, the trucks back at the house. My baby is down there," as I point to the far end of the lot. She turned and looked at me as if to say why? "Before you say a word... Yes, I could have parked closer to your building, but I didn't want to park under all these trees or too close to all those cars," I pointed out to help defend my rational. We only had to walk down a small hill to where my baby was parked just out of view. Someone had parked their SUV next to me while I was in Cyn's apartment. Once we reached my baby, and she could finally see exactly what I was driving, the small talk ended pretty quickly.

"Damn Girl! Playing with dead men must really be paying well. I know you don't think we are going to park this and take my car tonight? Oh, hells no Miss Thang! We are definitely taken this pretty little thing out on the town tonight!" as she glides her fingers down the side and peers through the window.

"I kinda figured you would say that. So stop drooling and let's go," I laughed as I opened the driver side door only.

"I'll follow you to the hotel so that you don't have to bring me back here tonight," she says so Cynthia perky, as she stands there obviously wanting me to unlock the door so she can ride back up the hill to her car.

"Okay," I said as I got in and dropped the top. "Well, what are you waiting for?" I asked. She didn't say a word as she smiled and pulled the door handle a couple of times without any results. I couldn't help but laugh as I unlocked the door and she slid into the passenger's seat. "Are you comfortable?" I asked with a smirk on my face.

She crossed her arms and said, "I sure am. You can go now," pointing towards the exit. I couldn't help but laugh at her again as I finished tying the scarf around my head, then slowly backed out of my spot and drove back up the hill to drop her off at her car. She backed out of her space, pulled around me, and proceeded to lead me out of the parking lot.

Because we were so pressed for time, we jumped on GA-400 to get off on Lenox Road, instead of taking the surface streets. As we made our way to the toll booth, I couldn't help but notice the scenery. I had forgotten how beautiful this city could be. Although it was much faster this way, it took me forever to find the correct change for the toll. It's a new car. I haven't had a chance to collect change in here yet. As we pulled up to the hotel, a fine, chocolate, young man came running out to open my door.

"Good evening ma'am. Welcome to the Ritz-Carlton of Buckhead. Will you be checking in today?" the young man asked with a big smile on his face.

I popped the trunk as he was opening the door. He was very well-spoken and easy to understand, even with such a heavy southern drawl, as well as being easy on the eyes. I just smiled at him as I thought, *"It doesn't get any better than this. Uhmm, uhm, uhm... and what a pretty, white smile."* What? Just because I'm with a white man doesn't mean that I don't still enjoy a fine chocolate man when I see one. When I'd finished taking in all there was to see, I finally responded as I read his name tag. "Well yes Christopher, I am."

As he reached out his hand to assist me out of my car, he asked, "Will you be needing the car again tonight ma'am?" as he handed me a claim ticket.

"Yes Sir, I will. I will be right back, as soon as I get checked in and drop off my bags."

"Well then I'll just pull it up for you so it will be close ma'am," he said as he removed my luggage from the trunk.

"Thank you, Sir."

I was so engaged with young Mr. Christopher that I didn't even notice Cyn walking up.

"Well you can park mine and put it on her bill," she said as she dangles her keys in midair, pointing at me.

"Yes ma'am. That won't be a problem," Christopher answered as he glanced back over to me to make sure it was okay.

I just smiled and nodded okay as I walked around to get my purse off the passenger side floorboard. "One of these days, you are going to stop being a leech," I announced as I reached over the door and gathered my things.

"Well not today sista," she retorted as she swung her arm around my shoulders and neck, pulling me close. "You know you love me, so let's get a move on. Chop, Chop," she continued as she pulled me through the front doors of the hotel.

Young Mr. Christopher already had my bags out of the car and inside waiting for me at the registration desk, when Cyn and I finished our little tete-a-tete. Did I mention how fine he was?

"How may I help you ladies?" asked the lady behind the counter.

"I have a reservation for D.J. Morgan."

"Yes, Dr. Morgan. I see it right here. I see that you are a Platinum Elite member. Would you prefer to leave this on your personal account, or will you be using your corporate account today?"

"Personal is fine," as I passed her my credit card. A few quick keystrokes and she gave my card back to me.

"You will be in Suite 1604. I just need you to sign here and initial here. Will you be needing a wake-up call in the morning?"

"No, thank you," signing and initialing the papers she had given to me.

"Will you require 1 key or 2?" she asked in between keystrokes.

"Just 1... I wouldn't want someone else to think they can stay," as I motioned towards Cyn with a quick head tilt. She was too busy talking to someone on her cell to notice, so I thought. The registrar and I laughed as she handed me my room key, and I passed her back the papers and her pen.

"I heard you. And you're still not funny by the way," Cyn said as she hung up her phone.

"I figured you were listening, nosey. Just let me drop this stuff off, and we can go. Is everything okay?" We both picked up a bag and turned to head over to the elevators as the clerk interrupts.

"The bellman can take your bags up for you if you'd like."

"Thank you, but we can handle it," as I turn to go back to what we were doing.

"Why not let them take your bags up? We need to get on the road. Our guests are already there waiting," she said, pulling the bag out of my hand.

"What guests and where are we going?" I ask again as I pick my bags up and smiled off the bellman. "We can handle it, thank you Sir." Shaking my head at her while we wait for the elevator to come. "Again, what guests and where are we going Miss Busy Body?"

"Boy the artwork in this place is really exquisite," Cyn says, looking around still trying to avoid answering my questions, as she pushes the up button repeatedly.

"Oh No! Don't get all professional on me now. Who and where? That's all I want to know." DING!

"Nice elevators too. The marble floor is a very nice touch. It kinda reminds me of the entry at Brian's house. Speaking of Brian are you two shacking up yet?" she asks.

"Nice...you're not special, you do know that?" I rolled my eyes.

"Whatever do you mean?" batting her eyes at me like she's innocent.

"Way to change the subject. That was pretty smooth," I admitted. "And that's really none of your business," I continued, looking up at the digital numbers change.

"Don't get so defensive. I'm officially off duty," she says with her hand over her heart.

"Pa-lease... a reporter is never 'off duty,'" I say sarcastically.

She giggled, "Yeah, that may be true, but this is just between you and me. Besides no one in Atlanta would care less if the White Police Chief in Mulberry, Tennessee, was dishing it out to a sista anyway," Cyn replies.

DING! The walk to the room was relatively short since there were only 6 rooms on this floor. When I tell you the artwork and decor were breathtaking, it's not saying enough. And the view...what a view. You could see to downtown Atlanta.

"Oh, you'd be surprised at who cares and who's watching. For a minute, we thought he was going to lose the election when people found out about our relationship 2 weeks before Election Day. As a matter of fact, his political advisors told him to walk away from me and quickly. It's one thing to have the Black communities support, but it's another thing to get caught tasting the forbidden fruits of the Black community, especially in public. Racism is still well and kicking in America today little sister. Especially in the South," I explained as I waved the keycard across the panel to open my suite door and let us in.

"So is that a yes or a no?" she asked pushing past me looking very annoyed because of my answer and due to my lack of giving her a yes or no answer to her question.

"It's none of your business, and you can quote me on that," I told her as I took my bag out of her hand and took it into the bedroom, dropping them all onto the bed for now. I adjusted the thermostat and started to close the curtains in the bedroom as I became lost in the view. I was taken back at how beautiful it was as the sun was beginning to set over the city, casting a soft glow over the buildings below. It was so serene; I couldn't help but get lost in all the warm colors mixing so perfectly until you know who brought me back to reality.

"Come on, come on! We have to go. Stare out the window on your own time. We're late," she said with her hands on her hips standing in the bedroom door. She stopped tapping her foot and turned and walked away.

"Late for what?" I asked, turning to see what she was doing now.

"You'll see. Now come on!" she said, waving her arm around, while holding the door open, trying to usher me back into the hallway.

As luck would have it, the elevator was still on my floor, so we made our way back downstairs and through the lobby fairly quickly. Christopher was waiting with my Precious as we walked out of the lobby. He was standing there with my door open and ready for us to just hop in and ride. I didn't even need to adjust the seat or drop the top. He closed my door, and we were off.

The air was getting a little chilly but still not cold enough for me to even think about letting the top-up. Cyn navigated us down Peachtree and onto Piedmont, then right up into Sambuca's parking lot. I couldn't believe it. She knew I've always wanted to go to this place, but I'd never had the time. I'd only heard good things about it, good food and great live jazz, you can't beat it. I let the top up while the valet helped Cynthia out of the car.

"Good evening ladies. Welcome to Sambuca. You're just in time for the first show," the parking attendant announced as he opened my door. He handed me a valet ticket and jumped into my baby. I hesitated for a moment as I watched him drive my Precious away, and it disappeared around the corner.

Cyn grabbed my arm and literally dragged me inside. The hostess greeted us with a warm smile and informed us that our party was already seated. She guided us to a side table to the left of the stage, but upfront, on the second row. Through the crowd, I could make out Shanice, we call her Niecy for short, sitting there talking with a man, but his back was to me so

I couldn't make out who he was. Niecy greeted me with a hug and then the man slowly stood up and turned around to face me.

"Tre!? It's been so long since I've seen you! What are you doing here?" I exclaimed obviously excited.

You would have thought he was my long lost love by the way we were hugging and rocking. Tre was a trainer back at A&M when I was in med school. I was still working the sidelines at the football and basketball games as he was working his way up through the student trainer ranks. We rehabbed many a player together.

"Sit down, sit down!" he said, pulling out my chair. We were kinda blocking the walkway, so I let him go and took the chair between him and Niecy. "Cyn told me you were coming to town, so I decided to surprise you. I'm working on my Ph.D. at Albany State, so I drove up to see how you were doing for myself. She also told me you're getting married. WOW!"

"Yeah, the love bug finally bit me. Decided I'd give this marriage thing one more try," I said, still smiling. My face was beginning to hurt from grinning so long.

Tre was not only a really good friend to me and the twins, but he'd also become like a little brother to me. He also had to run blocker for me on occasion, when one of the athletes would try to get just a little too friendly and didn't want to take no for an answer. We had some good times together on the sidelines, in the training room, in the operating room, and even after hours. See I'd cook, and he and some of the other trainers would come over to eat. They'd also come over and watch the away games at my house when they didn't travel with the team. I had a big screen TV, so my house was definitely the place to be, not to mention the food and drinks were free, and you could sleep it off if you had a little too much to drink.

We finally stopped talking long enough to order our drinks and some appetizers just as the show was beginning to start. We settled down to listen to one of my favorite jazz singers' sooth away all my stress. I just love me some Lalah Hathaway. Apparently, Cynthia had called in a favor from one of her contacts, 'Niecy' when I called about coming to town yesterday. I sure love my sorors sometimes. They definitely came through for me tonight. We all rocked and laughed the rest of the night away, to the smooth sounds of Lalah Hathaway, live.

Niecy said her goodbyes after the show was over, but Tre and Cyn brought the party back to the hotel with me. Christopher was still on duty when we arrived back at the Ritz, and like Johnny on the spot, he had my door open for me almost as soon as I put my Precious in park.

"Good evening Dr. Morgan. Will you be needing the car again tonight?" he asked with that award-winning smile and hand out, ready to take mine.

"No Sir. I'm in for the night, but thank you for asking," I replied as I took his hand and stepped out from behind the wheel.

"Very well then. Enjoy the rest of your evening, and I will see you tomorrow," he said with a smile.

"Thank you, and you have a good night too. Oh and Christopher..." I turned back to say.

"Yes ma'am?" he said, turning back around.

"Please be extra careful with my baby. She's new," I smiled, almost blushing. "And also the truck behind me, put that on my bill as well please," as I handed him a $50 tip.

"Not a problem Dr. Morgan. I'll take care of it. Goodnight!" he smiled as he handed Tre a valet ticket.

"Thanks Doc, but you don't have to do that," Tre says.

"I know I don't have to do it, I wanted to do it Doc." I winked at him as I grabbed his arm. The three of us turned and walked arm in arm, laughing and talking all at once, into the Ritz lobby and on up to my suite to continue our reunion. I asked Tre and Cyn if they'd like me to order up something from room service as we began settling in and of course they both wanted something to snack on and a few beers. So I ordered up a fruit tray, an assortment of sandwiches, a few Coronas, and a bottle of wine for me, as we laughed and talked. It was really great hearing the old stories and catching up on all the present-day events. I excused myself once the food had arrived to get a little more comfortable, for what looked to be an all-nighter. When I returned, Cynthia was sprawled out across a chair & ottoman with a plate of food, and Tre was kicked back on the couch doing the same. They were still laughing at the others pledging dramas when I took my place on the chaise lounge with a glass of wine and a small plate of fruit.

As interesting as their stories were, my pledging experience was totally different due to the simple fact that I pledged in a Graduate Chapter of Delta Sigma Theta Sorority, Incorporated, DST or Delta for short, and they both pledged as undergraduate chapters, of Delta and Kappa. Kappa Alpha Psi Fraternity, Incorporated, respectively. They basically endured things in undergraduate that would never have happened on a female graduate line. So, for now, I'm more than content to sit back, sip on my glass of Moscato, and listen to the sounds of their voices. Laughter heals the soul you know, and reminiscing about good times is great for the spirit as well.

But actually, when I think about it, there is nothing about my education that most people would consider to be "typical." See I wasn't your typical college student. I was what they liked to classify as a "non-traditional" student. I kinda took a 5-year break after my sophomore year at A&M, Texas A&M University to those who don't already know. Basically, I was too pregnant to go anymore and then in my infinite wisdom, or lack thereof, I got married and thought I didn't need to go back to school. My babies' father was a professional ballplayer. Why on earth would I need to finish my education? He could afford to take care of us for the rest of our lives... or so I thought. Thinking like that was the first of many mistakes I'd come to make. Needless to say, eventually the marriage and the pro career both went south. The harsh reality was that I'd never be able to depend on him for support, of any kind. So after my divorce, I did what I should have done right after the twins were born. I went back to school and finished my degree.

While Tre and Cynthia were talking, I faded back to my own memories of A&M. The good, the bad, and the ugly. Now don't get me wrong, for the most part, my time on campus was pretty good. It's only the first go around, that first couple of years out of high school that I would love to get a do-over. Better yet to totally forget anything to do with dating one Mr. Selkie Nathaniel Black, AKA "Selk," (pronounced the same way as silk – don't ask me it was his mama's creation), or our marriage, except for the twins of course. And don't ask me how that would work exactly because I have no idea.

Anyway, I spent a lot of time at A&M. First, I just hung out there a lot, then I was a student, then I was a pregnant student, and then I was the wife of an A&M superstar athlete who went to the pros. What a fairy tale, right? Well, it would've been except for the part where I became the divorced dropout with 2 small children, trying to work and go to school full time, without any help from the babies' daddy and very little help from my family after my mom passed away. And finally, as if that weren't enough, I up and decide to go to Medical School. I'm not complaining I was very blessed to have been able to accomplish so much with all the responsibilities I had, mostly on my own. If it hadn't been for an extraordinary group of friends, family, and professors, I know I never would have made it through.

It's funny how many people you meet in school and get to know, but they really never get to know your true story. I have to admit the people in my life, then and now, for the most part, have only general knowledge about my past, but nothing substantial. Nothing about the things that I'd been through or the decisions that I had to make that could affect my life or those I love. Only if they really knew the true story of me.... I wonder what they would have to say. I closed my eyes and laid back replaying my real-life story for what felt like only a minute, but I must have drifted off to sleep in the process. The next thing I knew, I was being snapped back to the present by the sound of Cynthia's high-pitched voice and Tre's hysterical laughter.

"Hey you! No sleeping over there!" she yelled.

"What? I'm not asleep," I explained as I nearly jumped out my seat. "I just got lost in my own thoughts," I said knowing that was only partially true.

"Yeah, sure you did," he replied, and both of them began laughing again. Tre excused himself to the bathroom while Cyn finished off the fruit tray. To be so little, she could sure eat a lot. Some things never change, I guess. Come to think of it that's how she and I met, at a pre-game meal.

I was classified as a senior when I met Cynthia and Tre. I was a physical therapy major who worked as a student athletic trainer, and I also had a work-study job in the Athletic Director's Office. If nothing else my marriage taught me, it's who you know and not just what you know. So I used my connections in the Athletic Department to wrangle myself a work-study job and a TFW (tuition fee waiver) from the Head Athletic Trainer. I was an older student who was a quick study, dependable, loved sports, and best of all... I had absolutely NO desire whatsoever, to date any of the athletes. So basically I was a dream come true for the Athletic Department and the Head Trainer. It was cheaper for them to pay for my education and train me the way they wanted, rather than have to pay a Certified Trainer and another secretary a full salary and try to retrain them to do things their way. So it was truly a win, win for everyone concerned.

Cynthia was a journalism major who doubled as a reporter and DJ at the campus radio station. So on occasion, she would do the pre and post-game reports for the men and women basketball teams. She was only a freshman when we first met, but over time, we became friends. I was always amazed at her energy level and her appetite, you couldn't miss either. In a short amount of time, she appeared to be as seasoned as the upperclassmen reporters, with 50 times the energy. She reminded you of a gerbil going around and around, on one of those wheels but on speed. She just never stopped moving. She was always poking around for her next exclusive, so we got to know each other well over the next few years. Being in the same sorority didn't hurt either.

Now Tre on the other hand, he and I hit it off immediately when we first met. He too was a freshman, but he was also a student athletic trainer. He and I spent so much time together, days, nights, and many a weekend, working in the training room or on the sidelines of a game. He became more of a brother to me and the twins because we all spent so much time together. By the end of my 1st year of medical school, Tre had made quite a name for himself in the Training Department. He had been assigned to the women's basketball team permanently, second only to the Head Trainer, and as a sophomore no less.

Yes, even in medical school, I worked as a student trainer to help make up for what my scholarship didn't cover. Like clothing, food, gas, daycare, treats for the boys, car payments, and shelter for 2 growing boys, but I digress. The truth is I had a little backup financial assistance if I really needed it, but I was determined to take care of us on my own. Besides, working as a trainer was also a great stress release believe it or not.

Tre finally returned from the bathroom looking more tired than when he went in. "Well ladies, it's been fun, but I really must head back home now. I'm beat, and I've got a nice little ride ahead of me," he said as he walked over and started massaging my head. I laid my head back and enjoyed the quickie message for just a moment. I smiled up at my friend as I lifted my arms above my head to get in a good stretch before I rocked forward to stand up. We came together for one more hug before he turned to walk towards the door, stopping just enough to pat Cyn on the head as he passed by her. "So D.J., when are you headed back home?" he asked.

"Sometime Monday I think," I responded as I followed him to the door. "Tre you don't have to go. You know you're more than welcome to stay the night. I'd hate for you to be driving tired and intoxicated on my watch," as I reached out to grab his arm and pull him back.

"I don't want to overstay my welcome. I'll be okay," he responded as he turned and smiled at me.

"There's plenty of room, and there are some extra blankets and pillows in the closet. What do you say?" as I continued to hold onto his arm, gently pulling him back.

"If you're sure it's no bother, I am a little twisted," he smiled.

"You know it's not, and I wouldn't have offered if it was," I poked at him. I glanced over at Cyn who was already half asleep and laughed as I asked as if there was any question as to what the answer would be, "So I guess that means you'll be staying too?"

She had figured out that the ottoman was a bed and had pulled it apart and stretched out to get a little more comfortable... "Oh, you know I'm staying. I wasn't even gonna ask," she responded matter-of-factly.

"You are a trip. You know that, right?" I laughed.

"Do you mind getting me one of those pillows and a blanket too? I mean, since you're going that way anyway..." she said with a silly grin on her face as she peeked over the edge of the couch.

In my best old English accent, "Noooo, it's not a problem at all Madame, would there be anything else I can get for you before I retire?" I asked as I curtsied and walked backward bowing as I left the room. The entire room erupted in laughter. I retrieved the blankets and pillows and distributed them throughout the room. They both immediately covered up in their positions and settled in for the night. I said my goodnights and quickly closed the French doors separating the two rooms and turned the lights out.

I gave my phone the once over before I turned it off. The boys had already called once and text twice, all is well in the Lone Star State. Brian had left a message summing up the events of his meeting as well. It was too late to call any of them back now, so I guess I will be safe lying down and closing my eyes for some much-needed rest. As I lay there waiting to fall asleep, I thought back to our days at A&M once again. I'm not sure who suggested it that night, but somewhere in the conversations, homecoming came up and the fact that I hadn't been back in years. In fact, I hadn't been back to A&M since I left Texas to do my residency at Vanderbilt Hospital and then a fellowship at Johns Hopkins, over 10 years ago. Those were the days; sometimes I do miss them, I thought to myself as I drifted off to sleep.

CHAPTER 4

I was awakened to what sounded like someone knocking at the door. As I tried to get my bearings, I could smell the aroma of coffee and heard what sounded like Tre laughing, both of which were out of place for me. Especially since I don't like or buy coffee and my house is usually quiet when I get up in the mornings. The twins don't get up til after 7am, and I'm usually up by 5am. I glanced over at the clock, 12:55PM. WOW! It's a little late. I rolled over and noticed the light flashing on the suite phone. How on earth did I sleep through the phone ringing? I must have really been tired because I know I wasn't that drunk. Oh well, I guess it's past time to get up. I rolled over and sat up for a second before I dangled my legs over the side of the bed. Just as I was about to stand up, someone knocked on the French doors, it had to be Tre because Cyn would have just barged in without knocking.

"Wake up sleeping beauty. Time to rise and shine," he said as he opened the doors before I could open my mouth to invite him in.

I couldn't help but laugh, some things really don't change. "Come on in you nut!" I said as I walked over to the window to peek out.

He was halfway through the door when I noticed he was balancing a glass of OJ, a bagel, and a bowl of fruit. All while flossing that award-winning smile of his.

"I just thought you might like a bite to eat," he explained as he sat it all down on the desk, next to where I was standing.

"Thank you Sir. How are you this bright and sunny afternoon? I can't believe I slept that long," I said as I sat down to eat.

Tre walked back out to the sitting room as he answered. "I'm good. Slight headache, but I've had worse that's for sure," as he came back with his own food and plopped down on the end of the bed eating. "So I guess you haven't slept this late in years?" he said laughing as he took another bite of a huge apple.

"No I haven't. You're absolutely correct. I really must have needed the rest." In between bites, I asked, "Where's Cynthia? And who were you laughing with?"

"I was laughing at the food that just showed up at your door. And you know Cyn... she was gone when I woke up to the knocking at the door. There's a hot story out there for someone to catch. Might as well be her."

We both laughed at his statement because it was so true. I glanced over at the light that was still flashing on the phone and decided to see who had called. I held the receiver to my ear and secured it with my shoulder as I ate from the bowl of fruit Tre had brought me. I entered the room code, and that lovely computer voice informed me... *"You have one call from a phone in the lobby..."* now this should be interesting.

"Hey girlie, it's me. I'll catch up with you later. I've got a meeting this morning. I ordered up some food. Talk to you later, bye." I heard a click, and the computerized voice returned... *"You have no more messages. To erase this message press 7, to save..."* I pressed 7 and hung up.

"It was Cyn. She had a meeting this morning, and she ordered the food," I laughed as I turned my attention back to my bowl of fruit.

"That was nice of her," Tre said as he headed back out to the sitting room. He quickly reappeared with a cup of coffee and a bowl of cereal. "So what's on your agenda for today Miss Lady?" he asked, taking a seat across the desk from me this time.

"Absolutely nothing I'm very happy to say. I might go to the mall later, but that's a big maybe," I answered as I walked across the room to turn on my cell since I did tell everyone it would be on. I heard the swooshing sound, so I released the on button and waited for the AT&T logo to disappear. There are my men...the screen saver is a picture of the twins and Brian. "WOW! Now, this is a surprise," as I kept waiting for a symbol to pop up saying I had messages or texts.

"What's up sis?"

"I don't have any voice messages, and there is only one text from Brian."

"Well, that's a good thing, right?" Tre asked, still eating his cereal.

"Yes it is, I guess," I said as I opened the text... *Good Morning Love of my Life! I tried calling u but got your voicemail on the 1st ring. WOW! I'm impressed Doc! I'm on my way 2 a meeting. I'll try u later. Have a Great Day! I LUV U!*...what a sweet text.

"Well I guess that's a great message," Tre commented in between bites of his cereal.

"Why do you say that?" I asked as I floated back over to the desk chair. "Just because I'm smiling doesn't mean a thing."

"Woman, please! Even the sun just put on some shades because you are shining so bright. So that text, was that from Mr. Brian? At least I hope it was," he finished as he almost choked himself from laughing with a mouth full of cereal and milk.

"That's what you get," I said, moving back to get out of the line of fire in case he sprayed his food all over the place. "Yes, it was Brian. Tre, I never thought I'd ever love anyone as much as I LOVE this man." I couldn't help but twirl around in my chair. I stopped short of a full turn when the desk phone started ringing, startling both of us. "Hello?" I said, still smiling.

"Hey Doc! Just wanted to check in and see what you were up to. Did you get some rest?"

"Yes Cynthia, I did, and thank you for asking. I'm talk'n to Tre and eating the food you had sent up. What's all that noise in the background?"

Tre walked into the bathroom as I turned the TV on to try and catch the news.

"I'm leaving this meeting; it was at the airport of all places. They were releasing the name of the new Director of Operations. Wait a minute! I know you are not just getting up! That food ought to be bad by now. Just sad... you go out of town and lose your mind! It's lunchtime..." she rattles off before I can get a word in edgewise.

"If you'd allow me to get a word in mother... I have no place to be, thank you very much." In the background, I hear the TV announcer say, "And your weather is up next on 5 Alive News..." "And how many washes do you think...?" TV commercials...as I pushed the mute button.

"Now how can I help you, Miss Dubois?" I asked as I leaned back in my chair.

"What's on your agenda for this evening? I've been invited to a little get together around 6 this evening. Wanna go?" she asked.

"Sure I guess. What's the attire?" I ask as my cell starts playing *Sexual Healing* by Marvin Gaye. "Hold on Cyn my cell is ringing, it's Brian." I laid the phone down & pushed the chair over to the bed and grabbed my cell. "Hi Baby! I got your text. How's your day going?"

"It's already been a long day, I'm headed back to my room for a while. Not sure if it was the meeting or the food, but I'm not feeling well. My head, chest, and stomach are killing me, it's probably just gas. But it's nothing for you to worry your pretty little head about Doc."

That got me to my feet. I don't pace often, but this doesn't sound good to me. I'm basically walking in circles coming up with worse case scenarios in my head. Brian's pretty healthy, but he has lost his father and 4 brothers to heart attacks, and all 4 brothers were in their late 20s to early 30s. Brian is in his late 40s.

"Baby, what's wrong exactly?" I asked. My mind is now racing a mile a minute at all the possible causes for his symptoms. He doesn't have the most stress-free job in the world and to add this trip to D.C. on top of everything else hasn't made his stress level decrease any.

"Don't worry Doc, just a little indigestion and a headache. I got some stuff back in my room. I'll be fine. I don't want you to worry baby. Walking seems to be relieving some of the pressure," as he releases a loud, long fart.

"I heard that! You are so nasty!" I laughed at him. "I hope nobody was around you."

"Naw, I'm all alone," another loud waaaaamp! "And Doc..."

"Yes dear?" I reply, trying not to laugh.

"That's a good thing. I hate to admit it, but I stink!" Now we are both laughing uncontrollably.

"Well don't cut through any parks. You'll kill all the wildlife with that deadly gas of yours," I said, still laughing as I relaxed and flopped down across the bed.

"Is that right you? Well, I tell you what, that would be the easiest hunt I've ever been on, miss smarty pants," he responds still laughing and passing gas.

"Be careful, you might need to check your shorts if you're not careful. What on earth did you eat?"

"Now that's not funny! I don't know, but whatever it was it doesn't like me very much," he answered still passing gas.

"Oh wait a minute baby! Hold on a sec I left Cyn on the other phone, Shit!" I told him as I rolled over and picked up the hotel phone next to the bed. "Hey Cyn, you still there?" all I heard was, *"Baa! Baa! Baa! Baa!"* Oh well, she'll call back later I thought as I hung up the phone. I glanced over to the receiver still off the hook, on the desk phone. I'll hang that one up in a minute; I don't feel like getting up right now as I rolled back over onto my back.

"Hey sis, I'm gonna go," Tre says as he comes out of nowhere, scaring me to death.

"OH SHIT!" I yelled as I grabbed my chest and jumped up off the bed, dropping my cell. "Boy, you scared the shit outta me! I forgot you were still here. I know you didn't blow up my bathroom!" I said loudly, but starting to giggle as I bent over to pick up my cell off the floor. Both Brian and Tre were talking at the same time.

"Baby! Baby! Baby are you okay?! Who's there with you?!" Brian is yelling.

"I saw you on the phone, so I got my stuff together and cleaned up my mess from eating. I really didn't mean to scare you. I just wanted to tell you I'm about to go," Tre said apologetically.

Now I'm talking to both of them...

"Do you mind hanging up the phone on the desk please?" as I pointed over to the desk. Tre nods okay and heads over to put the phone back on the hook.

"Sweetie it's just Tre. I forgot he was still here, he was in the bathroom so long," I try to explain as I start laughing.

"Who's Tre and what do you mean, he's still there?" Brian asked.

"Hold your horses, Sheriff. Let me explain, but first, you have to hold on for a sec," as I pull the phone away from my ear.

Tre gives me a tight hug and says, "Bye-bye Sis. It was great seeing you, and it has been way too long," he finishes as we walk over to the door. "And you really should think about going to homecoming if you can make it next weekend," he turns to say again with that devilish smile.

I give him another hug as I say, "I will cutie. I really will think about it. Talk to you later."

"Okay, I'm gonna hold you to that. See you later," as he pulls away and then turns and walks out the door.

"Bye-bye," I say as I closed and locked the door behind him. "Okay baby. Are you still there?" I ask as I put my cell back up to my ear and walk back into the bedroom.

In his 'let me stay calm voice,' "Yes. Now who is this Tre and why is 'he' in your room?" Brian asked.

"Tre was a trainer at A&M when I was finishing my bachelors and med school. *He* is like a little brother to me. I must have fed him as much as I fed the twins back in the day. He came back to my suite, along with Cyn, after we saw Lalah Hathaway at Sambuca last night. I insisted that he stay the night because he'd been drinking and it was so late when he tried to leave. Plus he had a long drive to get back home," I began laughing at him as I finished explaining.

"Oh really? So when do I get to meet this long lost brother?" he asked still obviously agitated.

"Not sure dear. He's here at Albany State working on his Ph.D. in Kinesiology. I told him he's more than welcome to come to visit anytime he wants, so he will let us know. But he's definitely coming to the wedding for sure," I told him as I cleaned up the dishes from my late breakfast and moved the near-empty food tray closer to the door.

"What was he saying about homecoming?" Brian asked much calmer now.

"Oh, he and Cyn have some silly idea about me going to A&M's homecoming next weekend because I haven't been back to campus since I graduated from Med School," I explained as I get comfortable in front of the window, overlooking the city again.

"Baby I think that's a great idea. Why not go? You deserve a week off. The office will be fine, and I'm sure Sammy can handle covering the office for a few more days. Go! Have fun! I insist."

"Oh really? You insist, do you? What are you trying to do, get rid of me or something?" I say in a teasing manner. "I'll think about it sweetie. I'll let you know if I do decide to go," I giggle. "Well, I hope you get to feeling better soon."

"I will Doc. I already feel better from just talking to you. And let me know what you decide to do, but I think you should go. I just wish I could go with you. I miss you, and I Love you baby."

"I Love You more," I replied.

"Well, I gotta go baby. I'll call you later and please enjoy your time off," he says still passing gas.

"I will. Bye my Love," I say as we both hang up the phone. Well, now I definitely need to charge this silly phone before I get out today as I noticed the near-empty battery. I forgot to plug it up last night, but since it was off, I guess it really didn't matter. As I went to the closet to find my charger, I noticed that all of a sudden, my neck and shoulders had stiffened up on me. Even my head was beginning to hurt like a migraine was coming on, and I hadn't had a migraine in years. Actually, now that I think about it, the last migraine I had was right before I graduated from Medical School.

I definitely feel a leisurely soak coming on as I finally locate the charger in the side pocket of my suitcase. Now that I think about it a little smooth jazz and a whole lot of bubbles sound really good to me right now. I start my bathwater and add a few bath beads for good measure before I go plug in my phone. I set up my iPod and climb into my nice big Jacuzzi tub and start soaking away any stress I still have remaining in my body at this moment. I never would have believed that I was holding on to so much anxiety over a simple trip back to Texas for homecoming. I hadn't been back to A&M since I graduated from med school, but I very rarely visited Texas period, for reasons unbeknownst to anyone in my life, at this time. As stressful as the mere idea of going back was, I had no idea, that in less than 3 days, I would be reliving all of the disappointments, pain, death, and piece that my marriages brought to my life.

I turned the jets on low to help relax away the migraine that was building up in the base of my skull, but even as I tried my best to relax, it hit me how much I truly feared going back to Texas. Back to the place that held some of the best times, but even more of the worst times of my life. The very place that drove me into the line of work I'm in today. The place that makes me so good at my job and drives me to prove who the bad guy is so that he, she, or they can be punished to the fullest extent of the law. What I now do for a living, is my own private way of atoning for my own silence, when telling the truth was too deadly and concealing the truth was the only way to set me free. Before I knew it, I had dozed off.

For the second time today, I was awakened to a strange voice. This time it was housekeeping coming in to clean my room. Actually, it was a good thing she came by. I'd been in the tub for nearly 2 hours, it was almost 4 o'clock. At least now my headache and stiffness were gone. I composed myself and prepared for the evening out with Cyn.

CHAPTER 5

I'm not sure what came over me, but when I returned to work Tuesday, my heart and my mind just were not into my work. This was really unusual because I am so passionate about what I do. But for some reason, I just wasn't feeling it today. Luckily, the only interesting things going on were all of the childish jokes being told about how much trouble I was going to be in when Brian got back next Monday. As I said my goodbyes for the day, I decided to take the rest of the week off.

I hadn't been able to let the top down since I'd gotten back to Murfreesboro due to the rain and the forecast here for the rest of the week didn't give me much hope of letting it down anytime soon. As I closed the pages on my computer, I couldn't help but check the weather forecast in Texas. Just so happen the forecast was for clear skies and in the upper 70's to low 80's. Sunnier skies are what I needed, maybe I did need to go to homecoming. Seeing the old gang might just be what the doctor ordered. No pun intended.

Before I left the office, I gave Sammy, one of the doctors under me, a call to see if he minded covering the office for the rest of the week. He didn't mind, especially since he was the one on-call this week and the weekend anyway. Funny how these things work out for the best. I gave mamma M a call on my way out the door, to let her know I wouldn't be in the rest of the week and that I would be out of town for the weekend. She'd already gone for the day, like most of the office staff. I was always one of the last to leave the office, especially when the boys were out of town. With them gone, I really didn't have any reason to rush home.

"Well when are you leaving and where are you going?" she asked.

"I'm going to Texas for homecoming at A&M. I'm not quite sure when I'm going to leave yet. Cyn and Tre are going too, but I don't know if they are driving or flying. I'm going to check in with them first before I make my final decision," I replied.

"Well, I hope you're not going to drive. You really don't need to be going that far all alone. And I know who Cyn is but who is Tre?"

"It's not that far, and I've made that drive more than once. It'll be fine. Tre was an athletic trainer at A&M when I was working there. And I'm going to call them next to see what their plans are for getting there," I explained as I pulled onto my street.

"Well, okay then sweetie. I'll let you go then, I know you have a lot to do. I won't keep you, but I really think you should fly. I don't want to sound like a broken record, but that would be so much safer."

"I'll figure it out soon, but I promise that I will let you know before I leave."

"I know you will do what's best. I'll talk to you later baby," she said.

Bye-bye, love you," I answered. As always she thinks and worries like a parent. I wonder if I'll ever be grown-up enough that she won't. Probably not... I pulled into the garage and collected my things. I dropped everything on the kitchen counter and made my way upstairs to get comfortable before I started my activities for the evening. As I made my way back downstairs, I began thinking about who I should call first? I glanced over at the clock and knew that Cyn hasn't made it home from work yet, so I guess Mr. Rambler is the winner, as I flip through the address book on my cell looking for Tre's number.

A man with a deep sexy voice answered, "Hello...?"

"Hello. May I speak to Tre please?" I asked, looking at my phone to check the number.

"Sure, one minute please," I hear him lay the phone down, but his voice is still clear, deep, and smooth as he calls out for Tre. "Yo man, telephone!"

A few seconds later, "Hello? This is Tre," he answers as there's a click on the line.

"Hey cutie! It's D.J. Were you busy?" I asked as I moved around the kitchen, fixing my dinner.

"No, not at all. What are you up too?" he asked.

"Just checking to see when you were headed out to Texas and how you were going?"

"I'm driving. I can't leave until Thursday morning though. I have a late class tomorrow and an even later client that I can't cancel on, so I plan on leaving early Thursday morning. Why? What's up? Are you thinking about going?" You could hear the anticipation in his voice.

"Yeah, I was thinking about it. Just trying to decide how I'm gonna get there if I go," as I put the finishing touches on what I must say is a beautiful seafood salad. A glass of Verdi and I'm all set. I didn't realize how hungry I was. I didn't really eat lunch, and I had a very light breakfast after my morning workout.

"Well I considered flying, but then I'd have to either bum a ride everywhere or rent a car. And since I don't wanna depend on anyone else or be cramped in some sub-compact that will cost an arm and a leg, I'm driving my truck," he said and then started laughing.

"I thought about that too, and a ticket at this late date is probably gonna be unreal. I guess I'll be driving too. How about a caravan?" I asked in between bites.

"Sounds like a plan. I'll call you when I leave here," he said.

"Cool. Do you know how Cyn is going?" I asked as I sipped on my glass of Verdi.

"She's driving too, I think... but don't quote me on that. I called her, but she hasn't called me back yet. I was gonna call her again tomorrow," he replied.

"Don't worry about it, I'll give her a call. Well, you have a good night, and I'll see you on Thursday, Sir."

"That's what's up. Talk to you later Doc," he finished. And then he was gone.

I guess I'll call her after I finish my dinner. Knowing Cyn, she's not home from work yet anyway, and I'm starving. I usually don't call people after 10pm, but you can't catch her until the news is off and since she's an hour ahead of me, it will be close to midnight before I can catch her at home. Anyway, this isn't important enough to bother her at work, or I'd just call her on her cell now. Oh well, that just gives me time to finish my dinner, start packing and let Brian know I'll be going after all.

After I had the kitchen cleaned up from my meal, I made my way upstairs to finish unpacking from my Atlanta trip so that I could start packing for my Texas trip. I started a load of clothes then gave Brian a call. As I figured Brian was happy to know I was going and wished me well. His only regret is that he wasn't able to join me. He loves his job, but he hates the politics that it involves. I'd attempted to start packing while we talked, but I couldn't focus in on what I might need in Texas, listening to him fuss about the 'bureaucratic idiots' as he called them, that he was dealing with in D.C.

I can't decide what to take and what to leave behind anyway. This is the worst part of last-minute personal trips for me; even if it is somewhere I know well...what do I take? I know my brothers will want to go out to dinner or the club. My father and step-mother will expect all of us to get together at least one evening for a family dinner. Especially since I have no plans on coming back that way anytime soon or for the holidays, which I know they will give me flack about the entire weekend. This is too mind-boggling right now. Packing will just have to wait until tomorrow. I collapse on the bed until Brian and I got off the phone.

As much as I would have loved to stay in my bed the rest of the evening, I have to get up and moving because I have so many things I've got to get done before Thursday. I guess I need to book a room too; I have no patience for my family 24 hours a day. I finally roll out of bed and make my way back downstairs to the kitchen, while I scanned the internet on my phone for a room. I can't believe there's not a decent room within 80 miles of College Station, at least not one that I'm willing to pay that much for or lower my standards enough that much for. Well, I guess I need to go to plan B. I hate begging people at this late date for a favor, but I have no choice, as I flop down in my favorite chaise lounge on my balcony with another glass of Verdi.

As I sip on my glass and soak up the evening calm, I know there's only one person I'd call at this late date to crash at their house this late in the game. She's more like a sister than just a girlfriend, which anyone paying attention would know. Especially since I can dial her number from memory, I barely have my home number memorized.

"Hello?" It's obvious she just answered the phone without checking the caller ID, by the questioning sound of her voice.

"Hi Pammy. How are you doing?" I asked without saying exactly who it is on the line.

"Hey there Doc! I'm good. What are you up to?" she happily asked after recognizing my voice.

"Not much, just trying to be nosey and a bum at the same time," I giggled. "What are your plans for this weekend Madame?"

"Nothing special really. I haven't decided exactly what I'm going to do for the game. Why what's up? Are you coming in for homecoming or something?" You could hear the growing excitement in her voice.

"Well actually, I am trying to come down for homecoming, but at this late date it's near impossible to find a room at a reasonable price, and all of my normal digs are booked solid," I explained.

"Damn a room! You know you are more than welcome to stay at my place. I know you're a big-time doctor now, but you can still slum it with the common folks on occasion," as she erupted in laughter.

"I don't want to be a bother and what slum? Your ex gave you that big beautiful house on the edge of town and the house in Austin. If that's slumming, sign me up now!" We both let out a long, heartfelt laugh.

"Gave?! Did you say 'gave'?! He owed me that, at least for all the bullshit he put me through," as her laughter turns into a much more serious tone. "I thought I told you..."

Cutting her off, "Told me what?" I asked.

"I sold the house in Austin and College Station and bought myself a wonderful little condo with a doorman and a view," you could feel how proud she was through the phone without even seeing her face.

"You did what?! No you didn't! When did this happen?"

"Last month. It was a quick decision and an even quicker sale. I don't need all that room, and the upkeep was killing me," she said, trying to explain.

"What do you mean the upkeep was killing you? They were paid for ..." she cut me off.

"Yes, but they have to be maintained. And you know I never liked to keep house. So I sold them to a sucker..."

"Wait one minute. Don't act like you didn't have people taking care of all that for you. I can't remember the last time I saw a broom in your hands," both of us had to laugh at that. As bad as her marriage was she married very well, an older man. He owned one of the largest construction companies in Texas. "Hold on, hold on, a sucker? What sucker?" I asked.

"My ex-husband of course," as she breaks out in uncontrollable laughter again. "He loved those houses. So I gave him a call and offered to sell them back to him."

"You aren't kidding?" now I'm laughing uncontrollably. "And he bought them, Both!?" I asked.

"Yes ma'am and for a pretty penny, I might add. You might just say that I'm set for life," as she starts laughing again.

"You Go Girl! That asshole can afford it. No telling how much he had hidden away from you and your lawyer before, during, and after your marriage was over."

Pam was so in love with him she signed a prenup before having a lawyer of her own look at it, which of course screwed her out of basically anything. But lucky for her, he was so in love with her that he failed to have his lawyer question her age. And since she had been lying about her age the entire time, she was too young to legally sign into any contract, so the Judge eventually threw out the prenup. But by then he'd hidden most of his assets, so she only got the 2 houses and enough alimony and child support to just keep her head above water.

I met Pam at A&M also. She was working on her master's degree in physical therapy while I was working on my MD. We both had young children so we learned to depend on each other to get through exams or when we needed a sitter so we could get in some extra studying, or even when we just needed a break. I don't know if I would have survived med school if not for her.

"Anyway, that's why I had no problem raising the price each time he sent one of his minions to try to buy them from me in secret. Can you believe he sent agents to offer me insulting amounts of money for those properties? Like I wouldn't have the sense God gave a turnip to figure out A: he was behind it and B: to go have the property appraised for myself. My Mama didn't raise no fool," she said as she held back her laughter. "So finally, I showed up on his doorstep, unannounced of course, and you know how he hates that. And I told him exactly what it would take for me to even consider selling those houses and the land."

"You are too crazy! I bet he was shocked," as I started laughing again in disbelief.

"You could've bought him for a penny. I only wish I had had a camera to record the silly expression on his face when I showed up at his house, then the even crazier look on his face when I told him how much I wanted to even consider selling. Giiiirl, I thought I was gonna have to dial 911. He was still recovering from his 3rd heart attack when I showed up and dropped that bomb on him."

Now we are both laughing hysterically. I didn't know about her, but I had tears streaming down my face. I could even picture him turning beet red and then stark white. Once we both regained our composure I said, "3rd heart attack huh. I guess even the devil don't want no parts of him cause we both know heaven ain't an option," I giggled. "Well you know I'm dying to know what you took him for, but that's not proper so I won't. But I'd love to have been there to see his pompous face."

"Girl please... I have no problem telling you, you're like a sister to me..." there was a long silent pause then she dropped the bomb on me... "150," she said giggling.

"MILLION?!!!" I said, cutting her off, as I slid off my lounger onto the floor.

"Yes million. Are you alright? It sounded like you just fell?" she starts laughing again.

"You're kidding! Stop playing! Was he smoking crack to agree to that?" The fact that my butt was hurting from my fall hadn't fully sunken in yet.

"I know! I know! It didn't hurt when I told him I was considering leveling both houses and selling the land to a developer... his major competitor of course," she started laughing again.

"Now wait... The house in Austin is the one he'd built for his parents, right?"

"Yes, about 10 years before they both passed away, so it held a lot of sentimental value for him. Hell, he campaigned like a mad man to have the

Judge in our final settlement, removed from the bench in that next election after he gave it to me. That was one of the first houses he designed and built himself, over 30 years ago."

"Well, I guess the old bastard does have a heart somewhere deep in his body," I said as I ease myself back onto my lounger and off of the floor.

"Yep! So I quit my job and bought me a penthouse overlooking Sherrill Stadium," she was so excited she just started talking a hundred miles an hour... "It's over 3500 square feet, marble and hardwood floors, 4 bedrooms, 5 1/2 bathrooms, an office/library, a fully equipped gym, and a game room. So yes, I think I can make room for you. Will Brian be joining us?"

"No, he's in DC on business. You'll have to settle for just little old me," I informed her.

"Well, where are my nephews gonna be? There is more than enough room and plenty of things for them to do here," she said.

"Oh there on their yearly pilgrimage to Texas to see their donor. I'm afraid I'm flying solo this time dear. Think you can put up with me for a couple of days on your own?" I asked teasingly.

Without any hesitation, "Well, of course, I can my dear. I hadn't quite decided what I was going to do for the game, but now that you're coming I guess I'll keep the 2 tickets I have if you want to go, they sold out months ago." Before I could answer, "And if you don't want to deal with the crowd, we can always watch from my balcony," she said so proudly.

As I sat dangling my leg over the edge of the lounger I told her, "As tempting as your balcony sounds, I was gonna make a call and try to get a sidelines pass. You remember Dan right?"

"Yes, he's the Head Trainer again. I've worked on a few of his kids over the years," she answered. Dan had stepped away for a while to work on his Ph.D., but now he's back in charge again.

"Well, I was going to give him a call. I think I may still have just a little pull around that place." I had to laugh at myself with that one.

"Well that's fine with me. 2 sideline passes on Dan then," she chimed in, in agreement.

"Great. Well then I'll see you late Thursday night then," I said.

"Will do. You wanna take my address now or later?" she asked.

"Can you send it to my cell? Then I can Google it from there if I need to, but I think I still know how to get to the stadium. It hasn't moved right?" as I started laughing.

"Now that you mention it, it is in the same place," now she's laughing too. "That won't be a problem. Well, I gotta run, so I guess I'll be seeing you on Thursday lady."

"I'll call you when I get close ma'am. Bye till later," as we both hung up the phone.

Now that lodging is taken care of I guess I'll check on Cyn. I dialed her up as I made my way into the kitchen for a snack. Nope, that silly voice mail.

"Hey girlie, it's D.J.. Well, I decided I was going to homecoming, so I wanted to know how you were going. I talked to Tre, and we're going to caravan on Thursday. Call me if you wanna join in. That's if you're driving. So call me anytime, I'm off the rest of the week. Later."

As I make my way back to my office to check out my emails, I nibbled on the bowl of mixed fruit I'd just made as I waited for the computer to boot-up. And since I really didn't feel like talking to each one of my brothers right now and having the same conversation over and over again, I decided to just text them all at the same time to let them know that I'll be in town for homecoming this weekend.

Send to: JR; LJ; MJ; PJ; dad

Message: Hi all! I'll b n town 4 A&M's homecoming this weekend. Won't get n til late thur so mayb we can get 2gthr sum X on fri. Luv Ya.

As you can see my parents were big on initials. None of us have a full name, just the initials and a period. Only in America...

WOW! As I answered the phone ringing back immediately, it was J.R. "Well that was quick," not bothering to hold back my amusement.

"Hey Sis. So are you flying in?" he asked.

"No, I'll be driving," as I scanned over my inbox.

"Well, you know y'all can stay with us if you want to. We can put all the kids down in the basement together. They'll love having access to the game room 24 hours a day," he laughed.

"It's only me, and I'm good. I'm staying with Pam in College Station," bracing for his reaction.

"Pam? The white lady you met when you went back to school? Why not stay with your family?! We'd love to have you!" he insisted.

"J.R., she has plenty of room and you and L.J. both have enough people in your houses already. And we both know there's not a snowball's chance in Hell that I would stay at your daddy's house. Besides, she's in College Station so I won't have to do so much driving and why does it matter that she's white anyway?" as my phone beeped letting me know I had received a text.

"I'm just saying. Well at least plan to have dinner with us on Friday. I'll see what L.J. and dad have planned."

"I can tell you already what they will say, but I'll let y'all work out the details and then you let me know," as I flipped through the texts, everyone had responded.

"Okay, I know you are a Super Doc, but now you're a mind reader too?" as he starts laughing.

From LJ: Glad 2 hear. Can't wait 2 c u. Call when u get 2 town no matter the time. Luv u 2.

Reply: Will do.

From dad: Can u get tickets 4 us 2? Need @ least 2... c u when u get here. Must do dinner b4 u leave.

Reply: I can't make any promises on the tickets but JR will confirm dinner & let me know when & where.

"What cat got your tongue?" he asked, laughing.

"No smart ass I'm reading your daddy and L.J.'s texts. L.J. just wants to get together, and your father wants 2 tickets to the game, of course. Some things never change," I say sarcastically.

"Well, he probably feels you can get better tickets than he can. You know the deal."

"Yes, I do unfortunately. I'm going to be on the sidelines anyway, I hope. I won't need a ticket," as I read M.J. and P.J.'s texts...

From MJ: Hay big sis. Finally going back 2 the homestead...it's about time. LOL Hope u have a great time. Wish I could join u but I have a business meetn up in Seattle I can't miss. I'll have 2 catch u on the next go around. XOXO ttyl

Reply: Ha Ha Ha...u r not fun e Sir. B safe n the land of rain & good luck on whatever u r workn on ☺. Luv u 2.

M.J. lives in Westlake, a little town just north of Fort Worth. He's an engineer for a defense contractor, so I've learned not to ask what he was working on or with whom. I'm impressed he even told me where he was going.

From PJ: Great Doc! I'm sneakn n2 town fri...guess I'll have to let the fam kno since I kno a get2gthr is now a must. Was tryn 2 just kick it with my frat bros but since ur cumn I'll make time.

Reply: Guess I should feel honored. I kno how u & frat get caught up... LOL Get with JR hes getn it all 2gethr. C u there baby bro.

P.J. is the baby of the group and the only other one of us that graduated from A&M. If I have a favorite, he's definitely it, but we have always had a special connection. It doesn't hurt that he's not only my brother; he's also my fraternity brother as well. Delta & Omega all the way, as if there were any other.

"Hell if that's the case hook yo brother up too!" as he starts laughing. "And you know if you tell him that, he will be calling you and waiting at the gate, no matter what you say," he's still laughing.

"Yeah, I know. I gotta take this call, but I'll let you know about the tickets & by the way P.J. was sneaking in town so get with him on dinner plans too. Love You."

"That punk... I'll take care of it. Be safe," he was chuckling as I clicked over.

It was Cyn, "Hey girlie, you got my message I take it?"

"Yes and no. I haven't listened to my messages yet. I saw you called, so I just called you back. So what's up?" she asked.

"Tre and I are going to caravan to Texas on Thursday, so I was checking to see how you were going?"

"Glad to hear you're going, but I'm flying out Thursday morning," she says.

"Oh okay, well Tre thought you were driving so I was just checking."

"I was, but my car doesn't need to go that far, so Troy said he'd get me a ticket. He's so sweet. I know he's the one for me," she added.

"The one you say...well okay then." I couldn't help but giggle as I took my dishes back into the kitchen. "I thought he was moving out of state and you two were gonna take a break."

"He was but not anymore, so there's no need to take a break anymore," she explained as I head back into the office with a glass of water. "So where are you staying and where are your seats?" she asked.

"I'm staying in College Station with Pam, and I'm not sure about the seats yet," as I settled in in front of my computer again.

"You know tickets are gonna be hard to come by? Even my old connections barely got me 1 ticket, and you can forget about sidelines passes."

"Oh yeah, why is that?" I asked nonchalantly as I clicked on another page?

"Well apparently they are also doing the induction to the Hall of Fame this year too, so the sideline is heavily restricted due to the volume of people that will already be down there."

"That's not good. Well worse come to worse I have a balcony overlooking the stadium with my name on it," I said, still flipping websites.

"A balcony with your name on it? Hold up...The only building high enough to see into the stadium is the Sherrill complex and do you know what it takes to get into that place?! Security is craaazy tight! You'd swear the President lived there. I know you're big time and all but who do you know in the Sherrill?" she asked sarcastically.

"Pam lives there," I said matter-of-factly.

"Wait... did you just say Pam lives in the Sherrill complex?" she asked. I could tell she was completely paying attention now.

"Yes, I did," as I started swinging around in my computer chair like a little kid because I knew this was getting ready to be a good one.

"Pam lives in the Sherrill complex... Do you know what it takes to get into that place?!!! Only the who's who can even get an application to fill out! And that still doesn't guarantee them a condo! So who did she kill to get a 'balcony' high enough to even see into the stadium?!?!" as she gasps for air.

I couldn't help but laugh at her towards the end of her tirade. "Is that all?" I asked nonchalantly.

"Just answer the question!" she snapped, obviously getting irritated now.

"Well, if you have the money, I think that trumps who you know sometimes," as I start laughing at her again.

"Money? She's a physical therapist. How much could she possibly make, $80, maybe $90 thousand a year, with overtime?" she said matter-of-factly.

"Maybe, but she retired. So her profession has nothing to do with it," I responded as I took a sip from my glass.

"Damn. I really need to roll with you. Think she'd mind if I came by after the game? I know y'all are gonna be partying this weekend," she says.

"I'll ask, but I can't make any promises. Well enjoy your flight, and I'll catch up with you later," I say quickly, trying to get off the phone.

"Okay. I'll call you on Thursday. When are you two headed that way?" she asked.

"Thursday, early afternoon," I responded.

"Well, be careful on the road, and I'll see you there, so keep your phone on D.J.," she said as if my phone would be off trying to avoid her.

"I will. Well, have a good night, and I'll talk to you later," I told her.

"Later Doc," as the phone went click.

Well, now it's time to see if I can actually get into the game as I log in to my personal email, to shoot Dan a quick message. I know he's still at work, as I glanced over at the clock, 10:45PM.

Send: D.Dodson@sptmedA&M.edu
From: DocDJ14@gmail.com
Subject: Lost child coming home...

Message: Close your mouth. Yes, I'm coming in for homecoming... no joke. Any chance your wayward child could score a couple of tickets and/or join you on the sidelines? Sidelines preferred...

I will get to town late Thursday night. I figured you were busy, that's why I didn't call you. Call me if you want, I'll be up late. Talk to you soon.

D.J.

Click, click...
Message sent....

As I scan the rest of my emails, there are no real messages I need to worry about right now. And since there's no one else that I really need to tell I'm coming to town, I clicked on my media player and select random play to listen to some music as I surf the web. Oh damn, I forgot to put those clothes in the dryer. I make my way to the laundry room and put some clothes in the dryer and lay others out flat to air dry. I went on back to my office and rocked back in my chair, closing my eyes and enjoyed the stillness of my house. I started giggling at the thought of what the rumor mill will come up with when the word gets out that I'm coming to town.

Baaring... letting me know I have an instant message on my computer. I lean forward wondering who'd be IMing me at this late hour, glancing over at the clock again. It's well after midnight now.

From DanD: Will Miracles never cease??? My lost foal is returning to the fold. Before I could answer. Baaring...2 what do we owe this honor???

From me: Need a vacation... -- send

Baaring...NO ticket available 4 U...

From me: That's okay....can I come by 4 a visit Friday? – send

I jump as the phone started ringing. "Now who would be calling me at this time?" as I followed the sound to find my cell. Here it is still in the kitchen. Not recognizing the number although it is a Texas area code.

"Hello?" I asked, trying not to sound annoyed.

"No, I don't have a ticket for someone who falls out of sight and never comes to visit me anymore. Why would I? Especially at this late date..."

"Hi Dan!" recognizing his voice immediately, even if it has been forever since we've actually talked. "It's great to hear your voice! Texting and email have really changed the way we all keep in touch. It really is sad," as we both share a light laugh.

"Of course I can get you a pass. I can't believe you asked me that. And if you don't come by before Saturday, I'll have you banned from College Station...FOR LIFE!" he explains as he starts laughing again. "Do you need 1 or 2 passes?" he asked. He knows me so well, I rarely travel alone.

"2 would be great. You remember Pam don't you? She was in the PT program, she'll be coming with me if that's okay?" I asked sheepishly.

"Sure I do. She takes really good care of my kids who require more extensive rehab than I can supervise here, free of charge I might add. But she already has primo tickets. I know I saw her name on the list."

"Yeah, but being on the sidelines is a whole other thrill," as I began laughing again. "Besides, it'll be nice to get a little hands-on care with living patients. By the time these get to me, the world has probably chewed them up and spit'em out," I said, bringing me down a little.

"I understand. It would be an honor to have you back by my side. We'll have to do lunch on Friday. Come by around 10:30 if you can. And Pam's welcome to come too if she'd like," he insisted.

"Will do. I'll check with her, but I will definitely see you for lunch," my cheeks were starting to hurt from grinning so much again.

"And I still have 4 tickets if you need them," he offered.

"You are the man! That would be great Dan! My dad and brothers would love to come. You know how that is..." I giggled.

"Well, then it's a date. You take care, and I'll see you Friday," he agreed.

"Okay Dan, I can't wait. And tell Jen I said Hi," I said. Wrapping it up, "Bye then."

"Will do. See you soon. Bye."

Still grinning from ear to ear as I hung up, I couldn't help but laugh. *'How about that...? Cynthia doesn't know as much as she thinks she does. Or maybe my contacts have just a little more pull than hers.'* I couldn't help but giggle as I sent Pam a text.

Send to: Pam

Message: Got the sidelines passes if you'd like 2 join me. Dan also invited you to lunch Fri @ 10:30. Don't get caught scalping your tickets. LOL! Ttyl – send

I get cozy under my favorite blanket and chair up in my room, as I scanned the preview guide. Cool, a M*A*S*H marathon. It doesn't get any better than this. Before I forget, I guess I'll send my brothers a text.

Send to: JR; LJ; PJ
Message: Scored 4 tickets in choice seats if u want 2 go 2 game. Let me no b4 I tell yo dad. LOL Might hangout @ Pams after... Very Nice Digs... let me kno ASAP 😊 - send

WOW, they must not be working tomorrow. That was quick, as messages started popping up.

From LJ: Thanks! But cant, have peeps coming over. Will c u fri. Luv Ya! Reply: K

From JR: Good looking out! Me & the kidz will b there.

Reply: K. Tell yo dad I have 1 ticket if he wants...

From JR: LOL!! U kno he'll want 2

Reply: 1's all I got left if u & both your kidz r going...he can take it or leave it. 😊

From JR: Thaaanks...I'll tell him n AM. LMBO Ttyl

Reply: K. LOL!

From PJ: Thanks but the bros have me covered... always the big sis lookn out.

Reply: I figured as much but just wanted 2 b sure. U kno me. LOL

Since I have no other pressing business to handle, I guess I can relax with the TV. Well M*A*S*H it's just you and me tonight, as I click on the TV Land marathon. As I settled in, it hit me... I've never noticed how quiet the house is without the twins. I really do miss them when they're not here.

CHAPTER 6

I can't believe how quickly I got the car packed this morning, but I guess it wouldn't take long since I consolidated everything into 1 large suitcase instead of 3 small bags and an overnight suitcase. It's still hard for me to pack for personal trips, I don't know why. If it were a business trip, I wouldn't have any problem. So sad I know. Now all I have to do is wait on Tre to get here. I guess I have time for a quick brunch before we get on the road. I just need to check in with Mrs. Melody. Maybe she can sneak out early and grab a bite with me too.

"Medical Examiner's Office. How may I direct your call?" Mrs. Melody answered as always.

"Hi Mrs. Melody. It's D.J. just checking in," as I sit bored, draw imaginary circles on the countertop. I'm not used to not being drowned in some type of work. This much idle time on my hands was killing me. I don't know what to do with myself. It's only 9:30AM, and I'm ready to lose my mind. I'm usually up and in the office by 8AM at the latest.

"Hello baby. You about to get on the road?" she asked.

"No ma'am. I'm waiting for a friend to get here from Georgia. We're caravanning to Texas later today," I explained.

"Well, that's a relief. The thought of you out there in that little car of yours, by yourself, for so long worried me," she says in her mama voice.

"I know. But I was calling to see if you might like to grab a bite to eat with me before I leave?" as I rolled my eyes. She worries too much.

"It's slow around here, so I don't see why not. What time and where did you have in mind?"

"How about the Country Club Café, in 30 minutes?" as I picked up a pen and started drawing real circles on the note pad by the phone.

"That sounds like a winner to me sweetie. I will see you there."

"Ok. I'll see you soon," as I hung the phone up. As I made my way to the garage, I noticed how brightly the sun was shining through the clouds. It seems like it's been raining since I returned from Atlanta. This may give me a chance to drop my top before I get on the highway this afternoon.

I had to snap myself out of the daze I was in as I sat inside my baby listening to her purr. I let the top down and slowly backed out of the garage for what I knew would be a delightful brunch. Brunch with Mrs. Melody was always eventful, one way or the other. I hit the garage door opener and slowly backed down the drive as I watched to make sure the garage door closed completely before I drove away. Lately, the silly door has been jamming halfway down & going back up. Brian was supposed to fix it before he left, but of course, he was busy with work and time got away from him, so it will have to wait until he returns next week. He'd have a cow if I called a repairman out to fix it.

It didn't take long for me to reach the Country Club. As beautiful as the day was, I wish it had taken me a tad bit longer. As I pulled into the valet area, I recognized a very familiar car directly in front of me... Mrs. Melody, I smiled. Just as we were about to say our hellos, my phone rang, 10:00 on the dot.

"Hi Tre. How's it going out there?" I inquired as I let the top up on my Precious.

"I'm good, I'm pulling into Atlanta now. I should get to you in about 2 1/2 hours."

"Only 2 1/2? That means you are going to be flying. Well, be careful, and I will see you when you get here."

"Cool. See you soon. Bye for now," as he hung up the phone.

"Well, I see you finally got to let the top down on that pretty car of yours," she said with the biggest smile you've ever seen. Like I didn't know what that was all about. Still with the jokes I see.

"Yes ma'am. I guess the heavens are smiling down on me this morning," as I finish locking the roof down in its proper place, so the valet wouldn't do it and possibly harm my baby.

As we locked our arms and walked each other into the café, it was interesting to see the lack of interest others had in us entering together. Or better yet me entering at all. A year ago every head in the place would have watched me come in, with open mouths. Sad to say even in this day, separation of the races is still a thing.

Me and mama M settled into a shaded area out on the veranda and ordered our drinks. As always she ordered a sweet tea and I ordered water, no ice as usual. As expected brunch with Mrs. Melody was a treat. We ordered our food and sat back enjoying each other's company. It's funny how much spending time with her, makes me miss being able to just sit back and relax with my own mom so.

I took my time getting back home so I could enjoy the clear sky and the warmth of the sun on my face. To be the middle of October, it was just warm enough that I could truly enjoy riding around with my top down. I pulled into the gas station to fill up, one last thing I had to do so not to hold us up when Tre got here. Next, I stopped by the Starbucks next door even though I don't drink coffee, and even if I did, I wouldn't spend $5.00 for a cup to save my life. I did, however, order a Tazo tea with a touch of honey. Although Passion is my favorite, I decided to go with something lighter this afternoon, a Green tea will have to do. Wasting time isn't as easy as it seems when you're used to going 90 to nothing all day long.

As I slowly made my way back home, I decided to stop and give my baby a bath. Actually, I stopped at the Benz dealership and asked for a detail, which they did without hesitation. In fact, they checked all my fluids and tire pressure since I mentioned that I would be taking a road trip. Full service is a beautiful thing; hopefully, it's just as good when the warranty expires. Just as I got back in my car, my phone started ringing again. This time I was able to answer it on my Bluetooth.

"Hello?" I asked as I pulled out of the dealership parking lot on to Murfreesboro Road.

"Hi D.J. It's Cyn. Have you talked to Tre today? I can't seem to catch up with him."

"I talked to him about an hour ago. Why what's up?" I asked her.

"I was hoping I could catch him before he got past Atlanta. Troy got me a family pass ticket instead of a regular ticket," she said.

"Okaaay and that means what exactly?" I asked.

"That means I'm flying standby, so I only get a seat if someone doesn't show up if the flight is full. I've been at this airport since 6 this morning, and all the flights into Houston are overbooked. Can you believe that? Of all the weekends for this to happen. And to buy a 'real' ticket for today is well out of my price range. It's just not going to happen," she went on. You could hear the distress in her voice.

"Well, I'm sure sorry to hear that. What are you going to do?" I asked as I pulled into my driveway.

"Well since I can't find him, do you think y'all could wait for me there, and then I can ride with one of you?" she asked.

I didn't answer immediately… "Well, I guess that won't be a problem. But I thought you said your car wasn't roadworthy. Is it safe to drive it this far?" I couldn't help but ask.

"It won't be a problem. I will be on my way as soon as I can get home to get my car. Thank you so much D.J. you are a lifesaver."

"Okay. Just be careful, alright," I added.

"I will. And thank you again," she answers, sounding much happier.

"See you soon then. Bye." I can't believe this is happening as I hang up the phone. I just sat in my car on the driveway listening to my baby purr and soaking up the little bit of sun that's still peeping through the clouds. The silence was broken by a loud clap of thunder. That instantly snapped me out of my daze and got me too moving. I closed and secured the top and pulled into the garage. I'm just hoping that it doesn't rain all the way into College Station as I go in the house and lay down for what I know will only be a cat nap.

I was awakened to the nonstop ring of my cell phone and the doorbell. As I gathered my bearings, I glanced over and saw it was a few minutes after 12, which quickly woke me up. I called out as I scooped up my cell and headed down the stairs to answer the door.

"I'm coming! I'm coming!" I shouted as I made my way to the front door. My cell startled me as it began ringing again.

"Hello?" I asked, still waking up.

"Yo Doc, what's the deal? You sleep'n on me huh?" Tre asked, trying not to laugh. And guess who was standing at the door when I opened it up. None other than A.C. himself. His parents did the initial thing too, but he is A.C. the III, which is why everyone calls him Tre. "So it looks like someone fell asleep," he grabbed me cracking up. "You ready to ride out? Let's get on the road Doc."

"I'm packed and ready but there's a slight snag in our plans," I began, as I invited him in.

"What kind of snag?" as he pushed past me. "And where's your bathroom? I'm about to bust."

"First door on your right," I directed him as I closed the door and followed him down the hallway. "So I got a call from Cyn like an hour after you called. She was try'n to catch you before you passed through Atlanta, to see if she could catch a ride with you. Her plane ticket kind of fell through," I explained as I went back to the kitchen while he handled his business.

"So what's the snag?" He asked from the bathroom.

"I told her I'd wait for her while she drove up," I explained as the water came on in the bathroom.

"Well how long will it be before she gets here?" he asked, coming into the kitchen.

"I don't know? But she should be here soon, I can call her and see exactly where she is," I said as I thumbed through my cell.

"Hello?" she answered on the first ring.

"Hey Lady, where you at?" I asked. "Tre's already here."

"I'm just leaving Chattanooga," she began.

I put the phone on mute, "She's just leaving Chattanooga," I told Tre. I unmated and put the phone on speaker.

"Troy couldn't come pick me up from the airport, so I had to take MARTA back to my apartment. MARTA! I'm trying to get there as fast as I can," she continued.

"Hi Cyn, its Tre. Sorry I missed your call, or I would have come and got you. But I have to get back on the road now. It's my parents' anniversary, so I was sneaking in to surprise them at their anniversary dinner tonight. I'm already running late," he explained.

"I'm so sorry Tre. I didn't mean to hold you up." Cyn said before I could say a thing.

"Tre don't worry about it. I'll wait for her, and you go on. I hope you make it there before it's over. Just be careful. And watch out for the police on the other side of Nashville. They get really bad just outside of the Ville and then again about 20 miles outside Memphis," I explained.

"I wish I could wait for you, but I really want to try to get there if I can," he explained again.

"Cyn come on to my house. I'm waiting for you. Just be careful," I told her.

"Okay, I'll hurry. Be careful out there Tre," she said again.

"Just be careful Cyn. I'm not going anywhere until you get here, Okay." I told her as I walked Tre out to his truck.

"I'll be there soon. And thank you again D.J.," she said as she hung up the phone.

We hugged again, and then Tre climbed up in his truck and closed the door. He let the window down after he started up the engine. "I'm sorry Doc, but I really can't afford to get any further behind. I already need to shave at least an hour from my drive," he explained even further.

"Tre. Don't worry about it. I completely understand. You just be careful and call me if you need to. We will be about an hour behind you so just be careful and don't get too crazy out there," I said as I patted him on his arm. I waved at him as he backed out of the driveway and drove away. I went back inside the house and waited for Cyn.

A little over an hour later, I heard a car pull up in the driveway. I glanced out of my office window to see Cyn getting out of her car. I shut everything down and went down to meet her and have her move her car to the other side of the driveway. Of course she'd pulled up on the side my car is parked in the garage. I met her as she reached my side door. "Hey Cyn, glad you made it here safely. And in record time I might add," I smiled as I gave her a hug.

"I was trying to get here as quickly as possible. I knew I'd inconvenienced you and Tre. I'm sorry again," she apologized.

"Again, don't worry about it. Do you need to go to the bathroom before we go? If not, I just need you to move your car to the other side of the driveway, and we can get on the road," I explained as I got my things together.

"I could stand to use the bathroom. Isn't it down this hall on the right?" she asked as she made her way down the hall towards the bathroom.

"Yes ma'am it is," I laughed as I checked the front door, to make sure it was locked. I quietly, sat in the kitchen waiting for her until she came out of the bathroom.

"So you ready to get on the road Doc?" Cyn asked as she came into the kitchen and struck a pose.

"Just waiting on you ma'am," I answered. I followed her out of the side door, locking it behind us after I set the alarm. She moved her car to the other side of the driveway, and when she had cleared out of the way, I back my Precious out. You know I haven't named my baby yet, so maybe that's gonna be her name...'Precious.'

Cyn loaded up her bags and some CDs, and we were off. It was 12:55 and we had at least 12 ½ hours ahead of us. It was time to make some time. You would think that I would know better than to speed after all the fatal accidents I've had to work, but I still tend to be a speed demon on the open road. All I really wanted to do is get there as quickly and as safely as possible.

Since I would be doing all of the driving, Cyn's only job was to keep the music flowing, but she also ended up navigating the conversation too. Of course she offered to help me drive, but there is no way she or anybody else is driving my Precious around unless I'm completely out of my mind and half-dead on top of that. That may sound crazy to you, but this was my brand new, only driven by the guy who took it off the truck, the valets, and me, dream car. I was already prepared to fend off my brothers. In fact, I hadn't decided yet if I was going to even allow them to test ride in it around the block, which I knew would be the argument of the weekend because they will insist on driving it. So there wasn't much else that could possibly go wrong? I was doing the driving and Cyn was to take care of the music and occasional conversation. Sounds like a win, win to me. I could sit back and let the music and scenic background sooth out all my anxiety as the landscape passed us by. Isn't it funny how the best laid out plans always seem to hit a snag?

Those were my plans for this trip at least. It never occurred to me that

Cyn would inadvertently change those plans by getting me to relive some of the most painful moments of my life as we headed back to the place that I dreaded most in the world... Navigate the music was all she really had to do, I never even saw it coming.

CHAPTER 7

We were driving along making really good time I have to admit, but Cyn was really starting to get on my nerves. Why is it when you're trying to relax and enjoy the scenery of the open road, someone else wants to hold a never-ending conversation? It's not like I had planned to take this trip, but since I agreed to go what could possibly go wrong with some company and a little small talk? Besides, maybe the conversation would make the next 9 hours on the highway go by even faster. At least that's what I told myself 3 hours ago.

Cyn had no problem manipulating the conversation, and I allowed her to. All I had to do is drive and listen to her ramble on about who was coming to homecoming and how surprised everyone would be to see me. I hadn't been back to A&M since I left 10 years ago. Boy how time flies when you're trying to forget your past.

Somewhere past Memphis we lost any decent radio stations, so I actually had to participate in the conversation. Cynthia was going on about her boyfriend and how she just knew he was the one she was supposed to marry, but sometimes he didn't seem very interested in marriage. They also had some significant differences about how to clean a house, and their bathroom habits were always a point of conflict. As content as I was to just listen, I knew deep down that eventually she would ask me what I thought.

I did everything I could think of to steer the conversation back to her and away from me when it seemed my opinion was being sought out more than before. As long as I kept her focused on her issues and what she wanted from a marriage, I was able to keep the conversation off me and on her. Some things are better left in the past, and my marriages were definitely one of those things. I had become an expert over the years at giving very short, sterile answers when the subject of my marriages came up. So I kept it very light and off me until we passed through Little Rock. Then somewhere along I-30 W, all my old secrets just started streaming out. As much as I never really discussed my past, somewhere in our conversation, I decided that maybe my story would give her some type of clarity with her own relationship. The questions and answering, the back and forth, had pretty much worked my last nerve. Then out of nowhere, Cyn asked the one question that started it all...

"I know you were married, and you ended up divorced, but wasn't it great in the beginning? Wouldn't you do it again if you could avoid whatever happened to split you up before?"

Before I realized it, I blurted out, "Hell No! And no one could ever pay me enough to ever do that shit again with him!" I don't know who was more stunned at my reaction, her or me.

After that unexpected outburst, we rode in silence for several miles before anything else was said, by either of us. I decided I was going to have to say something to her first or nothing else would be said for the rest of our trip. I just had to figure out exactly what to say and how to say it without further hurting her feelings.

"I'm sorry I didn't mean to snap at you. You just caught me off guard with that question," I explained as I quickly glanced over at her with a wimpy grin.

"I didn't mean to pry. I was just trying to get the opinion of someone who has been married before. I'm sorry if I upset you," she said. Constantly staring out the window but never looking over at me.

I've hurt her feelings, and I never intended to do that. "I know we've never really talked about my ex or my marriages, have we? It's not something that I choose to think about, let alone talk about," I explain as I glance over at her again, still unable to make eye contact. I guess she didn't know what to say to me at this point, so we just rode along in silence for a couple of miles before she decided to start up another conversation. Or maybe she was just sitting there coming up with a strategy to get me to talking about my marriage again, I don't know. I spent the quiet time deliberating on what to say to her next too.

"So...was being married really that bad?" she finally asked.

"I can't speak for other people, but for me yes and no. One of them never should have happened," I explained.

"Why? Didn't you love him? Or did he not really love you...you were pregnant, right?" she asked quickly. Obviously getting more comfortable with her question selection and rattling them off faster than I could answer. I could feel her staring at me now.

"Yes and no, no, and yes," I said. I had to laugh as I glanced over, finally making eye contact.

"What?" she said obviously lost.

"See we had a shotgun wedding, but not like most people think of a shotgun wedding," I started.

"Why is that because you were pregnant?" she asked before I could really get into my explanation.

"Nope, the twins were already here. The gun was at my back, not his. There was no way the only living daughter of Lisa and James Morgan was going to be an unwed mother, so I was forced to get married again."

"Wait, wait, wait! You were the one forced to get married, not him?" she asked, obviously confused.

"You got it! In fact, he had asked me to marry him twice before I ever got pregnant and I'd told him no both times...go figure," I responded.

"WOW! That is different. So you *didn't* love him?" she asked.

"Not exactly. He was actually my best friend for a while, and I loved him very much. We always had a lot of fun together, and the sex wasn't bad either, in the beginning. Then things changed, he changed. And then I fell *in* love."

"Okay, you've lost me again," she admitted with a puzzled look on her face.

"See the problem was that I 'Loved' him but I wasn't 'In Love' with him. And then by accident I met and fell 'In Love' with someone else," I tried to explain.

"What?!" she gasped. "Someone else....I'm completely lost now, but I get loving someone but not being in love. But in time don't you think maybe you could have fallen in love with him. You know God doesn't make any mistakes," she said proudly.

"God doesn't, but we do. I wholeheartedly believe God didn't put my marriage together. In fact, God did all He could to keep me from marrying Selk. I just wouldn't listen because I didn't want to disappoint my parents any more than I already felt I had."

"You're kidding?" she said obviously astonished at what I'd just told her.

"No ma'am. I wouldn't joke about something as serious as this," I explained.

"That's hard to believe D.J.. I mean, you are such a spiritual person. How can you sit here and say God didn't have a hand in your marriage?"

"I never said God didn't have a hand in my marriage. If it weren't for God covering me while I was married to Selk, I wouldn't be sitting here next to you now. Truthfully, if it wasn't for God, I never would have lived through my marriage," I explained.

"And what is that supposed to mean?" You could tell her wheels were spinning in every direction now.

Still trying to be somewhat vague, I added, "Sometimes things aren't always what they seem, and people aren't always who they appear to be.

And just because you live with someone for a while before you get married, things still seem to change once you decide to get married, is all I'm trying to say."

"I don't want to just live with him...I want to marry him. I know God has chosen this man to be my husband, and I'm ready to be married," Cyn starts again.

"That's all well and good, but is *he* ready to be married? Is *he* ready to be *your* husband? Even more important, does he want *you* to be his wife?" I asked her.

She took a moment to answer, then said, "I feel he will be a great husband and father one day. And why wouldn't he want me to be his wife? I mean I'm perfect for him, God selected me," she said it so matter-of-factly.

I was shocked at her naivety. I wanted to ask her, *'Are you fucking kidding me?'* But I knew better than to go there. I glanced over at her, still trying to figure out what to say to her, so as not to hurt her feelings. To be such a great reporter, I have to wonder how she could be so blind when it comes to love and affairs of the heart. How do I just come out and say to her, *'Now look Cyn, this man is just not feeling you the same way you are feeling him.'* As I kept one eye on the road and the other on her I finally came up with, "Have you two ever really had a serious conversation about your individual wants, needs, and expectations of what marriage is, or what you feel you desire in a mate?"

"Of course we have. It's just he doesn't go into depth about his needs. He just glances over things and expects me to figure out exactly what he means. Then on the rare occasion that we are out together, he doesn't always act like he's happy with me or happy to be seen with me," she explained.

"Wait a minute....he's fine behind closed doors, but he's angry or distant when you're out in public together? And by your own account, you two very rarely go out with each other. Does he go out a lot with other people?" I asked, still not believing what I was hearing.

"He's a musician...he's always out with other people, but he mainly goes out with his boys," she frowned. "My issue is that he very rarely invites me along. Granted I'm usually working late or on the weekend when he typically goes out. But if I show up where I know he'll be, he just seems distant sometimes. That is until we get back to my place, then he's the loving, touchy person I love him to be," she actually said that with a smile.

I'm floored by what I'm hearing. Someone as intelligent as she is can't really be sitting here telling me this with a straight face. She can't be that lost. OMG! She really is a sex toy and nothing else. This man obviously has no intentions of marrying her. Hell, by the sound of it he really isn't even seriously dating her. She's just a friend he likes to have sex with. Now I'm going to be the bad guy when I bring this to her attention.

"Cyn, has anyone ever told you that he isn't really that into you? I'm not trying to hurt your feelings, but as I've listened to you, he's just having a good time with you. It sounds like you are in a monogamous relationship, but he's just casually dating you. Troy is not that interested in getting married and even more specifically, getting married to you, dear." And before she could answer, I finished with, "You've spent the last 5 years of your life on this man...please wake up. If he avoids talking to you about his marriage desires, he's not opening up with you because he doesn't see you as someone he wants to marry. It doesn't take any man 5 years to figure out if you are the one for him."

And with that, she snapped... "And what makes you such an expert? You can't even have a simple conversation about your marriage or your ex-husband, without shutting down or taking people's heads off. And for you to be so spiritual... I can't believe that you feel God won't work it out in my favor," she rattles off obviously hurt and pissed off. She's obviously pouting as she turns and stares out the window. The way she flipped around and put her back to me would have been funny if this conversation wasn't so serious.

"Cyn look...I really didn't mean to hurt your feelings. But from all you've told me and what I've seen of the two of you together, I can honestly say from the bottom of my heart, we sometimes put things on God that He hasn't done. I can't imagine God blessing you with a husband who only wanted to be kind to you when you are behind closed doors. This basically means he's buttering you up to have sex with you, no more, no less. When God blesses you with a husband, a true mate, you will be loved in every area of your lives together. Now don't get me wrong, you will have your good days and your bad days as a couple, but you won't feel like the only time your man wants to be with you is when he wants to have sex or needs a hostess for one of his events. Sweetie, I learned this the hard way. And if you get *you*, into a marriage that isn't very loving or peaceful, it may just take 'God' to get you out of it. And believe me when I say to you, regaining that peace may just be deadlier than you ever expected, that I've already proven. So yes Cyn, I do consider myself an expert when it comes to relationships after what I went through with so much death trying to regain my life and some semblance of peace. Peace is deadlier than you know and sometimes peace of mind and heart can be a deadlier journey than you expect when you marry the wrong person," I explained as calmly and plainly as I possibly could. I could feel the anger in me bubbling up again, so I kept my eyes on the road and meditated until I felt myself start to relax. After a few minutes of self-meditation, I was finally able to glance over at her and was surprised to see her sitting there with her mouth wide open, staring at me.

"What cat got your tongue? You should be happy that I don't have the top down or you would have a mouth full of bugs right now," I said, trying to lighten up the conversation a little.

"Uhmm, what does 'deadly peace' mean? Exactly what happened to you during your marriage and why do you keep saying marriages?" she asked, finally closing her mouth.

"What happened to me? What happened to me is that I learned what it really means to have God on my side. I became the person I am today because of my marriages, the good, the bad, and the ugly. I learned how to truly stand on my own two feet and do what I feel and think is best, no matter what anyone else says because even though they may have your best interest at heart, *they* don't always know what's best for you," I explained to her. I glanced over, and she was still staring at me with a bewildered look, so I continued. "I had to learn the hard way that you can get yourself into serious trouble when you don't listen to God. I thought maybe the people I trusted most, knew what was best for me when my gut told me not to get married. I learned how games can blow up in your face. I learned that when you are completely out of control, God is still in control. That's what my marriages taught me. And I keep saying marriages because technically I've been married twice. My first was a very private affair and ended almost as quickly as it began. Technically Selk was my second husband," I finally finished hoping that this would satisfy her and it would be the end of this conversation, but deep down inside I knew better.

"Twice! You've never told me that. Who was the first, and what happened to him?" she said more excited than she probably should have, but I understood where she was coming from. "I can't believe what all you're saying right now with these 2 husbands, but I really don't get what deadly peace means. What's that all about?" Cyn replied as she adjusted around in her seat to comfortably get a better look at me.

I couldn't believe that after all of that, all she focused on was the death and peace part. That's what I get for dealing with a reporter. It's like she had taken mental notes and knew what I had and had not covered. As I drove along all I could think is, *'this is what I've tried to avoid since I left my ex-husband...a detailed conversation about my marriage history.'* I always knew that one day I would have to finally tell the story of my life before I became a successful doctor, but I just never dreamed it would happen this way. It was obvious that she wasn't going to let it go, so I took a deep breath and began narrating the events that led up to my marriages and the events that led to the fatal demise of my marriage to Selk.

"Selk and I had been going out for almost a year when he asked me to marry him the first time. Instantly I said no without even having to think about it." Before she could say anything, "And don't ask me why. That was just the first thing that popped into my head," I said, shutting her down before she could start asking questions. "Just let me tell you the story uninterrupted, please. You can ask me questions when I'm done. Okay?" as I glanced over at her. And before she could respond, I added, "And so you truly understand how we ended up together I have to give you some background info that may seem like it has nothing to do with what we're talking about, but you will completely understand when I'm done."

"Uhmmm, well okay if you insist," Cyn responded obviously not sure what else to say.

I took a deep breath, and I slowly began again to tell her my story, as I tried my best to stay calm. Now I have to be perfectly honest, the little voice in my head was screaming at me to keep my mouth shut. I was nervous as hell and kind of afraid that I would see this conversation in print one day... I am talking to a reporter.

CHAPTER 8

See Selk was my cousin Wyndale Jr's roommate at Texas A&M. We call Wyndale Jr., Dale for short. They were both on the football team and 1st string superstars, but to me, they were just cool guys to hang out with. I'd come down to see them play or just to hang out for a little while when I didn't have a lot to do myself. My mom didn't put up much of a fuss since I was a senior in high school. They were both sophomores and College Station was only about an hour away from Cypress. Besides, I was with Dale, and one or more of my girlfriends always made the drive with me, so as long as the weather wasn't bad and the streets were clear, she never put up much resistance.

Although I had fun hanging out with my cousin and his teammates, he and Selk kinda cramped my style. Everyone knew I was Dale's younger cousin, so they had no problem partying with me, but no one would cross that line and try to date me. I even had a couple of them tell me that they couldn't wait until I was on campus all the time next year after I graduated from high school. But anyone that seemed interested quickly lost interest when Dale or Selk showed up at the party. Everyone was excited about me graduating soon and expected me to attend A&M next year, especially my mother. I was her only daughter and the first to be going off to school, so keeping me close was her top priority. I think that's why she didn't mind my frequent trips down to visit A&M. That and the fact that Dale was there so there was only so much I could get into.

I received full academic scholarship offers to the 7 schools I had applied to and several others that I had never even thought about going to, so everyone was completely surprised, and not too happy, that I decided to attend Spelman College after I graduated and not A&M. Everyone but Dale that is, he had just been given a gift from God. It was one thing for his baby cousin to come down for a visit every once in a while, but it was a complete other for his baby cousin to be on *his* campus, cramping *his* style for his last 2 years in college, on a full-time basis. And if I was in school there, you could guarantee even more family visits from my parents and his. Needless to say, he was happier than me about my decision not to attend Texas A&M University.

What they weren't prepared for, especially my parents, was the fact that Spelman only offered me a partial scholarship because I applied so late in the year they'd already given away their big money. I had just turned down full rides from Texas A&M, UT (University of Texas), Baylor, Rice, Texas Tech, Texas Southern University, OU (Oklahoma University), OSU (Oklahoma State University), Tulsa University, Oral Roberts University (also in Tulsa, Oklahoma), MIT, Stanford, Tulane, Southern University, Grambling University, and an automatic appointment to West Point, just to name a few. That last one really broke my dad's heart, he was basically career military. He'd already retired from the Air Force and then snuck back in through the Army Reserves.

So off to Atlanta I went leaving everything and everyone I knew behind. I had a ball of course. I traveled up and down the east coast partying and having a good time. When I was on my campus it was to go to class and sleep, the rest of my time in Atlanta was spent on Morehouse's campus. I played cards and drank until the wee hours of the morning Monday through Thursday most weekdays and occasionally on Friday and Saturday too, as sad as that sounds. But with 4 more kids at home, my parents couldn't afford to pay my tuition and bankroll my partying, so I played cards against the men of Morehouse for money to keep my social life very social. That was the only way that I could run the streets and coastline with my roommate and all the other rich kids.

The only reason I stopped partying so much and began to settle down before my grades came out was the fact that I answered a flyer for open auditions to join the glee club. No sooner had I been invited to join the glee club, there was an announcement posted that Spelman would be conducting tryouts for their very 1st basketball team. I tried out and won the starting point guard position. So most of my partying had to be put on hold, but I still made my occasional run over to 'the house' that's what we called Morehouse for short, to make some money.

I only got to come home for Christmas, but I made the most of that time to reconnect with old friends and family. Our families always got together for dinner during the holidays, but this year Christmas dinner was at my parents' house. We were the only ones who didn't live in a black neighborhood on the black side of town. We lived in a white neighborhood across town in a much larger house than the rest of my mom's brothers and sisters that still lived in Texas.

A&M's football team was playing in the Orange Bowl, so Dale kept popping in and out of town with teammates from all over the country. When Dale finally showed up around 4 PM Christmas evening, he brought 7 huge football players with him. All but 2 of them were from out of state. As unexpected as it was that he made it, no one really complained when he showed up with 7 extra mouths to feed. That's how our family was, the more, the merrier. No one left the table hungry, and there was still enough food leftover that people took home to-go-plates.

We all sat around laughing and catching up the rest of the evening. Dale and his teammates had an 11 o'clock curfew so around a quarter to 10 they started saying their goodbyes and heading to their cars, each with a plate of food of course. Somewhere during the evening the guy from Spencer, Texas had left so there wasn't enough room in the remaining cars to get everybody back up to College Station comfortably. It was funny watching such big guys standing around 2 cars, 1 of which was a 2-seater, arguing about who was going to squeeze in where. Since I'd really had enough family time for one night, I volunteered to drive someone back to campus so they wouldn't get into trouble for missing curfew.

You guessed it, Selk ended up in the car with me, and we argued most of the way over to College Station. He complained about my driving at first, but then he started complaining about my music. He was from a tiny town called Paris, Texas and hadn't ever really left the state of Texas, except for traveling with the football team, so he just couldn't get into the music that I had come to love. Being in Atlanta and running up and down the east coast, I had fallen in love with House, Go-Go, and Reggae music. He was into Country, Rap, and Rock if you can imagine that. When we finally made it back to College Station, I was informed that he and Dale lived in an off-campus apartment and not the football dorm. I called myself dropping him off when he got a 911 page from Dale. He didn't have to twist my arm when he asked me to come in for a minute to see what was going on.

A couple minutes later Dale pulls up with some girl passed out in the backseat of his car and another one in the front seat. Selk helped get the one passed out in the apartment and then they carried her upstairs to his room just as someone knocked on the front door. Like an idiot, I answered the door, and there stood one of the coaches to check and make sure they were home. Once the coach was sure I was Dale's cousin and not some girl they were getting ready to party with, he left without checking the rest of the rooms.

Turns out the girl who was passed out was the Defensive Coordinator's daughter. Apparently, she was secretly dating one of the guys on the team and ended up drunk in the football dorm. They couldn't hide her and her friend anywhere safe in the dorm that the coaches wouldn't find them during their room checks and Dale was dropping off the guys who'd come home with him so they shoved them in his car since they knew the apartments would be the last place checked. Turns out it was a good thing I came down or else they'd all been in major trouble.

Needless to say, my Christmas vacation turned out to be almost as entertaining as my 1st semester at Spelman. Due to my party lifestyle the 1st semester, I received a letter a few days before I was to return to Atlanta that I was on academic probation and would lose my scholarship if I didn't bring my grades and GPA up to the academic minimum by the end of the next semester. My mom then put me on notice that they wouldn't be able to afford the full tuition at Spelman, so if I lost my scholarship, I would have to come back home to finish up my education. What a depressing tone to end my Christmas break on but I couldn't blame anyone but myself.

I did handle my business that semester, and by the end of the term, I'd ended up with a good friend from home that was never expected. As a matter of fact, my new friend came out to see me for a couple of days during his Spring break. It was Selk of all people...we had a good time, which was a pretty big surprise seeing as how we argued most of the time we were together back in Texas. I wasn't the least bit attracted to him, and he never let on that he was the least bit interested in me, but we became pretty good friends in those few days nevertheless.

Unfortunately, at the end of the semester, I hadn't achieved both things I had to, to return to Spelman the next year with my scholarship. My grades were back to what I'd been making in high school all A's and one B, but that wasn't enough to overcome the piss poor job I'd done the 1st semester. My overall GPA was still less than 2.5, so I lost my scholarship, which meant I would not be returning to Spelman in the fall. So when my dad and uncle showed up to pick me up, I said my goodbyes and never returned to Spelman as a student again.

I didn't know what I wanted to do with myself after that major failure, so I got a job and basically visited my friends that were somewhere in school in Texas. My parents put up with that for almost a year and then insisted that I go back to school. As an incentive to get me back in school, they offered to help me buy a car. Apparently, my colossal failure a year ago was just a fluke, and I had too much potential to just be wasting it. I'm paraphrasing of course. So what did I do next? I agreed that I was wasting my talents, and I took them up on the offer of a new car, but it wasn't what they expected in the least. I didn't go out and get just any old car now... I went out and bought a brand new candy apple red, Nissan 300ZX of course. And then I joined the Army. Hey, that move shocked the shit out of me too, especially since I'd turned down an appointment to West Point just 2 years earlier. But in my defense, it was the Army Reserves, and they would help me pay for school, and also I was going in on the buddy system, so I wasn't going in alone.

6 weeks later, I reported to Fort Jackson, South Carolina. It was like taking a step back in time. Everybody spoke to everybody else, and nothing seemed to be moving that fast. That is until I arrived at the intake center. Some people were screaming at anything that moved, and everyone else was running all over the place like their lives depended on it. Me and my buddy ended up in the same platoon, which was a definite relief. I'm not sure if this was as much as a culture shock to her as it was to me, but I have to admit that by the end of the 1st night I was seriously rethinking this choice. I don't know if you remember that movie Private Benjamin, well that was me kinda. I wasn't clumsy like her, but I was a spoiled princess of sorts. I wasn't an early riser, and there was no way I was trying to eat all the food that past by my face, especially breakfast. Luckily I was an athlete, or I would have completely fallen flat on my face.

I survived 8 weeks of basic training by the skin of my teeth and looked forward to going on to my advanced training down at Fort Sam Houston in Texas. I entered basic training thinking that after we finished there, we would go on to AIT to become medics. The joke was on me. Come to find out my buddy didn't score high enough on the science section to go to medic school and because we came in on the buddy system we had to stay together throughout our training. So I would be staying at Fort Jackson and learn to be a Computer Specialist, which was the military's way of training me to be a secretary. All I kept thinking was, *"Are you fucking kidding me! Not only did I hate computers I had to stay in South Carolina for 8 more weeks.... HELL NO!"*

My mom came up for my graduation, but right after the ceremony, we had to report to our next training post that afternoon, right across the base. Once we checked-in, the Commanding Officer gave us all 3 days of leave though. My mom checked us into a hotel and immediately took me to go get my hair done, then shopping at the mall. Funny thing is I really enjoyed it. I'd never liked to shop, and I hated getting my hair done, but I loved the time we were able to spend with each other. For the 1st time in my adult life, I was actually homesick. And that feeling only got worse as those 3 days past. In fact, my mom had to literally drag me back to post. I was more than willing to go AWOL (absent without leave). They could have locked me up for all I cared I didn't want to stay there another minute of another day, let alone 8 more weeks. Needless to say, I cried myself to sleep in my bunk that night and many nights after that.

I guess my mom saw it in my eyes when she left and could hear it in my voice when I'd call home, basically every day, how miserable I really was. So when I called her on that first Friday after she'd left, completely off the hinges because we had just been informed that the group coming down from New Jersey had been delayed so we would not be graduating on time, I'd had all I could take. That meant I would be spending my 21st birthday here, with these people, in this place. That was the straw that broke the camel's back. I'd just called to let her know on my next leave I wouldn't be coming back here, I was coming home. As always, my mom told me to pray about it, then started praying over me and pulled me back off of the ledge.

When the phone monitor informed me that my time was almost up on the phone, she dropped a little piece of news on me. A couple of people had asked about me so she gave them my address so I should be expecting letters from them any day now. Of course, she didn't tell me who, that was how she left me to focus on something other than my present situation. As cruel as that might seem, she knew exactly what she was doing and how to keep me preoccupied.

The next day I got my weekly letter from my mom keeping me abreast of what was going on at home along with a care package that I so desperately needed, but I also received a letter from my baby brother and another one from a military address in New York. I didn't recognize the sender's name, so I opened it first. I didn't know the writing, so I skipped to the end to see who this was... Oh My God, it was Fitzgerald, Fitz for short.

Fitz was a guy I went to high school with, and we graduated together. We also were born into the same church and were technically both still members of that church. We knew each other but were not that close in high school or at church. We hung out with different people, but since we were both athletes, we knew each other's closest friends. Actually, I always seemed to know where he was and what he was up to, but we never really hung out together on purpose probably. He hung out with a group of girls that I couldn't stand, and until our senior year, I basically hung out with upperclassmen.

Fitz had gone into the Coast Guard after high school, so we really lost touch after that. Apparently, when my mom got back from my graduation, he was home visiting his family, and after church, she told him what a rough time I was having getting used to the military life and being here at Fort Jackson. He asked if she thought it might help if he talked to me since he'd been through it and completely understood what I was going through. She decided that just might be what the doctor ordered, so she gave him my info.

Since we weren't really that close, it may seem silly, but just sitting there reading his letter did make me feel so much better. By the end of his letter, I was in tears, but they were happy tears. He told me to keep in touch and asked if it is okay if he called every once in a while, to check up on me. I immediately wrote him back, even before I read my mom and my brothers' letters, or before I opened my care package. After that, we wrote once or twice a week, and he usually called me on Sunday night when he knew I would be back from my weekend pass.

Believe it or not, he even called when he was out to sea or a temporary port. When he pulled into a temporary port is when I usually got a second letter in a week. That was so I'd get to see where he was from the postmark, even though he couldn't always tell me where he was or what he was doing. This didn't stop when my 8 weeks were up either. Once I got back into my routine at home, my first trip after I left Fort Jackson was up to visit him at the Coast Guard Station in Montauk, New York. Fitz and I were pretty inseparable after that.

In the meantime, I'd gone back to school, this time to Texas A&M. My job was kind enough to transfer me to College Station, so it was a win-win for me. I could afford both school and an apartment close to campus. In fact, my apartment wasn't far from the football stadium or the track. I still had plenty of friends in school, so I had the best of both worlds, a freshman with lots of upperclassmen as friends. And since I waited to go to A&M until after Dale had graduated, I didn't have him breathing down my neck all the time either. Nor were the male athletes afraid to talk to me, since my big cousin wasn't around anymore, one football player in particular. He was the writer of the second surprise letter back at AIT... Mr. Selkie Black, my cousins' old roommate.

We talked about what was going on at A&M and his decision to forgo his senior year and enter the NFL draft. Apparently, this choice was the real reason he popped up on me during Spring break at Spelman. He was in town seeing a sports agent on the down low, I was kinda his cover. He was a redshirt freshman, so he still had another year of eligibility left when he entered the draft. But because he entered the draft, he couldn't go back to A&M and play when he wasn't drafted as high up as his agent had promised him that he would be. He was the 2nd to the last person picked in the final round of the draft by the Dallas Cowboys, my favorite NFL team. Although he went so late in the draft, he actually made a name for himself during the camps and preseason and made the team.

Even though we spent time writing and talking every week, I never took him very seriously, but Fitz on the other hand, he was quickly becoming my heart. The problem with that was that I hadn't learned patience. I wanted to get married to Fitz, and he wanted to be like his Uncle Eugene. Eugene was in his mid-50's and had never been married, he was the ultimate bachelor. This was unacceptable to me. Here I am working, going to school, playing soldier one weekend out of the month, and playing wifey whenever Fitz calls or sent for me to come to stay with him on his base. What does he mean he doesn't want to get married? I'm acting like your wife, but you don't want to officially make me your wife? So, what do I decide to do in my infinite wisdom? I decide that I'm going to cut him off until he changes his mind. I'm too busy to hold a conversation for any length of time, or I just don't answer the phone at all.

Meanwhile, I'm hanging out with Selk, more and more. We're not officially dating, but when he'd send tickets to a game, at home or away, I went. He'd call the week of the game to let me know if he had tickets and I would let him know if I could go. Be it Dallas or some other state, he'd give me game tickets, a hotel room, and a plane ticket when needed. To me, it was just a good time, but to him, it was something much more, I guess. His feelings for me may be part of the reason why he came back to College Station to live, workout, and hang out, mainly with me, after the season ended.

As more time passed, Fitz grew tired of being put off, so he called to let me know he'd be coming to visit for a couple of weeks. I was so excited, but I couldn't allow him to know this, so I acted like it was no big deal to me. A few weeks later Fitz shows up, and I avoid him the first 2 days he was home. The 3rd day he just showed up at my apartment unannounced. As happy as I was to see him, I acted annoyed and still played the, 'who cares if you're here' game. I sat and talked for a while, but when Selk called to confirm dinner and a movie, I quickly ended our catching up and ask Fitz to leave because I had plans and need to get ready. He was obviously hurt, but I had to show him what he would be missing out on since he didn't want to marry me. Which I informed him of as he collected his things.

"You know, it's funny. You actually have the nerve to look hurt because I have plans with someone else, but you made it perfectly clear that you had no interest in a serious relationship with me," I told him as I changed my clothes.

Fitz stood in the doorway of my bedroom and said, "I came all this way to see you D.J., not my family or anyone else. Doesn't that say something about how I feel about you?"

"No. Actually, it doesn't. I'm just a booty call to you. You call, and I drop everything and deliver the booty. I'm basically safe sex by phone and flight," I continued as I put on some makeup.

"Look D.J., you know it's not like that. Spend the week with me, and you will know what I mean," Fitz responded, now sitting on the end of my bed.

"Look Fitz I have dinner plans tonight, and I'm not sure why you would expect me to drop everything for someone who I've invested my time, energy, and heart in, but has told me repeatedly that he just wants a friend, not a wife. Do you really think that at this point in my life I want to just be a girlfriend, forever? I want to get married and spend the rest of my life with my husband, not my boyfriend. And you have made me painfully aware that you have no plans to get married for oh say another 30 years like your Uncle Eugene," I said. "Do you really think I'm going to wait 30 years for you to decide it's time for you to start thinking about settling down?" and went back to putting on my makeup.

Fitz came into the bathroom and pulled me in close to him, "D.J., if you don't believe anything else I say, believe this, I do love you, and I miss you very much. Just spend the week with me and let's reconnect. Please..."

I have to admit he almost had me... then the doorbell rang and brought me back. 'No pain, no gain,' I thought to myself. I pushed past him and said, "Look Fitz, I wish I could, but I've gotta put me and my needs first. My date is at the door, so I've got to go," and proceeded to leave my bedroom with Fitz following closely behind. As I reached for the door, he whirled me around and kissed me. I couldn't help but kiss him back. The doorbell rang again and snapped me out of his spell again.

I pushed him away and recomposed myself. I loved this man with every fiber of my being, but I had to stick to my plan and let him see me moving on with my life, with another man. I straightened up my lipstick and opened the door. No one said anything for a moment then Fitz dropped his head looking devastated as he moved past me. "Hay, its Selkie Black... Sorry to hold up your evening," he said, and that's the last I saw of him during his visit home.

Selk just stood there with a stupid look on his face. I didn't feel like answering any questions, so I grabbed the rest of my stuff and said, "Let's go."

The entire night I was distracted, but finally, we went to the movie where I didn't have to look at Selk or fake like I was paying any attention to him. Honestly, all I wanted at that time was for our date to be over. I had a night of crying ahead of me, and I was tired of fighting back my tears.

The next day I received a much need surprise, the grade check I'd requested had come through, and I wasn't doing too bad. To keep myself from tears every day that I didn't hear from Fitz, I'd reapplied myself to my classes, and in return, my grades looked really good by the time summer rolled around. I was maintaining above a 3.5 GPA, and I'd recently received a promotion on my job. As good as things seemed to be going, I was pretty sad most of the time. I hadn't heard from Fitz in several months, and Selk was getting more touchy-feely. I was actually relieved when he left to go workout with a teammate out in California. It gave me more free time to try to get me together and not have him underfoot all the time. He was nice company, but he was no Fitz.

The summer rolled along uneventfully until the 1st week of June. Out of the blue Fitz called and that's all it took for us to start talking every day like before. After 2 weeks of us catching up, he invited me down to Florida to spend some time with him at his new duty station.

"I'm telling you D.J. you'd love it down here. I'll even get the ticket if you'll just say yes. Please say yes," he said.

"As much as I'd love to Fitz, I just can't take off my job right now," I explained, which was actually the truth.

"D.J., I'm not going to beg you anymore. I miss you, and I want to see you. So please come," he said.

I thought to myself... *'I've got him just where I want him now, just a little bit more and he will do whatever it takes to marry me.'*

"Look Fitz, here we go again with you calling and expecting me to drop everything to please you. I'm not going to do it. I'm not going to open myself up to the pain of loving and missing you all over again, knowing full well we want different things from this relationship." I explained fighting to hold back my tears.

"One last time I'm asking you. D.J., please come visit me for a few days, just one little weekend?" Fitz pleaded.

"This just isn't a good time for me as much as I'd like to, I can't right now," I told him. Still thinking to myself, *'In a couple of weeks he'll call asking me again, and I'll say yes.'* Unfortunately for me that call never came.

What did finally come is an announcement during the secretary's report at church, that the congregation was invited to join Mr. and Mrs. Fitzgerald James Anthony Sr. in celebrating the upcoming wedding of their son Fitzgerald James Anthony Jr. to the daughter of ...blah blaah blaaah was all I heard after that. I was in shock at what I was hearing. I felt my mom slide her arm around my shoulder and squeeze me tight. Then my aunt reached across from the other side and closed my mouth. Apparently, it had fallen open during the announcement. I looked at my mom shaking my head back and forth, trying to shake off my shock and speak. For the life of me, I couldn't figure out what that hissing sound was then I realized it was my mom whispering in my ear...."Shhhhhhhhhhhhh."

I was so busy trying to fight back the tears that I still couldn't wrap my head around any words being said, which was probably for the best. When I was able to see straight again, I realized that all eyes were on me. I literally mean everybody in the church was staring at me. It was all my mom and Aunt Claudette could do to keep me in the pew and not allow me to run out of the church during the middle of service screaming, but as soon as church let out, I made a beeline for my car. Fitz's parents, along with my mom, were all hot on my heels. Mrs. Anthony tried to explain that they had warned my mom before service and wanted to warn me too, but I came in after the service had already started.

"Oh so now this is my fault!" I yelled as I fumbled to open my car door to get in.

They kept talking, and I shut them all out. I finally got the door open and got in and started my car, but when I tried to close the door, my mom wouldn't let me. She proceeded to take me out of the driver's seat and had my brother J.R. get in to drive me back to her house because she didn't feel I was in any shape to drive back out to my apartment in College Station. I couldn't help but notice that not a single car had left the parking lot yet and people were just milling around watching what was playing out in front of them. They didn't even have the courtesy to act like they weren't being nosey. As my mom and the Anthony's talked to me, I zoned out more and more. I could have cared less what they had to say or anyone else for that matter. All I wanted was to get the hell out of that parking lot and away from everyone standing around, staring and whispering about me.

On the quiet ride out to my parents' house, I realized that my game had blown-up in my face. The only thing that I had succeeded in doing, was proving to Fitz that he didn't want to be alone for the next 30 years, but I was just so stubborn and so focused on breaking him that he decided to get married without me. What was really killing me is the fact that I would never know if the invitation to come to Florida was to break the news to me in person or to ask me to marry him. Needless to say, I ended up calling into work sick for the next few days and sleeping in my old room at my parents' house.

Part of me was happy Selk wasn't in town for all of this drama because I really didn't have the energy to explain what was going on with me. On the rare occasion that I did answer my phone when he called, I tried to keep up my spirits while we talked until that fateful day he caught me off guard with the question that changed our entire relationship. Our conversation was drawing to the end when out of nowhere, Selk asked me, "D.J., will you marry me?"

I was totally taken back. What was he thinking? Why was he asking me this question now? After what seemed like an hour of silence, I finally figured out what to say...

"Are you serious? No, I will not!"

"You're kidding right D.J.? Seriously, I'm asking you to be my wife," he said again.

"No, I'm not kidding, and NO, I won't marry you," I said again, matter-of-factly. As mean as that may seem, that's the first thing that popped into my head. Basically, I couldn't believe it. The man I wanted to marry was engaged to be married to some other broad, and the man that I was using to make that man jealous was asking me to marry him. How screwed up was this whole situation? Unbelievable, that's what it was. Next thing I knew, I was listening to a dial tone. Now that actually was believable.

Before I realized it, it was only a few weeks before school started again, and Fitz's wedding was only a couple weeks away. This was so boldly thrown back up into my face once again during the announcements at church the Sunday before the unhappy event. But this time the announcement was in regard to the caravan that would be leaving the church parking lot on Friday afternoon, going down to New Orleans for this unholy wedding on Saturday. At least that's how I felt about the situation, even if no one else did. I stoically sat through the whole thing sneaking a peek out of the corner of my eyes to see if people were staring at me this time. I caught a couple of people eyeballing me, but for the most part, people had gotten over the fact that Fitz and I wouldn't be the next set of members to get married in our church.

That week flew by without a hitch. I'd called my mom on Thursday to see if she'd babysit my dog for a couple of days while I was out of town. She agreed to keep him, so I finished packing my bags, and then I packed my car. I drove up to the city early Friday morning to drop off Tink, my beloved Cockapoo, expecting to immediately head over to the church for the caravan. But of course, my mom wanted to talk and began asking 101 questions. I answered what I could, the best I could, then she asked the question that hurt me to my heart.

"Why would you subject yourself to the pain of watching someone you love so much marry another woman?" she asked.

"I was invited. It would be rude not to show up, don't you think?" I answered, trying not to show any emotion.

I noticed the time and told her I had to go. I got up to put my glass in the sink, and she asked me to run upstairs and get her tweezers from her bathroom before I left. As irritated as I was with her, I ran up the stairs taking 2 at a time, to get her stupid tweezers. It took a minute for me to find them because they weren't where she said they'd be. When I finally got back downstairs, I said my goodbyes and turned to get my car keys and leave. Problem is my keys were no longer on the table where I know they were before I went upstairs, at least I thought that's where they were. I looked around for them downstairs then decided maybe I'd left them in the car when I came in with Tink and all of his stuff. When I came back in the house, my mom suggested that I go back upstairs and look around her room since I'd just been up there too, but they weren't. After looking around for almost an hour, it hit me... my mom has the spare set of keys to my car. No biggie I'll just take her set of keys. I go back downstairs again and asked her for her set of keys as I picked up her purse, expecting her to fuss because it always irritated her when we just went rifling through her purse. But this time she didn't say a word. I moved everything around and couldn't find them, which was obviously upsetting me, so she told me to have a seat and calm down while she searched through her purse looking for them.

She finally looked up with a surprised look on her face and said, "I don't understand. I can't find them. They're not here."

I was devastated. I spent the remainder of the day tearing the house up searching for both sets of car keys. No one was there but my mom and me but as soon as my brothers started coming in, I interrogated each one of them about my keys. They all had to think I was a stark raving lunatic by the way I was acting, but no one ever said it to my face. I finally gave up when the sun started going down. I had long missed the caravan, and even if I could get away with driving 200 miles an hour to try to catch up to them, if I didn't catch them, I had no idea where the stupid wedding was anyway.

I felt like a house had been dropped on my chest. I went outside and shot baskets on the goal in our driveway and cried. Growing up, shooting hoops always made me feel better when something was bothering me. I spent the next 2 days on that driveway just shooting hoops by myself all day and all night, with a steady stream of tears rolling down my face. When I got tired of shooting the ball, I'd sit next to the pole and just cry. On day 3 of my mental and emotional breakdown, my mom finally made me come in the house to take a bath and go to bed. I cried myself to sleep that day and the next few days that followed. I didn't get out of bed the rest of the week, who knew anyone could cry so much.

My brothers took turns bringing me something up to eat, but I didn't have an appetite either, so it just sat there until someone came to get the tray and dishes for the next meal. Basically, I was a complete wreck. He was married now, so there was nothing I could do to get him back. When I could finally hold it all together, I decided it was time to go home. I took a much-needed shower and then went downstairs for lunch. I was finally able to eat something without it nauseating me, which was a good thing, I guess. I got Tink ready to go back home and went upstairs to get my stuff. When I came back down a miracle had happened... my keys were right there on the table again. I said goodbye and never really thought much about it until years later.

Sometime later, basically after my marriage to Selk had failed, I finally found out that my mom had hidden my keys to keep me from disrupting Fitz's wedding and embarrassing me as well as my family and everyone from the church. Even if I didn't say it, my mother knew me well and knew exactly what would have happened if I'd gone to that wedding.... I'd have turned that place out and ruined what I heard was a very lovely ceremony.

CHAPTER 9

In the meantime, classes started again, and I spent most of my time studying or working. I found keeping busy was the easiest way to ignore the pain that still hadn't subsided since Fitz got married. Things were going along just fine, and then Selk started sniffing around again. I put up with it since I really didn't feel like getting to know anybody else right then. He called to see if I wanted to come up to Dallas for a game and since I didn't have anything better to do, I went. Maybe a good football game would help take my mind off of everything else that had happened over the summer. Little did I realize this would be the beginning to my end.

I chose to drive up to Dallas instead of fly this time because I felt the drive would clear my head. I went to check into the hotel only to find out I didn't have a reservation. That surprised me since this was always the hotel he put me up in when I came to town. I called him from the bar phone, but there was no answer at his house. I didn't bother to leave a message because I looked up, and there he was coming through the front doors.

"Hi baby! I was hoping to get here before you," Selk explains as he reached out to hug me. "How was your ride up?" he continued as he kisses me on my forehead.

'Baby? Whatever,' I thought before I responded, "It was actually relaxing, I needed that time alone," I explained. "I was just calling you. I tried to check-in, but they didn't have a reservation in my name," I finished as I pulled back so I could look him in the face.

"Yeah, I know. I didn't make one," he explained as we walked back over towards the lobby.

"Why didn't you do that?" I asked, stopping in front of the registration desk.

Selk took my arm and pulled me closer to him and said, "Because you are staying at my house. If you'd flown in like usual, we'd already be there," he smiled as he took my hand and grabbed my bag off my shoulder as he tried to lead me out the front doors.

I hesitated for a minute, and then I let him lead me out of the hotel and to my car. I followed him to his place for the first time in our relationship, if that's what you want to call it. The entire ride over I kept having an argument with myself. *'Why not stay at his place? How many straight men do you know that would keep coming around over a year, spending their time and money on you, when you keep refusing to sleep with him? None that I'd ever met before. That in itself should speak to his character,'* I thought.

It was time for me to put up or shut up and I didn't have any reason not to anymore. Fitz was married so it wasn't like I needed to save myself for him. What would it hurt if I really opened myself up to this man? He was a nice guy, he treated me right, he'd put up with my hot and cold attitude with him. It was the least I could do to actually pay attention to him and return the attention and emotion that he'd been extending to me. As we pulled up to his building, I finished my self-pep talk with, *'D.J. you go in there, and you act like you're having a good time. Stop being so standoffish when he makes his move, and you know he's going to make his move tonight, so be ready.'*

Selk opened my car door, and the valet jumped in and drove off just like that. I was surprised at how nice of an apartment building he was living in. The country boy from the backwoods of Texas had really come up. This building was nothing like any place I'd ever seen him living in College Station. I have to admit, I was extremely impressed, and I hated that I was a little turned on too, to boot. He escorted me inside the building, looking like a proud peacock. We went up to his place arm in arm and when he opened the door there were rose petals everywhere and candles flickering in every room.

As we entered the dining room, a man dressed as a chef appeared and welcomed us and pulled out my chair for me. It really looked like something out of a Romantic Movie; I didn't know what to say. We sat and enjoyed the first 5-course meal I'd ever eaten. The food and drinks were incredible. After dinner, we took our drinks out on the balcony and talked next to the fire. Before I knew it, the sun was coming up, and we were enjoying a beautiful sunrise.

That night was nothing like what I had imagined it would be. He had been a complete gentleman the entire night, and the conversation flowed like it never had before between us. I couldn't help but finish our night off with a kiss that was more intense than the sunrise we had just witnessed. He scooped me up like I didn't weight more than a feather and carried me back inside his apartment. He carried me all the way from the den to his beautifully furnished bedroom, kissing me the entire way. He laid me across the bed ever so gently, and I just knew this was going to be the first time we'd make love.

We slowly undressed each other and began rubbing each other, touching each other, caressing each other, and when I couldn't take it anymore, I pulled him in close enough to be my second skin and whispered in his ear, "Please make love to me, NOW."

He pulled away and kissed me on the forehead. He stroked my face and outlined my lips with his finger. He kissed me again and said, "Baby as much as I would love to, I can't right now. I've got a team walkthrough in a couple of hours, so I really need to take a nap, and then get to the field. I promise you we will pick up right where we left off tonight." And with that, he wrapped his arms around me, pulled me in close, and fell asleep. I couldn't believe it. I just laid there in total shock. He had to be kidding... this is a joke, right? No ladies and gentlemen, he was fast asleep, leaving me in the wet spot and horny as hell. Unbelievable! I laid there in total disbelief for almost an hour before I drifted off to sleep. When I woke up, I thought maybe it had all been a dream, but no such luck. I was butt naked in a strange bed, all alone.

There was a note, and a rose on the pillow next to me...

D.J. I didn't want to wake you, you looked too peaceful to disturb. My house is your house so feel free to treat it like it's your own. Chris is my chefs' name, he'll make you whatever you want to eat, and Sonya is the maids' name. Should you need anything, just ask one of them to show you where it is. I should be back around 6 if all goes well at the walkthrough, so relax and enjoy the rest of your day. Love Selk

What a sweet note. Even though the night didn't end the way I expected, I'm kind of glad it didn't. He was turning out to be more than I expected, and the way things had been playing out in my life that was a good thing. Like they say, you shouldn't read a book by its cover...this book was a whole lot more complicated than what it had initially seemed. I wrapped up in the sheet and made my way over to the window. I pulled back the blinds to another beautiful surprise. His bedroom had a gorgeous view and another balcony. I found my way into the master bath and instantly fell in love with the sunken Jacuzzi tub where I spent the next hour of my day.

As uncomfortable as it was at first, Sonya popped in and asked if she could bring me anything. I thanked her and said I'd get something a little later. She smiled and said nonsense, it's well after noon. I'll have chef whip you up something. And then she was gone. A few minutes later, she returned with a Mimosa and a fruit plate. They made me feel like a Queen in Selk's absence, and I made sure I made him feel like a King when he got home that evening. Before we drifted off to sleep, he told me if he didn't play well tomorrow night, it was my fault. I had definitely given him a thorough and unexpected workout, not that he was complaining in the least. To his surprise and my relief, Selk had his best game of the season that Sunday night.

Even though it may have looked like Selk and me were a serious couple to the outside world, to me he was really just a great friend with benefits. To be completely honest, Selk had managed to become my best friend, the sex was just an added bonus. We continued on with this routine without too many hitches for the next few months. If the game was in Dallas, I stayed at Selk's place, and if I attended an away game, we worked it out where I stayed in his hotel room. On the rare occasion that wasn't going to be possible, he still got me a room in the hotel they were staying in, so we still got to spend the night together. My traveling so much didn't interfere with my schoolwork or my job, for the most part, so I enjoyed what I affectionately began to call my weekend pamper sessions.

I should have known the good times couldn't continue to go on this way, but I was having too much fun to worry about it at the time. The season came to an end when Dallas missed a 40-yard field goal to beat the Eagles and not have to go into overtime. The Eagles won the toss and ended up kicking a 29-yard field goal to win the game. And once again Selk got a place in College Station to be closer to me.

If it hadn't been for the family pictures on the walls you would have sworn we lived together because we spent so much time at each other's apartments. This was a mutually beneficial arrangement for both of us I thought, until that Valentine's Day. Selk had a beautiful meal catered in for us to have a quiet, romantic night at his place. He'd already had a dozen long-stemmed red roses delivered to me at work, so I wasn't really expecting any other presents that night. Again, I would be wrong. When dessert was being served Selk got down on one knee and for the second time in the less than a year, asked me to marry him as he slipped what turned out to be a 3 1/2 carat diamond engagement ring on my finger. Again, the first thing that came to my mind was no, but this time I asked him to let me think about it. That seemed to satisfy him for the moment, so we went back to enjoying our evening.

I knew that I would eventually have to give Selk an answer, but I avoided giving him an answer as long as I could. Unfortunately, that lasted maybe two weeks before our relationship really took a turn for the worse. Daily he started asking me why I hadn't given him my answer yet. We won't discuss the multiple long worrisome messages he left on my phone or the fact that he was now calling my job and tracking me down on campus. And God forbid if he saw me talking to another man, he was becoming more and more paranoid. It felt like all we did anymore was argue and have sex. After a couple more weeks of that drama, I couldn't take the arguing anymore, and I started avoiding him altogether.

"D.J. if I didn't know any better I would think that you are trying to avoiding me. I don't know who you think you're playing with, but I'm not the one to be toyed with do you understand me! Call me back sooner than later! I'm not playing with you!" was the last message he left before I bumped into him coming out of the Chemistry lab.

Next thing I knew someone was grabbing my arm and whirling me around. "Who the fuck do you think you are?! I've been calling and leaving you messages all week!" he yelled as he shook me like I was a rag doll.

I snatched away from him and pushed him with both hands as hard as I could, partially because he scared the crap out of me but mostly because I wanted to put some distance between us. "Have you lost your got damn mind?! Don't you ever put your hands on me again!" I yelled as I began walking away.

In hindsight, that was the beginning of the abuse that I would come to expect in our daily lives together. Selk followed closely behind me all the way to my car and then proceeded to follow me home where we continued our argument. I knew he was following me and I really didn't feel like having this argument in the middle of the parking lot, so I parked my car and immediately headed for my apartment, not looking back. As I unlocked my door, I could hear his footsteps coming up quickly, so I stepped inside and attempted to slam the door behind me, but he caught it just as it was closing infuriating him even more.

"YOU EVIL BITCH! I can't believe you did that! Do you know what would have happened if you had injured my hand?" he yelled half looking at me, half looking at his hand.

I dropped my bookbag and my purse on the floor and blocked him from coming any further into my house. "I don't know what kind of silly-ass women you are used to dealing with but let me explain to you who you're dealing with right now. I am not afraid of your big ass, and I will not be treated or disrespected that way! Does your country ass understand me?" I yelled with my hands on my hips, my foot blocking the door from opening any further, and my, *'don't fuck with me,'* look on my face. "How dare you speak to me that way and call me out of my name? You must be crazy because you sure got the wrong one baby!" I continued, still partially blocking the door from opening.

"I've just been trying to talk to you for a couple of weeks now, and I'm tired of you avoiding me. Hell, I'm tired of waiting for your answer or did it slip your mind that I asked you to marry me?" he said as he finally pushed past me and took a seat on the couch. But he continued before I could respond, "I see you're still wearing my ring, but you haven't felt the need to give me an answer yet. You haven't even returned any of my phone calls or made it a point to spend any time with me in almost 2 weeks. I miss you D.J., and I just want you to be my wife. I'm tired of these games."

"I'm not playing games and why on earth would I agree to marry you after the way you just treated me today?" I said as I walked back over to the front door and opened it. I raised my hand as to show him back out the way he'd just come in.

"So what exactly are you trying to tell me D.J.?" he asked as he laid his face in his hands and didn't move to get up from his seat.

"I'm saying it's time for you to leave. So please just go. Don't make me call the police," I said as I stood there still holding the door open.

Selk looked up and finally stood up, slowly making his way over to me. He gently took my face in his hands and tried to kiss me, but I turned away. He pulled my face back around to look me in the eyes and then bent down just enough to whisper in my ear, "You know you are getting ready to blow the best thing that ever happened to you. I know we've said some things in the heat of the moment, but I forgive you. I love you D.J., don't you see that? All I want to do is marry you and make you mine. Don't you want to marry me?" he asked, pulling back far enough to look me in my face again. His eyes looking so sad, like a lost puppy dog, but you could also still see the anger just under the surface, waiting to erupt.

I laid my head back on the door for a moment then look him in his face and said, "No Selk, I don't want to marry you. I thought about it and I just don't think you and I should go down that road. I had lots of fun with you, and I enjoyed spending time with you, but I'm just not ready to get married to you or anyone else. I'm sorry if that hurts your feelings, but that's how I feel," I said being as honest and sincere as I possibly could. I looked down at that beautiful ring and slowly slid the ring off of my finger and placed it in his hand. I was bracing myself for the explosion that never came. Selk kissed me on the forehead and just turned and walked out the door.

I later heard through the grapevine that Selk moved out of his apartment that week and back into his place in Dallas. Turns out that that would be the last time we spoke to each other for over 6 months.

I went on with my classes and work routine for a month or so and then it hit me that I hadn't had a period in some time. It was normal for me not to have a regular cycle; in fact, I could go months without having one. See I was 14 years old when I was diagnosed with cervical cancer. After a year of treatments that included multiple cervical scrapings and radiation, I was told that I would never be able to have children due to all the scarring I'd sustained. Yet and still, I decided to go get a home pregnancy test and make sure my body was just doing its normal funky thing and that I wasn't with child. The test came back negative, and my anxiety level significantly decreased for the first time in weeks. I made it to the end of the semester without any other major issues.

Since I was truly single for the first time in years, I needed something else to fill my time, but I just hadn't figured out what that was going to be just yet. It had spread like wildfire around campus that Selk and I weren't together anymore, and that's all it took for the suitors to start sniffing around. Shortly after our breakup even Dale started checking in on me again. I wasn't interested in spilling my guts to him, and I really didn't feel like starting up another relationship, so I did the next best thing...I started traveling again. I accepted a position at work that would require me to travel more so that worked right into my plans.

About a month into my new position, I noticed that I didn't have as much energy as usual. I figured it was because I had been traveling so much and I hadn't taken a break this summer as I usually did. So, I started making it a point to slip in a nap whenever I could and went on with my new routine without a second thought. As time passed, I did get worried about how exactly I would be able to keep up with this routine when school started again in the fall, but I shook it off and kept doing what I was doing.

Just because I was getting nervous again, I snuck in another pregnancy test at a local testing center to make sure my fatigue and strange appetite weren't because I was pregnant. Again, it was negative, so I had to laugh at myself for being so paranoid about something I knew wasn't possible anyway. Hell, I had to go to therapy for almost a year about not being able to have kids when I was a teenager. So why was I so worried now?

By mid-July, I was really dragging my ass, so I decided to make an appointment with my gynecologist, especially since I still hadn't had a period yet. I expected to be told it would be a month or so before I could get in, but they had a slot open in 2 weeks. I gladly accepted it and called my mom to find out what she would be doing that day. Because of my hectic school and work schedules, I didn't make it home to visit as much as I would have liked even though home was only about 35 minutes away the way I drive. She said that she'd be home by the time I left the doctor's office, so she totally expected me to stop by for a visit and dinner afterward. Basically, that was code for I better stop by and give her a full report on my doctors' visit, and I was to wait for her if she wasn't home yet.

Things went on as usual for the next 2 weeks, and before I knew it, it was time for me to go to the doctor. As usual, I was a few minutes late, but I'd already called ahead to let them know. The receptionist informed me that he was running behind due to an unexpected delivery so that would not be a problem. I only waited around 20 minutes before Dr. Cleveland's nurse, Mrs. Kathy, called my name. I barely had time to fill out all of my paperwork before I was called back. As always, she took my weight and asked for a urine specimen. When I came out of the bathroom, she escorted me into a room and gave me a gown to put on. I proceeded to get undressed and thumbed through a magazine while I waited on Dr. Cleveland. A little while later, he and Mrs. Kathy came in for my exam.

When all the poking and prodding was done, he began to ask me questions that were a little out of the norm for one of my visits. He asked me when I'd had sex last. That was a first, but I told him it had been about 5 months since I'd had sex last. Next, he asked if there was any chance, I could be pregnant? I reminded him of what I had been told years before, but just to be sure myself, I had taken 2 different pregnancy tests over the past 5 months and they were both negative. Mrs. Kathy had stepped out of the room before we started talking but had just returned with my urine test results before we got too deep into our conversation. The pregnancy test was negative again, but there was a trace of white blood cells and my ketones where low.

Dr. Cleveland then informed me that I had another tumor about the size of a medium-sized rock he suspected, as he showed me his size estimate on the tip of his index finger; it was mid-way between the second and third line. I just sat there numb with my mind racing as he gave me the best and worst-case scenarios. After what felt like an eternity, he then informed me that he wanted me to go to the lab and have my blood drawn to find out what my white count was along with my other levels. All I could do was smile as I explained to him that I would be declining that request.

"I understand what you must be feeling D.J., but we must get the ball rolling and find out exactly where we are. I will put a rush on your pap smear, but we really need to find out exactly how compromised your immune system really is," he continued to explain.

"Dr. Cleveland I fully understand everything you just explained to me, but now I need you to hear me out," I said as I got up and started putting my clothes back on with him sitting there, which was highly unusual and actually startled him. I could tell he was completely dumbfounded from that move, as he just quietly sat there with a blank look on his face. "See doc, I can vividly remember what you *all* put me through as a teenager when I went through this before. I had no say as to what took place and how long I had to endure the hell *your* so-called 'treatment' put me through. I suffered through the reoccurring surgeries to remove the tumors and then the pain from those God awful freezing and scrapings. Oh, and let us not forget the nausea and vomiting from the chemo treatments," I said as I bent over to put on my shoes. "And this horror went on for over a year before you decided that I was 'cured' or should I say, 'in remission?'" I said matter-of-factly as I finished straightening up my clothes as I sat back on the examination table.

"That's all true, but the treatments have greatly improved since then, and we need to get on this now before it gets worse. The sooner we catch it, the better the chances of a full recovery," he tried to explain.

I glanced over at Mrs. Kathy, who was obviously tearing up. I smiled at her as I took Dr. Cleveland's hand and said, "Look...I understand everything you just said, and I so appreciate your concern. The problem is I'm not willing to go through that horror show again. This time I'm in control," I said so proudly. "And I say that I'm going to enjoy the rest of my life for as long as I can, without being poked or prodded, or living in a hospital room for weeks on end, ever again," I calmly explained. I could tell by his silence and the shocked look on his face that he was at a loss for words and that this was the last thing he ever expected me to say. I tried to reassure him by remaining calm and maintaining a smile on my face as I continued even though every fiber of my being was exploding on the inside. "So, no Dr. Cleveland, I won't be going to the lab, and I'm not concerned with my tumor. At this point I'm not in any pain and other than being a little more tired than normal I'm good. So even though I may be broken, I don't choose to be fixed. That might sound crazy, but that's how I feel. Life is too short to be cooped up in some hospital that causes you to get sicker and sicker, trying to cure what in all actuality, can't really ever be *'cured.'* I pray I have a lot more time but in case I don't, I'm getting ready to party like it's 1999. I don't plan on wasting another minute more of my life worrying about this. Everybody has to die eventually, so maybe this is a sign that it's just my time to go Doc," I finished as the tears I'd been fighting back started streaming down my face.

Mrs. Kathy handed me a tissue and took one for herself because she was now free-flowing tears too. I stood up and gave both of them a hug and left the room. I patiently waited at the receptionist desk for Dr. Cleveland to fill out my paperwork so that I could check out. He walked up to the counter and handed my file to the receptionist and placed his hand on my shoulder as a friend would do. Then he said, "D.J., I realize that this is a very emotional time for you right now, so take your time and think about what we discussed. Call me at any time, day or night, if you change your mind and I will get everything set up for you." He handed me a business card with his home phone number written on the back. "Just promise me that you will sleep on it before you decide not to treat this because it is completely treatable. We beat it once, and I know we can beat it again," he finally finished, obviously getting emotional because of my situation.

"I will do that Dr. Cleveland. Just for you. But don't be upset when you don't hear from me," I said as I gave him one last hug before I left his office.

I took my time driving over to my parents' house because I dreaded the conversation I was going to have with my mom. She wouldn't be as calm and understanding as Dr. Cleveland was that's for sure. I wasn't surprised that the only people at the house when I arrived was P.J. and my mom, but actually I was relieved. My mom was obviously waiting for me even though she tried to keep that cool, calm look she had perfected over the years.

"So how did it go?" she asked without even saying hello.

I let out a little laugh as I walked over to the fridge and got me a bottle of juice before I answered her. "Well hello to you too mother. And how was your day?" I asked as I took a seat at the kitchen table next to her. I could tell how impatient she was by the way she stared at me the entire time, so I took my time responding until she said hello to me.

"Hello D.J. Now how'd it go at the doctor?" she asked with her don't test me voice and side-eye.

"Well mother, I'm going to die," I calmly said as I took a sip of my juice and waited for the eruption in 3, 2, 1...right on cue.

"That's not the least bit funny D.J.! What do you mean you're dying!? Stop drinking that juice and tell me exactly what happened!" she said in a panic, pulling the bottle away from my mouth.

"Momma calm down, and I will explain," I began, trying not to laugh. "They found a tumor the size of a medium pebble and my urine had a trace of white blood cells and my ketones where low," I said.

She started bombarding me with questions before I could finish. "Well what was your blood count and your white cell level? What are we going to do next!? When are you going to have a biopsy? Does he think we should do a quick round of radiation or maybe even a little chemo? How about scrapings...did he do any?" she was rattling questions off so fast I don't think she ever took a breath.

"Mom, Mommmy! Slow down! Please..." I said, trying not to laugh as I pushed my juice away and reached over to hold her hand. "Can I please explain?" I continue.

"Okay. Well, what happened and don't leave out any details," she said finally relaxing just a little. I could tell because her fingers were loosening up the death grip she had on my wrist.

I took a deep breath and began, "Well, like I said, he found a tumor while he was doing my pelvic exam. Because the urine test showed that I had a trace of white blood cells and my ketones were low, he was concerned, but I decided not to pursue it," I said nervously. I knew she wouldn't accept that without going off on me again.

She made a face I'd never seen before and don't ever want to see again, as she began to speak extra slow as if I wouldn't understand her if she said it at a normal rate of speed, "You... decided... not... to... pursue... it..." Through a tightly clenched jaw, she managed to ask, "What exactly does that mean young lady?" The death grip she had before was quickly coming back. And this time it was even tighter.

I re-adjusted in my seat, pulled my hand away from hers, and placed it on her wrist, as I began to explain. "See he asked me to go have my blood drawn and I thanked him and said no. I explained that I remember what happened the last time and that I vividly remember the hell *'your'* so-called treatment put me through. I suffered horribly through the reoccurring surgeries to remove the tumors, and the excruciating pain from those scrapings and freezings, and none of you would listen when I pleaded for you to stop. And let's not forget the nausea and vomiting from the chemotherapy treatments, which also made it a nightmare to swallow because my throat was so raw from throwing up so much. Which by the way is the number one reason I can't stand Pepto-Bismol today," I added trying to lighten the conversation just a little. Which I could see wasn't working by the look on her face, so I continued, "And this horror show went on for over a year before you all decided that I was *'cured,'* or should I say in remission? I had no say as to what took place and how long I had to endure that hell, mom. I begged you to make them stop, but *you* allowed it all to continue," I pointed at her. "I don't know how else to explain it to you but to say, I absolutely refuse to go through that hell again. And if I have to, I'll disappear before I ever let that happen again," I finished and went back to sipping on my juice to show her that I was serious about my decision.

I could tell she was completely taken back by what I was saying, so I slid my chair closer to her and took her hands in mine again, then continued before she had a chance to respond. "Mommy, I would rather die than go through that horror again. I'm sorry, but this time it's my choice and ultimately my decision. You might not like or approve of how *I've* decided to handle this, but mommy it's my decision to make. And I'm going to tell you just like I told

Dr. Cleveland... No, I won't be going to the lab, and I'm not concerned with my tumor. At this point I'm not in any pain and other than being a little more tired than normal I'm good. So even though I may be broken, I don't choose to be fixed. That might sound crazy, but that's how I feel. Life is too short to be cooped up in some hospital room that causes you to get sicker and sicker, trying to cure what in all actuality, can't really be *'cured.'* I pray I have a lot more time on this earth, but in case I don't, mommy, I want to go out happy. So mom, I'm getting ready to party like a Rockstar. Like it's 1999. I don't plan on wasting another minute more of my life worrying about tumors or white cell counts. Everybody has to die eventually, and when it's my time, it's going to be on my terms. I love you, but I won't be needing *you* to make this decision for me," I finished feeling more like an adult than I ever had when discussing serious issues with my mom. I got up, gave her a hug and kissed her on the forehead, then went back in the kitchen to figure out what smelled so good, I was starting to feel hungry now that the nervousness was going away.

"Well now that you have finished your little speech, it's time for mine. So sit your happy ass down and listen closely Little Miss." She stopped me dead in my tracks. All I could do is drop my head and return to my seat for the scolding I thought I had masterfully avoided.

"Yes ma'am," as I closed the pot lid and returned to my chair. And just like that, she managed to make me feel like that little girl who always bowed down to her mommy's wishes.

"I didn't get you to this point in your life to allow you to throw it all away. You are my first D.J., my only living daughter. I'll be damn if I let you dye on me now and at such a young age. You have too much life left in you, and as God as my witness, I will drag you kicking and screaming into another 50 years if I have to. So, don't come in here all high and mighty telling me what you are and aren't going to do young lady. I'm your mother, and I'm telling you now that you *'are'* going to do whatever it takes to live," she finished.

What really burns me up is that she was just so matter-of-fact, like she was the boss of me. And just like that, she picked up the phone and proceeded to call Dr. Cleveland's office. Within minutes, she had him on the phone, demanding to know what they were going to do to treat me. He must have told her that he couldn't discuss my case with her because her calm insistence became very hostile and irate in a matter of seconds.

"What do you mean you can't discuss her case with me? You've been my doctor for too many years for me to remember, and you delivered all of my babies! I brought my only living daughter to you when she started having female issues and needed a gynecologist! Oh, you are going to talk to me Sir!" she demanded.

I knew this was only going to get worse, so I hit the speaker button as I rubbed her back, trying to calm her down. "Dr. Cleveland, I give you my permission to discuss my situation with her and answer whatever questions she may have, okay?" I felt this was my chance to be my own person once again, so I cleared my throat and continued. "But before you do, I need both of you to understand here and now that no matter what '*you two*' decided, I'm the one who is making the decisions here," I said looking my mom in her eyes the entire time hoping she'd understand my position. But deep inside, I knew that was just wishful thinking. Who was I trying to kid? She is the boss. She's the boss of me and everyone else who dares to enter her orbit. Push come to shove, it was going to take God Almighty to come down and rein her in.

I went over to the den and turned on the TV while she and Dr. Cleveland discussed what he found and what he would like to happen from here on out. An hour later I overheard him tell her if there were any changes to call him immediately and he'd get me in to see him by the next day at the latest. And with that, they finally got off the phone. That was the longest dinner I'd had to endure in a very long time.

Things went on as usual for a while without any further discussion of my tumor or my sudden partying lifestyle. I was living up to my claim of partying like it was 1999, but no one really commented since I was still handling my business. About a month later, I went bopping into my parents' house after a party at Towne Lake. It was the middle of the summer so of course I had on my summer attire consisting of my favorite tank pulled up and tucked under to look like a crop top and my shorts, slightly rolled down. My mom was sitting in her customary seat at the kitchen table reading a magazine and sipping on a glass of tea when I came in the house. I'm not sure if it was out of habit or just to annoy her, but as usual, I came in and picked up her glass to take a sip, knowing she'd start fussing. She so hated us drinking out of her glass, but all of us kids did it. Before I could get the glass to my lips, she grabbed my shorts, pulling them down even further yelling at me...

"Your tummy has obviously gotten bigger, and you hadn't said a word!" she yelled as she picked up the phone and started dialing.

I quickly put her glass down, without ever taking a sip, and pulled my shirt down. I had noticed that my pants were fitting a little tighter, but I chose to ignore it. It didn't take long to figure out who she was calling. "Dr. Cleveland please. It's Lisa Morgan, D.J. Morgan's mother. Yes, I'll hold." After a few minutes on the phone, she hung up looking pretty content and asked what my plans were for tomorrow. I should have known then she was setting me up, but it didn't occur to me.

"I decided to take a summer class at the vo-tech so I will be there most of the day," I answered as I started poking through the fridge and then asked about my brothers. "So how are the guys doing?" I asked eating on a peach I'd found. She told me J.R. was off at college taking summer classes, L.J. was away at some math camp, and M.J. and P.J. were both off at football camps.

Unfortunately for me, that meant that my mom had plenty of time to focus on me. That was made blatantly obvious when both she and my dad showed up at my class the next day and insisted that I come with them for a doctor's appointment. I couldn't believe they just showed up and embarrassed me like that. I sat there, frozen in place with my mouth hanging wide open.

Finally, the instructor said, "Miss Morgan, I think you need to excuse yourself, don't you?" You could tell she was just trying to break-up the awkward silence and prevent any further possible outbursts. I collected my things as quickly as possible and headed for the door with my tail between my legs. I was mortified, to say the least. I didn't speak to them the entire ride over to the doctor's office or when we were all called back to his office and not an examination room.

Basically, they discussed how the tumor had obviously gotten bigger and needed to be dealt with immediately. I needed to go down to the lab and have my blood drawn so they would know exactly what needed to be done before he got me in to have an ultrasound. You would have thought that I was 14 years old again because when I told them what I wanted, it was like I hadn't said a thing. My parents escorted me downstairs to the lab like I was a violent prisoner, who might try to escape at any minute. They were each holding onto my arm as we left Dr. Cleveland's office until we walked into the lab.

The comic relief came when we walked into the lab, which was filled to capacity. The lab tech at the counter looked up and immediately jumped up saying, "OH NO! NOT YOU AGAIN!" I couldn't help but crack up, especially since both of my parents looked just as shocked and embarrassed as I did earlier at school. It served them right. The looks on all of their faces was downright priceless. My mom handed him the paperwork and he immediately took us to the back, but not until after he apologized to everyone in the waiting room for taking me ahead of all of them. He didn't wait to listen to the complaints or answer questions, he just told us to follow him. It was obvious he remembered me from when I had to come in as a kid. I have to admit, I was a terror back then. I guess that's why he wanted to get me out of the way since I was such a handful all those years ago. He showed me into a little room and hit a button on the intercom asking for assistance.

I sat down, still laughing, and told him as we waited, "I promise I won't be as much trouble as I use to be. I can't believe you still remember me 10 years later. I must have been the worst patient you ever had to deal with."

He put on his gloves as he let out a light-hearted laugh and said, "Yes dear. I totally remember you, and I could have gone another 10 years without ever seeing you again. It used to take 5 of us to hold you down to draw your blood, and you were a little bitty thing back then. I can't imagine how many of us it's going to take to hold you down now that you are a grown woman," he finished leaning up against the doorway.

"Well it won't take 5 of you today, I promise. I will try to keep it down to 3 of you today, how about that? *And,* I will do my best not to scream," I said with a smirk on my face.

We both laughed as his help arrived and let out a deep moan. And to everyone's delight and amazement, I was a woman of my word. It only took 3 of them to hold me down to draw my blood. My dad assisted the other gentleman with holding me down, but he doesn't really count, and my mom stood to the side with her, *'don't let me have to show you who's really in charge'* look on her face, as the lab tech drew my blood. And no, I didn't scream, not one time.

Before we left the lab, the lady at the front desk advised us that Dr. Cleveland had called down to reiterate that he wanted my lab work completed stat. He also wanted me to call him tomorrow afternoon for the preliminary results and to discuss what the next step would be. I just smiled and walked out of the door, but my mom stopped to tell her that she fully understood.

As we made our way back to my car, my mom advised me that I was to come by her office after my class tomorrow to call the doctor for my results. I told her I'd call when I got home and she quickly turned around in her seat to look at me as she said again, "You will come to my office as soon as you get out of class tomorrow so that WE can call Dr. Cleveland and get whatever lab results they have in. Do you understand me?"

"Yes ma'am," was all I could say. It's amazing how she could make me feel like a little kid when I'm nearly 25 years old.

The next day went without a hitch. Luckily no one in my class asked me what all the drama was about the day before, which was a major relief. In fact, they asked me to join them for coffee after we got out of class. Since I was in no hurry to get my results from the doctor, I agreed to go, even though I don't even drink coffee. I enjoyed the time I spent with my new classmates and after an hour or so we all went our separate ways. I finally walked into my mom's office around 3 o'clock, nearly an hour and a half after I was expected. Her secretary watched me come into the building and make my way over to the office suite. I could see that she was just shaking her head as I came inside the inner office. I tried to act like nothing was wrong, and it was just another day.

"Hello Mrs. Lee. How are you doing today?" I asked as if I was just dropping in and hadn't been ordered to stop by.

She was still shaking her head at me and said, "I'm just fine, but you are in BIG trouble Miss D.J. Morgan. She was expecting you almost 2 hours ago. Why must you push your luck all the time? You know how she gets," she frowned at me.

"I don't know. You know, sometimes things come up. She will just have to understand," I said as if I had no idea what she was talking about, but knowing full well that I was getting ready to get an ear full. I was standing less than 10 feet away from her office, and I still was in no hurry to go in and deal with her or the doctor.

"Well let's go. You know she's waiting," Mrs. Lee said as she got up to escort me down the hall to my mom's office like I'd get lost or something. She knocked on the door… "Mrs. Morgan, you have a visitor," as she opened the door and ushered me in.

I just stood there for a second. Then I took a deep breath and walked on in. Mrs. Lee closed the door so fast she almost clipped me with it.

"Hi mom! How are you doing today?" I asked, trying to sweet-talk her so she wouldn't explode on me.

She looked up from her paperwork just enough to glare at me over the top of her glasses and said, "You're late," as she reached over to the phone hit one button and handed me the receiver.

And just like that, I was on with Dr. Cleveland's office. I don't know why that surprised me, but it did. I just shook my head in disbelief as I told the receptionist who I was and that I was told to call to get the results of my lab work today.

She said, "Yes Miss Morgan, we've been expecting your call. One moment please," and she put me on hold. A few seconds later, I was on with Mrs. Kathy. She was doing a combination of laughing hysterically and crying thing as she told me about the results of the lab work they had received back at this point in time.

I just stood there with the phone to my ear saying, "Okay," as I watched my mom fill out paperwork at her desk. She was acting like I wasn't even in the room.

Finally, Mrs. Kathy asked me, "Do you have any questions for me right now?" I didn't know what to say and just stood there holding the phone to my ear. As I silently stood there, I realized that mom still hadn't looked up from her paperwork yet. I guess since I didn't answer, Mrs. Kathy asked, "D.J., are you still there?"

"Yes, I'm here. I don't have any questions right now. I understood you," was all I could come up with. I was still processing what I had just heard. Mrs. Kathy was still laughing and crying when she hung up the phone. The sound of the dial tone shook me back to reality. I hung up the phone and just stared at my mom, still trying to process, trying to decide what I should say next.

My mom was a cool customer. She looked up from her paperwork and said, "You're pregnant. When do we go see the doctor?"

I literally fell back into the chair next to her desk and softly said, "Tomorrow at 3." I was still in total disbelief as to what I was just told and in shock from the fact that she knew, without speaking to the doctor's office. Mrs. Kathy happened to mention that they were expecting to hear from my mom earlier today, but they hadn't. How in the hell did she know? I know her... she prayed this shit up on me. When I was able, I said my goodbyes and drove back to my apartment in College Station. It seemed like forever on the road, but I finally got there just about the time the first tear fell. I proceeded to walk my dog and then cry myself to sleep. All I could think as I finally fell asleep is, *'Why is this happening to me? How is this happening to me? This is so unfair!'*

That morning came faster than I expected, and my class was over even faster than that. But really, how long is a day going to take to get here, since I found out I was pregnant only 24 hours ago. I still hadn't fully accepted the news of my pregnancy, and honestly, I didn't completely believe it. For one of the first times in my adult life, I walked into the doctor's office 10 minutes early. And yes, that was only because my mother was with me. I think she wanted to be there more to see for herself that Dr. Cleveland was still mentally capable of being a doctor; he was getting up there in age. He'd delivered me and all of my brothers after all, so he wasn't a spring chicken as they say.

When Mrs. Kathy called us back, she had the biggest grin on her face that I'd ever seen. Once we got back to the inner office area, she gave me the tightest hug that I'd ever gotten from a non-family member. She exchanged pleasantries with my mom as she weighed me and had me give the customary urine sample. She showed us into an exam room where I changed into one of those lovely open front gowns, and we waited.

Not long after I'd sat on the exam table, Dr. Cleveland came in and started talking. After a few minutes it occurred to me that he wasn't talking to me, he was talking to my mother. Not once did he look at me or acknowledge the fact that I was sitting there, half-naked freezing my chi chi's off. I guess after he had reassured her that he wasn't too old to still be practicing and how he saw no indication a month ago that I could possibly be pregnant, he turned to me and began poking and prodding me as he questioned me all over again about when I last had sex. Now the fact that he has is hand so far up in my vagina that his fingers are coming out of my throat with my mother sitting here watching aside, answering questions about my sexual liaisons in front of my mom is totally embarrassing. But at this point, it's too late to ask her to leave, not that she would have anyway.

Throughout all of this, he's still talking to my mom, more than he is talking to me. I hadn't noticed that Mrs. Kathy had come into the room during all of this and was quietly standing in the corner holding a bottle and a small box with a microphone attached to it. When he was finished palpating my uterus, he took the bottle from her and explained that it was a gel used to help reduce the static that is often caused when using a fetal doppler. He then warned me that the gel would be a little cold, which was an understatement, as he squirted it all over my stomach. She then handed him the doppler, and to all of our amazement, but to their obvious delight, we instantly heard the whoosh-whoosh sound of a little heartbeat. I just silently laid there and listened to the whooshing sound coming through the speaker. It was amazing and terrifying all at the same time.

Dr. Cleveland listened for only a few seconds and then started talking to my mom again. He wiped the majority of the gel off of me and then hand me a washcloth to finish cleaning myself up, and he and Mrs. Kathy left while I got dressed. Mrs. Kathy soon returned with a slip of paper in hand. She advised us that I was scheduled for an ultrasound on Friday. I was once again completely flabbergasted and asked, "I thought that it took several weeks to get an appointment for an ultrasound?" as I found myself trying to process what I was being told once again.

I looked up from the piece of paper I was staring at so intently, but not actually reading, when I heard Dr. Cleveland's voice coming from outside the room. He was standing outside my door looking at a piece of paper laughing and finally said, "D.J. you're right. Usually, it does take several weeks to get in for an ultrasound but lucky for you, your doctor is this hospital's Chief of Staff, so I have just a little bit of pull around this place. And just for the record, your urine test just came back negative again for pregnancy."

Well, enough said. I just stood there looking dumbfounded, so my mom took the slip of paper and thanked him for the hundredth time. I couldn't believe it, in 2 days, I would be seeing my baby for the first time. A baby that I was told years ago that I would never be able to conceive. And in the unlikely event that I did, I would never be able to sustain the pregnancy, let alone carry it to term. We all had underestimated the praying power of one Mrs. Lisa Jean Morgan.

We rode in silence all the way back to my parents' house, which was completely fine with me, I didn't have much to say anyway. And on top of that, I had so much to process that I preferred not to have to participate in idle chit chat or answer any questions. As we pulled into the driveway, my mom took my hand and held it tight, not allowing me to jump out of the car as quickly as I had planned to. After she put the car in park and turned off the engine, she turned to me and asked the questions that I dreaded to have to answer...

"Is Selkie the father of this baby?" she asked.

"Yes ma'am, he is," I said as I continued to stare out my window.

"Well, you do plan on calling to tell him that you're pregnant right," she said. It was difficult to tell if that was a question or a statement, but I figured it was the latter.

"I'm not sure yet. That's what I've been sitting here thinking about," I responded still staring out the window at nothing in particular.

We just sat there in silence for a while, holding hands, not saying a word. Finally, the silence was broken at the sound of another car pulling into the driveway. It was my dad coming in from work. I said to myself, *'Oh great! Now I get to explain all of this to him and listen to his two cents worth.'* As if I need any more drama right now. Thankfully my mom took the lead and informed him about our visit to the doctor and what we had just found out.

Very unexpected to either of us, he began rattling off about how I wasn't supposed to be able to get pregnant and how much therapy they had to pay for because I was so depressed after I found out that I'd never have any children. How could the doctor be so sure that I was pregnant or that I would be able to carry this baby to term? Were we sure that I was pregnant because he couldn't believe that I was over 6 months pregnant as small as I still am? I barely had a tummy, and he'd never seen anyone who was supposedly that far along who didn't have an obviously large belly. Was I sure when I had had sex last? I gave him a dirty look and turned my head in disgust. I wasn't even going to dignify that question with an answer. He kept going on and on. I grew tired of the conversation and said my goodbyes and went home. I figured they would go back and forth the rest of the night and I had no desire to participate any further for today.

Without saying good-bye, I stood up and gathered my things, and then headed for the door. My mom quietly walked me out to my car, but before I pulled off, she asked me, "You are going to call Selkie and tell him the news, right?"

Again I told her, "I don't know what I'm going to do yet mom. Everything is upside down and backwards right now. I'm just trying to process everything okay." I honestly didn't know what I was going to do. I really didn't want to think about it right now.

I don't exactly know when I started crying, but by the time I pulled up in front of my apartment my shirt was soaking wet, my eyes were beginning to swell, and my head was pounding. I was so worn-out that I didn't even feel like walking Tink. I just let him out the back door and watched him run around on his own. I ordered a salad and turkey sandwich to be delivered because I didn't have it in me to cook anything tonight. After I fed Tink and stopped crying, I ate my dinner. Then I took a nice long bubble bath and cried some more.

As I was getting ready to go to bed, I decided that I would call Selk and tell him what was going on. If nothing else, he did deserve to make up his own mind as to what he wanted to do. After I'd psyched myself up and was able to remain calm enough to maintain my composure, I picked up the phone and dialed Selk's number. I knew he was already back in training camp, so I didn't expect him to answer his phone because he was probably in a team meeting. And even if he could answer, I figured he wouldn't after the way we ended things, so it was a complete surprise that he actually answered his phone, and on the second ring no less. I was shocked because I knew that he had to have seen my name on the caller ID, and he answered anyway.

After we exchanged pleasantries, I began telling him about my doctor's appointment and that I was pregnant. I told him about my ultrasound on Friday and what time that appointment was if he wanted to come. Surprisingly, he never asked if the baby was his and said that he would see me on Friday. I answered what few questions he did ask me like how I was feeling, and could we ride to the appointment together. I could hear the excitement in his voice and wasn't surprised that he wanted to just sit and talk. Unfortunately for him, I still didn't want to hold a detailed conversation about this situation, but I also didn't want to be rude. So I tried to politely explain that I was really tired and was about to go to bed and that we'd have to finish this conversation another time. He was reluctant but said he understood and would call me tomorrow. I hung up the phone thinking *'please don't,'* but I knew down deep that it was going to be near impossible to avoid him after this. I cried myself to sleep, which in hindsight would become a running theme in my life for some time.

Friday morning had finally arrived, and I was awakened by my phone ringing off the hook. It was Selk calling to make sure I was going to pick him up from the airport so that we could spend some time together before my ultrasound. I confirmed his flight information and said that I would see him later. No sooner than we had hung up the phone, it began ringing again. This time it was my mother calling to make sure I hadn't changed my mind about riding to my appointment with her. I explained that I was picking Selk up from the airport so we would meet her there. After she reconfirmed my appointment time, I was able to get her off the phone to get another few hours of sleep. I didn't know if it was depression or pregnancy, but suddenly I was more tired than I had been before I found out that I was with child.

I didn't have class on Friday's and had already taken off from work for the day, so I didn't feel the least bit bad about lounging around my house all morning. When I finally got dressed, I decided to go have a quick pamper session to help me relax. I went to my favorite nail salon and got a mani-pedi before I had to be at the airport. That turned out to be the best thing I could've done before having to deal with Selk because no sooner did he get in my car, I could feel myself tensing up. He hadn't been in the car 10 seconds before he reached over and put his hand on my stomach to see if he could feel the baby moving around.

I immediately pushed his hand away, "Excuse you. You're in my personal space," I said.

"Come on baby. I just wanted to see if my boy is kicking," he said. It would've been cute if it wasn't for the fact that I was still torn about this pregnancy. On the one hand, it was a miracle, but on the other hand, it was a miracle that happened with the wrong person. I couldn't help to think how different things would be if this baby belonged to Fitz and not Selk. I know, I'm wrong for feeling that way, but I do. This should be me and Fitz's baby not Selk's. Just one more instance of how cruel God was when it came to what I wanted for my life.

Selk finally accepted the fact that I wasn't really in a talking mood, so we rode in silence the rest of the way to the doctor's office. When we arrived at the radiology department, my mom was already there waiting on us of course. I checked in and began filling out a stack of forms. Before I completed all the forms my name was called, and we proceed to go back for my ultrasound. The technician calling me back looked at me and then back at her paperwork with a confused look on her face. She finally looked back up at me and said, "I'm sorry, I called D.J. Morgan."

"I am D.J. Morgan," I said.

She continued to look back and forth from the papers in her hand then back at me, "Again, I'm sorry, but you can't be D.J. Morgan."

I wasn't sure why she felt that way, but I nodded my head again and said, "Yes ma'am, I am."

She let out a little laugh and said, "Well, there must be a mistake here. This paperwork says that you are having an ultrasound to confirm a 6-month gestation," as she looked back up at me from the paperwork in her hand.

"Yes ma'am, I am," I answered again, still not understanding the joke.

She held the door open for us to come on back and she laughed as she said, "Well honey I bet you a million dollars you aren't 6 months pregnant. Nobody as skinny as you can possibly be 6 months pregnant, I bet my life and my bank account on that."

I laughed and said, "Well I don't take checks, so I hope you have that in cash."

I could tell my mom and Selk didn't find our conversation very funny as she took us into the ultrasound room, but I really could've cared less. She introduced herself as Tammy and instructed me to get up on the exam table and pull my shirt up. She had me unbutton my pants and then she pulled them down further to expose my lower abdomen as well. Ms. Tammy squirted the gel on my tummy, and I quickly thanked her for warming it up. She smiled as she turned on the monitor and said that was the norm in radiology, as she began moving the little wand around. She looked over at the monitor, still smiling, and then her mouth fell open. She just sat there in silence with her mouth hanging open, looking back and forth from me to the monitor. Finally, she turned the monitor so that we could see what she was seeing. I was watching my mom and Selk's' faces before I looked over at the monitor, and when I did, all you could see was baby everywhere.

"Well I'll be damn. I wouldn't have believed it if I hadn't seen it with my own eyes," Ms. Tammy finally said, turning the monitor back towards her. "I guess I need to start taking measurements to find out exactly how far along you are." And just like that, she started to measure everything she saw. She readjusted the monitor so that we could watch the monitor too while she worked. I glanced over at her again and noticed that she had a strange look on her face and that she was beginning to press a lot harder on my stomach.

I asked her, "Is there a problem?" and she looked at me like a deer in the headlights, not saying a word. My mom noticed how she looked and how quiet she had become, so she asked her if there was a problem too.

Ms. Tammy cleared her throat and said, "Well, I'm not sure how to tell you this, but not only are you pregnant, you're pregnant with twins. I can't see the entire baby, but I have 2 sets of feet here."

I laughed at her and said, "Yeah, right. Nice joke, but I'm not buying it." As I began twisting my head further around to see the monitor above my head.

She kept staring at us then started pointing out the extra body parts on the screen. I couldn't believe what I was seeing. I looked over at my mom for reassurance, and wouldn't you know it, she was staring at me with her mouth hanging wide open too. Selk was squeezing my hand so tight I thought he was going to break my fingers.

Ms. Tammy asked me to drink some more water to see if that would help push the second baby up so that she could see it better on the monitor. All I could do is nod my head, yes. She brought me a large cup of water and finished measuring the first baby while I drank it. By the time she had completed those measurements, the two of them had rolled just enough to completely make out the second baby. I think all of us were in total shock, especially Ms. Tammy. She immediately began taking measurements on the second baby while it was in a good position to see its entire body.

We all were eerily silent, but you could hear Ms. Tammy saying under her breath, "There is no way you should be this skinny with one baby let alone two. I can't believe this. I've never seen anything like this in my entire career."

As we all stayed focused on the monitor, she asked if we wanted to know the sex of the babies? I looked over at Selk as if to ask what he thought without actually asking and before either of us could answer her, baby A threw open its legs to show us that it was indeed a boy. And just like that baby B rolled over like he didn't want to be outdone and showed us that he was also a boy. We sat there watching the two of them in total amazement as they flipped and flopped around like they were suddenly having a wrestling match.

Ms. Tammy said she would be right back after she calculated the babies' sizes and let us know exactly how far along I 'really' was. Before she could get out of the door, I stopped her and asked, "Would it be okay if I went to the bathroom? I am about to bust." She giggled a little and directed me to the bathroom down the hall. I'd never felt such relief in all my life.

When I came back in the exam room, my mom and Selk were silently sitting there almost like they were in shock and still didn't believe what they had just witnessed. I sat there in total silence with them for a few minutes then I said, "Well Mr. Black, now you've gone and done it with that super-duper sperm of yours." That's all it took to break the silence and get everyone to laughing somewhat.

Finally, Ms. Tammy came back into the room, and she was even paler than she was when she realized there were two babies and not just one. She just stood there for a minute looking at her papers, shaking her head. By now the laughter had completely subsided and the room was dead silent again. She looked up at us and cleared her throat several times before she could speak. She finally said, "I guess I need to take on a second and third job because it looks like I owe you a million dollars. I can't believe it, but by these measurements, you are exactly 6 months and 2 weeks pregnant. Where are you possibly hiding 2 babies? And how on earth are they this big and you are that little?" as she leaned on the doorframe for support.

We all just sat there for a little while looking back and forth at each other, never saying a word. Finally, she added, "I notified your doctor, and he wants you to come upstairs to see him when you leave here. I've already sent him the video and the still shots and here's a copy of the stills for you," as she passed me two pages of what looked like photo negatives labeled baby A and baby B.

I thanked her as we left the room and she walked us back out to the lobby. Just as she turned to go back inside the office areas, I turned and said, "Ms. Tammy."

"Yes," she said as she turned back to look at me.

"When can I expect that first payment because I'm really going to need it since I'm having 2 babies instead of 1?" I said. We both instantly started laughing as she came over and hugged me and said, "Goodbye D.J. Morgan. And good luck. I'll be praying for all 3 of you."

I thanked her, and we all continued upstairs to Dr. Cleveland's office not quite sure what to expect. It was well after 4 so his office hours should have been over by now anyway. As soon as we walked through the waiting room doors, Mrs. Kathy was standing there with a Kool-Aid smile on her face and welcomed us back. I didn't have to weight in or give a urine specimen this time, she just took us all straight into an exam room. Dr. Cleveland came in before we even had time to sit down and asked me to lye back on the exam table so that he could listen to both heartbeats for himself.

For the second time in one day, I had all that goop on my tummy again. Dr. Cleveland then pulled out 2 dopplers and with a little manipulation there they were, two very distinct heartbeats. He just sat there listening for what seemed like forever. Finally, he handed the two dopplers to Mrs. Kathy, who was tearing up by the way, and pulled out the films and began explaining what he saw.

To his amazement, I was indeed pregnant with twin boys, and they were identical twins, as he showed us one placenta with the two umbilical cords attached to it. He then gave me a script for prenatal vitamins and explained his concern for my lack of weight gain. He also wanted me to consult with a dietician in the next couple of days because I hadn't had a drastic increase in weight gain as is expected with someone carrying multiple babies. I was already nearing the end of my second trimester, and I had barely gained 5 lbs. from the time I came in last month to this month. Also, he wanted to discuss possible due dates with us because now that we knew for sure that this was a multiple pregnancy, that would drastically change the due date from December 1st. It was very rare for multiples to go to 40 weeks, so we needed to be looking at delivering around the 36-week mark. All this was dependent on how my pregnancy progressed of course, but he was pretty sure that he would either induce my labor in early November or just by-pass that all together and perform a scheduled C-section.

I sat quietly absorbing all I was hearing, and once he seemed to be finished with his opinions and the options we had, I asked, "So are telling me that I absolutely won't be able to deliver these babies naturally when they are due?"

Dr. Cleveland sat staring at me for a second and simply said, "Honestly D.J. I don't care for natural childbirth."

We then discussed natural childbirth and the pros and cons of it. Basically, Dr. Cleveland didn't care for natural childbirth because he didn't feel there was any reason for a woman to go through that much pain on purpose while giving birth, especially with twins. Selk's main concern was that the babies would be coming in the middle of his season and he definitely wanted to be there for their birth. He wanted to know if it came down to me being induced could it be done Tuesday through Friday to ensure he was available and not away at a game.

"Are you serious?!" I asked, not really expecting or wanting an answer. *'This man is fucking incredible,'* I thought without any further outbursts on my part.

"What? That's an important factor. You and the boys' health and well-being are important to me, but I do have my career to think about too," he finished. Truth be told, his contract was up at the end of this season so he was concentrating on getting his numbers up to ensure he could ask for top dollar from Dallas or start shopping other teams. At that point, I was rolling my eyes again at the thought of scheduling my delivery to fit his football schedule. I just sat in silence, shaking my head in sheer disbelief.

We talked for nearly an hour with Dr. Cleveland answering all of our concerns. Finally, Mrs. Kathy gave me the information on my medical deductible and a possible payment schedule. Selk immediately took the papers from me and advised them, "Payments won't be necessary. I will cover any costs that her insurance doesn't cover. Matter of fact, go ahead and put me down as the father and the responsible party for all the costs, for all three of them," handing Mrs. Kathy his credit card and drivers license so that she could put them on file. My mom smiled at this grand gesture, but I let out a slight moan and rolled my eyes, to which she proceeded to pinch me for.

"OUCH!" is all I said, as I rubbed my arm. I knew better than to say anything else.

Selk jerked back around, "What's wrong? Are you in pain?" as he rubbed my stomach.

I knew better than to push his hand away with my mom standing there watching every move I was making, so I just shook my head no and pulled my shirt down as far as I could get it to go, without it looking like I was moving his hand away from my stomach.

As we prepared to leave Dr. Cleveland dropped the final bomb of the day on me. He was classifying my pregnancy as "High Risk." And because I had been deemed a high-risk pregnancy, they wanted me to come into the office every week to monitor the babies growth and my weight from here on out. I couldn't muster the energy for a civil response, so I just stood there shaking my head, fighting back any sign of the tears that were fighting to start streaming down my face. I just stood there rapidly blinking and rolling my eyes because this was going to drastically cut into my work schedule, and school was getting ready to start back in a few weeks.

"You look troubled D.J.. What are you thinking?" Dr. Cleveland asked.

"This is really going to cut into my work schedule, and school starts back in a few weeks," I said, obviously disgusted. They all just stood there staring at me before another major discussion took place.

"Baby I don't know that school is going to be an option for you this semester," my mom started as she stroked my head like I was a damn cat or something.

I snatched my head away and glared at her as Selkie offered up his two cents. "D.J. you really don't need all that stress or to be subjecting yourself or the babies to all those fumes and chemicals you use in all those science labs you take. Why not just relax and concentrate on you and the babies' health? Matter of fact I will hire you a personal chef and a cleaning service, so all you have to do is relax and grow my boys." You could actually see his chest puff out as he said that to me.

"Are you crazy? Grow Your Boys?! What am I? A damn garden?! Don't think for one moment this pregnancy gives you license to take over my life or tell me what to do! Thank you, but no thank you Selk!" I could feel my mom tightening her grip on my arm.

Dr. Cleveland cleared his throat and took my hand and began stroking it as if that would calm me down. "D.J., I really don't think you're going to feel like walking that campus this fall. Not just because you will be so extremely pregnant at that time, but mainly because the heat can be so draining and miserable at that time of year. It is your decision but remember, you were never supposed to be able to get pregnant, let alone stay that way. I think we need to err on the side of caution and do whatever it takes to make sure you have a safe and healthy pregnancy. I really need you to make it to 36 weeks if you can."

I stood there looking back and forth at all of them as I fought back the tears that were now welling up in my eyes, "Why are you all ganging up on me?" Of course they all denied that that was what they were trying to do, but they all still agreed that it would be in my best interest if I were to forgo this semester because it was doubtful that I would be able to continue going to classes in a few more weeks anyway.

This was becoming more of a horror show than I had anticipated. My life was basically over as I knew it. I was going to have to give up school and eventually give up my job because of this. All of a sudden, all of these other people were making my life choices for me. It was like I didn't have a say about what I wanted or what I felt I could handle any more. By the time we left the office, I was sobbing uncontrollably. The reality of my situation was finally fully sinking in, and I didn't like the view.

Because I was crying so much, Selkie and my mom didn't feel like I should be driving so they drove both cars back to her house & then she drove him to the airport. I didn't want to ride to the airport, but part of me wished that I had. I also wished that I could've been a fly on the wall for that ride because I had a sinking feeling nothing good would come out of them being alone. Only time would tell, but in all actuality, my fate was sealed the moment they pulled out of that driveway without me.

CHAPTER 10

Weeks rolled on pretty much as *they* decided they should. The chef came and prepared meals for me even though I objected in the beginning. The maid service came in twice a week to clean, and eventually, one of the ladies came by once a day to walk Tink for me. It was easier to just shut up and stop fighting them. Dr. Cleveland was very pleased with my weight gain and the babies' progress, something else we didn't agree on. I was looking more and more like Shamu every day. But as strange as it may sound, it didn't take long for us to fall into a pretty regular routine. Every Thursday night, Selkie flew into H-town (that's a nickname we call Houston) late at night, so that he could go to the doctor with me early Friday morning. That way he could fly back up to Dallas before noon and handle whatever team business he had to, without too much flak from his coaches. I'd drive to Houston to pick him up and then we'd stay in a hotel overnight instead of driving all the way back out to College Station.

I didn't end up going back to school that fall even though I insisted that I was, up until the very last minute. I finally had to admit that attending classes wasn't going to happen for me this fall. By the time classes got underway, I couldn't even see my feet anymore, and we aren't even going to discuss the frequent bathroom breaks, or how I was beginning to waddle already. But even worse I really couldn't handle all the walking that would be required to get from class to class in a timely manner since I could barely walk my dog for 10 minutes once a day without taking a 3-hour nap. And I had been in such great shape before this happened; at least I thought I was.

The only bright spot was the fact that I did continue to work, even though I couldn't handle the extensive traveling anymore, the more pregnant I became. Luckily my job graciously re-assigned me to an office position. Unfortunately, that too was a big waste of time because after 2 weeks into my new position, I was put on bed rest. It seems the extra exertion and the constant heat were causing me to have contractions, so the week after that, Dr. Cleveland decided that it was time to put me to bed, permanently. We were already discussing taking the twins early when we finally figured out that the motion required for me to shift gears in my car, is what was actually causing me to have contractions making the possibility of me going into labor a lot earlier than either of us expected or wanted, much higher, so the decision was made that I would give up driving until after the boys had arrived. Let me make it clear, *"they"* decided to take my car keys even though I protested. To try to calm me down about losing yet another freedom, Selkie hired a car service to take me wherever I needed to go. Again, they couldn't see or understand that having a car service wasn't the point. The point was that my freedom and ability to do what I wanted, when I wanted, without interference or supervision was quickly disappearing. Even worse, Selkie was slowly gaining more control over my life. That was actually the worst part of this entire ordeal. And since he had long started paying all my bills and personal expenses, he was becoming a permanent fixture in my home. He didn't even bother to ask if it was okay for him to come over anymore, let alone if he could spend the night. He'd just show up at my home and had a key made without me having any idea. When he was in town, he didn't bother renting a car anymore he just drove my car. I couldn't leave the house without him, he joined me on any and every outing. He even instructed my chef as what to prepare me for my meals, like I wasn't fully capable of doing that or what I wanted wasn't good enough. Basically, he did exactly what I didn't want to happen...he took over my life and became my warden.

When I tried to discuss the matter with my mom and how he was working my last nerve, my complaints just fell on deaf ears. She wasn't trying to hear it and would immediately change the subject or even go as far to tell me she didn't want to hear my complaints, my pregnancy was almost over, so I needed to just suck it up.

The final straw came the last Friday in September. Selkie didn't have to rush back to Dallas because they had a bye week, so he didn't have a game to get back to. We'd gone out to eat after my doctor's appointment and stopped by my parent's house before we drove back out to College Station. Everything was progressing better than planned, and Dr. Cleveland had decided to see how things went over the next couple of weeks before he made a definite decision on when and how these babies would be born. I was filling my parents in on my most recent doctor's appointment when the shit hit the fan.

When I looked up from our conversation, Selkie was down on one knee, holding up an enormous diamond ring. It was twice as big as the last one he'd presented to me. "D.J. Morgan, would you please do me the honor of being my wife?" he asked with the biggest smile I'd ever seen on his face.

"What? Are you serious right now?" was all I could come up with at the moment.

"Of course I'm serious. Why wouldn't I be? I love you and you're giving me not one but two beautiful sons. So what do you say D.J...... Will you marry me?" he said, looking a lot more nervous now.

"Excuse us for just one minute," my mom said as she jumped up, grabbing me by the arm, dragging me out of the room. When we were well out of earshot of Selkie or my dad, she lit into me.

"Now listen to me and hear me well young lady. Stop acting like a spoiled brat and think before you act. That man came back here without question when you called to tell him you were pregnant. Not one time has he questioned the paternity of those babies nor denied that they were his. He has stepped up to the plate and accepted responsibility for them as well as you from the very beginning. So don't you dare say something you can't take back, or you will live to regret. You swallow your pride and go back out there and say 'yes' to that man. Do you understand me D.J..." she finished. I could tell by the tone of her voice and the look on her face that that was more of a statement and not a question.

The tears were streaming down my face as I began to explain. "Mommy I'm not in love with him. How can I honestly look him in the eye and say I'll marry him knowing that?" I said nearly indistinguishable through my sobbing. "It's bad enough that I'm having *his* babies. Not baby, but *babies*. And now you're standing here telling me I have no other choices but to marry him? Really?" I continued trying not to get any louder.

"Let me make myself perfectly clear for you right here, right now my dear. You are going to straighten up your face, wipe away those tears, and go back in there and say YES to that man. I'm not asking you, I'm TELLING you. You're young and naive about what the real world is like. Until now it's just been about you and what *you* want D.J.. Now you are going to be a parent, so you have to put the needs of your kids ahead of your own. And what your children need is two parents loving them and providing for them. If that means that you have to marry their father to make that happen, then that's what you are going to do. Am I making myself clear? And I do mean 'crystal' clear?" still holding onto my arm and squeezing tighter now than she was when she snatched me up off my chair.

"Yes ma'am," was all I could say. I knew there was no point in trying to get her to understand where I'm coming from at this point. It was all I could do to hold my head up, so making eye contact with her was absolutely out of the question. I could feel her grip loosening when I didn't act like I was going to say anything else to her.

"Now go in that bathroom, wash your face, and get yourself together. When you come out, I expect you to tell that man you will marry him, with a *'smile'* on your face. You will thank me for this in the long run D.J.. Mark my words, you will appreciate what I'm saying someday," she said as she held my face in her hands and lifted my head so she could look me in my eyes.

I didn't say anything and just turned and went into the bathroom like I was instructed, to get myself together. I don't know how long I was in the bathroom, but it wasn't long enough for me. I washed my face and tried to calm down. I looked through the medicine cabinet and found some eye drops to help my eyes recover from my crying spell. When my eyes had more white showing than red, I took a deep breath and joined the others back out in the den. It was almost like I'd never left the room.

Selkie was still down on one knee in front of the chair I was sitting in. I sat down, and before I could open my mouth, he took my hand and slid the ring on my finger asking, "D.J., one more time. Will you please marry me?"

As I looked down at the ring, all I could think is, *'my mom is going to choke me if I screw this up.'* Suddenly my mouth dried up, and I couldn't seem to form words. I cleared my throat and swallowed hard several times, and with a barely audible response I said, "Yes."

And that's all it took for the room to erupt in cheering and some crazy dance involving everyone but me. As a single tear escaped my eye and ran down my cheek, all I could think is, *'this was a set-up from the word go.'* As I sat there watching my parents and Selkie hug and hop all over the room, I wondered if the deal had been made the day my mom drove him to the airport months ago. Had my own mother sold me down the river to the man she knew I was only using to get the man I was and had always been in love with? As I wiped away any signs of that lone tear, I knew in my heart that *'yes, my mom had made a deal with the devil and I was going to have to pay the fee.'*

The next morning, I woke up in a bed all to myself, so I thought maybe this had just been a bad dream. Then I glanced over and saw the rock on my finger and realized I was having no such luck. As I got myself together, it hit me that something else was wrong in my room this morning. Tink wasn't lying at the foot of my bed as usual. As I struggled to get all of me out of bed, the bedroom door opened and Selkie entered holding a tray full of food and flowers, along with Tink close on his heels.

"Good morning baby. You tossed and turned all night, so I decided breakfast in bed may be easier for you than going up and down the stairs this morning," he explained as he crossed the room and began setting up a small corner table to eat at.

"I'm really not hungry, but thank you anyway," I explained.

"You really need to eat something," he began as he came over and helped me to the table. As nice as his jester was, I really didn't want him touching me, so I pulled away as I reached the chair. You know you are eating for 3 now and my boys need to be fed," he said with a huge grin on his face.

That's all it took to get me fired up. "Look Mister! You don't have to tell me what MY boys need to grow big and strong, okay? Dealing with you, I've lost what little appetite I had! Are you happy now?" I barked as I crossed the room and slammed and locked the bathroom door behind me.

"D.J., I'm sorry. I didn't mean to upset you this morning. Especially after we had such a wonderful evening."

"You had a wonderful evening, not me. Matter of fact, everyone had a wonderful evening except for me, but why should that matter? It's not like my feelings matter in any of this," I screamed at the door.

It was quiet for a few minutes then he started knocking on the door as he jiggled the handle. "I swear before God, I will lose it if you open that door! Do you hear me? JUST GO AWAY AND LEAVE ME THE HELL ALONE, SELK!" I screamed at the top of my voice as the tears started running down my face. I can't tell you what exactly brought me to tears, but I do know that he was the reason for it all. "Walk away Selk, I'm not coming out! Just get out of my house and please don't come back! I don't want to see your face!" still crying and yelling but softer. "I'm done! I don't want to play this game anymore! I quit!" Although I was now engulfed in more emotion than I knew what to do with, I could hear Tink scratching at the door. I could tell Selk had moved away from the door so as quickly as I could wobble, I walked over to the door and opened it just wide enough for Tink to come in, slamming it again as Selk jumped to his feet racing towards the door when he noticed it was open.

He barely got out "D.J.!" as the door slammed in his face again. "Baby, what do you want me to do? I will do whatever you want me to do."

"Leave. That's all I want you to do. I promise I will send your ring back to you. All I want you to do is leave," I told him. As I sat on the toilet crying Tink jumped up on the chair at my vanity table and laid his head in my non-existent lap and began whimpering in unison with my sobbing. I'm not sure how long I was in there or where Selk went, but I still didn't come out of the bathroom. I had been in there long enough that I had cried myself out again, and my legs had gone numb sitting on that toilet so long that I had to slide down onto the floor and sit there leaning up against the wall, especially since my back was killing me. While I sat there with one hand rubbing Tink and the other rubbing my belly I could have sworn I heard voices coming from downstairs. I leaned forward as far as I could, straining to hear when someone knocked on the door.

"D.J. Morgan...get over here and open this door right now young lady."

That asshole had called my mom. But not only had he called her, she was now standing outside of my bathroom door. "Mommy, this really isn't a good time."

"I know it's not a good time. You know how I know it's not a good time? I know this because I'm standing in College Station, Texas talking to you through a bathroom door when I should be at your brother's science fair, cheering him on. So no D.J., it really isn't a good time for any of us, so get yo butt up and waddle your happy ass over here and unlock this damn door before I take it off the hinges."

I immediately responded, "Coming," as I struggled to get myself up off the floor and made my way over to the door and unlocked it. If looks could kill, I would have been dead 10 times over when I saw my mom's face. And who was standing behind her with stupid looks on their faces but my dad and Selk? She saw the ring Selk had given me on the countertop and never looking back over her shoulder, she told them, "Give us a minute." They quickly disappeared as she just stood there glaring at me.

"Get out here," she growled.

I simply hung my head and waddled past her and sat at the table Selk had set up earlier for my breakfast. Even Tink knew not to mess with her right now. He refused to come out of the bathroom and watched from the doorway. She sat down across from me and fixed us both a plate of fruit and yogurt. I honestly think that was the most scared I had ever been of my mom. She sat there eating the plate of food she prepared, not saying a word to me. She'd occasionally look up from her plate and look through me, not at me, but through me, and then go back to eating. Finally, she looked up and said, "You really need to eat something before you make yourself sick, it's almost 3 o'clock."

'Oh shit! I was in that bathroom for more than half the day.' I finally got up the nerve to say, "I really don't have an appetite right now, thank you anyway."

As she finished off the last piece of fruit on her plate, "Now see, once again Miss D.J. Morgan, you are obviously not understanding me even though I know that I'm speaking plain English, as clearly as I possibly can. I wasn't giving you a choice. I said eat, and I mean get to eating right now," she said through clenched teeth as she reached over and tapped the side of my plate with her fork.

I didn't like seeing this side of my mom, and frankly, it scared me. I picked up my fork and began eating random things on the plate, chewing but not actually tasting. As I ate, she still wasn't saying anything. Suddenly I felt sick to my stomach and began throwing up as I tried to get to the bathroom. My mom must have seen it coming because she grabbed a garbage can out of nowhere and held it under my face as she helped me into the bathroom. I dropped to my knees and emptied the entire content of my stomach plus some. I was still sitting there dry heaving when I felt a cold towel on the back of my neck and another on my forehead. As my body began to relax, she finally decided to talk to me.

"D.J. I thought I made myself clear last night, but I guess you had a momentary freak out this morning and disregarded everything we discussed last night," she said as she pulled my hair back out of my face and passed me a glass of water to rinse my mouth out with.

At that moment, I really didn't care what the consequences would be, and I cut in before she had a chance to continue. "Mommy, *we* didn't have a conversation. *You* told me what I better do and didn't bother to listen to what *I* want. If you had, you would have heard me say that I don't want to marry him. I never have, and I probably never will. If you remember, I've already told him no two times before this mommy. I'm not in love with *him*," I was almost begging her to hear me. "I'm in Love with Fitzgerald. I always have been, and as far as I can see right now, I always will be," I said as I started trying to lift my body off the floor.

For the first time in my lifetime, my mother was actually speechless. At least I think she was speechless. She had this surprised look on her face, and it took her a second to respond to me trying to get up off the floor. As she helped me up and steadied me as I brushed my teeth, she never said a word. I started feeling powerful again, the longer it took for her to say something. I stupidly thought that she was finally hearing me and would actually listen and support me in this.

Once she was sure I was okay, she went back into the bathroom to clean it up. I always kept a few Ginger Ale and other things in the mini-fridge Selk had put in my room so that I didn't have to go down the stairs to the kitchen at night, and got one out and started sipping on it as I nibbled on the saltines on the table. I must admit that he had been pretty attentive throughout this pregnancy, but that didn't change the fact that I still didn't want to marry him. Once she was through cleaning, she came and pulled her chair right up next to me and asked, "Do you feel better now?"

I hesitated because I wasn't sure if she really wanted me to respond. I slowly said, "Yes ma'am. I do feel better."

"Well good, I'm glad to hear it," she said as she picked up my hand and held it in hers. As she held my hand, she began to pat the back of it with her free hand. "Now, that you feel better here is what's going to happen."

My stomach immediately started turning again, but I knew not to let on, so I just sat there shriveling up on the inside because I already knew where this conversation was headed.

"D.J. you are going to put this ring back on your finger, and this will be the last time we are going to have this conversation," as she slid the ring back on my finger. "I heard everything you just said, and I understand how you feel, more than you know. But I will not watch you throw a great chance away, for a pipe dream. The time for you and Fitzgerald has come and gone, he's married, and he's not coming back, so you have got to get over him." The tears started streaming down my face again as I sat there dying on the inside. "Selkie has been patient, and he's taken care of you without hesitation. Most men wouldn't do that, especially after so much time had passed since the last time you'd been together. Selkie is a good man, and he is more than willing to take care of you and these babies so this will be the last freak out. This will be the last time you ever take this ring off without a damn good reason. This was the last time you will tell that man to go away and never come back," as she continued to softly caress my hand. "Now, I'm going to tell you for the last time...you are going to marry one Mr. Selkie Black so you might as well stop with the tantrums, suck it up, and grow-up. You will be a mother in a few more weeks so all of these theatrics are over and done with as of right now," as she stopped stroking my hand and grips my chin turning my head towards hers so that we could look into each other's eyes. "Do I make myself abundantly clear?" she said as our eyes locked. I didn't answer; I just continued to cry without allowing my body to move. "I'm waiting. That was a question D.J... Am I making myself *crystal* clear this time?"

I knew better than to keep her waiting, especially since she still had a death grip on my chin. "Yes ma'am."

"Good. That's what I wanted to hear," she held my chin and her gaze a few more seconds for effect. She had just put me on official notice that this was happening no matter what I had to say, so I had better get with *her* program. Remember what I told you earlier, *nobody* challenged her, especially one of her children. "Now get yourself together and come downstairs and apologize to Selkie. And by the way, we agreed that it's time for you to move closer to the family. It's not safe for you to be way out here by yourself, so effective immediately, you will be moving to an apartment that Selkie got for you in Houston. Dr. Cleveland has been informed and has agreed that it makes more sense for you to be closer and that it's a much better plan for when the babies come," and just like that she disappeared out of my bedroom.

All at once, everything in me began to explode. My face was on fire with the sudden stream of hot tears as the anger boiled inside of me, but at least this time I managed to make it to the toilet before I started throwing up again.

By the end of the weekend, my entire apartment had been packed and moved down to Houston. I was moved into a 3-bedroom condo on the 21st floor of a 25-story high-rise with a doorman and 24-hour concierge services, among other things I didn't really need or want. I realize that I might sound ungrateful, but maybe I would have been more impressed if I wasn't so depressed. Just as I suspected my life was no longer under my control and for a control freak that is as bad as a bullet to the brain.

The doorman's name was Charlie and he was very difficult to be cranky around. His smile lit up the room, and he was just so damn polite. I promise you that song *Happy,* by Pharrell was his theme music. I had waddled downstairs a couple of times already that Sunday afternoon and both times I didn't make it off the elevator good and he was standing there to assist me across the lobby to where I was headed. So no, it didn't surprise me when the elevator doors opened, and Mr. Charlie was standing there waiting on me. "Hello Mrs. Black. If you call down to the desk, I'd be more than happy to run something up to you," as he held my arm with one hand, with his other hand at my back as if I was in labor and needed assistance getting to the door.

"Thank you so much for your help Mr. Charlie, but I'm fine. I just needed to get out of that place for a little bit," by the look on his face I could tell he wasn't expecting that answer. There were boxes and people unpacking them in every room of the apartment, and both were getting on my last nerve. Again, I know that might sound crazy, but I was tired of being told not to pick anything up or that I didn't need to be bending over, especially by people I had never laid eyes on before. Now don't get me wrong, I appreciated the fact that people were concerned for my well-being, but I was not an invalid, and I know what I can and can't do safely. Selk had hired a decorator to come in and supervise the people unpacking the boxes. She was organizing everything, including my bathroom and the boy's nursery. I hadn't even had a baby shower yet, but the babies' room was already almost fully decorated. A sports theme, mostly footballs of course. It was all I could do not to toss everything in there out in the hall, so it was time for me to take a walk, again.

"Uhmmm, Mrs. Black, is it not to your liking? I can let Tina know, and she will work with you to change it to your liking."

'Hmmm, so that's her name...' I thought to myself. I hadn't even bothered to ask. "No, no, it's not that. It's just, I didn't choose to move here, so I guess I'm feeling a lot overwhelmed. I miss my old place, and I really don't have the patience to keep bumping into boxes and movers every time I turn around. And please, call me D.J., not Mrs. Black. And if you insist on being so formal, it's Miss Morgan, not Mrs. Black, I'm not married. Not yet anyway." I continued rolling my eyes, as he helped me lower myself into a chair in the lounge that was right across from the lobby. He helped me get situated next to the fire pit table with the perfect view of the little park across the street.

He gave a lighthearted laugh and said, "I understand, D.J.," as he fluffed a pillow he'd taken off one of the couches and situated it at my back. "How does that feel?"

"Great! You're hired," I said as he pulled another chair over for me to put my feet up.

"Miss D.J., if you don't mind me asking, what does D.J. stand for?" he asked as he took a few steps back. It almost seemed as though he was inspecting his work as he stepped forward and repositioned the chair at my feet and then placed a pillow under them.

I giggled and said, "It stands for D.J., that's all I can tell you. My mom never really gave us any explanation as to why we only have initials for our names," as I adjusted myself just a little to move further from the heat the table was putting off.

"You said we. I take it you have brothers and sisters?" as he signaled for someone at the front desk to go open the door for someone who approached carrying several bags.

"You are half right. I have four brothers. And they only have initials for their names as well. I'm the oldest, and then there's J.R., L.J., M.J., and bringing up the rear is P.J.," I said matter-of-factly. Before he could respond, I continued, "So we are the initial 5," I paused just to see if he got the joke, but it was obvious he didn't right off. "Get it?" as I did air quotes to help get my point across, without totally giving it away. "The 'Initial' 5."

He just stood there for a second then he said, "Oh! I get it. 'Initial,' because you all have only initials. That is funny," as we joined each other in a light-hearted laugh. "So if you don't need anything, I'm going to get back to work now."

"No, no, you're fine Mr. Charlie. Please don't mind me. Like I said, I just needed a break from the clutter. Thank you for taking such good care of me and listening to me whine. I don't intend to be any bother." I really didn't. I could do things for myself if people allowed me to.

"Miss D.J. you are not a bother and if you need anything, just let me know. Besides, it's nice to see someone who would fit right in at my house, if you know what I mean." You could tell he was being genuine, and I knew exactly what he was saying. I'd already noticed there weren't many people of my complexion coming or going from this building. *'Thanks a lot Selk... put me on an island in the middle of downtown Houston why don't cha.'* I thought to myself, trying not to tear up, again. As challenging as I tended to be, I instantly knew that would not be the nature of me and Mr. Charlie's relationship no matter what else was going on in my life. He just wasn't the kind of person you could be cranky with. "And please call me Charlie, you don't need to say Mr. No one else around here does that's for sure," he said with a smile on his face.

"Yes Sir, I'll try, but it won't be easy. I wasn't raised to call adults by their first name. In my family, you better put auntie, uncle, sister, or brother in front of any adult you address even if they were a close family friend."

"That's because you were raised right," he said as he patted me on the shoulder with a smile, then turned and walked away.

As I sat there rubbing my belly watching Mr. Charlie walk back to his post, I knew he and I would get along quite nicely. And for the first time during this move, I truly felt like I was being seen and my feelings actually mattered. I could feel my body finally relaxing as Mr. Charlie took a seat behind the small podium at the door. Unfortunately, that feeling didn't last long because a few minutes later, I noticed my mom's car pull up. I had to adjust my body as it began to tighten up as she barely spoke to Mr. Charlie when he held the door open for her, making her way over to the security desk, looking like she was on a serious mission. I stayed as still as I possibly could in hopes they would send her on up to the apartment, and she wouldn't notice me sitting over here before she got on the elevator, but no such luck. I watched her turn to look for me as the attendant point in my direction.

I could tell by her reaction to seeing me in the bar, this day was only going to get worse. She didn't waste any time coming over and starting in on me before she ever attempted to say hello. "Why on earth are you down here laying around like you're in your living room? You have a beautiful apartment up there, so why are you propped up down here like a visitor who can't get past the front door?" she kept going.

"Hi mom, how are you doing today? It's nice to see you too," making it obvious that I was not excited to see her, while also pointing out how rude she was being. I didn't give her a chance to respond to my snide comments, "I was tired of bumping into boxes and watching people I don't know organizing 'My' apartment like they know me, my taste, or where my things should go, so I came down here because I needed a change of scenery." I continued as I readjusted again, knocking the pillow that Mr. Charlie had spent so much time fluffing for me, to the floor. I began to bend over to retrieve it when she snatched it off the floor and put it back on the couch where it belonged.

"Get up from there and come on back upstairs where you belong. You're making a spectacle of yourself," she continued as she took the pillow from under my feet and put it back on the couch too. "Now get up and come with me," as she held the back of the chair that was under my feet, obviously waiting for me to move my feet. I slowly lowered my feet to the ground, trying to aggravate her as much as possible, then slowly leaned forward to stand up. I noticed Mr. Charlie coming my way and motioned for him to go back to what he was doing. He simply smiled and kept coming. My mom noticed what was going on and quickly adjusted her attitude before he reached us sweetly saying, "Alright now D.J., take your time and let me help you up," holding my hand and lifting my arm, making it seem like she wasn't just biting my head off. She looked up just in time to lay it on thick for Mr. Charlie. "Oh, you didn't have to come over here to help us. I can take it from here," she smiled.

"It's not a problem ma'am. I've enjoyed talking to Miss D.J. this afternoon, it helps to pass the time," he smiled down at me as he pushed past my mom and helped me up. You could tell he startled her, and she doesn't tend to startle that easy. It was a great thing to see as he helped me waddle back over to the elevator and rode back upstairs with me again. I could tell my mom was annoyed with me, but I also knew she wouldn't dare let on until Mr. Charlie was completely out of view. I thanked him again for his kindness as he closed the door behind us. I was even more impressed that my mom didn't light into me until she was sure that he was no longer at the front door. I left her standing there and made my way past boxes and bodies, over to the kitchen.

"Why do you have that old man waiting on you hand and foot? Helping you get back and forth can't be a part of his job," she continued before I could get a word in. "Look, don't get in these people's way and stay your happy self out of that bar. It's not a good look for an obviously pregnant woman to be *laying* around in a bar. You have your own apartment for that, and there are plenty of places for you to lay around in here with your feet up. I can't believe you sometimes D.J."

I knew better than to interrupt her, so I continued to sip on my juice and pushing stuff around on the countertop like I was trying to arrange things.

She finally stopped talking at me and asked, "Are you listening to me D.J., or am I just talking to hear myself speak?" I could hear her foot tapping on the marble floor.

"Yes ma'am, I hear you and no ma'am you're not talking to hear yourself speak," I said, looking over at her with a smile.

"Well, why on earth were you downstairs anyway?" as she pushed by me opening and closing cabinet doors.

"Can I help you find something?" I asked.

"No, I just wanted to see where you put everything," she said.

Don't ask me why, but that was all it took to set me off. "Where *I* put everything? As if..." I said half surprised and disgusted all at the same time. "Where 'I' put everything? 'I' haven't put '*anything*, anywhere!' If I touch anything, someone comes running in to tell me not to lift that, or not to bend over! 'Don't move that! Don't lift that! That looks better over there! I think this should go over here,'" mocking the people unpacking the boxes. "I'm not allowed to touch my own stuff! And speaking of *my* stuff...where is it? Most of this crap I've never seen before! And where did all these pictures come from? I can't remember taking this many pictures with Selk and by no means would I have put all *these* pictures of us in such prominent locations, all around *MY* apartment, as you keep calling it!" picking up a picture on the counter, trying to figure out when we even took that shot.

"D.J. we didn't want to bother you with all the details, we just wanted you to be able to move in and be comfortable," she began to explain. "We wanted to create a space for the both of you. You are going to be married soon. This is a shared space now, it's not all about you D.J.," pointing around the place. "Selk needs to feel comfortable and welcomed when he is here. It's not really appropriate for you to have all these pictures of you and other people, especially other men, sitting around for all to see. No man wants to see his woman all hugged up with another man," pointing at a picture of my roommate and me, from our freshman year at Spelman. It was of us in the park with several of our Morehouse brothers at Freaknik.

I slammed the picture next to it of Selk and me down and storming into the living room pointing down the hallway, "Go take a look in *my* bedroom. I didn't pick out that furniture! My furniture is in the 'guest bedroom' according to the decorator! So now, even my taste in furniture isn't good enough for *my* bedroom, in *my* apartment. Who picked that bedroom suit out? You or Selk?!" I stopped her before she could respond, holding my hand up to her, "NO, don't answer that! Because it doesn't really matter," throwing my hands up then putting one on my hip in disgust, dropping my head and massaging my brow line.

"D.J., listen…"

I cut her off before she kept going. "No mommy, for once you listen," I said, looking up at her as I made my way back into the kitchen. I leaned over on my elbows at the kitchen island, clasping my hands as I dropped my head like I was praying. I slowly raised my head and continued, "Mommy, there is a baby room down that hallway," now pointing down a hall on the opposite side of the apartment from my bedroom. "…that is fully furnished, but the strange thing is…I didn't pick out anything in there. It's like the baby furniture fairy came by when I was out and completely furnished the boy's room. You picked out all of that stuff, didn't you?" I asked, not really wanting an answer. "Did you even once, stop and think, that I might want to at least HELP put *my* babies' room together?!" I said, rapidly pointing at the side of my head. "I mean they are *my* babies, right?!" I kept going before she had a chance to answer.

"And for the life of me, I can't decide if I'm living in a museum or a jail! Or should I say a morgue?! Because mommy, I'm *dying in here!* I look around, and I'm sorry, but this isn't *'my'* apartment. This is a giant box in the sky that *'you* and my soon to be warden, picked out for me! I didn't even get to help decide where *'I'* would be moving to mommy!" as the tears that had long since welled up in the corners of my eyes began to free flow from the previous occasional drip that I had been doing my best to blink away. Showing signs of emotional distress in public view was never acceptable in my mother's eyes. Yes, I was inside my apartment, but there were at least 5 other people in here with us, unpacking, cleaning, and arranging things. "And, since we are on the subject of this place," I said waving my arms all around. "I wasn't bothering anybody, sitting downstairs in that lounge, minding my own business!" poking the cabinet top with each word. "What? I'm not even allowed to do that. It does come with the whole package for this place right," it was more of a statement than a question.

"I'm surprised I'm even allowed in this kitchen to fix myself a drink!" as I pushed a glass away from me and closer to her. It stopped moving just shy of going over the edge of the island top. "I can't even choose my own groceries," I yelled, snatching open the refrigerator door and pointing inside. "Who picked out this stuff?!" looking at her as I slammed the door. "I mean, look at that," still yelling, pointing at a bowl of fruit on the counter. "I haven't eaten an apple since I was 6! And oops…I'm *allergic* to bananas, and purple grapes make… me… gag!" I said as dramatically as I could swaying from side to side, giving it a more dramatic effect if that was even possible. "And anybody who knows me knows that I *detest* room temperature fruit!" I continued flipping the bowl of fruit over, startling her as fruit went flying everywhere, still staring her down, even after the glass bowl rolled off the countertop, crashing to the floor. "But I guess that doesn't matter because it looked good sitting here in this picture-perfect kitchen!" throwing my hands up twisting my neck and head all around not really looking at anything but her. Under my breath but loud enough for her to clearly understand me, "Where '*I*' put everything?" I finally finished my rant with tears and snot streaming down my face, no longer pooling as two small wet spots on my chest and stomach but quickly spreading out creating one big wet spot resembling something you'd see in a wet t-shirt contest.

My mom was just standing there with her mouth hanging open, hands still in the air from when she jumped back to avoid the flying fruit from hitting her. I could tell I had not only surprised her, I had seriously hurt her feelings, but I really could care less right now. I also noticed that everyone had disappeared that had been in the other room finishing up the unpacking and cleaning. I grabbed a Kleenex and blew my nose like there was no tomorrow as I squirmed my way up onto a barstool, trying to keep it from turning so as not to fall. Nothing else was said for some time. Other than my nose blowing and eye-dabbing, I don't remember my mom ever moving. She finally closed her mouth and lowered her hands when one of the workers tiptoed in to clean up the mess I'd made with the fruit and bowl. When the bowl hit the ground, it had to have shattered into a million pieces from the sound of it. We kind of just sat there in silence, glancing over at one another every few minutes but other than that there weren't any other noticeable movements or sounds coming from the apartment.

The awkward silence gave me time to reflect on what had just happened, which in turn caused me to start feeling a little guilty and a lot embarrassed at what I had just done and said. My tears had slowed down to a manageable drip again as I grew angrier with myself. I had never spoken or acted that way with my mother before, especially when other people were present. She was only trying to help; I really shouldn't have gone off like that. And the bowl... that was a really pretty bowl. As my inner embarrassment grew, my little voice snapped me out of the hole I had begun to dig for myself. *'Yeah, I may have gone a bit overboard, but honestly, what could she really say back to me when she knew everything I had just said to her was pretty much true?'*

After what seemed like forever in silence, she cleared her throat and simply said, "I am only trying to do what's best for you," as she walked over to me, gave me a hug and kissed me on my forehead. When she released me, she didn't say anything else and turned and walked away. She gathered up her things and left without as much as a goodbye. I just sat there in silence thinking about what had just taken place, in '*my*' new home.

CHAPTER 11

I believe everything happens for a reason and the argument I had with my mom the first weekend I lived in my new place was just a warmup for the way things in my life would go for some time. Almost every week Selk flew into town for my Friday doctor's appointments then flew back to Dallas that afternoon. In the few short hours he was in town, we always seemed to have an argument before he left and typically the argument was due to my lack of appreciation for all that he was doing for me. Sadly, this became our weekly routine and my weekly breakdown session.

After each appointment, I would have dinner with my old high school girlfriends Phaedra and Chandra. Other than Summer, my roommate from Spelman, they were the only other two people who knew what I was going through and how stressful dealing with Selk and my family were to me. The problem with my family is that I couldn't let them know what I was going through because whatever I told them would inevitably get back to my mother, which would have made things for me worse than they already were.

It was now at the height of summer, and we were having a record heatwave in Houston. I couldn't take being outside more than 5 minutes at a time, so when my car overheated heading to one of our weekly meetings, life with Selk changed forever. I called the ladies to let them know that I wasn't going to make it because of my car issues and Phaedra suggested that they would just meet me at my place instead, so I was to call them when I was in and settled. She offered to come and pick me up, but I had already called AAA so I told her that I'd just meet them later. Like I said, we were in the middle of a heatwave on a late Friday afternoon, so I wasn't surprised at how long the person on the phone told me that I'd have to wait for the truck to get there to help me. Thankfully I had been able to pull over to the side of the road as I called my mom to let her know what was going on even though I knew she was out of town already. She always attended our school events, and this is Texas, Friday night football rules. Once I convinced her that I was okay and explained why I was driving in the first place, I left the heat of my car and went inside a little coffee shop a couple doors down from where my overheating car sat, to sit in the air while I waited for AAA to show up. I was pleasantly surprised when after only 30 minutes the tow truck showed up since I had been given an original wait time of nearly 2 hours, but I was totally befuddled when JW's black and gold Escalade pulled up right behind it. JW or J. Dub, as almost everyone but me calls him, is Selkie's younger brother Johnnie Walker. As we say, his government name is Johnnie Walker Black. And yes, that is his real name. JW was a sophomore at Texas Southern University and was already one of the superstars on their football team. So at the least, he should have been on campus getting ready for walkthroughs for tomorrow's game.

He was talking to the tow truck driver when he spotted me in the window of the coffee shop and made a beeline for me. I made my way to the front door, but before I could get there, JW had me scooped up in his arms. "What are you doing here?" I asked, completely surprised. I thought to myself, *'What the fuck is going on? Why is he here? How did he know I was here or what was going on?'* as he hugged me.

"Hey baby girl! Are you okay?" he asked as he placed his hand on my stomach like he was checking on the boys too.

"I'm just fine. JW what are you doing here? How did you know I was even here?" I asked again stepping out of the coffee shop, looking back over my shoulder as I approached my car. He stepped in my way and started moving me away from the street and up further on the sidewalk.

"Selk called and told me to come check on you. He said you'd been in an accident so get here immediately and let him know what was going on," he said obviously worried about me and expecting the worse.

"I'm fine. We're fine. The only thing wrong with me is that my car overheated and its 110 degrees out here," I said, fanning myself as I started getting more frustrated. "Besides, how did he know anything was going on anyway?" I asked, showing him how annoyed I was.

"I can't tell you that D.J.. All I know is what he told me, so here I am." I could tell he was telling me the truth, so I left him alone. I'd be yelling at the source soon enough. JW must have noticed the sweat running down the side of my face and insisted that I either get in his truck and he'd turn the air on for me or I was to go back inside the coffee shop.

"I'm fine right here. Besides, I have to talk to him about my car," I explained, pointing at the tow truck guy.

"D.J. this heat can't be good for you or my nephews so for once, make this easy please. I'll talk to this guy while you settle down in the air," he continued without giving me a chance to respond. "So which one is it going to be, my truck or the coffee shop?" he said pointing between the two with a kind of, 'don't test me' look on his face.

"JW, that's *my* car, and I'm more than capable of taking care of this myself," I explained as the mechanic approached.

JW put his hand up, letting the mechanic know to hold on for a second. "D.J., it's hot as hell out here, and I'm not in the mood to fight with you so which one's it gonna be? I'll take care of the car," he just stood there waiting. So did the mechanic.

I let out a long exhale, "FINE! I'll wait in the truck. But this makes no sense! I'm capable of taking care of things myself," I continued as JW raised his arm, ushering me over to the truck.

He opened the door and reached over, starting the truck and turning the air up full blast, then turned and helped me up and inside. Before he closed the door, he smiled, rubbed my stomach and said, "Thank you D.J.," and then quickly closed the door and returned to the roadside guy. After a brief conversation, he handed the guy some money and returned to the truck tapping the hood as he came around to the driver's door.

He couldn't get in and close the door good before I started with all the questions. "So what's going on? Where's he taking my car? Did he say what was wrong with it? Why did you give him money? I have the money to pay for this," as I watched the tow truck pull out and then back in to lift my car up. It was impressive how quickly he pulled out in traffic and backed in to pull my car up the ramp without getting hit.

"Damn D.J., take a breath," he started laughing as he eased out into traffic. "I told you, I got you. All you need to worry about is what you want me to get you for dinner," he laughed as he reached over and patted my hand.

As I pulled my hand away, I gave him a quickie smile and said, "Ugh, thank you, but that's not necessary. You don't need to worry about that I have dinner plans already," as I pulled at the seatbelt. It was digging in, in all the wrong places. "This truck isn't built for pregnant women, and you never answered my questions," still pulling at the shoulder strap.

"Well that kinda makes me happy to hear since I'm not in the habit of transporting pregnant women," he started laughing as he glanced over at me at the red light. "Besides, this is a bachelor vehicle, and I'm not trying to have to transport any pregnant women any time soon, except for you of course," he smiled as he started picking up speed. "Anyway, as far as your other questions, he's taking your car to Ridley's over in the old 5th Ward. He said that just looking at it here he could tell your radiator hose had a big crack in it, but he couldn't tell if you'd damaged the radiator by just glancing at it. And I gave him the money for coming so quickly. If that's okay with you?" he continued as we pulled up in front of Triple J's BBQ spot.

"Well thank you. That was nice of you. But seriously JW, I already have dinner plans," I explained as I waved towards the building.

He turned the engine off, "So you're telling me you're going to pass up some of the best BBQ in Houston for who knows what... the queen of BBQ is passing on Triple J's?" he said obviously waiting for a response.

"Well....," as I looked over at the storefront. "I guess we can get something to go. We are already here," I smiled. We both started laughing as he jumped out and ran around to help me out. JW is a pretty good guy, I have to admit. And unlike his brother, he doesn't get on my last nerve within 5 minutes of being around him.

I waddled in thinking we were going to order and leave, but to my surprise, Phaedra and Chandra were sitting there waiting for us. I came to a dead stop with my mouth hanging open when I saw them. JW was obviously not expecting me to stop as he bumped into me hard enough that it startled everyone who witnessed the collision. People started jumping out of their chairs, hands extended, trying to catch me before I could fall.

I stumbled and recovered without assistance, even though I did drop my purse. "What? Y'all thought I was going to tumble over like Humpty Dumpty huh?" I started laughing.

"Girl! Don't scare us like that! We just knew you were going down on top of those babies," Chandra said as she grabbed my purse off the floor and everyone else went back to their seats.

"Thank you all for your concern, but I'm okay. That little tap isn't going to make me fall," I giggled. "Anyway, how did y'all know we were coming here?"

"Well, your mom called us, and we told her you had insisted on meeting us later, and she came up with this idea," Phaedra explained as she looked back and forth between Chandra and JW. They both just stood there shaking their heads in agreement. I should have known. My mom could orchestrate all of this in her sleep. I made my way to the counter to see what they had out to choose from as she continued. "So we decided to go along with her plan and just meet you two here then play it by ear from there," she paused. "Any idea what happened to your car?"

"Ask him," I nodded my head over towards JW. "He took care of everything. I'm just here for the ride," I continued still trying to figure out what I wanted. I could see JW roll his eyes as Phaedra and Chandra looked over towards him.

"Hi. May I have your 3-meat special please."

———————

"Of course baby! Which 3 meats? And you get 2 sides with that too," the old lady at the counter said. And before I could answer, "One of y'all give her a chair. She don't need to be standing up here waiting on my slow self," she laughed as she shewed them in the direction of a bar stool that was over in a corner.

"Ma'am that's not necessary. I'm fine standing for a little while longer," I smiled at her. "It's nice to stand some. All it seems like I do anymore is sit, lay down, and sleep," I continued with a laugh.

"Baby, everybody calls me Mama J, and I remember those days. I had 8 chillen, and everyone of'em took a little more out of me. Specially them last 2," she smiled, showing nothing but gums where her top front teeth should've been. "My oldest and my two youngest boys own this place. John, Jeremiah, and Joshua," she giggled.

"WOW! 8 kids...I can't imagine. I don't want to imagine that," I started laughing right along with her.

"Yeah. 6 boys and 2 girls. John, Jordan, Joel, Jered, Jessie, Jessica, Jeremiah, and Joshua. I thought I was done till that last surprise," you could feel how proud she was by the huge smile on her face.

"All those J's. How on earth did you keep up with who was who? And I'm sensing a theme," I smiled at her.

She laughed, "Yeah, it was never dull. But God gave me my babies for better or worse, so I had to give them all names from the *Good Book*. They all been to some kind of college and got good jobs and own their own homes. They ain't never been in trouble with the police, and they all living good lives. I ain't never had to want for nothing since they all got grown either." She was absolutely beaming with pride. She continued before I could say anything, "Who would've ever thought I'd be working for my chillen? I've retired twice, and now here I am again working here, for them," she laughed.

"Yes ma'am, I can see why you are so proud." It really was impressive.

"Mama! Whatcha doing out here on your feet? We agreed you would *'sit'* at the register if you're gonna be here," a young man shouted as he came through the double doors holding a pan of freshly smoked meat for the serving line.

"Aww hush it up now, ya hear! I'm not kill'n nobody. If I'm gonna be here, I might as well help out," she said as she shuffled back to her seat at the register.

"Sorry about that. She's as hardheaded as the day is long," he said as he wiped his hands on the towel draped over his shoulder. "Now how may I help you pretty lady?" he managed to say with a toothpick hanging on for dear life from the corner of his mouth.

I rolled my eyes as I sighed, "As I was telling your mom, I'd like the 3-meat special. I think I want the turkey, ribs, and hot links with your hottest sauce on the side and…"

He cut me off before I could continue, "I've got to warn you, the hot links are really hot, and in your condition, you might want to choose something else and a milder sauce as well." He had absolutely no idea the firestorm he had just brought down on himself.

"My condition? And what condition would that be? Hungry?!" I started getting louder as I slid off the stool.

"Well," he stood up straight and looked a lot surprised. "I just meant, with you being pregnant and all it might be too hot for you. Heartburn and all," he was trying to explain.

"What does my being pregnant have to do with the heat of your food? What, pregnant people can't eat spicy, hot food?! Oh, well maybe I should just have a couple slices of bread and a glass of milk instead!" I yelled at him. You could tell he wasn't expecting what was happening. He was standing there part deer in the headlights and part looking for the nearest exit. JW had begun to pull me closer and closer to him until I stopped my attack and turn my attention to him.

"Damn it! If you squeeze me one more time, I promise you, you won't be using that arm the rest of the season boy!" as I pushed him away. Phaedra and Chandra didn't want any part of my rant by the looks on their faces and how far they had stepped away from me. I really could've cared less at the moment.

"Move, boy! Why you go and upset this nice lady?" Mama J snapped at him as she snatched the tongs out of his hand and bumped him out of the way. "Baby don't mind this fool. He just a silly man who 'thinks' he knows everythang, but don't know nothin bout nothin. Especially when it comes to pregnant women," rolling her eyes at him as she piles my requests onto the plate. "Boy, pregnant women don't eat what they want. They eat what that baby wants," as she points towards my stomach. "And if she says she wants it hot, don't be making comments about her being with child, say something like, 'maybe you wanna taste that before you leave?'" she explained as she handed me a spoon full of the sauce I'd requested. "Anyway, yo job is to sell the food not talk folks out of buying it. At this stage in the game, you know what you can, and cain't eat," she paused and smiled at me. "You lucky she's still standing here after you said that to her. That's almost as bad as folks walk'n up rubbing yo belly like you one of them Buddha dolls or something," she said to me, still shaking her head while giving him a side-eye.

You could see the embarrassment all over him as he began to apologize, but the look on his face when he noticed how much meat his Mama was piling on that plate was hilarious. "Uhmmm ma...you wanna take it easy there?" he nervously said as he glanced up at us.

I was laughing on the inside, but my outside definitely didn't let on. Honestly, I'm not sure why I was so upset with him, he was only looking out for my well-being. Heartburn was nothing to play with. It could mean the difference between a few hours of sleep and no sleep at all. We all settled in to eat, but I really didn't feel like eating anymore. I pushed my food aside and just sat there, listening to the conversation at the table. After everyone else in line had ordered and paid for their food, I went back up to the counter and asked the young lady who was now serving people if she would call the man I'd yelled at, back out front.

You could tell by the look on her face she was a little hesitant to go and get him. "Uhmmm, Mr. Jeremiah stepped outside to the smoker, I think," she looked around for reassurance, but Mama J was ignoring her.

"I promise, I'm not going to yell at him again. I actually want to apologize for the way I just acted." The smile on her face was all the response I needed as she turned toward the kitchen without saying another word to me. "And, please don't tell him what I'm going to do. Just tell him that the crazy pregnant lady wants to speak with him again," I gave a light-hearted laugh as I rubbed my stomach.

"Okay, I understand," she said as she disappeared through the double doors.

I glanced over at Mama J sitting at the register taking in all that was happening, as she simply smiled and gave me a quick head nod and wink as if she was saying, *'Good job, you know you were wrong, but I'm glad you decided to swallow your pride and do the right thing and apologize.'* I simply dropped my head with a slight smile in response and waited for her son to come back out to the lobby.

I knew the young lady didn't tell him what I was up to by the way he poked his head out and peeked around before coming all the way out from the back with a sheepish smile, minus the toothpick this time, "Uhmm, how may I help you ma'am?" he said cautiously.

"I just wanted to tell you that I'm sorry about going off on you earlier. I had no right to take out my crappy day on you, so please forgive me," I said, offering him my hand as a gesture of solidarity.

He just stood there for a second, then finally walked from behind the counter and gave me a hug. "No, thank you! You don't know how much I appreciate you taking the time to offer me an apology," he said still squeezing me tightly.

I wasn't sure what to do, so I hugged him back and finally said, "Well, you're welcome."

"Most people wouldn't have thought twice and kept it moving," he said as he finally released me. When he backed up, I was finally able to get a good look at him for the first time. He was taller than I realized, standing a good 6 foot 4 or better. He had a beautiful smile, now that he wasn't chewing on a toothpick. And his eyes were a beautiful brown, and they were clear, shining, and kind. All in all, he was a very nice-looking man, too nice to be covered in smoke and barbecue sauce. "I'm sorry, I probably shouldn't have hugged you like that, but with the week I've been having, I couldn't help myself," he continued.

"Well I can completely understand where you're coming from. This day, week, hell the last couple of months has been one thing after another for me, and I find innocent bystanders are taking the brunt of my fury," I said as I glanced over to my table of friends, who all seemed to be taking very little interest in my conversation. "My name is D.J. by the way," I said, extending my hand again.

This time he took my hand, "Well hello Mrs. D.J. I'm Jeremiah. It's very nice to meet you," he said with a big smile.

"Nice to meet you as well. And it's Miss., not Mrs.," I corrected him. I found myself doing that more and more lately, but don't ask me why. I guess it was my way of passively letting the decision-makers in my life know, I haven't been pushed down the aisle yet.

"Oh, okay, Miss. D.J.," he laughed. "I'm not sure if I should ask after what happened the last time I asked you a question, but I have to," he said, still shaking my hand. "Why on earth is a beautiful young woman such as yourself, NOT married?" as he glanced down at my obviously large stomach and bare ring finger.

"Now, twin! You know that ain't none of yo damn business!" his Mama yelled over the counter. "When you gonna learn to keep yo mouth shut?" she said slapping a towel on the countertop like she was swatting him with it. Funny thing is he flinched like she actually hit him. "I declare! You can take the man out the uniform, but you can't take the detective out of him. She's not one of your suspects or perps or whatever you call 'em at the police station," she said, shaking her head.

Before I could respond, he glanced over at his mom and said, "I know that's none of my business," still holding my hand, "but I still have to ask." Now watching me again, "There's no way I'd have you walking around carrying my child and NOT have a ring on your finger."

I realized that I was blushing as I glanced over at my friends who were no longer eating or talking and were just watching my conversation. His mom had left her chair and was fake cleaning the counter behind us now as well. I could feel my face getting hotter as I smiled and lowered my head for a moment. I couldn't remember the last time a man made me smile, let alone blush. And the fact that he was obviously flirting with me actually made me grin on the inside. Lately, the sight of any man even looking at me made my blood boil, but I could tell my body was responding positively from his attention. Even the twins had decided to start bouncing around and making their presence known. "Ouch!" I said, grabbing my side.

"Are you okay?" he said, reaching for the same spot on my side that I had just grabbed. I could instantly tell that he was genuinely concerned, which made me even more embarrassed as his hand softly covered mine, startling both of us as our eyes met for the first time. Time seemed to stand still for a moment as we got lost in each other's eyes while *I've Been Searchin' (Nobody Like You)* by Glenn Jones softly played in the background. We got lost in each other's eyes as our fingers intertwined on my side, before we simultaneously snapped out of it, pulling away from one another like we'd just been caught playing spin the bottle in the closet.

"Here, take a seat," as he grabbed a chair from a nearby table and helped me lower my body down into the chair. That move startled JW and Phaedra as they both jumped up and were at my side instantly.

"Are you okay sis?" JW asked. "Do I need to call your doctor?" rushing back to the table and grabbing up his phone.

"No, no! Don't be silly," I said, waving them all off. "One of these hardheads mistook my ribs for a soccer ball is all. It just startled me and kinda hurt," leaning back, rubbing my side. I started talking to my belly, "I don't know which one of you it was, but somebody in there needs to settle down before you both get in trouble," I said as I continued to massage the spot and started giggling.

Phaedra and JW returned to their seats, but I suddenly realized that Jeremiah was not just holding my hand again, he was stroking my head as well. I felt my face heat up as he knelt beside me and started talking to my stomach. "Hey you in there, you need to settle down a little bit. It's not nice to kick your mommy like that," he explained ever so softly. "Wait," glancing up at me then back at my stomach. "Did you say 'one of *these* hardheads' like there's more than one in here? *And* they're *both* boys?" he asked, looking up at me with a look of surprise and utter joy. From his reaction, you would have thought he was the father and just found out what we were having and how many.

"Yes Sir, you heard me right. There are two little knucklehead boys in there, banging around like they are on a football field or playing soccer," I laughed until I felt his hand stop rubbing my stomach and rest on top of mine again. I noticed the look on everyone's faces and cleared my throat as I removed my hand from under his and sat up a little straighter in my chair. I felt like we needed a little more space between us, but I didn't want to be so obvious as to move my chair away from him. "Yeah, every once in a while, they decide to let me know they are wide awake and hungry," I said as I grabbed Jeremiah's arm and started pulling myself up to a standing position again. He grabbed my arm and leaned in with his shoulder and helped me stand up until I was steady on my feet. "Thank you, kind Sir," I said as I backed away from him and smoothed out my top. "I'm okay, I just need to eat. These two don't believe in missing any meals." I started patting my stomach as they both started rolling and kicking so hard that you could see the outlines of their bodies moving around through my top.

Out of nowhere, I grabbed Jeremiah's hand and placed it on my stomach. "See what you started," laughing as I held his hand on my tummy. Now maybe for some pregnant women, doing something like that was normal, but for me, it was completely out of the norm. If you wanted to piss me off, you reached out and touched my stomach and I very rarely, willingly stood by while someone did just that, especially a man. I didn't even allow Selk to sit and rub my stomach, let alone sit still long enough for him to talk to the boys.

He silently stood there with an ever-growing grin on his face, as he felt the boys toss and turn for a minute then he started laughing, "Oh man, they're having a serious wrestling match in there." I found myself just watching him, taking in how he smiled, how he laughed. I stood there and simply enjoyed the moment as he eventually morphed into a sidelines broadcaster, "Let's get ready to rumbleeeee...." and then started a hilarious commentary on who was flying off the top rope and what wrestling move the other was trying. As I stood there watching him, I couldn't help but smile and take in all of his expressions, his warmth, how gentle he was for his size, and his smell. I realized underneath that hickory smoke odor, he was wearing one of my favorite colognes on a man, Lagerfeld. I closed my eyes and absorbed all the positive energy he was giving me through his touch, his voice, and his scent.

We were all laughing at what he was saying, but I could tell by JW's silence that he wasn't too happy with how comfortable and friendly me and Jeremiah had gotten. He finally came over and took my hand away from Jeremiah's and said, "Yeah, come on sis. I think it's time we get the 3 of you home." He gave Jeremiah a look that screamed '*Back off, or there's going to be some furniture moving in here.'* He gently created more space between the two of us, causing Jeremiah to move his hand away from my stomach.

But to my surprise and delight, Jeremiah didn't back down from JW's look and never broke eye contact with him as he took my other hand and said, "Well Miss. D.J., it looks like the tribe has spoken. Your brothers' right. If you've had such a long day, it's time to go put your feet up and relax." He giggled and finally looking away and focused on me. "Two boys huh. Well, give me a second and let me wrap your food up for you, then you can be on your way," as he squeezed my hand.

My hand melted into his. I looked down at our hands then smiled, all the while hoping that I was only imagining what I was feeling, "Thank you so much. I'd appreciate that." I could feel everyone watching us as my face began to warm up again when I heard Sade's *Your Love Is King* playing in the background. I didn't typically embarrass easily, but I was in full blush mode, and I found myself liking it. I didn't want to let go of his hand, which became obvious to him, if no one else when he tried to pull away, and I didn't let go.

Mama J didn't miss a thing even if everyone else did, "Never mind you two, I'll take care of it," his mother said as she shuffled over and grabbed the plate of food off the table as we continued to hold hands and gaze into one another's eyes.

He smiled and gave my hand one last squeeze, talking to me with his eyes as he said over his shoulder, "Let me go help her. She's really not supposed to be on her feet," as she walked away. "She has a heart condition, so she's really supposed to be taking it easy," he said, shaking his head. "It's like running a business and babysitting all at the same time. I promise you, next week I'm taking the trailer to the football game and letting one of my brothers stay here and keep an eye on her." I could tell he was making light of the situation, but you could also tell he was really worried about her.

"I heard you twin. What does that old doctor know anyway? I feel great! The only time I'm really tired is when you and yo brothers and sisters keep trying to keep me in a chair or laying down or..." her voice trailed off as she went through the double doors. We could tell she was still talking, we just couldn't understand what she was saying behind the doors.

I finally loosened my grip and slid my hand out of his and said, "Well I can see you've got a lot on your hands so please, don't let me keep you. Like I said before, I'm sorry for acting a fool with you. It really had nothing to do with you, it's just been a really long and frustrating day." I tried not to make eye contact, but I couldn't help but get lost in his eyes, again. They were so kind and gentle, all of which I had already figured out from the time he hugged me. He stood there a few more seconds and just smiled at me with Sade's *The Sweetest Taboo* now playing in the background. I thought to myself, *'I can't buy a break,'* as I felt my face get all hot again. He gave me another heart-melting smile as he rolled my hand over and kissed the back of it then finally turned and disappeared in the back. I continued to stare at the double doors with my heart racing until Phaedra cleared her throat and snapped me out of my trance.

With a soft, "Yeah," I said, looking over at her like, *'What did I do?'*

She slid up next to me and looped our arms and just above a whisper said, "Ummm, what was that all about?"

"I don't know," I whispered back. And I honestly didn't.

"I haven't seen you mesmerize a man like that in awhile, or vice versa in forever. If I didn't know better, I would have sworn you two were long lost loves."

I glanced at her out of the corner of my eye and gave her a sheepish smile and hunched my shoulders without saying anything. I could tell JW was still paying close attention to us even though he was talking to the young lady behind the counter. I shifted so that he couldn't read my lips but tried not to make it so obvious that I was trying to avoid his gaze.

"Giiiirl, I've never seen that man before in my life. I don't know what that was, but whatever it was, it sure felt good. Was it that obvious that there was a connection? Or was I just imagining that?" I nervously asked. I was hoping that I was reading and seeing more into what had just taken place than there really was. I turned again so as not to be so apparent that I was avoiding peering eyes.

"Well little mama, if I were you, I'd steer clear of that man because he wasn't trying to hide the fact that he saw something in you. And since we're on the subject, where is your ring?" she said glancing down at my hand as she rolled it over to see if it was there. She turned and looked out into the street as if we were just chatting about nothing. JW must have decided that we were talking about nothing because when I turned to look in his direction, he wasn't looking in our direction anymore.

"My ring is in my pocket. After sitting in that hot car my fingers started swelling so I took it off before it got too tight," as I reached in my pocket and pulled it out to show her, but wouldn't you know it, Jeremiah returned with the bag of food at that very moment. He was standing there before I had a chance to react to his presence.

"WOW! Now that's a big beautiful ring!" he said, staring at the ring.

I went to slide it back in my pocket, but JW chimed in before I had a chance to get it back in my pocket or respond.

"Yeah, my brother spent a pretty penny on that ring. I was wondering where it was?" he said, staring at me like I'd done something wrong.

"Ohhh, so you're her fiancé's brother. Well now it all makes sense," he chuckled as he shook his head.

"And what's that supposed to mean?" JW stepped closer.

I knew I had to do something. This conversation was getting ready to take an ugly turn. I reached out and grabbed JW's arm, "Hey, it's not that serious. Chill out." As nice as JW could be, he still had a quick temper, just like his big brother. They both have the personality of a linebacker on and off the field at times. I guess that's part of the reason why they were both so good at their position.

"D.J. stay out of this. I was talking to '*twin*' here. We're just having a civilized conversation," he smiled. Problem is, it was one of those devilish smiles, not a smile that said that it really was a peaceful conversation.

I stepped further between the two of them and turned my back to JW. "Jeremiah, thank you so much for everything. And since everyone is making such a big deal about *this* ring," as I twirled it onto my finger again. "The reason I didn't have it on is because my fingers started swelling while I sat in my car when it broke down earlier, so I had to take it off before it got too tight to take off." My fingers were still a little puffy, but I was able to get the ring back on without too much difficulty, as I held my hand up for everyone to see.

Mama J stepped up and took my hand. "Oh, my Lord. That thing is huge! Is it real?" you could tell she caught herself after she asked the question.

"Mama! And you say I ask too many questions. That's *really* none of our business," you could tell he was embarrassed enough for the both of them as he spanked the back of her hand and took my hand out of hers almost all in the same motion. Still holding onto my hand, "That man must love you to death Miss. D.J." He made my entire body quiver when he called my name. I closed my eyes again and simply trembled.

"Yeah, he does. Very much," JW said as he took my hand out of Jeremiah's. "We *all* care about her very much and will protect her with our LAST breath," he smirked. Looking over to Mama J, "And to answer your question, Yes ma'am it is very real. 6 carats real," with the same smartass smirk on his face, but now looking at Jeremiah again.

I snatched my hand away. "Who cares how big it is. It's not like I asked for it!" I turned and stormed out the door.

"Now look what you did!" I heard JW yell.

"What I did?! Boy what the hell are you talking about? I didn't do anything but admire a beautiful woman and a *nice* ring. You're the one acting all butch." I don't know if anyone touched the other, but I heard a chair screech as it moved across the floor.

I could tell by Phaedra's voice she was struggling to keep them apart and get JW out the store. "Let's go! Let's go now JW!"

I heard Mama J yell, "Yeah, it's time for y'all to be gone! This a place of bi'nass, not no boxn ring!"

"D.J., come back here!" Chandra yelled after me. She caught up to me as I reached the corner. "And where do you think you're going Ms. Messy Boots? What in the hell was all of that?!" she yelled at me as she reached out and grabbed my arm while pointing back towards the restaurant.

I snatched away and held my hand up to hail a taxi I saw approaching. "I have absolutely no idea what you're talking about," I said, giving her a go somewhere and die look. Between her and Phaedra, she was definitely the one who was still more loyal to Selk. "And you've sure got you're nerve Miss Thang. If anyone is messy, it's definitely you," I turned to look at her so she could see my eyes rolling into the back of my head.

As the taxi pulled up, she grabbed me again, this time tightening her grip on my arm, "I'm not messy, I'm complex. Maybe even calculating but not messy," she insisted.

I snatched away from her again, "Yeah riiight." as I opened the door to the taxi glancing over my shoulder.

"D.J. wait!!!" I heard a man's voice calling, and it wasn't JW.

I jumped in the back of the cab and yelled at the driver to drive before I could even get the door closed. "Drive! Go! Go! Go! Now!" as I slammed the door and the taxi pulled away from the curb sharply, slinging me to the middle of the seat. When I regained control of my body, I looked back to see Jeremiah and Chandra standing there waving at the cab to stop. He was holding the bag of food he'd fixed for me to go. 'DAMN! Now I'm going to starve on top of everything else,' I thought to myself. I turned back around and told the cabbie where to go thinking, 'What a day. What a day.....'

I finally got home to a worried doorman and 20 plus not so nice messages on the house phone. I had long since turned my cell off, so I guess they decided to start giving the house phone a try in hopes that I'd pick-up. After I stood there listening to the first couple of messages, I took a wild guess as to what the next several messages were going to be like, so I let them play as I went to my room to get comfortable. The house was so quiet that their voices clearly carried throughout the place, even though my room was so far removed from the kitchen. Among the couple of sales calls, were my mom's 7 calls, Selk had called at least 10 times, and then JW, Chandra, and Phaedra had all called multiple times, along with the repair shop, but it was the last message that got my full attention though.

"Hi D.J., its Jeremiah. Please don't be angry, I made Phaedra give me your number. I have to admit I thought she was giving me your cell, but I guess this will do. I just wanted to make sure that you made it home okay and apologize for my part in upsetting you today. I know better, and when I saw that you were uncomfortable, I should have walked away, but something just wouldn't let me. I have to admit, I hadn't felt whatever happened between us since before my wife passed away four years ago. She went into preterm labor and had complication giving birth to our twin boys and died before they were delivered. Neither of the boys survived the night. Today, was the anniversary of their deaths, so when I saw you, I didn't mean any harm with what I said. I just remembered how bad my wife's heartburn would get after she ate spicy foods, so I guess I automatically assumed you did too.

Again, I was wrong for that, but I'm also sorry if I offended you because I kept touching you, but when you apologized to me, a wave of emotion hit me that I wasn't expecting. And when I hugged you, I felt something in you that I hadn't felt since well before I ever got married. I don't know how to explain it, but my spirit woke-up when I touched you. It sent a shock through my body that warmed my heart and my soul. My wife wasn't one to apologize, even when she was in the wrong, and the last time we spoke, it wasn't a very nice conversation. Actually, it was probably what caused the accident that led to her death. I'm a detective with HPD in the gang unit, and I was working late as was typical. We had planned a romantic dinner to try to reconnect. We had drifted apart before we found out she was pregnant, and the only thing that was holding us together was the pregnancy.

I don't know why I'm telling you all of this, but I guess I feel like you're someone I can open up to, be myself with. I know we just met, but I can't help feeling the way I feel about you. Although I was sad to find out that you are in a committed relationship, I will completely understand if I don't hear back from you, so don't worry, if you don't call me back, I'm not going to stalk you or anything," he let out a light-hearted laugh then paused for a moment. *"But D.J.... I just wanted you to know what I felt. I know it's not right, you being engaged and all, but I know you felt it too..."* after an even longer pause, *"...at least, I hope you did."*

And with that, he was gone.

I sat on the barstool staring at the phone so long my legs went numb. I hate to admit it, but I knew exactly what he was talking about because I did feel it too. I hadn't felt that way since Fitz, and that really made me sad. I just knew I'd never feel that way about another man, but somehow this chance encounter changed all of that. I was feeling things that I thought were dead in me and that I'd never have in my life again. I'm not sure when I started crying, but the sound of the phone ringing brought me back from wherever it was I had drifted off to. As I wiped my face off, I answered the phone without even looking at the caller ID.

"Where in the hell have you been?! I've been calling and calling you! Your cell is going straight to voicemail! Damn it D.J. I don't have time for your bullshit!" Yeah, it was Selk. I just sat there while he berated me, not really hearing what he was saying or even caring about what he was talking about. It all faded into what sounded like Charlie Brown's teacher when she was talking. I really don't know what he was saying, but suddenly I heard, "D.J.! D.J.! Do you hear me?!?!"

I didn't say anything and just hung up the phone. When it rang back I immediately knew exactly who it was and had absolutely no desire to talk to him, or should I say listen to him calling me names, so I decided to go back to ignoring the phone and started digging around in the fridge for something to eat. It suddenly hit me that maybe I was so nauseous because I hadn't eaten anything since breakfast time. I couldn't find anything appealing in the fridge, so I decided to order out.

I nibbled on a few saltines as I looked for my cell, finally finding it in the one place I should have looked first...my purse. To my surprise, I had 12 voicemails. There was no telling how many missed calls it would have shown if it had been on, but at the moment none of that really concerned me. The only thing on my mind at the moment was food. I called a couple of my regular go-to spots but for some reason, their delivery times were going to be longer than an hour, so I had no choice but to waddle myself downstairs to the bar.

As always, Charlie greeted me as the elevator doors opened, shaking his head and asked me where I was headed this late at night. We had become more like daughter and father than tenant and doorman, so it didn't bother me the least bit when he started questioning me. It was actually the type of relationship I missed not having with my own father.

"Well good evening to you too Mr. Charlie. How are you doing this fine evening? I'll be heading to the bar Sir." I giggled as I stepped off the elevator.

"Well, I'm doing just fine Miss. D.J. I was a little worried about you though. I understand you came back this afternoon, upset and riding in a taxi. What happened to your car? And why were you driving in the first place?" he asked as he hooked his arm in mine and led me over to the bar area.

I started to explain what had transpired throughout the day, and Mr. Charlie had lots to say as always. He was not a Selkie Black fan by any means. He'd witnessed one too many Friday aftermaths for his liking and didn't like the way Selk talked down to me when he was here. We found a quiet table in the corner next to one of the faux fireplaces. I tended to get too hot next to the real ones. Once he had me all situated, he kissed the back of my hand and told me to have the hostess come and get him when I was ready to go back upstairs. Now you'd think all of his doting on me would irritate me, but it really didn't. I knew it was coming from a kind place, with the best intentions, so I agreed as always and watched him take his place at the front desk.

It wasn't long before the waiter showed up with my usual. A ginger beer with a couple wedges of lime and a whiskey glass full of green olives. It's not what you think, there's no beer in it. It's just a very strong carbonated ginger drink. I've been hooked on them ever since I had one in a Jamaican restaurant.

I still wasn't sure what I wanted to eat so I asked him if there were any new specials tonight and he smiled and said, "Well since you asked, yes there is. Tonight we have smokehouse ribs, with country style potato salad, and cucumber salad."

'What's the chance of that?' I thought to myself with a little laugh. "I tell you what, I'll take that but instead of the potato salad can I have a baked potato with butter and chives?" I asked.

"Now you know how Chef frowns on substitutions, but for you Miss. D.J., I think the Chef will make an exception," he winked.

"Thank you. Also, what's in your cucumber salad?" I asked quickly.

"It's just cucumbers, cherry tomatoes, and onion slices in vinegar," he explained.

"Well that sounds harmless enough, I'll take it," I laughed, knowing the onions might not agree with me later.

"That will be right up," as he turned and walked away laughing with me.

I noticed that the bar was pretty empty for a Friday night, but after the day I'd had, quiet was just what the doctor ordered. As the lights outside faded, the fireplaces in the bar gave off a calming glow that I found easy to lose myself in thought. What was only a few minutes seemed like forever as I got lost in the day's events. I was replaying the message Jeremiah had left on my machine over in my head for the second time when the waiter appeared with my food.

"Here you go Miss. D.J.," as he laid out everything in front of me. "Is there anything else I can get you?" he asked.

I took a nibble of one of the sauceless ribs. "Do you have any sauce for these? Preferably something...."

"Something hot and spicy," a deep voice cut me off.

The waiter and I were both startled, as I looked up to see a very cleanly dressed man standing behind us in a tailor-made suit. Drink in one hand and the other in his pants pocket. It was Jeremiah.

"What are you doing here?!" I said, trying not to seem overly excited. "But yeah, what he said," I motioned at the waiter as I started laughing while I was squirming to get out of my seat.

"Don't get up. You're fine, so very *fine*," he said, smiling down at me.

'Is he flirting with me,' I thought as I stopped struggling to my feet.

"I'll see what we have in the back Miss. D.J.. Sir is there anything I can get for you?" he asked.

"No, I'm good. Thank you though." Jeremiah said, still standing beside my table.

"Please, sit down," I smiled up at him, *'please, please sit down for a while,'* I thought to myself.

"I don't want to disturb you, but I had to come over to say hello when I realized it was you," Jeremiah explained, still standing as he gave me a peculiar look.

"Okay, well please join me, and what are you doing here?" I asked, pushing the chair out so he would sit down.

He unbuttoned his suit coat and took a seat. "Only because you insisted," he laughed.

My mind was racing with the how's, what's, why's and where this man came from, so we sat in silence, just staring at each other for a moment. I must have had a crazy look on my face because the next thing I knew the silence was being broken by the sound of a very familiar voice.

"Miss. D.J., is everything okay over here?" Mr. Charlie asked as he patted my shoulder, startling me. He had a concerned look on his face as he looked Jeremiah up and down.

"Ouch!" as I bumped the table with my knee. "Hi Mr. Charlie. Yes, yes, everything is fine. This is the gentleman I was telling you about from my adventure earlier today. The man from Triple J's," I continued as I rubbed my knee.

Jeremiah had immediately stood up when Mr. Charlie startled both of us, appearing out of nowhere. "Hello Sir. I'm Jeremiah Thomas," reaching out to shake Mr. Charlie's hand.

Mr. Charlie immediately began to smile in a way I can't ever remember seeing him smile at very many men he'd seen me with. "Well, hello, Jeremiah Thomas. You are my favorite man right now," he said, shaking Jeremiah's hand and smiling down at me. "It's good to know that there are still some men out there who know how to treat a woman," as he continued to shake Jeremiah's hand with a big Kool-Aid grin.

Jeremiah looked down at me with a look of surprise, "So you've been talking about me, have you? Good things I hope," he said with a big smile. I could feel my whole face go flush. I hadn't been this embarrassed in a long time.

"I care about this young lady a lot, like she was my own daughter, so any man who can put a genuine smile on her beautiful face is a winner in my book. It's really none of my business, but she needs a lot more of that if I do say so myself," Mr. Charlie continued. "She doesn't smile enough, and that's a damn shame."

I really hoped they didn't notice me dab my eye with my napkin. I know Mr. Charlie meant well, and what he was saying was probably true, but crying in public was still not something I did willingly, and this was definitely not the time for tears.

"Aww sweetie, I didn't mean to upset you," Mr. Charlie said, kneeling down beside me.

"No, no, you didn't Mr. Charlie. I just got something in my eye," I said, turning my head away from them to conceal the water welling up in the corners of my eyes, as I wiped away another tear as it escaped before I could blink it away or had a chance to catch it with the napkin.

"I know it's not my place to say, but you know that man don't treat you right. And nobody but me seems to care is all. I get you don't want to disappoint anyone, but you need to think about *your* needs and stop thinking about everyone else's D.J.," he said pausing for only a moment. "I don't care if he can provide for you and those babies, he's not a good mate for you, and you know it. You just need to have the courage to stand up to him and your mama and tell them how you really feel baby," he said, pulling me in closer.

I tried not to respond, but when Jeremiah moved his chair right up next to me and took my hand, it all came pouring out. All the pain and frustration came rolling out, and it was like I couldn't stop once I got started.

"Mr. Charlie, you know I have! I've told her more than once, and she is

Deadly Peace

not hearing me. NOBODY hears me. Nobody but you, Phaedra and a couple of people who live too far away to help me even if they wanted to," I started babbling with tears now free-flowing down my cheeks. "I told him twice," holding up 2 fingers, "before I found out I was pregnant that I didn't want to marry him, but once I found out I was pregnant, that changed everything. My mom isn't having it. You've even heard her say it, *'Lisa Morgan's ONLY living daughter will NOT be pregnant and NOT be married.'* What else am I supposed to do? THEY moved me out of my apartment, without my permission, and moved me into this place," I continued throwing my arms up waving them around at the building. "I don't want to marry him! I've even told him that recently, but nobody is listening!" I said looking between him and Jeremiah as I gripped their hands tighter, "But what am I supposed to do? My mom calls me spoiled and naïve, my dad just wants me out of his pockets, and we both know Selkie has deep pockets and the ability to wrap everyone around his little finger," I said as I blew my nose into the table napkin. I know that is gross, but it was all I had nearby.

I'm not sure when my food got wrapped up, but I was still talking a mile a minute when I realized that I was being ushered out of the bar and across the lobby, towards the elevators. Mr. Charlie had me wrapped in his arms, steadying me as we got on the elevator, and there was Jeremiah, bringing up the rear with my keys, wallet, and holding the plate of food.

"Well not everyone has fallen for his fake charm. Especially me! I know the devil when I see him and Miss. D.J., that man has the devil in him."

As embarrassed as I was, I still continued to talk and cry all the way up to my apartment.

"You don't have to tell me! I'm the one who has to deal with him even though he's never in town. He's always here even though he's not here. I have no control over my life anymore! I rise every morning under the roof he pays for, and you best believe, I'm reminded of that almost every day. I can't even enjoy my favorite sport let alone my favorite team anymore because of him," I said, still shaking my head, barely holding it up anymore.

"What do you mean, 'he's *not* in town?' He's not here taking care of you?" Jeremiah said louder than he intended by his startled reaction. "Wait... did you say 'Selkie?' As in Selkie Black, the all-pro linebacker for the Dallas Cowboys, Selkie Black?" Jeremiah asked with his mouth hanging open.

"Oh, she didn't tell you who she's engaged to did she son?" shaking his head more in solidarity with me than as if he disapproved. I just stood there crying as we exited the elevator and made our way down the hallway to my apartment. "Yes, that would be the one. Would you mind unlocking the door for me son? That key right there," he pointed with one finger as he still held me in his arms. "And no, he doesn't live here, for the most part, he lives in Dallas and comes back and forth each week to keep her all upset and anxious. He pays for this place and makes sure she gets whatever she wants, but No...he doesn't take care of her. Not the way that matters to her at least. She's not one of those gold diggers trying to land a pro athlete, you young people talk about. She's a good girl, with a good heart, and great moral values. She just has more respect for her parents and the folks at her church than she should," Mr. Charlie explained as he made me comfortable on the couch.

"Take care of me? Take care of me?! He pays the bills around here, but he doesn't take *care* of me. He puts on a great front for everybody else and makes it seem like he's so loving, but he doesn't know how to love me, and I absolutely DO NOT LOVE HIM! I GOT PREGNANT, AND NOW I'M BEING ORDERED TO MARRY HIM! I'm just another trophy to him. Something to conquer and keep for himself on a shelf," I rambled on through a waterfall of tears and constantly blowing my nose.

At some point Mr. Charlie stopped my ranting, "D.J., over these last few months I've grown to look at you more like a daughter than anything else, you know this. And as much as I wish I could shake some sense into your mama and knock the hell out of your daddy, I can't. But what I can do is be here whenever you need me, for as long as you need me, understand?" I don't think he was really asking me, but I said yes, as he kissed me on the forehead and then turned to Jeremiah and said, "Son, I don't know you, but I know people. And I can tell that you are a good man. I've got to get back downstairs, so I'm going to trust that if I leave you up here with her, she will be safe and you won't take advantage of her in ANY WAY," holding out his hand towards Jeremiah.

Jeremiah jumped to his feet, "Yes, Sir. I will take care of her and no Sir, you don't have to worry. I already know how special she is," as he glanced down at me for a moment, pausing as we made eye contact. "I make my living off reading people as well," he gave me a slight nod and a wink. I could feel myself beginning to blush as my tears suddenly dried up. He smiled as he turned his attention back to Mr. Charlie, "I promise you on my honor and my sworn duty to serve and protect the citizen of this great city and state, that D.J. and these babies are totally safe with me Sir," he responded with an obviously firm handshake.

"I'm going to hold you to that Mr. Thomas," as he turned for the door. "And will you try to get her to eat something please. I don't think she's had much to eat all day."

With a big smile on his face, "Yes Sir, I will make sure she eats something before I leave." He smiled back at me over his shoulder, reaching out to shake Mr. Charlie's hand again but this time, Mr. Charlie wrapped his arms around him and gave him a big hug, startling both me and Jeremiah.

"Good man. I know you will." And with that Mr. Charlie left this complete stranger alone with me in my apartment and returned to his post downstairs.

CHAPTER 12

I came to a little foggy but quickly realized that I was in my bed and not out on the couch, which is the last place I remembered being. As I fully woke-up, it also became painfully clear that I wasn't alone. I could hear music and a man's voice in the distance, both of which were totally out of place and not something I was used to in my apartment. I rushed in the bathroom to get myself together when there came a light knock on the door, just as a man appeared in the doorway holding a glass of orange juice and a plate of fruit and a muffin. To my surprise, it was Jeremiah.

"What are you doing here?" I asked downright bewildered, but before he could answer, I realized that I was only wearing a t-shirt and I grabbed a towel off the counter and quickly wrapped it around myself as much as it would, to cover up with.

"WOW...okay, I see how you're going to act. You sleep with me, and the next morning you act like you don't know me."

"What the hell! We didn't sleep together! You need to leave. Leave now!" I started yelling as I pushed him out of the bathroom and across my bedroom towards the door.

"Hold your horses D.J., let me explain," he said, digging in his heels and refusing to be pushed anymore.

"What's to explain? You just need to go!" I finally stopped pushing him and just stood there, pointing out the door.

"D.J. I'll leave but tell me something. Are you really that upset about me being here or are you worried someone else will find me here?" he asked.

He caught me off-guard with that question, which totally disarmed me. After a few seconds of silence, I finally responded with, "Why would you ask me that? I don't care what anyone else thinks," I said, obviously searching for my answers.

"D.J., please don't lie to me, but you really shouldn't lie to yourself," he continued. He went and sat the juice and plate of food down on the end table and came back over to me, still standing in the middle of my bedroom. He held my chin in his hand, and gently lifting my head to look him in his eyes, "Now you tell me... why am I still here D.J.?" I couldn't speak while looking him directly in his eyes, and he wouldn't allow me to break eye contact with him. When I didn't say anything, he let my chin go and took my hand and led me over to the Chaise lounge by the window.

"Have a seat please," as he held his hand out to the chair. I slowly complied with his wish, still not saying a word. He lifted my legs so that I was stretched out, and there was enough room for him to sit down next to me. I turned to stare out the window, and he leaned around me to make me look at him again. "D.J., I'll ask you again. Are you really that upset about me being here or are you really worried someone else will find me here?" he didn't say anything else and waited for me to respond.

I turned to look out the window again as a tear rolled down my cheek. We sat there quietly as he gently wiped my tears away. After what seemed like an eternity, I turned to look him in his face as I began to answer his question. "I'm really not upset with you because of the reason you're probably thinking," I said as I twisted my body to face him more comfortably. "I'm upset with you because you make me feel. You make me feel things that I never dreamed I would ever feel again, and that is not a good thing," I explained, now gripping his arm.

As he continued to wipe my tears away, "Go on."

"Last night, I opened up to you about things that I've had buried deep inside of me for some time now. Not even my best friends know how many times Selk has grabbed me or how isolated I am in this place. He monitors who's coming and going. He monitors my phone calls and where I am, and who I'm with. I honestly wouldn't be surprised if there were hidden cameras and bugs all throughout this place. Everyone keeps saying enjoy all the luxurious things he has to offer me and that it's probably my hormones that has me so cranky, but it's not all hormones. Some, but not all. My girlfriends' say, get his name on the birth certificates and then put him on child support and refuse to marry him. But it's not that simple," I paused as I began to stare out the window. He quietly sat there watching me and gave me time to continue in my own time uninterrupted, "My *mom,* she is completely on his side, and nobody goes against her. What she says is the law. Besides, I tried to stand up to her and look where that got me...here on the 21st floor," I finished as I continued to stare out the window at absolutely nothing.

We sat in silence until I leaned forward as far as I could and laid my head on his chest. "I'm sorry. I wish I could say I love him, but I can't. I am not in love with him now, nor have I ever been. In all honesty, I was using him to make another man jealous, and it blew up in my face," I paused as I tilted my head up to look at Jeremiah in his face. It was amazing how calming his eyes were to me. He simply smiled at me as I continued, "He married someone else leaving me alone and completely destroyed. After that, Selk became a distraction to help me feel better, so my heart didn't hurt so much anymore. Don't get me wrong, we did develop a very warm and caring friendship, but at no time was marrying him on the table." He began to stroke my head as he turned so that we were both lying on the Chaise lounge, now with me wrapped in his arms again. "Jeremiah, I can't have you here. I can't start feeling things again. Me being numb is how I'm going to have to learn to survive if I'm going to make it down the aisle and live as Mrs. Selkie Nathaniel Black from here to eternity. I'm sorry, but you can't be a part of my life. So yes Jeremiah, *I* want you to go because you are a problem for *me*. Not because I'm afraid of what someone else would say if they found you here, although that would be a problem too."

I didn't realize how much I had been crying until I moved my head and saw the enormous wet spot I'd left on his shirt. He pulled my head back to his chest and simply rubbed my head saying, "Shhhh, shhhhh. It's okay. Everything will work out the way it's supposed to in the end."

I didn't try to fight him. I just laid there, allowing him to stroke my head like I was a cat and listened to him as he reassured me that everything was going to be okay. As he told me about his late wife and the final days they had together, I began to melt into his chest. His heartbeat was so relaxing, and his voice was hypnotizing. I hate to admit it, but I liked how I felt in his arms, and I loved the calming effect his heartbeat had over me and the twins for that matter. I rolled over a little bit more and crossed my leg over his and snuggled in. He placed his hand on my stomach and gently rubbed it, and the boys began to settle down as well. It was like his hand was a conductor's wand, and they were swaying to the motion of his fingertips as they moved back and forth, up and down, without doing a number on my ribs like they usually did.

"As much as I love the way it feels when you do that, *this*, all of this, is a problem for me. Even the boys know something's not right."

"What do you mean by that?"

"When you touched me yesterday, they got even more excited like they are doing now, but it's like they are dancing to your touch and your voice. They've never done that with Selk. When he touches me, they either get eerily still, or they get painfully, violently active. They are calm with you. I can't explain it any different than that, but your touch affects them differently than anyone else, and that can't be good," I explained as I laid my hand on top of his while he continued to rub my stomach.

He gently brushed my hair out of my face and kissed my forehead as he said, "D.J., they know the difference between a calming spirit and a troublesome spirit. Pay attention to their reaction to people's touch, they'll tell you everything you need to know about a person. And I'm not telling you that to pump me up as the good guy, I'm telling you that because kids and animals have a sixth sense about people and their intentions. They will always be a great radar when it comes to the people you come in contact with. Always remember that okay," he tilted my head so that we could make eye contact.

"Okay," I calmly said as I laid back in his arms and finally allowed myself to relax in the safety of his spirit.

He went back to telling me about his life and his late wife. He explained to me that he and his wife had been having marital issues before they found out that they were pregnant, and although things did get better in the beginning, those happy days didn't last long. The night she and the boys died they had gotten into a huge argument that morning. They said some very hateful and hurtful things to one another, and when she threw the mug that she'd been drinking her morning coffee out of at him, he knew that it was on him to walk away until they both had time to calm down. She chased him out of the house, yelling and grabbing at him until he drove away. Unfortunately, later that morning, she was in a terrible car accident and went into labor in the ER. Because of her injuries, she was rushed to the OR to have an emergency C-section but went into cardiac arrest before the boys were born. Apparently, they were only 30 weeks, and both had suffered severe trauma from the car accident as well. One baby was stillborn, and the other only survived a couple of minutes after that.

I could feel how much he was still hurting from what happened and how much he blamed himself for their deaths. My suspicions were confirmed when he told me that their deaths were on his head. It didn't help that he had stormed out of the house and drove to a bar where he spent the rest of the day and evening. He was so drunk when he got out of the cab that night that he never even noticed that his wife's car wasn't in the driveway and since he slept in the guestroom he had no clue that she wasn't even in the house that night. It wasn't until the next afternoon when the banging on the front door and the telephone constantly ringing woke him up that he found out what had happened over 24 hours ago.

I wiped the tears from his face as he explained how he had not only not been there for them, he had missed his only chance to say he loved them, and how sorry he was for the things he'd said to her in the heat of the moment. He explained what a valuable lesson that was and how he tried his best never to leave a heated conversation saying things he'd regret if he never saw the person again. Listening to him, I understood why he reacted the way he did when I apologized to him for screaming at him when we met yesterday. Apparently, his wife tended to be quite stubborn and refused to apologize even when she was in the wrong.

As he talked about his likes and dislikes, what he wanted out of life, and how he never dreamed he'd ever meet someone who could ever make him feel again, I began to imagine myself getting to spend my days and nights with him. I could actually see myself falling asleep in his arms on a regular basis, listening to his heartbeat, enjoying the warmth of his touch, allowing myself to feel safe in the bows of his arms. As I laid in his arms, listening to his heartbeat, I began to image me, Jeremiah, and the twins playing in the park and laughing under the summer sun. I simply drifted off to sleep with images of the four of us living out our lives as a blissfully happy little family. The next thing I knew, I was sitting straight up in my bed, in a panic.

"D.J. Morgan! What in heaven's name is going on in here?! Who is this MAN!?"

Jeremiah must have picked me up and put me in the bed again when I dozed off, and apparently, he dozed off too because he nearly fell off the bed when I jumped up in a panic, startling him awake.

"Momma, what are you doing here? And how did you get in here?" I asked as I scrambled to my feet. "It's not what it looks like, let me explain," grabbing the robe off the end of the bed and quickly covering up. My stomach felt queasy as I glanced over to see Jeremiah struggling to put on his shirt. How was I going to explain that there was nothing going on and more importantly, who Jeremiah was?

"What it looks like, is that you're in bed with another man! How can you possibly explain that to me?" she just stood in the doorway with her hands on her hips with an expression that was part mayhem and the other part pissed off to the highest of pisstivity. How could you really argue that point? I was, in fact, in the bed with another man. As I started to explain Jeremiah jumped in. Crossing the room with his hand extended, "Hello Mrs. Morgan. My name is Jeremiah Thomas, and I'm simply a friend to your daughter. She was upset, and I sat here giving her a shoulder to cry on and in the process she fell asleep, so I brought her in here to be more comfortable so that she could get some rest. The only reason I was in here with her is that I simply dozed off trying to calm the babies down so that she could get some rest."

His words surprised both of us, "To calm the babies down? What do you mean, to calm the babies down?" she asked, loosening up a bit. He could tell by the look on my face I was not only surprised, I was also mortified.

The look on my mom's face though was almost peaceful, if not happily impressed, but I knew that I had to be reading her wrong.

"Well see they get pretty riled up when she's upset, but they are like karate experts when she hasn't eaten on top of that. So I was trying to get her to eat a little, but she didn't eat very much before she fell asleep," as he nodded at the food on the table. "So when I put her to bed, I could see how much they were moving around, and she started whimpering a little," as he glanced over at me. "So I sat here and talked to the boys until they calmed down. Problem is when I'd stop talking they'd start kicking again, so I simply laid down beside her and started singing to her tummy. I guess I fell asleep like all of them," he finished with a quirky smile on his face. The entire time he had been holding his hand out to my mom, but she hadn't attempted to shake his hand yet.

We all stood there in silence, me with a silly grin on my face and happy tears in my eyes, my mom with her hands back on her hips, and Jeremiah with his outstretched hand. I can't tell you how much time passed, but it felt like forever went by without a peep or visible movement from any of us. My mom and Jeremiah stood there, staring each other down like two kids on a playground when my mother finally broke the silence and reached out to shake Jeremiah's hand.

"It's nice to meet you, Mr. Thomas. I appreciate what you did for my daughter and my grandchildren but let this be the last time we greet each other this way. As you can tell by the sizeable stone on her ring finger, she is spoken for and soon to be married."

"Yes, ma'am. I can see that," as he glanced over towards me. "I didn't…"

"I'm not finished yet, so please don't interrupt me again," she quickly said, looking very stone-faced.

Jeremiah simply nodded yes to her and then turned to look at me. I was standing there with my head down, now staring at the ground, not making a sound. It was painfully clear that I wasn't going to be any type of help to him. Basically, he was on his own. I knew that no matter what she said to him, it didn't half compare to what she was saving for me.

"D.J. is in a vulnerable state right now, so she doesn't need anyone trying to confuse her or give her any silly ideas. You two are very lucky it was me who found you like that. What do think would have happened if her fiancé had been the one to walk in, to find you two curled up together, in *their* bed?" Before either of us could respond, although we both knew better than to interrupt her again, "I can tell you what would've happened. The police and an ambulance would have been up here trying to revive someone and arresting someone else. So how about we *not* put anyone in that situation, shall we Jeremiah Thomas. I'm sure you're a kind man and that you were only trying to help, but let me give you a free piece of advice," she gave a long pause to give the full effect and weight to what she was about to say. "The next time you want to help, DON'T! D.J. is a big girl, and she can take care of herself. If she needs a shoulder to cry on, she has me, her dad, or her fiancé's shoulders to cry on. All she has to do is pick up the phone and call one of us," she continued burning a hole right through me with her glare. "So thank you Sir, but I can take it from here. Let me show you to the door."

She didn't give him a chance to respond, she simply turned, walked out of my bedroom and towards the front door. Jeremiah just stood there staring at the empty space that she had once occupied and slowly started shaking his head. He finally turned to look at me and just stood there watching me, without saying a word. We stood there in silence, staring into one another's eyes holding a full conversation without a word ever being spoken.

'WOW! Now I see what Mr. Charlie was talking about. She's worse than a Texas twister.'

'Jeremiah, I'm sorry about all of this, and I'm sorry for not being brave enough to stop her from berating you like you were a child.'

'D.J it's okay, I totally understand what you're going through now. I'm sorry you are having to deal with this but believe me when I say, I don't blame you. I understand, and I wish there was something more I could do to help you.'

I felt what was the first of many more tear to come, welling up in the corners of my eyes, and then quickly roll down my cheeks, *'I wish you could help me. She's not going to listen even if we both tied her to a chair and gagged her, to make her listen. She is totally team Selkie, and that means anything, and anyone who interferes with her plans for me is enemy number one. Even if it's obvious that I'd be better off without him...and with you,'* as I felt myself blushing and I dropped my head again.

As always, he came over and gently wiped away my tears and gently raised my head by lifting up on my chin. Once our eyes were locked onto one another again, he silently continued, *'Oh, my dear, dear D.J. don't cry. I can't stand it when I see you cry. If you want me to, I will gladly take you away from all of this,'* he placed his free hand on my stomach, instantly calming the boys down. With all of the commotion, my stomach was jumping hard enough that it was easy for him to see it, even from a distance and through my robe.

And with that, I finally broke our nonverbal conversation. I softly said, "I think you need to leave. It would be better for both of us if you go. And Jeremiah..." I paused for a moment.

"Yes, D.J." as he continued to stroke the side of my face while he gently rubbed my stomach at the same time.

"Please don't come back," as I cupped his hand to my face and dug my cheek into his palm.

"D.J., if that is what *you* want. I'll leave and never contact you again, but ONLY if that's what you want," he said as he grabbed me up in his arms and gave me a hug.

I held on for dear life, as I allowed his aroma to engulf every part of my being, but I knew that I had to let him go. I released him and softly pushed away from him. I could feel how hard and fast his heart was beating with my hand when I touched his chest and everything in me wanted to disappear in his arms again, but I knew that that wasn't possible.

"Yes, I need you to go. My life is complicated as it is, and this, whatever this is, can only complicate it more." I felt the first tear fall, and as he moved to wipe it away, I stopped him blocking his hand. "Please don't. I can't handle you touching me like that."

He took my hand and softly kissed my palm. "Your wish is my command, beautiful lady." As he turned to leave my room, he stopped for a moment and said over his shoulder, "D.J., you know how to find me if you need to. But just in case, here's my business card. Call me day or night if you need me, for anything," quickly crossing the room taking a pen off the desk. "Here's my pager number and my home number. Call me if you need me, and I do mean for anything or at any time D.J." He turned and came back over to me and placed his card in the palm of my hand and closed my fingers around it. He kissed me on my forehead and walked away.

I sat on the end of my bed with tears streaming down my face, holding on to the card for dear life. I was so lost in my grief that I didn't even notice that my mother had returned to my room. I just happened to look up to see her quietly standing there in the doorway, watching me with a look of utter fear across her face. Honestly, I could've cared less what she had to say right now, but for the first time in a very long time, I felt like she actually could feel my pain and cared that I was hurting.

She simply came over and sat beside me, turning my face to her breast and said, "It's okay baby. You can cry on my shoulder as long as you need to. I truly understand."

I looked up at her in complete disbelief, "*Whaaat?*"

"Shhhh, shhhhh. Cry all you want. Mamma understands." She sat there holding me in her arms and didn't say anything else to me as she began humming my favorite song from when I was a child and stroking my head.

In that moment we connected in a way that we hadn't in years. She held me like she would protect me from the world with her last dying breath. She stroked my head and allowed me to cry on her shoulder until I couldn't cry anymore. She never scolded me. She never said a word. She simply sat there holding me tight, rocking me, as she sang my favorite song. She also never spoke of what happened in my room that day to anyone, not even to me.

CHAPTER 13

Life after that continued with a whole lot of closely monitored routine. Selkie was not happy with me hanging up on him or the fact that I had snuck out to drive my car when it stopped, so as I suspected I not only received a new car, I got a new car with...a permanent driver. Also, anyone who visited me had to be on *his* approved visitor list. All deliveries were left at the front desk, and someone brought them up to me. For the most part, I saw no one that he didn't know, and I went nowhere that he wasn't very quickly made aware of. Basically, I was on his leash, and my collar was getting tighter and tighter.

I'd like to tell you that I'd forgotten about Jeremiah, but unfortunately, I hadn't. I honestly tried too, but I just couldn't get him out of my head, even worse, out of my heart. Even though it was becoming more difficult for me to get around, due to my size, not my transportation, I still managed to peek in on him on occasion. Friday's after my weekly doctor's appointment became BBQ Friday's for a few weeks. Jeremiah put an end to that though. He always disappeared around the time me, Chandra, and Phaedra would show up. Mama J was there every once in a while, and she always greeted me with a hug and a smile, like we were best friends and she hadn't seen me in years. She explained to me that seeing me was too painful for Jeremiah, but he always asked her or the staff how I looked, how I was doing, and did I look happy. Apparently, the reports always seemed to make him happier, but the fact that no one could honestly say that I looked happy, even though I always had a smile on my face seemed to bother him. I didn't realize how much it bothered him until Mr. Charlie delivered a special package to me one late afternoon.

In October I was given the news I had been hoping would never come, Dr. Cleveland was putting me on complete bed rest. The only time I really left my apartment after that was for my doctor's appointments, which were increased to twice a week. And to make sure I didn't go anywhere else, Selk hired Taylor to be my full-time nanny. Wherever I went, she went. Then he also started riding back to the apartment with me on Friday's and then the driver took him to the airport. I didn't dare ask to stop for BBQ with Taylor or Selk in the car, so those little rays of light came to an abrupt end. The girls didn't even come around on Friday's anymore because of Selk. Apparently, I was getting too riled up with them on the weekend, so they weren't allowed up anymore unless he said it was okay.

The only time my friends could get past the front desk was when the 3 women who staffed the desk weren't around. I guess that should have set-off some type of warning bells, but there was so much going on that I just added that to the growing pile of Selkie's rules and regulations. My mom wasn't much help either when I told her what was going on. All she said is that she'd talk to him, but I didn't see much change if she did. And once Taylor came on board, she would simply tell me, '*Try to make the best of the situation, for now, you won't be pregnant forever.*'

I spent more and more time alone, crying in my room, and praying for a way out of this mess. God had to have a plan for me, but I couldn't see it, nor did I understand why I had to go through all of this misery. I was never supposed to be able to get pregnant let alone pregnant with twins, so why was God punishing me so? Being pregnant was starting to make me lose my family and everyone else who ever cared about me. And to top it all off, I was way past beginning to have feelings for a man who I couldn't be with and didn't expect to ever have these kind of feelings for, ever again. Feeling this way about a man had died when Fitz married another woman, so why would God allow me to feel this way again, especially now under these circumstances, and for a man I barely even knew? A man who probably wasn't even giving me a second thought anymore. I was at the end of my rope and needed some kind of lifeline. My outlook on life was getting darker and darker, even the babies weren't moving around as much anymore. So when Mr. Charlie showed up with a special delivery, I not only found out how much Jeremiah still thought about me and how much he really did care about me, I also figured out that maybe God was paying attention and had sent me the lifeline I desperately needed, although completely unexpected and totally inappropriate. It gave me a shimmer of hope and a much-needed tickle, that my "on time God," could also be just as inappropriate as me.

I was resting in the den when the doorbell rang, but before I could get up, Taylor appeared out of nowhere. "Sit down, sit down Miss. D.J... I'll get it. Remember that is what I'm here for," she laughed as she went to answer the door. Taylor was my newest gift from Selk. She was to keep the place clean, so I didn't have to do it, be my companion on the very rare occasions that I did leave the apartment, and I guess to be my new "friend," since he managed to run my real friends off. Basically, I felt like she was his cleaning spy to make sure I wasn't doing anything or seeing anyone that he didn't approve of. So basically if you weren't family or one of his friends, you didn't get up to see me, and I couldn't sneak downstairs anymore, so he finally had me where he wanted...on a deserted island all alone, and he was my only way off.

I could tell by the sound of her voice she was annoyed, "It's Mr. Charlie. He has a package for you." He must have told her that he had to deliver whatever he had to me personally. Anyone else would have left what they had with her but my friend, he didn't worry about her or Selk's feelings for that matter.

"Well, let him in," I said as I immediately began fixing my hair and making space on the couch for him.

"Hello Sunshine. How are you feeling today?"

"I'm maintaining," I smiled. He was holding the most beautiful bouquet of flowers and balloons that I'd seen in forever. "Oh my God! How beautiful!" I scrambled to stand up.

"Miss. D.J., you're not supposed to be getting so excited and moving that fast isn't good for you either," Taylor said as she scrambled to help me to my feet while giving Mr. Charlie a death stare that he completely ignored.

"I'm fine! I'm fine!" I swatted her away.

"Well, I'll take those then," as she reached for the vase and the balloons.

"No you won't," I reached out to hold her back. "Mr. Charlie, you put them right here on the end table," I gestured as I tossed the picture of Selk to the side to make room. "If you want to help, put *that* somewhere else please," I told Taylor. You could tell she was annoyed, but I really didn't care. "Don't worry about us, you can go now," I said without ever looking in her direction.

Mr. Charlie was just standing there with a slight smirk on his face as she picked up the picture and left the room.

"Well, I see you still have a way of commanding the room young lady."

"Yeah, the apple doesn't fall too far from the tree I guess." I glanced over in the direction Taylor had disappeared in, "I get tired of my keeper. I'm surprised she isn't trying to wipe my behind to keep an eye on me behind closed doors," I explained. I looked around to make sure the coast was clear, "Never mind her, sit down. Since you wouldn't release these to Taylor, I take it they are not from Selk?" I whispered, returning his smirk with a much bigger smile.

"That would be correct," he smiled as he removed the card from his breast pocket. "I knew that she would be the one to open the door so I kept the card so that if you were asleep or otherwise disposed of, she wouldn't be able to report back to him who sent this to you or get rid of it before you saw it," he smiled as he passed me the card. To my delight, it was a note inside of it from Jeremiah.

Hello Beautiful Lady!

I heard through the grapevine that you were on bed rest and didn't get out much anymore, and you don't get to have many outside visitors either. It hurts me to imagine you being so isolated from people who really care about you. D.J. I know I said that I'd keep my distance, but I couldn't let another day go by without saying something to you. Since I know that you are not ready to stand up to your mom or Selkie, hopefully, this small token of my feelings for you will help bring a little bit of sunshine to your day and put a smile on your face, even if only for a little while.

So, D.J. Morgan, you are the recipient of the 1st, All You Can Eat Unlimited Coupon, for all the Triple J's BBQ you care to eat, heavy on the hot & spicy sauce, your heart can handle and a bouquet to remind you that you are worthy of beautiful things, meant for no one else but you.

I don't know where the box was hidden, but I looked up for a moment and realized that Mr. Charlie was presenting me with a plain white box with a beautiful velvet ribbon and bow on the top. I stopped reading and began opening the box. Inside was something I never expected. It was a hand-carved African puzzle box. The box was the most exquisite thing I'd ever seen. It was trimmed in gold, with onyx and mother of pearl inlay adorning the carvings of children playing by a river and women pampering a pregnant woman not far away from them. The men were close by, some holding spears and others playing the drums. The box was a beautiful representation of a village protecting life while also celebrating it.

Mr. Charlie handed me a tissue as tears began to well up in the corners of my eyes.

"It's beautiful," I finally managed to get out as my fingers gently swept across the box.

"Well open it up," he smiled.

Inside was a card explaining how to set the lock, but that wasn't the only thing in the box. There was something wrapped in a pretty paisley tissue paper. I sat the box to the side and removed what turned out to be a leather-bound diary. It wasn't like any diary I'd ever seen before. This book had a lock on it as well, but not the typical key lock you usually find on a diary. This book had a lock on it that resembled that of a small lockbox, but instead of numbers, it had letters that I could create the combination for as well. Trouble was there was nothing to explain how to lock in the combination for the book.

I flipped through the pages looking for another tag or something with instructions when Mr. Charlie interrupted me, preventing what was developing into a full-blown panic attack.

"D.J., finish reading the note," as he took the book away from me and softly patted me on the back of my hand. I picked the note up and continue reading as I was instructed to...

D.J. I know you don't feel like there is anyone who is 100% on your team so just know, this box contains something that you can consider your confidant. There is enough room to keep small items that are important to you, and the book is secure enough to hold onto thoughts and ideas that you want to keep private from anyone else. So choose your combinations wisely for you are the only one who will have the ability to gain access to either lock. When your book is full, just let me know, and I will have another dispatched over to you PDQ.

D.J. just know, if I had realized that I wouldn't get to see you anymore, I never would have avoided seeing you in the first place. I didn't realize how much I looked forward to my Friday reports about you until they stopped coming. I miss you D.J. I know I shouldn't, but I do. So I'll say it again. If you ever need anything, call me day or night, for anything. And I do mean anything D.J.

My gifts may seem silly, but sometimes simply writing out your feelings can be the difference between life and death. Let go of the things that you can't tell anyone else on the pages of this book. It may not make sense to you right now but bottling up your feelings can only end in disaster, take my word for it.

I pray all is well with you and the babies, and please don't be mad at Mr. Charlie for helping me reach out to you like this. He means well, and I can tell he really cares about you. We both do D.J., more than we probably should, but we do.

Peace & Love,
Jeremiah

Mr. Charlie handed me another tissue. "I sure hope those are tears of joy and not because you're upset," as he twisted his head to look into my eyes.

"*No*. I love it. I absolutely love all of it," I said as I gripped the letter to my chest and motioned towards the flowers and the balloons.

"Well, I'm glad to hear that because there's one more surprise. Now I hope you don't get upset, but it's going to take a moment for me to get it together," he said as he gave my hand a pat. Mr. Charlie quickly jumped up and crossed the room, picking up the phone.

"Okay..." I wasn't sure what else to say.

He listened for a second then dialed a number, "Hi it's me. We're a go. Yes, now would be a good time," he hung up the phone and took a seat as if nothing was going on.

The phone startled me when it rang, and the smile on Mr. Charlie's face told me that he had something to do with it. A couple of minutes later Taylor came out from wherever it was she'd gone, to explain that the food that I had ordered from the bar needed to be picked up because their runner called out sick and they were short-staffed today so no one would be able to bring it up to me. Since I hadn't ordered anything from downstairs, I knew this surprise had to be a doozy for Mr. Charlie to be going to such lengths to get Taylor out of the way.

I played along, "That's fine. Take your time. Mr. Charlie won't mind keeping me out of trouble while you're away."

"No, that won't be a problem at all. I'm on my lunch break anyway," he smiled as he waved her off.

"Okay, well it shouldn't take me but a few minutes. I'll be right back," she responded. You could tell by the way she was looking at us that she was suspicious, but short of calling me and whoever was on the phone a liar, what else could she do but go down to the bar.

No sooner than the door closed, Mr. Charlie sprang from his seat and was looking out the peephole. I guess he was waiting for Taylor to get on the elevator because he immediately ran over to the phone to make another call. I had no idea he could even move that fast.

"What's going on?" I held my hands up all but pleading for an explanation.

"Patience my dear. *Patience*," he calmly said as he made his way back over to the door. A few seconds later, there was a light knock at the door.

Mr. Charlie looked over and smiled at me as he opened the door. There to my surprise and utter joy was Jeremiah. I surprised all of us jumping to my feet and rushing over to him, burying my face in his chest and crying.

I could feel Mr. Charlie moving us on inside so he could close the door, "How about we take this inside shall we."

"D.J., calm down. And you have no business running like that," Jeremiah laughed. Now typically, anyone trying to tell me what I shouldn't be doing, even if they were right, would irritate me and set me off on a tirade, but not today. Not this time.

As I held on tighter and tighter, all I could muster up to say is, "You're right." I held onto him like there was no tomorrow and this would be the last time we'd ever see each other again. As I expected, he hushed me as he rubbed my head and held on tight. We stood there together for what felt like an eternity even though it had only been a few seconds. As we made our way to the couch it hit me, *Jeremiah was in my apartment and Taylor would be back any minute!*

"Oh no! I can't have you here. Selk hired a full-time nanny for me, and she'll be back any minute!" I could feel my heart beating out of my chest as I began to push him back towards the door.

"Calm down D.J. I've taken care of Taylor. The kitchen will keep her busy for a while," Mr. Charlie smiled ever so slyly with a wink. He was still standing at the door and waved as he went to leave. Before the door closed, he peeked his head back in, "Oh yeah, I'll call you when she's on her way back upstairs," he gave me another wink as he excused himself. I nodded ok as the door quickly closed behind him.

I started patting his chest and arms as if to make sure he wasn't a dream. "What are you doing here? Which one of you two came up with this plan? Thank you so much for the flowers and the balloons! This box is absolutely beautiful, and I so appreciate the diary, but you really shouldn't have. You're doing too much. I'm..."

Cutting me off, "D.J., slow down. We have time. Everything is going to be fine," he explained as his eyes locked onto mine. I sat there, turning to putty in his arms. Other than Fitz, I'd never met a man who could shut me down so easily. Typically when I get all wound up, it takes a miracle to calm me down, but not for him. 'Slow down' was all he had to say to calm me down.

"Now, I spoke with Mr. Charlie last week when you didn't come into the restaurant the second week in a row. I was worried that something had happened to you and the babies, so I left a message downstairs asking him to call me when he had a chance. He filled me in on what was going on with you, the babies, and your life in general. He told me how little he saw you anymore and that you now had someone staying with you at all times, against your wishes, which didn't surprise me at all." He just sat there shaking his head in total disapproval. "D.J., you can't allow them to treat you this way, especially him. You're setting yourself up for a lifetime of abuse baby."

My happy tears were now turning into sad tears. Almost under my breath, "I know."

He suddenly pulled away from me, looking into my eyes again, "What do you mean, 'I know?' Has he hit you D.J.? Tell me the truth. This is not a game of words D.J.," he said.

I blinked away my tears as I scrambled to think of what to say to him. I didn't want to lie to him, but I really didn't want to have this conversation either. "No Jeremiah, he has never balled up his fist and hit me," I mumbled.

He watched me for a second, and then almost like he was looking at me down his nose, he said, "Why do I get the feeling that you're not being completely honest with me, D.J?"

We sat in silence for longer than we should have. Him watching me and me searching the floor for a response. The phone ringing startled both us. I knew who it probably was, and I wasn't happy about it in the least bit as I instinctively grabbed onto his wrist and stared at the phone. Since I didn't attempt to move, Jeremiah went over and picked up the phone. He handed it to me after he answered it, so it wouldn't go to the answering machine.

"Hello?" sounding sad and tired all at the same time.

"Hi Miss. D.J. I'm sooo sorry it's taking so long for me to get back. They keep messing up your order. I've never seen it this bad down here. I saw Mr. Charlie was back down here at the desk, so I just wanted to make sure you're okay." She really was trying to be nice. She just came along at the wrong time, in the wrong situation.

Jeremiah could tell by the huge smile on my face that it wasn't Mr. Charlie calling to tell me he needed to leave. The grip I had on his hand could have also given him a clue as well. We both let out a sigh of relief as I squeezed his hand tighter and tighter, finally pulling him back down on the couch beside me, "Taylor, don't worry I'm fine. Take your time, Mr. Charlie brought me a treat before he left," I smiled at Jeremiah.

Jeremiah giggled, and under his breath, I heard him say, "Oh I'm a treat am I?" he sat there a moment shaking his head at me then, without me asking, he got up and went to the kitchen. I knew exactly what he was up to when I heard cabinet doors opening and closing and the silverware and utensil drawers rattling. I could feel my face warming the bigger my smile got.

"I'll give the kitchen a call and see if I can speed things up so just wait there, it shouldn't be much longer. They just know how picky I can be about my food. Besides, if I need anything the phone is right here next to me, I'll call down for you."

"Well, okay if you're sure," she hesitated.

"I'm sure. Matter of fact, order you something and enjoy it while you wait."

"That's probably not a good idea Miss. D.J.. I don't think Mr. Black would like that."

"Mr. Black knows that you need to eat too. Why should you have to come back up here and cook when you can order you something down there since I've already ordered out? I should have thought of asking you what you wanted before I ordered anyway. So just order something and enjoy it, please. You'll make me feel so much better. I promise you it's not a problem at all."

"If you're sure it's okay Miss. D.J."

"Yes, I'm sure," I said, rolling my eyes at Jeremiah as he came back with a real snack. Jeremiah and I both had to giggle as he sat down with a plate of fruit, a turkey sandwich with all the fixins, a few chips, and a glass of cranberry juice.

"Okay, I will then. Thank you so much." I could feel her smiling through the phone.

"You're welcome Taylor. And again, take your time, I'm fine." I laid the phone down and took Jeremiah's hands in mine. "Jeremiah, I would never lie to you like that. Yes, I might slant the truth a little bit every once in a while, but I promise you, I'll *never* tell you a blatant lie."

He smiled and leaned in to kiss me on my cheek. "D.J., I'm not worried about you lying to me, I'm more worried about you lying to yourself."

Something that simple was enough to get the tears to flowing again. Jeremiah didn't say anything else for a few minutes as he allowed what he'd just said to fully sink in. In fact, the only movement that happened the entire time was him gently wiping away my tears.

"Jeremiah, it's not that I'm lying to myself, I'm fully aware of how I feel and my situation. It's just my mom. She won't listen, and they have taken over my life. They even took my dog from me. According to them, even he is too much for me to handle now. I can't go to work or school, so I'm dependent on others to take care of me financially. So what am I supposed to do?"

"D.J., I'm not trying to upset you. I'm just worried about you. And the fact that I know you are not being completely honest about how he's treating you really isn't sitting well with me. You are living like you're a prisoner, albeit a very nice prison with all the bells and whistles, but you're still being isolated just the same, and that can't be healthy for you or the babies," as he rubbed my stomach, calming the boys down some. "And if all you need to get out of here and away from him is money, all you have to do is ask. I would have no problem helping you find a place to stay, or you can come stay with me. I even have plenty of room and a huge back yard for your dog," he smiled. He took me by the chin and said, "D.J. don't ever let money control your happiness," as he began to stroke my cheek.

"It's definitely not about *his* money, I do my best not to touch his money. I do have some savings left, and I haven't maxed out all of my credit cards, not yet anyway. You just don't get my family or my church. *Me* getting pregnant before I got married has NEVER been the plan for my life and my mom just isn't having it. I wasn't supposed to even be able to get pregnant, so now that I am, my parents are dead set on me being married. You don't know how hard it's been to keep them from getting me down the aisle before these boys are born," I explained as I glanced down, rubbing my stomach. "I have to choose my battles, and right now, I just don't have it in me to keep constantly fighting with all of these people, especially my mother," I explained still looking down at my stomach.

Jeremiah just nodded as he picked up the plate, "No worries for right now. Here try this," as he lifted the sandwich up to feed me.

The fact he surprised me was 100% obvious by the look on my face, but I didn't fuss and did as I was told. I took a bite of what turned out to be a very good turkey sandwich. We sat there enjoying each other's company, sharing the real snack he'd made me. I fed him, and he fed me. It was the best impromptu date I'd ever had in my life. We sat there talking about any and everything. He couldn't believe my brothers all had initials for their names just as I did. He was also shocked to learn that I was taking 2 distance learning classes that no one else knew about. Like I said, I was fighting battles in my own way.

He told me how he became a police officer, how he got into the BBQ business, and about his brothers and sisters. He explained why Mama J had given them all biblical names and why they all started with the letter J. His oldest brother was 24 years older than him which was a big surprise because I was 24 years old. His brothers and sisters also followed a 2, 3, 4 years apart pattern until it came to him and his twin brother, they are 10 years younger than the closest sibling. John is the oldest brother and one of the partners in Triple J's BBQ. He was 53 years old and had been married for 30 years to a police officer. He was retired military, with 4 kids, and 3 grandchildren.

Jordan was 51 years old and the oldest girl. She had been married for 28 years to a Police Lieutenant in Major Crimes, and she was now a retired Meter Maid. They had 6 kids, 2 set of twins, and 4 grandkids. Joel was 48 and had only been married 12 years. He and his wife both worked for the fire department, he was a Captain, and she was a dispatcher. They only had 2 children, but they were 10-year-old twins, a boy, and a girl. Jered was 44 and had been married for 24 years, and they had 3 children. He and his wife were both in the military until they started having children and then she got out, but she still worked for the Air Force as a civilian employee. They didn't have any grandchildren yet.

Jessie was a 41 year-old pilot for United Airlines, and his wife was a ticket agent for the same company. They'd been married 10 years and had a 6-year-old daughter and a 3-year-old son. Next was the baby girl, Jessica. She was 39 years old and had just become a Jr. Partner in her husband's family law firm. They had only been married for 2 years. Now Mrs. Jessica was somewhat of a rebel and had not only married a man 20 years her senior, but he was also white. They didn't have any children, and apparently, Jessica had no desire to have any children. Her husband had 3 from a previous marriage so, he wasn't pushing to have any more kids either, so the only person who wasn't happy with this arrangement was Mama J, of course. She liked the husband, not the plan to remain childless.

Next were Jeremiah and his twin brother Joshua, also known as 'the twins.' Jeremiah was the oldest by 5 minutes and as I already knew he'd been married 3 years when his wife and sons passed away. Joshua was the baby, but he had been married much longer than Jeremiah. He and his wife were high school sweethearts and had a set of twins their senior year in high school. When they graduated, they got married, and Joshua went to school to become an electrician, and she became a bus driver for the city. They'd been married 11 years and have 5 kids now, and apparently, the BBQ business was Joshua's great idea and talked Jeremiah and John into running the restaurant as a family business. He talked all of his siblings into investing something, even if it wasn't money. He'd already been smoking meat and selling plates out of one of the local gas stations, and they just grew the business from there.

Joshua found their present store location by chance. He was working on the electricity on the store next door and found out that the person who owned the building had passed away recently, so his family was trying to sell the entire property because there were so many electrical problems and they didn't want to be bothered with all the repairs to bring it up to code. Joshua took it upon himself to reach out to the family and ask them what it would take to sell him the property. After a couple months of back and forth, they reached a price and Joshua convinced his twin brother to take a chance and help him run the place. John offered to come in as a silent financial partner and took out a loan to help make it a cash sale as the owners had insisted. Other family members helped to do the work on the building or buy the things necessary to furnish the place. And of course, Joshua did all the electrical work, so the building was up to code in no time.

Jeremiah and his wife met when he was in the military, during his basic training. She was actually one of his drill sergeants. After he graduated and went off to Ranger school, they ended up at the same duty station and began to date. She was 6 years older than him when they met and when he returned from his tour in Desert Shield they got married. She left the military and became a consultant with a security company, and he finished out his 4 years as an MP, which means military police. When he got out of the Army, he became a police officer and quickly rose through the ranks after being recruited as an undercover officer, because of his baby face.

It was during the year as an undercover cop that his marriage began to suffer. He didn't go into much detail as to what he was doing undercover other than to say, some of the choices he had to make will haunt him forever, but he also learned life lessons that he'd never forget. He knew that the time he spent undercover changed him and his wife wasn't happy with those changes. She felt he had become softer and much too sensitive for her. He wasn't the larger than life, hair on fire, take no prisoners man that she had fallen in love with and didn't like the settled down, cautious man that came back to her. They were actually on the verge of separating when they found out that they were pregnant and decided that they should try counseling and stay together if for no other reason than for the sake of the baby, which they soon learned were actually babies, twin boys. He explained to me what happened leading up to the accident and why he now spent his time focused on work and his business.

We found out how similar our wants and desires were, how much we appreciated a calm walk in the park, but would both lose our minds over a good football game. He didn't judge me when I explained to him about Fitzgerald and Selkie and how we got to where we were today. He was surprised when I told him that I was in the Army Reserves and that my brother JR had a set of twins his senior year in high school, both girls. The really interesting thing is that my mom didn't force him to get married to their mom. Only relevant because of the push for me to get married since I was now pregnant.

To have grown up so differently, we had so many things in common. Although he never was much of a dog person, he understood why I didn't lock my dog outside and loved animals so much. He found it funny that I was a city girl, who he felt, had a country girl locked up inside of her as he saw it. I begged to differ, but it was okay that he felt that way. Most people laughed at me when I said I wanted a couple of horses and more than a few house dogs, on a few acres of land but he didn't. Come to find out he lived on 15 acres of land outside of Houston and owned a couple of horses. After his wife passed, he sold his house and used a chunk of the insurance settlement from his wife's accident, to build a house in Missouri City off Flat Bank Bayou and helped to pay for Triple J's. He had lots of open space with a nice woodline that the deer disappeared into as they crossed his land and drank from the pond on his property. We both got a cold shiver when I described my dream house, and he pulled out his phone to show me pictures of his house. What I described was almost a complete replica of his house, right down to the color and the oversized wrap around porch, that included a porch swing of course, and the deck off the master bedroom.

As we sat there, absorbing everything the other had to say, I fell head over heels in love for the first time in my life. Understand me when I say, I was in love with Fitz, but this here was nothing like I'd ever felt before. He was everything I'd ever dreamed about and more. And not once did I come up with ways to "fix" him, for my satisfaction. He was perfect exactly how he was. I could feel a cloud of sadness creeping over me as I wondered why now? How could God be so cruel as to send someone who gave me so much hope, gave me peace, and gave me the encouragement to become the person that 'I' wanted to be? He wasn't trying to control me or make me a trophy in his life. We even agreed on the perfect number of children we wanted to have. We both wanted 4. It was more than 2 but less than the number of siblings we both grew up with. I was okay with only having boys, but he insisted that he needed a daughter. We even agreed that it would be our luck to have a girl and then get pregnant with twin boys again. I wasn't laughing as much as him on that because I felt like it would be my luck to get pregnant with twins both times. It seemed like they ran pretty strongly in both of our family's.

So this time when the phone rang, it took everything for us to let each other go, but we knew that we didn't have a choice and finally said our goodbyes. As much as I wanted him to kiss me, it didn't happen. We simply held each other tightly, and finally, he kissed me on my forehead. I could feel his arousal as we clung to each other, so I knew I wasn't the only one feeling this way. It made me smile to know that he wanted me as much as I wanted him, but he always respected the fact that I was engaged to another man and wouldn't cross that line of physical intimacy. He knew as well as I did, that if we crossed that line, we'd never be able to unring that bell and neither of us wanted to add another complication to our already complicated relationship. I walked him to the door and watched him as he walked the short distance to the elevator. No sooner than he pushed the elevator button, the doors opened, and Taylor stepped out.

"Oh, I'm sorry I wasn't expecting anyone to be standing there," she said.

He quickly glanced back over his shoulder and moved to block her view of my door as I quietly shut the door, but I heard him say, "No worries. I should've been standing to the side anyway. You have a nice day ma'am."

It was a little too close for comfort, but Taylor had no idea who he was or where he was coming from, so nothing else came of our blind date. I wish I could tell you that Jeremiah and I continued having our secret dates, but we didn't. Mr. Charlie kept him abreast of how I was doing, and he kept his distance. After all the feelings and coincidences during our conversation, we decided that it was best for us to keep our distance from one another. Nothing good was going to come from the feelings we had developed for each other, nothing good at all.

CHAPTER 14

My birthday was right around the corner when I started having my first episodes of Braxton Hicks contractions. I had just left my Tuesday checkup when I began hurting but decided not to say anything until we were on the elevator on the way back upstairs to my apartment. Taylor had asked me 20 times already if I was okay and of course I had kept saying that I was just fine. I don't know what happened in the elevator, but I'm fine, turned into crying hysterics somewhere between the 10th and 15th floors. By the time the elevator reached the lobby again, Mr. Charlie was standing there with a rolling chair and had emergency services on the phone. Soon after that, the ambulance pulled up in front of the building, and they had me and Taylor loaded up in the rig in a matter of seconds and hurrying towards the hospital.

After a round of pain meds, I agreed with Dr. Cleveland that natural childbirth was not for me, which he got a good laugh out of it even though I saw no humor in it at all. Before I knew it half of my family and friends were at the hospital trying to check on me. Selkie was on the phone with JW trying to run things from Dallas and figure out how to get Hazel Mae there, to which I wanted no parts of. It was bad enough to have my own mother hovering. To have to endure his loud, country twanging mother too, would drive me absolutely nuts. After a couple of hours, Dr. Cleveland informed us that I was actually having false labor pains, but since I was so close to the 36-week mark, it was time to think about scheduling a C-section or at least inducing labor.

On the one hand, I was relieved, but on the other hand, it started the next nightmare to rolling. Opinions began to fly about the room as to what should happen now, but no one seemed to be listening to what I wanted. Selk was insisting that I waited until he could get there on Friday and Dr. Cleveland and my mom thought that we should go ahead and get things going since I was already in the hospital. After listening to everyone else's opinions for longer than I cared to, I informed all of them, rather loudly, how I felt about the subject.

"EXCUSE ME! I'M GOING HOME!" The room instantly grew quiet.

"What do you mean, you're going home?" my mom asked.

"Just that. Unless Dr. Cleveland has a really good reason to make me stay, I want to go home."

"Didn't you just hear the doctor say that you might as well stay and start the ball rolling on this?" she asked impatiently.

"NO! I can't get to Houston this evening. Wait til Friday so I can be there!" Selk screamed into the phone.

I laid there hearing the chatter going on around me but not really listening. I had already made up my mind, so there wasn't really any voice I wanted to hear other than Dr. Cleveland's, and he hadn't said anything to make me think there would be a serious problem if we waited.

After several minutes of arguing amongst themselves, I asked Dr. Cleveland, "When can I be discharged? I'm getting kind of hungry and I'm really craving some barbecue." I heard what I thought was someone bust out laughing in the hallway, but I couldn't see anyone, so I didn't give it a second thought. Even if I did hear laughter, it probably had nothing to do with me anyway. My question brought the entire room to a screeching halt, again.

"Well young lady, I guess you've made up your mind then," Dr. Cleveland said with a huge smile on his face as he crossed his arms across his chest.

"No she hasn't. She's not going anywhere," my mother chimed in as she grabbed onto his arm.

"Lisa, I hate to tell you this, but what you think really doesn't matter at the moment," as he loosened her grip on his arm. "This is D.J.'s decision, and since the babies are in no distress, I really don't have just cause to make her stay."

"Are you serious right now?! She's just a child! You're her doctor, and if you say she needs to induce or have a C-section right now, she needs to induce or have a C-section today," she said holding onto Dr. Cleveland's arm again like he needed her guidance.

"I understand how you feel, but D.J. is an adult and fully capable of making this decision for herself," prying her hand lose again. "And yes, I would like her to seriously consider staying and getting a jump on any possible complications arising while she's at home, but I cannot keep her here against her wishes without a very good medical reason," he explained. My mother was obviously livid, but he continued before she had a chance to speak. "D.J., I will let you go home, but when I see you on Friday, we need to have a serious discussion on when we are going to meet these two boys face to face. As I told you earlier, they are both getting close to 5 lbs. each, and there is no reason not to think they won't be perfectly fine if we go ahead and start your labor process now."

"I understand all of that, but is there any reason I can't wait to see if they decide to come on their own? At least if I'm not having any complications along the way?"

"No, there's not. But when you're looking at multiple babies, I'd prefer to err on the side of caution and take them sooner than later."

"That right there is my hesitation. *'Take them.'* Babies are supposed to *come*, not be taken. Now don't get me wrong doc, but 10 years ago didn't you tell me that not only would I never be able to get pregnant, but in the unlikelihood that I did, I wouldn't be able to sustain a pregnancy beyond a week or so?" I said as I sat up straighter in bed. The room had grown quiet again.

"Well, yes D.J., I did tell you that. Who would have thought that after all the damage caused by the scrapings and radiation that you would be able to get pregnant?" he said with a surprised look on his face.

"That's what I thought. I have already defied the odds, so how about we keep it going and allow them to decide when they want to *come*?" I gave him the most satisfactory smile I could muster as I leaned back and rubbed my belly.

Nobody said a word after that. Dr. Cleveland simply nodded and left the room. A few minutes later, a nurse came in with my discharge paperwork and instructions on things I need to watch out for. She took out my IV and asked me if I had any questions for her.

"No ma'am, I sure don't," not waiting to get my top back on so I could go.

"Well, then let me get a wheelchair, and I will take you out."

My mom jumped in on me no sooner than the nurse had stepped out the room, "I can't believe you are doing this. I don't understand why you have to be so damn difficult and headstrong." And that caused everyone else to leave out in unison which didn't slow her down a bit, "I just pray you and these babies all survive *your* bad choices young lady," she finally finished her rant.

I fought back my tears as I slowly pulled my pants on. Not 20 minutes ago, I'd felt so empowered like I was on top of the world and queen of my own destiny, but now all I felt was beat down and completely drained. As I managed to look up I could've sworn I saw someone at my door again, but I figured I just caught a glimpse of someone passing by. Before I could figure out what to say, she continued.

"D.J., I love you, but sometimes I just want to shake some sense into you."

"Don't worry, Selk will do that for you when he gets here on Friday," I said so matter-of-factly before I realized it.

"What did you just say?" she asked, grabbing my arm.

"Uhmm, nothing," I said as I pulled away from her and slid my shoes on.

"No, you said 'not to worry about it because Selk will do that for me when he gets here on Friday.' Has he hit you D.J?" she actually sounded like she cared as she grabbed both of my arms this time. "Stop fiddling with your shoes and answer me! Has Selkie hit you!" she looked around like she heard someone coming in, but there wasn't anyone there.

"NO! Selk has never *actually* hit me." I turned to get my purse, and under my breath, I said, "Like it would actually matter to you if he did anyway."

"Yes, D.J., it would matter to me," as she followed me across the room. "I'm not giving him my only living daughter to mistreat. So if he's hitting you, tell me now." I just stood there looking at her with my mouth hanging open. She was actually concerned. Don't ask me why I was so surprised, but she really was being sincere.

As much as I hated to say it, "No ma, he's never actually *hit* me," I said as I lowered my head. He hadn't ever hit me, but he did yell at me all the time, grab me and hold on way too tight, and then there's the occasional shaking me like a ragdoll, that's happened more than once. I guess I should have told her all of that, but I didn't want to hear *'suck it up and stop being a baby,'* so I decided to keep it to myself. As the door swung all the way open, I got a shiver up my spine again, like someone was there other than the nurse but again there was no one there but her and P.J. giggling as she wheeled him through the door.

I sat down in the wheelchair and didn't say anything else on the ride home. I rode in silence as my mom drummed into Taylor's head what to look for and to call her if anything happened, especially if I refused to go back to the hospital. As we pulled up in front of the building P.J. screamed, scaring all of us.

"Mama STOP!"

"What?! What's wrong?!" she said slamming on the break, jerking all of us forward.

"Ouch!" I yelled as the seat belt tightened, and I struggled to pull it off of my neck and chest. It locked in place when she slammed on the break and was squeezing way too tight. "P.J. what is it?!" I yelled at him.

I could tell I hurt his feelings as he lowered his head and in a barely audible whisper, "I'm sorry Sissy but you said you were hungry and we didn't stop to get you anything to eat is all."

Now I really felt bad. He was only thinking about me. I sniffed back a tear as Mr. Charlie came outside and opened my door. "I'm sorry P.J... I shouldn't have yelled at you like that. You were only trying to help me, and you're right, I did say I was hungry munchkin. Thank you for taking such good care of me and the babies."

He jumped over the seat and hugged me around my neck. "Sissy, I've got to take care of you. You're making me an uncle. I've got to be a good example for them," as he squeezed me tighter and buried his head in my neck.

"Give me a second to park, and I'll help you upstairs D.J."

"Mrs. Morgan, I've got her. You go on and get little man something to eat. I'll wrangle up something for Miss. D.J. to eat so she can get some rest. She's had a long day," Mr. Charlie smiled at my mom as he closed the car door and sent Taylor on ahead. My mom didn't argue with Mr. Charlie and told me that she'd call to check on me later, letting the cracked window up before pulling off with P.J. waving like a madman through the back window.

"It amazes me how easy it is for you to get her to agree with you and she gives me and everyone else the blues. I'll never understand why she hates me so much," I dropped my head.

"She doesn't hate you Miss. D.J.. She just wants what's best for you, and to her, a man with lots of money is what's best. See, in my day, sometimes you married for necessity and learned to love the one you were with along the way. She just wants to make sure you and those boys are properly taken care of is all," he softly patted my hand as we slowly walked arm in arm across the lobby towards the elevators. As we reached the elevators, a young man ran over and gave Mr. Charlie a package.

"You don't want to forget this Mr. Curtis. If it had sat here much longer one of us would have eaten it, it smells so good," the young man laughed as he turned and went back to the front desk.

"What's this?"

"Apparently, it's the barbecue you requested," he smiled.

"What barbecue?" I was completely shocked and stopped moving forward. "Please explain to me where this came from Mr. Charlie because I know that none of the people at the hospital picked it up for me, so how did you know that I wanted barbecue?" I impatiently asked.

"Get on the elevator please and I'll explain," he glanced around like someone might be listening. As the doors closed, he explained everything to me. "When they got you in the ambulance, my next call was to your mother and then Jeremiah. He was there before you got there but stayed out of sight because your folks got there before he got a chance to see you. He didn't want to leave until he knew you were okay, and apparently, he overheard you asking for something to eat. Jeremiah called me when you were being discharged and told me what had happened and that the food was on the way. Once he knew you were okay, he ran by the restaurant and picked this up for you and dropped it off a few minutes ago. D.J., I know you are dealing with a lot but when I say that man loves you, I mean that man is 100% *in* love with you. He will move heaven and earth for you, you gotta see that girl."

I squeezed Mr. Charlie's hand as a tear started running down my cheeks. "So I'm not crazy. He was there. I felt like someone was there, but every time I looked out the door, there wasn't anyone there. I felt him Mr. Charlie. I actually felt him there." I turned to him with a huge smile on my face, "And just for the record. I love him too, but that doesn't change anything. My mother doesn't want to hear about me being in love with anyone but Selk and no matter what I do or say, you know she's not going to accept any different," I said as the smile slowly turned into a frown.

"D.J., there comes a time when you have to shit or get off the pot and baby girl it's your time to choose, no matter what your Mama thinks, says, or does. Now ordinarily I wouldn't tell a child to disobey their parents, but in this instance, I've got to say something. This is your life, not your Mama's. You're the one who is going to have to live your life, not your Mama. The bed you make is the one you're going to have to lie in, next to the man you say 'I do' too. Not your Mama," he finished just as we reached the door and Taylor opened it.

Thankfully I wasn't crying, or she would have definitely had my mom on the phone, and I would have been on my way back to the hospital or even worse, they would have forced Mr. Charlie to stay away from me.

"I was getting worried, it was taking you so long for you to get up here. Is everything okay?" Taylor asked as she took my other arm like I needed that much help getting around.

"Yes, everything is just fine. I'm just moving a little slower than usual is all, I'm a little stiff from the hospital bed," I tried to reassure her as they lowered me down onto the couch.

"Here let me take that, and I'll make you a plate," as she grabbed the bag from Mr. Charlie and headed off into the kitchen.

"How'd I know she was going to do that," he said with a frown on his face. "Here D.J.. Jeremiah included a note that I took the liberty of holding back just in case Ms. Nosey Body got to the bag before you," he said still shaking his head as he handed me a neatly folded piece of paper then kissed me on the forehead and turned for the door but stopped as he reached for the knob. "D.J. Morgan, I'm gonna pray for you," he said over his shoulder.

I could tell he was choked up, which is probably why he didn't turn around and look at me when he said that. Before I could respond, he had opened and closed the door behind him.

I ate a little quicker than I normally do so I could get to my room and read the note that Jeremiah had left for me. It took a minute to convince Taylor that I didn't need any more help for the evening but just to be safe I went inside my bathroom and locked the door behind me to ensure Taylor didn't come in and interrupt me. That's all I need for her to walk in on me with a note from another man in hand.

D.J.,

You really scared me tonight. I'm relieved to know you and the babies are okay, but we need to talk, sooner than later. Get rid of Taylor so we can talk, please. I will meet you tomorrow at noon. So, for now, enjoy the barbecue and please take it easy and get some rest.

With all my love,
Jeremiah

P.S.

I loved the way you stood up for yourself today. I'm glad to see you didn't let them bully you into doing something you didn't feel was right for you or the boys. Didn't it feel good?

Til tomorrow,
XOXO

He was right. It really did feel good to stand up for myself. Problem is, the doctor has to take his directions from me unless I am incapacitated so it doesn't really matter what my mother decides I should do. But outside of the hospital, I have no backup when it comes to dealing with her, or Selk. If only I could get her to understand how I feel and allow me to make this particular decision for myself. Only if that could actually happen.

CHAPTER 15

I wasn't able to meet Jeremiah the next day because my mom decided that she was going to spend the day with me, which wasn't as bad as I had originally thought it was going to be. She took off work and gave Taylor the day off. She organized a pamper party, in house of course, for the two of us and invited Phaedra and Chandra over as well. Thing is, my mom always has something up her sleeve, and this turned out to be just another way for her to disarm me before she dropped a bomb.

We began with full-body massages and facials. Then to my surprise, they had Triple J's BBQ delivered and served by one of the owners... Joshua, not Jeremiah.

"Can I get you something else Miss. D.J.? I have baked beans if you don't want the potato salad," Joshua told me. He gave me a look that caught me off guard for a moment. Although he and Jeremiah were obviously fraternal twins, when he shot me that look, he looked just like Jeremiah for a moment.

"Uhmm, yes please thank you," I gave him an inquisitive look. I could tell he had something more to say to me, but he also had obviously been warned about my mother. As I sat there picking at my plate, I wondered just how much he did know about me and my situation.

I set my plate down and went to get up, and of course, everyone tried to stop me.

"D.J. what do you need? Don't get up!" my mom said, jumping to her feet.

"I'll get whatever you need," Chandra chimed in.

"Well unless one of you can go pee for me, I've got to get up," I said giving them all a now what you gonna say to that look. I could see Joshua out of the corner of my eye and could see he was fighting back his laughter.

"Oh, well yeah you're going to have to take care of that one on your own," Phaedra said. She was trying not to laugh as well.

"Where are you going with your plate? One of us can get that for you," Chandra said as she got up to take the plate from me.

I slapped her hand away, "Nonsense. I can use the bathroom off the kitchen, so it's right on my way."

"Well when you get back, I have one more thing to talk to you about D.J. So hurry back," my mom quickly added.

"Yes mother...I'll make it quick," I rolled my eyes, with my back to her of course. They all seemed to relax and go back to their conversation as I exited the room. I glanced back as I rounded the corner to make sure I wasn't being followed when Joshua pulled me on inside the kitchen.

"Shhhh. Hurry up. I have a call for you," he whispered as he handed me his phone.

I whispered, "Hello?" as if I didn't already know who it was.

"Hello Miss Morgan. How are you feeling today?" Jeremiah asked.

"Well I'm doing just fine Mr. Thomas. Thank you for asking. And to what do I owe this surprise call too?" trying not to act as excited as I was to be talking to him. I motioned to Joshua that I was going to take the phone in the bathroom with me and he nodded okay in agreement with a huge Kool-Aid grin across his face.

"I know you can't talk long, but I just wanted to touch base since I won't be able to see you today. Did you get any rest last night?"

"I actually did. It helped to know that I wasn't crazy and just imagining someone was watching me, because there actually *was* someone watching me at the hospital, go figure." I giggled as I flushed the toilet and then turned on the water like I was washing my hands in case someone came to check on me.

"Yeah. When Mr. Charlie called, I was coming back from checking on mom, so I threw on the lights and siren and came by the hospital before I headed home."

"I see," I kept giggling.

"I know you have to go but I just wanted to let you know I've got to go out of town for the next few days on business, but you are to call my office or Joshua at Triple J's and leave a message for me if you have to stay in the hospital, okay? I'm serious D.J. This is not the time to play 'I can handle this on my own card,'" he said. I could tell by his tone he was not playing with me.

"I will, and I understand, but we feel great right now, and we've already discussed this. They are going to stay put until they are supposed to come," I laughed. "I hear Joshua talking to someone in the kitchen I've got to go. Be careful wherever it is you're going and watch your six Sarge." I was being so serious right now. "All jokes aside. I know you can't tell me where you're going or what you'll be doing, but I know it's dangerous. So please be careful."

"D.J. are you okay?" It was Phaedra.

"Yeah, I'm fine. I'll be out in a second." I quickly responded. In a whisper, "Okay, I've got to go now. Be safe, and I don't care if he's in town or not, call me when you can and let me know you're okay," I told him as I drew little hearts on the countertop.

"Yes ma'am. Take care of yourself D.J.. I'll talk to you soon." And with that, he was gone.

I took a few deep breaths to get myself together before I returned to the others, but as I came into the kitchen I realized, I really did need to go to the bathroom and immediately turned to go back in when my mom turned the corner.

"D.J., what's wrong? Are you having pains again?" she asked, rushing over to me before I could pass Joshua his phone.

"Nothing's wrong," as I slid the phone in my pocket. "I feel like I need to go again, is all," I tried to smile. She held on a little too long, "Geez mom, cut the umbilical cord already," I said, rolling my eyes as I turned back towards the bathroom, pushing her hands away. Joshua turned to clean a spot on the counter that didn't need to be cleaned. My mom just stood there looking between the two of us like she knew something was up but just couldn't put her finger on it. When I came back into the kitchen, she was still standing there talking to Joshua. I could tell by the look on his face, he needed to be rescued.

"Mom, what's going on?" I asked cautiously. I've seen her in investigation mode many times before, and when she gets that way, she's like a dog with a bone. She won't give up asking questions until she's fully satisfied.

"I was telling Joshua that he looks so familiar to me. I can't quite put my finger on it, but I know I've seen him somewhere before," she looked over at me like she knew who he was but wanted me to tell her.

I acted like I had no idea why she was looking at us so suspiciously. "Oh really. So have you gone through who his people are yet?" I asked with a sarcastic laugh, slowly waving my hands back and forth in front of my head. This was a question I had learned to dread when I was finally allowed to start dating. It was a question I soon learned, was something all older black folks asked when you started dating someone, or they met someone they didn't know but wanted to figure out where they came from. It was also to ensure you didn't start dating your long-lost cousin too. Once someone asked 'who are your people,' by the end of the conversation you have told them everyone in your family going back 3 or 4 generations, so I knew if she'd asked him that question she already knew that Jeremiah was his brother, so why should I play her game.

"No, I haven't asked him that. Yet," looking at me. "Do I need to?" she asked, still staring at me.

"I don't see why you would. I'm not trying to date him, so it really doesn't matter," I said as I walked over and patted him on the shoulder and gave him a quick wink. He started giggling, but my mom didn't flinch or relent.

"I know you think you're being cute, but I'm really not in the mood D.J."

"Momma, I have absolutely no interests in this man whatsoever. So why on earth are you concerned with who his people are? In fact, this is the first time I've ever met this man before. I swear you can be so embarrassing for no reason sometimes." I let out a long sigh and slowly passed behind Joshua, sliding his phone into his back pocket as I passed him. "So unless you have a specific question for him, how about we get out of his way while he's trying to clean and pack everything up. Okay?" I kept going on into the living room where the others were getting their nails and feet done.

"WOW! You two are really loving all of this pampering, aren't you?" I laughed while praying on the inside that my mom would follow me out of the kitchen. As I sat down, Phaedra shot me a *what the hell is going on look.* I bucked my eyes at her and signaled into the kitchen. She immediately knew what was going on.

Getting up from her seat, "Excuse me for a minute please," she said to the manicurist. "Hey Momma Morgan, do you need some help in there?" she asked as she went after my mom in the kitchen.

"Okay, what am I missing," Chandra asked. She could sometime be so about self that she had no idea the drama about to go down under her nose.

"Nothing. We'll talk about it later," I explained to her trying to act like nothing was going on.

Phaedra stepped back around the corner, "Uhmm D.J., can you come in here for just a moment?" looking at me like, *'HELP!'*

I slowly got up, knowing I was walking into the fire. At that point, nosey Chandra knew something was up and followed me into the kitchen as well.

"Yes?" I asked, looking back and forth between Phaedra and my mom. I couldn't look at Joshua right now. I was too nervous to look at him.

"D.J., who is Joshua to you?" Phaedra asked me. By the look on her face, I knew the jig was up.

"Again, I have never met this man before today."

"That's not what she asked you. What she asked you was *'Who* is this man to you?'" my mom asked.

"Mother, I did answer the question. I met this man for the first time when he showed up at my front door. What else do you want me to say?" I said with my hands up.

"Then how does he know you D.J.? And before you answer, just know the word games, they are done as of right now," she said as she raised her finger at me and slowly lowered it to the countertop.

"Mom, what do you want to know?" I threw my hands up in the air like I was giving up. "Like I said, I met him at the same time you did. I fell in love, and he is here as a special surprise for me." Everyone in the kitchen, except for my mom, was shocked by my explanation. You could tell by the way all of their mouths fell open when the word 'love' came out of my mouth, none of them were expecting me to say that. "Mom, He's the owner of the barbecue place I've fallen in love with. I've never met him before today like I've said multiple times, but I've met other members of his family including his hilariously funny mother, maybe a niece or two, and a couple of his brothers."

"Ah ha! That's what I was waiting on. And who is his brother?" she asked like she didn't already know.

"Ma'am let me explain," Joshua interjected.

"NO!" she held her hand up to him. "I want my daughter to explain," she stood there burning a hole through me with her eyes.

"Again,..."

"D.J. Morgan! Don't play with me right now, I'm not in the mood!" she growled before I could even finish my statement.

"Momma, can we discuss this in private please? He has nothing to do with this," I pointed at him, while I begged her with my eyes.

"Oh yes. He has a lot to do with this. Apparently, *all* of you have a lot to do with this," she shot Phaedra and Chandra a deadly look as well. "Now, I want to hear it from you. Who...is...this... man...to...*you* D.J. Morgan?"

"Mommy, he is the owner of the place I like to eat at. We have never met before today! Why are you doing this?!" as tears began to well up in the corners of my eyes. Joshua leaned across the island to hand me a paper towel. "That's all I can tell you!"

"I don't know who you think you're raising your voice at. I don't care how grown you 'think' you are, raising your voice at me is NEVER an option. You better get it together young lady. Do I make myself clear?"

"Yes ma'am." I was so humiliated right now all I wanted to do is curl up and die.

"Is this man related to Jeremiah?" she asked, staring at each of us, one at a time but beginning and ending with me.

After a deep breath, "Yes, he...." I started to answer.

"Yes ma'am I am. I'm Jeremiah's twin brother Joshua," he explained as he stepped forward with his hand extended.

Of course, she just stood there with her hands on her hips, staring at his extended hand like she didn't know what it was. They all stood there in silence as I sat down on a barstool dabbing at my eyes.

"And in what universe did you all think this was the least bit appropriate?!" she yelled. They all jumped and started mumbling at the same time, but I knew that they were wasting their time, she was only getting started. "Like I told your brother when I met him. D.J. is spoken for and doesn't need anyone in her ear as to otherwise."

"Momma Morgan, we weren't trying to talk D.J. out of anything," Phaedra started.

"I wouldn't finish that statement if I were you young lady," she snapped, immediately shutting Phaedra down. "Like I was saying. D.J. is spoken for, and her fiancé would not appreciate you or your brother being in his home, knowing how your brother feels about my daughter, his soon to be wife, and the mother of his children I might add. I don't know you or your brother, but I do get that he cares about my daughter, and she might *think* she cares about him, but there is no future in those feelings. D.J. is engaged to be married, and before those babies get here, she will be marrying *their* father. So young man, thank you for all you've done here today, but it's time for you to leave and please don't come back here again. But before you go, please give your brother a message from me..." Even though she paused, we all knew better than to open our mouths. "Please tell Jeremiah that I'm sorry he got you caught up in this love triangle, but he needs to go on with his life and stay far away from my daughter. He is not to call her or send anymore barbecue her way. Don't get me wrong it's really good barbecue, but we can't afford for D.J. to fall in love with anything or anyone, other than her fiancé," she said looking over at me. "Chandra, go in there and get my purse."

"Mrs. Morgan, me nor my brother meant any harm. And you're right he does care deeply for your daughter, but ma'am I know my brother well and can vouch for his character. He's not a homewrecker, and he would never try to break up a happy relationship. He's just not that type. As D.J. has said several times, this is the first time we've ever met, although I have heard a lot about her, I can't leave here without saying...." he paused as he looked over and smiled at me. "Mrs. Morgan, if she feels half of what my big brother feels for your daughter, she has no business marrying Mr. Black. Even if he is the father of those babies. Marriage is hard enough without going into it with such low expectations. Even you have to see how she lights up when my brother's name is even mentioned, let alone when she talks to him. Engaged is not married, and in my humble opinion, she has no business getting married to a man she obviously isn't in love with."

My jaw was on the ground, but now there was no doubt in my mind that Jeremiah had thoroughly told him about me or that he and his brother were on one accord. As terrified as I was as to how my mom was going to react to the things he was saying, I was seriously praying that she would not only hear what he was saying, she would actually listen to what he was saying because what he was saying was 2000% true.

"Mommy, I know you don't want to hear this, but I am NOT in love with Selk. And I really don't want to marry him. I didn't a year ago, and I don't now. I don't know how many different ways it's going to take to get that through to you, but I just don't." I got off the stool and walked over and held her hand. "I know this isn't what you expected to happen today but since you insist on having this conversation, let's have it." I could feel me gaining strength as I opened up to her with all these witnesses. Out of the corner of my eye, I saw Joshua lift his phone up and lay it on the countertop. I figured he had called Jeremiah when this conversation first got started, but now he was making sure he could truly hear what was going down.

Through clenched teeth, "D.J., don't you dare say another word."

"No ma'am. You wanted to have this conversation, so we're going to have it. Right here. Right now. I've never met this man, but you keep asking me 'who he is to me,'" I smiled at him with a nod. "Since you won't let it go, I'll tell you exactly who he is to me…" I hesitated for a second but never taking my eyes off him, "He is the twin brother to the man I have fallen madly in love with."

Joshua's mouth fell wide open, but he finally smiled and nodded back. Phaedra and Chandra were both standing there in shock with their mouths hanging open just as my mom was when I looked back over to her.

"Joshua, I'm sorry you got caught up in all of this, but thank you. Thank you for having your brothers back when I didn't. And mommy, I'm not trying to hurt you, but I am *in* love with Jeremiah. I don't know how it happened, I wasn't even looking for it *to* happen, but it did and honestly…I don't want to change that. I know you don't want me to have to struggle trying to raise these two as a single mother, but mamma, I won't be alone. I can't tell you where Jeremiah and I will end up, but for right now we both want to explore what we feel more openly and honestly. He's a good *man* mom. *You* just need to give him a chance. He loves me, and he loves these boys like they were his own," I looked down for just a moment rubbing my stomach. "Isn't that more important than money? And yeah, Selk has a whole lot of money, but he doesn't have my heart mommy. I promise you, I've tried to make myself love him, but I just can't, and I don't."

She threw her hand up as she turned away from me, "I'm not listening to this nonsense D.J."

"Well, maybe you'll listen to this," as I grabbed her arm to turn her back towards me. "Both you and Jeremiah have asked me if Selk is putting his hands on me, specifically, if he is 'hitting me,' and I've told both of you more than once that he has never hit me, which technically he hasn't. But he has grabbed me and squeezed really, really tight while shaking me like a ragdoll, or he's pushed me down and wouldn't let me get up." I could tell everyone in the room was shocked at this little revelation.

"I knew it! I'm going to kill that bastard!" came from the phone. Joshua snatched it up from the counter and turned his back as he started rambling.

"Look Zeke, you're not gonna do no such thing. You're not gonna throw your life away for him or for love. Do you hear me?!" he shot me a look that told me he was scared for his brother.

"Jeremiah, no you're not! Do you hear me?! You're not gonna touch him!" I yelled, reaching for the phone. Joshua quickly brought it over to me. "I do love you, and there's no way I'm going to lose you because of him. He's not worth it! Do you hear me?! He's not, worth it!" I said, crying into the phone.

"D.J. why didn't you tell me? I knew something was wrong, I just knew it!" he pleaded.

"And you were right. But he has never actually hit me, and you keep asking me if he's *hit* me."

"D.J., I'm with your mom on this one. You and these damn word games has got to stop! You knew what we were asking when we asked you if he's put his hands on you! This isn't a game! That man can seriously hurt you, and those babies. D.J., sometimes you can't handle everything on your own," Jeremiah pleaded. I could feel his pain coming through the phone.

"Mamma, I love you, but I don't *need* you to make this decision for me. I know you want what's best for me, but Selkie is NOT what's best for me. And before you say this is because of Jeremiah, don't. You know I felt this way before I ever met Jeremiah. So mommy, look at it this way, you got what you wanted for me. A man who really does love me and *I love him back*. I know I can be happy with Jeremiah for the long haul. And mommy, even the boys can tell the difference between the times I spend with Jeremiah versus the time I spend with Selk. So mommy, I'm begging you. Please don't be mad, but I can't do this anymore. I'm miserable here! I appreciate everything Selk has done but mommy if he really wants to be a father to these two, to be the man he wants everyone to believe that he is, he will keep taking care of them, and he can be an active part of their lives still. I'd never keep them from him, but I don't want to marry him. I'm NOT going to marry him." For probably the first time in my life, I stood there, relentlessly staring my mother down.

We all stood there in silence for the longest time. I didn't realize it until Phaedra reached over and wiped a tear away from my mom's cheek that I noticed that she was even crying. At that moment, everything in me turned a flip. I had finally gotten through to her. *We* had finally gotten through to her! I was so happy I didn't have words. I wrapped my arms around my mom and buried my face in her chest, crying uncontrollably. I was so happy I just couldn't control it. I felt free. I could finally breathe. Joshua made his way around the kitchen island and squeezed my hand as he pulled me around and gave me a hug like I had just made his year. When he released me, I wiped my mom's face and kissed her on the cheek, which wasn't hard to do since I was taller than her, but I still felt like I was stretching up, to reach her face. I pulled back from her and sat back down on the barstool. She still hadn't said anything as she turned and went into the bathroom without saying anything to any of us.

I picked up the phone and couldn't help myself, "Jeremiah, I LOVE YOU! And I'm sorry you had to hear that for the first time this way, but I really, really am *in love with you*."

"Nonsense D.J. I'm just glad you finally admitted it," he laughed. "Because Miss D.J. Morgan I have been in love with you since the first time I touched you. I just didn't know how to tell you once I found out you were engaged, but D.J. you are so right. You're not in this by yourself, and I'm not going anywhere. No matter what Selkie decides to do, you and those boys will be taken care of, do you hear me? You will be taken care of. I LOVE YOU WOMAN!"

I squeezed Joshua's hand so hard he jumped. "Well man, I can tell you she loves you just as much if the way she just squeezed my hand is any indication of how she feels about you," he laughed shaking his fingers out.

We were all laughing and talking when my mom came back into the kitchen just as I was sliding Selk's ring off my finger and laying it on the island countertop.

"D.J., what do you think you're doing!" she yelled, startling all of us.

"Huh?"

"Don't huh me! What did I tell you before? You better put that ring right back on your finger young lady! What? You thought all of those tears and theatrics in front of your audience had changed something? Nothing's changed! You are still getting married, to Selkie. In fact, you're getting married on Friday morning, before we go in to have those babies. It's all been arranged."

We all stood there in disbelief. This couldn't be happening.

"Wha...wait, what?" I stuttered, shaking my head, trying to make sense of what I'd just heard.

"Don't wait, what me. I told you, nothing's changed. You are marrying the father of those two boys on Friday morning. Nothing's changed except the timetable. SURPRISE!" as she looked around the room at each of us with a look that said, *'don't test me.'*

"But Mrs. Morgan, she's told you. She's in love with my brother, not Selkie. How can you say that?" Joshua said, shaking his head back and forth, trying to understand what he was hearing.

"You young people and all of your foolish ideas. D.J. is marrying the father of her children, and that's all I have to say on the matter," as she slid Selk's ring back on my finger.

I sat there with my mouth hanging open staring at my hand. When I looked up at Phaedra and Chandra, they both had their heads down and wouldn't make eye contact. I sat there shaking my head trying to comprehend what was going on right now. I know I heard Jeremiah's voice, but I can't tell you what he was saying. As the tears started free flowing down my face, I looked up at Joshua whose mouth was still hanging open. As our eyes met, he pulled my head into his chest, and that's all it took for me to start howling in pain as my heart broke into a million little pieces.

"It's okay D.J., it's okay. Don't cry sweetie. As soon as Jeremiah gets back, we will deal with this. We've got your back," he whispered in my ear as he tried his best to console me.

"No, it's never going to be okay. She's never going to let me leave Selk. She's never going to let go," I cried into his chest. "OW!" I screamed, doubling over in pain.

"What's wrong?!" I heard Jeremiah yell through the phone.

Everyone was instantly standing around me, holding me up. I was still doubled over when the pain came again.

"UHHHHH! It hurts so BAD!!" I cried.

"Phaedra, my car is in the garage. Go bring it around to the front, and we will get D.J. downstairs," my mom said, just as calm and collected as ever. "Just go in my purse and get the keys and we will meet you in a minute."

Phaedra started rambling through her purse and took off running when she found them. Joshua grabbed the phone and told Jeremiah he thought I was going into labor, and they were taking me to the hospital.

"NO! We'll take care of her. You don't need to come," my mom shot back.

"Look Mrs. Morgan. I don't mean any disrespect, but I'm not going anywhere but to the hospital unless D.J. tells me to stay away. Then when *we* get there, I'm not leaving the hospital until I know she and these babies are okay. You may not care, but my brother is under a lot of stress right now, and he needs to focus on his job, and he can't do that worrying about what's going on with *your* daughter. I expect to see him in a few days, so I need him to focus, and he's not going to do that unless he knows she and these babies are okay, so until further notice, just look at me as part of the family." And with that, he turned his attention back to getting me to the elevator. "Chandra go get the elevator, and we will be out there as soon as possible." He'd taken Jeremiah off the speaker, so I don't know what he said to Joshua, but Joshua responded with, "Zeke, don't worry bro, I got this. You take care of you, and I'll take care of her. Love ya bro! Now go focus on your job and come home ALIVE!" and put his phone in his pocket as he balanced me.

My mom was scrambling around, gathering up my things when my knees buckled in the living room from the pain.

"D.J.!" my mom yelled as she lunged at me to help keep me from going to the ground, but before she could actually help me, Joshua scooped me up in his arms to carry me the rest of the way. My mom was obviously startled from this move and was frozen in place, just watching.

"Come on Mrs. Morgan! We've got to go!" he yelled back at her as he rushed me into the hallway.

"Hold on! Her ring came off again!" You could tell she was down low looking for it by the way her voice trailed off.

He wasn't waiting for her. He told Chandra, "Let the door go. She'll have to catch the next one." You could tell Chandra wasn't sure what to do as she hesitated for a minute. "Let it go, NOW!" he said again, and with that, the doors closed just as my mom came into view.

Mr. Charlie was standing at the elevator when the doors opened and said he was on the line with emergency services. Apparently, there was a major accident on the highway, and it would be at least 20 to 30 minutes before an ambulance could get there.

"Is my truck still out front?"

"Yes, I had the valet pull you forward instead of parking you."

"Well I'll take her then, if you'll get me my keys."

Mr. Charlie didn't say another word and sprinted across the lobby and met us at the front doors.

"But wait a minute. Mama Morgan is on the way down. She's not going to be very happy about this. You need to wait for her." Chandra explained as she held on to my hand.

"If you want to wait, that's just fine. But I'm taking D.J. to the hospital right now. So are you riding with us or you waiting for her mother?" Joshua asked as he and Mr. Charlie carefully slid me onto the back seat of his truck. He only hesitated a minute before he closed the door, "So are you coming or not?" he gave her a disgusted look.

Chandra looked around for a second and then ran around the truck and jumped in on the other side and laid my head in her lap, "Yeah, yeah! Let's go!" And just like that, we were off.

By the time my mom and Phaedra got to the hospital, I was already in a bed and hooked up to the fetal monitor. Even Dr. Cleveland made it to my room before my mom did, and when she got there, she was fit to be tied. The nurses had given me a shot of pain medication in my arm because I wouldn't keep still enough to start the IV. I was known to be a difficult stick already and the fact that I had hit the nurse who tried to start my IV when I got to the hospital, didn't help matters in the least little bit. Joshua was standing at the foot of the bed when hurricane Lisa blew into the room.

"Get out! Get out of here! Right now!" she yelled at Joshua, who simply looked at her like she wasn't even talking and continued to rub my foot to comfort me.

"Lisa! This isn't the time or place for that," Dr. Cleveland barked back at her over his glasses. He was looking at the strip coming out of the fetal monitoring machine when she stormed in. When he knew he had her attention, he went back to watching my contractions and the babies' heartbeats on the monitor.

I was sure she was going to go off again, but she didn't. She handed Chandra her purse and walked up to my bedside and took my hand, still staring at Joshua, who by the way never flinched and kept one eye on me and the other on the monitor.

"D.J. baby. How are you feeling," she said, moving my hair out of my face as she began to stroke my head. It was really scary how she could turn it on and off so easily. Anyone who came in my room at that moment would never have believed that she was trying to rip Joshua's head off just 10 seconds earlier. I just laid there shaking my head at her, I really didn't have anything to say to her.

"Are you okay D.J.? What's wrong baby?" she asked again.

"What's wrong?" I paused as I began to well up with more emotions than I knew what to do with. "You're what's wrong! You're always what's wrong mother! I can't with all of this," I flung my arms out to the side, snatching away from her, "I just can't," as I dropped my head back and the tears started rolling down the sides of my face. Alarms started going off from every monitor in the room.

"What? What do you mean? What did I do? Somebody tell me what's happening!" She actually sounded surprised as she stood up looking all innocent. I just laid there, shaking my head looking at Joshua as the tears flowed down my cheeks.

"Okay. I think I know what's going on," Dr. Cleveland announced as the alarms on all my machines continued going off even after they were silenced multiple times. "I need everyone to leave," he looked around at each person in the room, one at a time over the top of his glasses, stopping the longest time on my mother.

"Well, why? I'm going to stay, but the rest of them definitely need to leave," she retorted as she burned holes through Joshua with her eyes.

"No. I said *everyone* needs to leave, that means you too Lisa," Dr. Cleveland said so matter-of-factly, as the nurse came in to get set up to try to start another IV.

The alarms started fading when she didn't respond and just turned and walked out of the room with Chandra and Phaedra close on her heels. Joshua hesitated for a second as I reached for his hand as he went to leave.

"Would it be alright if he stayed Dr. Cleveland?" I asked, wiping away the last few tears on my face.

"No D.J. I need to examine you, and we need to talk without any interference this time. He can come back later if he likes, but right now, I just need you to relax and focus on calming down."

"That's fine doc. D.J. I'm not going far. But I have to ask you doc. Is this happening because she's stressed out? I've been through this 4 times with my own wife, and I can tell by the monitors, that she and these babies started running on high again when her mom came in," he stood there holding my hand waiting for an answer.

"Well, I don't know who you are or how you've played into this drama, but yes. You're on the money young man. She's not really in labor according to the monitor, and the babies aren't in any real distress, *IF*, she stays calm, but I still need to check and see if she's starting to dilate, so I do need you to step out for just a few minutes. If that's negative, my diagnosis is going to be stressed induced Braxton Hicks again young lady," as he turned to look at me. "D.J., we need to have a serious conversation concerning the direction this pregnancy is headed and decide when we are going to deliver these babies. You can't keep doing this to the 3 of you, it's just not safe."

"I'll give you two some privacy," Joshua said as he patted the back of my hand. "But D.J., just remember a couple of things. You're in control, not your mom. And I'm here until *you* don't need me to be. I'll be right outside, and I promise, I'll steer clear of your mother," he said as he gave me a wink and chuckled a bit.

I smiled at him and finally exhaled for the first time since the meltdown in my kitchen got started. "Thank you so much. And I'm sorry I've gotten you and Jeremiah involved in all this mess." No sooner than I'd said that, an alarm started going off again.

"Son, you need to go," Dr. Cleveland explained as he turned off the alarm.

"Yes, Sir. I'm going. I'll get word to Jeremiah, so he knows what's happening," he told me as he kissed the back of my hand and then turned and left the room.

For the next hour, Dr. Cleveland and I discussed my health and what I should think about when it came to inducing labor or just having the C-section. We weighed the pros and cons and came up with a plan that I felt like I could live with. I didn't want to have the babies on or around my birthday, so we decided to schedule the induction for after Thanksgiving. He wanted to do it tomorrow, but I was able to convince him that I'd be able to relax and keep my BP out of the danger zone.

After I'd told him what had happened at my place, he decided that all of that stress is what caused my blood pressure to go so high. He also decided that he was going to admit me into the hospital to keep me for observation for a couple of days, just in case my visitors caused my blood pressure to spike again. He informed the nurses and my visitors that I was not to have more than 2 visitors at a time and if the nurses felt like I was becoming too agitated, they could reduce that number or not allow me to have any visitors anymore until further notice. As I listened to him put and keep my mother in her place, my blood pressure came down to what was well within the normal range. Even the boys settled down and gave my ribs a rest. I swear they took turns kicking them to see if they could make them vibrate.

Phaedra and Chandra decided to take a cab back over to my place to get their cars, so they made a quick exit immediately following Dr. Cleveland's announcement. I really couldn't blame them, they had had a long enough day trying to keep my mom and Joshua apart. Joshua had excused himself to make another phone call right after they left, leaving my mother and me alone for the first time since she figured out who Joshua was. Even then, we didn't really get a chance to discuss much. She had to leave to go pick P.J. up from school, and M.J. had a dentist appointment to get to, so she needed to be on her way as well. She told me she'd come back later to check on me and of course, I told her that wasn't necessary.

As I laid in the darkness, the only thing I really had on my mind was Jeremiah and was he safe. I drifted off to sleep concerned about nothing other than him, where he was, what he was doing, and when I would be able to talk to him about what had taken place in my kitchen that afternoon. I probably should have been more concerned with my health and how the boys were doing, but we were the least of my worries at the moment. I knew in my heart that the boys and I would be just fine. Jeremiah on the hand, not so much.

CHAPTER 16

I woke up a little foggy, but I knew I wasn't alone. As I struggled to regain my bearings, I saw a shape standing in the corner behind the baby monitor but couldn't really make it out in the darkness. I felt along the bed rail trying to find the button to turn on the lights in the room, as I finally asked, "Who's there?"

Without a sound, the figure began to approach. I could feel my heart beating harder as the alarm started going off on the pulse monitor I was still attached to. The person still hadn't said anything, and I still couldn't make out who it was as the door swung open and the nurse entered, turning the lights on as she hurried over to my bedside. It was Selk.

"D.J. are you feeling okay? Your heart is racing."

"Yes, I'm fine. I just panicked a little when I couldn't get the lights on," I looked over at Selk searching for some signs of what could possibly be going on in his head. "My friend here startled me in the darkness," I continued.

She silenced the monitor and stood there for a second, just watching us. "Well, if you're sure you're okay, I'll go then." She straightened up my covers a little then pulled my handheld call light up from between the head of my bed and the wall. "Hun, how'd your call light get way back here? You'da never found it back there," she explained as she looped it around the bedrail and laid it by my side.

"Thank you. That's what I was looking for to turn the lights on," I explained to her. Selk still hadn't said a word.

"Okay then. If you need anything just hit the light, and someone will be in, *quickly*," she said, looking directly at Selk. Finally, she turned back to me, smiled, and said, "Don't hesitate to use your call light dear."

"Thank you. I won't." I could tell she was letting me know she didn't like the vibe in the room and that I was safe. My pulse rate had returned to normal, and it did make me feel better to know she could tell something wasn't quite right in my room. She gave Selk another wary look before she turned and left the room.

I immediately lit into him when the door closed. "Why didn't you tell me it was you?"

"Who else would it have been D.J.? Were you expecting someone else?" he said with a smirk on his face.

As I let the head of my bed up higher, "I sure wasn't expecting to wake up to a shadow in the dark that's all. What time is it anyway?" I could tell it was either very late or very early because there wasn't any light coming in from behind the curtains.

"It's after 11. You must be worn out, I've been here since about 6 o'clock, and you hadn't attempted to wake up. You even missed your dinner," he continued as he moved a little closer to the head of my bed, dragging his hand up the bed rails as he got closer to me.

"Well, why didn't you wake me when you got here?"

"I figured you'd wake up eventually, so I waited. And frankly D.J., I'm glad I did," he gave me a devilish smile.

"Really, and why's that?" I asked as he stood right up over me, staring down on me.

"I learned a lot just watching you. And listening to you," he said as he dipped his head to the side and glanced over at the door. In one quick motion, he had me by my throat and pinned me to the bed. "Who's Jeremiah D.J.?" he growled from somewhere deep and dark inside of him.

I grabbed his wrist and began to kick and struggle as all the monitors in the room started screaming. He was squeezing so tight I could barely breathe so there was no way I could scream. As I flopped around in the bed trying to release myself from his grip, he suddenly released me. Almost as quickly as the attack started, it was over. I was coughing hysterically, gasping for air when I finally realized what had just happened.

"D.J., you have to be more careful," as he wiped the water off my chin. "You're going to choke drinking so fast," he said.

I took in a deep breath and coughed a couple more times when I realized that there were 2 nurses standing at my bedside. He stood there playing the doting fiancé when they moved him aside and began turning off alarms and checking me over.

"I don't know what happened. She was drinking her water, and all of a sudden she started choking," he explained in a panic.

I could feel my eyes getting wider and wider as I listened to his lies. I let out one final cough, holding on to my neck, trying to fully process what had just happened.

"D.J. talk to me! What's happening? Are you okay?" Susie asked as she adjusted the baby monitors on my stomach. Mary was still pushing buttons on my monitor as my high blood pressure reading set off another alarm.

I could see the look on Selk's face as I turned to answer her. I knew better than to tell them what had really just happened, but for the first time, in a long time, I didn't care. I grabbed her arm and pointed at Selk.

"He just choked me! He grabbed me by my throat and wouldn't let go!" I yelled as the tears started streaming down my face. "When you came in he must have splashed water on my face to make it look like I was choking on it," I cried as I turned my head away from Selk and held Susie's hand even tighter.

"Sir, you've got to leave. NOW!" she told him as she pointed to the door still holding on to my hand. "You're fine D.J. Calm down. You're going to be just fine," she told me as she leaned over me as if she was going to lay on top of me to protect me from Selk.

Julie hit the emergency call light, "Call security NOW!"

"D.J. are you crazy! Why would you tell them that? You choked on your water! I didn't touch her! Look at her, she spilled water all down her front! She's soaking wet," he pointed over Susie's shoulder as another nurse came in the room and took Susie's place over my bed as she began pushing Selk towards the door.

I turned my head into the pillow still sobbing as security stepped into the room and escorted Selk out still pleading his case.

"D.J.! Tell them the truth! I never laid a hand on her! I was only trying to help her!" he yelled out as the door closed.

There was a constant rush of people in and out of my hospital room for several hours after that, including my parents, Dr. Cleveland, Mr. Charlie, and the police. It was taking everything they had to bring my blood pressure down, and Dr. Cleveland kept threatening to take me for an emergency C-section right then, which was only making my blood pressure go higher. The boys were not in any distress when I wasn't so upset, so I didn't see any reason to deliver them now. I hadn't even started to dilate, so I saw no reason for surgery. Not yet anyway.

I pleaded with him to just wait a little while longer before he made me go to surgery. Finally, he relented, saying, "D.J., I'll give it an hour. If your blood pressure and their heart rates aren't where I want them at the end of 1 hour, you're delivering these babies today, whether you want to or not. We didn't come this far for everything to go to hell because of your stubbornness. Understand me, 1 hour," he held up his finger at me.

"Okay, I understand. 1 hour," I repeated. Trying to force a smile on my face through the tears that were still somehow streaming down my face. I'd been crying so long you'd have thought they'd all dried up by now, but they didn't. They kept coming and coming. At this point, I don't even think they were all sad tears anymore. In the back of my mind, all I could think is *'I'm free. I'm finally free.'* At that moment, in all my relief, I just didn't realize how untrue that idea really was going to be.

An hour later, we had settled down enough that Dr. Cleveland decided that I didn't have to deliver the boys at that very minute, but he also refused to discharge me either. It looked like I was going to make this room my home until the boys made their debut. All I knew was I wasn't going to surgery and change of shift was coming soon. Susie finally ran everyone out of my room and gave me something to rest. I so appreciated her and all the other nurses who had been taking care of me in the wee hours of that morning, so giving them a hard time about anything they told me to do was not an option.

I remembered my nurse for the day shift coming in to check on me and the nursing assistant, but that's about all I remembered doing when I woke up fuzzy again to a very familiar smell. It took me a few minutes to get focused again, but I had the feeling that someone was in my room again. The hairs on my arms started to stand up, but that smell calmed me down just enough that I didn't set off any of the alarms on my monitors.

"Who's there?" I asked, trying to turn the clock around so that I could see the numbers. Suddenly a figure came rushing over to my bedside.

"D.J. calm down. It's only me," a very familiar and much-needed voice cut through the darkness as he clicked on the light just as my heart rate shot up.

I grabbed his hand and pull him into the bed with me, as I buried my face into his chest, and the tears began streaming down my face.

"Jeremiah! When did you get here? Why didn't you wake me up? I'm so happy to see you!" I cried into his chest as all the alarms started going off.

Without warning, the door to my room flung open, and 4 nurses came rushing in.

"D.J. are you okay? Who is this? Do we need to call security?" as two of them turned off the alarms, and the others scrambled to put space between Jeremiah and me.

"No! No! No! Joy I'm fine! He's fine! This is Jeremiah, not Selk! This isn't Selk! I'm just so happy to see him," I tried to explain.

"I didn't mean her any harm. I just didn't want her to panic when she woke up and saw a shadow in here," he explained.

My nurse gave me a wondering look as she checked my IV sight and adjusted the straps on my belly. "Okay then," she let out a deep breath holding her chest. "Just please, don't scare us like that again D.J.," she swatted at me. "Girl we thought that we were going to have to get security back up here again," she said. "Let them know it's a false alarm before they call out the troops," she told one of the other nurses. "And what is that heavenly smell?" she said, looking around the room, finally smiling.

"Oh, I brought her some barbecue, but there's plenty if you'd like to have some," Jeremiah explained as he went back over to where he'd been sitting and picked up a large bag of food and brought it back over to my bedside table and began to empty the sack.

"No, we can't," she said with a laugh. "But it does smell so good."

"If you want some, please feel free to get some. I guarantee there's more than enough for all of us. And if we run out, I'm in pretty good with the owners of the store, so I can always get some more," I laughed as I gave Jeremiah a wink.

"Well if you insist," she smiled as she went over to the sink to wash her hands.

"Here just take these 2 boxes. There's a variety of meats and sides in there. It should be enough for everyone at the desk to get a taste," Jeremiah explained as he handed her the 2 boxes of food.

"No, no, now this is too much. We can't take all of this," she barely insisted.

"Yes, you can. And yes you will. I guarantee there's plenty of food in this box for me. He kinda spoils me like that," I laughed.

"Well if you're sure," she said with a huge smile on her face.

"We're sure," Jeremiah and I said at the same time. We both looked at each other with a look of surprise on our faces as the room exploded into laughter. Joy said her thank you's and finally left the room.

"What are you doing here? You weren't supposed to be back until the weekend." I started again patting at a space I'd just made in the bed for Jeremiah to sit down beside me.

"Well Miss Lady. I heard through the grapevine what happened to you last night, so I cut my business short to get back here to you. How are you feeling?" he asked as he rubbed up and down both sides of my neck where it had begun to bruise, as much investigating the damages as he was consoling me, I think.

"I'm better now that you're here," as I lifted his hand off my neck and kissed his palm. "You really shouldn't have done that ya know. You have important work to do. You can't be dropping everything because of my little tiff," I continued as I snuggled my face in his hand.

"Little tiff! The police report says that fool tried to choke you D.J. I'd call that a bit more than a tiff," as he lifted my chin up to look into my eyes. "How long has this been going on D.J.? And don't play word games with me because anyone bold enough to try something like this in such a public place would definitely have no problem doing worse in a private one," he said as he wiped away a tear before it had a chance to run down my face.

"Jeremiah, I'm fine. That's all that matters," I explained as there came a knock at the door. "Come in."

"Hi. I have a delivery for D.J. Morgan," a young man peaked in the room as he held onto two huge vases of flowers for dear life. One was a dozen long stem yellow roses, and the other was 2 dozen long stem red roses with one white rose in the center.

"How beautiful! You can put them over there in the windowsill," I pointed. Pulling Jeremiah's arm hard enough to pull him back in the bed again and giving him a kiss. Our first real kiss.

"Here are the cards ma'am. Have a nice day," as the young man turned his head, obviously blushing, as he hurried from the room.

"WOW! What was that for?" Jeremiah said with a big smile on his face.

"For the flowers silly," as I swatted at him.

"Thanks, but they're not from me this time," he said with an awkward smile.

"They're not? Well, who else would be sending me this many flowers?" I said with a puzzled look on my face.

"Well open the cards and find out already," as he sat down on the edge of my bed.

I quickly opened the first envelope and immediately froze when I saw the note on the card.

"What's wrong D.J.? Who's it from?"

I just looked at him in disbelief. As he snatched the card out of my hand, I said, "They're from Selk's agent."

Jeremiah read the card as his smile turned to a deep, angry frown. He didn't even wait for me to open the other envelope as he snatched it out of my hand and read it as well.

"Who in the hell does he think he is? I can't believe he's got this much nerve to attack you and then turn around and threaten and all but blame you, for him putting his hands on you!" Jeremiah was fuming. "I'll give the precinct a call and let them know about these cards so they can enter them into evidence," as he whipped his phone out and began to dial.

"Evidence?" as I took the second card from him so that I could see what it said.

"Yes, evidence. He and his *'agent,'* all but admit to him choking you so the prosecutor won't have much of a problem getting a conviction when this goes to trial." I didn't say anything at first as Jeremiah started pacing and fussing. I just sat there reading the cards for a second and third time as it finally hit me what Jeremiah was saying.

I heard him talking to someone on the phone when I reached out to him and said, "Wait, what? Conviction? But, I told the detective that I wasn't pressing any charges."

"You did WHAT?!" Jeremiah said as he stopped dead in his tracks and turned to face me. He came back over to my bed and sat down beside me, staring down at me with a look he'd never given me before. "What do you mean, 'You're NOT pressing any charges?'" he paused only for a second, "D.J.! Be serious! Let me call you back!" as he hung up the phone and began pacing again.

I pushed myself up in the bed before I answered, "I am being serious. If I press charges, I will ruin his career. This is a contract year for him, and he can't afford any bad press."

"Damn, the bad press. He should have thought about that *before* he put his damn hands on you!" as he came over and gently rubbed the bruised areas on my neck. "You can't let him get away with this! He could've killed you D.J.! And what about what could've happened to the babies? Cutting off your oxygen cuts off their oxygen too."

"I... I know this sounds crazy, but I don't want to take his livelihood away from him. I just want him to leave me alone. And he'll do that now. I know he will," I pleaded my case reaching for Jeremiah's hand.

He pulled away from me shaking his head, "No, I'm not with you on this one D.J.," still moving away from my bed. "You can't tell me his job is worth more than you and those babies' lives," he pointed back at me. "You don't give any man a pass for putting their hands on you in a violent matter. I don't give a damn what they do for a living! He chose to attack you, and he should damn well pay the piper for it! If his career was so important to him, he would've thought about that before he put his hands on your throat and tried to squeeze the life out of you," he motioned with his hand with each of his points. Before I had a chance to respond, he came over and started rubbing my belly, as he asked me, "Do you even realize how much damage he could've caused if he'd cut off your air just a little too long? Those babies are dependent on you for everything, including their oxygen. Was he thinking about them when he attacked you? I'd say NO!" as he backed off and began to pace back and forth across the room again.

I just sat watching him pace as he became angrier and angrier. My focus on him was finally interrupted when my pulse monitor began to alarm. I'd never seen him like this. He was as livid as he was on the phone in my kitchen a few nights ago. Only this time Joshua wasn't here to calm him down.

My door opened without a knock.

"Is everything okay in here? We can hear voices up at the nurses' station," Joy said, giving Jeremiah a stern look as she turned the alarm off.

"Everything's fine," he said, waving her off as he continued pacing and shaking his head. "I just found out that she's not pressing charges against Selkie... and I got a little riled up," he threw his arm up over his head again, still waving her off as he continued to pace and talk to himself.

"Well, I really don't need her getting all excited...wait. What did you just say?" she stopped being so nurse like and just stared at me in disbelief.

"Yeah, you heard me right. She's not pressing any charges," he continued to pace and mumble under his breath.

"D.J., what does he mean 'you're *not* pressing any charges?' That man could've killed you *and* these babies. He's at least three times your size!" she started waving her hands around in the air.

I could tell this was going to be a long night as I laid my head back and thought about my decision not to press charges against Selk. Was it some misguided loyalty I had to him or was it because I had gotten so used to his outbursts that I thought I could truly handle him on my own? Either way, nobody in this room at the moment, was going to be happy about me not pressing charges against Selk. I figured since I had finally exposed him, he'd keep his hands to himself, so there was no real reason to take things any further. I laid there hearing their voices but not really listening, thinking about all that had happened and what I was hoping would happen until I dozed off.

I woke up to an empty room, which did make me sad, but it was also what I expected. Selk was back in Dallas, and Jeremiah was probably still pissed off because he couldn't change my mind about filing charges against Selk. So yes, I expected to wake up alone. I figured this would be the state of my life for some time to come since the only two men in my life had great reasons to stay away. As I laid in the darkness thinking about how screwed up my life was, I could hear my mother's voice saying, '*I told you so. You had to do things your way, and now you're all alone raising 2 babies on your own....I tried to warn you, but you wouldn't listen. I told you so D.J., I told you so....*' kept playing over and over again in my head.

I whispered to myself, "What have I done?" as a tear escaped from the corner of my eye before I could blink it away. At some point, I gave up and just allowed the stream of tears to free flow down the sides of my face. I didn't realize how upset I'd gotten until one of the monitor alarms went off. I quickly wiped away my tears and tried to regain my composure before someone came rushing in the room to check on me.

Right on cue, the door flew open without a knock, "D.J., are you okay?" as she scanned the room obviously expecting to see somebody. It was Susie, I'd slept the entire day. The night shift was back on duty.

"I'm okay," I sniffed, turning my head away from her so she wouldn't see my tears.

A voice from the doorway chimed in, "What's going on? D.J. are you okay?" as Jeremiah rushed in the door. I jerked around totally surprised but immediately happy. It was Jeremiah. He was here.

"I'm okay. What are you doing here? I thought you'd left.... for good," I said with a huge smile on my face as he rushed to my side.

"Now why would I leave, when my heart is here," he smiled as he took a seat on the side of my bed and wiped away a tear. "Why are you crying D.J.? Are you in pain?"

"No. I was just laying here thinking my mom was right. I'm all alone, and I'm going to have to raise these boys all by myself," I said, feeling awful embarrassed at the moment.

"Silly, I'm not going anywhere," he smiled as he continued to wipe my tears away.

"Well, you must be the infamous Jeremiah," she smiled. "D.J. I see you're in good hands now, but don't hesitate to call me if you need me, okay?" she said as she winked at us and turned and left the room.

"I can't believe you're here. You were so mad at me so when I woke up and you weren't here, I figured you'd left and probably wouldn't be coming back," I said as I snuggled into his chest. As I began to relax to the sound of his heartbeat, he threw his legs up in the bed and curled up alongside me and held me tight.

"D.J. my dear. It's going to take more than a disagreement to send me running for the hills never to return," he said as he stroked my head. "I don't agree with your decision, but it's just that, your decision. All I can do is voice my opinion and support you, however you need me to, for as long as you need me to," he paused for a minute. "But D.J. I need you to understand me when I say, if he ever puts his hands on you again, you won't get a chance to press charges. Do you understand what I'm saying?" as he gently pulled my chin up so that he could look into my eyes.

"Jeremiah don't say things like that. He's not worth you getting into trouble over. Please don't do anything crazy. Promise me you won't do anything to him," I could feel my heartbeat picking up as the tears started flowing again, and I buried my face into his chest.

"Shhhh, shhhh D.J.. Calm down baby. I won't do anything crazy, but I can't promise you that I'm not going to put my hands on one Mr. Selkie Black if he harms you in any way. We will be having a man to mouse talk sooner than later, that I can promise you," he whispered as he kissed my forehead and began to stroke my head. "D.J. a real man would NEVER put his hands on a woman, under *any* circumstances," as he moved his head to look into my face.

I lifted my head so that I could look him in his eyes, "Jeremiah, I know that. And I know that you would NEVER touch me in a way that wasn't loving."

We laid there, losing ourselves in each other's eyes when I finally got up the courage and pulled his face closer to mine. I expected him to stop me, but he didn't. I hesitated for a second and simply enjoyed the feeling of his breath on my lips before I stretched my neck just a little more for our lips to finally meet. My body exploded from the inside out as I slid my tongue between his lips and felt the warmth and wetness that eagerly greeted me. Our tongues embraced in a way that I'd never experienced before. It was like they became one but still moved at their own pace and rhythm.

He pulled my body closer as he gripped my leg and gently pulled it over the top of his. His hand gently massaged up and down my back, across my hip, and down my leg. I could tell I was getting very moist and hoped that he would reach under my gown to massage the throbbing going on between my legs. My hand ventured lower and lower until I felt a thick mound of him, hard as a rock. He was more than I could wrap my hand around through his pants, so I worked to loosen them enough to slide my hand down them and inside his underwear to touch his manhood to discover more than I could have ever imagined. I began to massage and pull at him, wanting to feel him inside of me more and more, with every stroke.

He pulled me in closer and gently slid his hand down my tummy and under the covers, slowly lifting my gown as his fingers began to strum on my clit like the strings on a guitar. He was so gentle, as he flicked and messaged the heart of me, causing my body to explode and melt all at the same time. I gripped him harder and tugged with all my might, getting him to give me a deep primal moan as he slid a finger inside of me and my body vibrated in total ecstasy. Our tongues made love to the rhythms and vibrations of the beautiful music that our fingers were creating as we massaged one another.

Suddenly an alarm went off, jarring us both back to reality. He scrambled from the bed with my juices dripping from his fingers and silenced the alarm like he'd done a hundred times before, with his dry hand of course. I sat up all wide-eyed and in a near panic knowing that anyone could walk in at any minute and instantly know what we had been up to with one sniff of the air, but to our surprise, nobody came in. The quick knock and body coming through the door never happened.

After a few tense seconds, we both threw our heads back, laughing uncontrollably. When we settled down, Jeremiah simply slid his sticky fingers in his mouth, closed his eyes, and slowly pulled them back out letting out a thick and warming moan.

"Uhhhhhmmm. Baby, you taste soooo good." He gave me a million-dollar smile as he leaned down and forced his tongue in my mouth for another beautiful, passionate dance. I reached out trying to pull him back down to me, but he grabbed on to my wrist saying, "No D.J....As much as I hate to say it, we need to stop. This is the wrong place, and it's definitely the wrong time."

"Please don't stop. I didn't' know I could feel this way. I've never felt this way when a man touched me. Don't stop. Please don't stop," I begged him.

"D.J. as badly as I want to oblige you right now, we can't. Not here. Not like this," as he rubbed my hair back and leaned down to kiss me on my forehead. "Baby, I haven't felt like this before either, but I know we are totally out of order for what we almost let happen." He could tell by my body language and the sad look on my face that I wasn't happy with what he was saying, even if I did know what he was saying was completely true. "I'm just as disappointed as you," as he opens his palm up and waves it towards his still very erect penis. "So if I'm willing to wait, surely you can hold on a few more weeks," he said with a sheepish grin.

"Weeks! Why weeks?!" I said, startling him.

He just looked at me for a moment then started laughing.

"And what may I ask is so damn funny." I saw nothing funny. Not in the least little bit.

"D.J. if you could only see the look on your face when you said that," still laughing as he turned to go into the bathroom. He turned the water on and continued to explain, "I said weeks because you're not supposed to have sex for at least 6 weeks after you have the babies. That's why." He came out of the bathroom with a washcloth in hand. He pulled my gown to the side and began to wash me off. "Didn't your doctor tell you that?" he asked, still washing away any evidence of what had just transpired a few minutes ago. I wasn't able to respond at first. I was still shocked at what was going on right now. It was amazing how gentle he was and how careful he was getting all the sticky goo my body had released, off of me. He disappeared into the bathroom again before I could muster up the words to respond.

"No, no he didn't. Why would he? I haven't had sex since these two were conceived," I caught myself after I'd said the words. I flinched as I thought to myself, *'Idiot! Why did you say that of all things?'* with my eyes tightly shut.

When I opened them, I saw Jeremiah standing in the bathroom doorway with his hands dripping wet and his mouth hanging open, just staring at me.

Finally, he said, "Come again?" twisting his face up like he couldn't believe his ears.

I held my hand over my mouth, shutting myself up as I dropped my head and closed my eyes, shaking my head back and forth. I was hoping he wasn't standing there when I finally opened my eyes again, but he was. I let out a sigh and began to explain to him that Selk and I hadn't had sex since we broke up long before I had found out that I was pregnant.

He just stood there watching me and then started laughing. "Well that explains a lot," and returned to the sink that he'd left running. He quickly returned to my side, only this time to rinse the soap off of me. I laid back, closed my eyes, and enjoyed the gentle message of his fingers through the washcloth.

"I'm glad I could be your late-night entertainment," I said sarcastically.

He leaned down and kissed me on the forehead, then said, "Uhhh, D.J.?"

"Yeah..." I replied, finally looking up at him.

"This would work so much better if you would stop enjoying this so much," he smiled.

"Huh? What are you talking about now?" I asked, not realizing what was happening.

He started laughing, "Well it's obvious to me that I'm doing too good of a job....at getting you off anyway. You're getting all gooey again. At this rate, I'll never get you cleaned up," he laughed even harder.

I could feel my face heat up as I sat up straighter and pulled my gown down as I pushed his hand away. I turned away from him, "Ohh, I'm sorry."

He reached out and took my chin, pulling my head back around towards him. His eyes were so soft and loving as he spoke, "Don't be ashamed. That's the best flattery a man could ever get. It makes me happy to know that you want me to touch you. That you enjoy me touching you....," he paused for a moment. "Even if it is with a washrag in the hospital," he busted out laughing.

"That's not funny!" I swiped at him. It hit me, I was actually sitting here pouting. Realizing that only made things worse, not better. "Stop laughing at me! I see nothing funny!"

Jeremiah went back to cleaning me up and finally stopped laughing, but not before saying, "Yeah, this is worth all the tea in China. You are too adorable for words," as he leaned over to kiss me on the cheek and took the washcloth back inside the bathroom. He returned with the aroma candle I had asked Mr. Charlie to bring from my place, lit it, and sat it on my bedside table. I glanced over at him as he turned back towards the bathroom and couldn't help but notice the rather large bulge still protruding from his pants, which made all of the embarrassment and laughter worth it. He stayed gone a little while this time, finally closing the bathroom door, which was probably a good thing. Because no sooner than he closed the door good, my room door opened without much of a warning.

"It's just me coming to check on you. Your monitors were doing some interesting things a few minutes ago, but they've settled down nicely now," Gail said. "Susie's in with another patient, and it's taking longer than she thought it would, so she asked me to come check in on you."

I hoped she couldn't tell how embarrassed I am right now. I tried to calm myself, praying that Jeremiah straightened up his clothes before he came out of the bathroom. "I'm fine. We're fine. Thank you for checking on us," I finally came up with the words to say, just as the toilet flushed.

"Oh, I thought your friend had gone home. It's way after visiting hours," she said as she adjusted the baby monitors we had accidentally moved out of position in our frisky state.

"I didn't realize it was so late. He will probably be leaving soon."

"Woman, didn't I tell you earlier? I'm not going anywhere," Jeremiah said with a huge grin on his face and arms crossed, standing in the bathroom doorway.

"I didn't see you there," I smiled, shaking my head. "It's late, and you need to go home and get some rest Sir."

"Yeah, yeah. This recliner looks pretty comfortable to me. If there's a chance I could get a blanket from this wonderful nurse, I'll be just fine right here, with you," he smiled and gave the nurse a wink.

"Well, I think I can manage a blanket for you, but the window box might be a little more comfortable...not much, but a little," she smiled as she turned and left the room.

"Jeremiah. You don't have to stay. I'll be fine. Go home and get some rest," I said as I reached out for his hand.

"Look Little Mamma. I'm here, and I'm not going anywhere tonight," he kissed the back of my hand then looked at his watch. "Oh, my. You've got to be starving." And with that, he picked up the phone, dialed someone, and walked away talking. As he walked out the door, Gale walked in the door with a pillow and a blanket.

"Here you go. These should help a little. I don't know how comfortable he's going to be in that chair, but at least he won't be cold," she laughed. "Where's he off to anyway?"

"Food, I think. We didn't realize how late it was."

"That makes sense. We were holding your dinner tray for you, but I bet whatever he brings back is better than what we served tonight. Beef stew...." she jerked forward with her hand over her mouth like she was getting sick. That's all I needed to agree with her that whatever Jeremiah found, had to be better than that. "Well if there's anything else you need, just let us know."

"I will and thank you for the blanket and pillow," I waved to her as the door closed.

He was gone quite a while, but when Jeremiah finally returned, he came back with a large pizza and a salad.

"Where on earth did you get that, this time of night?" I giggled.

"I have my connections. Besides, it's the weekend. Some places stay open later than they do during the week," he gave me a wink as he set the food up and handed me the salad.

"And what made you think I'd want a salad?" I gave him a half-smile with my arms crossed over my chest.

"Well, I remembered you saying that sometimes you like the salads from here, better than the pizza, so I was covering my basis and got both," he gave me a wink and a smile as he handed me the salad dressing and silverware.

"Nice....a man who actually pays attention," I grinned. "Well thank you so much for covering your basis Mr. Thomas. I do sooo appreciate that." As I pulled him in closer for a kiss. I could feel my body start to tingle again so I let him go and grabbed a slice of pizza and took a much larger bite than I probably should have, but I didn't really care because I was actually starving. "Mmmm...either this is really, really good or I'm just super hungry right now," I smiled as my eyes rolled back in my head. Then I started eating it like it was a cookie, and I was the cookie monster.

He started laughing, "Slow down! You're going to choke," as he reached out to pull my hand away from my mouth. "You don't have to eat like you're in the military you know. It's not going anywhere, and you don't have a time limit," he laughed.

"Funny," I gave him a twisted smiled as I took another slice of pizza. "Stop starving me, and I won't eat like I've never seen food before, how about that." I couldn't help but laugh as he shook his head at me, then started eating his slice in slow motion, mocking me.

We sat there talking and picking at each other over the next hour. He took the leftovers out to the nurses' station to ask permission to put what was left in the refrigerator. When he returned, I was already fast asleep. Being around him made it so much easier for me to relax and get comfortable, even in this hospital bed. Even the boys calmed down and stopped kicking so hard, giving my sides and ribs a break. Needless to say, we all had a very comfortable night's rest. At least as comfortable as one can get in a hospital bed. We actually had such a nice couple of days after that that Dr. Cleveland decided that I could go home until we induced labor after Thanksgiving, under certain conditions. We agreed that I would go home on complete bed rest and with limited visitors, to keep my activity level down and prevent any undue stress. He also didn't want me taking the stairs, which I quickly explained to him was going to be a problem.

"But my bedroom is upstairs. If I have to stay in bed at all times, I'm completely cut off from the kitchen."

"Come on D.J., you have an assistant who can get you whatever you want," Jeremiah interjected.

I shot him a cross look, "I know but…"

"No butts D.J." Dr. Cleveland cut me off. "Either you stay in the bed, or you stay here. The *ONLY* thing you are allowed to do is go to the bathroom. I don't even want you taking hot baths or very long showers. Do I make myself clear?" he asked.

Before I could answer, "Yes Sir, she does," Jeremiah answered, smiling at me. "And to make sure she follows your directions, she's coming home with me."

"I'm *(She's)* what?" me and Dr. Cleveland said at the same time.

"You heard me. You're coming home with me," he said with a big smile on his face. "I have plenty of space, and everything is on one level, for the most part anyway. I was already taking off next week, so I can take off this week too and take care of you," he smiled like he had just saved the world.

There was an uncomfortable silence for just a moment when Dr. Cleveland finally spoke.

"D.J., it's up to you where you go, but from what I've been told and what I've seen over the last couple of days, with him is where you ought to be," he said pointing at Jeremiah, looking like a hitchhiker with his thumb out.

I sat there trying to maintain my composure at the excitement of the possibility of going home with Jeremiah, but that excitement quickly turned to sadness as the reality of the situation began to weigh on me. I guess they could tell what was going on inside of me, because after a few more minutes in silence, Dr. Cleveland spoke up again.

"Again, D.J. it's really none of my business, and I know this is an awkward situation, but you and those babies are my only concern so I could care less what it might look like or how anyone else, especially your mother, might feel about the situation. So because I can see how torn you are, I'm giving you two choices."

I finally found the strength to speak, barely looking up, "What two choices?"

"You go home with this nice young man and allow him to take care of you while keeping you safe and calm, or you stay here in the hospital."

"That's not really a choice," I said as I dropped my head again.

Jeremiah gently lifted my head by my chin, smiling at me, "D.J., deep down, you know what you need to do. Like I told you, I'm not going anywhere and even if I don't like your choices, my job is to support you as much as I can," he explained as he wiped away the tear rolling down my cheek. "I made the offer because I love you and these babies, even though I know this here between us," he motions back and forth between us, "was never in either of our plans, it just happened. But no matter what, we were brought together if for nothing more than to give these babies a better chance at a healthier and safer pregnancy. Now, your doctor agrees that it would be the best choice for you to come home with me but what we think doesn't matter if you don't agree. So what do *you* want to do?" he finished as he wiped away another tear.

"I..." I rapidly blinked back many more tears. "It's not that I don't want to come home with you, it's just..."

"Go on D.J., you don't have to be afraid, say whatever it is you're feeling," Jeremiah interrupted as he handed me a tissue.

"I know I need, no, *we* need to come home with you, but I also know that there is going to be hell to pay if I do and my mother *will* come for her pound of flesh, and I don't want you caught in her crosshairs any more than you already are. She's only stayed away this long because she'd *NEVER* allow the staff to put her out and she knows that if an alarm goes off because of her, the staff would do just that. She's way too proud for that. She'd die first. So she's playing nice for right now but if I leave this hospital with you, and go to *your* house until these boys are born... the wrath we will all face from that woman would be beyond biblical proportions, and I don't want to do that to you, or to you Dr. Cleveland," I explained looking back and forth between the two of them.

Dr. Cleveland started to laugh as he crossed his arms and leaned up against my bed. "D.J., I've known your mother longer than you have. I've seen her at her best and at her worst, and I've seen her at her most vulnerable state, especially when it comes to you kids. You forget I delivered you and all your brothers. I was also there when her pregnancies didn't go as expected, and she lost a baby or two. Your mother is a very determined force to be reckoned with, especially when it comes to you, but so are you. Have you ever asked why your mom is so protective of you?"

"No. It's just the way it's always been."

"How many times have you stared me down in the last week alone, with her in your ear siding against you, with me? And every time you stood your ground and the sun came up the next day. The world is not going to come to an end if Lisa Morgan can't control every aspect of her daughter's life."

I just sat there staring at him, but I could feel the bed moving as Jeremiah tried his best to stifle his laughter.

"It's not funny," I moaned as I laid my head back and closed my eyes.

"D.J., come on. That was one of the best encouragement speeches on why to live your life for *you* that you've probably ever heard," Jeremiah said poking me in my side to try to get a giggle out of me. I shook my head no and let out another moan and rolling my eyes.

"D.J., listen to what I have to say. I'm breaking a confidence now, but I think it will bring you a whole lot of clarity."

I didn't know where this was going, but I sat straight up in bed and gave him my full attention.

Looking a little surprised, Dr. Cleveland said, "You really don't know why your mom is so protective of you, do you?"

"I always figured it was because she almost lost me to cancer at such a young age," I hunched up my shoulders with my hands raised.

"Well, that does have a lot to do with it, but it's not the only reason," he paused. "Has your mom ever explained to you why your name is D.J.? I mean really explained?"

"Again, not really. When the subject came up, she'd just say, *'Because that's what I decided.'"*

"Well, the real reason she *'decided'* that is because you were a twin my dear."

An alarm immediately went off, "Wait....WHAT?!" I shouted as I sat straight up in the bed, nearly knocking Jeremiah off of it.

"Calm down, calm down," as he reached over and silenced the alarm. "Yes, my dear D.J., you were a twin," he smiled.

"Why have I *never* heard this before? There's no way she would have told me that, but somebody should have!" I sat there shaking my head like I was trying to get something off of me. Jeremiah was patting my hand trying to calm me down, with his mouth hanging open.

"What do you mean she was a twin doc? What happened to her twin?"

"Your mom went into labor around 24 weeks. Once she realized that something wasn't right and finally made it to the hospital, we were unable to stop it in time to prevent your sister from coming. But because you were fraternal twins, we were able to stop you from coming and sewed your mom's cervix closed until time for you to come. She spent the next 12 weeks in bed, with her feet elevated."

I jumped in, "Wait. Let me get this straight. I have a sister I've never known about.... Why wouldn't she tell me that?"

"D.J. you know your mom. She doesn't let people know when there is something wrong with her, not like that anyway. But yes, your sister was stillborn. She was just so tiny, there wasn't really anything we could do for her, but you. We fought like hell to get your mom to term then the damndest thing happened..."

"What?! What happened?" I said a little louder and more excited than I probably should have, as an alarm went off.

He let out a light-hearted laugh as he silenced the alarm, "You didn't come. You were actually 3 weeks late. We ended up inducing labor and then still had to go in with forceps and pull you out."

"You're kidding? She was that stubborn early on huh?" Jeremiah laughed as he hugged me and gave me a kiss on the forehead. I just looked at him for a moment. "What....I'm just kidding," he shrugged.

"No you're not," I lifted a finger up to him as I turned my attention back to Dr. Cleveland. "And I'm still confused. Why is this the first time I'm ever hearing this? When people asked, *'do twins run in your family,'* she would always get this distant stare but never responded. I'd always say, yeah on my father's side." I was still in shock with what I was hearing. "Is that why I've always been so attracted to twins?!" I said, nearly jumping out of bed.

"What do you mean, 'you've *always* been attracted to twins?'" Jeremiah asked.

"It's not exactly what you think. See when I was little if I ever saw twins or heard someone talking about twins I would follow them around like a stalker. Seriously...people started thinking something was wrong with me. Then when I got older, I only wanted to date a twin, so when I got married, I'd have a better chance of having twins."

"You're kidding, right?" Jeremiah asked with the same shocked look on his face that I had when Dr. Cleveland started this conversation. I just shook my head no.

"Could be. You never know. Twins have a strange connection that we still don't fully understand. But you decided you didn't want to come. It's like you remembered your sister going out that tunnel and never coming back. In fact, we had two nurses trying to massage you down while I tried to grip you with the forceps. Young lady, you ran up to the farthest corner you could and balled up so tight I was about to give up and do a C-section. I felt so bad for your poor mom. I induced her, and 36 hours later, you still weren't here, and she still wanted to give you a chance to come on your own without any more medical intervention. It was actually an inspiring thing to watch. She fought for you like a mother lion D.J.," he finished shaking his head. You could tell by the way he was looking out the window that he was going back to that day.

"This explains so much…. She always refers to me as her 'only LIVING daughter,'" I put in air quotes. "I never put two and two together," I said, shaking my head. "It has always bothered me to hear her say that, but I never questioned it. Any of it. And to think….my dad never said a word, nobody did." I was still trying to process what I was being told.

"Now D.J., the short time I laid eyes on your dad, even I can see that there's no way on God's green earth he would *ever* challenge your mom. Matter of fact….is there anybody in your family that will challenge your mom?" Jeremiah asked.

Almost over my shoulder and very matter-of-factly, "No," quickly turning my attention back to Dr. Cleveland again, "Now Dr. Cleveland, you're telling me that I'm really a twin, but I'm still not clear on where the initials come in."

"Well, that was your mom's way of paying tribute to both of her babies. You are basically named for 2 people, your name is derived from the first initial of the name she had already picked out for you and your sister."

"So are all of my brother's twins also?"

"No, not all."

Jeremiah jumped in, "What do you mean, 'not all?' One of her brothers was a twin too?"

"Yes, but that's not the point of this conversation."

"The point of this conversation was lost when you told me that not only am I a twin, so is at least one of my siblings," I said obviously upset.

"D.J., the point of this conversation is that your mother did what she felt was best for her even when no one else understood or had something negative to say about it. I told your mom that she should not have any more children after she lost another baby, but she obviously didn't listen. This was my way of telling you to do what you feel would be best for you and *your* children."

"Yeah, well you lost me at my mother has been lying to me my whole life. And which of my siblings was a multiple too? It has to be either J.R. or L.J. because I remember when she was pregnant with M.J. and P.J."

"That's not important D.J.. What is important, is that you do what's right for you and the two babies you're carrying right now," Dr. Cleveland explained.

I turned to Jeremiah, "I can't believe what I'm hearing. How could she not tell me, US! Someone else was a twin as well." I shook my head, trying to understand what I was being told. "I've always known my mom could be hard, but this...this is just cruel. I had a right to know. All of us have a right to know," as tears began to roll down my face, and soon after the alarms began going off again.

Jeremiah pulled me in close, "It's okay baby. It's okay," as he rocked me and rubbed my back. "Doc, when the paperwork is ready, I'll be taking her home with me."

Dr. Cleveland simply nodded in agreement, patted me on the arm, and then turned and left the room. A few minutes later, my nurse came in and discharged me with another list of things to watch for. I still hadn't said anything since Dr. Cleveland left my room and didn't until we were comfortable in Jeremiah's truck.

"Thank you for being here with me, I don't know what I would do without you."

"D.J....."

"No, let me finish," I said, cutting him off. He smiled and simply nodded his head in agreement. "Jeremiah, you came along so unexpectedly at a very low point in my life. You have become the calm in this storm that has become my life. I don't know anyone, especially a man who would step up and take on so much drama that had absolutely nothing to do with him, particularly from an overly pregnant woman who isn't carrying his child. You are a great man Jeremiah Ezekiel Thomas. You are truly a God's send, and I don't deserve you," I finished, squeezing his hand tighter and tighter, trying my best not to start crying again.

I could tell my words had really touched him. He didn't say anything as he pulled away from the curb, but he tried to clear his throat more than once, as he tried to blink away a tear. I reached over and wiped another tear from his cheek as we road in silence. We continued down the road without any spoken words for a few more minutes when he finally looked over at me and kissed the back of my hand at a red light.

"I love you more than I ever imagined possible D.J.. You opened a door that I closed years ago. I didn't save you D.J. ... you saved me," he explained as he gently kissed the back of my hand again to *Come Into My Life* by Joyce Sims playing in the background. I smiled as the tears began to well up in the corners of my eyes, and the butterflies flickered around in my stomach.

We drove without saying another word until we pulled up in front of my apartment building. You would have thought the silence would have been awkward, but it wasn't. There were no more tears along the way, but we still held on to each other as we made our way down the city streets. It felt like we were the only two people on the road, even though there was a steady flow of traffic all around us. We fell more in love with the other as we held hands and returned the occasional squeeze.

I insisted on packing my own things even though Jeremiah constantly fussed about me being on my feet and moving around so much. I knew he meant well, but this was something I had to do for myself, and there was no way he was going to go rifling through my underwear drawers just yet. It didn't take long for me to gather up my clothes and few personal effects, but I couldn't find the beautiful puzzle box Jeremiah had given me or the diary, which sent me into a panic. After several minutes of searching, Jeremiah called out to me letting me know that he'd found them both.

"Well, what's taking you so long? Bring them up here so I can pack them up and then we can go," I yelled down to him as I grew more impatient waiting on him. I was sitting on the edge of the bed putting a few more things in a bag when Jeremiah entered with a worried look on his face. I barely glanced over to him asking, "Where'd you find them?" Finally noticing that the hand I could see was empty and the other was behind his back. He was just silently standing in the doorway with a sad look on his face. "What's wrong?" I could tell something wasn't right.

"D.J. please stay calm..."

"What's wrong? Just tell me!" I yelled at him as I grabbed my chest and started digging in with my nails, turning my body to look at him square on.

He slowly moved the hand at his back around so I could see what he was holding. He never said a word or took his eyes off me as he revealed what was left of my puzzle box and diary. The box had been smashed into multiple pieces, and the diary had been burned almost beyond recognition.

"NO!!!" as I slid off the bed onto the floor crying hysterically. Jeremiah dropped what he was holding and rushed to my side, scooping me up as if I didn't weigh more than a feather, and laid me on the Chaise lounge.

"D.J.! Are you okay?" as he gently rubbed up and down my body like he was checking for broken bones, finally stopping at my stomach softly rubbing from the top, around the sides, and back to the middle, finally resting one hand on my stomach and the other on my cheek. I had buried my face in my hands and was crying hysterically talking to no one really.

"Why would he do that? He had no right? How could he?" I cried as I kept talking.

"Shhhhh. It's going to be okay," he said as he pulled me close and rubbed my head.

"Whyyyy? I can't believe he did that. Just evil, pure evil," I cried into his chest.

"D.J., I don't care why he did it, but I need you to calm down," he explained as he gently rubbed my head. "Baby, you are going to end up right back in the hospital if you can't calm down and this time Dr. Cleveland isn't going to let you leave again, even with me" he whispered.

"I, I...can't believe he did that. I know he was angry with me but this.... this is inexcusable. No more...no more," I cried as I tried to regain my composure.

"D.J., they're just stuff. They can be replaced. They will be replaced. But this is a sign of a very disturbed man. If this doesn't make you see how dangerous he really is and what violence he's capable of, my God. Baby, what would have happened if you had been here when he found these?" He pulled me out of his chest to look me in the face. He gently moved my hair out of my face and wiped away the tears still streaming down my cheeks. "D.J., you can't protect him anymore. The man needs professional help, and you and these babies don't need to be anywhere around him until he gets serious help. I know you want him to be a part of these boys' lives, but not like this. He's just too volatile and unpredictable right now. It's just not safe."

I didn't know what to say right now because I had so many things racing through my head at the moment. For the first time in my life, I kept my mouth shut, and I just sat there looking into Jeremiah's eyes. My mind began to slow down as I saw how much he was hurting right now. I suddenly realized, he was hurting for me. I sat there getting lost in his eyes and calmed down as the feeling of safety I felt through him, began to sink in. My thoughts quickly went from what Selk had done to how safe I felt with Jeremiah's arms wrapped around me. He finally pulled me in closer, and all of my fears and anxieties floated away to the rhythm of his heartbeat. It was at that moment that my heartbeat synced up with his, and we truly became one.

I laid on his chest, enjoying the calmness that had engulfed me when a voice inside said, *"It's time."* I pushed back from Jeremiah and gave him a smile as our eyes locked for a moment. I looked down at my hand and removed the ring that my mom had warned me more than once to never take off again. I held it in my hand looking at it one last time as I pushed up on Jeremiah to get to my feet. He never said a word as he helped steady me, but he stayed seated and quietly watching me as I crossed the room and knelt down beside the shattered puzzle box. Jeremiah jumped to his feet and steadied me as I picked up what was left of my beautiful box and then help me stand back up. When I had regained my balance, I smiled up at him and took the broken box and the ring over to the window and sat them both down on the windowsill with my ring sitting squarely on top of the pile. I turned back to Jeremiah and reached out to him. He quickly took my hand, and I gently squeezed his hand and said, "Please take us home."

Jeremiah grabbed me up in his arms and laid his head on top of mine, "Let's go home." He held me for a little while, and without another word, he gathered up my things, and he led me out of my apartment.

To our surprise, Mr. Charlie was standing at my door as we entered the hallway. He explained that my mom had called him looking for me when she realized that I had been released from the hospital. They told her that I had left with Jeremiah, so she was in a panic trying to find me since I wasn't answering my phone. I don't even remember hearing either of my phones ringing, but I really didn't care at the moment. There was nothing she had to say that I cared to hear right now. I was in a good place, and her negativity and lies were not going to disrupt this feeling. Not now, not today.

I explained to Mr. Charlie what was going on and what we'd discovered in the apartment on the way downstairs. It felt like the elevator took forever to get to the lobby as I rattled off the day's events but when the doors finally opened Mr. Charlie had tears welling up in the corners of his eyes, and he was holding on to my hand tighter than I can ever remember him holding it before. He didn't say a word as he squeezed my hand one last time and relieved Jeremiah of a couple of the bags he was holding on to.

I finished my story as the attendant brought Jeremiah's truck around and said my goodbyes to Mr. Charlie. The doorman took care of all my bags as Mr. Charlie opened the truck door for me to get in. I hesitated for a moment and smiled at Jeremiah when I heard *You Should Be Mine* by Jeffrey Osborne playing softly in the background and thought to myself, *'what perfect timing.'* Mr. Charlie reached for my hand to assist me up into the truck, but Jeremiah quickly stepped in and said, "Let me." Mr. Charlie smiled and backed away as Jeremiah helped me get in, then dropped to his knee on the side rail and took my hand. He reached into his pocket and pulled out a tiny velvet box.

I heard Mr. Charlie say, "Oh my God!," never losing focus on the box as Jeremiah slowly opened it up to present the most beautiful ring I'd ever laid eyes on.

"D.J. Morgan, will you marry me?"

"Yes."

You could tell that I startled him and Mr. Charlie. They both looked like they couldn't believe what they heard as Mr. Charlie squeezed Jeremiah's shoulder.

"Are...D.J. are you sure about that?" he asked in a soft voice.

I giggled at him, he was so cute, "Yes silly. I've never been more sure about anything in my entire life," I smiled at him as I held my hand out waiting on him to put the ring on my finger.

"I know it's not much, especially compared to what you've been wearing, but I hope you like it," as he slid the infinity knot ring on my finger.

The tears began rolling down my cheeks as I stared at the ring. Jeremiah quickly stood up and gently wiped the tears away as they rolled down my face. "Like it..." reaching out, taking his face in my hands and bringing him closer, "It's perfect. I love it," as I gave him a long, passionate kiss.

The ring was a white gold infinity knot filled with Sapphires, surrounding a round 2-carat diamond that was absolutely flawless. It wasn't only unique, it contained my favorite color, blue. This man knew me like we'd known each other our entire lives. As I stared at my ring through a veil of tears, I told him, "This is a ring I would have picked out for myself. It's absolutely perfect."

Once we were able to get away from Mr. Charlie, we drove by Triple J's and gave Mama J and Joshua the good news. Before I knew it, his entire family was there, brothers, sisters, their spouses, and their children, laughing, crying, and celebrating. They didn't ask any questions. There were no snide baby daddy comments or judgment. They simply welcomed me with open arms and agreed that they couldn't wait to spoil the twins. I couldn't believe how happy they were for us even when his sister Jessica, let it slip that they already knew all about me and Selk. As happy as I was it also saddened me to know that he would never receive this warm of a welcome from my family...at least not from my mother. Maybe in time, but not initially at least.

Jeremiah could tell something was wrong with me and made his way back to my side. He kneeled down beside me, and simply smiled at me for a moment then finally said, "Baby don't worry. She'll come around eventually. Your church family will come around too," then he took my hands and kissed them on the back.

'I can't believe he knows me so well,' I thought to myself as I simply nodded at him, trying to blink away my tears. I didn't have to say a word to him, our mental connection was already taking over when spoken words didn't need to be shared.

'D.J., how can I not know you? To not know you is like not knowing myself. You are the rhythm to my heartbeat. I feel you when you're happy and sad, I know when you're up to something and when you're scared, even when you're acting brave. Baby, I LOVE YOU like I've never loved anybody before. So yes my love, I know you very well.' he smiled at me.

He wiped away the single tear running down my cheek, *'How did I ever get so lucky to find you? Your heartbeat is my heartbeat. You make my soul smile, and I know God is listening every time I look into those beautiful brown eyes of yours. I'm not scared to open up my heart anymore. I didn't think I'd ever love again or could ever love anyone this much and out of nowhere, you appeared. What am I going to do with you?'* I simply smiled back.

'Well, hopefully you will keep loving me even when I get old and stinky. But if we're talking right now, I can think of several things I look forward to you doing to me,' his eyes said with a very devilish look on his face. *'But for now, just love me D.J., just love me,'* he smiled.

I chuckled as I slightly shook my head, *'You are so bad.'* I smirked back. *'Oh my God! I've got a dirty old man on my hands.'* I rolled my eyes and laughed out loud. *'But no worries. I gotcha babe,'* I winked back.

'Awww shucks!' as he rocked my legs back and forth.

"Hey you two," Joshua shouted at us over the noise of the crowd. "Stop making moon eyes at each other and join the party!" he laughed as others started to join in.

"They're probably working on their vows," a female voice said.

I started laughing as Jeremiah yelled out over his shoulder, "Mind ya business," never taking his eyes off me.

"Yeah, he's over here harassing me!" I yelled out. Jeremiah's mouth fell open, and he looked completely shocked. I tapped his arm and motioned for him to help me up.

"Harassing you! This coming from the woman who walked into my establishment and handed me my head over some damn barbecue sauce and hot links," he said as he helped me to my feet. "I'm slightly offended," he laughed.

"Only slightly?" I asked, rather seductively as he rubbed my stomach. He gave me a wayward smile as I pulled him closer so that I could whisper in his ear, "Well take me home Mr. Thomas, and let's see if I can *seriously* offend you," I patted him on the butt as I turned to go to the bathroom.

"Well then...." He said as he jerked forward. "I think it's time for me to get this beautiful young lady out of here. She's supposed to be on complete bed rest, so it's about time for me to take her to bed."

"I bet it is!" rang out from someone in the crowd as the room erupted in laughter.

"That came out all wrong. What I meant to say is she's supposed to be on bed rest so she needs to get home so that she can get some..." He tried to clean it up, but he was making it so much worse. He was so flustered when I returned that he didn't even notice me standing behind him.

I tapped him on the shoulder, "Hay gravedigger, wanna stop working on that hole and just take me home. I'm beyond worn out, and these two are getting ready to start acting up," I said, trying not to laugh. "Okay now. All of you give big daddy a break. He's just excited to be getting me to bed," I paused as he gave me a wide-eyed look with his mouth hanging open. "Without any nursing interference," I explained, now cracking up myself and not trying to hide my amusement in the least little bit. The look on his face was priceless as we all burst into laughter. Everybody but him anyway.

"That wasn't funny D.J.," he quietly said as his face turned red. He was so embarrassed he didn't know what to do as he began to squeeze behind me.

"Well that's not what your body is saying little bro," someone else said above the laughter.

I only stopped laughing when I glanced down as he tried to squeeze by me and realized, Jeremiah had a very noticeable erection. "Oh my...." I said as I felt my face get hot. I snatched my jacket off the back of the chair and stepped in front of Jeremiah as I began to give my goodbyes. He simply wrapped his arm around my neck and shoulders, keeping me between him and everyone else as we made our way through the crowd. Everyone had settled down by the time we made it to the front door, that is until one of the boys kicked me extra hard, and I doubled over in front of Jeremiah, and he naturally grabbed me from behind. Unfortunately, after the conversation that had just been going on, that's not what it looked like, causing the crowd to erupt in all-out laughter again.

"That's the perfect position when you're having pregnant sex! Just don't get too excited and start pumping too hard, you might break her water!" one of the male voices yelled out.

Me and Jeremiah turned beet red at that comment. Once he was sure I was okay, he eased us both out the door but not before he yelled back, "Very funny! How about you act your ages, not your shoe sizes!" as the door closed behind us. We could still hear their laughter as we pulled out of the parking lot. It didn't take long for us to start laughing ourselves, you have to admit it was rather funny.

CHAPTER 17

We laughed and talked, holding hands all the way home, except for the few times he rubbed my stomach to try and settle the boys down. They were more excited than I was about our new living arrangement by the way they were bouncing and kicking me during the drive home. And for the first time, it was even difficult for Jeremiah to get them to settle down. Being with him felt so natural like we had known each other for years. The only interruption came when he convinced me to answer the phone when my mom called for the umpteenth time.

"Hello."

"D.J. what do you think you're doing? I can't believe you left the hospital with him! I don't care where you are, you need to have him bring you home, right now young lady!"

I had her on speakerphone, so Jeremiah was able to hear everything she was saying.

"Mamma, I love you, and Jeremiah is taking me home."

"Good! What time will you get there?" she said, obviously relieved.

"Mamma, I'm going to our home. Jeremiah and my home. He asked me to marry him, and I said yes," I blurted out. Jeremiah squeezed my hand as he glanced over at me with a surprised look on his face. I air-kissed him, and he gave me a quick wink and a smile. I wasn't expecting to blurt it out that way, but I really didn't care what she had to say anymore. I was happier than I'd been in a very long time.

Without taking a break between questions, "YOU DID WHAT?! D.J MORGAN HAVE YOU COMPLETELY LOST YOUR MIND?! WHAT HAVE YOU DONE?! YOU'RE ENGAGED ALREADY TO THE FATHER OF YOUR BABIES! WHAT ABOUT SELKIE? HOW DO YOU THINK HE'S GOING TO TAKE THIS NEWS?" she said.

"Mom, I honestly could care less. I'm doing what's best for me and *my* children. Selk can be a part of the boys' lives....after he gets some help with his anger issues, and we feel they will be safe with him. As far as me and Selk are concerned, it's over momma."

"What's that supposed to mean D.J.? I swear I don't know what I'm going to do with you. I try and try to help you make better choices…"

"Mommy let me stop you right there," I cut in.

"EXCUSE ME!" she said, half shocked and obviously annoyed.

"Mommy, I mean no disrespect, but I can't do this anymore. I've allowed you to make some VERY important decisions concerning my future that has absolutely nothing to do with you. I am not *in love* with that man, never have been, and probably never will be, so why do I have to live in a loveless marriage where I'm being mistreated? Mom, you say you want the best for your kids, but why am I the only one who has to up and get married because children are on the way? You didn't make J.R. get married when his twins came along, so why do I have to get married and to someone you know, I'm NOT in love with?"

"It's just different D.J."

Cutting her off quickly, "No ma'am, you always told us and everyone else how you pride yourself in raising all your kids the same, boys and girl alike. So if J.R. didn't have to marry the twin's mom, why do I have to marry Selk? Especially when I'm in love with a man who treats me the way I want and deserve to be treated. And frankly mom, he treats me the way you should want a man to treat your *ONLY LIVING* daughter," I rolled my eyes as the tears began to free flow down my face. I didn't even bother trying to blink them away like I typically did. I turned away from the phone and Jeremiah, and quietly stared out the window mumbling to myself.

Jeremiah had been quiet up until that point, but he took the phone from me and took over the conversation. "Hello Mrs. Morgan. I mean no disrespect, but I can't allow you to upset D.J. like this. I promised Dr. Cleveland that I would keep her calm and in a low-stress environment and right now I can tell if we don't end this conversation, I'm going to have to turn this car around and take her right back to the hospital."

"Son, I know you think you're protecting her, but you two are making a big mistake. I really appreciate what you've done to keep her calm, but my daughter is just in an overly hormonal state right now, and I fear when everything settles down, she will see what a mistake she's made," she calmly explained. She actually sounded like she sincerely cared about his feelings.

"Well Mrs. Morgan, that's D.J.'s choice to make. And if she decides that she's made a mistake after things 'settle down' as you say, I'll be fine with that. I love your daughter, and I only want her to be happy," he explained as he wiped a tear from my cheek. "I pray that day never comes, but if it does, I will do my best not to stand in her way."

I turned and gave him a quick smile then went back to looking out the window. My tears had stopped, but I was still bubbling with emotions. Which became very apparent when she went back to explaining why we were making a mistake.

"You think you'll be able to let go but you won't son. Listen to me..."

"AND THAT'S A FANTASTIC THING MOTHER!! YOU'D THINK YOU'D WANT ME TO BE WITH A MAN WHO IS WILLING TO FIGHT FOR ME WITHOUT PUTTING HIS HANDS ON ME!" I erupted startling Jeremiah.

"D.J., it's okay sweetie, calm down," he said quickly.

"NO! I'VE HEARD ALL I CARE TO HEAR FROM HER TODAY! EITHER SHE'S GOING TO SUPPORT US OR SHE'S NOT! IT'S HER CHOICE!" as I snatched the phone and ended the call. "Uhhh," as I grabbed my side doubling over in pain.

"D.J.! What's wrong!" as the truck came to a screeching halt on the side of the road. In one motion, Jeremiah had his seatbelt off, one hand was on my stomach, and the other was on the back of my neck. "Baby talk to me! Did your water break? Hold on! We're going back to the hospital," as he put his seatbelt back on and began to turn the truck around.

"No. Please don't," I reached over to touch him and finally looked over at him with tears welling up in my eyes again. "I'll be fine I promise. My water didn't break, that's just the cup I had when we left Triple J's. I must have knocked it over," I tried to giggle as I patted his hand to try to comfort him. "Please just take me home. That's where I want to go right now, not the hospital, not my parent's house. I want to go home, to *our* home," I explained as I placed my hand on his cheek and stroked it.

Jeremiah pulled over again and kissed the palm of my hand. "D.J. are you sure?"

His eyes were so full of love and emotion; it was all I could do, not to try to kiss him. "Yes my love. I'm sure." I reached over and took his hand and kissed his palm then laid my face in his hand and snuggled in. He simply smiled at me, leaned over and kissed me on the forehead, then looked around as he pulled back onto the road and took us home.

A few minutes later, we pulled onto what I thought was another road, but it turned out to be the driveway to the most beautiful house I'd ever seen. There was a large circle driveway with a fountain in the very center. The porch wrapped around the front and the sides of the house as far as I could see. There were beautiful plants hanging along the front of the porch and a beautiful flower bed all the way around it. The porch swing was long enough for at least four people and was covered in cushions, alongside a couple of matching chairs, and a table with a centerpiece of candles. The fountain out front had rose bushes surrounding it. I figured to keep animals from drinking from it, but I still asked when he came around and helped me out of the truck.

"The roses are absolutely beautiful. What made you put them around the fountain?" I smiled at him as I made my way around the truck towards the roses. I could tell he wasn't expecting that when he dropped my bag and ran around the truck to catch up to me.

"You move pretty fast for a pregnant lady," he laughed. "I have several reasons for the bushes. I planted one for each of my sons and my wife when I built this house and each year on their anniversary I've planted another bush. Then when my dad past, I planted one for him. Last year when my mom saw it, she suggested that I put the gate up and fill in the rest of the "rose wall" as she called it, to keep the deer from drinking from the fountain and eating the grass. Then I decided that it would be nice to have somewhere to sit, so that's when I put the benches out here."

"Wow! I figured it was to keep the animals out, but it's even more special knowing how it all started," I smiled at him as I squeezed his hand and took a seat. He took a seat alongside me, and we sat there for a while enjoying the silence as a gentle breeze kissed our faces, filling the air with the scent of the roses. I don't know when I leaned over on him, but at some point, I dozed off wrapped in his arms as my head nestled into his chest.

I woke up to him gently shaking me and calling my name, "D.J., D.J sweetie, wake up."

"Oh my. How long was I out?" as I tried to gather my bearings.

"Not long. I would have let you nap longer, but a storm is moving in, so I decided you'd probably prefer not getting drenched out here," he smiled and kissed me on the forehead. I snuggled in and then leaned my head back and pulled his head down to kiss him. Once again, my body exploded from the inside out and a rush of heat filled places that hadn't had any type of reaction in months. A light drizzle is the only reason we let each other go as we rushed back to the house just as the heavy rain started.

We stood in the doorway laughing our heads off as the boys decided to join in the party with a kick to my ribs.

"OUCH!" I exclaimed, grabbing my side in pain.

Grabbing my side as well, he steadied me. "What! What's wrong?"

I looked up at him panting with a tear rolling down my cheek. When I could breathe normally, "One of your sons just decided to use my ribs as a kickboxing dummy," I finally replied, taking one last deep breath as I stood up straight again. I wiped another tear away when I realized that Jeremiah was just standing there all wide-eyed with his mouth hanging open. "What's wrong? Why are you staring at me like that?" I asked.

He began to smile at me, rubbing my stomach as tears started to well up in his eyes.

I wasn't sure what to say as I reached up and wiped away a tear as it escaped from the corner of his eye. "What? What's wrong baby?" as I cupped his face in my hand.

"You...you called them 'my sons,'" he said with a huge smile on his face. "You've never referred to them as, 'my sons' before." In one motion, he scooped me up in his arms and carried me inside the house, whirling me around and kissing me all over my face.

I couldn't help but laugh at his reaction, gripping him around the neck and joining in with his laughter. Finally, I regained my composure enough to say, "Okay, okay! You need to stop before we fall over," as I kissed him on the cheek.

He stopped spinning and plopped down on the couch in what looked like a formal living room, still holding me in his arms. He turned my face to his and said with tears still welling up in his eyes, "D.J. Morgan, you just gave me the best gift you ever could have. For you to consider me to be their daddy. I mean, WOW! Next to saying you'd marry me, this is the most wonderful thing you've ever said to me. Thank you! Thank you!" as he kissed me again.

"Well you are. You've been more of a dad to them than their father has already. And the smile you put on their mother's face and in her heart is more than they could ever ask of their daddy," I said wiping away the tears that were now free-flowing down his face. "Man, you really don't know how much I love you," I said, holding his face in my hands. Before he could respond, I continued, "Listen Jeremiah. You are my heart. I knew you were meant for me the first time you held my hand. I just didn't understand what was happening or how this could be happening under these circumstances. Baby, you are my strength and my light. God knew I was at the point of giving up and because He loves me so much, He sent me you. I'm convinced of that. You, Mr. Jeremiah Ezekiel Thomas, are God's gift to me and these boys," I explained as I covered his hand that was rubbing my stomach. "None of us would have survived if you hadn't come along. I'm convinced of that kind Sir," as I wiped the last tear away gazing into his beautiful brown eyes the entire time. I kissed him again as he gently slid from underneath me and kneeled down beside me, wrapping his arms around me as he moved down my body, stopping at my tummy.

"Listen you two. This is your daddy talking," he smiled up at me. "I need you two to settle down for a few minutes because I need to spend some adult time with your mother right now. I promise you I won't hurt you or her, but you might be a little uncomfortable for a little while," and then he kissed my stomach twice.

I didn't say a word as I watched and listened to him talk to the boys. By the time he was finished, the boys had settled down, and I couldn't feel them moving at all. He gently lifted me off the couch and carried me back to an enormous bedroom with one of the biggest beds I'd ever seen before. He carried me past the bed and into a bathroom made for a king. He gently lowered me down onto a rot iron vanity bench with a super soft white cushion and went over to the oversized tub and ran a bath.

As the tub filled with lukewarm water, a light foam of bubbles began to form. He slowly removed my clothes as he began kissing me from the top of my head down to my stomach. With one sudden jerk, he had me up in the air and was removing my pants and panties. He continued to kiss my stomach as he carried me to the tub and slowly lowered me into the water. Surprisingly it was the perfect temperature. He knelt by the bathtub and began to wash my body with a sponge.

"Lay back D.J. and just relax," he smiled.

I did as I was instructed and laid my head back on the towel he'd pulled down and rolled up to make a pillow for my neck. I loved the way he washed my body and caressed my breasts and flicked my clit along the way. Before I realized it, he was in the tub with me, and it hadn't overflowed, nor did I feel cramped up with both of us in it.

I took the sponge away from him and began to wash him as he steadied his body over mine, sucking on my nipples. I felt my body relax even more as I began to purr like a cat as his tongue glided over each nipple, tugging ever so lightly. I started massaging his engulfed penis, stroking him as I pulled him closer to me.

"D.J. Morgan, may I make love to you?" he whispered in my ear as he nibbled at my earlobe and circled my ear with his tongue.

"Man, if you don't, I'll never forgive you," I whispered back pulling him down on top of me.

With one swift motion, he was inside of me, without any assistance from either of our hands. It was like his body knew exactly where it was supposed to be and knew how to find my spot without either of us having to guide him to the essence of me. He was so gentle but forceful all at the same time. I wrapped my legs around him and rode his strokes like a cowboy gripping a bronco. I can't explain how good that man felt inside of me. He was what my body had always been craving in a mate. He kissed me so passionately as I rode him, and my walls gripped his penis more with every stroke. It only startled me for a moment when I began to hear music playing, but I quickly realized the music I was hearing was his penis singing to me. I'd heard stories of that happening, but I never really thought it was possible, but his dick was actually singing to me. With each gentle stroke, he'd play a new cord that my body responded to in ways I never imagined possible. We made passionate love for the first time without any interruptions or interference, not even from the boys. We made love so long the water had become ice cold, but even that didn't affect the love we made.

As his pace quickened, I felt an explosion inside me and gripped his back, digging my nails in like I was holding on for dear life. We both moaned and pulled each other in tighter as he simply whispered in a low, deep, growl, "That's it baby. Let daddy have it."

In one swift motion, he had rolled us over, and he was on top of me again. I laid my head back and moaned from a deep carnal place that I'd never known existed. I gripped his back, dragging my nails up and down him, and finally reaching down, grabbing his butt, and pulling him in deeper. "Uhmmmm, baby, you feel so damn good," I moaned.

"So you like that do you?" he whispered with a hard thrust of his hips.

"Yesss, baby. I love it."

The pace quickened again as our bodies melted into one fluid motion and a rush of pure exhilaration came over both of us as we exploded simultaneously. I could feel him vibrating inside of me as my walls gripped him and pulled him in tighter and deeper with every movement of his penis as it slowly became smaller. Somehow he lifted us both up out of the tub without missing one final stroke and softly kissed me as he carried me over to the free-standing shower and turned on what turned out to be a double-headed shower. We continued to make love with our tongues as the warm water quickly ran down our backs. He reached for the shower head above me and began to gently rinse me off, from head to toe, caressing and kissing me along the way, still holding me firmly up against the sidewall.

When he reached my tummy, he kissed my navel and whispered, "Thank you two for being so quiet while me and your mom spent this time together. I'm so very proud of you right now," as he smiled up at me while he lowered me to the bench below. He had a devilish look in his eyes and a crooked smile on his face as he continued. "But as quiet and well-behaved as you two have been, I really need you to stay quiet for just a little while longer. Daddy and mommy aren't quite through yet."

I turned my head slightly as my eyes tightened, and I returned his devilish grin with an inquisitive smile of my own, "What are you up too?" I asked with an ever-growing smile.

"Shhhhhhh. Just sit back and enjoy this baby." And with that, his tongue began to dance around with my clit in a way it had never been danced with before. The explosion from earlier was quickly coming back as I arched my back and began to grip the wall behind me, moaning from a deep and primal place, once again. I couldn't help myself as I grabbed the back of his head and pulled him in closer, as I wrapped my legs around his head. I could feel the explosion happening again and screamed out in utter joy as my essence began squirting all over his face. He took it in stride as he licked and sucked on me until there was nothing left.

When I was able to regain control of my body again, I pulled him up to me and kissed him like this would be the last time our tongues would ever meet. He finally pulled away from me and sat down beside me as he pulled me in close.

He held me in his arms as he began to explain, "D.J., I've been dreaming of this moment since the very first time I held you. I hope that I didn't disappoint you," as he pulled my wet hair out of my face and kissed my forehead.

I looked up at him with tears in my eyes, "Are you kidding me right now? I've never felt this way in all my life. Jeremiah, you just made me feel things I've never felt with anyone else. You made my body do things I never knew it would do," as he wiped away my tears. "Baby, you are more than I ever dreamed possible or even thought possible for my life," as I pulled his head down and stretched my neck up to kiss him again. Now I don't know what kind of water heater he had because the water was still warm as it trickled down our bodies.

"Sweetie, you're all I've ever wanted in a wife. Every time you touch me, my heart flutters, and I can't control myself."

I glanced down and saw he was standing erect yet again. I gave him the same devilish grin he had given me earlier before I commanded him to stand-up.

"What?! What are you up too Little Miss?" he returned a questioning grin.

I ran my hand down his sculptured thigh to his engulfed penis and gently pulled him up over the top of me. I massaged him as he stood at attention in front of me and slyly looked up at him as he smiled down at me.

"You better hang on to something," I suggested as I slid my tongue up and down his shaft, finally taking as much of him as I could into my mouth where my tongue caressed him as I sucked and released, moving him in and out until I felt him relax and allow me to really go to work. The more he moaned, the harder I sucked and massaged his penis, gradually taking more and more of it in. This man was definitely blessed in the man meat department.

I'd never been one for oral sex before, but even though he was a lot to take in, I was really enjoying having him under my control. I realized that I was moaning just as much as he was as he slowly began to move his hips in unison with my head movement. He gripped my nipples, massaging and pulling on them as I inhaled his dick deeper and deeper into my wetness. He released my nipples and grabbed on to the back of my head, arching his back, and moaning from so deep inside that I could feel the vibrations through his stomach. As his body tightened up and his legs began to quiver, he began to thrust at his own quickened pace as he exploded inside my mouth. Just as he'd done for me, I continued to suck on him until he collapsed by my side. He was kissing me before I realized it, mouth full of cum and all. So for the first time in my life, I swallowed.

We laid there in that soothing stream of water until it started getting cold even though he was periodically adjusting the temperature. I reached for a washcloth and commenced to washing his body as he sat there next to me. I washed him from head to toe, gently stroking his body and moving his manly parts from side to side, squeezing and stroking every now again.

"Uh uhm," he cleared his throat. "If I didn't know any better, I'd say you were trying to get something started again Miss Lady," he smiled at me as he sat back enjoying his bath.

"I have no idea what you're talking about, and frankly I think I'm a little offended by your tone Dear Sir," I explained with an, I'm so appalled that he would even suggest it look on my face. At least as long as I could hold it until I started giggling. I snatched the shower head from his hand and rinsed him off, but just before I handed it back, I gave his penis one final kiss on the tip.

"I knew you were up to no good young lady," as he grabbed the hose and the washrag and began to wash and rinse me off just as the last of the hot water gave out.

He took my hand as we stepped from the shower and simultaneously dried each other off. I'd like to tell you that was the end of it but fortunately, I can't. That kiss on the tip of his penis had already caused him to begin to swell again and rubbing and kissing him didn't help matters much. We rubbed and kissed our way back into the bedroom where our lovemaking started again for the rest of the night.

I woke up to a familiar heartbeat and arms wrapped around me, but a very unfamiliar room, although it still felt like home. Jeremiah was laying there with me in his arms, just smiling down at me. He moved a few loose strands of hair out of my face and gently kissed me on my forehead.

"Good morning Sleeping Beauty. I can't believe how beautiful you are," he smiled at me.

"How long have you been awake," I asked as I moved higher in the bed.

"Oh, I've been up for a while now. At least since the sun came up."

"Why didn't you wake me? I would have gladly watched the sunrise with you," as I leaned into his chest and gave him a kiss.

"You were sleeping so peacefully I didn't want to wake you," he kissed me on the forehead again and then threw the covers off as he crossed the room and opened the curtains, exposing a beautiful set of French doors that opened up to a deck and his gorgeously sculptured naked ass.

I moved the covers off of me and began to get out of the bed, but stopped when I realized that I was up higher than I had originally thought. "Uhm, a little help here please."

He jumped back from the doors and ran around the bed and took my hand. "Be careful. We don't need you to fall," as he helped me ease from the bed. All at once it hit me, we were both standing there completely naked and with the deck doors wide open. I looked around and grabbed the sheet off the bed to cover myself up with. He could sense that I was embarrassed and pulled the blanket out of the way so I could cover up with the sheet.

He lifted my head up and smiled down on me as he said, "Baby, you never have to be embarrassed about being naked around me. I love your body. And no matter what you look like in between pregnancies, I will always love your body," as he caressed my face.

I just stood there for a moment gazing into his eyes, before a slight frown formed on my face and I said, "In between pregnancies. So what, you're already planning to knock me up again?" as I began to giggle.

"Well, yes. I look forward to making more babies with you my love," as he pulled me in tighter and kissed me.

I could feel him rising through the sheet and pushed back just enough to put a little more space between us. "As much as I'd like to oblige you right now, I've really got to go pee," as I tried to gather up the sheet as I began to scurry off towards the bathroom.

"Damit woman! Just drop the sheet before you trip and hurt yourself," he called out after me.

Just as I reached the bathroom door, I turned and stuck my tongue out at him and dropped the sheet as I disappeared into the bathroom. I didn't have time to close the door as I hurried to sit down before I had an accident all over the floor. I barely got to the toilet before a gush of water began to flow. It was so much at first that I thought maybe my water had broken, but when I didn't see any blood and the stream stopped without leaking, I felt pretty confident that I just needed to pee really, really bad.

I could instantly tell the boys were happy that my bladder was empty because they immediately began to bounce around as usual. As I washed my hands, I finally noticed how large the bathroom really was. There was a double vanity with his and her sinks and medicine cabinets. A vanity desk and the chair he had sat me on last night was next to what had to be a linen closet. The tub was much larger than I had realized initially, and the shower not only had two shower heads it also was equipped to double as a steam room. There was a large window beside the tub that looked out onto a huge lawn and tree line. I had become so consumed with my surroundings that I didn't notice Jeremiah standing in the doorway watching me. As I turned from the window, I caught a glimpse of him in one of several mirrors startling me.

"Oh my God! How long have you been standing there?" I asked, holding my chest.

"Not long. I didn't mean to scare you. When I heard the water turn off, but you didn't come back, I got worried that something was wrong and just came in to check on you," he explained. "And I would have knocked first, but you didn't close the door," he smiled.

"What are you grinning about?" I smirked at him as I took a towel off the rack and wrapped it around me. I quietly stood there as the smirk turned into a smile, and I instantly began tearing up.

"I was just getting a kick out of you wandering around with that look of amazement on your face," he said as I finally looked up and he was able to see the tears forming in my eyes. "What's wrong baby?" as he rushed over to me.

I looked up at him and said, "This towel...it fits all the way around me."

He just stood there for a second and then threw his head back and began to laugh as he pulled me in close and rubbed my back. "Oh sweetie. I thought something was wrong. I take it, that's a good thing," as he leaned down and kissed me on the forehead.

"It's not funny," as I swatted at him. "You don't understand."

"What don't I understand baby?" as he began to rock me in his arms.

"I haven't been able to find soft, thick towels that fit *all* the way around me since I got so big," I looked up at him with happy tears in my eyes.

"Oh baby. If only everything I do could make you this happy, I'll be the happiest man on the planet," he laughed again as he sat down on the side of the tub and pulled me in close.

"It's still not funny," as I snuggled into his chest once again.

"Ouch!"

"What's wrong," I asked, looking up at him.

"Even I felt that kick. You're telling me you didn't," as he moved to rub my stomach.

I sat on his lap and began to laugh. "Oh that was nothing. That was a warning shot," as I covered his hand with mine and watched as our hands moved back and forth across my stomach. "Your boys are trying to tell us that they are hungry," I laughed.

He looked around the room, "Well look at the time. I guess they should be hungry. Especially after the night we had," he lifted my hand and kissed the back of it. I hadn't noticed the clock hanging above the door. This bathroom was absolutely magnificent.

He bumped me up off of his lap and swatted me on the behind. "Well woman. I guess it's time for me to feed you. All of you," he laughed as he moved from behind me. "Give me a second to shower, and I'll wrestle us up something to eat." He walked over and turned only one shower head on and turned back to me as he stepped in. "I'd invite you in, but I have a feeling that we won't make it out anytime soon if I do," he winked at me as he closed the door laughing.

"Ha, ha, ha mister. Very funny," I said, crossing my arms, slightly disgusted. "I bet you won't be laughing if I flush that toilet."

The shower door popped open, "I could care less. Go ahead and flush away," he laughed as he closed the door again.

"Don't tempt me. I'll do it!" I yelled back over my shoulder as I turned and walked away. I didn't flush the toilet, but I did turn on the sink for a moment so I could wet my toothbrush. As I stood there brushing my teeth in the mirror it hit me, *'my toothbrush and toothpaste are in the bathroom.'* I looked around for a second and noticed that my other bathroom items were sitting around the sink, and when I opened the medicine cabinet, there were the rest of my things. *'When did he do all of this?'* I asked myself.

The last time I saw my bags, they were still sitting in the middle of the floor in the foyer. I quickly finished brushing my teeth and went back into the bedroom. I opened up the first door I came to and to my surprise there was a walk-in closet big enough to be a very nice size bedroom, complete with shoe racks, a tie rack, and a middle cabinet that contained multiple drawers on all sides. I was so busy investigating the room that I didn't hear the shower cut off or notice Jeremiah once again standing in the doorway watching me. As I pulled out one of the doors in the cabinet, he let his presence be known.

"So what do you think?" he asked, standing there with a towel wrapped around his waist.

"Okay, I'm going to have to put a damn bell around your neck if you don't quit sneaking up on me like that," I said, holding my chest again. He just stood there laughing as he watched me investigate the room. I finally looked over at him as I opened a drawer containing my things. Already separated by color. "It's breathtaking, but when did you do all of this?" I asked with a huge smile on my face.

"I did it when I built the house," he smiled. He knew what I was asking, but he was being a smart aleck.

"You know what I'm talking about," I shot him a cynical look. "This closet is absolutely beautiful, as I ran my hand along the top of the cabinet. You planned for pretty much everything, I think. I know women who would kill for this closet," I continued.

"I put everything away after you fell asleep on me. One minute you were talking, and the next minute you were snoring."

I cut him off before he had a chance to say anything else, "I beg your pardon. I do not snore," I explained.

"Oh yes, you do. And quite loudly I might add," he said as he began to laugh. I just rolled my eyes at him as he continued. "Like I was saying. You fell asleep, and I was too wired to sleep, so I got up and put your things away," he explained as he came out of the doorway and hugged me from behind.

"Wow! What a thing to say. Make me feel bad why don't cha," I said as I elbowed him.

"What?! I just meant I was so excited that you were actually lying here in my arms, in my bed, I couldn't sleep," he pulled me in tighter and began kissing me all over my neck and shoulders. I held on and giggled while he rocked me from side to side, kissing me.

"Stop it before you make me dizzy or shake these two loose," I laughed as I smacked his hands.

"Anyway, you were sound asleep, so I brought your bags in and unpacked your things. I figured that I'd get it out of the way, especially since I knew you'd try to do it this morning," he explained as he kissed the back of my hand. He started pulling out drawers. "These two sides are yours, but if you need a couple more, this side has a few empty drawers." He pointed to a panel on the wall and began to explain. "Now this button dims the lights, and this button turns on the ceiling fan."

"Why on earth did you put a ceiling fan in the closet?" I laughed.

"In case my wife was hot-natured and needed the extra cool air," he said matter-of-factly staring at me.

All I could do is drop my head and draw circles on the dresser. He knew he'd just shut me down, and I couldn't argue with him, "Well, I guess that makes sense." The joke is that I'm a hot body and had ceiling fans installed in every room of my condo, including a small fan I kept by the sink in my bathroom.

As he showed me the ins and outs of the rest of the house, it was almost like he had designed this house specifically for me. All the things I ever dreamed or wanted in my house were here. From the other 2 huge Jack and Jill bathrooms to the other 5 bedrooms, the office, the formal living room, and dining room, along with a den and eat-in kitchen with an island and wrap around bar big enough to seat 8, and a tv/game room. The outside deck did wrap around the entire house, but the deck off the master suite was slightly elevated, which he would have to explain to me how at a later time. There was a four-car garage and a tack room, already filled up with his tools and workbenches. And finally, we made it back up to our bedroom were behind the other door in the room, that I assumed was another closet, was actually a very nice sized sitting room with a big screen tv and minibar and fridge.

"I figure we can use this room for the babies until they are big enough to go to their own rooms," he smiled as he pulled an oversized bassinet from out of the closet.

I didn't know what to say as I covered my mouth with a surprised look on my face.

"Woman, you're going to make me start buying stock in Kleenex with all these tears of yours."

I quickly wiped my tears away and skipped over to him, jumping up into his arms as I wrapped my arms around his neck. "Oh my God! Jeremiah, it's beautiful!" I cried as I bounced up and down. "When did you buy this?" I finally asked after I let him go and stopped bouncing. I kneeled down beside it and rubbed it from one end to the other. "Seriously sweetie, when did you buy this?" I asked, with tears welling up in my eyes again.

He just laughed and knelt down beside me. "I didn't buy it. I made it."

Looking up at him in amazement, "You what?" as I wiped away my tears. "When?"

He kissed me on my forehead. "I originally designed it when I found out my wife was pregnant but never seemed to find the time to make it. Then there was no reason to make it. But after Mr. Charlie helped me surprise you that day I sent you the flowers and the box, I came across my designs and revamped them with you in mind and started to build it. For the most part, it went pretty smoothly. I only had a couple of hiccups. But I knew, no matter what happened between us, I was going to finish this and give it to you no matter what."

As I watched him stroke the bassinet and rub my back, I could feel how proud of his accomplishment he was. And he had every right to be. I'd never seen a bassinet with all of the detail and carvings along the sides. And it was big enough for two babies to sleep in comfortably.

"Jeremiah, I love it. And I love you even more for building it for us," as I turned around to kiss him. Somehow we got off balance, and I ended up on top of him which I instantly thought was funny, but he didn't join in on my laughter until he was sure me and the babies were all okay. "This right here, is why I love you so much. I know you will never do anything to hurt me and will always protect me, even when I don't really need protecting," as I began to kiss him.

He gently moved my hair from my face as he took my face in his hands, "D.J. I love you more than I've ever loved anybody else in my life. I not only love you Miss, I am so *'In Love'* with you," as he returned my kiss.

I pulled away and tried to get up on my own, which didn't go over very well. After he helped me to my feet, I took him by the hand and took him back through the bedroom and out on the deck. During our tour, I noticed a couple of Chaise lounges under an umbrella and led him over to one. I gently pushed him down on it and leaned over him to kiss him. I stood back up and slowly dropped my towel and climbed over him to straddle him as I removed his towel, exposing a very erect penis.

I lowered myself down on him without any help and smiled as I began to kiss him while I rode him. He gripped my waist as he joined in, and our rhythms synced up yet again. We kissed so passionately as our body juices mixed one more time.

He pulled back for a moment, "You know if we keep it up like this, we're never gonna get to eat, and we're gonna make these babies come sooner than later, ya know."

"Shut up and kiss me man," as I pulled his face back to mine, and our tongues began to dance just as the music began to play again. I could tell he heard it too as he pulled away and looked around for a minute trying to figure out where the music was coming from. I giggled for a second and pulled away just enough to whisper in his ear, "I know you hear it too. The music our body's make when they become one. Nice huh..."

He pulled back, and I simply smiled at him. He looked down and watched his penis disappear and reappear from between my legs then looked up and gave me the biggest smile he'd ever given me before as he pulled me close and said, "I LOVE YOU D.J.! Let's make beautiful music together," grabbing my face and kissing me so deeply my body began to quiver. Again, without breaking our rhythm, he lifted me and rolled me onto my back as he took over and how the music played as he filled every inch of space inside me. We made love on that balcony over and over again.

You would have thought I'd be starving by now, but I wasn't. It was like he was feeding us with every thrust of his hips, with every flick of his tongue, with every orgasm, with every kiss and caress, he was definitely feeding us – body, spirit, and soul.

CHAPTER 18

The week flew by and before we knew it, it was Thursday morning. I did manage to sneak in a few meals and quick showers in between our lovemaking sessions, but not once had I had any signs of contractions. While Jeremiah was out making a quick grocery run, I made a call to the doctor's office. I was showered and dressed by the time he got back home, and I greeted him at the garage door with my purse ready to go.

"What's going on? Where do you think you're going Little Lady?" he chuckled as he sidestepped past me holding two armfuls of grocery sacks. I followed him into the kitchen and began putting the groceries up when he came in with the last load, placed them on the counter before he took me by the hand and led me to a chair and sat me down. "You sit right here and relax while I put the groceries up. You're not supposed to be on your feet remember," he winked as he began putting the things away.

"I didn't hear you telling me to stay off my feet the last few days," I said as I popped a grape in my mouth and gave him a smirk.

He only stopped for a moment as he looked up from the refrigerator door. "Ha, ha. Very funny," as he closes the door. "And if I remember correctly, you haven't been on your feet. Your back, your knees, your sides, and even your tummy a time or two, but nope...never on your feet. Or was that someone else I kept picking up and carrying around the house?" he said with a wicked grin on his face as he began to chuckle.

"Oh, you think you're funny Mr. Man," as I threw a grape at him expecting to hit him, but he was obviously expecting me to do that as he wiggled his head around just enough to catch the grape in his mouth.

"Mmmmmm, it tastes almost as good as you do. Almost," he winked then burst out laughing.

"I really don't like you very much right now," I shook my head and crossed my arms.

He came around the counter making kissing noises at me, "Awww there, there. What's wrong with my little gumdrop today. Too much protein in your diet?" as he lifted my chin and kissed me.

I jerked my head away and pushed his hand aside, "That's not funny. See when I swallow again," I huffed. Knowing he was still having too much fun with me right now to really care about my comment, especially since we both knew it wasn't the least bit true. We were like two teenagers who had the house to ourselves for an unlimited amount of time.

He walked back over to the last sack, and when everything had been put up, he fixed us a snack as he continued to poke fun at me. He finally brought the plate over to the table and pulled up a chair next to me and then lifted my feet into his lap. "Would you like to bless the food, or would you like me too?" he smiled and waited for me to respond.

"You can, Mr. Smarty Pants," as I grabbed his hand and bowed my head.

After a pretty quick prayer, Jeremiah picked up half of the sandwich and offered me a bite, which I took of course. "So, I'll ask you again my darling. Exactly where are you trying to run out to?" he asked as he took a bite of the sandwich too.

"Well, while you were out, I called the doctor's office…"

He instantly dropped the sandwich and grabbed my stomach. "Why is there something wrong?"

"No, no, no. If you'd let me finish," I laughed as I shook my head at him and motioned for him to give me another bite of the sandwich we were sharing.

He smiled and shook his head, "I've created a monster. You're rotten, you know that right?" as he lifted the sandwich again so I could have another bite. "So go on. You called the doctor's office…," he giggled.

"Okay," as I wiped my mouth before I continued. "I called the doctor's office while you were out, and I moved my appointment up to this afternoon."

He just sat there looking at me, breaking his stair only long enough to take another bite of food. Finally, he asked in an extra calm voice, "And you did this why?" as he continued to chew and stare at me.

I took a bite of the sandwich on my own, and after I swallowed it, I said, "Because I don't want to run into Selk should he decide to show up tomorrow." I could tell by the expression on his face this wasn't sitting well with him. "And before you say anything, it's not because I'm afraid of him or what he might do if he sees us together."

"Oh no," turning his head slightly to the side. "Then why the sudden change?" he asked, with that same disgusted look on his face.

I lowered my feet out of his lap and moved my chair closer to him. I smiled as I held his cheek in my palm and then pulled him down just enough to kiss him on the nose. When I finally allowed him to pull away, "I'm not worried about Selk. I'm trying to protect you." I could tell by his reaction he wasn't expecting that answer. "Jeremiah, I know you better than even I can believe or understand in this short period of time, but I do. And if Selk has the audacity to show up tomorrow and act like nothing ever happened, as we both know he will, you my Dear Heart, you are going to lose it. And neither of us want to see you get hurt or even worse, arrested," I continued as I caressed his cheek. "So yes. I moved my appointment up to avoid the inevitable fight that is bound to happen if you and Selk end up in the same room together."

We just sat there staring into each other's eyes for a few minutes. The staring match finally ended because Jeremiah picked up the last piece of sandwich and said, "Do you want this, or can I have it?"

"You can have it Dear Heart. We need you to keep up your strength now don't we," as I patted him on what behind I could reach in his chair.

He finished off the sandwich and the last of the fruit without saying anything else to me. As he gathered the dishes, he looked down at me and gave me a quick huff, and shook his head as he loaded the dishes into the dishwasher. Once he'd wiped down the cabinet he'd prepared the food on, he leaned up against the cabinet and turned to me and asked, "So what time do we need to be at the doctor's office?"

I smiled as I crossed the room and pulled him down to kiss me. "2 o'clock big daddy so chop, chop," as I gave him a firm slap on the butt.

"Look out there now Miss Bossy. I'm the only one who gets to give out the occasional slap on the ass," as he pulled me in close and kissed me on the top of my head and then slapped me on my butt.

"Ouch! Now, do you feel better? Can we go now?" I laughed as I rubbed where he'd just spanked. "That was kinda hard ya know?" I looked back at him with a frown on my face as I left the room, still rubbing my butt.

"I meant for it to hurt," he yelled back from another room. I could hear him laughing the further he went away from me.

The ride to town took less time than we expected so we had a little time to spare. We'd road most of the way in silence, but as we pulled onto the parkway, Jeremiah lifted my hand and kissed the back of it. "So, I guess we just had our first argument in our house huh?" he watched me out of the corner of his eye.

I continued to look out the window when I finally answered, "Yeah, I guess so. Let's hope they all go that peacefully."

"I'm sorry if I hurt your backside. I wasn't really trying to hurt you."

"I know. I could tell by the way you reacted when I jumped," I finally looked over at him with a slight smile.

"Oh, could you now?" he said as he kissed the back of my hand again. "D.J. I'm sorry that I hurt you. I really didn't mean to."

I took a deep breath and turned to look at him, "I know you didn't. And I'm sorry I made the decision to change my appointment without discussing it with to you first... Even if my decision was the right decision," I threw in at the last moment with a little smirk.

He just looked at me with his mouth hanging open for a second. "Oh really," as he tickled my side.

"Stop it! Stop it!" as I wildly slapped at his hand. "Watch the road and quit picking at me," as I slapped his hand one last time as he went back to driving with both hands on the steering wheel again.

We rode in silence again until we came to a red light. "D.J."

"Yes, Dear."

"Thank you for changing your appointment today. And thank you for already knowing me so well," he said, never taking his eyes off the road even though we weren't moving.

I could tell by his body language he was holding back his emotions from spilling out. I reached over and caressed his cheek with the back of my hand. "Ohhh, my Dear Heart. You don't have to thank me. It's my job to be smart enough for the both of us when the time calls for it. It was one thing for him to destroy the things that you gave me, but it is a complete other for him to put his hands on me. You still haven't let that go...even if you haven't said anything else about it. You still haven't let it go. So for now, keeping the two of you away from each other is the best thing for all of us," I smiled.

He took my hand and kissed my palm then snuggled his cheek into it as he began to sing along with the radio....

The first time I looked in your eyes I knew
That I would do anything for you
The first time you touched my face I felt
What I've never felt with anyone else

I wanna give back what you've giving to me
And I wanna witness all of your dreams
Now that you've shown me who I really am
I wanna be more than just your man

I wanna be the wind that fills your sails
And be the hand that lifts your veil
And be the moon that moves your tides

The sun coming up in your eyes

Be the wheel that never rusts
And be the spark that lights you up
All that you've been dreaming of and more
So much more, I wanna be your everything

When you wake up, I'll be the first thing you see
And when it gets dark you can reach out to me
I'll cherish your words and I'll finish your thoughts
And I'll be your compass baby, when you get lost

I wanna be the wind that fills your sails
And be the hand that lifts your veil
Be the moon that moves your tides
The sun coming up in your eyes

Be the wheel that never rusts
And be the spark that lights you up
All that you've been dreaming of and more
So much more, I wanna be your everything

I'll be the wheel that never rusts
And be the spark that lights you up
All that you've been dreaming of and more
So much more, I wanna be your everything

I wanna be your everything
I wanna be your everything
I wanna be your everything[1]

I quietly listened as he sang his way into my heart.

'That was Your Everything by Keith Urban. You're listening to KYND 92.9 FM. We'll be right back after these important messages...'

I can't tell you what else came on the radio the rest of the ride into Houston that day, but I can tell you with all certainty, that if I wasn't totally in love with that man before he sang to me... Jeremiah Ezekiel Thomas owned my heart and soul by the last run of *'I wanna be your everything'* came floating out across his lips.

My doctor's appointment couldn't have gone any better if I do say so myself. Dr. Cleveland was totally pleased with how I was doing both physically and mentally. The fact that I hadn't had a single contraction since I'd left the hospital was also to be celebrated, especially since we'd spent so much time making love since we got home. Dr. Cleveland was happy with my progress and let me know that I had indeed begun to dilate. I gave Jeremiah a quick sheepish glance trying not to let on as to how I'd been spending my days and nights lately. As we finished up, Dr. Cleveland asked us if we had any more questions.

"Well yes Sir. I have a question," Jeremiah said.

I looked at him wide-eyed begging him with my eyes not to ask what I knew he was getting ready to ask about.

"Is it okay for her to have sex or does she need to refrain from that type of activity until after the babies come?" he asked it so innocently it was almost cute, but I just lowered my head trying to hide my embarrassment.

You could tell Dr. Cleveland wasn't expecting that question as he looked back and forth between the two of us with a surprised look on his face for a minute, before he burst out laughing. He reached out and gripped Jeremiah's shoulder as he said, "Son, if she feels like having sex, I'd say go for it as long as she's comfortable and she doesn't start leaking fluid. But I must warn you both, don't be surprised if you accidentally break her water and speed up her labor. It's getting a lot more crowded in there so if you push too hard, those boys may push back," as he started laughing again.

Jeremiah smiled and said, "Thank you Sir. That's good to know," as he reached out one hand to shake Dr. Cleveland's and rubbed my back with the other one. I just sat there embarrassed, hanging my head. "What? What did I do?" he leaned over and whispered as he kissed the side of my head.

"Oh D.J... Don't be embarrassed. He's not the first man to ask me that question, or woman for that matter," as he started laughing again. "It's probably the main question I get when we get this close to the delivery date. So don't be embarrassed and most definitely don't get to fussing at him when you leave my office," he said as he reached out and squeezed my hand.

"Thanks for saying that Doc cause I think that maybe I'm in a little bit of trouble right now," Jeremiah admitted as he nodded over towards me.

"D.J., it's not like I can't tell that you've been having sex and lots of it already. Did you really think I didn't know?"

"Oh my God! What?" as I dropped my face in my hands.

"Young lady I've been doing this much longer than you've been alive. Of course, I can tell. And besides that, I've never seen you so happy and relaxed when you've come in here to see me. So as far as I'm concerned, keep doing what you're doing and let's get ready to have some healthy babies," he said with a huge smile on his face.

All I could do was shake my head at the both of them as they smiled at me like a couple of Cheshire cats. Finally, I had to laugh myself, knowing that we would probably end up making love when we got home because Jeremiah would say something like, *'It was your Doctor's orders,'* as we cuddled tonight.

"Now, I wanna see you back in here on Monday next week to check you again, okay."

"Is everything okay?" I asked as my embarrassment quickly changed to nervousness.

"Yes, yes. Everything is just fine. Next week is Thanksgiving, and since you're already dilated to about a 2, I wanna monitor you more closely over the next few days is all. Don't worry D.J., we're in the homestretch, and I just wanna get us to the finish line without any problems is all. I will check you out on Monday and again on Wednesday next week, and then we will let Mother Nature take her course after that until Saturday when we will induce your labor if you haven't gone into labor before then, as we agreed."

"Yes, I remember our agreement. That'll be fine," as I smiled at Jeremiah.

"Okay then. If there's nothing else. Get dressed, and I'll see you next week young lady," as he patted me on the arm.

I looked at Jeremiah before I answered, "No. I don't think we have any more questions," I smiled.

"Well, have a great weekend and try to get some rest in," he smiled at me and then gave Jeremiah a wink as he turned to leave the room, giggling.

"Yes Sir, she will," Jeremiah called out right before the door closed behind Dr. Cleveland.

I just shook my head at him and then climbed down from the exam table to put my clothes back on.

"What? What did I do wrong?" he quickly asked as if he'd done nothing wrong.

"I can't believe you asked him if it was okay to keep having sex," as I struggled to pull my pants on.

"D.J., please sit here and do that. You're making me nervous hopping around like that," as he helped me to the chair he once occupied. "Besides, we needed to know if it's safe or not," he explained.

"And what would you have said if he'd said it wasn't safe?" as I dropped my top over my head.

"I would have said okay, and that would have been all she wrote Little Mama," he smiled.

"Why don't I believe you right now," I started laughing.

"I don't know because it's the truth."

"Suuure…." I said giggling and shaking my head as we made our way to the front desk to check-out. We didn't continue this conversation until we were sitting in the car.

"I could sure use some barbecue," I said, flashing him a tremendously big smile.

"Oh could you now?" he glanced over at me. "Well, what if I'm not in the mood for barbecue?" he asked with a big grin on his face.

"That's fine. After we stop and get me some barbecue, we can stop and get you whatever it is you want," I laughed.

"Oh, is that right? What if I don't feel like making 2 stops?"

"Then don't. After we get the barbecue we can go home," I quickly respond.

"Well that's mighty big of you Little Mama. Selfish much?" he laughed, shaking his head.

"I wouldn't call it selfish. I'd say I was looking out for self," I smiled.

"You truly do love those word games don't cha?" as he shook his head.

"I'm not playing word games, I just choose to choose my words very carefully and strategically is all. I say what I mean, and I mean what I say. Are you having trouble keeping up?" I asked, twisting my body so I could watch his facial expressions more comfortably.

"Oh no. I'm keeping up just fine. My point is when I ask you a direct question, I'd prefer a direct answer. You tend to play around in the gray areas more than me is all," he explained. He reached over and took my hand and gave me a light squeeze before he kissed the back of my hand.

"Well, everything isn't always black and white ya know. Sometimes the detective in you overrides your brain and doesn't allow for the maybe factor is all."

"What is the 'maybe factor'?" he laughed. "I've never heard of such. And it's not that I only see black and white, it's that I don't play the 'what if game.' What if no one was in the habit of coming to your room so quickly when the alarms went off? What could've happened if they played in the gray areas deciding, 'Oh that's not a very serious alarm' when Selk attacked you, not really knowing what was really going on in there?" he finished. I didn't have an immediate comment, and after a few minutes of silence, Jeremiah reached over and took me by the chin to turn my head from the window. "D.J. the gray area can get you killed. There is a time and place for everything, but you need to realize that black and white keeps everyone on the same page and with a clear understanding of the situation. Baby, I don't mind you being coy when we are talking about food, or what we are going to do for the evening, but when it comes to serious things. Things like, is he hurting you, or medical issues, or how we raise our kids....no D.J., I won't join you in the 'gray area,' or how you tell your 'half-truths.' Things like that are very black and white to me. It's either yes or no, right or wrong. I'm not big on maybe's and justifications."

He wiped away a tear that had escaped from the corner of my eye before I could blink it away. I suddenly realized that for the first time in my life, I was dealing with a man who I wasn't going to be able to talk circles around and leave in a state of wonder. He wasn't going to change much which meant most of the changing was going to be on me to do, and I wasn't quite sure if I liked the direction that he was taking me in. To me, life had always been about pushing the boundaries and blurring the lines. This man here, he was definitely a stay in the lines kinda guy, and I could see now that my fast-talking him, was not going to fare well for me. I still hadn't come up with a response as he pulled into Triple J's parking lot, pulled into a spot, and turned off the engine. We just sat there in silence for what felt like forever before he finally decided to say something.

"D.J. are you okay? Are we okay?" he was being so gentle and sincere. It was oozing from his voice and his eyes. I still had no verbal response for him, but I did squeeze his hand. As we sat there in the silence, I finally figured out the best thing to say.

"Jeremiah, I love you. And I can see your point..."

"I hear a but coming," he said, cutting me off.

"But, I need you to understand something about me. The gray area has kept me sane, so I can't promise you that I won't play in that area at times. When I was 14 and basically lived in the hospital when I had cancer, the gray area is what I learned to live for. The 'what if' became my best friend. I learned to ask, 'what about C' when everyone around me was always about A or B. And as someone who is now carrying not 1, but 2 babies to term at the same time, after being told over and over again, that it would NEVER happen," I broke eye contact with him only for a few seconds as I looked down at my stomach and gently rubbed it. "I'm in no hurry to operate in a totally black and white world. I get what you're saying, and I completely understand why black and white is how you have to live to survive in your line of work, but I'm a science geek. We live in the realm of 'what if's' and the gray." I continued before he had a chance to respond and I lifted his hand to my cheek. "My Dear Heart, I mean this with all sincerity and conviction. I will not hide anything from you, important or not so important. So please believe me when I tell you, from here on out I give you my solemn vow that I will not half-truth you to death, but I cannot promise that I won't still dabble in the gray areas from time to time. Please understand that, and I pray you can accept that ungrudgingly," as I kissed his palm.

When I finally looked up again, Jeremiah was just sitting there staring at me with tears building up in the corners of his eyes. Again, we sat there in silence just gazing into each other's eyes when he turned to open the door and got out of the car. For the first time since we'd both professed our love, I got a sinking feeling in my gut that this might be the other shoe dropping, and definitely not dropping in my favor. He took my hand to help me out of the car, and once I was clear of the roof, in one swift motion, he had me up in the air-kissing me all over my face. I started giggling like a little kid and relaxed as he began to spin me around.

"D.J. I Love You so very much! I'm so happy we had this conversation. I've been worrying about this for a while and wasn't sure how you were going to take it. I didn't want to upset you, so I left it alone, but after the conversation in the doctor's office, I knew I couldn't wait any longer. And don't get me wrong, your gray area balances out my black and white, sometimes. I just needed you to know that I do tend to play by the rules and when I'm told by an expert not to do something or that I should do something, I listen to that advice. That's what you're paying them for," as he lowered me to the ground.

"Jeremiah, I appreciate that about you. I think we are a wonderful balance and compliment to one another. That's probably why we work so well together," I hugged him with everything in me.

"We are going to have to work on your greedy nature though," he laughed as his chin rested on the top of my head.

Pulling back from him, "What greedy nature Mister? I'm not greedy in the least bit," I told him as I turned to reach for my purse.

"Here, let me get that," as he moved me out of the way. I just stood there smiling at him, watching as he grabbed what he thought I needed. He closed the door as he swung my purse over his shoulder. I couldn't believe how willing he was to touch my purse let alone carry it, and in public no less. "And I beg to differ young lady. You are very greedy. That's why you were going to have a fit if the doctor had said that we couldn't have sex anymore."

I just stood there with my mouth hanging open. I couldn't believe the way he had just weaved sex back into this conversation the way he did. By the way, he was cracking up at my expression, you could tell he loved picking on me. He was laughing so hard he had begun to cry. I had started walking away from him before he realized it, so he had to hurry to catch up to me. Not that I was moving all that fast, just with a purpose.

As I reached for the door handle, he swatted my hand away, "Ouch! What was that for?" I asked as I rubbed the back of my hand. He really didn't hurt me, it was more for effect than anything else.

"Uhmm, that's my job young lady. Don't you ever reach for any kind of door handle when you're with me. Understand?" as he stood there with his hand on the handle but not opening the door.

All I could do is say, "Yes Sir. I understand." I could feel myself blushing as he opened the door for us to go inside.

You would have thought we were celebrities by the reception we received when we walked through the door. Employees and customers greeted us with hugs and how are you's as I was quickly ushered to a chair to sit down. It felt so comforting to be there with people who were genuinely happy for us. Accepting of us.

"We're fine. We're all just fine," Jeremiah said as he lowered me into the chair and made his way behind the counter. "Where's Mama J at?" as he peeked behind the kitchen doors looking for her.

"She wasn't feeling so well, so Joshua called around for someone to come pick her up. Jessica actually just left with her not 5 minutes ago," Cynthia explained as she worked the register.

"Well, why didn't anyone call me?" he asked as he checked his phone. "And where is Joshua? What's going on?" he looked around, obviously concerned as he began dialing someone's number.

"Well, I guess no one wanted to bother you. You have kinda had your hands full lately," as she motioned towards me. "And Joshua had to go get something to fix an outlet he decided needed attention," she explained.

For the first time since I'd met Jeremiah, I felt sorry for all the drama I had brought into his life. In all my happiness, I'd forgotten he had so many responsibilities before I came along. I turned away from him as I sat there rubbing my stomach, so he couldn't see me tearing up. One of the customers reached over and handed me a tissue as I was reaching for a napkin to dab my eyes before any tears escaped.

"Thank you," I smiled at her.

"You're welcome sweetie. Chin up," she replied.

Jeremiah had walked into the kitchen talking on the phone. I assumed it was with Jessica since that's who picked his mom up.

"What can I get you Ms. D.J.?" a little voice asked, startling me.

"Oh! I didn't see you there," I explained as I tried to hide my tissue from her. It was Jeremiah's niece, Jered's youngest daughter. I remembered her from all the family pictures at the house. "No thank you. I seemed to have lost my appetite."

"Oh no she hasn't," a very familiar voice exclaimed out of nowhere. Before I could respond, Jeremiah was pulling up a chair alongside mine. Dee Dee sweetheart, get your Aunt D.J. a few ribs and smoked turkey, along with the turkey greens and roasted carrots please," as he leaned over and kissed me and then my tummy.

"Okay Uncle Jeremiah. And what would you like?" she asked so eagerly, not writing anything down.

"I'll fix me something once this fine lady here starts eating. Thank you baby," he smiled at her.

"Okay. I'll be right back with Aunties plate," she smiled and took off like a shot.

"What are all the tears about?" he asked as he wiped a tear off my cheek.

I blinked another tear away and wiped across my face before I spoke. "I didn't want you to see me crying, again," I gave him a sheepish look. "But it just hit me how much I've interfered with your life. Your family and your business need you, and I've taken you away from all of that. Your mom needs you, and you haven't been around much lately," as the tears began to stream down my face.

"Oh baby. Don't cry," as he grabbed a handful of napkins and started wiping away my tears. "You haven't interfered with anything. If nothing else, you've given me back my life. Besides, its past time that some of my other brothers and sisters have to handle my mom's issues."

"But they didn't call you. What if something terrible had happened?" I sniffled as I tried to quietly blow my nose. Dee Dee gently slid my plate and a glass of water in front of me. I could tell by the look on her face she was worried.

"Thank you Dee Dee," as I tried to give her a convincing smile.

"Aunt D.J., are you okay?" she asked, still looking worried as she moved closer to Jeremiah.

"Yes, she's okay Dee. She's just having a moment," he explained as he patted the back of her hand. His explanation must have put her at ease since she smiled and went back to her seat behind the counter and began reading her book again.

"Honey, my mom is fine. They didn't call me because there wasn't really anything wrong with her other than being her typical, overly dramatic self. Apparently, someone came in the store that she couldn't stand in her younger days and she caused a scene, that's all. I promise you, if it had been something really important, I would have gotten a call," he explained as he pulled me in close and kissed me on my forehead.

"Are you sure?" I asked.

"Yes honey. No gray areas here. She got upset for no reason and needed to go home. That's it. Jessica was in the area, so she stopped by and picked her up," he said as he twisted his head so that he could look me in my eyes, as he gently moved my hair out of the way and continued to hold me close.

"Thank you," I said and kissed his chest, on the area of his heart, and laid my head back onto his chest again.

"What was that for?" he giggled.

"For being you," I said. "Just for being you."

"Well okay then," he laughed. "Well, would you do me a favor then Miss D.J.?"

"Sure, anything for you," I smiled looking up at him.

"Please eat before it all gets cold."

All I could do is giggle as I turned and began eating the wonderful smelling food that was on the table before me.

CHAPTER 19

After a couple of stops, we made our way home to find something rather unusual waiting for us. There was a very large snake curled up on the front porch by the front door. Upon further inspection, Jeremiah figured out that the snakes head had been partially cut off, which was completely out of order. As he went into investigation mode, all I wanted to do was get in the house and as far away from the snake no matter if it was dead or alive.

Jeremiah was outside so long that I had dozed off on one of the couches in the den. I woke up to multiple voices in the house, and after a quick stop in the bathroom, I followed the sound of their conversation to the hallway leading to the garage. Jeremiah was talking to two men, one was in a police uniform, and the other was wearing plain clothes, but I noticed the badge hanging on his waist. You could tell by the look on their faces that whatever they were discussing was not good and when they realized I was there, it became completely clear that their conversation was not meant for me to hear.

"Is everything okay?" I asked.

"OH! Hi Sweetie. We didn't see you there," Jeremiah said as he reached out and pulled me closer and kissed me on the top of my head. "Gentlemen, this is D.J." and reaching down to rub my stomach, "and these are the boys," he said with a forced laugh. "This old fart here is my Lieutenant and old partner Keith Williams and this young man in the spiffy uniform is Patrolman Donny McGee.

"Hello, D.J. we've heard a lot about you," Lt. Keith said as he extended his hand to shake mine.

"Hello. It's nice to meet you."

"Ma'am," is all the patrolman said as he gave me a quick head nod.

"Baby, you should go back in the house and put your feet up. You're on bed rest remember." It was more of a statement than a question.

I could tell I was being rushed out of the room even though what he was saying was true. I patted his hand, never taking my eyes off Lt. Keith. "Yes,

Love. I know. But I have a feeling there is something going on that I need to know about, so just tell me already. What's really going on? Is it about the snake?" I asked, looking from one to the other waiting on an answer.

"Baby, it's nothing for you to worry about. I'll fill you in later."

"No. You're going to tell me now. What's going on?" I said as I stopped looking at their expressions and rested my gaze on him. The other two men kinda lowered their heads and began staring at their feet.

"D.J., let me help you back inside. You need to get off your feet," Jeremiah insisted as he turned me back towards the kitchen. "Gentlemen let me take care of her, and we can pick up where we left off in a minute," he called back over his shoulder.

I stopped us in our tracks and turned back to the two men watching us make our way back into the house. "Gentlemen, please come in and have a seat. It seems we have a lot to talk about." You could tell by all of their expressions that they were not expecting me to say that nor did they have any intentions of letting me in on what was going on.

"Uhm, we're fine here but thank you for the invitation. Jeremiah, we'll do some checking around and get back to you later. It was nice meeting you, D.J." as Lt. Keith kinda saluted me and then patted McGee on the shoulder as they turned to walk away.

"Hold on guys. I'll meet you out front."

"Jeremiah, what's going on?" I asked as he helped me get comfortable on the loveseat and put my feet up on the ottoman.

He gently moved my hair off of my forehead and kissed me on it and said, "D.J., give me just a minute, and I promise you I'll be back in a few minutes to explain everything." He turned to leave, and I grabbed his hand.

"Zeke, whatever it is I can handle it, I promise. Don't feel like you need to hide anything or lie to me please."

He kissed the back of my hand and said, "I had a feeling you'd say that. Let me finish up with them, and then we'll talk. I love you Little Miss," as he squeezed my hand then turned and walked towards the front door. "And you know I really don't like it when you call me Zeke...I always feel like I'm in trouble when you call me that," he gave me a sheepish grin over his shoulder. I'd started calling him Zeke whenever he went into drill sergeant mode. It was like he took on a whole other personality. He was typically calm and understanding, a real tenderheart, but when Zeke came out... he was much more no-nonsense and aggressive, a firecracker, but with a protective force of nature about him.

I have to admit I started getting very nervous waiting on him to return. It was one thing for him to start poking around the snake but for him to call in backup meant something was seriously wrong. And the longer I sat there coming up with scenarios on my own, the more anxious I got. By the time Jeremiah returned I had started having contractions. I was panting so hard that I didn't even notice that Jeremiah had come back in the room.

Rushing over to me, "D.J.! You've worked yourself into a frenzy," as he knelt by my side. As he gently rubbed my stomach, he finally said, "I really think we may need to go to the hospital."

I grabbed onto his hand and began to squeeze as I managed to say, "No! I'll be fine now that you're here." And sure enough within 15 minutes, everything was fine, and the contractions had stopped. "Now, what's going on Sir?"

"I think this can wait awhile. You need to stay calm right now."

"I will stay calm if you tell me what's going on," I said.

"You are so stubborn," he let out a little laugh as he took a seat next to me on the couch and pulled me closer. "D.J. when I got to looking at the snake closer, not only was its head nearly severed there was a rat tail sticking out of its mouth. I knew that was a message and had to call in backup. It could be nothing, but that is highly unlikely. My gut is telling me it's definitely something," he finished as he closely watched my every move.

"So, is someone coming after us?" I calmly asked.

"Us? Highly unlikely. Me….only time will tell," he said and then kissed me on the forehead. "D.J. I don't want you to worry yourself with this and don't be afraid. You and the boys are perfectly safe here."

"I believe you, what if someone comes back when you're not here? What am I supposed to do then?" I asked, looking up at him.

We sat in silence for a few minutes, and finally Jeremiah moved from under me and reached for my hand. "D.J. come with me. I want to show you something."

I took his hand, and he led me through the house back to our bedroom and into the closet. He never said a word as he walked over to the panel on the wall and pushed a button that I hadn't noticed the other day on my initial tour. He then walked over to the cabinet and began pulling out random drawers and then something clicked. He opened one last drawer, and the top edge of the cabinet that was so beautifully carved out, popped open, and a hidden drawer of guns and ammunition slid out. I just stood there frozen in total shocked as to what I was seeing.

After a few minutes in silence, Jeremiah closed everything up and then said, "Come over here so you can try to open it by yourself." I didn't say anything as I followed his every instruction from beginning with the panel on the wall to how to feel the ever so subtle clicking of the drawers as they were pulled out to the proper distance and the order in which they had to be moved. To his surprise, it didn't take me long to get it right.

"WOW! It only took you 3 times to do everything by yourself. That's impressive," he smiled.

"I'm a quick study my dear," I gave him a light-hearted laugh and wink back.

"Okay now. I know you trained on an M16, but have you ever had any training with a handgun before?"

I started laughing and said, "Yeah, I've used a handgun a time or two and a shotgun and a rifle with a scope," I smiled at him as I lightly stroked the 9 mm in front of me. "I may be a city girl, but I come from a family of hunters. I can't think of any household in my family that doesn't have at least 1 gun, including my parents," I admitted. "In all actuality, I'm probably the only adult in my family who doesn't own a gun."

"Oh really. Well that's good information to know," he laughed. "Remind me never to piss you off, or anybody else in your family for that matter."

"You my love, don't have to worry," I gently kissed him. "I'd never pull a gun on you. Truth is I don't really like guns or having them in the house."

"Well other than you and Joshua, no one else knows this drawer even exists or how to get into it, so I feel like they are plenty safe here. My service piece is secured in a safe and lockbox over here," he moved to the shoe wrack closest to the door and pulled on the lower half of the wrack, and it swung open to reveal a safe in the floor.

"You really have a thing for puzzles I see," as I shook my head in amazement. Now the diary and puzzle box he'd given me was beginning to make total sense. "Are there any more secret compartments or trap doors I should know about?" I said with a big smirk on my face.

"Well now that you mention it, there is another gun with ammo in the safe room in the library behind the desk," as he closed up the gun draw and took my hand leading me down the hallway into the library. "This room is actually the room most centrally located in the house. Most people don't realize that it's not as big as it should be compared to where the walls are." He walked over to the desk, opened the center drawer, and pushed a button causing the far end of the bookshelf to open up, exposing a panel. He entered a code and a door slid open, revealing a set of stairs going down.

"That makes total sense!" I exclaimed, obviously startling him.

"What do you mean?" he asked.

"I've been trying to figure out why the deck off of our bedroom was so much higher than the rest of the porch that wraps around the house. There is a room below our bedroom!" I don't know why I was so excited, but I was bouncing around like a kid dying to go trick-or-treating.

Jeremiah just stood there watching me for a moment then finally he threw his head back and began laughing hysterically.

"And what's so funny may I ask?" I asked, obviously not amused.

When he regained his composure, "The excitement on your face and the way you started bouncing around was too funny. You looked like a kid in a candy store who just found out that they could have anything and everything they wanted," he started laughing again.

"Whatever...," I said as I pushed him in the chest and turned to leave the room.

"Aww Little Mama, don't be like that. I'm only have'n a little fun," as he closed everything up and caught up to me as I reached the kitchen. "And what do you think you're doing, may I ask?" as he wrapped his arms around me, bringing me to a dead stop.

"I was going to fix me a snack. We're hungry, if that's alright with you," I replied, patting his arms.

"Well actually, that's not alright with me. You've been on your feet too much already today so how about you rest yourself over here," as he guided me to the table and put my feet up in a chair. "And I will be your beckoned snack maker," he flashed that beautiful smile I'd grown to love as he kneeled down beside me.

"Alright beckoned snack maker," I laughed. "Well nothing too fancy Sir. How about some vanilla ice cream, a slice of that pizza from yesterday, and a little bit of that spicy sauerkraut you were putting on those sausages the other day. Yeah, that ought to do it," I smiled back.

"It's going to do something alright," as he shook his head. "That combination sounds really nasty, but your wish is my command, as he kissed me on the forehead and went to preparing my request.

"No comments required from the peanut gallery thank you very much," I laughed.

"Would you like that kraut warmed up or do you want it cold?" he asked over his shoulder.

"Warm please," I said with a huge grin on my face.

"You know D.J., it's really hard for me to believe how small you still are by the way you eat. Don't get me wrong, I'm glad you are eating but oh my," he said as he put the final touches to my order.

"It must be the company I'm keeping. I didn't ever eat this much before I moved in here with you, my dear," I fluttered my eyes at him with a big smile on my face.

"Oh is that right? I wonder why that is?" Before I had a chance to respond, "....spoiled much," as he began to laugh.

"I resent that remark. I'm not spoiled. You just force food on me every time I turn around is all. Besides, who wouldn't love to have their own personal chef at their beck and call?" I asked as I pulled him down closer to me so I could kiss him. "Besides, a girl can't live on protein alone," I gave him a wicked smirk and patted him on the behind.

After he fixed him something to eat, we sat and talked and laughed for the next hour or so. Neither of us mentioned the events from earlier in the day as we enjoyed one another's company, but I could tell it was still weighing heavy on his mind. As he loaded the dishwasher, I decided to bring up the snake again.

"Jeremiah Love."

"Yes my dear."

"What did you all do with that snake and rats' tail?"

By the way he stopped cleaning, I could tell he wasn't expecting that question, and by the way he hesitated, he really didn't want to start that conversation up again.

"Baby, it's not for you to worry about, okay. But since you asked, they took it with them for evidence," he said as he laid the towel he was wiping his hands on down on the countertop and came back to sit by my side. "D.J., like I said before, I don't want you to worry about that. I'm not expecting anything to happen out here, but just in case something does, is why I showed you where my guns are and how to get into the safe room, should it come to that," as he held my hand and caressed my cheek.

"Has anything like that ever happened before? I mean, before I moved in?" I asked, already knowing the answer.

"No. No it hasn't, but why did you ask that?" he asked with a puzzled look on his face.

I lowered my head and barely above a whisper I asked the question that had been nagging at me since I found out what was going on, "Do you think it has anything to do with me and Selkie?" not wanting to make eye contact.

"Oh no baby," as he gently gripped my chin to lift my head up. As our eyes met, he said, "D.J. I'm going to be honest with you. My Lt. asked that very same question, but I honestly can't see how. I haven't seen anyone following us when we've come back from town, and this place isn't listed in the phone book. I don't know how he'd know where you were," he said not only reassuring me with his voice but through his touch and with his eyes as well.

I cleared my throat and said, "Well I do," staring down at the floor.

"What do you mean, you do?" he asked, lowering his head and slowly lifted my head as that gentle look took on a sterner gaze.

I turned my head away for a moment and finally said, "My cell phone. We're on the same account." As I made eye contact with him again, I asked, "Can't you track those things?" He didn't say anything immediately, but I could tell by the look on his face that I was right. He tried to play it off, but I could tell what I had asked was right on the money.

After a few moments of silence, he dabbed me on the nose and said, "Well, we're not going to worry about that right now. How about we get you to a more comfortable seat. Your backs got to be hurting you by now," as he helped me to my feet and carried me to the tv room in our bedroom, never really answering my question. "So, what would you like to watch? We can watch a movie or just watch tv," he explained as he opened up a cabinet full of movies. As badly as I wanted him to answer my question, I left it alone. It's not like I already didn't know the answer anyway.

I'm not sure when I fell asleep, but I woke up in the bed by myself. I could hear Jeremiah talking in the distance, but instead of calling out for him or going to see where he was, I just laid there in the darkness, straining to hear what he was saying. I knew he was on the phone since I didn't hear any other voices, but I could only make out a word here and there. He was obviously pacing by the way his voice would get louder then drift off in the distance, but from what I could make out he was discussing the snake and my cell phone. As I looked around, I realized my cell phone was not on the nightstand where it usually was. As I laid there in the darkness, tears began to stream down my face as reality hit me. This was all my fault. I was the snake and Jeremiah was the rat. Selk was sending us both a message. I don't know who he had doing his dirty work, but this had Selkie written all over it. As I laid there crying, I listened to Jeremiah's voice echoing throughout the house as I drifted back off to sleep.

The sun had been up for some time when I finally woke up to an empty bed again and the unmistakable sound of drilling. Once I had gained my bearings, I went to the bathroom to freshen up a little and then followed the noise through the house to see what Jeremiah could possibly be drilling on. As I stepped out onto the front porch, I realized that it wasn't just Jeremiah making all that racket, Joshua was here too. They were installing cameras and running wires around the house.

Jeremiah saw me before Joshua did, which was probably a good thing by his reaction. I must have been standing there with a look of mayhem on my face by the way he reacted to my presence. He almost stumbled coming off his ladder as he hurried over to me.

"I'm so sorry we woke you. But don't worry, everything is okay," he smiled at me as he gave me a hug and then bent down to kiss my stomach.

"Hey you two! Stop all of that! We got work to do man!" Joshua yelled out as he came around the house and caught Jeremiah talking to my tummy as he always did, first thing in the morning.

"Yeah, yeah. Let me get her situated, and I'll be right back."

"Don't get lost," Joshua laughed as he went in the back of his van for something.

"I'm fine, don't mind me, but what's all of this?" I asked, not really wanting to hear the answer.

Jeremiah wrapped his arms around me as he turned me back towards the door and ushered me back inside the house. "How about I whip you up something to eat while you go take a leisurely soak in the tub." He continued before I had a chance to respond, "You tossed and turned all night. And I could tell you'd been crying when I touched your pillow last night, it was soaked from all your tears," he said in a very soothing voice.

"I'm fine," as I swatted at his hands. "Please don't treat me like a child and just answer my question," I protested.

"And what question would that be pretty lady?" he acted like I hadn't asked him a thing.

"Stop it! I'm not stupid or blind. Why are you two putting up all these cameras all of a sudden?" I insisted.

"D.J. I need you to stay calm. I'll tell you what's going on but first how about I draw you a bath and get you set up with some food before I explain," he insisted with his eyes. You could tell he was really worried about how I was going to react to what he had to say so not to make things worse I took him up on the bath and breakfast in the tub.

"You lay back and relax, and I'll get you something to nibble on while you're soaking," he kissed me on the forehead and immediately left the bathroom before I had a chance to respond. But when he returned with the bowl of fruit and a couple of muffins, I made sure he explained everything before he went back to work.

"I got a call while you were asleep and apparently there is a new player in town who likes to leave a snake and rat tail as his calling card. Now don't get upset because I don't know that Selk has anything to do with this, but I can tell you that he is fit to be tied," he paused obviously waiting on my reaction.

I sat straight up in the tub, "What do you mean, 'Selk is fit to be tied.'" I didn't even realize I'd started fidgeting until Jeremiah said something.

"Calm down D.J. and stop fidgeting," as he stroked my head and held my hand. "Your phone rang this morning and I tried to silence it so it wouldn't wake you, but when I saw who it was, I answered it."

"You did what?! Why would you answer my phone?" I was sitting straight up again. "Who was it?" I asked as if I already didn't know.

"Calm down. Let me explain," he said as he put the towel behind my neck and pushed my shoulders back until I was laying back, again. "I know I shouldn't have, but when I saw who it was, I couldn't help myself."

"So, who was it," I said much calmer than before.

"It was Selk."

I didn't say anything at first. I just moaned as I rolled my eyes to the back of my head and laid my head all the way back. Those few seconds of silence felt like minutes, but finally I mustered up the energy to ask, "What did he say?" not really wanting to know.

"Nothing nice and nothing I care to repeat to a lady. D.J. if he says half the things to you that he said to me, I can't believe you've been putting up with that. I mean, you don't seem the type to take that kind of abuse."

I laid there with my head back and my eyes closed, as the first of many tears began to run down the sides of my face.

"Oh Love, please don't cry. I wasn't trying to make you cry," he explained as he tried to wipe my tears away.

When I didn't respond, he continued to tell me what all Selk had to say to him and to me. He showed up for my doctor's appointment just like I figured he would, only to find out that I had already seen the doctor yesterday without him and without letting him know. He called both of us all sorts of names and how he wasn't going to take this lying down. Apparently, there was no way another man was raising his sons, not over his dead body. Jeremiah sponged off my tummy as he finished telling me about their conversation and how he said he knew exactly where Jeremiah lived. That's what prompted him to take action and do what he could to fortify the house and grounds more than it had been. Again, he tried to reassure me that he couldn't connect Selk to the snake, but he wasn't taking any chances either way.

"That's enough. I don't want to hear any more right now," I tried to muster up the best smile I could as I patted him on the hand. "Go on, I'm okay here. Go get back to work before we look up and Joshua is standing in the middle of the bathroom with us," I smiled as I kissed the back of his hand. "I'll be fine here for a while. If I need you, I'll just call you…if you bring my phone in here," I continued.

"I don't know that I like how calm you are right now, but okay," he gave me a wary look as he slowly turned to go retrieve the phone. He placed it on the stand next to the tub, gently kissed me on the forehead, and turned to head back outside to his project with his brother.

But before he could leave, I said, "Miah..."

Rushing back over to my side and kneeling down beside me, "Yes my love."

"You can answer my phone whenever you want to. I really don't care if you see who I'm talking to," I kissed the back of his hand and smiled. He smiled down at me, gave me a wink, and then kissed my forehead before he returned to his work. I laid there with my eyes closed until the water was too cold to stay in it anymore. I didn't feel like eating, and I tried my best not to even think, but that part was almost impossible to pull off. I didn't worry myself to the point of having contractions, but I did shed a tear or two as I begged God to explain to me why this was happening, all of this.

After my heart was broken when Fitz got married to someone else, I never expected to be able to love again, but here I was, more in love than I'd ever been before. I was never supposed to be able to get pregnant, yet here I was pregnant with twins. And finally, why on earth would you allow me to get pregnant and fall in love but not make both of those things happen with the same person? I'd like to tell you that I gained some sense of clarity as I soaked away my anxiety, but I can't.

When I got tired of letting the cold water out and refilling the tub with hot water, I decided that it was past time to get out of the tub and go back to living my life. It was like Jeremiah and I had some type of telepathy because no sooner had I finished rinsing the last few bubbles off my body there he stood in the doorway.

"Now I know you weren't about to try to get out of that tub without calling me. I just know you weren't going to do that Little Miss," he said with his arms crossed and a smirk on his face as he leaned up against the doorframe of the bathroom.

"Well, see what had happened was....." I laughed.

He just shook his head as he came over and helped me out of the tub.

"What are you smiling at Mister?" as he wrapped the towel around me. Let me say again, he wrapped the towel all the way around me. And yes, I have a thing for towels that will completely cover me up.

"I could enjoy this view all day every day," he smiled as he opened up my towel and gave me a wink.

"Is that right now? I learn something new about you every day," I giggled.

"Oh yeah. And what have you learned today pray tell?"

"That you have a thing for beached whales," I started laughing.

"Beached whales....you are nothing like a beached whale. I've never seen a Shamu look as beautiful as you with the water glistening on its skin," he started laughing, and of course, I stopped.

"Shamu...are you serious right now?" I huffed.

"You're the one that called yourself a whale. I'm just adding to the conversation," he flashed that brilliant smile that I'd grown to love.

"Uhh.... I can't with you," as I finished drying off and made my way over to the closet. "So how's it going out there? You almost finished?" as my dress fell over my head.

"We're done my lady. Would you like to come take a look at the system to see how it works?"

"That's a silly question. Of course I do," I laughed.

"Well come on then slowpoke," as he picked me up to carry me to wherever the monitor was.

"You know, I can walk right?" I asked as I wrapped my arms around his neck and swung my legs like a little kid on a swing.

"You've done quite a bit of walking already today Little Miss. Remember, you're supposed to be on bed rest," he gave me an awkward grin.

"Yeah, yeah."

He sat me down in the chair behind his desk in the study and pulled out the keyboard to his computer. With a few swift keystrokes, there were live feeds of all the cameras, 10 in all. He showed me how to see all the cameras at one time, or I could pull up a single camera. 5 of the cameras actually rotated whereas the other 5 were all still cameras. They had installed cameras on all sides of the house, in the garage above the door to enter the house, behind and inside the tack room, at the front door of the stable, in the back of the house off of our bedroom deck that watched the tree line, and one in the bushes on the road as you turned onto the driveway.

"WOW! You weren't playing around were you?" as I looked at all the views in front of me. I hesitated to ask, but I couldn't help myself, "Was all of this really necessary?" I could tell by the way he reacted to my question it was.

"D.J., I just want my family to be safe when I'm here and when I'm not. You never know what people are thinking, so it's best to plan ahead and not wait and see what happens and then react. It's like in chess, you need to be thinking 3 moves ahead at all times," he explained.

"Maybe that's why I don't like chess," as I watched the monitor. "It's all just a little overwhelming is all," I turned to look at him as he squatted beside me. "Jeremiah, I need you to be honest with me. Do you regret me being here? I mean look at all of this, all you've had to change in your life because of me," I said as I blinked away the first of many tears.

"Oh baby, please don't cry," as he wiped my tears away and gently caressed my face. "Don't you ever doubt how much joy you've brought to my life or how much I want you here? Besides, who's not up for a few upgrades anyway," he laughed as he pulled me in tight.

It was amazing how at ease I felt wrapped in his arms. I'd never felt so safe with anyone like that, not even my parents. Being with him was a new experience in all aspects of life for me. I never knew a man could be so strong but also be so nurturing as well. Jeremiah was definitely cut from a different cloth and a welcomed gift from God.

"Well, how about some lunch?" I asked.

He started laughing, "Alrighty then. Mind if I get cleaned up first?" as he tried to pull away from me.

"Nope not at all," I started fanning the air like he smelled bad. Funny thing is, he smelled like he'd been working out, but it wasn't an unpleasant odor. In fact, it was kinda turning me on as I kissed him on the neck and started working my way down. He stretched his head back as I kissed my way down his neck, to his chest, with the occasional nibble. I could feel his body tightening up as I rubbed his shoulders and his chest as my hand slowly made its way down his body to a very engorged penis.

"You know, if you keep this up, you're not going to get to eat any time soon," he moaned as I caressed his penis in my hand and began to give him a slow massage.

At that moment I decided that my actions would send a much stronger message then my words as I pushed him, causing him to fall back on his butt. I gave a devilish look as I lowered myself down on top of him and slowly pulled his pants and Under Armour down to his ankles. I began kissing him up his legs stopping only a moment to caress his knees with my tongue as I continued up his leg with gentle kisses and elongated tongue strokes until I reached the place we both wanted me to be.

I gave him one more quick stroke with my hand as I took all of him I could in my mouth and began to suck and stroke him with my tongue. It was surprising to even me how much I enjoyed having him in my mouth, this was never my thing before. But it was something about the way he tasted and the way he feels that just keeps me coming back for more. As his hands gently gripped the back of my head, helping to pace my strokes, I could tell he was about to orgasm. With one last long stroke, he let out a deep moan as his body quivered and my mouth filled with all of his essence. I continued to suck just a little while longer to make sure he enjoyed every last second of our midday delight.

As he laid there breathing heavy with one hand on his chest while the other stroked my head, I slowly kissed him from his navel up to his neck until he pulled me on up to his face with one swift move. He held me over his face smiling at me for a moment before he lowered me enough so he could kiss me. As our tongues made love to one another, I felt a tug at my dress as it began moving on up my body until it reached my chest. I was notorious for wearing what I called drop dresses. You simply drop them over your head and you're done.

He sat up, with me on top of him, lifted my dress up over my breast as he began sucking and circling them with his tongue. My dress came up over my head and dropped to the side as he caressed my breast with his other hand and continued to massage me with his tongue. As I sat there enjoying the warm feeling of his tongue gently ministering to my nipples, I began to get a tingling sensation as his fingertips began to slowly slide down my body until he found my very wet, very hot, spot. As soon as he made contact with my clit, I jerked, arching my back and dropping my head back as I released a long and sensual moan.

"Yes baby. Yessss," as I vibrated with every flick of his fingers.

He teased me with the tip of his finger for what felt like an eternity, but by no means was I complaining. As he played with me, I could feel my insides begin to contract, trying to pull his fingers in deeper and deeper.

"That's it baby, that's it. Give it to me D.J. let go and give it to me."

I continued to moan and grip his back as I felt myself turning upside down and just like that he had flipped us over and was inside of me. Stroking me every so gently but with all the force I could stand. With each thrust, my walls gripped on tighter and tighter as if I was holding on for dear life. He felt so good sliding in and outside of me as he continued to tickle my clit with his finger. As the music played, I lost myself in our rhythm when I felt a drop of water on my cheek. I opened my eyes expecting to see sweat building up on his brow only to realize it wasn't sweat at all, it was a tear. He was smiling at me with tears welling up in his eyes.

All of my emotions exploded at that very moment. I pulled him down closer as I forced my tongue between his lips and added another melody to our symphony. We rolled to the side as our lovemaking continued and the tears freely flowed down both of our faces. Our bodies melted into one as we consumed each other in a passionate dance that lasted the rest of the evening. I can't tell you how many times we made love that day, but I can tell you that our bodies did things that would have made the Kamasutra blush and then take detailed notes. We made love like there was no tomorrow. We electrified one another's body like we were the only source of energy and we needed to provide the world with light. In that moment, there was no need for cameras, there wasn't anyone who didn't want us together. In that moment, we were the only two people on the planet capable of filling the entire world with love.

Before we knew it, it was time to head into town for my next doctor's appointment. The weekend had flown by and Thanksgiving was creeping up on us faster than I could believe. Our life was perfect when it was just the two of us and none of the outside negativity was able to touch us. Problem is, that's not reality.

Although we made plenty of time for making love, we actually spent a lot of time talking about us and our future. Sunday, Jeremiah had finally talked me into calling my mom to try to start mending our shattered fences. Our conversation went well enough that I actually agreed to come out to the house after my doctor's appointment. It didn't hurt that she put P.J. on the phone to beg me to come by the house too, he missed me and really wanted to see me.

So Monday after a very good check-up, we made our way to my parents' house in Cypress. As we pulled around the corner, I was shocked at what I was seeing. Jeremiah noticed the look on my face and immediately pulled over and asked me what was wrong.

"Keep driving! Don't stop! Keep going!" I yelled at him before I realized it, not really expecting to react that way.

"What is it D.J.? What's wrong?" as he sped up and drove past the house before anyone saw us.

When we were clear of any possible eyes, I patted him on his arm as I laid my head back and simply exhaled. As he waited for an answer, I could feel the tears welling up in my eyes and tried my best to blink them away. He pulled over to the side of the road and reached over and began wiping my tears away, still waiting on an answer.

After a few minutes in silence, I took a deep breath and said, "It was a set-up."

"What do you mean 'it was a set-up?'" he asked as he handed me a tissue.

"All those cars....my pastor was there, my aunties and probably uncles were there..."

He laughed, "So what. Maybe they just wanted to meet me," he said, cutting me off.

I shook my head as I turned to look at him. "No, you don't understand. That was Selk's truck parked in the driveway."

The look on Jeremiah's face could have melted ice. We sat in silence for a few more minutes and then he finally said, "You've got to be kidding me."

I knew it was more of a statement than a question so I didn't respond, but it wouldn't have mattered anyway because before I had a chance to answer Jeremiah went off. "Your mother! I've NEVER in my life met someone so manipulative and determined to have their own way. What good would've come from having *us* in the same room together? She has said more than once how disastrous that would be. Does she not care that you aren't supposed to be stressed out? What's she going to do? Have someone knock me over the head and force you to marry him right there in the living room?"

He rattled on that way for at least 15 more minutes before he finally settled down, never giving me a chance to respond, not that I could have anyway. I honestly didn't know what she could've been thinking. This move was completely off script even for her. Once he finally calmed down, he turned to me and said, "Well D.J. I'm going to leave it up to you. We can go back and find out what's really going on, or we can go home."

And just like that, he placed the decision squarely in my lap. I sat there trying to decide what to do and read his face all at the same time, but the two emotions didn't mix in the least little bit. As he waited for an answer, he took my hand and kissed my palm.

"Everything in me is screaming 'LET'S GO HOME....' but if you are up to it, let's go back and see what's really going on," I finally mustered up the strength to say.

"Only if you're sure D.J." he replied, squeezing my hand tightly.

"I'm sure. We're going to have to deal with them sooner or later and maybe with my pastor there, everyone will be on their best behavior," I said with a sheepish grin on my face.

"Well alright then. Here we go."

I'd love to tell you that everything went smoothly and we all got along. I'd love to tell you that everyone was on their best behavior in front of our pastor and that Jeremiah and Selk shook hands like men and squashed this beef. I'd love to tell you that my mom and I made up and everything that had happened over the last few months was water under the bridge, or that by the end of that meeting, Selk accepted the fact that I'd chosen Jeremiah, and my family, namely my mom, had accepted me and Jeremiah's relationship with open arms....but I can't. What I can tell you is that there was more pushing and shoving than there should have been and some feelings were seriously hurt, but no one got arrested, no bones were broken, nothing of great valuable got broken, and more importantly, I didn't go into labor. And most importantly, Jeremiah and I left there more determined and devoted to one another than when we got there. Basically, when all was said and done, we all walked away in one piece, able to argue another day.

CHAPTER 20

A line of thunderstorms moved in late Monday afternoon, and it continued to rain all day and into the evening on Tuesday. Jeremiah learned first-hand how scared of storms I am even though I try not to allow anyone to see anything but a strong and independent woman. The first time I screamed after a clap of thunder, I nearly gave him a heart attack. We were in separate rooms of the house so when I screamed, he must have thought I had fallen, or I was going into labor by the way he sprinted into the room and jumped up on the bed with me.

"What's wrong baby? Where does it hurt?" he panted with a panicked look in his eyes as he felt up and down my sides and stomach.

I dropped my head to hide my embarrassment and explained, "I'm not in any pain. The thunder woke me up and scared me. I'm actually terrified of storms."

He just stared at me with this shocked look on his face, then he finally said, "You're what?!" but before I could respond he continued, "You're telling me that Ms. Billy Bad Ass is afraid of a little storm." He could tell by the look on my face that I was telling him the God's honest truth, but after a few moments of silence, the room erupted in laughter, his laughter.

I just sat there feeling even more embarrassed, listening to him laugh at me as I simultaneously jumped and screamed with another clap of thunder, landing in his chest. "I'm sorry for scaring you like that," I managed to say as I looked up at him. "But it was cute how you rushed to my side and with one leap you were up in the bed checking me out," I finally giggled.

"You're not kidding, you're actually scared," he said as he wrapped his arms around me. "D.J., baby you're really trembling." My only response was to snuggle in closer as he held me tighter. Eventually I dozed off, but apparently, even in my sleep I still jumped and made some type of whimpering sound with each clap of thunder, but Jeremiah never left my side.

It was very late in the evening when I had the first twinges of pain, but I did my best to hide it from Jeremiah. I figured it was the stress of the storm taking its toll on me and I had absolutely no desire to spend Thanksgiving in the hospital, which is exactly what would have happened if I told him what was going on. It was well after 10 as we sat in the den all curled up watching *Jurassic Park* when there was a deafening clap of thunder that shook the entire house and then all the lights went out. Of course I screamed and buried myself in Jeremiah's chest as he did his best to calm me down.

"Calm down baby. The storm must have taken out a transformer somewhere." Since we lived out in the country and couldn't really see any other houses from our property, he was just guessing. "Here, let me get some candles going, so we have a little light in here," as he gently slid out from under me. I could hear drawers in the kitchen opening and closing very quickly, and he soon returned with a big flashlight and several candles that he began setting up around the room. As he finished lighting the last candle, a pain hit me that was bad enough that I couldn't hide it if I'd tried.

"Uuuhhhhhh!"

"Okay that was a pain scream and not an, 'I'm scared of the storm scream.' What's wrong baby?" as he dropped the lighter and was immediately kneeling at my side.

"Uhmm, I'm not sure, but this doesn't feel like before."

"Well was it like the pains you had in the hospital?"

"Honestly.....it was much WORSE, than...." as another pain hit me in mid-sentence causing me to double over again.

"Alright, that's it. We're going to the hospital."

I tried to grab his arm as he moved to stand up, "NO! Pleeease! I don't want to spend Thanksgiving in the hospital, and if we go now, they'll never let me come back home," as a tear ran down my cheek. Before he could respond, another pain hit me nearly knocking me off the couch. "UUUUHHHH!"

"I'm calling your doctor, and we're going to the hospital. I'm not arguing with you about this D.J." He slid me further back on the couch and off the edge, and then grabbed the phone and the flashlight as he headed off in the direction of the bedroom. I don't know how long he was gone, but I was sure happy when he came back. I could tell by the look on his face something else was wrong.

"What's wrong?"

"I just spoke to your doctor and he wants us at the hospital immediately. He'll meet us there."

I rolled my eyes as another pain hit me, "Uhhh! I guessed that," I began to pant. "But that's not the reason you look worried," I managed to say through the pain.

"I don't know what you're talking about D.J., I'm fine. Now let's get you to the car," as he picked me up and headed towards the garage with me in his arms and my overnight bag and purse thrown over his shoulder.

"Don't lie to me Zeke. Something else is bothering you, so tell me what it is," I was able to say almost pain-free.

As he slid me into the car and fastened the seatbelt around me, "I don't want you to worry, but it's not just the lights that are out, the phone is out too," as he closed the door before I could respond. It took a minute for him to get in the car because he had to manually open the garage door. No power means no garage door opener.

I did my best to use what I had learned in Lamaze class, but it was so much easier to do with the instructor talking me through it and no pain. Jeremiah was finally in the car with me after getting the door down, so I could finally ask, "What do you mean the phone is out? When did the phone go out?" I managed to get out in between shots of pain.

"Like I said, don't worry about it. The storm must have knocked down some phone lines as well. How are you feeling over there?" he asked as he eased out onto the main road. It was darker out than I ever remembered it to be at night, and there were no lights coming or going in either direction. "D.J. talk to me. How are you doing over there?" he calmly asked as he reached over and rubbed my stomach.

"I'm okay. The pain is actually easing up." I patted his hand then said, "Two hands on the wheel please Mister. I appreciate your calming touch, but right now I'd feel better knowing you are in complete control of this car," I smiled.

"Well yes ma'am," as he held the steering wheel at 10 and 2. He glanced over at me and then started laughing.

"And what may I ask is so funny?"

"You are. It's not like I haven't driven a car in much more stressful situations than this and I haven't been in any unintentional accidents. Not yet anyway," he winked at me. "I'd knock on wood if I had any," he paused for a second then suddenly reached over and tapped me on my forehead as he began to laugh.

"I don't think that's very funny.

"Oh come on now...it was a little funny," he smiled.

Uuuhhh!" as I grabbed my side and held my breath.

"Breath through it baby...don't hold your breath," as he started doing my Lamaze breathing.

When the pain subsided, I looked up with a terrified look on my face. "Miah..."

He immediately stopped panting when he saw the look on my face, "What's wrong? What happened?"

"You mean besides the fact that one of them just Judo kicked my ribs?" I reached underneath me best I could, "...I think my water just broke."

"You're playing right?" he asked with huge eyes.

"No sweety. I'm so serious right now," as I lifted my hand to show him my wet fingers with a terrified look on my face.

"Oh my God! It's okay baby. Stay calm, everything's going to be okay," he tried to reassure me.

"I think I'm really in labor this time Miah," I managed to say as a tear ran down my cheek. Another pain hit me, and I began to do my Lamaze breathing like he'd told me earlier as I tried to stay calm, but that didn't last long when we both jerked forward as the car swerved a little. It felt like someone had just hit us from behind, but there were no lights behind us, and in the darkness and rain, we couldn't see anyone behind us either.

"What was that?" I asked, grabbing on to his arm.

"Baby, I'm not sure," as he stared at the rearview mirror after regaining control of the car. "I don't see anything, but I swear, something just hit us from behind." Just as he said the last word, something hit us again, this time sending the car into a tailspin. "Hold on D.J.!" he quickly glanced over at me as he struggled to regain control of the car.

I grabbed onto the door handle and reached up to the ceiling and pressed as hard as I could screaming, "What's going on?! Who hit us?!" as the tears began to stream down my face.

Jeremiah reached over with his arm and pinned me to the seat, startling me. I looked over at him just as the car began to tumble and roll. Everything was moving in slow motion as glass began to fly and everything that wasn't tied down began to fly around our heads. I felt a sudden jerk, and everything went black. The next thing I remember was the sound of running water, excruciating pain, and feeling upside down. It took a minute to gather myself, but when I was finally able to focus, I realized four things...I was in the car by myself, I was upside down, the back end of the car was in the water, and it was beginning to pour in from all sides.

"Jeremiah! Jeremiah, where are you?! Please help me. I'm stuck!" I cried. I pulled on the seatbelt, but it had me pinned to the seat, and I couldn't get it undone. I cried and struggled to free myself as I continued to call for help. "HELP! PLEASE, SOMEBODY, HELP ME!" But the only sounds I heard was the water rushing around the backend of the car and the rain. I don't know how long I'd been out or where Jeremiah was, but I knew for sure that my water had broken, I was feeling a whole lot of pressure between my legs that I'd never felt before, and I had absolutely no idea what I was going to do. I must have sat there stuck to the seat and in pain for hours before a much-needed voice cut through the darkness.

"D.J.! D.J. baby talk to me! Call out!"

"Jeremiah! I'm over here!"

"I can't see very well. Keep talking."

"I'm over here!" as I struggled to find him in the darkness. "I'm still in the car. It's upside down and water is coming in!"

"Can you reach the steering wheel?!"

I thought that was a strange question, "Yes, barely! Why?" as the tips of my fingers touched the wheel.

"Well honk the horn!" he yelled.

My eyes got wide as I now realized why he asked me that. I struggled to touch the center of the steering wheel, but when I reached it, 'HOOOOOOOOOOOOOOOONK!!!!' I didn't even think about letting up, I just laid on the horn until my arm and body hurt too badly to continue.

The water was now touching my back as I felt an arm grab me out of nowhere.

"I've got her! I've got her!"

It wasn't Jeremiah's voice, which made me cry even harder. I knew it was bad if he wasn't the person coming to save me, but I didn't even worry about who it was as I held on for dear life. "Please, help me," I cried as the arm lifted my head out of the water.

"Calm down. I got you. I promise I've got you." And with one swift jerk, my body fell to the ceiling of the car.

I began to flail around grabbing and kicking at any and everything when I heard Jeremiah's voice coming from the other side of the car.

"D.J.! We need you to stop fighting! Calm down so we can get you out!"

"Where did you go?! Why did you leave me?!" I cried as I tried to twist my body around and reach for him, but a sudden excruciating pain made me stop moving altogether. "Ahhhhh-ahhhhh! STOP!" I swung at the man who set me free. "THAT HURTS! STOP PULLING ME PLEASE!" as I broke down crying again.

"Hold on. Your leg is stuck," he explained as he reached around me and moved my leg from between the seats. Instead of trying to move towards Jeremiah, I just allowed him to maneuver me out of the window on his side.

As my body landed in the water, I felt a warm sensation running down my leg. I reached for the warm spot and immediately knew the warm feeling was from my blood mixing with the water. He pulled me up the embankment just as Jeremiah grabbed me and held me in his arms crying into my chest.

"I'm so sorry! I don't know what happened. One minute we were okay then the next minute all hell was breaking loose. As I climbed out of the car, the embankment gave way, and you and the car went with it."

"Well why'd you leave me? I called for you, and you didn't answer," I slapped his arm.

"Believe me when I say I had no choice." I could feel him stiffen up as he pulled me in tighter, "Baby I just couldn't." We laid there holding each other as the faint sound of a truck engine got louder and closer. A sudden flash of light caught Jeremiah's face, and I saw why he couldn't see me.

"OH MY GOD! JEREMIAH YOUR FACE!" I pulled his shirt up to try to wipe away some of the blood. His left eye was completely swollen shut, and the gash above his right eye still had blood running down into his face. "You look like you've been in a fight," I told him as another contraction hit me. "Uhhhhhh!"

"Baby it probably looks worse than it feels," he managed to smile as he kissed me on the forehead.

"Miah I'm in labor. Somethings coming out and I don't know what to do," I cried into his chest.

"You promised to help me get her out. SO HELP ME!" he yelled. I forgot there was someone else there. He hadn't said a word the entire time.

"I remember" he said, a little to calm for my liking. Then he suddenly yelled out, "We're over here!"

"Thank you so much for your help," I reached out to grab his hand.

He knelt down beside me, "You don't need to thank me. I just happen to be in the right place at the right time," he smiled as he stood up again. As the lights got closer, I could finally make out his face for the first time. I knew his face from somewhere, but I couldn't remember from where, but those gold teeth... those gold teeth. I know I'd seen them before. A chill went up my spine as he stood there and smiled down at us as the voices got closer.

"I know you, don't I? Who are you?" I asked as another contraction hit me. "Uhhhh!"

There was a loud cracking sound as the ground around us began to move. Jeremiah held on to me tightly as we both slid back towards the water with all the dirt and branches around us. I reached out to the man standing at my side. As our fingers touched, he stepped away and watched us slam into the car.

"They're over here. Get down here now!" he yelled.

"Hold on D.J.! Don't let go! Keep your head down and stay still!" Jeremiah explained.

"I can't," I cried. "It hurts too much to be still anymore."

"D.J. I need you to remember that I'm doing this for you, to keep you and the babies safe," Jeremiah explained to me as he struggled to push me up on top of the car and then laid a broken branch over me.

"Doing what? It's not your fault this happened. It was an accident."

"D.J. I love you. NEVER forget how much I LOVE YOU!" he kissed me for a moment then he pushed the car, and it began to move with the water as Jeremiah suddenly disappeared underneath it.

"JEREMIAH!" I reached for him in the water, but I couldn't feel him anymore. I heard another crackling sound then the car jerked and started moving faster before it came to a violent stop as it slammed into something. All I felt was a sharp pain as I struggled to hold on as everything went black again. At some point, my face must have fallen into the water because I was suddenly wide awake and choking. I heard men's voices screaming at me as I tried to get my body back out of the water and free my legs. Something heavy had them pinned down.

"Ma'am don't move!"

"Stay still! We've almost got you free!" another voice yelled.

"Jeremiah! He went under! Please find him! He went under the car!" I cried.

"We have rescuers that will look for him, but right now I need you to remain as still as possible. The more you move, the more this car moves, and it's not going to stay still much longer, so we've got to get you free quickly. So please stay still, so we have time to get the rest of the tree off of you and get you into this basket."

I laid my head down crying, as I tried to stay as still as possible. I felt something hit my back and started screaming again, but even through the pain, I could tell my legs were finally free.

"It's just our ropes! You're okay! I promise you, you're okay," another voice cut through the darkness out of nowhere. I felt a hand on my arm and began wildly grabbing at the arm attached to it thinking it was Jeremiah, but it wasn't. It was one of the firemen that had swum over to me to secure the ropes on the car. "Now I need you to help me. Do you think you can do that?"

Through my tears and cries of pain, "Uhhhhhh! I think so."

"I need you to hold onto me as I work this harness around your body."

"Okay, I'll try." I don't know how he did it with me holding onto his arm with a death grip, but he managed to get the harness on me and rolled me into a basket of sorts.

"Oh my God! She's pregnant!" another voice called out as they hooked my harness to the basket and another rope. With a sudden jerk, I could feel the basket moving across the water as the men on the embankment pulled, and the men by my side pushed us all safely out of the water.

Once I was back on land, I began begging them, "Please find Jeremiah! He can't see. One eye is swollen shut and the other had a gash above it bleeding into his face. Ask the man who was helping us! He knows exactly where he was last," I pleaded.

"What man? There's nobody else here but you ma'am?" a fireman said.

"There was a man here! A black man with gold teeth. Find him he knows. And PLEASE just help Jeremiah! Please find him! Ask the man!" I cried as they carried me up the side of the hill, back up to all the flashing lights. "Uhhhhhh!" I screamed as I grabbed my stomach.

"Ma'am, I need to check you. Can you tell me how long you've been in labor?" the EMT asked as they got me out of the basket and onto the stretcher.

"Since around 4 o'clock. We left the house a little after midnight headed to the hospital," I explained. I grabbed the officer standing by me, "PLEASE, PLEASE go find Jeremiah! He's still out there," I cried out in pain as I gripped his arm.

"That can't be ma'am. We've been on the scene for more than 2 hours," he looked confused.

"I know it was well after midnight when we left the house! It was pouring down rain, but the clock in the car said 12:30 when we got hit," I screamed out in pain again. "Find Jeremiiiaaaah! Pleeeeez!"

"Ma'am, we're looking for him. Can you tell us what he was wearing?" an officer asked.

"What's she talking about? It stopped raining 2 days ago," someone said just above a whisper.

I grabbed the police officer standing closest to me. "What do you mean 2 days ago? It's Tuesday night, right? Find Jeremiah....uuuuhhhhhhh!"

"No ma'am. It's early Thursday morning," he replied, just as another sharp pain hit me. "UUUUHHHHHH!"

As I screamed out in pain, the EMT yelled out, "There's a problem. I see a lot of cord but no baby. Get her in the rig now!" I felt a jerk and was suddenly up in the air, then inside the ambulance and all the brightness of its lights.

"Please save my babies! I don't care about me, but you've got to save my boys!" I cried as I heard the doors of the ambulance slam shut. I was holding the officers uniform so tight that I drug him in the ambulance with me, more from the pain than anything else I think. Through back to back deep breaths, "Jeremiah, he's a detective in the HPD Gang Unit. Find Lieutenant

Keith Williams, he's his LT and old partner." Another pain hit me, sharper than the last one. "UUUUHHHHHHHHH!"

"He's what?" he pulled away from me.

"Jeremiah is a COP! NOW FIND HIM!"

I could tell he opened the back door by the sudden draft in the back of the ambulance. "ATTENTION EVERYBODY! WE'VE GOT AN OFFICER IN THE WATER!!!" as he mumbled something into his mic.

Another voice quickly came back over the radio, "JEREMIAH THOMAS IS A DETECTIVE IN THE GANG UNIT. WE'RE SENDING YOU MORE HELP! WATCH COMMANDER IS IN ROUTE!" The back door slammed again, and I felt a jerk as we started moving, sirens blaring.

As much pain as I was in a wave of relief came over me. I turned my attention back to the EMT, "I don't understand. It can't be Thursday. We left the house Tuesday going into Wednesday."

"Ma'am, are you carrying twins?"

Through clenched teeth, "Yes! 2 boys." The pain was coming from everywhere now. I tried to pay attention to what was going on, but I couldn't, I hurt too bad to even think.

I can't tell you when we got to the hospital or what all happened after that. I just remember hearing lots of voices and bright lights all around me. There were people everywhere, I didn't feel wet anymore, but I was still freezing cold. As I closed my eyes, I whispered to the nurse holding my hand, "Tell Jeremiah and my boys that I love them."

"We're losing her!" she yelled, as I closed my eyes and drifted away from all the lights, the noise, and even the pain.

CHAPTER 21

I came to feeling very groggy and hurting more than I had ever hurt in all my life. I really couldn't focus well, but there were little green, red, and yellow lights flashing above my head but not making any type of noise. I could hear a tv on in the background and could see shapes moving around on what I assumed was the screen, but couldn't really get the fuzziness to go away to see what was really going on. Through the foggy haze, I managed to say, "Hello. Who's there?" as I reached for the thing in my nose, I heard a voice call out to me in a very calming voice as a hand grab mine.

"No D.J. don't pull on that. You're okay. You're in the hospital," she explained as she put the nasal cannula back in its place.

"D.J. baby, it's mommy. How are you feeling?" she held my hand and began patting it, leaning over my bed so I could see her better.

It hurt to turn my head, so I stopped trying, "Mommy? What happened? Why can't I move?"

"You were in an accident, honey. Don't you remember?"

"An accident?" I just laid there for a minute trying to remember. "No, I don't remember that."

"Well, don't you worry yourself about it then," with a worried look on her face. I wasn't used to seeing my mom look scared. She always had such a poker face unless she wanted you to read the emotions on her face.

"Mommy what's wrong?! What happened!?" I yelled in a panic. Suddenly alarms all around me started going off.

Before I realized it, there were multiple people standing around my bed, pulling at something or another and asking me questions.

"Hi D.J.. I'm Dr. England. I'm a neurologist, and I need to take a quick look at you if that's okay?"

"Yeah, that'll be fine I guess," I said as my free hand finally rested on my stomach causing me to panic all over again, "Where are my babies?! Somebody tell me! What happened to my babies?!" I screamed as the first tear ran down my cheek as I grabbed the doctor's coat.

"Shhhh, shhhh. The boys are holding their own. They are in the NICU, being taken care of, very well," he calmly explained as he loosened the grip I had on his coat.

"The NICU! What's that? Where's that?" I wildly looked around the room for answers as I tried my best to get out of the bed. You would have thought I committed a crime the way people dove on top of me to keep me down.

"D.J.! You need to stay still and get your rest so you can heal and take care of them. They're going to need you in one piece," a very familiar voice said. It was Dr. Cleveland. I don't know when he came into my room but hearing his voice had an instant calming effect over me.

I reached out for him, "Dr. Cleveland. What's happening? Why is my chest and throat so sore? Why can't I see very well? Why can't I move? I don't remember what happened. What happened? When did we get here? How..."

He cut me off, "D.J. calm down dear. Let Dr. England check you over, and we will explain everything to you," he said as he took my hand from my mom.

Dr. England started out by flashing a light in my eyes, but that did nothing more than set my head on fire. My head immediately felt like it was going to explode.

"Please STOP! That hurts so bad," I jerked my head back and immediately started crying.

"Okay, D.J. Okay, I'm stopping, but I need you to try to calm down," he said. "I need everyone out of here immediately."

"I'm not leaving my baby. Not again."

"Yes ma'am. You're leaving too. Right now. I'll let you know when you can return," Dr. England told her matter-of-factly.

"Come on Lisa," Dr. Cleveland said as he gripped her shoulders. "The nurse will come and get you when we are through."

"Then you stay and promise me," as she whirled around and hugged him like her long-lost friend. "This is my only living daughter, and I'll be damned if she's going through this with strangers."

"Lisa, I promise you I won't leave her side," he hugged her back. After standing there staring at each other for a moment, she finally turned to leave the room.

"Mommy..." I reached out for her.

"Yes my love?"

"Please don't go far. I'm scared mommy. I'm scared," as tears continued to run down my face and alarms began going off again.

"I'll be close baby. I'll be..." I didn't hear the rest of what she had to say.

I guess they gave me something to relax me as I closed my eyes and went back into a deep sleep.

I could barely move when I woke up again. After a short struggle, I realized that my wrists were tied to the bed. The nurse noticed my eyes were open before my mom, who was asleep in the reclining chair in the corner.

"D.J. I'm your nurse, my name is Amy. You're in the ICU."

I cleared my throat a couple of times before I could speak, "Why am I tied down?" as I tried to lift my arms again.

"We had to restrain you because you started pulling out your IVs and tubes. You were still combative after that, so we sedated you to keep your blood pressure down," she continued as she patted me on the arm for comfort. "If you promise me that you won't pull on anything, I can let your hands go," she waited for an answer.

"I promise that I won't pull on anything," I managed to say. "Why does my throat feel so bad," I asked as she let my hand go and I could finally rub at my throat.

"You gave us quite a scare young lady. You stopped breathing on us, so we had to intubate you again. Did you know that you are very allergic to latex?"

I shook my head no.

"D.J. sweetie. How are you feeling?" my mom jumped in stroking my head.

I struggled to turn to look at her, "Why is my neck so stiff?"

"Because you have an IV in your neck, so they have you in a neck brace to keep you from pulling it out. Between that and the accident you're probably just really stiff all over," Amy explained.

"A few hours. What happened? And what time is it?" as a tear ran down my face. "Where are my babies? Please tell me they're okay," I pulled at my mom's sleeve.

"Slow down, slow down. It's 4:30, Saturday morning, and you were in a car accident on Tuesday night. And the boys are fine baby. They're just fine. They're in the NICU being very well taken care of. I've checked on them while you've been sleeping."

"Did they get hurt in the accident? I don't remember driving anywhere. I wanna see them. I wanna see them now." I didn't realize how upset I'd gotten until the first alarm went off.

"D.J. I understand that, but I need you to calm down, or I'm going to have to sedate you again. I need your blood pressure to stay down and your stitches to stay in."

"Stitches?" as I lifted my arms, trying to see what she was talking about. "Please, I just want to see my babies," I begged as the tears began to free flow.

"I'm sorry but right now you can't. Maybe tomorrow, but not today D.J.. Honey, you almost died yesterday. Your heart has stopped twice, they had to repair a laceration of your liver, and you have a badly bruised kidney. You have staples and stitches pretty much from head to toe, you have at least 2 broken ribs, and several others are fractured along with a fractured fibula, and a nicely broken ankle that now has 3 screws in it, along with multiple bruises and contusions, internally as well as externally. So no ma'am, you cannot go anywhere tonight. We need to monitor you very closely for a little while longer." I wasn't trying to hear what she was saying as I turned my head, what little I could, and started crying into my pillow. "I understand how you feel, but if all is well come this time tomorrow, we might be able to transfer you to a step-down unit and then you will be able to go visit with them. But for now, I'm sorry D.J., you've got to stay in this bed."

My mom held me as I continued to cry and beg to go see my boys. But my pleading was falling upon deaf ears. Dr. England, Dr. Cleveland, and Dr. Ortiz, the orthopedic surgeon, all stopped by to see me and all of them refused to allow me out of the bed so I could go be with my boys. In an attempt to help calm me down my mom turned the tv on thinking watching the highlights of the football game would help, after all, I had always looked forward to Thanksgiving and the Dallas Cowboys playing. With all that was going on football was the last thing on my mind, especially since I didn't want to see Selkie on TV.

"Mommy..."

"Yes, my love."

"What happened to me? I mean did I hurt somebody in the accident?"

"Sweetie you weren't driving. You didn't hurt anybody," she pulled my chin up so she could look into my eyes.

"Well if I wasn't driving, who was? Its obvious Selk wasn't driving, he wouldn't have been in town with the game and all. Was Kevin driving?" Kevin was the driver Selk hired for me.

"Shhh, shhhh D.J.. We'll discuss it later. It doesn't matter right now," my mom replied as she pulled my head in close to her chest and rubbed my head.

"Please tell me. I gotta know," I pulled away.

I saw the look Amy shot her as she shook her head at my mom and said, "D.J., you really need to rest. In time you will probably remember on your own."

"Someone tell me now!" I yelled, immediately causing alarms to start going off.

"Okay, okay D.J. calm down baby. I'll tell you what we think we know," my mom said as she pulled me in tight and began to rock again. "You went into labor at home during the storm on Tuesday night, and somehow the car ended up going down an embankment and into a canal. Emergency crews found you passed out, clinging to a tire of the car after midnight, Thursday morning and brought you to the hospital. They had to do an emergency C-section on you when you got here. Your water was broken, and you had a fever over 104 degrees when you got here. You and the babies were all in distress and very toxic from exposure and infection. The only reason they even knew it was you is because Dr. Cleveland was in the ER with someone else who had come in, in labor. When he saw you, he notified us they'd found you."

"But why did you think I was lost in the first place. Mommy tell me! Don't leave anything out."

"D.J., Jeremiah had called to tell Dr. Cleveland what was going on and he'd told him to bring you in immediately. When you all didn't show up, Dr. Cleveland started calling around looking for you. Finally, someone noticed the skid marks in the mud and the damaged trees along the side of the road and put two and two together."

"Wait...I was with Jeremiah. Why was I with Jeremiah?" I looked at her with wide eyes.

Apparently, Amy had stepped out and called the doctor because my mom didn't get a chance to answer me.

"D.J. what is the last thing you remember?" Dr. England asked as he began giving me the once over.

I cautiously looked over at my mom before I answered. "Well...I remember being in the hospital after having an argument with my mom in my kitchen."

"What else do you remember? Take your time," he said.

"I remember Dr. Cleveland telling me he wasn't allowing me to go home and wanting me to agree to surgery to deliver the boys."

"Anything else?"

I glanced over to my mom, and the look of surprise on her face worried me. "What is it mommy? Why do you look like that? What else happened?" I panicked. I started crying and began hyperventilating.

Alarms began going off and Dr. England quickly put an oxygen mask on me and grabbed my hand, "D.J. I need you to calm down. You're fine. You're safe."

"No….something's not right. I can tell. And where is Jeremiah? What happened?" I squeezed his hand a lot harder than he expected.

"We don't know D.J. You were at the car by yourself. They haven't found him yet."

"Yet?! Why were we together in the first place? This doesn't make sense!" I cried.

Dr. England looked at my mom and finally said, "Tell her."

"D.J., you left the hospital with Jeremiah. It was the only way Dr. Cleveland would agree to let you go home. You've been staying with him these last few days."

I pushed away from her and just laid back, staring up at the ceiling as the tears began rolling down my face again. After a few minutes of silence, I slowly pulled the mask off my face and closed my eyes, "Is he dead?" Neither of them answered me immediately, and I didn't dare open my eyes to look them in the face.

Finally, my mom responded, "D.J., they're still out looking for him, but they haven't found him yet."

I turned my head away from her and began sobbing loudly.

"D.J. baby, that's a good thing sweetie. That means he still may be alive baby."

"Call Joshua please. I need to talk to him," I said, barely above a whisper.

"D.J. I understand how you feel, but I don't know that that's a good thing right now. Maybe tomorrow when things settle down a bit," Dr. English said.

I turned to look at my mom as if I hadn't heard a word he'd said, "Mommy, call him now."

"Baby I don't know his number. And you heard what the doctor said. You don't need to be getting all riled up. You need to rest."

"Call my phone. If we were missing for almost 2 days, I know he had to have called me. Get his number from the voice messages." The look on both of their faces said it all. You could have bought them both for a penny. Neither of them expected me to come up with that solution and so quickly.

I dozed off while waiting for Joshua to show up, but I woke up when I heard him outside of my room talking to the doctor and my mother.

"Please let him in," I called out startling all of them.

The glass door slid open, and Joshua stepped in with an obviously forced smile. My mom quickly followed.

"Mommy, will you give us some privacy please."

You could tell she was surprised at my request. "Uhhh, baby I don't think that's a good idea."

"Mommy, it'll be fine. Please just give us a minute," I said as I squeezed her hand. She gave in pretty quickly because none of the alarms went off.

"Okay, I'll go check on the babies." She gave Joshua a stern look as she turned to leave the room.

I reached out for his hand. "Please, tell me what's going on."

He squeezed my hand as he took a seat next to me on my bed. "D.J. first I need you to stay calm okay? You've had a very rough time, and they don't want me to get you overly excited."

"Joshua, I'm fine. Now tell me what's going on? They aren't telling me everything I can feel it."

"D.J. we're all still trying to piece it together. The way the car looks, it's hard to tell exactly what happened. All we do know is you were clinging to life when they found you, and there was no sign of J. They have boats and divers in the water looking for him, but they haven't found anything yet. We've all been walking down the sides of the canal looking for any signs of him, but we haven't found any tracks yet. But we aren't giving up D.J. I promise you we aren't giving up. We will stay out there as long as it takes," he squeezed my hand tightly.

The tears were streaming down my face again as I cleared my throat and asked, "Joshua, what happened here?"

"D.J. I swear that's all I know right now."

"No, I mean what happened for me to end up going home with Jeremiah. My mom said that I have been staying with him for the past few days. For that to happen, something really bad had to have happened," I reached over and squeezed his hand with both of mine.

He looked away, then gently wiped away my tears. "D.J., you're getting worked up, and they warned me not to get you overly excited."

"Joshua don't do that. Something happened! What happened?! Please tell me!" I pulled his arm hard enough to make him jerk forward, as the alarms began to go off.

He glanced over his shoulder as the door to my room slid open, "Calm down D.J. Why not just give it some time and let your memories come back on their own. The doctor feels like that would be better than us giving you all these details. You just need to rest for now, I promise we'll talk tomorrow," Joshua explained.

"Joshua please. I've got to know. I feel like part of me is missing."

"Sir, I think you should go now. She really needs to get some rest," Dr. England softly said.

Joshua raised his hand up to the doctor and nodded, then he let out a very light-hearted laugh. "Well D.J., part of you, is missing. You had two babies, so you've lost a lot of pressure."

"Uh uhh, don't do that Joshua. Don't patronize me. It's not that. I feel like my heart isn't beating right."

He dropped his head and then slowly looked up at me as he gripped my hand, "D.J. your heart did stop, more than once. Your body is just trying to begin the healing process. You've gone through a lot of trauma in a very short period of time."

"I'm telling you that's not it!" I turned away from him audibly crying again. I calmed down a little when I saw the nurse stand up and look into my room. "I'm sorry for yelling at you but this feeling, this feeling is something else I'm telling you."

He just dropped his head and let out a long sigh. "D.J. this is going to sound crazy, but you are actually giving me hope. You and my brother have as strong a connection as we do, if not stronger. I feel the same way. My heart's not broken, but it feels like it's offbeat too. That tells me Jeremiah is still alive. We've just got to find him," he squeezed my hand tighter. "My brother loved you more than I've ever seen him love anyone. The time he's spent with you has been the happiest I've ever seen him. So for now, we both just need to pray, while you get some much-needed rest so you can heal up, and I'm going to go back out there and help find my big brother."

I kissed the back of his hand and then pulled it into my cheek, "Joshua," I paused just a moment. "I love your brother more than I understand how, but I love him with everything in me. I don't remember how we got to this place, but I know something important has happened that you all aren't telling me about. I appreciate you trying to protect me, but you saw what happened in my kitchen and for me to leave the hospital with your brother, something major had to have happened after that." I realized there were tears welling up in his eyes and instantly knew I was on to something. "So what am I missing? What happened at the hospital that caused me to leave there with Jeremiah?"

It took a second for him to clear his throat and regain his composure before he could respond. And when he did, he stood up, and said, "Baby girl, I think we've talked enough for tonight. You really need to get some rest." Then he kissed me on the forehead, and he turned to leave.

"Joshua, don't do me like that! Please? Tell me!" alarms began going off again.

As he stood motionless at the door with his back to me, Amy slid open the door and said, "Sir, visiting hours are over, and she's got to calm down and get some rest now. You're more than welcome to return in the morning," patting his shoulder as she passed him.

Joshua never turned around to look at me, but he said over his shoulder,

"He really wanted to be here when the boys were born. He truly loves you, but you were also his chance for redemption," as he slowly left the room, closing the door behind him without looking back.

Alarms continued to go off as my tears began to flow down the sides of my face. "JOSHUA COME BACK! PLEASE COME BACK!" I screamed out. Before I realized it, Amy was injecting something into my IV, and I was out like a light.

I slowly opened my eyes to, "D.J., D.J., wake up." It was Dr. England with that damn light flashing it in my eyes again.

"Ya know, when you do that, my head explodes all over again," I slowly explained as I tried to adjust myself in the bed. My body hurt so badly when I went to move that tears immediately began running down my face, even though I never cried out in pain. My lips started quivering as I slowly moved my body up in the bed, as I kept pushing my PCA button. I dropped my head and let out a long sigh as I turned to look at Dr. England.

"You are an interesting case D.J. Morgan, I must say," he stood there looking down at me with his arms crossed over his chest.

"Yeah, how so doc?"

"I've never met someone so bound and determined to do everything I tell them NOT to do."

"What did I do this time?" I asked nonchalantly as I continued to try to get comfortable.

"Are you trying to tell me that you don't remember last night? Or are you just pulling my leg?" he asked with an anxious look on his face.

"For once I can honestly say, I have absolutely no idea what you're talking about doc," I said as I closed my eyes and let out a long breath. The pain was finally getting better. "You know, whoever created this PCA pump should receive a Nobel Prize if you ask me," I managed to give him a slight smile as I opened my eyes. The look on his face panicked me and alarms began to go off as my heart rate suddenly increased. "What! What's wrong?!" I asked in a near frenzy. Nurses were quickly moving around the bed shutting off alarms, and someone gave me a quick injection in my arm before I realized what was going on. I quickly relaxed, but I didn't fall asleep this time. I felt like I was floating around the room and all the voices seemed to be coming from a distance. I tried to focus on their conversations, but there was so much going on it took a moment to hone in on one voice, Dr. England's voice.

"D.J. tell me what's the last thing you remember from last night?" He said it so calmly that it was creepy.

"I remember asking to go see my babies and being told NO by everyone."

I paused for a minute expecting to get a reaction from everyone, but when I didn't, I got a cold shiver up my back and continued with what I could remember. "I, I remember my mom telling me that I was in a car accident and that I got pretty banged up, but I didn't hurt anybody else." A wave of panic came over me and I grabbed Dr. England's hand startling him. "I didn't hurt anybody, did I? Please tell me I didn't hurt anybody," as the tears began to race down my cheeks again as an alarm went off.

"Calm down. Calm down D.J. You didn't hurt anybody. I promise you. Now slowly, what else do you remember?" he said as he gently rubbed my head.

"Well....that's it. That's all I remember."

"I want a head CT STAT and get me the results of her last MRI immediately."

"What's wrong? Tell me....what's wrong?!" I demanded as multiple alarms began going off again. I tried to move my entire body again, but the immediate rush of pain stopped me in my tracks.

"D.J. I really need you to try to stay calm, but I also need you to try to focus and answer my questions, and with a little less sass if you can," he said with a smirk on his face.

I took a deep breath, "Okay. What is it you want to know?"

"Do you remember having any visitors last night?"

"Only my mom. They won't allow very many other people to come in here," I sighed.

"Any new memories of what led up to the accident or what you were doing before the accident?"

"No. Not a one. I've been trying, I promise you I've been trying," as a single tear slid down my face. "I really have been trying..." I closed my eyes and just laid there listening to the sounds around me.

"Dr. England, they're ready to do the CT when you are," the nurse interrupted our silent moment.

"Come on in," as he stepped aside for them to bring the machine into my room. "D.J., just hold still and this will only take a moment."

Just as he said, it only took a few minutes for them to get what they needed and leave. While Dr. England went out to study my scans, Dr. Ortiz came by to check on me and so did Dr. Cleveland. They were both happy with what they saw, but they weren't brain doctors either. They both joked about the screws and stitches holding me together, but when it came to my brain and getting my memories back, all they had to say on the subject was give it some time. Funny thing is, time was the one thing I didn't feel like I had.

While I laid there trying to remember what everyone else seemed to know, a new doctor came in to visit with me. She was the pediatric specialist from the NICU, Dr. Rozalyn Livingston.

"Dr. Livingston, please be honest with me. How are my boys doing?" as I struggled to move up in the bed.

"First, call me Dr. Roz or Mama Roz, everyone else around here does. And second, you have two strong boys. They are both fighters and doing much better now," she smiled as she patted my arm.

"Please have a seat. I've been trying to get down to visit them, but they won't let me come down and see them. Any chance they'll be able to come see me soon?"

She just looked at me for a moment then suddenly started laughing. "You're joking with me, right?"

I wasn't sure if she was asking me a question or not, so I quickly answered, "No, I'm not joking."

"After the scare you gave everyone last night, you're lucky they don't have you tied to that bed in four-point restraints." When I didn't respond, she realized something wasn't right and composed herself as she made eye contact with Dr. England coming through the door. The anxious look of surprise on her face was enough to tell me something happened that no one was bothering to tell me about.

"Okay, what gives? What happened last night?" I asked, obviously irritated.

"Well D.J., you snuck out of here last night. We figure you were trying to get to your babies, but they found you passed out in an elevator young lady," Dr. England explained.

"I what?!" causing my head to explode in pain. "Uuhhh!" I grabbed my head as I felt around for the button to the PCA pump. "I don't remember that!"

"And that's what has me worried. Your short-term memory seems to be affected, but only sporadically, which is highly unusual," he explained.

"So wait. You're trying to tell me I got past all those nurses out there, without being seen, with all these tubes attached to me and made it onto an elevator where I passed out?" It was so unbelievable I started laughing, which no one expected by their reactions, but their lack of reaction spoke volumes and stopped my laughter.

After a few minutes of very uncomfortable silence, "Yes, that's exactly what I'm telling you, except for the attached to all these tubes part. You pulled out your IVs, your foley, and ended up pulling out several of your stitches and even managed to pop a few staples young lady. The only thing you didn't tear up was that bionic ankle. Your screws and stitches are just fine there, but we put you in a hard cast just to be safe," he said with a slight sigh.

We all sat in silence as I went back and forth from each face in the room, expecting one of them to break out laughing at any moment, but the laughter never came. As the gravity of what I was being told began to weigh on me, the first tears started to well up in the corners of my eyes. My mom came over and held me in her arms as they explained to me what work they had to repair in surgery last night before the conversation about my babies finally got started.

Dr. Roz explained to me that the boys were both very septic and in distress when I came in, due in part to the infection that was going on and the other part to our hypothermia. They were both delivered via C-section although baby A had to be pulled back out of the birth canal first. So she warned me, "Don't be surprised at how long his head is. He was squished in that space for quite some time, so that is to be expected." She went on to explain that his umbilical cord had prolapsed, but luckily, they hadn't found him to have any cognitive defects as of yet, but they were still monitoring him very closely. She was surprised at how well he was doing after his umbilical cord had been compromised for so long, but the amazing thing about that was that his prolapsed cord is probably what saved both of their lives. Instead of pushing babies out into the cold water, I pushed the cord out, slowing down my labor.

I laid there crying in my mother's arms as she explained what medications they were being given and how much air they were on. Luckily, they were both breathing on their own even though they still had oxygen going in their incubators. Baby B had to have a minor procedure to repair a hernia, but he was doing fine. Apparently, he was a real pistol. He was definitely the ringleader the way she described him.

"D.J., do you have any questions for me?" she asked as she rubbed my arm.

I let out a cynical chuckle as I answered, "Why does it matter? I'm probably not going to remember this conversation come morning anyway."

No one expected that comment. You could tell by how quiet the room was even though several people were sitting and standing around, watching my every blink and flinch. You could also tell no one knew exactly what to say to me as long as it took for someone to say something.

"D.J. you can't think that way," my mom finally responded as she rubbed my head.

"I appreciate your honesty D.J., and since you brought that up I need to ask you, have you considered giving someone else power of attorney to make medical decisions, at least for the babies, until you're able to care for them and your memory comes back?" Dr. Roz asked.

I wasn't sure what to say to that, so I just sat there for a minute going over what she'd just asked me. "Well, I honestly hadn't thought about it," as I looked at all the faces staring back at me, obviously waiting for a response. "I don't really see the need for that right now but if I decide to do that, what do I need to do?"

"It's just a matter of filling out some forms is all. I can have someone bring them in for you to take a look at them if you'd like?" she replied.

"I guess taking a look at them couldn't hurt, but let me ask you this…. if something were to happen to me right now, who would have the right to make decisions on their behalf?"

"Legally, their next of kin would be. So, their father would be the legal guardian and decision maker at that point." As she looked around the room, "Matter of fact, if you don't mind me asking…where is their father? I don't remember meeting him," she asked.

"Yeah, I was wondering the same thing. Momma where's Selk? There's no way he hasn't heard about this already," I turned to look at her while keeping an eye on Dr. Cleveland and the others in my room. "What's going on? Why hasn't Selk been here yet? Or am I forgetting that too?" I said with a sound of sarcasm.

"Well, that's the other thing D.J.," my mom started slowly.

"Just tell me already!" I said louder than I meant to causing an alarm to go off with my elevated heart rate.

"Okay, stay calm. There's no need to yell," as she gave Dr. Cleveland a help me look.

"D.J., Selk was hurt in the game on Thursday night. He's in the hospital in Dallas, so he hasn't been able to get down here yet," Dr. Cleveland jumped in.

You could tell they were all waiting to see how I took the news, so I let them wait a little while before I responded. And a response it was. I bust out laughing, "OH! Is that all? I thought you were going to say he'd been here, and we were married now, and you were trying to figure out how to tell me," I continued to laugh. It was blatantly obvious no one else thought that was funny. Other than my laughter, the room was completely quiet.

"D.J.! I can't believe you!" my mother said.

I rolled my eyes, "MOTHERRR….PLEASE! I do remember you telling me I was getting married before we left my kitchen," I said with all the disgust I could muster, also making sure it was written all over my face. By the way she looked away, my shot had hit the target, and she was definitely embarrassed.

Finally, Dr. Roz giggled and said, "Well now that we've got that cleared up, take a look at these papers and let me know what you'd like to do," as she handed me the forms. "Also, there is the matter of names. Do you have anything snappier than Baby A and Baby B picked out for them?" she asked with a heartwarming smile.

"I actually do, but I'd really like to see them to make sure they feel right. If that's okay?" I quickly added, looking around the room.

She patted me on my arm, "Yes, yes, of course that's fine. When you're ready, your nurses have all the papers you'll need to fill out for their birth certificates and social security cards."

"Thank you for all your help Dr. Roz."

"You're more than welcome D.J." Her smile just made you feel safe. Like nothing could harm you. I could tell the boys were in great hands, but I still had this anxiousness about me that she immediately picked up on. "Is there something else D.J.?" she looked at me with a worried look on her face.

"There is, but it's nothing you can help me with."

"Try me," she smiled.

"I just feel like something is missing. I can't shake this feeling like a part of me is out of sync," I explained as I made a circling motion over my chest, then simple exhaled and gently patted my heart. No one said a word. They all just sat there watching me and quickly shot each other looks as if asking one another what they should do.

"Well for now just get some rest D.J. That's all you need to worry about right now," my dad said.

I jumped when he spoke. I don't know why, but he startled me with his words and the simple fact that he opened his mouth at all. My father finally had something to say. And shockingly enough, he was actually comforting. I tried to hide the surprised look on my face, but I failed miserably. I finally smiled at him and gave him a slight nod as I tried to get comfortable in my bed.

It didn't take long for the nurses to run everyone out of my room, which I didn't mind. I was more tired than I could ever remember being. I dozed off pretty quickly that evening, but in the middle of the night, I woke up in a panic, screaming to high heaven.

"HELP ME! HELP ME! JEREMIAH....PLEASE HELP ME!" I cried. With a sudden rush, I had multiple nurses at my bedside and every alarm that could go off was going off. I was engulfed in tears, and my pillow and gown were soaking wet from my weeping. It was obvious that I'd been crying for a while in my sleep.

"D.J., you're okay. You're okay," my nurse Minnie explained as she rubbed my head and rested her arm across my chest, as much to comfort me as to hold me down.

I looked up at her all wide-eyed and slowly calmed down as she hushed me. When I realized where I was, I let out a deep gasp and collapsed in her arms crying.

"Call Dr. England stat," she called out over her shoulder as she allowed me to cling to her sobbing uncontrollably.

Through a steady stream of tears, I kept mumbling, "He disappeared under the water. He disappeared under the water…."

I had settled down by the time Dr. Cleveland and my mom arrived a little after midnight, but amazingly, I was still crying and whimpering as I clung to my pillow, rocking, and mumbling.

"D.J. baby are you okay?" my mom softly asked as she moved my hair out of my face.

"NO, I'm not okay! He went under the water and didn't come back up! He left me! He left me…" as I began to cry harder again.

"Who left you D.J.?" Dr. Cleveland asked.

"Jeremiah," I said into the pillow. "He was there and then he wasn't," I sobbed.

Dr. England silenced the alarms and took a position right over the head of my bed. As always he flashed that light into my eyes then calmly said, "D.J., first, I need you to calm down. Take a few slow deep breaths with me." Once my heart rate had come down and I was breathing more regular, he continued, "Now, tell us what you can remember."

I startled them all when I suddenly jerked forward with wild eyes, "Where is Jeremiah?!"

"Well, we're not sure. They haven't found him yet…." a voice called out from the corner. It was Lieutenant Keith. I don't know when he got here or how long he'd been sitting there, but the look on his face sent me into a full-blown panic attack causing all the alarms to go off simultaneously.

"But they haven't given up looking," my mom quickly added as they tried to calm me down again.

"D.J. can you tell me what you remember? What happened to you that night?" Lt. Keith asked as he moved closer to my bed, taking my hand.

"What are you doing here? Please tell me where Jeremiah is? Why isn't he here?" I rattled off through my tears as an alarm began to sound off again.

"She really needs to calm down. I don't think it's a good time to do this," Dr. England said as he silenced the alarm.

As defiant as ever, I wiped the tears from my eyes, took a deep breath and asked, "Where do you want me to start?" For the first time in a long time, I was being humbly sincere. There wasn't an ounce of smartass in my tone or disposition.

"If I might interject, D.J. start with the night of the accident," Lt. Keith said. Looking at each person in the room like he was in charge now.

"Okay. I can do that," as I wiped the remaining tears from my face and slowly pulled myself up higher in the bed. I took a deep breath and just like that, I began to tell them what happened that night as more and more of my memories came flooding back. "And the next thing I remember is being shoved in the back of the ambulance and coming here," I finally finished.

For a few moments the room was completely silent. No one asked any questions, and everyone just stood there with this look of horror and disbelief on their faces. Lt. Keith would furiously scribble something in his notebook, then give me this look of surprise for a moment, then go back to scribbling again. Everyone else just stood there watching my every move.

"Now D.J., the man with the gold teeth. Do you think you can describe him if I get someone in here to draw his picture?"

"Yes, I think so. I don't know how good it will be, it was very dark, and it was still raining, but I'll do my best."

"How many voices do you remember hearing?" But before I had a chance to respond, "I mean before you woke up on top of the car?"

"They were kinda in the distant, but there were at least 3, maybe 4. I'm not sure it was hard to tell," I shook my head out of frustration. "And nobody else saw them?"

"No. And after all the people moving around on what was left of that bank, we really couldn't tell who had been where or what exactly happened that night."

An alarm went off again, and Dr. England decided it was time to let me get some rest.

As he closed his notebook, Lt. Keith said, "That's fine doc. I think I have enough for tonight," sliding his notebook into his coat pocket. He gently took my hand and squeezed it as he smiled down at me and said, "You did good young lady. I'll bring that sketch artist by later in the day if you're up to it."

"Yes. That's fine. Whatever it takes to get some answers and to find him. Whatever it takes," I managed a slight smile as we continued to squeeze hands.

Before Lt. Keith left for the night, he advised us that he was putting an armed guard outside my room and the NICU, just to be safe. Needless to say, every alarm that could go off in my room went off. Dr. England insisted that everyone leave so that I could get some rest. Of course my mom wanted to stay just like she'd been doing since I woke up in the ICU, but I insisted that she leave. With all the memories came all the emotions along with them. And as much as I wanted and needed her with me when I couldn't remember, it hurt me even more, to have her hovering like she cared so much about my well-being now that I could remember all she'd put me through and all she hadn't said over the last few days in the hospital. She was still protecting Selk no matter how you looked at it. I appreciated all she'd done, but it was time for her to go.

"Congratulations young lady, you've got your memories back," Dr. Cleveland winked at me as he turned to leave the room.

"Dr. Cleveland, can I ask you a quick question before you go?"

He let out a light-hearted laugh, "Well D.J., I wouldn't expect anything less of you. I'll try my best to give you a good answer," he smiled.

"Is there any chance I can go see my babies?" I asked as tears began to well up in the corners of my eyes again.

He simply smiled and said, "Give me a few minutes. I think I can help you out with that."

A few hours later, my nurse had me and all my tubes in a wheelchair, on the way down to the NICU. I held my breath the entire time they helped me scrub my hands and put the isolation gown on. I was so nervous I could barely keep still, but I managed not to jump out of the wheelchair when they pushed me up alongside them. As dark as it was in the room, I could still tell that they were both in the same incubator, side by side.

Out of nowhere, a very familiar voice said, "I'd like to introduce you to Baby A and Baby B, the Morgan twins." Dr. Roz stepped over to the incubator and held her hand out like one of the models on The Price is Right, standing there with a Chester Cheese smile on her face. "I heard through the grapevine you were headed this way, and I knew I couldn't miss this moment," she continued to smile.

I scooted closer to the edge of my seat until my nose finally made contact with the glass, "They are the most beautiful babies I've ever seen before," I glanced up at her with huge tears in my eyes for only a moment.

"Here, you can reach through these little portals to touch them if you like."

"If I like..." it wasn't really a question, "Of course I want to touch them, to hold them," I sniffled. "Can I hold them? Please tell me I can hold them?" I glanced up again.

Dr. Roz smiled down at me, "I thought you'd never ask," as she removed Baby A from the incubator as she explained what each tube and cord attached to him was for. When she finished explaining how they were doing, she finished up with, "They are definitely fighters. And, they're progressing faster than any of us could have imagined."

No sooner than I had snuggled up to Baby A, Baby B threw a screaming fit.

"And right on cue, Mr. Morgan B shows us just how good his lungs are," Lisa laughs. She's the boys NICU nurse.

"Is this why they're in the same incubator?" I asked, watching her every move as she removed Baby B from the incubator. "Here give him to me too," as I carefully shifted A to one side making room for B.

"You did that like you're a pro," Dr. Roz said as she helped me move a couple of cords out of the way. "And to answer your question, YES. This is his reaction whenever he is away from his brother, or he feels like he's not receiving enough attention. This one here is definitely your fireball. He lets you know immediately when something is wrong with him or his brother...,"

"Or when he's just not happy," Lisa said, cutting her off.

As soon as I had him secure in my arms, I leaned down and said, "Hush little boy. I'm here now, and I'm not putting up with these shenanigans. Understand me?" And like that he quieted down, even though his little lip continued to poke out just a bit.

"Well I see you've got everything under control here," Lisa said as she and Dr. Roz began to laugh. We will give you 3 some privacy. If you need anything, just call out and someone will be right over," she smiled as she gently tapped me on the shoulder.

"Okay, thanks. And thank you for looking after my boys," I smiled up with happy tears forming in the corners of my eyes.

"It's our pleasure," Dr. Roz said as they walked away.

For the next hour, I sat there falling in love with my sons.

CHAPTER 22

I t had been a long time coming, but early Tuesday morning I was moved to a regular room on the postpartum floor. As happy as I was to be out of the ICU it was still bittersweet because I could hear the faint cries of babies when my door was open, and knowing that some mommy down the hall was enjoying her baby, but I wouldn't get to experience that bonding time with my babies, not in the same way. Before they had a chance to really get me settled in, I was already bugging my nurse about going to the NICU.

"D.J. give your nurse a break already," Dr. Cleveland laughed as he stepped in my room.

"What? I'm just trying to get to my boys. She should be happy to get rid of me for a little while," I smiled innocently.

"D.J., you just got here. How about you get settled in and get some rest first. You are still recovering young lady," he smiled as he looked at my incision. "Healing nicely, I must say. Even though you tried to undo my fine stitch and staple work," he gave me a wayward look.

"Yeah, about that," I smiled.

"Stop right their young lady," he put his hand up. "I really wouldn't have expected any less from you to be honest. I'm actually surprised it took you so long," he smiled. All I could do is drop my head a blush. He was so right, there was no denying it. He pulled up a chair, "We need to talk."

I was a little startled by his tone, but I pulled myself up higher in the bed, "Okay, what's on your mind?" I asked like I was the one running the show.

"D.J., we need to discuss what's going to happen when I send you home."

"What? You're getting ready to send me home? When?" I was excited and worried all at the same time. "What about the boys? Are they coming with me?"

"Slow down, slow down. D.J. you can't go home yet, and you sure can't go home alone. Not with that broken ankle and all your fractures. We need to start coming up with a plan that me, Dr. Ortiz, and Dr. Roz are all happy with," he explained.

"Well, Dr. Ortiz should be happy with the house since there aren't any steps except for the front porch and as for you and Dr. Roz, what do I need to do to convince you both that I'm able to take care of me and my babies?"

"Honestly, we haven't discussed it, but I feel like I can speak for her when I say that we both would be more comfortable if you didn't go home alone." I didn't respond as I thought about what he was saying. "D.J. I know you and your mom have your issues but what's the chance of you burying the hatchet long enough for you to at least get to a walking boot and off the crutches?"

He was obviously waiting for me to respond, but I still didn't have anything to say. We sat in silence until the door creaked open. "Oh, Dr. Cleveland. I didn't realize you were still here. D.J. just give me a call when you're done," as she backed out of the room. It was the lady who files the birth certificate paperwork.

"Dr. Cleveland, I hear you, but I can't honestly tell you that right now. With all that's happened over the past several months, even now she's still trying to push me and Selk together," I shook my head.

"D.J., I understand, but she loves you, and you're going to need a lot of help with two babies to take care of."

"I get that, but I can't give up on Jeremiah. I feel it in my heart he's still alive and I want to be at 'our' home when he comes back to me. I doubt very seriously she'd be willing to come stay there with me and not bring her sarcasm with her. And I know for a fact Jeremiah would only let her come stay IF she swore on her life that she wouldn't bring up or invite Selk over. After all he's done, we have already agreed that he's not allowed anywhere close to me or the boys without Jeremiah or someone of authority around. And my mother isn't to be trusted when it comes to Selk. She's proven that time and time again," I explained without tearing up for the first time ever.

Dr. Cleveland stood up and patted my good foot as he gave me a gentle smile, "D.J., I totally agree with you and Jeremiah, but as sad as it is, I need you to think about what you're going to do if Jeremiah isn't back when you are ready to go home." He walked over to the door and turned back for just a second, "D.J. I know it's not going to be easy, but I really think your mom is going to be your best bet. Just think about it is all I'm saying."

I laid my head back and looked out the window, "yeah, I'll think about it," I said just as the door closed behind him.

I laid there in my room, listening to the occasional baby cry and watching the shadows dance across the wall. As much as I hated depending on other people, I knew that Dr. Cleveland was right. I was going to need some help. And that fact really was driven home when I tried to go to the bathroom on my own. It was bad enough to have my foot in a cast, but unfortunately for me, it was the opposite leg that was fractured, so I had a cast on my other leg as well. Basically, no matter which leg I tried to put pressure on, the end result was the same...me lying in the floor calling out for help.

As they helped me off the floor and back into bed, all I could do is apologize profusely. Once I was comfortable, I explained to them what I was trying to do and how I couldn't believe I made it past the nurses' station and all the way onto an elevator, but I now understand why I passed out. Dr. Cleveland just stood there shaking his head in disapproval as he listened to my explanation while he checked my suture line. You could tell he wasn't impressed with my lame attempt at a joke. Once he was done, Sydney and the nursing assistant began to help me into the wheelchair so that I could go to the bathroom, but just as we got me situated in the wheelchair, Dr. Ortiz and Dr. England burst into my room giving orders.

"As soon as you get her back to bed order a head CT," Dr. England said as he flashed his little light in my eyes as Sydney turned me towards the bathroom door.

"And get another x-ray of both her legs and her torso as well," Dr. Ortiz followed up. "And don't put any more pressure on her legs."

"Where are you going? The bed is that away," Dr. England pointed.

"Well I was on my way to the bathroom when everything went to hell," I said looking at the two of them as Dr. Cleveland stood to the side, silently leaning on the wall with his arms crossed.

"Matter of fact we may need to consider putting her on the bedpan for a while," Dr. Cleveland chimed in with a silly grin on his face.

I gave them all a concerning look as we entered the bathroom, closing the door behind us. "I can't believe he's serious with that bedpan crack," I said to Sydney.

"I think that might be a good idea for a few days," she smiled.

"What?" I looked up at her in disbelief.

"There's a lot we need to consider D.J. We want you to be safe as well as keeping us safe," she added. "Just pull the cord when you're ready." I just nodded in agreement. "And D.J...please don't try to get back in your wheelchair by yourself," she winked as they left me to handle my business.

Shortly after I returned to bed, my room was full of x-ray equipment, and soon after that, I was whisked away for a CT scan. On the way back, I asked to stop by the NICU, and reluctantly the tech took me there instead of my room.

I got washed up by myself and only needed help getting the gown off the shelf so I could go in with the boys. Once the nurse gave me an update on how they were doing, she asked me if I wanted to help feed them since it was nearly their mealtime. I got so excited that I almost came out of my wheelchair when she asked me that.

We decided that it was best for me to stay in the wheelchair for now and simply propped a couple of pillows at my back and under my arm with the IV as the nurse handed me Baby B and a bottle of formula. I read the label and thanked her for bringing me soymilk for them. "But how did you know that I would prefer soymilk for them? I planned to breastfeed," as I watched him suck down a 2-ounce bottle without taking a breath. "Oh my God! He's starving!" I looked up at Jackie as I pulled the empty bottle from his mouth.

She just laughed and said, "No, he's not starving." I just sat there shaking my head in disbelief. "Go ahead and burp him," as she prepared another bottle. "They kept spitting up with the regular formula, so we put them on the soy which seemed to do the trick."

I did as I was instructed thinking that she was getting the bottle ready for Baby A. It didn't take but a few firm pats on his back for him to let out a belch that would make an old man blush. She started laughing at the surprised look on my face. "What's wrong? Never heard a baby burp like a grown man before?"

"No. No, I haven't," as he began to scream bloody murder. I put him back on my shoulder and began to rock him and pat his back again. "Shhhh, shhhhh. You're just fine. You're just fine."

"Yeah, you're wasting your time doing that," as she handed me the next bottle. "Here, he's ready for round 2. He drinks two bottles every 2 hours on the dot, so no he's not starving."

"WOW! Does his brother eat like that too?"

"No, not at all. We can barely get him to take one whole bottle, and he definitely takes his time drinking that, but I guarantee that one," she laughed as she pointed at the baby I was watching, inhale his second bottle, "He is going to eat you out of house and home."

I was burping him for the second time when my nurse tapped on the glass with a not so happy look on her face. I tried to smile at her as she waved me out of the room. I tried to ignore her after that, but the boy's nurse came back in the room and cleared her throat as she took the baby out of my arms.

"He hasn't burped again," I explained as I reached for him back.

"I'll take care of it. You didn't tell me that your nurse didn't know you were down here." She gave me a disappointing look as she finished burping Baby B.

Before she had a chance to react, I had reached into the isolate and taken Baby A out of it.

"D.J., what do you think you're doing?" she asked as she reached for my wrist.

"I'm going to change and feed my other child," I responded matter-of-factly.

"Young lady, it's time for you to go back upstairs so that your nurse can take care of you," she responded as the door opened.

My nurse had grown impatient and had gowned up to come in and get me. As she began to chastise me, Baby A began to cry uncontrollably. I ignored her as I thought to myself, '*Just as I suspected...he's my soft-hearted child. My child that doesn't care for conflict, especially when it comes to his momma.*' They allowed me to quiet him down before I was rushed out of the room like I was going into witness protection or something.

On the way back to my room I received an ear full from Sydney. She'd been waiting to give me my meds and pain meds which I truly needed. The pain meds I received after my floor experience had long since worn off, but I knew if I had complained, they would have cut my visit with the boys short. Not that it wasn't cut short when she finally figured out where I was, but at least I got to spend more time with them and get to experience for myself how they acted and responded to their environment.

Once I was back in bed with all the tubes reconnected, I commenced to filling out the birth certificate information for each of the boys. Funny thing is, "the boys" is how they would come to be referred to most of the time. The top of the page for each set of forms was marked with Baby A or Baby B to ensure that there would be no confusion as to which forms went with which baby. When I was done filling the papers out, I called the number on the top to let the records clerk know that I had finished. A few minutes later, a young lady came in to go over the forms with me.

"Hello Ms. Morgan. I'm Shirley and I'll be taking care of the forms you've filled out for your babies."

"Hi Shirley. Sorry it took so long to get these done," as I pushed the papers in her direction.

"You're fine. As long as they're done before the babies are discharged, we don't have a problem," as she looked over the papers. I could tell she was taken back by their names when she looked up at me after reading the name lines on each set of forms. I quietly waited for the inevitable questions that were coming my way.

"Uhm, I don't usually question the names parents pick out but...." as she looked at me with a completely confused look on her face.

"Yes," I said with a smirk on my face.

"Well, there are only initials on here for their names. Wouldn't you prefer to give them a real name and then just call them by the initials?"

"Those are 'real' names. Did you happen to notice their mother's name? And I guarantee you my name is very real," I paused, but before she could say anything else, I continued. "So are their uncle's names, J.R., L.J., M.J., and P.J.," I said matter-of-factly.

She cleared her throat, "Please forgive me if I offended you. I see a lot of names come across my desk so when I see something that is extremely different or possibly offensive I try to help the parents select something less controversial, but I see this is a family tradition, so I do apologize for upsetting you." You could tell she was being sincere, which made me soften my tone and body language.

"I didn't mean to be so rough on you. I've had to listen to people questioning my name my entire life so I shouldn't have reacted that way to your question. Please charge it to my head and not my heart," as I reached out and patted the back of her hand.

She smiled at me as she squeezed my hand in response. "So Baby A will be JT and Baby B will be EJ. Now, will there be a period after each initial or not?" as she scanned the papers again.

"There's a period after each initial," as I tried to see what I'd put on the papers.

"I'll make the periods a little darker so that there won't be any questions," as she made the periods much darker. "J.T. and E.J.. Now, the only other issue I see is their last names. Since your last name is Morgan and you are giving them their father's last name, he will have to sign an affidavit that he is okay with them having his last name and that he is confirming that he is okay with being the father of record on the birth certificates."

"He will if that's necessary, but I'm just not sure if he will be here anytime soon though...he's in the hospital himself, I think."

"Oh, well that is a problem. Well, we have until the babies are being discharged to get this paperwork submitted," she explained in a reassuring tone.

"I don't know if it matters, but their dad has already signed a bunch of paperwork saying that he is legally taking responsibility for all of our doctors' bills and hospital care. The papers acknowledge the fact that he believes that he is the father of my boys. It's all in my medical records if you need to see them."

"Oh! Well if that's the case, I'll take a look at your records, and if everything you're telling me is there, I can attach that to this paperwork, and there shouldn't be a problem with them having Black as their last name," she smiled. "Wait," as she looked over the forms again, "Selkie Black, the all-pro linebacker is their father?"

I laid my head back and stared at the ceiling for a moment before I responded. I let out a long breath, "Yes, Selkie is their biological father," as I looked at her again with an obviously sad look on my face. Then quickly added, "Can we leave the present name cards on their crib until I let everyone know what their names are going to be?" I frantically asked. I knew there was going to be hell to pay when it got out what I had named them, and I was secretly hoping that Jeremiah would be back in time for the fireworks so that I didn't have to weather that storm alone.

"Why that look? You should be the happiest woman on the planet right now. Selkie Black...half of Texas is in love with him," she explained trying to contain her excitement. "My husband is going to die when I tell him I almost got to meet Selkie Black," she smiled, but just as quickly, she began to shake her head with a sad face. "It's a damn shame he tore up his knee during that Thanksgiving game...on a busted play no less."

"Yeah, I should be," I frowned blinking away my tears. Then it hit me what she'd just said, "What do you mean a busted play? What happened exactly?" I asked as I pulled myself up in the bed.

"Well, he was on the sidelines when someone, the announcers identified as his younger brother, called him over to the side and whispered something in his ear. You would have thought their mother died by the look on his face," she explained.

"Go on..." I said, anxiously waiting on her to continue.

"His brother handed him a phone. He actually took a call on the sidelines," she shook her head again, "And while his head was turned the play suddenly came to his sidelines and wiped him out. He wasn't paying the least bit attention to the field. Who does that? Especially that close on the sidelines," she asked, but I didn't have an answer for her.

I instantly knew deep down that he had something to do with our accident. I was shocked at what I was hearing as tears started streaming down my face before I realized I was even crying. I vaguely remember Sydney at my bedside calling my name, but it sounded like she was far away, in a tunnel of sorts. I finally came out of it when Dr. England clapped his hands together again for the umpteenth time, bringing me out of my trance.

"D.J., D.J., come back to me!" as he slapped his hands together. I shook my head and simply stared at him for a moment. "D.J., can you understand me," he asked?

"I need to talk to Lt. Keith. I know he had something to do with it. I'm telling you, he had something to do with this!" I gripped his arm as I began crying hysterically, "Selk had something to do with this!" The next thing I knew, I was out like a light.

I woke up to a very familiar smell that sent me into a tailspin. I was a little groggy, but from the aroma, I just knew everything was going to be better from here on out. As I regained my bearings, I realized that I was in a different hospital room, but that didn't matter because I could smell Triple J barbecue. I rubbed my eyes to help get them to focus better as I came too, calling out to Jeremiah.

"Jeremiah, you're back," I smiled as I could finally focus in on the person sitting at my bedside. To my sadness, it wasn't Jeremiah at all, it was Mama J. "Well, isn't this a wonderful surprise," I reached for her hand as I noticed Lt. Keith and Joshua huddled up in the corner.

"Hi baby. I been want'na to come see you and the babies, so when I heard that one over there whispering on the phone about ya, I insisted on tag'n along," she motioned toward Joshua.

I tried to put on a straight face and straighten myself up in the bed so that she didn't worry because I knew they hadn't told her why they were really here. "That's fine. I'm glad you gotta come," I gave them a slight smile. Joshua just hunched his shoulders and raised his hands as if saying, *'What was I supposed to do? You know how she gets.'* As he cleared his throat and made his way to my bedside.

"Hey little sister, how are you feeling today?" as he leaned down to give me a hug.

"I could be better, but I'm not complaining," as he fluffed my pillow. "Anything new to report," I asked, looking at him and Lt. Keith.

"Sorry to say, no. We haven't seen any sign of him yet," Lt. Keith responded. I took a deep breath and stared at the ceiling for a moment. "But D.J., we haven't given up. Okay, we haven't given up," he added, stepping closer to my bed.

I sat there smoothing out the covers for a second trying to regain my composure. It's incredible how much energy I was using trying not to cry on a daily basis. Mama J continued to hold my hand as Joshua began to explain why they were all here. "After what happened yesterday, I wanted to be here when you talked to Lt. Keith again. Like he said, we aren't giving up, but we're running out of leads D.J.." he paused for a second. "And it's not looking good," as he dropped his head.

I reached for his hand and squeezed it as I begged him and everyone else in the room, "Please don't stop looking for him. I know in my heart he's still alive. Joshua, he's out there." Looking around the room in a near panic, "He's out there I'm telling you!"

"Calm down D.J., or they're gonna kick us out of here," Joshua patted me on the shoulder as he looked towards the door.

I took a few deep breaths and said, "You're right," lowering my head, slowly shaking it from side to side. "It feels like I'm going to explode every other minute these days. I've got so much emotion churning away inside of me that sometimes it just overwhelms me." I grabbed his hand again as I squeezed Mama J's as well, "I'm going to get it together," looking between the two of them. "Besides, this isn't a time for tears with that fantastic smelling barbecue over there," I finally smiled.

"So D.J., what was the big emergency?" Lt. Keith asked as he pulled out his notepad.

I wasn't expecting that as I watched his every move, "Well, the registration nurse was helping me fill out the twins' birth certificate information and began to explain to me exactly what happened to Selk at the game, and it hit me like a ton of bricks," I explained.

"Go on," Lt. Keith said.

"Don't you see," reaching out towards him, "He had to have had something to do with what happened to Jeremiah and me," I continued looking between him and Joshua.

The room got quiet as they all just sat there watching me without saying a word until finally Lt. Keith asked, "Well what makes you think that?" as he leaned forward in his chair motioning towards me, balancing on his crossed legs.

I explained to them how she explained to me that he got hurt after taking a phone call on the sidelines and that there was no way on God's green earth that Selk would ever take a call during a game unless it was something urgent, life-altering in fact. Even if I had gone into labor during a game, I was to call the team doctor and leave a message with him. So, the only reason he would ever take a call on the sidelines is that someone was calling him to let him know that me and the babies were still alive. The room was dead silent again, but the looks on all of their faces spoke volumes without them ever saying a word. I knew I had their complete attention and total curiosity up.

Finally, Joshua broke the silence, "But D.J., just because he took a call doesn't mean he had anything to do with your accident."

"Joshua, you know how upset he was and how he threatened me and your brother," I explained.

Joshua's face turned to stone as Lt. Keith jumped to his feet and said,

---

"What are you talking about?" But before either of us had a chance to respond, he asked Joshua, "What is she talking about?" staring at him as he pointed at me. We both hesitated for a second as Lt. Keith continued to shake his pen at us.

Joshua just stood there shaking his head and finally looked down at me and said, "D.J., that can't have anything to do with the other. That all happened days before you went into labor."

"I know Joshua, but you know how angry he was, and I know Jeremiah told you what he did to the puzzle box and diary he gave me. He and Jeremiah had that huge argument only a few days before the accident when you put all the cameras up, and then that shoving match on Monday before the accident. And we both know he was in a rage both times. Joshua, he point blank told us that there was no way he'd ever allow Jeremiah to raise his boys and that he'd see us both in hell before he ever let that happen!" I said a little louder than I probably should have.

Lt. Keith jumped in, "What are you saying, Selk threatened you and Jeremiah after you left the hospital?" grabbing on to Joshua's arm. "You never told me any of this! What is she talking about?! What argument?! What fight?! What did he do to you?!" he said in a flurry of emotion.

"D.J...." Joshua hesitated as he began to pace the room. "I never put it together. That argument was what, a week before your accident? And they just did a lot of pushing and shoving at your mom's place, but..." He stopped pacing to look at me for only a second, "Surely he was just blowing off steam," as he shook his head, staring at the look of horror on his mother's face, rushing to her side. "Hey, he didn't mean anything with all of that. It was all in the moment," as he pulled his mother in close. "Ma, maybe you should go wait in the waiting room while we finish up here. You don't need to hear any more about this," as he tried to help her up out of the chair.

She slapped his hands away, "Nonsense boy. If this has anything to do with my baby and why he's not here with us today, I wanna hear it for myself." By the look on her face and the way she slowly turned to look at each one of us, we all knew that she wasn't going anywhere.

"Joshua, was it all in the moment when he choked me in the hospital, then went back to my apartment and destroyed the puzzle box and diary your brother gave me," as I pointed at him. "Was it all in the moment when he crushed the box into small pieces and burned it and my diary?" I asked him. "Was it in the moment when he threatened our lives and your brother had you help him install 10, not 1 but 10 cameras around our property the very next day?" I pleaded with him. As he stood there with a horrified look on his face as I continued before he had a chance to verbally respond.

"Joshua, that man set a fire, inside my apartment. And I don't have a fireplace anywhere in there. You know that."

Everyone just sat there with their mouths hanging open. Joshua snapped out of it and quickly explained, "Jeremiah never told me all of that. He told me that Selk had trashed his gifts, but he never told me to that extreme."

"He didn't want to worry you!"

"Wait a minute! Are you telling me this man carried out another attack on you AFTER he attacked you in the hospital the first time, and then they actually had a physical confrontation?" Lt. Keith asked nearly crawling up in the bed with me.

"He didn't attack our person, per se, his agent did send me flowers with notes apologizing for what Selk had done, while also blaming me for it. And then when we went back to my apartment to gather up my things, we figured out that he'd found the things Jeremiah had given me and destroyed them. And that was the point of no return for me. I placed them in the windowsill and took my engagement ring off and placed it on top of them and we left," I explained. "And we haven't been back since."

"So Selk could have seen the ring you left behind?" Lt. Keith said as he began pacing and tapping his mouth with his pen. He suddenly stopped and began to furiously scribble in his notebook, then quickly turning to look directly at me. "Okay, D.J. Let's walk through this again. When did you get the notes and when did he burn your stuff?"

"Well, the cards came late Friday night and my things were burnt up when we got there from the hospital, so it had to be that Friday before he flew back up to Dallas," I explained to him.

"Okay, so what is this you're talking about, him threatening you and Jeremiah?" Lt. Keith asked as he looked back and forth between Joshua and me.

"That was a week later. Apparently, I was still asleep when he called on Friday morning after he'd gone to my doctor's appointment, only to find out that I had been there the day before, with Jeremiah and without him," as I looked away for a moment. "Without telling him about the change," I added. "So he called my cell phone and Jeremiah answered it. They got into a very heated argument. After that," I glanced over at Joshua, "Jeremiah called Joshua, and they commenced to setting up cameras all around the house and property."

Joshua just stood there with his mouth hanging open, barely breathing. He was just shaking his head like he didn't understand what all I was saying. He reached out like he wanted me to stop. "Wait a minute, wait one minute," as he kept shaking his head back and forth like he was trying to clear his mind, "I never dreamed that that had anything to do with this," as he began pacing the room again. We all remained quiet as he began mumbling to himself, finally stopping at the foot of my bed and continuing, "D.J., what he didn't tell you about that conversation, is that he threatened Selk," he said as his eyes welled with tears and a look of fear engulfed his face.

"He what?!" I sat straight up in the bed.

"What did you just say?" Lt. Keith grabbed Joshua's arm a whirled him around to face him.

"What do you mean he threatened Selk?!" I yelled.

Jeremiah slowly wrapped his arms across his chest and let out a long sigh before he began to explain as he slowly turned to face me. He held out his hand as he began to explain, "Selk told Jeremiah that he'd meet you both in hell before he ever allowed Jeremiah to have anything to do with raising his boys. And that he knew exactly where you all were and what your routine was, so if Jeremiah wanted to continue to breathe, he needed to back up, and send you back to where you belonged. Jeremiah told me, that he told Selk, that if he caught a glimpse of him anywhere close to you or the boys, walking down the street, sitting at a light, or anywhere close to the house, he'd shoot first and ask questions later." The tears were running down my face uncontrollably as Joshua came and took my hand, "D.J. he told him that he was an expert marksman and had the entire HPD at his back so no one would ever question his actions in a court of law."

I snatched away from him as I held my own head as I shook it from side to side, "No! NO! He wouldn't do that. He's too controlled for that," I pointed my finger at Joshua. "He's too controlled to let Selk take him there," as I continued to shake my head while trying to wipe the tears away. "Even when they argued at my mom's house, Jeremiah never said anything like that." I disappeared into my own thoughts, mumbling to myself. If it hadn't been for Mama J squeezing my hand and pulling at my arm, I don't know how long I would have been out of it, but I snapped back to alarms going off and Joshua and Lt. Keith arguing in the corner. Dr. England was standing over me with that damn penlight again flashing it into my eyes as the nurse tried to silence the alarms going off.

"D.J., D.J. are you alright," I finally heard him ask as he continued flashing the light in my eyes.

I pushed his hand away, as I jerked my head away from him, "I'm fine. I'm just fine."

"You all are going to have to leave now. You're upsetting her too much, and she's still in a very fragile state," Dr. England explained as he waved them all towards the door.

I threw my hand up, "But wait! Wait, wait, wait!" I yelled as the room went silent. "Joshua," I sniffled, "Why didn't you tell me any of this?" I reached for him. "Why didn't *he* tell me that?" as I dropped my hand and laid my head back, slowly shaking it from side to side as the tears streamed down my face again. "Nobody threatens Selk. That's not the kind of guy he is," I said barely above a whisper. I jerked forward startling everyone in the room, "It's one thing for me to leave, but it's another thing for your brother to threaten Selk with bodily harm." I reached around Mama J and grabbed his arm, "Joshua, what did he do?! What did he do?! Selk would never take that lying down!" as I let go without a struggle. My body began to go limp as I started crying hysterically, "This is all my fault! This is all my fault!" as I began to drum on my chest, crying.

Mama J stood up and scooped me up in her arm, "Baby calm down! Please calm down. This ain't none of yo fault, and none of us blame you," she rubbed my head as she rocked me from side to side. "This ain't none of yo fault. My child knew exactly what he was doing. There ain't no way he would'a ever let somebody hurt you or them babies. Just calm down D.J., baby just calm down." As Dr. England had the nurse give me something in my IV.

I started fading out as I squeezed Mama J's hand and whispered, "He did it," looking up at her. "He did it. I'm telling you. Selk tried to kill us. He did it," as I drifted off to sleep with tears rolling down my cheeks.

CHAPTER 23

"**W**ake up D.J.! Wake up!" as little arms wrapped around my neck, squeezing tightly.

It took a moment for me to focus and my mouth was really dry, but I knew that voice anywhere. As I cleared my throat again, I finally managed to say, "P.J., not so tight, okay," as I patted his arm, "I'm awake little man. I'm awake," as he loosened his grip from around my neck. He was so excited he could barely sit still. "So what brings you here today?" I asked as I pulled myself up higher in the bed and then let the head up.

"I just saw my nephews! They know who I am Sissy! They both squeezed my fingers," he smiled.

"Is that right?" I smiled at him as I finally noticed that all of my brothers were scattered about my room today. They'd been to visit many times but never all at one time.

"Yeah sis, we all got to go in and meet them today. They let us go in a special room one at a time with momma, and we got to touch them," M.J. explained with a huge smile on his face.

"They squeezed our fingers as we talked to them sis. It's like they know who we are already," L.J. added.

I smiled at them and kinda giggled, as I said, "Oh really. So you're telling me they know which voice goes to what peanut head uncle already?" I asked.

"Hay! That's not funny," J.R. said as he hung up his phone. "Now look here sis. I didn't drive all the way back down to Houston to be insulted," he continued. "I could be on campus working on a project I've got to get in before the semester ends.

"That's like what? A week away," I gave him a sideways grin, shaking my head.

"Yeah something like that," he shrugged me off.

"Well, I'm glad they finally let you in to see them. They are almost 2 weeks old now."

"But sissy. They are 2 weeks old," P.J. insisted. I gave him a slight frown

296

as he continued, "They are 2 weeks old today," as he exaggerated his statement with his hands flopping open.

I just sat there staring at him as I thought about what he'd just said to me. "What?" I looked to the side thinking, "That can't be," as I looked around the room. "It's only been...." I trailed off still thinking about it.

My mom walked over and took my hand in hers and said, "Sweetie, he's right. It's been 2 weeks now," as she gently squeezed my hand. "And isn't it about time my grandsons were given proper names? What are you thinking Selkie Jr. and..."

I just sat there staring at her as I tried my best to blink away my tears so as not to upset my brothers. After a few moments of silence, I was finally able to put on somewhat of a smile and say, "Well happy 2 week birthday to the twins."

"Yes, sissy. And I'm going to be the best uncle they will ever have." P.J. gave me a smile warm enough to melt an iceberg.

"Come here you," I reached for him and helped him sit up in the bed with me. "You are already the best uncle they will ever have," as I pulled him in close and kissed him on the forehead. He gave me a big hug and then jumped from my bed and went over to watch M.J. play a video game.

I let out a long exhale as I settled back in, "So, they let all the peanut gallery in today huh," as I smoothed out my covers. "I don't see dad anywhere," as I twisted up my mouth at my mom.

"D.J., you know how your dad is about hospitals," as she turned and walked away. She lifted P.J. up onto her lap so that she could sit down. "He stood in the window and watched for a while, but no, he didn't want to go in right now. He said they're still too little for him to fool with. He can wait until they're able to scoot around on their own and pulling up on stuff."

I gave a little laugh as I shook my head, "Well, that sounds like him."

"Now look here young lady. That sarcasm isn't necessary today, okay," she said as she adjusted P.J.'s position on her lap.

I didn't have a response other than to roll my eyes as I looked away from her steady gaze as a very familiar voice rang out in the hallway. It was a voice no one could ever forget, with that high-pitched squeak and country twang. I looked at my mom, and with my mouth hanging open wide I said, "Oh my God she's here!"

My mom was busy tying P.J.'s shoe. Without looking up, she said, "Who's here?" finally looking up at me.

With wide eyes, I said, "Don't you hear her voice?"

My mom stopped for a second and strained to hear what I was talking about. And finally looked back at me and started laughing. "Oh. That's Selkie's mom, isn't it?"

"Yes, that's Selk's mom! Who else sounds that way?" I barely got out before the door burst open with a huge teddy bear coming through followed by a bouquet of balloons and low and behold, in stepped Hazel Mae Black, Selkie's mom.

"Hey baby! How you do'n?" she asked, smiling from ear to ear, with a nurse following close behind her with a huge vase full of flowers. She stood still just long enough to look around my room before she started barking out orders. "You can put those right here. Yeah, right here. This will be a good spot for them," as she pushed my things to the side to set the flowers on my bedside table.

I gave my mom a sideways look as if to say, *'Do you see this? She's got her nerve! Are you serious right now?'* I quietly sat and watch the show known as Hazel Mae, rearrange my room to her convenience. My mom gave me a look that told me not to open my mouth, so for once in my life, I didn't.

"I tried to see the babies, but they told me my name wasn't on the list and that there was someone in with them already."

I looked over at her with a concerned look, "What do you mean there's somebody in with them already?"

"I dunno. All I saw was a man's figure. But there's some man in there with them. I just figured it was somebody close to you," with a smirk on her face.

"There's only one person I know that can get in without me or my mom and I don't think that he is here," I quickly continued before anyone could ask me any questions, "Momma did you leave someone in with the babies?"

"No. Your dad is down in the waiting room watching some old movie. There wasn't anyone else down there when we left to come up here."

"Well there's some man down there now, and he's sit'n there talking to the babies," she explained with her hands on her hips. "I couldn't see his face, his back was to the window."

I picked up the phone and called down to the NICU to speak to the boy's nurse. When Rose finally came to the phone, I asked her who was in with the babies and she quickly responded, "There's no one in with the boys D.J. what are you talking about? Your brothers were here with your mom a little while ago, but there's no one in with them now," she explained.

"Well their dad's mom came down, and she said there was a man in with them."

She suddenly started whispering as if Hazel Mae could hear her, "Oh! That loud lady is related to you then. We didn't know her, and her name wasn't on the list, so we didn't let her in, but now that you explained it, she's right. There was a man in with them when she came. He was a police officer here just checking on them."

"A police officer. What police officer?" I asked pulling myself up a little higher in the bed. She explained to me that he told her that he was a very close friend of the family and he was just checking in on me and the babies, so of course, they allowed him to come in.

"Okay, and he's gone now?" I asked, trying to remain calm.

"Yes, he actually left as you were calling."

"Okay, well that's all I guess. I'll be down shortly to check on them myself."

"Call down before you come. Doc Roz has ordered some tests on them so give us a little while to get done first, okay dear." It really wasn't a question, but I responded anyway.

"Okay, but is everything okay," I nervously asked.

"Yes, yes. Just doing some routine lab test and some cognitive testing is all. Everything's fine. Don't worry yourself about it okay."

"If you say so. I'll be down later," as I hung up the phone. My mind was racing so I didn't even notice Hazel Mae flapping her arms around like a crazy woman.

"What's wrong?" I finally asked her.

"You didn't tell her to put me on the list D.J.," she said, tapping her foot in disgust.

I lowered my head and tapped on my forehead for a second, "Oh, I'm sorry. I forgot about it that quickly," lifting my hands as I hunched my shoulders as if I was saying sorry. I noticed the disappointed look on my mom's face and then realized that she was gathering my brother's things up as if they were about to leave.

"Get your coat baby, it's time to go," handing P.J. his hat.

"Mom, where are you going?"

"It's getting late D.J. I need to feed your brothers before J.R. gets back on the road."

"But, you don't have to go now," I pleaded with my hands. "Surely y'all can stay just a little while longer?" I pleaded with my eyes.

As she reached down to pick up her purse, she looked up and gave me another disappointing look, shaking her head at me. She knew exactly why I wanted her to stay, and it definitely wasn't because I missed her. There was no way she was leaving me alone with this woman.

"Now D.J., we've been here for over 3 hours and it's time for us to go, besides you have company," pointing over at Hazel Mae with a crooked smile on her face. "I need to get your brothers fed before they decide to eat one of us. So I'll check on you later." On cue, all of my brothers started laughing as they finished putting on their coats.

"But mom..."

"D.J. don't but mom me. Remember," as she waved her hand in the air at me, "You're a grown woman. So, I'll check on you and the babies later. You have a great evening and Hazel Mae it was good seeing you, I hope to see more of you soon," she continued as she ushered my brothers out the door.

"Well yes, it was good seeing you too Mrs. Lisa. It's been way too long. Too bad we didn't spend no time together for Thanksgiving...even though I was at the game with my babies. I can't believe what happened to his knee," as she plopped down by the oversized Teddy bear shaking her head.

Finally breaking her gaze from Hazel Mae, "Well D.J., like I said I'll check on you later and do NOT give these nurses a hard time. You just got to this floor, so try to stay longer than 24 hours this time why don't cha."

I just looked at her knowing it was a statement and not a question, as I watched her walk out the door, stopping only long enough to turn and give me a sly smirk before she closed the door behind her and my brothers.

Hazel Mae sat there for the next 45 minutes talking nonstop until she finally took a break. Unfortunately, it didn't last long, but thankfully she continued only to say, "Well, I guess I'll gone and go since it don't look like I'm gonna get to see the babies today. My ride ought to be here anyway."

"Well I'm sorry. Like I said the doctor was doing some tests on them and they were gonna call me back before we tried to come down there."

"Okay, well I'll be back soon. Hopefully Selkie will be with me next time. He got out of the hospital a few days ago, but we're still trying to figure out how to get him down to Houston comfortably."

"Uh-huh," was all I said.

As she gathered up her things, "Those planes just ain't built for people in a full leg cast and need'n to keep it up ya know."

I didn't respond immediately, knowing I had nothing good to say, so I simply watched her fight with her coat with a sly smirk on my face. When she had finally gathered all of her things, I said, "Well, I'll probably be here a few more days so y'all will probably figure it out before they discharge me."

"Well okay. You have a good night D.J.. And I'll be sure to tell Selk you send your love."

"Oh wonderful," I rolled my eyes. "Please do that," sounding as sarcastic as I possibly could, shaking my head at her. That woman was clueless and never even noticed.

Once she was gone, I called Joshua to let him know what had gone on with the mystery visitor. He decided that Lt. Keith needed to know and that he'd give him a call immediately and for me not to worry. Once I got the okay, I went down to visit the boys and began questioning the nurses about the mystery man, trying not to be too obvious about what I was doing.

"So, what did this man look like?" I asked as I changed E.J.'s diaper.

"Oh, he was nice looking. Even though he would have probably looked better without the beard. He was fairly tall, very well-spoken, and had a pretty brown eye."

My mind was racing, but I was able to compose myself enough to let out a little laugh, "A pretty brown eye. What, he only had one eye?" I asked.

"He wore an eye patch so I can't really answer that question."

"He wore an eye patch?" I looked up at her as she helped me move to the rocking chair and get my legs propped up on the little foot ottoman that went with it.

"Yeah, he said he'd just had surgery on his eye, so they had him wearing it for protection. They do that sometimes to make sure nothing gets in it after surgery," she explained as I began to feed E.J.

"So, was there anything else about this man you noticed?" I asked as E.J. watched me, and I watched every move he made as he inhaled his bottle.

"Not really. He was very gentle with them as he changed their diapers."

"You let him change their diapers?" I asked more than a little surprised.

"Well, yes. I had stepped out for a moment, so he let Amanda know that he thought J.T. had a dirty diaper and offered to change him. She told him that wasn't necessary, but he insisted, so she supervised him as he took care of it."

I did my best to conceal my excitement as I finished feeding E.J. and finally got him settled down long enough to take care of J.T. In my heart I knew it had to be Jeremiah, but for the life of me I couldn't figure out why he would visit them and not me. And furthermore, why would he not tell us all he was alive and okay? That was the only thing I couldn't figure out. If it was him, he'd never worry his mother that way.

As I calmly contemplated these things, Dr. Roz came in, and we began to discuss the tests they had done on the boys and the results. The boys were coming along very nicely, and she was happy to report that she hadn't found any neuro or cognitive deficits with the boys, and their blood work was looking great. They were both maintaining their body temperatures now without any assistance, and their lung function was obviously okay. She would like to see J.T. pick up just a little more weight, but they should be ready to leave the NICU in another couple of days. I thanked her for all of her help before she left, trying my best not to cry.

"Oh D.J. don't cry," Rose said as she handed me a tissue. "We're in the home stretch now," she continued as she patted my shoulder.

"Yes, I know. I just can't believe it's been 2 weeks already," I explained, shaking my head. A tear escaped me before I could brush it away before it dropped onto J.T.'s face startling him. He jumped so hard that he kicked through the blanket he was wrapped in exposing his long legs and feet. Rose took him from me and began wrapping him up again as I composed myself. I blew my nose as I started giggling. "Little boy, you are definitely going to have to grow into those feet," as I strained to get to the hand sanitizer on the stand by the wall.

"Here, let me help you with that," Rose said as she moved the portable stand closer. "I must say D.J., you are a definite clean freak."

"Why do you say that?" as I propped my foot up a little higher with another pillow.

"We have to remind parents and visitors time and time again to wash or sanitize their hands once they get cleaned up to come in here but you, you do it any time you touch anything related to the babies. It's like it comes natural to you. Have you ever thought about a career in medicine?" she asked as she helped me get comfortable again.

I laughed and told her, "I'm more accustomed to working in a science lab to be honest. I've never thought about working with people...medically that is."

"Well I think you should. You picked up everything we taught you in a matter of minutes. That's not typically how it works in here."

Once I had both of the boys comfortably in my arms, I looked up at her and said, "Thanks for all your help and I hope that I haven't taken up too much of your time."

"No, not at all. These two are a handful," she laughed. "Fortunately, they are my only 2 patients tonight," she smiled as she leaned on the door. "Is there anything else I can do for you before I leave?" she asked as she moved the crib closer to me in case I needed anything off of it.

"No. We should be fine for now," as I looked around. "By the way," I hesitated for a second. "Was there anything else about this man that caught your eye?" I gave her an innocent look.

"No, not really. He just sat here talking to the babies. We really didn't listen in since we didn't think that it would be a problem."

"No it's not a problem, I just wasn't expecting anyone to be visiting the boys is all," as I masterfully moved E.J. to the same arm as J.T. so that I could get a sip of water from my cup.

"Well, we figured since Lt. Keith called to let us know to expect him, you already knew about it," she said as she turned to leave.

"Wait. Lt. Keith called to let you know he was coming?" I asked with my mouth hanging open.

"Yes. That's why no one gave it a second thought," she smiled as she turned and closed the door behind her.

I just sat there in shock. Lt. Keith called to give them a heads up that someone was coming to see the babies. I wondered if Joshua knew about this when I called him. Was that the reason he insisted that I didn't worry about it and why he reassured me that he would talk to Lt. Keith for me? I was replaying how Rose had described this mysterious visitor and the final bombshell about Lt. Keith letting the staff know that he was okay to come in. Who was this man? My heart began to flutter as I convinced myself that it was Jeremiah who had visited the boys. I was so lost in thought that I didn't initially hear E.J. begin to whimper. Before I realized it, he was having a full-blown meltdown. I nearly dropped J.T. when I jumped, trying to console him.

Rose rushed in the room, "Is everything okay?"

"Yes, yes. I must have drifted off for a second. Everything is fine," as I laid J.T. across my lap to get E.J. under control.

Rose just stood there for a moment watching me. I could tell she knew something was wrong. "D.J., are you sure you're okay," as she took the sleeping baby from my lap and put him back in the crib while I settled E.J. down.

"I'm fine. Nothing's wrong. Just thinking harder than I should be," I quickly smiled at her as I tried rocking E.J. "Rose..."

"Yes, D.J...," she said slightly over her shoulder as she changed J.T.'s diaper.

"I understand why I couldn't breastfeed the boys before but now that we are all off so many antibiotics and I'm only taking oral pain meds now, would it be a problem if I tried to breastfeed them." My heart was pounding in my ears as I tried not to look too eager.

She turned and smiled at me, "Well, I can't make that call, but Dr. Roz is still here so I will go and ask her for you."

"Would you please?" I smiled much bigger than I probably should have.

"Yes I will, that won't be a problem at all," as she left the room in search of Dr. Roz.

A few minutes later, Dr. Roz came to speak with me herself. "So what's this I hear about you wanting to breastfeed?" she asked with a sly smirk on her face as she pulled up a stool next to me.

"Before, Dr. Cleveland told me that I wouldn't be able to breastfeed for a while because of all the meds me and the boys were on and how they could become toxic due to so many drugs if we weren't careful," I explained. "Sooo, now that I've been off of all but 1 of my antibiotics for a couple of days now and the boys aren't on any antibiotics anymore, would it be okay if I gave it a try?" I asked sheepishly.

"I took the liberty of calling Dr. Cleveland, and we went over you and the twin's labs from this afternoon. We both feel like your levels are low enough that your milk shouldn't cause any overload issues with the babies at this point," she smiled at me. The way she was dragging it out, I just knew she was about to tell me I still couldn't.

I hugged E.J. tighter than I probably should have by the squeal he let out, but I was so excited I couldn't help myself.

Dr. Roz gave me a moment to compose myself. "So Ms. D.J. Morgan, would you like to try it right now?" she asked as she stood up to help me get in the proper position.

"Dr. Roz I don't mind helping her," Rose stepped in when she saw Dr. Roz getting a washcloth to help me clean my nipples.

"No, don't be silly. I have time to help her," she smiled back. "Now let's see if I remember how this works," she took a slight step back and placed her hand on her chin, slightly tilting her head like she was trying to figure something out. The look of surprise on my face made her and Rose burst out laughing immediately. "Don't worry D.J., I've done this so many times I could do it in my sleep," she giggled as she began to help me adjust my breast and body in a way that was comfortable for the both of us.

My eyes were as wide as saucers when he latched on like his life depended on it. I jerk back unexpectedly at the force in which he began to suck. Rose and Dr. Roz let out a light-hearted giggle, "You weren't expecting that I take it?" Dr. Roz said with a smile on her face as she held my breast, guiding me and E.J. back into the proper position.

Finally shaking the surprise away, "No, I wasn't. That didn't feel anything like the way it does when they suck on my finger," I quickly said, shaking my head in disbelief.

"Yeah, things tend to change when it's dinner time," Rose said as she gently stroked E.J.'s head. "He's really taking to that well," she added.

Looking up at them like a deer in the headlight, "I have to admit, I was afraid that they wouldn't take to the breast well," I bashfully grinned.

"Oh yeah? And why is that?" Dr. Roz asked.

"My friends warned me that they can get confused when they use a bottle nipple for too long. Apparently, they don't tend to like the breast much after that. Something about it being easier to get milk from the bottle nipple, I think." I glanced up on occasion, still keeping my eyes on the little person that seemed to be permanently attached to my chest as he continued to watch me and suck away.

"People always say that, but in my humble opinion nipple confusion is just a fancy term to say you have a lazy baby," Dr. Roz said so matter-of-factly. "Yes, it is much easier to get the milk to come out of a bottle nipple than it tends to be a real breast nipple, but most babies will adapt to having to suck a little harder...that is unless you have a finicky baby who just doesn't have it in them to work that hard or you just have a lazy mommy. You my dear, definitely aren't going to have that problem with this little guy," she laughed. "Now his brother on the other hand," as she picked J.T. up as he began to stir about. "Now this little guy here," as she held him to her shoulder and softly patted his back, "Only time will tell."

"Why do you say that," I asked.

"Don't get me wrong," as she began to slowly bounce up and down as she patted J.T.'s back, "When you can get him to eat, he's a good eater. It's just he's nowhere as greedy as his little brother," she laughed. "So, it might take a little more patience on your part to get him accustomed to the breast, but if he's anything like his brother, he'll do just fine." Her smile was all the reassurance that I needed.

E.J. wasn't very appreciative of our conversation by the way he swatted at my breast all of a sudden. "Well, I guess he wants all of my attention right now," I laughed, shaking my head as I glanced over at Rose and Dr. Roz cooing with J.T.. The only reason I could tell E.J had finally drained my breast dry is by the look on his face when he'd suck and stop and then suck again even harder like he wasn't getting anything anymore and he couldn't believe it. Just as he decided to audibly let us know something was wrong, I said, "I think maybe this side is empty and he needs to latch onto the other side.

Rose stopped what she was doing to come and help me, but before she had a chance to show me the squeezing my breast technique again, E.J. clamped down like a vice grip. Even Rose jumped back when I yelped as he attacked the tip of my nipple and sucked the entire thing into his mouth. I looked up at her with wide eyes and finally said, "I think he might need to stick to the bottle," as I mouthed the word *'OWWW!'* still shaking my head at him.

"Like I said, you don't have to worry about nipple confusion with that one," Dr. Roz said as she handed J.T. over to Rose with a laugh. "Well D.J., I'm going to go finish my rounds, but you're doing great," she smiled as she gently patted me on the shoulder.

I blushed a little as I said, "Thank you Dr. Roz. I truly appreciate all you've done for all three of us."

She gave me a nod as she turned to leave the room, "Oh by the way, if it's okay with you I think that they might be able to come visit you in your room for short periods of time starting tomorrow," as she gave me a wink.

I got so excited I snatched E.J. off my breast by accident. "Are you playing with me right now?" I jumped forward. "That would be great!" as tears began to well up in the corners of my eyes.

"No need for tears. It's time," she smiled as she turned and left the room.

Once E.J. was finally satisfied and dry, Rose and I switched babies. I looked up at her with a worried look as I tickled J.T.'s cheek to get him to wake up for me.

"What's wrong D.J.? Why the sudden frown?" Rose asked as she laid E.J. down in the crib.

"E.J. eats so much. If he emptied me out, how will J.T. ever get enough?" I asked in all sincerity.

Rose just stood there watching me for a few seconds and then threw her head back and began laughing uncontrollably. I just sat there watching her getting more and more annoyed at her because I felt that that was a legitimate concern.

Finally, "Oh D.J. my dear, your body will know how much milk to make and once you really get into a rhythm, you will have more than you ever dreamed," she said then slowly frowned up.

"Then why the frown?" I asked as J.T. finally opened his eyes for me and let out a big yawn.

"Well, now that I think about it, the way your number two son eats, let's hope you can produce enough milk to keep up," she gave me an awkward smile as she patted me on the shoulder.

"Well here goes nothing," I said as I held my breast the way Dr. Roz had shown me earlier and offered it to J.T.

After a few minutes of him not latching on Rose could tell that I was beginning to tense up and said, "D.J., just relax. If you get anxious, he's going to get anxious, and this is going to end before you begin. So relax your shoulders and just sit back. Keep rubbing your nipple to his mouth...." And just like that he latched on and began to suck, much softer than his brother I might add. "See, he's got it," Rose said as she gently rubbed his head in approval.

I looked up at her with a huge smile and a sigh of relief at first, but it was obvious by the way I began to bite my lip that something wasn't quite right...

"Is there a problem D.J.?"

I looked up at her with my face all crooked. I had one eye open and the other one closed like I'd just bit into a lemon, "Okay should I be feeling pins and needles in my breasts," I asked as I rounded my shoulders in pain.

Rose blinked a couple of times then threw her head back again and started to laugh. This time it didn't last as long as her and Dr. Roz's laughing outburst from earlier, but from the tears running down the sides of her face, I could tell that this definitely tickled her more. This time I didn't wait to be included in the joke. "And what is so funny, pray tell?" I asked still wincing from the sharp feeling of multiple pins sticking me in both my breasts, all at the same time.

Trying to get herself back under control, Rose laid a hand on my shoulder as she inhaled one more time and let out a huge sigh, "D.J. my dear, that's how you will know you have milk." I just sat there looking at her with a look of horror and mayhem on my face. "Young lady, your milk is coming in," she smiled at me like she just struck oil.

I looked down at the angelic face looking back up at me as he began to suck harder and harder, then I slowly looked up at her in sheer terror and slowly said, "You mean every time my milk comes in I'm going to feel this way," as my mouth fell open.

She simply smiled at me and gave me a deep nod and said, "Yep. Every time...." We didn't say anything else for a few minutes as I sat there and let the idea of feeling like a hundred needles pricking me all at once each time my milk came in, marinate for a second, with my mouth still hanging open.

I looked back down at my beautiful baby boy as he suckled from my breast like he'd been doing it his entire life, then I looked back up at Rose with a tear in my eye and said, "I don't think I can handle this. They might need to take the bottle instead." And right on cue, Rose broke out in tears and laughter again.

The next day flew by as I waited impatiently for my nurse to tell me when the boys would be coming up to see me, in my room. I'd already been down to the nursery several times to spend time with them, but now it was time for 'us' to spend some much needed alone time, on my turf. I called down to the nursery again and asked for Lisa, and this time she just so happened to be the one who answered the phone.

"Hello again D.J.," she said a little sarcastically.

I quickly shook that off and said, "Hi Lisa. I know you're probably sick of me by now, but I just wanted to know when the twins would be coming up to see me?" I anxiously replied.

She chuckled then said, "D.J., just like I told you 5 minutes ago. Dr. Roz is doing her rounds and as soon as she's done, I will bring them up to you."

I thought to myself, '5 minutes...is that all it's been?' I laughed as I said,

"I know you're tired of me. But come on now…it's been a lot longer than 5 minutes," now looking at the clock trying to remember when I called her last.

"That would be a no D.J. You called me at 3:30 on the dot and it's now 3:35," as she began to laugh out loud. I could tell that she was shaking her head at me even through the phone. "Why on earth did I tell you that they would probably be able to come see you after their 3 o'clock labs were drawn?" she asked.

For the first time in our conversation, I wasn't sure if that was a question for me to answer, or just her thinking out loud so I answered her. "Because you like to keep your patient's family's well informed and you could tell how excited I was to get to finally have them in my room," I finished with a huge smile on my face.

There wasn't an immediate response, but suddenly all I heard was laughter and then a very familiar voice, "D.J. Morgan, if you don't stop giving your nurse a hard time and give me time to finish my rounds, I promise you that I won't write the order for them to do a room visit today." And before I could respond, Dr. Roz said, "Do you understand me young lady?"

All I could do is drop my head and softly say, "Yes ma'am," into the phone.

"Now as soon as I'm done, J.T. and E.J. Black will be up to see you." She said it so sternly that all I could manage to do is sit there and hold the phone to my ear. "Are you still there?"

"Yes, I'm here," I replied.

Again, there was nothing but laughter coming through the line. After a few seconds, "D.J. the handfuls that we know as the Black twins are on their way up."

Tears began to run down the sides of my face as I wrapped my arms around myself and rocked in the bed. I was clutching the phone with my ear and shoulder as I began the, thank you! Thank you's! I quickly hung up the phone and tried to prepare myself for my 2 bundles of joys. As I nervously watched the clock there came a light knock on the door and without me answering, Lisa popped her head in my room.

"Surprise!" she said with a huge grin across her face.

"Hi!" I said, pulling myself up higher in the bed returning the same huge, silly grin. And to my surprise, she wasn't alone. Dr. Cleveland and my nurse came in right behind her, and then a few minutes later, Dr. Roz came in. You would have thought I was a long lost relative, and we were having a family reunion with all the hugs and tears that were flowing.

After several long minutes of excitement and compliments on how long they were, how big they were getting and so fast, how much hair they had, how curly it was, and how alert they were, we finally found ourselves completely alone. Part of me was terrified that no one was an arm's length away, but the other part of me wanted to barricade the door to keep everyone out. Of course Dr. Roz told me, with everyone present as witnesses, that they could only stay for a couple of hours this time.

When I was done counting fingers and toes, we snuggled in together with my back to the door, and them propped up on a pillow facing me, as I turned down the lights and had my first heart to heart with my sons. I kissed each of them gently on the forehead as they both watched every move I made, like they knew something important was getting ready to happen. I said, "Boys, I need you both to listen to me very carefully because I have a secret to tell you. And I can't promise you that I will ever say this to you again, so I need you both to listen well," as J.T. began to doze off. I gently stroked his cheek until his little eyes popped open wide again before I continued. I hesitated only a second when I thought someone was at the door, but when no one entered, I continued on. "Boys, this has to do with your daddy. The man who loves us more than life itself, who would protect us with his last breath if it came to that. Your biological father may be Selkie, but your true daddy is Jeremiah Ezekiel Thomas. And I guarantee you that no one will ever bring this up in your presence, but he is who I've chosen to name you after," as I smiled down on them with tears streaming down my face.

I began to regale them with stories of Jeremiah, from how we met, to the last day we were all together. If you hadn't known better, you would have thought that they really understood every word I was saying as they both watched me intently and paid close attention to every movement of my mouth, every twitch of my face, every tear that filled the corners of my eyes. I'd never seen newborn babies pay such close attention to someone for so long, but they did that night.

I pulled J.T. close and began to breastfeed him while still laying on my side. I took this special bonding moment to tell him, "My tender heart, I'm naming you J.T. Black. I'm giving you those initials because Jeremiah Thomas is so much like you," I explained to him as I stroked his cheek and he kept his eyes on me. "He's so gentle, he's very kind, and he's a great protector," as I let out a light giggle. "He's so laid back, kinda like a cool breeze on a warm summer's day. He's a true tender heart just like you, my precious son," as I kissed the back of his hand. I continued to tell him about the man I was naming him after, and when I felt like he had had enough to eat and he was good and dry, I moved him over so I could focus on his brother.

Once I was sure we were all safely in my bed, I began to feed E.J. He had never taken his eyes off me, even when I was feeding his brother. As I gave him all of my attention, I explain to him how I came up with his name. "And my demanding, number two son, I'm naming you E.J.," as I wiped away a tear as it rolled down my cheek. "See there's a part of Jeremiah that is just as feisty as you," I smiled down at him. "Zeke is a firecracker. He's a natural protector, who's just as fierce at every turn and demands that you pay close attention to him. And that side of him is what makes me call him Zeke, short for Ezekiel. So, your initials stand for Ezekiel Jeremiah because you're still as loving as Jeremiah is, but you are definitely going to be a handful, just like he is when Zeke comes out," as I kissed his little nose. Just as I'd done with J.T., I continued to regale E.J. with stories of his dad and the love we had both come to know.

As I finished changing his diaper, I scooped them both up in my arm and gave them a family hug before I continued. "So understand me, my dear sons, that even though he may not be here with us right now, you are forever wrapped in his love and blessed to carry his name," as I paused to regain my composure for a second. I shook away the final tear I would shed over this subject and told them, "I know in my heart he is still out there and I promise you that he's doing everything in his power to get back to us right now. He loves us all so much, and one day soon, I pray he's back here with us so our family can be complete again," as I managed to kiss them each on their forehead. "So, unless he comes back to us, this subject will never come up again."

I managed to safely get both of them back in their crib as I noticed the time, before I continued our conversation, still amazed that they were both still wide awake for such a long time. "And God forbid, he doesn't come back to us, I need you both to understand that from here on out, it's just you and me boys." I began rocking them to sleep as I whispered to them, "Jeremiah Ezekiel Thomas will forever be a part of our lives to the end of our days and beyond.

CHAPTER 24

I was preparing myself for the firestorm that was sure to come down on me when word got out as to what I had named the boys, so I did my best to simply smile. I had been smiling so much by noon that my face was beginning to hurt, but at lunchtime that forced grin took on an unexpected life of its own when I had a surprise guest come to visit me around lunchtime. The boys were back in my room again, with their new name tags on their crib, when my door creaked open and my nurse Bridgette and Lt. Keith stepped in my room, along with a nurse I'd never seen before.

"Excuse me D.J., this officer needs you to come with him," Bridgette explained.

My heart immediately sunk, and I got a queasy feeling as I collapsed back in my bed. I reached for the baby's crib to pull them closer to me as I watched Lt. Keith, silently standing to the side with a blank expression on his face and his hands behind his back. He wasn't even trying to make eye contact with me. I began to shake my head faster and faster and finally said, "No...I don't think that would be a good idea," never taking my eyes off of Lt. Keith.

He finally stepped forward and said, "D.J., trust me when I say, you really do need to come with me."

I continued to shake my head no as Bridget eased herself over to the far side of the bed and forcibly removed my hand from the crib so that the other nurse could take the boys away.

"No! Why are you taking my babies?" I yelled at her as I grabbed her arm.

Lt. Keith quickly moved in to intervene and finally revealed what he had hidden behind his back. As he grabbed my wrist, he slid a box onto the end of my bed and said, "I need you to put this on D.J." His face never gave any hint of what was going on in his mind. I'd never seen someone keep such a straight face and give off no signs of emotion whatsoever.

Bridgette quickly pushed the boys over to the mystery nurse and turned and said to me, "Here D.J., let me help you get changed," as she quickly came back to my bedside and helped me into the wheelchair. She scooped up the box and handed it to me, all while the nurse that never identified himself disappeared out the door with my children.

"No, I don't like this," I said as my hands began to shake uncontrollably.

Lt. Keith simply laid his hand on my shoulder and look down at me and said, "D.J., I can't do this without you, so I really need you to come with me."

I sat there looking at him thinking, *'That's it! You just want me to trust you?'* I slowly calmed down and said, "Just like that. You come in here without even a hello and have my children whisked away, without any explanation as to what's going on," as the tears began to well up in my eyes.

"Well...yes," he replied.

Bridgette was pulling me towards the bathroom to change when I whirled around with a face full of tears and snapped, "If he's dead just tell me! You don't have to do all this cloak and dagger stuff! JUST TELL ME HE'S DEAD ALREADY AND GET IT OVER WITH!" I grabbed his arm nearly pulling him down into my lap, startling both him and Bridgette.

He struggled to keep his balance as he pushed back against the arm of the wheelchair and chuckled, "WOW! I wasn't expecting that at all," as he pulled on his coat to straighten himself up. "D.J. I had no idea you were that strong," he gave me a half-grin. "Just go inside there, get changed and come with me please," he said, again without giving me any type of indication as to what was going on. When I tell you he gave me a blank stare, his face was completely blank.

Bridgette quickly wheeled me on into the bathroom and helped me get cleaned up as I opened the box to reveal the outfit he brought for me to put on. She pulled out this long silk powder blue gown and a jet black hooded cape that was big enough to cover up what I was wearing and then some.

When I came out of the bathroom, Lt. Keith finally gave me a slight grin and said, "There, was that so hard?"

I jerked my head and gave him a frown as I replied, "No, it wasn't, but what is really going on? And why do I look like Little Red Riding Hood's dark alter ego?" I asked holding up the oversized black cape.

For the first time, Lt. Keith broke character and actually gave me some heartfelt emotion. He started laughing almost to the point of tears and finally said, "Oh my D.J., that was a good one." And without another word, he peeked out into the hallway to make sure it was clear, and then the three of us were off like a shot. We didn't take the main elevators, we took some service elevator I'd never even seen before, down to a back hallway on the main floor and then quickly into the chapel.

When Bridgette turned me backwards to enter a nearly dark room, I quickly asked, "What on God's green earth is going on?" But before either of them answered, Lt. Keith took over the wheelchair and pulled me down the aisle of the chapel, backwards while Bridgette stood guard at the door. "I'm not kidding, Lt. Keith what the hell is going on!" I yelled, causing my voice to echo in the dark empty room. My yelling did get an immediate reaction though, just not from whom I intended. Both J.T. and E.J. immediately began to cry which let me know we weren't alone as voices began to hush them. Lt. Keith whirled the chair around as the lights slowly came up. Standing there consoling the babies was Mama J and Joshua along with all the rest of the Thomas siblings and spouses, Mr. Charlie, and Phaedra.

"What are y'all doing here?" I asked, trying to hold it together. They all looked back and forth between themselves, but no one said a word.

As we all looked at each other in silence, a distant voice cut through me like a knife. My heart skipped a beat as the voice got closer and a hand reached out of the dark from behind me and slid down my arm as I held my breath. Out of the corner of my eye, I watched a man's body slide past me and kneel down beside me. I was afraid to turn and look into his face as he kissed the back of my hand. All I could do is close my eyes as the tears began to stream down the sides of my face. My body quivered as he gently wiped my tears away and finally pulled my chin around so that we would be face to face.

"Open your eyes, it's okay," he said as he wiped another tear away.

"No...this can't be real," I softly replied, shaking my head back and forth.

He let out a light-hearted laugh as he kissed my cheek and said, "Does that feel real to you?"

"Yes, but..."

"No buts Little Mamma. It's really me."

I could hear the giggles and the aahhh's as I took a deep breath and slowly opened my eyes to see Jeremiah's smiling face, hidden behind an eyepatch and a beard. "It was you," as I stroked his cheek not realizing how badly my hands were trembling. The tears began streaming down my face like a flood.

"Don't cry," as he tried to wipe away my tears. "Ohhh baby, please don't cry," Jeremiah said as Mr. Charlie stepped forward with a handkerchief.

"Why were you gone so long? We've been missing you so much," I cried into his chest.

"I know, and I'm sorry. There're things you don't understand right now, but I'll fill you in soon."

"What things?" I finally loosened my grip on his neck.

"Later. Right now is for something else," as he took a knee again and picked up my hand. "D.J. Morgan, will you marry me?"

I giggled as I wiped my face, "I know my memory has been a little spotty since the accident, but I do believe that I already said yes to that question Sir," as I smiled at him.

"Well what I meant to say was, will you marry me, today?" he asked as he opened up the velvet box that he'd given me outside my building when he first asked me to marry him. I'd asked about the whereabouts of my ring several times, and no one could seem to find it. But there it was, as beautiful as the day he first slid it on my finger.

I looked up as tears began to form in the corners of my eyes again, "Are you serious? Of course I will," I latched onto his neck so quickly that he didn't have a chance to adjust his balance, as we both tumbled to the floor. You should have seen how everyone scrambled trying to catch us, but I could've cared less. The man I loved was back, and we were getting married. Now the outfit and all the secrecy made perfect sense. I knew that I might be sore later, but as I held onto Jeremiah and he kissed me, I didn't have a care in the world.

Once we were all standing upright again and my nurse was sure that I hadn't injured myself again, they wheeled me up to the front of the chapel as a minister stepped forward. The tears began to well up in the corners of my eyes again when I realized it was my pastor, Reverend Clive. He was standing there with a smile on his face so wide that I knew he was excited to be here, to be a part of this celebration.

I was able to stand now with a little help as I looked over at Jeremiah and asked, "How did you do all this?"

"Shhh woman. That's not a question asked during a wedding, and you're talking out of tern," he laughed as he held my hand. I just giggled as I shook my head at him. I could feel my face getting hot and knew he had me blushing as I slowly dropped my head to help conceal my smile.

"If everyone's ready, let's began," Pastor Clive said as everyone took their seats. "D.J. I have a few words to say first so why don't you sit until we get to the vows." It was a statement and not a question, so I did as I was instructed without any hesitation. Once everyone was settled, he began.

"Dearly beloved, we are gathered here today, in the presence of these witnesses, to join D.J. Morgan and Jeremiah Ezekiel Thomas in Holy matrimony. Today we come together to celebrate one of life's greatest moments. The moment when a man and a woman come together to become one...united in love, trust, and honor. Vowing to cherish one another to the ends of time. Now, D.J. and Jeremiah, I have to admit this is a first for me. It's the first time I've performed a wedding in secret, and it's the first time I've performed a wedding without several weeks of marriage counseling," as he gave us both a solemn glance and followed it with a heartwarming smile. "But let me tell you all. When I met this young man for the first time, I was initially skeptical. Her mother had already filled me in on what was going on and I met him already giving him 2 strikes. But after speaking with him and watching the way he protected her from everyone standing there trying to convince her what a mistake she was making leaving with him, I knew in my own heart that he was the perfect man for you D.J.," as he touched me on the shoulder.

I smiled up at him and slowly exhaled knowing he was on my side, as a tear fell from my eye and I mouthed, *'Thank you,'* to him.

"See I've known this young lady since she was a little girl and I've been there through her ups and her downs, but the one thing you all need to know is she's a special gift from God. She's a true fighter. In her short 24 years, she's dealt with many battles that would have crippled most, but she's kept her eyes to the Lord and fights her fight no matter what anyone else says or thinks. So Jeremiah, just know you are dealing with a diamond so always let her shine," he said as he gripped Jeremiah's shoulder and gently shook him.

Jeremiah nodded in the affirmative, as Pastor Clive continued. "Now here is where I'd usually ask, 'If any person can show just cause why these two may not be married, let them speak now or forever hold their peace?' But since I know, no one here has any objections, we can move on," as he slightly nodded his head.

I don't know why but something inside of me said, *'He's nodding at someone in the back,'* so I took a deep breath as I slowly looked over my shoulder. My eyes grew wider as my mouth fell open, and I slowly tightened my grip on Jeremiah's hands and quickly looked from the back of the room to him. He could tell something was wrong and followed my gaze. He didn't make a move at first as Pastor Clive continued.

"Please take each other by the right hand. We didn't have a lot of time to prepare, so would you two like to say something in the way of vows?"

I sat there quiet as a church mouse, not sure what to say. I was frozen in my seat as I began to tremble, worrying about what my mother was about to do to embarrass me now. Jeremiah could feel my hands shaking and slowly bent down and quietly whispered in my ear, "It's okay, don't worry, I had your Pastor bring her along with him," as he squeezed my hands. "So don't worry, today is all about you, so go on and say whatever you want to say. The floors all yours Little Mamma," and then he kissed me on the cheek.

Everyone could tell something was going on as they took turns looking behind them and quickly whispering amongst themselves, "Who's that in the back?"

"Who's that lady back there on the wall?"

"Is that her mother?" I heard someone else ask as I tried my best to blink away my tears.

Mr. Charlie finally whispered to them, "Yes, that's her mother."

The entire time she just stood there, never saying a word, never making a move. I just continued to sit there half looking over my shoulder, half staring at the floor, still completely afraid to move or utter one single word because I just knew she was waiting to pounce. After what felt like forever in silence, I felt a slight tug on my hand, pulling me out of my hypnotic stupor. I took a deep breath and slowly exhaled as I turned my attention back to Jeremiah and quickly got lost in his beautiful brown eye, and finally gained the courage and the strength to speak up, "Yes, please," reaching for help to stand up, sending Phaedra and Joshua scrambling. It was a sight to watch me balance myself on my wheelchair with my broken ankle bent under me trying not to put too much weight on my fractured leg. I could see my nurse shaking her head at me out of the corner of my eye, as I took one final look back, before completely focusing on the man standing next to me.

"Jeremiah, I knew the minute you held me that you were the man for me. You were an immediate calming spirit in my life. You gave me hope when I had just about given up, you calmed those two rowdy boys down even inside my womb," I glanced over at the boys, surprised to see that both of them were wide awake, as quiet as they were. "You filled my heart with more love and trust than I've ever known in my life. You are God's gift to me Jeremiah Ezekiel Thomas, and I promise you that I will forever cherish you, love you, and protect you with every fiber of my being. God is love, but you are the heartbeat. I love you with all my heart and soul," as I squeezed his hands. "You are my rock and my protector. I know that no matter what this life may bring, I will always be able to depend on you and my heart will forever be yours. I vow to love you to infinity and beyond. I promise to protect your heart just as I know you will protect mine. You are the mate that God has created for me, the love that makes life worth living. Your heartbeat is now my heartbeat, my soul belongs to only you and the Lord. I can't wait to create a family with you and grow old with you as we watch our children grow and go off and have their own children. I look so forward to being the gray area in your black and white world," as I kissed the back of each of his hands.

"Jeremiah...do you want to say a few words to D.J.?" Pastor Clive asked as he brushed away a tear.

Jeremiah gave him a quick smile and said, "Naw. I think she said enough, don't you?" By the stunned looks on everyone's face, you could tell none of us expected that. Even Pastor Clive was standing there with his mouth hanging open. Jeremiah surveyed everyone's reactions and then burst out laughing. "Of course I have something to say," as he shook Pastor Clive's arm still giggling.

"D.J. Morgan, you blew into my life so unexpectedly and turned everything upside down and inside out....all over an order of hotlinks and spicy barbecue sauce," he smiled devilishly at me. I could feel my face heating up, but I did my best not to break eye contact for very long. "You are the reason I look forward to another day, you are the sunshine in my mornings and the moonlight in the night. Your light shines so brightly that it guided me back to you through the pain, the darkness, and the rain," as a tear ran down the side of his face, I gently wiped it away. "You make my heart smile D.J.. You've given it a new rhythm that just didn't beat the same when we were apart. You've given me the gift of life. Not just my own but these two beautiful babies that carry my name."

My eyes grew as big as saucers as my mouth fell open. "You...you know about that?" I sheepishly asked.

"Of course I know about that," he softly replied along with a wink. Then without warning turned to the audience and said as he lifted his arms in the air, "And again, she's speaking out of turn," he said loud enough for everyone to clearly hear him, as he made a face like he was fed up towards our small crowd, causing them all to start laughing. All I could do is drop my head and smile.

"Anyway, like I was saying," as he took my hands again with a Kool-Aid smile. "I loved you from the moment we touched. I fell in love with our boys at first kick. I know you are going to be a handful, but I've got pretty big hands if I do say so myself." You could hear the moans and giggles from our guests. I just smiled and shook my head as he continued. "You also came into my life when I was positive that I'd spend the rest of my life alone. D.J., I'm not ashamed to say I was a broken man even if nobody else really knew to what extent, but you have managed to seal up all of my cracks, bang out all the dents, and restore me to a luster that even I never dreamed possible. You are the melody to my music and the rhythm to my heartbeat. My soul would be lost without you or my boys," he smiled as he softly wiped away a tear that escaped my eye before I could blink it away. "D.J. I love you with all of me, now and forever, into eternity and beyond. I promise you that I won't hold it against you when you play around in the gray areas...but don't press your luck or you'll have to have a long talk with Zeke," as he kissed the back of my hands.

As much as I didn't want to, I had to take a seat, the pain was becoming unbearable trying to keep my balance on one knee and the heel of my other foot. The only thing you could here for a moment was the "aww's" and "how beautiful" from the crowd.

Finally, Pastor Clive spoke up, "After that, there's not much more to say," as he covered our hand. "Do you have the rings?"

I began to frown as I shook my head no, even though I noticed Jeremiah turn to Joshua and take something from him. I couldn't believe it. He had a wedding band for me that actually matched the ring he had given me.

"Now repeat after me Jeremiah. With this ring, I thee wed, and all my worldly goods I thee endow."

A tear rolled down my cheek as Jeremiah smiled and slid both the new band and my engagement ring on my finger and said, "With this ring, I thee wed, and all my worldly goods I thee endow."

I stared at the rings on my finger, shaking my head back and forth in disbelief. "How did you? Where did you find it?"

"Shhh. That's not the next line," Jeremiah snapped, causing my mouth to fall open even wider as everyone in the room burst out laughing.

"In sickness and in health, in poverty or in wealth, till death do us part," Pastor Clive continued.

"In sickness and in health, in poverty or in wealth, till death do us part," Jeremiah smiled holding my hand.

"D.J. please repeat after me."

I could feel me blushing as I dropped my head and softly said, "But I don't have one for him."

Jeremiah began to laugh as he lifted my chin up and said, "Oh ye of little faith," as a tear began to roll down the side of my face. He quickly wiped it away then opened my hand, as Phaedra reached around me and placed a matching men's ring in my palm.

My eyes got as big a saucers again, "You really took care of everything," I sniffed as tears began to stream down my face.

"Again, that's not the next line," he said, smiling as he used the hanky to quickly wipe my tears away.

Pastor Clive giggled as he cleared his throat, "Now D.J., repeat after me. With this ring, I thee wed, and all my worldly goods I thee endow."

"With this ring, I thee wed, and all my worldly goods I thee endow," as I slid the ring on his finger.

"In sickness and in health, in poverty or in wealth, till death do us part."

"In sickness and in health, in poverty or in wealth, till death do us part," I repeated with a huge smile on my face.

After he wrapped a golden rope loosely around our wrists, Pastor Clive then said, "By the power vested in me by the Great State of Texas and the Lord Almighty, I now pronounce you husband and wife. Jeremiah, you may now kiss your bride," with a smile on his face bigger than I'd ever seen on him before.

I braced myself for what I knew was about to come, as Jeremiah whisked me up out of my wheelchair and kissed me like it was the first time. I simply wrapped my arms around his neck and returned the favor as everyone began to cheer, clap, and whistle. Even the twins joined in with their high pitched wailing for a few moments after being startled by all of the loud noise.

As everyone settled down, Pastor Clive slowly raised his arms to the side, still gripping his bible in his hand and said the words I had been dying to hear, "I present to you Mr. and Mrs. Jeremiah Ezekiel Thomas!" as he wrapped his arms around the both of us, giving us a tight hug.

I was so engulfed in all the joy and tears that I barely caught my mom sliding out the back door. As our eyes locked onto each other for a short moment, she simply smiled as she gave me a head nod, then blew me a kiss as she creeped out the door. For just a moment, a tear of sadness slowly crept down the side of my face, as the hugs and kisses began. I tried to keep up appearances and smile and thank everyone for coming, but even through my smile and laughter, Jeremiah knew me so well. He knew that as happy as I was, my heart was still heavy. He gently sat me back in my wheelchair as he whispered in my ear, "At least she came baby. That says a lot," as he kissed me on my forehead, gently moving my hair out of my face, and wiped my sad tears away.

I squeezed his hand, gave him the best smile I could muster up at the moment and said, "My Dear Heart, thank you for making this the best day of my life." We disappeared in each other's eyes and soft kisses as our friends and family celebrated our new life together. We loved on each other and the boys until we all had to go back to our rooms.

I woke up in a panic, feeling hazy, and very sore. I was frantically patting around for the call light when a soothing voice cut through the darkness and reassured me that I wasn't dreaming, as the table light clicked on, "Hey beautiful. What's wrong?" as he began rubbing his eyes, trying to focus on his watch. "Are you still in pain?" Jeremiah asked as he stretched his arms wide and then moved closer to my bed.

"Oh my God! It wasn't a dream," as I wildly reached for his hand, noticing the rings on our fingers.

"Well by the smile on your face, if you were dreaming, I take it, it was a good dream at least," as he leaned down to kiss me on the forehead.

I surprised him as I pulled him down in the bed with me and hugged him tightly until he pulled back a little, starting to cough, "D.J. not so tight. I can't breathe," as he pulled on my arms from squeezing so tightly around his neck.

"I just can't believe it's you," as the tears began to flow down my face. "Where were you? Why were you gone so long? What happened out there?" as I buried my face in his chest.

"Slow down, slow down," he laughed. "One question at a time please," as he gently rubbed my head and rocked me.

"Jeremiah, I missed you so much," I cried softly.

"Ohhh, don't cry. It's okay, it's all going to be okay," as he reached over for a tissue and began drying my face.

Through my sniffling, I asked him, "What do you mean it's going to be okay?" as I looked up at him.

"Shhh, shhh, not now. We will talk about it later. I promise," he swept my hair out of my face as he kissed me on the forehead again.

"But..."

He cut me off before I could say anything else, as he softly pressed his fingertips to my lips. "No but's. Right now, just let me hold you. I want to hold my wife," as he scooted under the covers alongside me and curled up next to me. I quietly laid my head on his chest, and for the first time in weeks, I actually got some sleep.

I woke up to voices in the corner of my room discussing something about suspects and leads as the nurse came in to check on me startling all of us. Lt. Keith and Jeremiah suddenly ended their conversation and Lt. Keith politely said his goodbyes and congratulations again as he quickly left the room. I asked Jeremiah what that was about and as what was becoming his usual reaction to my questions, he hushed me up and said that we'd talk about it later.

Once my nurse finished checking me over, and I received my morning meds, she gave us my daily report on my progress, in the eyes of all my doctors of course. She explained that there had been several notes written concerning my discharge which made me very happy to hear but still worried me nonetheless. It wasn't because I wasn't ready to go home, because I was. And now that Jeremiah was back, I felt better about getting around in the house without depending on my mother. What had me worried is the fact that I still hadn't heard anything about when the boys would be released. I wasn't trying to leave the hospital without them. Seeing as how she now had 2 people asking her questions, I feel like she was still in and out of my room pretty quickly.

I called down to check on the boys and asked for them to be brought up to my room. After a brief discussion, I agreed to an hour or so, so that Dr. Roz had time to give them a thorough physical this morning. Once I'd convinced Jeremiah that there was nothing going on that out of the usual, we had a moment to spend more time catching up.

To my surprise, Jeremiah answered all of my earlier question and more over the next couple of hours. He explained to me what he and Lt. Keith were so busy discussing in the wee hours of the morning and why all the secrecy of our wedding, which I was still tearing up over by the way. He sat next to me playing with our wedding bands as he, in very great detail, explained what happened to us the night of our car accident and where he had been ever since. As I sat there taking in all the information he had to give, I finally understood what it meant to be in a partnership with someone.

I was an expert at telling half the story or just the parts that I felt were relevant. But Jeremiah held nothing back, as he explained to me why he was now under a protective detail because of the accident and the beating he'd taken on the side of the bank that night. He explained to me how lucky he was that the current swept him down the canal fast enough that our attackers couldn't keep up on foot in all the mud and slipperiness along the bank. How he must have passed out and come too, clinging to a downed tree that provided enough cover that no one would have noticed him unless they were coming at him from just the perfect angle. Then how he slowly made his way back to the house through the woods and hid out in the tree line for a few hours to make sure no one was waiting at home for him to show up. He even told me how men did arrive at the house and began poking around before he had finished getting cleaned up good, so he went to the safe room, where he passed out again.

As he explained to me all he'd been through, I truly learned what it meant to trust someone with everything you had and everything you were. Over those few hours, the investigator in me was born. I told him what I could remember and the conversations I'd had with Joshua and Lt. Keith over the past couple of weeks, before and after I got my memory back, I left no detail out. I wasn't even the least bit surprised to find out that the night that all of my memories came flooding back is the exact same night he made contact with Lt. Keith. I felt his energy that night, I felt his spirit. The bond Jeremiah and I shared became more solid than I ever dreamed possible with anyone. I not only bonded with my husband, but I had also officially grown up.

CHAPTER 25

Lt. Keith came and whisked Jeremiah away that afternoon, so I decided to take a much needed nap. Both my nurse and the boy's nurse were shocked when I asked for them to be taken back to the nursery so that I could get some sleep. The funny thing is I only slept a couple of hours, which didn't surprise either of them when I called for assistance to go down to the nursery.

I hadn't gotten comfortable in the chair trying to feed E.J. when I heard the unmistakable voice of one, Hazel Mae Black. I could instantly feel my back tighten up, which immediately upset young Mr. E.J.. I guess he sensed the tension in the air. I managed to get him quieted down and latched on again when I heard Selkie's voice as well. I could hear him talking to the nurses and then a few seconds later Rose popped her head in our little room to let me know that he and his mom wanted to come in with the boys.

"Uhmm D.J..."

I slowly looked up at her and said, "Yes..." quickly looking back down to continue my conversation with the little person attached to my chest.

"There's a gentleman in a wheelchair and his mother out here who would like to see the twins. And he says that....he's the twin's daddy," she announced, awkwardly shuffling from one foot to the other. She already knew Jeremiah and had given him the other armband to get in anytime he wanted to see the boys, so I understood her awkwardness as she waited for me to okay this other man coming in, who is now identifying himself as their father. And even stranger after all this time of no daddy's showing up, they've now got 2 men showing up saying that they are the twin's daddy. Even if only one of them actually fit that title.

I didn't respond immediately, but it soon hit me...she wasn't here the night Hazel Mae came to see the boys, so she had no idea who she even was. I slowly shook my head and finally said, "Sure. Let him come on in," I shrugged as I masterfully moved E.J. from one side to the other side.

"Okay. If you say so," she said, almost as if she was questioning my answer. Just before she closed the door, she added, "Are you coming out so that his mother can come in too?"

I looked up at her as my top lip slightly rolled up and I puckered my mouth as a deep crease formed in between my eyebrows, almost like I had suddenly got a whiff of something that repulsed me, "Not on your life," as I slowly looked back down and started cooing at E.J. again.

I already knew Selk was going to have an attitude when he finally came in the room after the way he reacted to Rose's news that I'd said he could come in, but refused to come out so his mom could come in with him. I don't know for sure, but I think Rose held him up even longer because of the tone he took with her out in the changing room. I really didn't care. Besides, it was enough time to give me a few more minutes alone with my boys. I was about done feeding E.J. as he finally wheeled himself in.

He didn't even bother trying to look happy to see us, well at least me anyway. "Have you completely lost your mind?" he huffed.

As I removed E.J. from my nipple and covered myself back up, I dipped my head slightly to the side and gave him a shit-faced grin, "Well hello to you too. How're you doing today Mr. Black?" as I stared at him with the stupid smirk on my face as I proceeded to burp E.J.

He gave me a frown as he slowly moved his wheelchair closer to me. "You really have lost your fucking mind," he growled. I didn't really give him much mind until he reached up and grabbed me by the wrist, pulling me down towards him.

He completely caught me off guard with that move. Luckily I was cradling E.J. tight enough that I was able to hold onto him with my free arm, as I instinctively snatched my arm back catching him off guard as he jerked forward, nearly knocking his own leg down off the elevated extension plate of his wheelchair. You could tell by the surprised look on his face he wasn't sure what to do or say next.

As I held on to E.J. for dear life, now cradling his head with my newly freed hand, I thought to myself, *'Where is Jeremiah? I wish he were here...'* as my other little voice said, *'Oh no you don't! He'd choke the life out of Selk if he saw that.'* I quickly regained my composure and calmly said, "If you ever put your hands on me again, I'll kill you," steadily glaring at him with all the hate, anger, and truth, that I could muster up, without actually exploding.

It was obvious he was taken back for a moment as he tilted his head and looked at me like he had absolutely no idea what language I was speaking. He just sat there watching me as I finished with E.J. and picked J.T. up to begin my feeding routine all over with him.

Although I was acting like I didn't have a care in the world, I had to actively talk myself through how to breastfeed my more relaxed child. Finally, I took a deep breath as I told myself, *'D.J. get it together! You can do this! Just be careful and don't you dare drop your guard again, but if he so much as twitches in a way that worries you…. scream your motherfucking head off until help arrives.'* I caught myself giggling at myself as I noticed Selk fiddling with the nametags on the side of the babies crib.

"What the hell is this?" he asked, now holding one of the crib cards in his hand waving it at me.

"It's a crib card to identify who these two little guys are," I said sarcastically, already knowing exactly what he was talking about.

"Real cute D.J.. I know it's a fucking identification card," he said, still waving the card at me. "I want to know what the hell these names on here are all about?" he asked, reading the card in his hand out loud. "E.J. Black."

"Well, I'd think that would be obvious," I said as I moved J.T. to the other side still trembling slightly. "That's his name," I sighed as I looked over at him for the first time since I'd threatened him. "This here is J.T. Black, the baby formally known as Baby A. And that inquisitive little man in the crib is E.J. Black, the baby formally known as Baby B," as I realized that E.J. was not only wide awake, he was watching every move Selkie made. It was almost like if Selk did anything else out of pocket, he was going to crawl up out of that crib and kick his ass himself. Before I realized it, I had a smile across my face as I watched my little protector keep an eye on his biologic.

"What the hell are you smiling about? I don't see shit funny about this?" he said louder than he should have, as he gave me a crazy look. Who told you that it was up to you, what their names were going to be? This is some kind of joke, isn't it? J.T. and E.J…really D.J.?! What the FUCK!?" I didn't say anything back initially as I kept one eye on him as I talked to J.T. for a few more seconds while he finished his meal. Before I could respond, the door swung wide open, and Rose was standing in the middle of the room, with her hands on her waist. There wasn't much space after that, but I felt so relieved to have someone else standing in between us.

"*Excuse me,*" she said, exaggerating her words as she glared at Selkie for a moment before looking over at me. "This is a quiet area. If you are going to stay in here," as she pointed down towards the ground. "You will use your quiet voices at all times. Do I make myself clear?" as she stopped looking back and forth at us and rested her eyes on Selk.

I rolled my eyes and finished burping J.T. as Selk snapped into his "Mr. Charm" mode. "I'm so sorry for raising my voice. It won't happen again, I promise you," he smiled up at her.

She pursed her lips together as she crossed her arms across her chest. He never relented from his sudden case of niceness, but I could tell she could see right through it. "Uhmm hmm," was all she said.

"D.J. was just about to wheel herself out so that my mother could come in. Weren't you D.J.?" he continued to smile, barely taking his eyes off Rose.

I had managed to stand up as I began changing dirty diapers and continuing to ignore Selk. After a couple of seconds of silence, I looked over and said, "No," and went back to attending to the twins.

"What did you just say?" he said through clenched teeth, as he bumped my leg with his wheelchair.

I began to sway a little but caught myself pretty quickly, "I said, No. I'm not going anywhere," as I gripped the side of the crib. "If you want her to come in...you are more than welcome to leave, but I'm not going anywhere," I shot him a quick, *'you can go straight to hell look.'*

Rose instinctively jumped in, "D.J. sit down before you fall down," holding my wheelchair in place so that I could sit down safely. Suddenly she began moving the room around and opening up the privacy curtains so everyone could see in as she continued. "Here, let me help you get more comfortable," as she moved me over to the rocking chair and ottoman next to the observation window closest to the nursery. I could have easily changed seats on my own, but I understood what was going on even if Selk didn't. Rose could feel the tension in the room without me saying anything, and she'd also heard the rumors about Selk choking me before the babies were born. She had moved all the furnishings around to put more distance between Selk and me, while also making it nearly impossible for him to touch me without someone seeing or having to drag the crib and changing table out of the way first. "There, that's better. Now if you need anything, don't hesitate to call me," as she hooked up the extension call light and laid it over the edge of my chair.

I smiled and gave her a head nod to say, *'thank you,'* as she turned back to Selk.

"Sir, if you like, I can help you out so that your mother can come in now." She stood there looking like an angel as she gave Selk the same syrupy sweetness back that he had tried to give her.

He just sat there with his mouth hanging open for a second before he kicked back into sweet-talking mode. "Is it possible for her to come on in so that we can spend some time with the twins as a family and so that I can introduce her to her grandkids?" he said with big puppy dog eyes and a smile.

Without missing a beat, "No Sir. I'm afraid we have pretty strict rules back here in the NICU. We're only allowed to let 2 people back here at a time, and one of those people has to be wearing an armband, identifying them as an authorized visitor of the infant or in this case infants that they're visiting. So when you are ready to step out, your mother is more than welcome to step in," she smiled back.

By the look on Selk's face, you could've bought him for a penny. He was so used to getting his way all the time he really didn't know what to do with himself. It took everything in me not to fall out in the floor laughing, but I held it together just for Rose's sake.

Selk truly looked like a lost puppy now, "But, but I'm their father. I should have an armband anyway," he pleaded his case.

"That may be the case, but since you two aren't married, it's solely up to the mother as to who receives an armband and the limit is two."

"Okay, so her and me. That makes two."

"That you'll have to take up with D.J., but at this time Sir, the Morgan twins, excuse me, I meant to say the Black twins have reached their authorized limit. I'll give you two a moment to discuss it," as she turned to help me pick up the second baby. "If that's okay with you D.J.?" she quickly added as we all settled into our rocker comfortably.

I grinned at her and said, "Yes, that'll be fine," still cracking up on the inside. And with that, she left the four of us alone in the room.

The door didn't close good before he began his rant. "You're enjoying this I bet. You think you're in control, but you're not. I'm the one paying your bills, did you forget that? I can pull the plug on this little gravy train anytime I want too. And then what are you going to do? You can't afford to pay for this on your own," he said so matter-of-factly.

I didn't bother to respond because I knew he wasn't through yet, so I simply rocked the boys and waited for him to continue. Besides, I wanted to see how deep down the rabbit hole this tantrum would go. It's amazing how badly people slip up and say the wrong thing when they're upset. It didn't take long before he picked up where he left off.

He huffed, "Stupid bitch. You don't even have anywhere to go. If you think I'm going to let you back into that apartment, you're crazier than you look. And if I do decide to be nice and allow you to move back in, it will definitely be alongside me, back in Dallas," he said with a devilish grin on his face. I glanced up at him as a shiver went up my back at the mere idea of that even being suggested let alone a possibility, but still, I remained silent and didn't flinch. Besides, I'd just learned that he had no idea that Jeremiah was even alive...at least I knew that I could kind of trust my mother when a life was truly on the line.

"And who the hell did you give the second armband to anyway?" as he stared a hole right through me. "If you even try to tell me they aren't mine I swear that will be the last thing you ever say," he leaped forward bumping the crib.

It was a miracle, but I never flinched. However, I did take this opportunity to say my peace. I slowly adjusted the boys in my arms so that he could get a good look at their faces, thinking to myself, *'As if they could possibly be anyone else's. How I wished to God! They were someone else's.'*

"Now you take a long look at these two little faces and tell me who they look like?" pulling their blankets down well under their chins to make sure he could get a good look at them. I removed their little caps and said, "And who's fat head do they BOTH have?" as I watched his every move. After I was sure he'd gotten a good look at the two heads that were an identical shape to his and the two little faces that unfortunately looked more like him every day, I continued on. "So if you want to challenge their paternity, go for it! And while we wait on the results, I will give them the last name that I would love for them to have before the results come in...and no that ain't Black if you were wondering," I paused for a moment to let that sink in. "And as for the bill. Don't pay it. Best believe it will be paid, in full and on time. And you think me moving in with you is some prize or lifelong goal?" I paused, "Boy please!" I flipped my hand at him. "Have I EVER asked to live with you? Have I EVER asked you to take care of me? Of US?" I continued before he had a chance to answer, "No I haven't! And I dare you to hold your breath until I do," I looked him square in his face as I slightly shifted into a more defiant posture. "I don't need you, or your money Selk. So do whatever the hell you want with it because me and mine, well we will do just fine without it or YOU. You best believe that," I said with a quick snap of my neck. "And, you may have my mother wrapped around your little finger but understand me when I say, as long as she has breath in her body, me nor my children will ever have to worry about a place to live," I paused. "And in the unlikelihood that we do, I guarantee you there will always be someone else there who loves me enough to pick up the slack."

He sat there with his mouth hanging open looking like he had just been sucker punched. I took his silence as a moral victory and decided to continue my onslaught. "And just for the record Mr. Black, they *are* named after their daddy. Not their father, their *d..a..d..d..y*." I spelled it out. "And as we both know there is a major difference between the two," I smirked. "But if you have a problem with them having their *'father's'* last name, I will have absolutely no problem changing them for you, like I said earlier. That too, you can take to the bank," I finished with my own devilish smile. After

I said it, I knew I'd probably gone too far, but at the moment I really didn't care. This was absolutely priceless and a once in a lifetime opportunity. I was getting to shut down the one, the only, Selkie Nathaniel Black. I knew I might have to pay for my slick tongue eventually, but right here, right now... I knew there was absolutely nothing he could do about it. And that gave me a confidence that I hadn't had in a very long time. My killer instincts were definitely back, and I was going for his jugular.

We sat there in silence for at least 20 minutes before another word was said, and as tired as I was, I made sure it wasn't me who gave in first. When Selk finally opened his mouth he almost sounded kind and loving as he said, "D.J., I apologize for the things I said. We'll talk again soon, and if you or the boys need anything, please don't hesitate to let me know."

I just sat there. I couldn't believe my ears or my eyes. Was he actually swallowing his pride for once and being nice to me? I just watched him as he finally asked me, "Would it be okay if I held them? One at a time though, I've never held two babies at the same time before," he finished with a sheepish grin.

I couldn't believe it. He was actually being humble. I blinked away the tears I felt forming and cleared my throat to speak. "Uhmm...yeah, sure." He moved the crib to the side, which caught Rose's attention. She just watched for a moment and then went back to what she was doing when she saw everything was alright. Once the path closer to me was clear, he wheeled up alongside me and I asked, "So who do you want to hold first," with a soft smile.

He smiled at me with that award-winning smile that had cheered me up so many times in the past and said, "My firstborn of course."

That was probably the wiser choice even though he didn't know, J.T. was the much calmer of the two and less irritable. I laid E.J. across my lap and then slowly passed J.T. to his father. Even though I knew Selk knew how to hold a baby, I still caught myself talking him through it. And like a champ, my oldest child screamed bloody murder when Selk introduced himself to him as his father. I know it's sad to say, but it warmed my heart to see my son's reaction to him. And unfortunately for Selk, E.J.'s reaction was a hundred times worse.

Oh yeah, he tried to explain it away, saying it was because they just needed time to get used to him, but down deep I knew the truth. What Jeremiah had told me weeks ago was totally true. They both immediately knew the person holding them had an unsettling spirit about him and they both had no problem letting the world know it too.

It took me so long to get them quieted down again, Rose had to come in and help me. While we worked to settle them down, I asked her if just this one time we could break the rules and allow Selk's mom to come in and meet her grandchildren...without him having to leave the room. After a little back and forth she agreed and asked one of the other nurses to bring her in. Funny thing is, even at a whisper Hazel Mae's high pitched, God awful squeaky, country twang voice was still really, really loud but when she picked the boys up. Not one sound did either of them make.

I was so comfortable with her being there with the boys that I told Rose to let her feed them since they wanted to stay longer. I was worn to a frazzle, and the pain was definitely setting in fast. It was way past time for me to go back to my room and I knew that I was going to feel it the rest of the night. As I said my goodbyes Selk reached out and grabbed my hand. He caught me so off guard that I instinctively snatched away before I caught myself. I instantly knew what I'd done and turned away for a second to regain my composure, then turned back and said, "What now Selk?"

He reached out to touch my hand again, and this time I let him. He gently squeezed it and said, "D.J....thank you. They're beautiful boys, and I thank you so much for having them for me." He could tell by the way I jerked my head and twisted up my face that he needed to clean that up and quick. "What I meant to say was, with me. Thank you for having them with me," he smiled, immediately letting my hand go. I slowly straightened up my face and gave him a slight grin and a quick head nod, as Rose wheeled me out of the room, leaving him and his mother, alone with my boys.

I tried to remain calm as the nurse's aide helped me to my room, but I was noticeably shaken. She kept asking if I was okay and of course I'd say yes, even though it was obvious that something was wrong. Even my nurse was concerned with how jittery I was when she brought me my pain meds, but once I reached into my bra and slid my wedding rings back on my finger, I was finally able to relax and calmed down. As I quietly waited for my pain pills to start kicking in, I couldn't help but wish Jeremiah had been here to see me finally stand up to Selk and defend myself.

When I finally woke up, it was to the familiar smell of barbecue, the sound of a baby crying, and horrible pain. It took me a second to get my bearings but when I did, there was a bag of food on the table and Jeremiah sitting in the corner trying to quietly console E.J..

"What time is it?" I asked as I rubbed my eyes and pushed the nurse call light.

"A little after midnight," Jeremiah hummed to me as he continued rocking and humming to E.J..

"May I help you?" came over the speaker.

"Hi yes. Can you let my nurse know I need something for pain please?" I asked the faceless voice.

"Yes, sure thing. She will be with you in just a few minutes."

"Thank you," as I turned my attention back to Jeremiah and E.J..

"Here, give him to me," as I reached out for my bawling child. I took a deep breath shaking away the rest of the fogginess I felt as Jeremiah passed him to me, but before he could say anything my nurse's voice came over the intercom.

"Excuse me D.J.," she said.

"Yes ma'am."

"I just wanted to ask you what your pain level is between 0 and 10?"

"Honestly, it's about an 8, 8 ½ right now."

"Okay, I'll be there in just a moment."

"Thank you."

"WOW. You must have had a really long day," Jeremiah said as he leaned in for a kiss.

I got E.J. settled on my nipple and then gave my husband the kiss he was waiting for.

"Now that's what I'm talking about," he said as he pushed the hair away from my forehead and gave me another kiss on it, as he smiled down at me.

"Yeah...it has been a very long day. You don't know the half of it," I said as I patted the space I'd created beside me in the bed. "You should have woke me when you got here. And where did Lt. Keith have you stashed away all day anyway?" I gave him a questioning look.

"Oh yeah, about that?" he said as he went to put his leg up on the bed. But before he could completely sit down, J.T. began to stir about. We waited for a second to see if he was going to quiet down on his own as we both watched the crib. "Well, what has you so tuckered out Little Mamma? Tell me all about it," Jeremiah turn back to me as J.T. let it be known, he was feeling left out. Jeremiah pulled the crib closer and quickly bundled J.T. up and rocked him in his arms as he scooted in bed next to me and E.J.. The bed was barely big enough for one person let alone four, but we made it look like it was just the right size for our family.

"Well, I was down in the nursery, and you will never guess who showed up today?" as I made E.J. a little more comfortable in our tight quarters.

"Well, it must be somebody good. So who was it already?"

"Selk and his mother." I could feel his body tighten up, which wasn't surprising, but I quietly waited as I watched him out of the corner of my eye.

"Oh really? And how did that go?" he finally asked without taking his eyes off J.T.

"Well, to be honest, it went better than I had imagined."

Jeremiah's head dipped a little lower as he slowly shook it from side to side. "So, is that all you have to say about it?" he looked over at me.

"Well, it did. At first, it was pretty tense but..." as the door opened.

"Hi D.J., I brought your pain meds," Janice said.

"Thank you so much. I see I'm not going to be able to keep going so long without them," I admitted.

"Well I'll be John Brown. Is D.J. Morgan admitting that she doesn't need to wear herself out?" she said with a hand on her hip and a twisted grin on her face.

I knew she was being sarcastic, so I just gave her a quick grin instead of saying anything back.

"I'm going to give you something in your IV since your pain level is so high. Once we get it back under control, we can go back to the oral meds, okay."

It was a statement and not a question, but I said, "That's fine with me," anyway.

"There, all done. I gave you a little something for nausea also...just in case. Is there anything else you need before I go?"

"No, that was it. *Thank you* Janice," I said, dragging out the thank you part with a big smile on my face.

She returned the sarcasm as she turned to leave the room, *"You're welcome D.J.."*

Nothing was said for a few more minutes. I finished up with E.J. and gave him to Jeremiah to burp so I could feed J.T.. As we sat there in our tight space, my little voices were going back and forth with how much information I should tell Jeremiah about Selk's visit. The silence was finally interrupted by the explosion taking place in E.J.'s diaper. We both screwed up our face and looked at him and then each other.

I spoke first, "You're going to have to handle that, I've got my hands full," I gave him a huge smile waving my free hand over J.T. and my breast.

He rolled his eyes, "Uhhhh, now you wanna cry help," he said as he moved over to the crib to change him. "Oh Nooo!"

"What? It's bad isn't it?" I said, trying to peek over into the crib to see exactly how bad it was.

"He's pooped all out of his diaper. D.J. it's all over his onesie and the blanket," he moaned. He looked back over his shoulder at me, begging for help with his eyes.

I hunched my shoulders up at him, "Sorry Big Daddy. I have a little person attached to my chest at the moment, but you know I'd help you if I could," with a big grin.

"Yeah *sure* you would," he chuckled as he turned back to the mess in front of him. "He needs a bath. These baby wipes aren't going to do anything but make it worse," he groaned as he began removing his clothes.

"I can call a nurse to help you if you like," I offered.

"No, no. I got this," he waved me off as he covered E.J. back up. "Where's that basin that was in here before?" as he moved things around under the crib.

"Check the very bottom shelf in the back."

"Ahh, here it is," he smiled up.

As he prepared a bath for E.J., I decided to fill him in on the events of my day. I started from the very beginning with hearing Selk and his mom in the reception area trying to get in, to him insisting that I leave so his mom could come in, to him grabbing my wrist and bumping me with his wheelchair. While Jeremiah bathed E.J., I gave him all the gory details of my encounter with Selk and how Rose treated him as well. Other than the occasional grunt, Jeremiah didn't have any comments as I told him what had taken place in the nursery. Somehow we even switched babies at some point, and he bathed J.T. too, while I explained to him why I was so tired and why I was hurting so much. By the time I finished my tale, we had given both of our boys their first full body baths, cleaned up our mess, and had all settled down again. The boys laid quietly in their freshly made crib as Jeremiah started fixing plates of barbecue for us. I told him everything. Every smirk, every flinch, every shady comment from both of us. I told my husband everything that had happened and everything I felt. For the first time in my life, I'd told the whole story, leaving nothing out, or playing in the gray areas.

Jeremiah didn't say much at first then finally said, "Wow. That was a long day. I see why you're in the shape you're in," as he reached over and gently stroked my wrist.

I knew what he was doing, even though I didn't say anything about it. He was checking to see if my wrist had any marks on it from Selk squeezing it earlier. I loved how caring this man was, but it was still a little unsettling how calm he could appear when I knew that every nerve in his body was firing on all cylinders at this moment. I couldn't take the silence any longer, "Sooo, you don't have anything to say to me?" as I bit into a rib, peeking over at him.

"What's to say? It sounds like you handled him well," he responded without looking at me.

"HUH?" I jerked to the side. "I sure wasn't expecting that," I said with big eyes before I went back to eating. We continued to eat in silence for a few more minutes. I kept looking over at Jeremiah, who wasn't giving me any hints as to what he was thinking. He just quietly sat there eating his food and occasionally looking over into the crib.

After Jeremiah had cleaned up our plates, he dimmed the lights and returned to the bed. Once he was happy with the arrangement of the crib next to the bed, he rolled over and held me in his arms. He pulled me in as tight as he could, then gently kissed me on the forehead and tilted my head up so we could look into each other's eyes.

"D.J. first, let me just say thank you."

"For what?" I tried to ask, but he put his fingers up to my mouth to silence me.

"Shhh. Let me finish," slowly lowering his hand. I just nodded and waited for him to finish.

"Thank you for letting me in. This is the first time that you have truly let me in. You told me everything that happened the exact way it happened, including everything you were feeling while all of it was going on," he smiled. He gave me a soft peck on the lips before he continued. "I have a confession to make D.J., and I hope you don't hold it against me," he grinned sheepishly.

I pulled back from him a little so I didn't have to strain my neck so much to look into his eyes, "Yeah, and what's that?" I asked, as expressionless as I could.

"Well D.J., see what I didn't explain to you is that because I have a special detail, you kinda do too," he twisted up his face a little.

"Uh huh," was my only response.

"See, we kinda track you and the boys' movements with the new armbands you all got last week," he winced again.

I didn't say a word. I glanced down at my armband as I twisted my wrist back and forth for a moment, so he continued again.

"We felt it was best to keep an eye on you and the boys after what happened that night, especially since they didn't have an officer at your door or the NICU anymore," he began to talk with his free hand. "And," he paused. "We kinda set up a few cameras and audio surveillance equipment in a few areas too," he pointed up at the smoke detector.

I jerked my head to the side as he quickly began to explain that the only time the audio on the video went active was when there was someone with us that they hadn't already checked out or if they felt like I was becoming too agitated. He explained that they knew Selk was in the hospital before he ever reached the nursery and they heard every word that was said from his first interaction at the reception desk, til the time he and his mother left the nursery.

I just laid there absorbing everything this man was telling me as he got so animated explaining to me how it took Lt. Keith and a couple of other officers to hold him down, to keep him from rushing back over to the hospital and choking the life out of Selk when he grabbed my wrist. Then again when he bumped me on purpose, to how proud he was that I finally stood up to him, and how impressed he was at the couple of cheap shots I took, as he started to giggle.

"D.J. I didn't think I could be any prouder of you than I was as I watched you stand up for yourself and finally put Selk in his place. At one point, I even told the folks watching what was going down with me, *'That's my wife,'* with my chest all pumped out," he smiled. "And my heart is about to explode right now, knowing that I don't have to worry if you're telling me everything anymore, especially when it comes to him," he pulled me in tight and rocked me as he kissed the top of my head.

"Is that all?" I calmly asked as I pushed my hair out of my face.

I felt his body get tense as he pushed back a little and cautiously said, "Yeah, that's all," obviously bracing for whatever I was about to dish out.

"Okay. I was just checking," as I snuggled back into his chest.

"Wait...What?" as he pulled me away so he could see my face. "Is that all you're going to say? No yelling, or fussing about the invasion of privacy, or how I should have told you about the surveillance sooner," he waved his hands around.

I pulled him back in closer and wrapped my arms around him and gave him a tight hug, as I simply enjoyed the sound of his heartbeat, "Nope. I'm good," I look up at him for a moment before I rested my ear over his heart again.

"Well, alrighty then," as he pulled my chin up and kissed me. I kissed him back, as we all settled in for a well-deserved night's sleep.

The next morning we got the best news ever. We were all being discharged. I couldn't help but start crying when Dr. Cleveland and Dr. Roz came in to give me the news. I was so happy I couldn't help but cry all over them, but it was totally obvious that they didn't mind it in the least little bit. Everyone in my room had tears flowing, even the twins. Once things in my room settled down, and the four of us were alone again, my anxiety level truly increased. I had 101 questions and scenarios for Jeremiah about what was going to happen when we got home. He finally just took a seat in the rocker and watched me until I had worn myself out.

"Now that you've taken a breath, how about this?" he smiled.

I just sat there with a dumb look on my face and motioned to him that he had the floor.

"Now, this is what's getting ready to happen. You're going to go in that bathroom and get cleaned up while I make a few calls. Then, you're going to get dressed while I dress these two. Once all the paperwork is signed, we are going to go downstairs, get into the car that will be waiting for us and I'm going to take my gorgeous wife and our beautiful babies home. When we get there, you're not going to lift a finger to do ANYTHING because everything has already been taken care of," as he took my hand and kissed the back of it, as he sat down next to me on the bed.

I leaned away from him and twisted up my mouth as I asked, "What do you mean everything been taken care of?" I looked at him with a frown on my face.

He quickly kissed me before standing up, "Just what I said. Everything's been taken care of. Security is in place, the refrigerator and cupboards are all full, the nursery is all set up and fully stocked, with the products you specified," he pointed at me as he took a small suitcase out of the closet and brought it over and sat it on the bed. He quickly opened it and turned it around for me to see what was inside. "See, I have outfits in here for them and a couple of cute choices in here for you," waving his hand like he was some game show model.

I sat there with my mouth hanging open as I saw all the things he had so neatly folded in the bag. As I thumb through the clothes, I wasn't sure what to think at first as I finally asked, "When did you do all of this?"

He reached over to close my mouth being funny, "Close your mouth, we wouldn't want anything to fly in there," as he started laying out the cutest baby outfits in front of me. "Now I wasn't sure what you'd want them to go home in, but I'm kinda partial to these two," as he pointed at the little Santa suits and holiday present t-shirts.

I looked up with tears in my eyes, "They're adorable."

"Ahhh, baby don't cry," as he sat down next to me and wiped my tears away. "What's wrong?"

"I've been looking forward to this day for so long, and now that it's here, I'm scared J. I'm really, really scared," I held the little outfits in my hand as I slowly looked up at him.

He pulled me in tight and gave me a much needed hug. "Oh, baby," as he kissed my forehead. "What are you afraid of?"

I looked up at him, "Jeremiah, they are getting ready to send us home… alone with them. No more nurses to cover us when I've got to get some sleep, or I'm in more pain than usual. And what's going to happen when you're at work? I can get around pretty well for the most part but come on now, our bed is much higher than this thing," I waved at my hospital bed.

"And what happens if someone comes by who shouldn't be there? I can't get me let alone the 3 of us into the safe room," I explained through a veil of tears.

"Shhh, shhh. D.J. we've got this. And believe it or not, everything is going to work out for the best. First of all, there is a security team at the house already, so you don't have to worry about anyone coming around uninvited. Second, we're going to have to make a schedule to keep all of our family from camping out, so I don't think either of us has to worry about getting overwhelmed. Third, after the way we handled that great diaper explosion last night," as he pointed at the crib, "My money's on us. We can handle anything after that," he smiled as he shook his head at me. "And finally, unless there is a national emergency, I'm officially off for the next 8 weeks," he gave me the most heartwarming smile.

"What..." I said, starting to calm down. "What do you mean you're off for 8 weeks? You can do that?" I asked with my mouth falling open again.

"Yes my love. I can do that. That was part of the reason I was gone so long yesterday. We had to get everyone caught up on my cases and try to tie up a couple of loose ends before I took off," he hugged me like he was never letting go.

"Jeremiah, I had no idea," I sniffled, as I snuggled into my favorite spot on his chest. "We can do this," I began to smile.

He leaned back and kissed me on the forehead, "Yes my dear, we can."

Amazingly enough, things were going pretty smooth, especially after having to talk to so many doctors and going over all the different instructions of care. Mine alone took a couple of hours and a few extra x-rays to make sure my bones were healing up well before they were ready to let me go. Then on top of that all the phone calls and questions from my family and friends as to where we were going, since the only people who knew Jeremiah was back was still my mom, Mr. Charlie, and Phaedra. I was still nervous as I signed the last of our discharge papers, but I did my best to hide it and keep a smile on my face.

As Jeremiah gathered the last of our belongings and all the free baby stuff the nursery was sending home with us, the time had come for us to go home. Several of the NICU nurses and nurses who had taken care of me before the babies arrived and after, stopped by to say goodbye and to take pictures. Dr. Cleveland stopped in one last time to say bye just as my mom showed up at the hospital, even though I told her she didn't need to come, and she brought my dad and P.J. along with her. Within a few minutes after that, Joshua and his wife showed up along with Mama J, of course. And so did Jessica, Joel's wife, Jessie and his wife, Phaedra and Mr. Charlie. By the time we all managed to get downstairs, you would have thought that I was the Queen of Sheba with all of my entourage.

We finally made it safely into the car when I had a moment to speak to Jeremiah alone, kinda. Technically there was a driver and someone from his protective detail in the car with us, but they were in the front with the partition closed. The boys were all snuggled up and strapped down tight in their matching car seats, as Jeremiah and I quietly sat there holding hands.

I squeezed his hand, and as he turned to look at me, I said, "I love you more now than I ever have before. And I'm so thankful that you're back to do this with me," as I kissed the palm of his hand and snuggled my face into it.

With a tear in his eye, he reached over and took my face in his palms and said, "D.J., you have officially made me the happiest man in the world," as he pulled me in closer and kissed me. He wrapped his arm around me as I rested my head on his shoulder.

We road for a while without saying anything, as he lightly ran his fingers up and down my arm and occasionally kissed my forehead. I was actually beginning to tingle a little when he moved away from me long enough for him to settle the boys down and quickly slid back in his seat right next to me again. We kissed for a minute, and then I looked up at him and said, "Miah?"

"Yes, my love," he smiled at me.

"I've never made love in a car before. Do we really have to wait 6 whole weeks?" I gave him a huge Kool-Aid smile as I stroked his leg.

He just sat there motionless for a second then threw his head back cracking up. "Yessss, D.J. we're going to wait the full 6 weeks," he hugged me.

As I continued to stroke his leg, "Well you know…there are other things we can do," as I accidentally on purpose brushed along his crotch.

He quickly grabbed my hand to stop me from going any further as he gave me a very stern look. "D.J., stop."

He surprised me with that reaction as I pulled away and sat solely on my seat. I didn't say anything as I adjusted my body so that I could comfortably lean up against the window and started watching the trees go by.

I saw him drag his fingers across his mouth, and then rub his chin for a moment before he reached for my hand, which I immediately pulled away. "Come on D.J., don't be like that," he whined and laid his hand on my thigh. Just as quickly as he touched me, I pushed his hand away again. "D.J.…. really?"

We rode in silence a little bit further until Jeremiah took off his seatbelt and got down on his knees in front of me. "What are you doing?" I asked, lifting my arms above my head making room as he wrapped his arms around my waist and laid his head in my lap.

"I love you D.J." was all he said.

I slowly lowered my arms when I realized that he wasn't immediately getting back up. I began to rub his back as he laid there in my lap without saying anything else. As we turned into our drive, I shook him and said, "Okay, J. Get up, where home."

He didn't move at first then slowly lifted his head up as the car came to a stop. The driver got out and opened the door, and was obviously surprised at what he saw, Jeremiah on his knees, laying in my lap. Jeremiah didn't attempt to get up as he instructed him to take our things in the house and to give us a minute. He said okay as he closed the door and went on about the task he was given. The other door was suddenly wide open, and there stood Joshua and Phaedra.

Jeremiah simply laid his head back down in my lap and asked them to take the babies inside and that we'd be inside to join them in a minute. They looked at me and then each other without making a sound. I know my face had to have been panic-stricken as they simply removed the baby carriers and quickly closed the door behind them without asking a single question as to what was going on.

Now I was getting worried. This was something new, and I wasn't quite sure what to do or say. As we quietly sat there I could feel Jeremiah take a deep breath then he slowly began to explain, "D.J., you remember when I went to your doctor's visit with you and at the end of it when Dr. Cleveland asked us if we had any question?"

"Yeah, I remember," I said as I rubbed his head and patted his back. I suddenly realized that I knew exactly where this was going.

"When I asked your doctor, the man you trusted above all others to get you to the finish line with a healthy pregnancy if we could continue to have sex, he said yes. So when we talked about it later, I explained to you that I would always follow the experts' advice no matter what else was going on. Do you remember that D.J.?"

"Yes, I remember that too."

"D.J. we just spent the last 4 hours listening to doctors and nurses tell us what we shouldn't do, what we couldn't do, and what we should seriously consider avoiding at all costs. Then they gave us paper after paper with written instructions for you and the boy's aftercare, did they not?" as he continued to lay in my lap.

I began to tremble a little as I said, "Yes they did," in a soft voice.

"So D.J., when I say that I would lay down my life for you I mean it.

When I tell you that I love you to the moon and back, I love you that far and more. But what I'm not going to do with you, is play these little childish games when you don't get your way. Baby, I would give you my heart if that was the only way for you to live, so please, I'm begging you. PLEASE... don't get all pouty and push me away when I tell you NO to something that we just spent the last 4 hours being warned against, if not straight up told, NOT TO DO by some of the best docs in the state!" he railed off at me in almost one breath.

I turned to look out the window and brush away a tear as he lifted his head out of my lap. He cupped my hands inside his and kissed them as he got off his knees and slid into the seat right up next to me. He pulled me in close and touched his forehead to the side of my head and whispered in my ear, "I didn't mean to make you cry but pushing me away about this, that I couldn't take. Not today. Not tomorrow. Not ever," as he turned my face to his and gently wiped away my tears. "D.J. I'll give it to your mother about one thing," he shook his head at me, "You seem to thrive on drama and putting on a show sometimes, and you are a master at getting your way. Don't get me wrong, that's okay sometimes. But baby, this just ain't one of those times. I almost lost you more than once, over a very short time span. And if not having sex with you so that your entire body can fully heal is what it's going to take to make sure that I don't have to worry about another medical crisis anytime soon, that's damn well what's going to have to happen. Do I make myself clear?" he watched me as I sniffled back my tears.

Before I had a chance to answer, the door opened again, and P.J. was standing there bouncing, "Sissy, come on! We're all waiting for you."

I hid my face as I wiped away my tears and cleared my throat...

"Hey little man, give your sister and me just a second, and we'll be inside in just a minute okay," Jeremiah quickly jumped in. "And make sure you save us some of that cake, okay?" he laughed as he patted P.J. on the shoulder to reassure him that everything was okay.

P.J. could tell something wasn't right, but he slowly agreed and closed the door, and then ran back to the house yelling, "Mommy, mommy D.J. is crying...."

"Well, we better go before everyone comes out here to see what's going on," as he dropped his head.

I grabbed his hand as he opened the door and began to step across me, "Wait a minute. I need to say something."

"Yeah...what's that D.J.?" he looked back over his shoulder with one leg already out of the car.

"Please. Close the door and give me a second," I asked, as I finally released his wrist. He just watched me for a second before he pulled his leg back in the car and closed the door as he took the seat across from me. "Jeremiah, I love you. And I'm not trying to hurt you. So I'm sorry that I just hurt your feelings and I love you for being smart enough for the both of us, this time," I smiled. "I know I can be difficult, but so do you. You all but said it in your vows...'I'm a handful,' those were your words, not mine."

"Really D.J.?" as he shook his head.

"Let me finish," I gave him a smirk. "I started getting that butterfly, tingly feeling I get when I'm close to you, and I just wanted to feel that connection again. I've been missing that physical connection with you. Baby, I miss the music and when we couldn't find you..." I hesitated for a second, "Well when we couldn't find you, I thought I'd never hear it again Miah," I smiled, trying not to blush. "So yes, when that tingly feeling came back, even through all this pain, I pushed even though we were warned against it. And I pushed you away when you told me no because selfishly, I need to feel that connection again. And for that, I'm not sorry, but I do apologize," I lifted his hands up in mine and softly kissed his wedding ring. "But that was a low blow saying my mother was right. You better take that part back right now Mister, or it's going to be a long night up in these parts," I quickly switched gears and snapped at him. Taking the opportunity to pull him towards me so that I could poke him in the chest.

He frowned up as he pulled back rubbing his chest. "Was *that* really necessary D.J.?" he asked, trying not to giggle.

"Yes, it was," as I pulled him close again and gave him a long passionate kiss. Before I realized it, he had me up in his lap, and we were all but laying in the seat, as the back door opened again with a large group of our guests, peering in at us.

My father of all people was the one to speak up, "Excuse us, but we're kinda having a party inside, and the other 2 guests of honor seem to be missing all the action," he smiled. Now the one thing you need to understand about my dad is that he is always up for a good time. He may be absent in every other aspect of your life, but when it comes time to partying, he's definitely going to be the life of it.

Jeremiah carried me in the house instead of pushing me in the wheelchair, which after second thought was actually the romantic thing to do since we were newlyweds. What woman doesn't want to be carried over the threshold for the first time after her wedding? The house was completely decked out in Christmas decorations and baby streamers. Our friends and families were throwing us a Welcome Home, Christmas Baby Shower.

I couldn't believe how many people were at the house, especially since hardly any of their cars were in the driveway when we arrived. Both of our families and several friends came to celebrate our coming home, and it wasn't even a weekend. His family turning out in mass was not a surprise, but mine...that was a shocker. And when I say my family came out, I mean my family came out. My parents and brothers, along with all of my aunts, uncles, and cousins, were all there.

I can't tell you how many boxes of tissue we went through either. There were tears flowing all night long. And surprisingly, everyone got along. Jeremiah laughed and partied, playing games with many of the same people who had ambushed him at my parent's house, just a little over 4 weeks ago. When I say water under the bridge, it was water under the bridge for both our families. His brothers and sisters knew exactly what had been happening with my mom and if you didn't know that, you would have thought that she had invited them all in with open arms the first time they met.

As I watched my mom and Jeremiah go down the Soul Train line together, I had to admit one thing to myself... Jeremiah was correct about one thing, my mother was right when she said that I could be a drama queen, but no matter what else anyone thought, you best believe that I learned it from the master.

The partying went on and on. I had already put the boys down twice when I finally had to turn in myself. There were several people still there when I went to bed, but amazingly enough, once we closed the door to the hallway and our bedroom door, much of the noise from the front of the house was drowned out. I didn't have to worry about getting up to take care of the boys throughout the night because my mom and Momma J were both spending the night to help us out, so I opted to take an extra pain pill so I could try to get a good night's sleep. And even though I insisted that Jeremiah returned to the party immediately after we got me settled in the bed, he stayed in the back with me until he was sure I had fallen asleep. I drifted off to sleep snuggly wrapped in my husband's arms and listening to the faint sounds of music and laughter thinking to myself, 'It really can't get any better than this.'

Unfortunately when I woke up the next morning, I found out exactly how mistaken I could be. In the distance, I could hear multiple voices and laughter, while the aroma of coffee, bacon, and wood-burning filled the room. As I sat there enjoying all of the sounds and smells filling my house, Jeremiah came in and slid across the bed and kissed me.

"Good morning Sleeping Beauty. I thought I heard you finally moving around," he smiled.

"Why'd you let me sleep so long?" as I re-wrapped my hair again, so it wasn't all over the place, and quickly threw the covers off of me so that I could get out of the bed.

"Oh no. Hold your horses Little Mama," he said as he rolled out of bed then came around to my side. "This time how about you wait for some help," he said as he moved the wheelchair closer to the bed. "And to answer your question, because you obviously must have needed it," as he reached for my hands.

I sat there squirming as I dangled my legs over the edge "yeah, yeah. Well, I've got to go bad," as I wrapped my arms around his neck so he could lift me over into the chair. "And what do you mean, 'how about I wait for help this time?' What happened?" I looked up at him as he pushed me into the bathroom. "I got it from here," I smiled as I pushed myself the rest of the way over to the toilet and pushed the door a little, so it wasn't wide open.

He smiled, shaking his head as I watched him hop up on the countertop to wait for me to finish using the bathroom. "Well let's just say, I learned 2 things last night...1st, I need to keep a baby monitor on you too and 2nd, I must reaaallly love you," he giggled.

"Oh nooo. What happened?" I asked as I flushed the toilet. I knew it was something really embarrassing when I opened the door, and he was still laughing. "Just give it to me straight. What did I do?" I said, shaking my head as I wheeled up to the sink.

"Did you not notice anything different this morning? What you're wearing or the sheets on the bed perhaps?" he asked with a huge grin on his face.

I looked down at what I was wearing, "This isn't what I had on last night," as I looked up with a terrified look on my face. "Please....don't tell me," as I bit my lip.

"Yep! You guessed it," he pointed at me. "You tried to get up on your own last night and let's just say you didn't make it to where ever it was you were trying to go," he leaped off the countertop and circled around me as he knelt down beside me. I just sat there like a deer in the headlights listening to what he had to say. "So when I came in to go to bed, guess who I found half-naked, curled up at the foot of the bed in a puddle of breast milk?"

"Nooooooooo," I said with a deeper voice than I would typically use. I laid my face in my hands, shaking my head. He just knelt there rubbing my back. Through clenched fists, "I am so sorry," as I sat up with tears in my eyes.

"Oh baby, don't cry," as he hugged me. "Who cares if I had to change the diapers in your bra and sop up all your spilled milk? It was kinda fun trying to pump you, reminded me of being a kid on a farm," he laughed. "Well at least milk doesn't really stain anything, and the mattress was still pretty dry since you were on top of all the sheets and blanket," he said with a giggle.

"That's not funny!" I said as I swatted at him. "How humiliating," I buried my face in my hands again.

"Oh, come on," he kissed me on the top of my head. "You would do the same for me, and we learned a valuable lesson in the process," he giggled as he pushed me out of the bathroom.

"Yeah, and what's that?" I asked, still shaking my head.

"We learned that you don't ever, ever, ever, ever, ever need to take more pain meds than prescribed. You become a complete fruit loop," he burst out laughing. I just sat there looking up at him with my mouth hanging wide open. I couldn't believe he just said that to me. When he finally got himself under control, he asked, "Do you wanna pump before we head in with our guests? Technically the babies have already eaten this morning but knowing E.J. he could easily go for another round," he shook his head. "D.J., I promise you that boy is going to eat us out of house and home," he laughed.

"You're right about that. I've never seen a baby eat so much." I was trying not to giggle. "I'll pump. If he gets to crying I'll fill up again anyway," I shook my head. "And who's still here anyway. I know I hear more than 2 voices out there."

"Well, it's kinda hard to say. A few people spent the night after tying one on. Let's just say it's a good thing we have so many bedrooms and bathrooms or there would have been a big mess and bodies lying everywhere this morning," he giggled. "Your younger brothers and my nieces and nephews hit it off, so they camped out in the game room for the night, our mothers spent the night in the babies' room, and I don't know what got into Jessie and his wife. They tied one on like I've never seen before, so they slept in one of the guest rooms. As I was coming to check on you I saw a car coming up the drive, so there's no telling who else is in the kitchen at this point," he explained while I finished pumping.

"Well, we both said that we wanted a house full, I guess we got it sooner than later," I smiled.

"Yeah, a house full of kids. Not hungover adults," he sighed.

"Well look at it this way," I looked up at him as he pushed me down the hallway, "At least we don't have to worry about whether or not our families are going to get along," I squeezed his hand.

"Thank God for that," he smiled as we entered the circus known as our kitchen.

Mama J was bouncing E.J. on her shoulder while fixing somebody's plate. My mom was scrambling eggs, while Jessica was making pancakes, and Jordon was slicing up a ham and frying it in a skillet. Even my brother J.R. was helping squeeze fresh orange juice from the oranges Jered's oldest daughter was busy cutting up. I was shocked at all the activity going on as I settled in next to Mama J and the bassinet, where J.T. quietly slept even with all the noise going on around him.

"Well good morning, Sleeping Beauty. We were beginning to worry about you," my mother smiled.

"I guess I overdid it, again," I smiled as I motioned to Jeremiah to fix me a glass of juice.

"Well, I'm glad you got some rest baby. See it was a good thing that me and your mama stayed and helped out," Mama J patted my hand.

I had to admit it, I kinda enjoyed having all these people in the house. It gave me a glimpse of what I hoped it would be like when Jeremiah and I added to our brood. Having a multigenerational home was more than I ever dreamed possible and having all of these babysitters was a dream. We sat laughing and eating so long, that before I realized it, they had started fixing lunch. I'd already fed my two a couple of times when I had to excuse myself to take a nap. This time I made sure that I pumped myself dry before I laid down to take a nap. I woke up to my mom and Jeremiah having a heated conversation on our bedroom balcony. They got quiet when they saw me sit up in the bed, but I already knew what this argument had to be about...Selkie. They quickly made their way back in the room while trying to put on happy faces, but I put an end to that before they had a chance to feed me some cockamamie story.

As I swung my legs over the side of the bed, "So what did Selk say?" I asked, watching the two of them fidget.

"Well baby, he called the house yesterday and left a message," she looked at Jeremiah.

"And," I said with a flat look on my face.

"Well, he was a little upset that no one told him that the babies were being discharged and he wanted to know where they were, that is all," she explained as she sat down next to me.

I just kept looking at Jeremiah as I rolled my eyes and said, "So what did you tell him?" as I looked over at my mom.

"Like I said, he called and left a message yesterday while we were all out here, so your father listened to it and told me about it."

I threw my hands up, "Please get to why you two were outside on the balcony arguing," as I pointed outside.

"Your mom took it upon herself to call Selk from our *house phone* to talk to him this morning."

"You did what?! Why would you do that?! If we wanted Selk to have our house number, I would have given it to him!" I nearly came off the bed.

She just sat there with her head down for a moment, "I wasn't thinking about it that way. I was just calling to ease his mind and let him know that you and the boys were okay and safe and sound at home," she explained.

"Mom, first of all, Selk couldn't give a damn how I'm doing, and second, you could have called him from your cell phone. Now he will be calling harassing me, day in and day out," I said as I reached for Jeremiah to help me into the wheelchair.

"Baby, he was concerned about you and who was helping you with the babies. I explained that I was here with you and that Jeremiah's mama was helping out too," she followed me into the closet.

"Yeah, I bet that went over like a ton of bricks," as I dug through a couple of drawers trying to figure out what I was going to wear. "Mom once again, you've overstepped. I could care less if you talked to him but calling him from our house phone and giving him details as to who is here," I shook my head, "That wasn't your call to make. You should have asked us first," I said as I slammed the drawer shut. I realized she was too quiet as I turned to see what she was doing and was shocked to see her just standing there, staring around the room. I rolled my eyes as I turned and bumped her as I wheeled past her.

"This is absolutely beautiful," as she ran her fingers across the center cabinet.

Jeremiah was leaning up against the wall shaking his head as I went into the bathroom to change my clothes. She was just coming out of the closet when I came out of the bathroom. "So what else did you tell him?" I asked as I stopped next to Jeremiah.

"Nothing else really," she waved me off.

"Yeah, I find that hard to believe," I frowned.

"Go on. Tell her what else you told him," Jeremiah said sarcastically as he took a seat beside me.

"Moooom! What did you do?" I asked, moving closer to her.

"D.J., he had a right to know," she snapped.

"Know what?!" I yelled, as Jeremiah reached over and closed our bedroom door.

"He had the right to know that Jeremiah was here taking care of you and the boys."

"Mom you didn't!?" I turned to look at Jeremiah with wide eyes.

"Yep, she sure did," he said, shaking his head.

"He was bound to find out eventually. And besides, he has a right to know who's taking care of his children," she said so matter-of-factly.

I wheeled my chair back around at her so fast it startled her, "His children? Did you say 'his children'?" I continued before she had a chance to speak. "Mother, understand me once and for all. The ONLY parents that have any say in the lives of those two children are me and their daddy. And if you need me to point him out to you, he's sitting right over there by that door," as I pointed back at Jeremiah. "I don't give a damn what Selk feels or what you 'think' he should know! The only man that I give a damn about how he feels or what he thinks is the one I'm married to, and if you spilling your guts to Selk, hurts him in any way, momma I guarantee you one thing's for sure..." I paused for effect, "Your loyalty to Selk will cost you any kind of relationship with your ONLY LIVING DAUGHTER AND HER CHILDREN! DO I MAKE MYSELF CLEAR?!"

She stood there like a deer in the headlights longer than I expected before she responded. "D.J. Morgan! Since when do you speak to your mother in that tone?" with her hands now on her hips.

No one was expecting me to stand up, causing Jeremiah to hurry to his feet and jump to my side to balance me. "Mom, when my mother puts the safety of my family at jeopardy, I will respond, however, I see fit. There are armed guards all over this property for a reason mother. And until we figure out exactly who tried to kill us, all of us," I waved. "Certain people are on a need to know basis, and that includes Selk!"

She acted like she was shocked to hear me say that as she gasped, holding her chest. "Surely you don't think Selkie had anything to do with that," as she looked back and forth between me and Jeremiah.

I just shook my head at her as I finally sat back down, "Momma, I love you, but right now, I think you need to leave."

"Fine, I'll go back and finish cleaning up the kitchen," as she started past me.

I reached out and grabbed her arm and kept her from storming past me. "No. I mean you need to *leave* our house. You need to get your belongings and go home."

"What?!"

"You heard me mom, go home. If you can't respect my husband and my home, I don't want you here. You knew full well why we hadn't said anything to Selk about Jeremiah's whereabouts, and you took it upon yourself without consulting anyone about it to tell Selk he is alive and well. So for now, I think you need to go," as I let go of her arm and turned away from her.

She quietly stood there, almost holding her breath. I knew I'd hurt her feelings, but I really didn't care at the moment. "If that's the way you feel about it, I'll get our things together and leave then," she said in a way I knew she was looking for me to respond, but I didn't. I laid my head on Jeremiah's chest and ignored her until she left our room.

Jeremiah didn't even say anything initially as I rolled myself over to the balcony and simply stared out the window. I quietly sat there going over what had just happened and all of the possible ramifications of what she'd just done without saying another word. I could hear P.J. protesting having to leave, but I still didn't move to intervene, even when Jeremiah asked me if I wanted him to go tell her it was okay for him to stay a while longer. I just shook my head no and remained in my own thoughts. It wasn't until I heard J.T. crying that I even came out of my room.

J.R. immediately began questioning me as to what happened and why our mother left so upset. Thankfully Jeremiah stepped in and simply explained that she and I had had a difference of opinion, and he decided that we needed some space. His explanation was fine with me as I tended to my boys and did my best not to start crying in front of everyone. Of course my brother knew something more than a simple disagreement had taken place, but for once, my family understood that I wasn't the same D.J. and that I wasn't going to kowtow to her every whim and for once in my life, I had put my foot down, and I meant it.

As the afternoon dragged on, the house emptied out of all of our guest, except for Mama J of course, but even she seemed to make herself scarce for a while. Jeremiah and I finally got a chance to snuggle in with our new bundles of joy, all alone in our home, kind of. We sat there half the night counting fingers and toes and playing rock, paper, scissors to decide who was changing the poopy diapers, especially E.J... When I tell you that boy could fill up a diaper, oh my.

It was amazing how quiet the house was now that all of our guests were gone and the babies were settling down for the night. I decided not to take so much pain medicine tonight even though my ankle was bothering me more than usual. But after what happened last night I think it was for the best. We finally got both of the boys down and began to settle into bed ourselves as we discussed what had happened with my mom. The funny thing is, although he understood why I did and said the things that I did, Jeremiah actually felt like I had gone a little hard on my mom. Needless to say, I was surprised that he felt that way, but I warned him not to be too sympathetic for her, the fallout from Selk's fury wouldn't affect her, it would fall squarely on us. And right on cue, the shenanigans began. The phone rang waking up both of the boys. Since they were in our room, Mama J came in to get one while I tried to quiet the other. The reality of what I had just said, fully sunk in with Jeremiah as he played phone wars over the next few hours. Each time we got the boys back to sleep, damn if the phone didn't ring again, only to hear a quick click and a dial tone. Finally he gave up and just unplugged the phone, so we could all finally get some sleep, but of course I had to let him know I was right before we both fell asleep.

He rolled over and wrapped his arms around me as I snuggled in as close as two different sized spoons could get. "Miah…"

"Yeah baby,"

"I told you so," I giggled and kissed his arm that was closest to my face.

"Haha, very funny," he squeezed me a little tighter. "Go to sleep woman," then kissed me on the head as we settled down until the next feeding.

CHAPTER 26

It's funny how quickly you can get into a routine, but thankfully, by Christmas Eve the boys were sleeping through the night. I was still breastfeeding for the most part, but a little rice cereal in their bottle at bedtime definitely did the trick. You would have thought the heavens had opened up the first night we tried it, even though I was still up multiple times throughout the night. It didn't matter that they weren't awake or trying to drain me dry at night anymore, my body was used to putting out a certain amount of milk at specific periods of time, and it still did it even though there was no one trying to eat in the middle of the night anymore. By the third night, Jeremiah didn't even wake up to keep me company while I pumped.

We hadn't talked about it, but Jeremiah knew that there was something wrong with me other than the fact that Selk and I had gotten into it earlier in the day. He caught me trying to make myself a snack when we finally slowed down long enough to talk about what was bothering me.

"Penny for your thoughts," he said as he swatted me on the behind.

"Ouch! What was that for," I said rubbing the spot I'd just been swatted.

"That was for walk'n around the kitchen when you know you're not supposed to be," he said as he kissed me on the forehead.

"Ya know, just because you kiss me on the forehead after you pop my butt doesn't make it any better," I said with a twisted grin on my face. "Besides, you were busy with the boys, so I figured I'd take care of it myself."

"Uhm huh," he returned the grin. "Have a seat and let me get what you need," he continued as he moved the wheelchair closer so I'd sit down.

"I was just trying to get the bread down to make a sandwich." I'd already gathered everything else I needed out of the fridge already.

"Here ya go," as he moved all of my things over to the table for me. "So what's wrong?" he asked as he picked at the bowl of fruit on the table.

"What makes you think something's wrong?" I asked as I smeared mayonnaise on both pieces of bread. "Would you like one?" I asked.

"Sure, since you offered," he smiled. "And I can tell when somethings wrong. You've been sulking all evening," he said as he started piling things on his sandwich once I'd prepared the bread.

I slowly shook my head then hesitated for a moment as I cut my sandwich in two. I exhaled quickly, "I've never spent Christmas away from home," I finally looked over at him even though I was embarrassed.

"Really?" as he took a bite of his sandwich with a surprised look on his face. "I can't imagine," he said as he watched my every move.

"I know that sounds silly, but I haven't. Even when I moved into my own place, I still went back to my parents' house on Christmas Eve and spent the night," I shrugged. "Then when we finally got the boys to sleep, me and my mom would wrap presents all night to put under the tree. We might have our battles at times, but Christmas became our time to call a truce and have fun together. And even though I'm still pissed at her, I still miss her," I explained as a tear rolled down my cheek out of nowhere. I tried to quickly wipe it away before he noticed, but of course, that didn't happen.

"D.J. stop being stubborn and call her. It's been 5 days already," he said as he took another bite of his sandwich.

"What good is calling her going to do? It's not like that's going to change anything," I said as I pushed my glass around the table.

"Well, do you want to go over to your mom's tonight?" he asked, watching me out of the corner of his eye.

I sat there staring at my sandwich for a moment, "No sweetie. This is our first Christmas together. I don't want to drag you and the babies out in the cold, in the middle of the night," I shook my head. "Thank you for offering though," as I leaned over to kiss him.

"Little Mamma, all you gotta do is say that you wanna go and we can pack a couple of bags and go," he explained as he backed away from the table and got him a beer out of the fridge. "Christmas is all about family so we can always go crash at your parent's place tonight and open presence there, and then go have dinner with my family and open presence there. Besides, we hadn't really discussed what we were going to do tomorrow anyway. It's not like the boys are big enough to know what's going on, so it really won't matter where we are come morning, as long as we're all together," he sat down beside me and kissed the back of my hand.

I leaned up against him, "I get all of that, but I don't know," I hesitated for a moment, shaking my head. He didn't say anything as he held my hand and finished his beer. "What about the detail?"

"What about them?" he asked so nonchalantly.

"Here they have beds to sleep in. That won't be the case over there."

"Technically that's not true D.J."

"How's that?" I asked as I leaned over into the bassinet to pat J.T.'s back to get him to stop whining.

"Doesn't your mom have that room in the back of the house and there's always the couch in the den?"

"The maid's quarters?" I asked with a surprise. As I looked around the room like he'd just said something so outlandish. "Well, I guess that could work. I don't know how my mom and dad would feel about some strange men wandering around their house, but I guess it could work," I shrugged.

He kissed me on the forehead as he got up and picked up the phone. "So, do you want to call her, or do you want me to?" as he held the phone out to me.

I just sat there a second and said, "Honestly, I'd prefer you call, but I guess I will," I frowned, shaking my head. "She'll never go for this," as I slowly dialed her number.

Jeremiah covered up the mouthpiece and said, "Baby, if you don't really want to do this. We don't have to. I just thought it would be a nice way to call a ceasefire and put a smile on your face."

'Hello. Hello, is anybody there?' came through the phone. 'Mommy, no one's there,' the little voice said on the other end.

"It's now or never," Jeremiah said as he leaned up against the breakfast bar.

'Hello, is someone there?' my mom asked.

I took a deep breath then said, "Yes. I'm here. It's me, D.J.. I wanted to talk to you about something," I explained as Jeremiah winked at me and walked out of the room. You would have thought we were old girlfriends who hadn't talked in years because nearly an hour later we were hanging up the phone and I had a huge smile on my face. I went to find Jeremiah to let him know what had happened and bumped into him coming out of our room carrying a suitcase.

"What's that for?"

"Aren't we going to your parents' house?"

"Well, yeah if you still want to," I smiled.

"Well, we'll need clothes don't you think," as he lifted the case up at me. I just sat there smiling at him, I swear I loved that man with everything in me. "What? Cat got your tongue?" as he squeezed by me and took off down the hallway.

I turned to follow him, "No. I was just thinking about what a lucky woman I am and how much I love you."

"Yes, you are. I totally agree," he laughed over his shoulder. I just sat at the garage door watching him load up the truck. When he finally turned to look at me, I simply stuck my tongue out at him and turned to go back in the house. Now if you've ever needed a good laugh, we could definitely give you one. The next thing I knew, he was chasing me back down the hallway yelling, "Oh, I got something for that tongue. Stick it out again, I dare you!"

We were like two big kids running through the house, well he was running, I was rolling for my life. But he had me giggling like I was 6 years old again and someone was trying to tickle me to death. The guys on the detail were used to us by now and didn't even pay us a second mind. I just happen to catch one of them out of the corner of my eye shaking his head at us as he passed through the kitchen, where Jeremiah had me pinned in a corner tickling me. Which inevitably turned into a mini make-out session that came to an abrupt halt when Mama J interrupted us.

"Y'all keep that up ya gonna have another set of young'ns to take care of...sooner than later," she giggled as she pushed the babies down the hall in their bassinet.

"It's his fault," I yelled back after her, as I straightened my clothes up.

He looked all wide-eyed, "Me? What did I do?" all innocent. "She started it!" he finally yelled out letting me out of the corner.

I swatted at him, "What?! That's not funny."

He hunched his shoulders really quick, "I thought it was," as he jumped out of the way of what he knew was another swat coming his way.

Once we had everything loaded up, we were off to my parents' house in Cypress along with one of the guys on our detail, while the other one took Mama J to Joshua's house for the night. That's where his family was getting together for Christmas dinner the next day. I have to admit, it was nice getting to spend the night with my mom and even though Jeremiah stayed up with us, more as a babysitter than anything else, it felt just as special as it always did.

When we finally went to bed, I whispered to Jeremiah, "I have a confession to make."

"Oh yeah, and what's that?" he asked as we cuddled closer in my old room.

"You're not the first boy I've had in my room," I giggled.

"Is that right? Do tell, Little Miss Hot Pants," he smiled.

"I twisted my ankle really bad at a basketball tournament my sophomore year in high school, and my boyfriend had to help my mom get me up the stairs. She left the room to go make an ice pack, and he kissed me before she made it back upstairs," I smiled.

"He kissed you, huh," he sniffed. "Well was it like this," as he gave me a quick peck on the lips.

"Nope," I smiled.

"Well, how about this," he pressed his lips against mine and just held that position a bit longer.

"Uh uh," I giggled.

"Hmmm, what about this?" as he gave me a softer, more passionate kiss.

"Hmmm, no wasn't like that either," I smiled.

"Well give," he said with a scowl on his face.

I pulled him close and said, "It was like this," and pushed my tongue in his mouth and flopped it all around uncontrollably, then broke out laughing.

"You've got to be kidding me," he shook his head.

"Nope! It was like his tongue was out of control and just attacked me in a wild frenzy," as I shuttered.

Pulling me in closer, "Well then, let's see if we can give you a better kissing memory in your old room shall we," he smiled.

"Yes, lets," I smiled back as we commenced to creating memories that my room would never forget.

The next morning, we woke up to P.J.'s giggles and babies laughing, which was a bit surprising.

"What are you doing monster man?" I asked P.J. as he stood over the babies in their bassinet, making goofy faces. "What time is it?" I rubbed my eyes trying to focus.

"It's time to get up," he smiled over at me. "Mommy told me it was okay to come in and wake you guys up," he bounced up and down on the side of the bed.

As Jeremiah pushed himself up, "Well, I guess we need to get to moving, don't you?"

I just giggled, "Yeah, I guess so. Give us a second to brush our teeth, and we'll be right down."

"Okay, well hurry up! We're all waiting on you!" he jumped around. "I can take the babies down if you want?" he asked with a big grin on his face as he went to push the bassinet.

Almost at the same time, Jeremiah and I both leaped for the bassinet to keep it from moving yelling, "NO!" as I patted P.J.'s hands.

"No sweetie, Jeremiah will carry them down the stairs but thank you for offering," I smiled at him.

He looked down at his feet with a sad face, "I'm big enough. I can do it. I take the twins down the stairs all the time," dragging his foot in circles.

"I know you do, but the twins are much bigger than the boys," I tried to comfort him.

Jeremiah quickly crawled over me and said, "We know you're plenty big, but we need to get them cleaned up too," as he patted P.J. on the shoulder. "Besides," as he sniffed the air. "At least one of them is overdue for a diaper change, and I know you don't wanna do that," he smiled.

P.J. took a quick sniff then backed up, "Oh no. I'm not touching that," and ran out of the room.

Jeremiah and I gave each other a blank look, then we both started cracking up. That was absolutely priceless. I made my way into the bathroom while Jeremiah handled the diapers. I quickly breastfed the boys while he was in the bathroom. I had gotten pretty good at feeding both of them at the same time, believe it or not. And when they were fed, and we were all freshened up a bit, Jeremiah took the babies down then came back up and carried me down. As much as I hated having to depend on others to get around, I did love him carrying me in his arms.

Once we were all situated, the calling out of the names began. It was usually a big production as to whose name would be called first, even though we all knew it would be P.J., but to all of our surprise, this year the first name my dad called out from Santa was to Jeremiah. Even my mom looked surprised. The box was passed down the line until it got to Jeremiah who took it with a silly, half surprised, half excited look on his face and quickly opened it.

I leaned in and whispered, "You must have been a good boy this year," and gave him a wink.

"I guess so," he smiled as he ripped the ribbon and wrapping paper off the box like he was a 10-year-old. Inside he found a Christmas sweater that read: *Daddy's 1st Christmas* above a picture of the twins and me, in our Santa outfits. He looked up with a tear in his eye and said, "This is the best present I've ever gotten from Santa," and leaned over and gave me a big kiss. After all the oohs and aww's from most, and a great big 'Yuck!' and 'Get a room' from P.J. and M.J., my dad went about his duty as the distributor of all the gifts.

As always P.J. made out like a bandit but both sets of twins made out like fat cats as well. It was funny watching Angel and Grace, J.R.'s twins, fascination with the boys and every move they made. They were more concerned with the babies than any of the toys that Santa brought them. And to my surprise, Santa even snuck me in a gift or two. All in all, it was a fabulous morning with my family and a fantastic evening with Jeremiah's family. It was a day I would never forget.

CHAPTER 27

had to pull over and take a break from driving for a few minutes when we finally reached Texarkana, but that didn't slow down our conversation one little bit as we stretched our legs....

"Not only did 6 weeks fly past, 6 months had flown by before we knew it. Things had gotten into a normal routine pretty quickly once I was cleared medically, and the protective detail was no longer required. I went back to work part-time at Service Merchandise until I finished the medical assistant program that I had been secretly working on while I was pregnant. After I graduated I landed a position as a forensic assistant to one of my old Anatomy professors from A&M who'd taken a job at the Medical Examiner's office in Houston, so I got to see Jeremiah even when we were both at work on occasion. Which was a great thing since Jeremiah was back working at the PD and Triple J's. Fortunately, we didn't have to put the boys in daycare as busy as we were because Mama J decided that she would much rather watch the boys than sit around the restaurant every day, so even that worked out in our favor. I have to admit, as busy as we were, we were happy with our active lives, and seemed to manage our routine pretty well. We were truly living into our family dream," I smiled. "We had even started talking about when we thought would be a good time to start trying to add to our family," I continued, as I paid for our drinks.

As we walked to my car, the weight of the things to come began to weigh on me. As I reached for the door handle I stopped for a moment and sadly looked across the car at Cyn as I continued, "But that's the funny thing about routine, you can get sucked into this false sense of security that can devastate you when your calm, perfect life is rocked to its core."

"What?! What happened D.J.?" she begged as we got back in the car.

"My life crumbled before my eyes. I ended up alone with two babies and remarried to a crazy man," I sighed as we pulled back onto the highway, to continue on our journey.

CHAPTER 28

It was late August, August 26th to be exact, but it had been raining on and off the entire week like it was early May, so it wasn't that big of a surprise when the tornado alarms began going off late that afternoon. I had already picked the boys up from Mama J and was going to meet Selk so that he could spend a little time with the boys when the first alarm went off. I'd already discussed my plans to meet up with Selk that afternoon with Jeremiah, who let it be known that he didn't like the idea of me meeting him so late in the day, especially with all the storms about. But I guaranteed him that we'd be fine, and I'd let him know when we were on our way home.

Selk was supposed to meet us at my parents' house but never showed up. My mom insisted that we wait to go home after the last tornado alarm went off, so of course I did when the weather report predicted the worst storms would pass through over the next hour or so. There was no point in being stubborn about leaving and get caught in the storm with the boys in the car with me, so I called the house to let Jeremiah know that we were okay and what had happened, but he didn't answer the phone and the machine picked up. I thought that was a little strange since he'd told me he wasn't feeling well, so he was going home early from Triple J's when we talked earlier, but I went on and left a quick message anyway letting him know Selk was a no show, and I'd call him when we were on the road.

My mom was still insisting that I wait to go home when I developed a sudden headache. I'd already waited a couple hours to go home, so I decided it was time to leave even though I wasn't feeling well. I called the house to let Jeremiah know we were on our way, and he still didn't answer the phone, so I called him on his cell. That's when I really got worried, he didn't answer it either. I called the store to see if he'd ended up staying later than he intended and they confirmed that he wasn't feeling well and had left hours ago. I called the PD to see if maybe he'd gotten called back in on a case, but even then I knew something wasn't right. Even if that had been the case, Jeremiah would have called to let me know something came up and he had to go back to work. It wasn't like him to be unreachable, which pushed me to get home even faster even though it was still raining cats and dogs.

As I pulled onto our road, my heart began to race. I could see that there were flashing lights down the road, but my heart sank when I got closer and realized that they were actually down our driveway. There were fire trucks and police cars everywhere as I went off the road to get around them so that I could get up to the house. Everyone was mostly down by the stable and tack house, but I couldn't really see the buildings until I made it all the way up the drive to the house. Lt. Keith was talking to someone on the phone on the front porch as I pulled up in front of the garage. When our eyes met, he quickly hung up the phone and made a beeline for me. I had started to get out of the car, but before he had a chance to say anything to me, I saw it. The coroner's van pulled around the side of the house, and that's when my life changed forever.

"What happened?! What are they doing here?!" I yelled, pointing at the passing van as Lt. Keith reached out for me.

"D.J. I need you to stay calm. There's been an accident," he said as he held onto my arms.

I was already trying to back away from him, patting my chest and shaking my head, "What kind of accident? Where's Jeremiah? I've been calling him all evening, and he's not answering his phone." I had backed up as far as I could, I had backed up against the car.

Lt. Keith's phone rang, but he ignored it as he reached for me again. "D.J. let's get the babies and go in the house out of the rain, and I'll explain," he said as he motioned to the officer who was with him on the porch to get the boys out of the car. The front door was already open.

"Why's the door open? Where's Jeremiah? Tell me please. Where's Jeremiah?" I began to cry as he sat me down in the living room.

"D.J., there's no other way for me to say this, so I'm just going to tell you straight," as he tightened the grip he had on my hands. "Jeremiah is gone. There was a fire, and he got caught in it."

I jumped up, "You're lying!" as I ran for the front door. I was out on the porch headed down the stairs when I ran into Joshua and John coming up the stairs.

"D.J. slow down! Where are you going?" John asked.

I pushed away from him with tears streaming down my face, "I'm going to find your brother!"

They pushed me back in the house, back into the living room again. "D.J. he's not out there," Joshua said softly as he held me in his arms.

"STOP IT! He has to be!" I looked wildly at them.

Lt. Keith had backed away and was whispering into his phone again as some woman in a firefighters uniform came over to talk to me. I honestly didn't hear anything she said as I sat there balling, talking to myself. They were all doing their best to console me, but none of them had even noticed that I'd taken off my shoes. Before they had a chance to reach for me, I'd taken off running again, and this time I made it down to what was left of the barn before they caught me. I was on my knees, crying in the mud when Joshua and Lt. Keith caught up to me.

"It's gone. It's all gone," I sobbed as I noticed the blue tarp covering something over to the side. They were trying to help me up off the ground as I shook loose from them and darted over to the tarp and pulled it back. "OH MY GOD!" I yelled as I collapsed to the ground throwing up. It was Beauty and Wizard, Jeremiah's beloved mare, and her foal. They were both burned almost beyond recognition.

I honestly can't tell you much else of what happened that night. I woke up in the hospital in a panic the next afternoon with my parents at my side. Before long, my room was full of family and police officers asking a hundred and one questions that I didn't have any answers to or giving me their condolences. People were explaining to me what they thought had happened and I really didn't want to hear it. All I wanted was to see Jeremiah, to hold my children, and to get out of the hospital.

After I was finally discharged, I insisted on going to see Jeremiah in the morgue. I refused to believe what they had just spent the last several hours trying to convince me had happened. I couldn't believe what they were telling me had happened because, in my heart, I knew it wasn't true. We kept arguing about me going home and getting some rest, but I wasn't trying to hear them.

"Look! It's up to you! I'm going to see him with or without you!" I snatched away from my mom as Joshua grabbed my other hand.

"D.J., you really don't want to see him like that. We've already taken care of everything."

"What do you mean you've taken care of everything? I'm his wife! I have a right to see him!" I grabbed Joshua's arm.

"D.J. calm down," he said as he loosened the grip I had on him. "We all understand that, but we felt it was best if we spared you all of that. He wouldn't want you to see him this way," he pleaded.

"Oh, it's okay for you to see him but not me. His wife?" I asked with my hand covering my chest as if I needed to point myself out.

No one said a word as we stepped off the elevator into a hallway that I'd come to know very well over the past several months. I made my way down to the viewing glass, with my mini entourage on my heels.

"D.J. are you sure you want to do this?" Lt. Keith finally asked.

I hesitated for only a moment as I stood there with my eyes closed, "Yes, I'm sure."

I heard someone tap on the glass and then multiple gasps and an, "Oh my Lord."

Joshua was holding me on one side, and I could feel my mom's arm tightening around my waist. I stood there with my eyes closed for a few more seconds, as I took a deep breath and slowly opened my eyes as I exhaled.

I simply shook my head, "That's not him," I said as I pressed my finger up against the glass.

"D.J., that is him," Joshua said softly.

"NO! That's not Jeremiah," I began poking my finger at the glass looking back and forth at the horrified looks on their faces. "I'm telling you all...that is NOT Jeremiah!" I had a smile on my face as I did my best to convince them that the severely burned body on the table in front of us wasn't Jeremiah.

Lt. Keith motioned for them to cover him up as I stood there begging them to believe me. "I know Jeremiah from top to bottom, and that's not him. I don't care how bad that body is burned, I'm telling you all that that's not him!" as they pushed me over to the chairs to sit me down, I became more and more agitated.

Lt. Keith cleared his throat, "D.J., the ME has confirmed it's him. He's burned so badly that we had to match his dental records to the body. I'm sorry to say, it's Jeremiah," he said as he dropped his head.

"I'm sorry, but it is baby," my mom finally added.

I just sat there watching them all as the tears began to well up in my eyes. I slowly stood up, walked back over to the window, and laid my forehead on the glass for a minute. I turned to look at them and said, "I don't care what you say you can prove, that is not Jeremiah," I pointed back towards the window. "Besides, if that was Jeremiah I'd feel it in my soul. My heart would tell me so, and my heart is just fine," I explained.

No one said anything for a minute, and yet again, my dad surprised me. He cleared his throat as he came over and took me in his arms and said, "D.J. my dear, it's going to be okay. Daddy's got you baby. Daddy's got you," and began walking me out of the building and to the car. I just kept telling them that it wasn't him, but no one would listen. We picked the boys up from Jessica's house and went back to my parents' house for the night. I didn't put up too much of a fuss that night, but the next day I insisted that they take us home.

When we arrived at the house, Jeremiah's brothers and Lt. Keith were already there with a couple of other people. As much as it irritated me that they were in my house, I did my best not to come off with an attitude.

"So what do I owe the pleasure?" I asked as I carried the boys in the house.

"Here, let me help you with them," Joshua offered, as he grabbed one of the boys out of my arms. "Man, they're getting so big so fast," he smiled.

"Yeah they are," I smiled. "Mommy, will you keep an eye on them for a minute?" I asked as I headed back out on the front porch where the others were still at before she had a chance to answer.

You could tell they were talking about something that they didn't want me to be a part of by the way they all got quiet when they realized that I was standing there.

"So, what's the meeting about and why wasn't I invited?"

No one rushed to respond at first, then finally Lt. Keith spoke up. "We were just going over the preliminary report from the fire investigator..."

"And this here is Kevin McCaw, your insurance agent," John jumped in. "He's insured all of our houses and cars for years," he gave me a sheepish smile.

"It's nice to finally meet you D.J.," Mr. McCaw said as he shook my hand. "I just hate it's under these circumstances," he added in a softer voice.

"Yeah, me too," I nodded at him as I quickly turned my attention back to the rest of the group. "So, what happened here? Or can't they tell?" I asked.

Lt. Keith took the lead, "From all indication, it looks like a lightning strike started the fire and the chemicals that were stored in the back of the building intensified the flames and accelerated the fire faster than Jeremiah expected. We figure Jeremiah was in the house when he heard the strike and went out to investigate and when he saw the smoke he called 911, but still went in the barn to let the horses out and got trapped. It looks like the fire started in the front of the barn but quickly spread with all the dry hay in there. And then caught the storage room and tack room on fire as well. J was able to let Beast out of his stall and get him out safely, but Beauty got trapped in the back, along with Wizard. We figure the little guy got spooked and bolted to the back of the barn and Beauty refused to leave without him, so Jeremiah stayed in longer than he should've, trying to get them both out and they all got trapped," he finished as he lowered the papers he was holding.

We all just stood there for a minute, then I realized that they were all watching me. I slowly walked over to the porch swing and sat down as I thought about what Lt. Keith had just told me. I turned to look at what remained of the 2 buildings that use to be there and just stared at the charred remains. Over my shoulder, I asked, "Where is Beast? Is he hurt?"

"He's at the vet. He needed a couple of stitches on his leg, but he's going to be just fine," Joshua said as he took a seat next to me. "We figure he cut his leg kicking, trying to get out of his stall," he said as he patted my shoulder.

I turned to smile at him, "He loved those horses so much," as I wiped a tear away. "He was so proud of that foal," I sniffed. "You would have thought he'd given birth to him himself," I chuckled as I turned to look at the people on the porch. "You're right about one thing that's for sure. There's no way he would've given up trying to get them out," I smiled as I laid my hand on Joshua's.

"No, he wouldn't. My little brother wasn't built that way," Jered added.

As I looked around, I realized that we all had tears in our eyes, including the insurance agent. I wiped both of my hands across my face and jumped to my feet. "Enough of this," I waved them off. "It's all a moot point anyway. That wasn't Jeremiah in the morgue," I shook my head as I made eye contact with each of them. I could tell by their faces they were worried about me even though they didn't say anything. I patted at my heart, "I'd feel it right here if he was gone and I don't," I explained. "Come on Joshua. You have to know. You'd feel it too if he was really gone," I pleaded with him as he stood up and took my hand. "Well, did you even bother to check out the surveillance video to confirm what happened?" I quickly asked. You could've bought them all for a penny. No one expected me to ask that question.

"D.J., I understand what you're saying, but I'm sorry, the video confirms what we suspected," as Joshua pulled me in close to hug me. "The storm knocked out a couple of the cameras, but we are sure that that was my big brother in that fire," as he pushed me away so he could look into my face. "Little sis, he's gone," he said to me as the tears began to well up in his eyes.

I just stood there with a lost look on my face, then pushed his hands off of me. "STOP IT! JUST STOP IT! ALL OF YOU...THAT WASN'T JEREMIAH SO STOP SAYING THAT IT WAS!" I screamed at them, slowly backing away. My parents heard all the commotion and came running out on the porch holding the twins.

"What's going on out here!?" my mother yelled as she passed E.J. to John. "Why is she crying like that? What happened?" she asked with a wild look in her eyes.

"They keep saying it was Jeremiah that died in that fire and it wasn't! Mommy, I'm telling you! I'm telling all of you, that wasn't Jeremiah in the morgue! I know my husband, and that wasn't him!" I ran past all of them and into the house. I ran to our room and jumped up on the bed crying my eyes out as I clung to his pillows for dear life, they still smelled like him.

My mom eventually slid in next to me and held me in her arms as she rocked me saying, "It's okay baby, it's okay. It is all going to be okay," as she held me tight. I laid in her arms crying, until I fell asleep.

The next couple of days, I walked around the house in a complete fog, like I was all alone, although the house was always full of people. My mom and Mama J had all but moved in with me along with Joshua and his family, Jessica, and Phaedra. I could hear them whispering about me as I brought the boys into the kitchen to feed them. They were probably the only link I still had to reality at the time and in all likelihood the only reason they all hadn't elected to have me committed, especially since the doctor had already prescribed me a heavy sedative to curb my frequent outburst.

I was finishing up with the boys when Mama J and Joshua came in to talk to me. My parents came over and took a seat on both sides of me and began to talk to me like I was the baby.

"D.J. we need to talk to you about something," she said as she looked around the room.

"Yeah, what about?" I asked as I wiped J.T.'s mouth and hands off.

"Here, let me do that," Aunt Mayvis said as she took over cleaning duties.

"Baby, we really need you to pay attention and try to stay calm okay," Mama J. added as she took my hand and led me into the den where the rest of the family was waiting.

"What's going on now?" I asked as they walked me over to the couch, and Mama J and my mom quickly sat right beside me, like we were some kind of sandwich.

"D.J. sweetie, we just got a call that the coroner is releasing Jeremiah's body today, so we need to start finalizing the arrangements," Mama J explained.

I didn't respond immediately as my body began to stiffen, and I sat up a little straighter. I looked around the room at all the eyes that were staring back at me before I could come up with anything to even say. After a few minutes of silence, I cleared my throat and said, "That's funny. I didn't hear the phone ring," as I glanced over at my mom.

"Well honey, see...we turned the ringer off in your room so the constant ringing wouldn't disturb you," she gave me a wimpy smile as she adjusted in her seat.

"Hmmm, is that right," I looked at her with a crooked mouth and the beginnings of a frown developing across my face. "And who made that decision?" as I looked around the room.

"Actually D.J., I suggested it. I felt like we needed to limit your outside stimulation," my Aunt Claudette admitted. Now out of everyone in the room, she was the one person that I wasn't going to challenge. My Aunt Claudette was the Assistant Director of Mental Health Services for Houston and the only reason my doctor didn't have me sedated and in the hospital.

"I know you all care, but a ringing phone isn't going to make me lose my mind," I smiled. There weren't very many smiles coming back my way. About that time the twins came racing in in their walkers, banging into everything. I quickly scooped them up into my lap and began rocking them. "So, what now?" I asked as I concentrated on them and not the conversation at hand.

"Well, we didn't want to just make plans without your input," Mama J explained.

"I see. So what do you need from me?" I asked, as I sat further back on the couch with a dead look on my face.

"Well, first we need to decide on a funeral home. We've always used Skipper Lee for funerals, but if there's someone else you'd prefer, we're open to discuss'n it," Mama J said.

"Nope, that'll be perfect cause that's who our family always uses too. One of the directors attends our church. He'll do a great job."

"I'll give them a call and let them know they can go pick him up," Jered said as he turned to leave the room.

"We need to go over and pick out a casket and start putting the program together...," Mama J started to say, but I cut her off.

"Actually, we don't," I said as I handed one child to her and the other to my mom and left the room. The room erupted in chatter as I walked out of the room. I wasn't gone long, just long enough to get a locked box out of the office safe. The room went silent when I came back and took a seat between my mother's again. I didn't say anything as I entered the combination and took out a pile of papers.

Once I found what I was looking for. "Here," I pulled out a stack of papers and dropped them on the table. Everyone was watching intently. "Here is what he wanted done in case something happened to him," I looked around the room.

The stunned looks on their faces was priceless. Joshua took a step forward and picked up the papers, "I was looking for these, but I couldn't find them," he said as he turned the pages.

"They were in the safe," I said as I started playing with the boy's tummies.

"What safe? I checked the one in your room, and these weren't there," he said, a little bit above a whisper as he took a seat and passed a couple of papers to John.

"I had it installed in the office and surprised him with it for his birthday," I answered.

After the brothers looked over the papers, "Well, it's all here," John said as he laid them on the table. "Everything he wants to be done is pretty much spelled out in these," as he points at the papers. "And to top it off, it's all paid for," he looked over at me.

I was busy changing E.J., "Yeah, before he went back to work we had a long, 'what if' conversation. We both voiced our wants and desires if something were to happen to either of us. We were even in the process of having him legally adopt the boys so if anything were to happen to me, he'd be able to keep them safe, here with him," as E.J. squirmed away from me, just as I got his diaper secure.

"You what? How were you going to do that? Selkie would never go for that," my mother railed off as she gripped my arm.

I yanked away from her, "What?! He was served with the papers last week. All he could do is show up for court and plead his case."

"What were you thinking? You know he'd never put up with that," she looked at me all wild-eyed.

I ignored her for a few minutes as I changed J.T.'s diaper, but as I got him cleaned up what she said finally sunk in. I slowly looked up at her, "Mom, you don't think Selk had anything to do with the fire, do you?"

The room went silent. "No, no I wasn't saying that," as she grabbed at her shirt shaking her head no. We all just sat there staring at her. She continued to shake her head as she made eye contact with everyone in the room, still saying, "No, no...he wouldn't. Besides, they already said it was started by a lightning strike," as she tried to put on a smile and continued to shake her head no.

Joshua quickly left the room as I whispered, "What did we do?" as the ocean of tears began to stream down my face. I remember being walked to my room, but not much else after that.

A few days later, the programs came for Jeremiah's service, and the family was very pleased with what they saw. Saturday morning, I got dressed in Jeremiah's favorite black dress on me and prepared myself for what was going to be the longest day of my life, Jeremiah's funeral. I don't recall much leading up to that day, but I do remember arguing with my mother about taking the boys to the service. Of course she won, and one of my cousins stayed behind with the babies. A funeral was no place for infants, even though they both looked more like toddlers than infants.

As the family car pulled up in front of the church, I had a meltdown of biblical proportions believe it or not. I kept asking, "Why are we going through all of this when Jeremiah is still alive?" No one in the car would answer me, as one by one, they dropped their heads to avoid eye contact with me. The longer it took them to speak, the more agitated I became.

Finally, Joshua said, "D.J., I know this is hard for you but think about it. Would we be going through all of this if that were true? Would we be putting our mother through this if it wasn't true?" he asked as he patted Mama J's hands.

No one else had anything to say, not even my mother. We all sat in silence for a few minutes until the driver finally opened the door at which point I broke down in uncontrollable tears and began to hyperventilate. It took my Aunt Claudette nearly 15 minutes to help me get my panic attack under control, which also included an extra dose of medication to calm me down.

It still wasn't common knowledge that Jeremiah and I were married, so the service was able to get started without me on the front row, without too much fuss about where I was or why the service was starting later than planned. Even though it was a closed casket I still didn't want to be that close to it, so I had no problem finding a seat in the back of the church with my mother on one side of me and my auntie on the other. For whatever reason, Mama J sent Joshua and John to get me from the back of the church to come and sit with her on the front row after the opening song and prayer.

I did a good job of holding it together until his eulogy. There was a slideshow that played as Joshua so eloquently eulogized his twin brother, that I didn't know was going to take place. I was fine until the pictures of us leaving the hospital with the boys flashed across the screen. That's what started the ocean of tears to streaming down my face again. And then the picture of Jeremiah holding the twins alongside Wizard the day after he was born was what broke me down to the point of having to be carried out of the service. I still have pictures of the police salute as they brought him out of the church, that's the only reason I was able to see how beautiful it was, because I missed it through all of my tears. My head was buried in my mother's shoulder as I cried uncontrollably when we returned to the cars to go to the cemetery.

My heart was breaking into a million and one-pieces, but no one realized how bad off I was until days later. They were more concerned with trying to console me while the services were going on and get me through the day. Luckily I didn't fall out in the floor crying but propping me up on someone's shoulder was the only way they could get me from point A to point B the entire day.

It was on the way to the cemetery that I truly began to self-medicate to get through stressful situations. Somehow I managed to take a few more anxiety pills without everyone in the car noticing as I sipped on the bottle of water someone had given me. By the time we reached the cemetery, my extra doses had fully kicked in, and I was as stoic as an opossum playing dead. I barely even flinched during the 21 gun salute. As I think about it, if not for the tears that began to slowly drip down my face as Lt. Keith handed me the crisply folded flag, you might have thought I'd died as still as I was. And even then I stared straight ahead, never really making eye contact with him or even acknowledging the fact that I was now holding onto that flag for dear life. It wasn't until the repass that I actually had a little bit of life in me. And to be honest, that was probably due to the bottle of wine I managed to consume without anyone realizing it. It was during this time that I learned how to alternate taking pills to calm me down and drinking alcohol to pick me back up, or so I thought.

I was tired of crying all the time, and it had been nearly a week since we'd buried Jeremiah, but my heart hurt so bad that I did whatever it took to make me feel better, and all under the watchful eyes of my mother and my aunties. It was nearly 2 weeks to the day that we'd laid Jeremiah to rest that they found me passed out in my bathroom, barely breathing. I woke up in the ICU hours later with the most God awful taste in my mouth, once again on a ventilator, and in wrist restraints. They realized that I was awake when the alarms on the vent started going off. I just laid there with tears slowly streaming down my face as the nurse explained to me what had happened, I had managed to overdose on my pill and alcohol combination. I couldn't believe it, I had almost killed myself. As I laid there trying to wrap my head around what was going on a doctor came in to talk to me and finally removed the tube from my throat.

Even though he wanted to send me home my aunt insisted that I be held on a 72-hour psych hold although I swore that I wasn't trying to kill myself, I just wanted to stop hurting. Needless to say, I spent 3 days in the psych unit being evaluated before I was cleared to go home, with the understanding that self-medicating wasn't an option. I was to be pill and alcohol-free, especially at the same time, and I had to attend therapy sessions twice a week with a therapist of my aunts choosing. It was during this time that my life took a turn for the worse if you can imagine that, and I learned the hard way that sometimes peace of mind and heart can be deadlier to get than you expect.

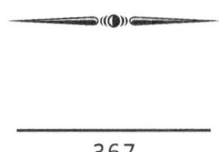

As we made our way down the highway, I explained to Cyn that I was in no state of mind to be making simple decisions, let alone life-changing ones. I was hanging on by the skin of my teeth for several months after Jeremiah's death, even with multiple weekly therapy sessions and all of the medications my therapist had prescribed for me. Probably the only reason I hadn't crawled off somewhere and died is because of the twins. They were the light that kept me getting up every morning. I had long since quit my job and school, so the only reason the bills were even getting paid was because they were automatically paid out of an account Jeremiah had set-up before I came along.

After weeks of begging, Joshua was finally able to get me to allow the executor of Jeremiah's will to send someone out to the house with his Last Will and Testament since I was refusing to accept the certified letters he had mailed me and refused to come by his office and pick it up. Everyone else had their copy except for me. I was in no hurry to accept a document that would make me finally have to accept the fact that the love of my life was truly gone. I didn't get why it was so urgent for me to receive his Will until I sat down with Joshua and John to read the papers. I couldn't believe my eyes as I read and re-read the pages. I learned that not only was I now a one-third owner of Triple J's, but I was also the administrator of a couple of scholarships that Jeremiah had set-up in his first wife and twins names, along with a trust he'd set-up for Mama J's care, and an education fund for our twins.

As I read Jeremiah's Will, I would occasionally pause with my mouth hanging open, and just stare at Joshua and John for a few moments before I would continue reading. The reason they were in such a hurry for me to read the Will after it went through probate is because they were in the process of trying to expand the business and needed my vote in the matter. Once I was finished, I still couldn't believe that Jeremiah had left me his shares of the family business, the house and land it was on, the majority of his life insurance money, and the majority of the money he still had from the payout he received from his first wife and children's deaths. So between the life insurance, the property insurance, and his original estate, which was worth much more than I ever dreamed, I wouldn't have to worry about money for some time, if I didn't run through it. When you added it all up, I was sitting on a little more than four million dollars.

"WHAT?!!!" Cyn yelled out. "I knew it! I just knew it!" she smiled with all of her teeth showing.

"You knew what?" I asked sarcastically.

"I've always guessed you had money."

"Yeah. Why is that?" I glanced over at her.

"You never complained about money in college, and I knew there was NO WAY you could afford your apartment, car payments, and taking care of two growing boys the way you did without having a little coin in the bank," she shook her head.

"Well Miss Detective, you're only half right."

"What's that supposed to mean? Half right."

"I had money, but when you met me, I didn't have that much anymore. Remember I was married to an idiot for a while, and I'd given a big chunk of it away by the time I went back to A&M."

"You're kidding!" she said with a gasp.

"Nope. Not at all," I shrugged. "I was in a very low place after Jeremiah died and an even lower place after I married Selk. I didn't feel like I deserved Jeremiah's money, especially after I married the one man we both despised and swore to protect our family from. So I gave my interest in the business to Mama J, and eventually turned the house and the land into a retreat to benefit abused women and children and made his family the controlling executors over it. I gave to charities and added to the twins' educational funds, along with a few more endeavors," I smiled.

She just sat there with her mouth hanging open.

"So when we met, I definitely didn't have that kind of money anymore, but you're right, I wasn't in dire straits either. But that's neither here nor there," I smiled. "Now back to what I was trying to get to," I winked at her as I got back to my story.

CHAPTER 29

After Jeremiah died, I didn't have it in me to fight with Selk about seeing the twins, so my mom took over visitation duty with him for me, which turned out to be one of the biggest mistakes of my life. It was during this time alone with Selk that he and my mom rekindled their original plan of us wedding, again. I was completely blindsided and didn't see it coming. I never would have dreamed that my mother would sell me down the river like that again, especially after all I'd already been through.

Selk was back at it on the field when the season started, but sadly he just didn't perform the way he had before his injury. I even found myself feeling bad for him when he lost his starting spot, and to a rookie no less. This was also when we began talking to each other again, kind of the way we did after Fitz got married. We'd talk several times a week, and I even went to a couple of games as his guest again. Me and the twins would fly up to Dallas and stay at Selk's place for the weekend and then go back to Houston. By the end of the season, I was spending more time in Dallas than I was in Houston.

I managed to keep it together through the twins 1st birthday and the holidays, but everyone could tell I still wasn't handling Jeremiah's death well. I was losing more and more weight, I wasn't sleeping well, and I'd begun to bite my nails again. The only thing I wasn't doing is taking more medication than the doctor prescribed, but my alcohol intake was on an upswing again, unbeknownst to my family and friends. I became very good at hiding what I was drinking and how much from everyone. It wasn't until I crashed and burned again that people began to realize how bad off I really was, and that's when they pounced.

It was the anniversary of Jeremiah's death when everything crumbled around me. My mom had picked the boys up from Mama J to go see Selk and his mom on Friday, so I had the weekend to myself. Somehow I had managed to drink myself silly and wandered out to the barn inebriated. When I didn't answer the phone for 2 days, people began to worry, so Joshua drove out to the ranch after he closed up the restaurant Sunday night to check on me and found me passed out in the back of Beast's stall. So back to the hospital I went, and this time I was there for about a week.

When I was finally released, I was discharged to my mother's care and had to move back into her house. A couple days later, Selk, had me served with papers demanding that I prove my fitness as a mother and asking the court to award him sole custody of the boys. I was so embarrassed that at first, all I did was cry and refuse to take anyone's calls. My mother took the liberty of hiring me an attorney who talked me into going to mediation with Selk to avoid going to court. He didn't think that I stood a very good chance of retaining custody of the boys after so many hospital stays due to what they called "suicide attempts," even though I wasn't really trying to kill myself, I just needed to dull the pain. Nevertheless, I went to arbitration, and when it was all over, I wished to God that I'd just taken my chance in court.

Basically, I had to move in with Selk for 2 years, while undergoing intensive therapy and random alcohol tests for the first year. If I failed a drug test, or refused to move in with him, or failed to stay with him for the entire 2 years, he would get sole custody of the boys until the court decided that I was well enough to not be a danger to my children, and even then it would only be joint custody with him being the primary caregiver. So a week later me and the twins were permanent residents in Dallas alongside Selk, his chef, and his maid, who became my keepers and Selk's eyes and ears when he wasn't around.

Although I was alcohol-free, my depression slowly worsened, and I had no privacy. Even though Selk did his best to isolate me once again, I still had to keep in contact with John and Joshua because we were in business together. That's how Selk came to find out how much money I actually had in the bank, which only made things worse for me. It was killing him that I wasn't actually dependent on him to survive and that the only reason I was even under his roof was to retain custody of the boys. He did everything he could to derail my sobriety and force me to be the submissive woman I once was.

The chef started using a lot of wine and cooking sherry in the meals he was preparing, so I started cooking for myself. If I tried to stay in Houston or anywhere else longer than he liked, he would have my doctor call and ask for me to come in to submit a urine sample, making me go back to Dallas within 24 hours to be tested. It got so bad that the only time I even got to visit Houston anymore was for the holiday's and even that was basically going down and back overnight. I was never a big fan of Dallas, and now I was learning to despise the city again. If I complained to my mom, of course, she would tell me, *'It's only for a couple of years D.J. Why don't you put more energy into becoming a real family and less time into figuring out ways to cause arguments with Selk? He loves you-you know. He'd do anything to make you all a family again.'* Problem was we had never been a family, and as far as I was concerned, we weren't ever going to be.

I was living my life, and I told Selk more often than necessary that he needed to live his. By the end of football season living with Selk had become almost unbearable because he knew that Dallas had decided not to sign him to another contract. The only reason I hadn't taken the boys and disappeared in the middle of the night is because he was spending the majority of his time either working out or with his agent shopping for a new team. And by March, Sonya and Chris had become more of my allies than my keepers because we were all walking on eggshells around him. He'd already threatened to bring in a new chef and housekeeper more than once so they did everything they could to keep one of us happy. Chef was even cooking for me again, minus the alcoholic versions that Selk had him preparing when I first arrived.

Although I was able to function, I was still sad most of the time and had begun to pray for God to either save me again or let me die. Even my poetry was starting to reflect on how depressed I was becoming. One night, in particular, I'd spent the day in my room crying and wrote what became the first version of my poem *Blue Daze*, as I began to recite it almost on cue....

———— ⋘(●)⋙ ————

Blue Daze

It's amazing how one event can so dramatically change your entire mood and your perspective on life. The "Blue Daze" is the mood that comes down on me when life's expectations and drama get to be too much for me. The blueness is deep, it's dark, and it's all-knowing.

My "Blue Daze" began with car troubles and quickly escalated into job troubles, school troubles, children troubles, husband troubles, and now baby daddy troubles and broken heart troubles. All of this translated into having the blues, dilemma, crisis, depression, legal issues, and whatever else you want to add to the list. Because I'm not one who asks for things or help very often, I've found myself in a very awkward situation causing more "Blue Daze" because I know I'm drowning. My "Blue Daze" is pretty much self-inflicted I would say. Being so proud is now making me "blue" too. The blueness is deep, it's dark, and it's all-knowing.

At times in my life, I've tried to put together a picture for a plan to enjoy brighter days and then try to walk myself through it. But I get so bogged down in so much emotion that I get lost in the vast depths of the "Blue Daze" that I just can't move. The idea of Death would be so sweet if not for what would be left behind. Scared to imagine what would happen to the lives I brought into this world, but to innocent to even allow me to consider taking out. My selfishness now has me "blue" too. The blueness is deep, it's dark, and it's all-knowing.

I've even attempted to put it down on paper, but lately, my writing has been very scatterbrained. It's all over the place with no beginning and no end. Trying to focus on one main goal is near impossible. I have so many ideas racing through my mind, and none of them seem to have anything to do with the other. Focus girl, focus, see what I mean? I dream a story and see it so vividly, but when I try to put it down on paper, it seems to lose most of its vitality. Those sparks that made it so exciting in my mind lose so much energy in the written interpretation. How to focus the dream into reality is the dilemma I seem to have. Focus on the idea, see the idea, and then write the idea. It sounds so easy to do, but again the transition becomes gray and fussy too. So difficult to see and work through the haze, now do you get why I'm so blue these days?

The blueness is deep, it's dark, and it's all-knowing. The rope is tightening, the stress is building, and the expectations are too high. For once, I wanted to do something for me without the expectations and pressure from the outside world interfering. But the world won't let me live in peace and calmness it seems. The blueness is deep, it's dark, and it's all-knowing. It's the "Blue Daze" I have become once again and no it's not a dream. It's the blueness I've succumbed to, the depression that's deep, dark, and bitter to the very end. I can't seem to escape the blueness I've created. The blueness is deep, it's dark, and it's all knowing.[2]

We rode in silence for a few miles until I was able to snap out of my trance. I was a little surprised that she actually gave me that time to regain my composer without one hundred and one questions, but I was grateful that she did even though I didn't tell her to. I just picked up the story where I had left off.

CHAPTER 30

As fate would have it, Selk was signed to a one year contract by the Houston Oilers, which was the best news ever to me, even though I was also riddled with guilt. See moving back to Houston meant that I was much closer to everyone I cared about, but I still wouldn't be able to go home, to me and Jeremiah's home. As happy as I was to be moving back to Houston, there was no way I was moving back into me and Jeremiah's home with Selk.

By the summer we had moved from Dallas to Houston, and back into the apartment Selk had purchased for me when I was pregnant. Selk just knew we were going to be in the same room together since my old room had a bathroom in it, but I was more than happy to move into the guest bedroom and use the bathroom down the hall from it. Besides, it was right next to the boy's room, so it made my life easier. We had the office converted back into another bedroom since Sonya decided to move to Houston with us as well did Chef, but he got his own place. As happy as Mr. Charlie was to see me, he wasn't happy to see me living with Selk. We had long conversations as to why we were living together and just as I suspected, he thought I should have taken my chances in court too. But as we caught up all I could say is what's done is done and right now I'm just trying to keep moving forward.

When I needed a break from Selk, I would go out to the ranch and lose myself in memories. I'd met a woman through my old therapist, that I'll call Maggie for now, that I'd been paying to keep the place up for me, but there was nothing like being there to do it myself. Maggie had been in a very abusive marriage and needed a place to go that her husband couldn't find her or her dog. She had gone to a shelter before to get away from him, but no shelter accepts animals, and she was deafly afraid that he'd hurt her beloved Rottie just to get back at her, so she had to go back to him. So when I was forced to move in with Selk in Dallas, my therapist approached me with the idea of allowing her to stay at my house since I had no plans on selling the place and I would need someone to keep it up for me.

It was actually a win-win for both of us. I needed someone to maintain my property in my absence and she needed a safe place for her and her dog to stay. Maggie had left her husband a couple times before, but no matter how far she ran, his people would find her and bring her back. He was a high-level politician and had lots of high-powered connections, so it was best for her to completely disappear. So, since she needed a new identity and the ability to earn a living without her husband finding her, and I had no problem paying her under the table or with her Rottweiler living in the house, her living at my place was the best option for both of us, especially since she loved animals to boot. She'd grown up on a farm, so she jumped at the chance to help take care of Beast as well. I simply set up an account that I transferred funds into each month that she had full access to through a debit card in her new name. Eventually, we did make everything legal, but at the moment, it worked for us.

My visits to the ranch were therapeutic for me and a God's send for her. Being a victim of abuse knows no color. It didn't matter that I was black and that she was white, we were both women trying to survive our abusers. Maggie and I became very good friends over time, she became my sounding board, especially when it came to Selk. Who better to understand what I was going through than someone who had gone through the same thing? Through some of our late-night conversations is where the idea of turning the place into a retreat for abused women and children came from. Eventually, I started a non-profit for the retreat and Maggie was the on-sight manager, and the Thomas family were among the Board of Trust members.

I could still feel Jeremiah's presence in the house when I was there. It gave me the strength to go back to the city each day, to that apartment with Selk. I could tell it truly bothered Selk that I was happier, and he did everything he could to break me down when he got a chance. He was really sneaky about it, so Sonya didn't see or hear the things he was doing, but every chance he got he had something negative to say to me.

One day, in particular, I was busy fixing the boys something to eat when he decided to be a thorn in my side. "Why don't you do something with your hair? It looks like a dirty wet mop," he said as he flipped my hair as he passed me in the kitchen.

I pulled my head to the side, out of his reach as I said, "My braids are not dirty, nor are they wet and I'd prefer to keep them that way, so please don't touch my hair." I rolled my eyes as he leaned on the refrigerator watching me, but not saying anything. "And I like my hair just fine, thank you very much."

He didn't say anything for a few minutes, he just watched me feed the twins. "What is that slop you're feeding them anyway? It looks like dog food," as he twisted up his face and stuck his tongue out.

I let out an audible breath as I answered him, "It's called baby food. Try some you might just like it," as I held up a spoon full of peas and carrots for him to try.

The funny part was the twin's reaction to what I was doing. E.J. and J.T. started babbling at me like they were fussing at me and finally E.J. reached for the spoon like he wasn't trying to share anything with Selk and said, "No! No! No! No!" as they both gave him the side-eye. It was the cutest thing I'd ever seen.

Selk caught their drift and immediately showed his disapproval. "No? Who do you two think you're talking too and looking at that way? You're not too young for me to put you both over my knee and show you who's boss around here, so you better straighten up your faces before I give you a reason to look at me crazy," as he came over and stood over all of us.

"I wish you would," I snapped back as I stood up and moved between him and the twins. "Put your hands on them if you want to, and I will break every bone in both your hands," as I reached my arm out, blocking him from my babies.

"Are you crazy?!," as he stepped back and gave me a crazy look. "Bitch I'll break your little ass in two," he smirked as he pointed at me. But he didn't move any closer to me or the boys. Finally, he just snorted at me and started laughing as he left us alone in the kitchen.

I let out a sigh of relief once I was sure he was gone. As I took my seat and went back to feeding the boys, I could tell they were afraid, I could see it in their eyes. I did my best to put a smile on my face and reassure them that everything was okay, but they still knew something wasn't right. That was the first time they heard Selk get loud with me and call me out of my name, but I'm sorry to say that wasn't the last time they witnessed that. That actually became the norm around the house, I'm very sad to say.

He was also very calculating as well. And of all days, he chose the 2nd anniversary of Jeremiah's death to really show his ass. I'd spent the day out at the ranch and Maggie had me in a funky headspace. She loved to turn the radio up blasting music throughout the house, which I usually didn't mind, but today a song came on that brought me to tears, and I hadn't fully recovered from it when I made it back to the condo. I'd just finished up some paperwork when a song called *Ghost in This House* came on, and by the end of it, I was curled up on the floor sobbing like a baby.

———»《◉》«———

"Hold on. What was the name of that song?" Cyn asked as she began fiddling with her phone.

Even though I really didn't want to hear that song right now, I knew what she was up to and told her anyway, *"Ghost in This House."*

"Aww, here it is. By Alison Krauss," she said with a smile as the song began to play before I could answer.

I don't pick up the mail,
I don't pick up the phone,
I don't answer the door,
I just soon be alone
I don't keep this place up,
I just keep the lights down,
I don't live in these rooms,
I just rattled around

I'm just a ghost in this house,
I'm just a shadow upon these walls,
As quietly as a mouse,
I haunt these halls,
I'm just a whisper of smoke,
I'm all that's left of two hearts on fire,
That once burned out of control,
You took my body and soul,
I'm just a ghost in this house

I don't care if it rains,
I don't care if it's clear,
I don't mind stayin' near,
There's another ghost here,
He sits down in your chair,
And he shines with your light,
And he lays down his head,
On your pillow at night

I'm just a ghost in this house,

I'm just a shadow upon these walls,
I'm living proof of the damage heartbreak does,
I'm just a whisper of smoke,
I'm all that's left of two hearts on fire,
That once burned out of control,
You took my body and soul,
I'm just a ghost in this house

That once burned out of control,
You took my body and soul,
I'm just a ghost in this house[3]

"WOW! That is powerful," she looked over at me with a tear rolling down her face.

I simply nodded in agreement and went on with my story....

I'd just got the boys down for a nap when Selk came home and struck. He came into my room and plopped down on my bed of all places, still wet and smelly from the gym. I completely lost it. I was yelling and screaming like a madwoman and eventually threw something at him that he mostly blocked, but the edge of it caught him on the side of his head. It left a tiny little scratch on his forehead, and that was all it took for him to call the police on me. And once they arrived, he truly put on a show for them. He made it seem like he was in fear for his life and that I was totally out of control. He told them about me being under psychiatric care and about the judgment against me. He even said that he was scared for the babies, who he had managed to wake up and get to crying to high heaven by the time the police arrived. He even told them about me threatening to break his hands.

I pled my case to the officers, explaining to them that Selk was making a big deal out of a simple argument and that the hand comment was made weeks ago after he threatened to spank the twins over nothing. My explanation was falling on deaf ears as they both sided with the great Selkie Black and handcuffed me. After talking with him a few more minutes, they proceeded to take me downstairs and walked me out the front lobby and put me in the back of their patrol car. The only reason I didn't end up in jail that day is because Mr. Charlie had called Joshua to let him know what was going on when the police arrived, and Joshua had immediately called Lt. Keith, who was pulling up as I was being placed in the back of the police car. After he talked to the officers, they agreed to release me into his custody, with a citation to appear in court and a guarantee that I wouldn't try to stay in the condo tonight.

I promised to leave as soon as I packed our bags, so Lt. Keith went back upstairs with me to keep the peace. I was surprised at how quiet he was and that he didn't give me a lecture on the way up, but I wasn't going to complain about it either. The boys were still crying hysterically when we walked through the door, but the real show was Selk's reaction to my return. He went ballistic when I walked back in the door.

"What the fuck are you doing back here, bitch?! They just arrested your crazy ass!" he yelled at me just as Lt. Keith stepped in the door behind me. The look on Selk's face was priceless.

I gave him a big grin as I waved Lt. Keith on in and closed the door. "Oh, Lt. Keith talked to them, and they decided to release me into his custody and write me a citation instead," as I waved the ticket at him. "I'm not allowed to stay here tonight, so I just came back up to pack our bags, and we'll be on our way," I smirked.

Selk hesitated for a minute then asked, "What do you mean 'our bags'? You're not going anywhere with my kids. You can go, but they're staying here," he explained.

I pushed past him, "Oh really? You can't even quiet them down. Do you really think I'd leave them here with you?" as I went to pack our bags.

"They're still crying because you scared them and their upset," he called after me but never moved to follow me. He knew better with Lt. Keith standing there watching every move he made.

As I left my room, I went in the nursery, and the boys immediately quieted down. I packed them a bag and carried them along with our things back out into the living room. You could tell by the silly look on Selkie's face that he wasn't happy that the boys had stopped crying for me so easily. But his pride wouldn't allow him to give up that easy.

"D.J. I said you're not taking them anywhere," as he snatched them out of my arms. He obviously didn't know what to do when I didn't try to stop him, as he almost flung them over his shoulders when I didn't resist. He expected me to fight him and play tug-of-war over them, but I didn't. And their reaction to him was enough for me to get my way without any further argument from him. In unison, they both threw an uncontrollable fit, and I did absolutely nothing to help him control them. They were screaming and flailing around like someone was attacking them. He actually broke into a sweat trying to control them and not drop them at the same time.

They fought to get away from him even harder when they saw me walked right past Selk and not reach for them. I walked over to Lt. Keith and said, "Would you mind holding these for a second please," as I gave him a goofy face and handed our bags over to him.

He smiled at me, even though he was obviously worried about what Selk was going through at the moment. "Sure, that's not a problem," as he took the bags from me and then glanced back over at Selk as he fought to control the screaming toddlers.

I walked back over to Selk, "May I?" as I held my hands out to take the boys, but remained far enough away that he would actually have to come to me to hand them off. As much as it was killing him, he finally took a step towards me and slowly passed them over to me one at a time. To add insult to injury, as I touched J.T., he immediately quieted down and held onto me for dear life as E.J. completely lost it when he saw me take his brother and not him. I intentionally hesitated in taking E.J. just to drive home my point. Selk was so flustered he nearly threw him at me just to get him out of his hands. E.J. instantly quieted down and clung to my neck for dear life too. Once I had them properly balanced, I looked Selk in his eyes and sarcastically said, "Unless we need to discuss them going or staying any further, we'll all be going now," as I smiled at him.

He stood there with his mouth hanging open for a moment then finally said, "No, we're good," as he slowly dropped his head in defeat and stepped to the side so I could pass.

I turned towards the door and couldn't help but giggle when I saw the look on Lt. Keith's face. He was so shocked he hesitated for a minute until I reached the door. I turned back and cleared my throat at him, then whispered, "Are you coming with us or staying here with him?" and started laughing.

He quickly shook his head like he was having to clear it and said, "Oh, yeah. I'm right behind you." As he closed the door, I heard him say, "Mr. Black, you have a wonderful evening now."

As the elevator arrived, we could hear Selk going ballistic in the apartment. He was cursing up a storm, and then we heard a loud crash.

"Do you think I need to check on him," he asked.

"Nope! He's a grown-ass man. He can take care of himself," I said as I pushed the button for the lobby. "But now that you mention it, if I call the police will they do anything to him for destroying the apartment?" The doors closed behind us before Lt. Keith closed his mouth. He never answered my question, but I didn't really care. Anything important to me was either out at the ranch or in the elevator with us. Selk could burn the building down for all I cared.

As always, Mr. Charlie was standing there waiting for the doors to open. He immediately took E.J. from me as I stepped into the lobby. I couldn't help but start laughing when I saw the surprised look on Lt. Keith's face when E.J. snuggled into Mr. Charlie's neck and didn't make a sound.

"That says a lot doesn't it?" I said to Lt. Keith as I nodded my head in Mr. Charlie and E.J.'s direction.

"Yeaaah," he said, obviously stunned. "I just knew he was going to pitch a fit when you let him go, but he's as quiet as a church mouse," he finally smiled.

"My boys don't respond well to Selk on most days, but when he gets them going like he did today, you can forget it," I waved.

"Yeah, that man needs Jesus," Mr. Charlie added as he shook his head with a frown on his face.

"He needs something," I agreed with a smile.

While we waited for the attendant to bring my car around, we discussed where we were going to stay tonight. I explained that I'd be taking the boys out to the ranch and that we'd probably be there until after I went to court in 2 weeks. I strapped the boys in and walked around the back of the car to get in myself. As I reached my door, I stopped for a moment and turned back and gave the two men a big hug.

"Thank you both for everything you've done for me. For being in my corner and keeping me out of jail tonight. Jeremiah has to be so disappointed in me," I sniffled.

"Look here Missy. Jeremiah couldn't be disappointed in you if he tried," Lt. Keith explained as he pulled me in tighter.

"D.J. you know how I feel about you, them babies, and that demon upstairs. And you are doing the best you can under the circumstances with the hand you've been dealt so I don't wanna hear nothing else about disappointing Jeremiah. Girl that man loved you up and down from the moment he met you, and we all know that none of this would be happening if he was still here. So pick your head up and take them babies home and get some rest," Mr. Charlie said as he held my chin higher.

I tried not to start crying, but I couldn't help it as I snuggled into his chest for a moment.

"Awww, there, there, sweetie. You're going to be just fine," he giggled as he held me tight.

"Thank you," I said as I wiped my face so the boys wouldn't see me crying. I smiled at them one more time as I ran around and got in the car and pulled off.

I called Maggie to let her know that the boys and I would be coming out to stay for a few days. Of course, she was okay with it and reminded me again that I didn't need to let her know we were coming, technically it was my house. I understood what she was saying, but I still felt like I needed to let her know since technically it was her home too.

I decided to stop by Triple J's to let Joshua know that I was okay and to simply touch base. He was happy to see me when I stepped in the back office.

"D.J.!" he said as he came around the desk and gave me a hug. "I was just getting ready to call Lt. Keith to see what was going on. What happened? Are you okay?" he asked as he pushed me back so he could see my face. "And where are the babies?" as he stepped back looking around for them.

"They're fine. There out front with Mama J," as I sat down. I laid my head in my hands and then slowly smoothed my hair back as I began to explain to him what happened. Needless to say, by the end of my explanation, I was balling like a baby. Joshua had come back around the desk to try to console me as I cried out, "Joshua, I just miss him so badly! Why did this happen? I don't understand," as the tears streamed down my face.

I must have been louder than either of us realized because Mama J came in and took me in her arms to hush me. "Baby it's hard I know, but you've got to pull it together if for no other reason than to take care of them babies," she rocked me.

"I'm trying to. I really am," I pushed back. "I don't know what happened. One minute I was fine, and the next minute I was yelling and screaming like a crazy person. I know I don't have any business throwing things at anyone, but I couldn't stop myself. And the more he talked about Jeremiah the madder I got. Why is he here and not Miah? Why does God hate me so much?" I cried out as I fell back into her arms sobbing again.

"Baby girl, God don't hate you. That ain't God's nature. And Jeremiah is gone because he had such a big heart and couldn't stand to see anyone or anything suffer," she began rocking me again as I felt Joshua rub my back as well. "Baby girl, God blessed you both to know a love that most people will never experience let alone understand. So stop all this wallowing and be thankful that you've felt the love of a good man. Besides, God won't ever give you more than you can handle," she finished.

At that point, I knew there was no point in me saying anything else to her about how I was feeling or how angry I was with God. She was old school, and she wasn't trying to hear any of that. So I cleaned up my face, pulled myself together, and went to the only real home I'd known as an adult, and did my best to keep a smile on my face…at least whenever the twins were around.

I spent the next two weeks loving on my boys and trying not to think about having to go to court again. I'd met with my lawyer twice and my therapist several times before my court date so we felt everything would be just fine. And just to dot our I's and cross our T's we did an alcohol and drug test the day after Selk called the police on me and a couple more over the next two weeks just for good measure.

And with all of that, I still got screwed over in court. I had to complete an anger management course, and for 90 days I was to be supervised at all times when I was around my own children, at my own expense of course. And the ultimate slap in the face was that Selk was granted temporary custody of the boys for 6 months. I promise you Selk lived for making my life a living hell. And to make matters worse, he purposefully did things to try to get a rise out of me when no one else was looking. So I was constantly on pins and needles whenever he was around. My mom wasn't much help either when I would tell her what was going on. She still sided with Selk for the most part.

The shit really hit the fan on my birthday. I was having a party at the ranch, and of course, Selk wasn't on the guest list but just happened to show up. He'd never been out to the ranch before and as far as I was concerned, he never needed to come. It was hollowed ground to me, and the devil wasn't welcomed. He caught me coming out of my bedroom with a male friend and proceeded to show his ass.

"Who the hell is this nigga?" he yelled, grabbing my arm. The music was so loud no one really knew what was going on as I struggled to get away from him.

"Let me go Selk! Are you crazy?! And who the hell let you in my house?!" I yelled as I finally shook loose from him.

"Hey man! Don't put your hands on her like that," Mark told him as he held his arm out blocking Selk. "And not that it's any of your business, we went to school together. Once upon a time," he smiled at me.

"Get out of my house! You're not welcomed here!" I yelled, pointing towards the front of the house. When he didn't respond, I should have known someone was coming closer, but it didn't click until I stepped out into the hallway. "GET THE HELL OUT OF MY FUCKING HOUSE SELK!" as I shoved him.

"D.J.! What are you doing? I can't believe what I just saw," my mom yelled.

"What you saw was me defending myself! You missed the death grip he just had on my arm, and Mark is my witness," I said, pointing at Mark.

"Yes, ma'am. Selkie started it by grabbing D.J. She was just defending herself, Mrs. Morgan."

"You know you can't be putting your hands on him D.J.," she pointed.

"Oh, but he can put his hands on me?"

"I'm sorry Mrs. Lisa. I wasn't trying to upset D.J., on her special day. I was just surprised to find her coming out of here with him," Selk explained like he was ashamed, but I knew exactly what he was doing. Playing to the crowd as always.

"It's none of your business who I'm with or where, especially in MY house. Especially since I didn't invite you here in the first place," I said as I stormed past him.

He reached out to grab me again, "D.J. wait," as he held my wrist.

I snatched away from him again as Mark grabbed his hand, "Man, the woman obviously doesn't want you touching her so please don't do that again," he gave Selk a wayward look.

You could tell Selk wasn't expecting that and knew better than to react with my mom standing there watching. He just dropped his head, "Yeah man. You're right," he said softly.

"Well, I think we need to join the others out front," my mom said as she pushed me on down the hallway. I just shook my head as I picked up my pace to get away from her too.

Joshua saw my face as I came in the kitchen and came over to check on me just as Selk stepped into the kitchen. Joshua had just opened his mouth to ask me a question when he saw him and stopped dead in his tracks. You could see him shake off his surprise as he pushed me to the side and behind him asking, "What is he doing here?"

My mom stepped in before any furniture got to moving. "Joshua, I told him about the party when he stopped by to pick the boys up today."

"That still doesn't explain why he felt he would be welcomed here, in my brother's house," he said, never taking his eyes off of Selk.

"Hey man. I don't want no trouble," Selk said as he took a step back and threw his hands up. "I just thought that maybe the mother of my children might want to bury the hatchet and get back to loving each other again."

My mouth fell open as Joshua turned his head to the side and froze. People who had no idea what was going on could tell something wasn't right and began to come in the kitchen to see what was happening, which ended up playing right into Selk's hands, so he thought.

"D.J., I know you've been really sad lately, but I just thought that maybe this would help cheer you up," as he took a small box out of his pocket and got down on one knee.

I rolled my eyes and turned my back as Joshua yelled, "Man STOP! And get up! Don't start that shit. Not here, not now," as he stepped closer to Selk, waving his hands.

Selk was actually surprised as he slowly stood up. "Man I don't know you, and I don't mean any disrespect, but this is between me and D.J."

"As my sister-in-law and someone I consider to be my little sister, she is my business," Joshua explained as he patted his chest as he stepped closer to Selk again.

You could tell Selk wasn't ready for what he'd just been told. Stuttering, "Your sister-in, sister-in-law...how's that? She's never been married," he said with a silly expression on his face.

Immediately my mom stepped in, "Now Selkie, maybe this isn't the time to get into this," as she began pushing him towards the front door.

"No ma, what does he mean by sister-in-law?" as he pointed at Joshua.

"What he means is I'm a widow. My *husband,* my one true *love,* the man the twins are named after, was his late brother Jeremiah Ezekiel Thomas," I paused. "J.T. and E.J...get it?" I smirked with a slight twist of my head.

"Woman, stop lying," Selk laughed as he waved me off.

"D.J. no!" my mom yelled, grabbing my arm. "Selkie, let's go son. This isn't the time or the place," my mom said again as she released me and started pulling him towards the front door.

"So wait. Are you telling me, she's telling the truth?" with a look of bewilderment. "She was married to that clown, the barbecue guy? And *my* fucking kids are named after *HIM,*" he said much louder than he should have, not knowing who was in the crowd.

"I know you're not calling my baby brother a clown," Jessica said, with Jered and Joel at her back.

As the angry crowd behind him grew, Selk knew he had stepped into something that he wasn't prepared for. "I don't want no problems," Selk waved off.

"Man, you were asking for trouble when you showed up here," Mark said as he opened the door. "I think it's past time for you to leave dude," he shook his head.

Without another word Selk left, but not before shooting me a very cryptic smile. As happy as I was to see him go, I knew this wasn't over. Not by a long shot.

Thanksgiving weekend, the other shoe dropped. I had planned the perfect birthday celebration for the boys when Selk decided to exact his revenge on me, in open view of all of my friends and family. We were about to sing happy birthday when Selk showed up with 2 officers and the social worker.

"I'm sorry, but there she is," Selk pointed at me.

"What do you think you're doing?" I asked as I passed Mama J the cake I was holding.

"Well, see you have my sons without my permission or the court-ordered supervisor," Selk said as loud as he could. "So, the police are here to make sure you don't cause any problems when I take my kids from their unfit mother," he said with a smirk on his face.

"Selk! I can't believe you're doing this," my mother pleaded as if he was going to listen to her. "We discussed this, so why would you do this?"

"Selk, I can't believe you right now. This is completely uncalled for," I said, reaching for his arm.

"Officer if she touches me, please arrest her for assault," he smirked.

"This is not happening! This is a bitch move man," Joshua said.

"What do you want Selk? Tell me? What will make you stop this?" I asked as the tears began to well up in my eyes as I stepped closer to him.

He stepped closer to me and leaned over to whisper in my ear, "D.J. you already know what I want, but today I want you to understand who's actually in control here," he kissed me on my cheek. I shrugged him off out of habit as he leaned closer again. "See, it's things like that that make me do the things I do."

I just stood there shaking as he bumped me on his way to try to pick up the boys. Once again, they lost it and began crying and flailing around.

"Please don't do this," I grabbed his arm. And right on cue the police grabbed me and handcuffed me. I tried to snatch away as I yelled, "Don't do this Selk! Please don't do this!"

That only made things worse for me. Of course, they pushed me to the ground and began yelling at me to stop resisting. At that point no matter what else happened the party was over, for me anyway. The boys were screaming bloody murder, and I was definitely going to jail. The only positive thing that happened was Selk allowed the boys to stay with my mom. He knew he'd never be able to control them or get them to stop crying. He got what he wanted anyway. To embarrass the hell out of me and get me under his thumb.

It was late Saturday night and not even Lt. Keith could pull enough strings to get me out that night. I was going to have to sit in jail until I was arraigned on Monday morning. That was the longest 36 hours of my life. When I appeared in court on Monday, the deal had been done, and my fate had been sealed. At my lowest point, my mom had sold me down the river, and for good this time.

As I stood before the Judge, the DA announced that he wanted to charge me with assault on an officer, resisting arrest, disturbing the peace, and unauthorized contact with a minor, all of which were felony offenses. I pled not guilty, and the Judge set my bail at $350,000 cash or bond and ordered me to stay away from my children without state supervision. You could tell by the look on his face that he thought that bail would be too high for me to get out, but I leaned over and whispered in my lawyer's ear.

"That won't be a problem your honor. I'll be posting the cash immediately."

The Judge and the DA's mouths actually fell open as they both looked at me in complete surprise. I just stood there with a slight smirk on my face as I gave the DA a wink.

"Ms. Thomas, you do realize that that amount has to be paid in full before you can be released? Not a payment plan... And how can you afford that?" the Judge finally asked.

"Yes, your honor. And I'm not sure why the court needs to know what I can or cannot afford. What I need to know is would you prefer I pay that in cash or will a personal check be okay?" I asked with a little more sass than I probably should have, as the courtroom gallery burst out in laughter.

Banging his gavel, "Order in the court! Order in the court!" as he glared at me with a beet-red face. My attorney grabbed my arm and whispered to settle down in my ear.

I nodded okay, then replied, "Yes, your honor. I understand the amount and all of your instructions. My lawyer will be paying cash as soon as he leaves your courtroom, Sir." My mom and Joshua were sitting right behind me, both of whom could access my accounts.

"Your honor the money won't be a problem, but we do have another issue that we'd like to bring to the court's attention."

"And what would that be Mr. Adams?" the Judge asked sarcastically.

"Well your honor, Ms. Thomas has been ordered to live with the father of her children so having someone from the state supervise her when she's around them is going to be a problem Sir."

"I don't see a problem. If Ms. Thomas can afford to pay the $350,000 in cash, surely she can afford to pay to have someone watch her as well," he smiled at me.

"Your honor. That's a bit excessive don't you think. And we both know that the state is not going to ask one of their social workers to move into Ms. Thomas's home until this case goes to trial," he added.

The Judge knew he was right and amended his order, "In light of Mr. Adams's very compelling argument, Ms. Thomas, you will obey the original supervisor order to a T or your bail will be revoked, and you will sit in jail until this case goes to trial," he glared at me.

Mark squeezed my arm as he said, "That will be fine your honor. Thank you." As much as I hated it, I remained quiet and let my lawyer do the talking. 30 minutes later, I was leaving the courthouse with a surprise guest in tow. Lt. Keith had been sitting in the back of the courtroom, quietly watching everything.

"Young lady, I don't know what to tell you," Lt. Keith shook his head. "I rarely say anything about a Judge's ruling, but I'd say that the DA and the Judge don't care for you very much," he reached over and put his arm around me as we walked down the courthouse steps.

"I noticed," I leaned into him. "You'd think I'd killed somebody," I shook my head.

"Well, in my humble opinion, if they offer you a deal, take it. Your lawyer shouldn't have any trouble getting the assault and disturbance charges dropped, and the resisting arrest knocked down, if not dropped, but that unauthorized contact with a minor charge," he shook his head. "That one is going to be hard to beat. If no one else heard Selk say it was okay for you to take the twins, that charge is going to stick, especially since the caseworker wasn't there."

We all just silently stood there as the weight of what Lt. Keith was saying sunk in. Finally, my mom broke the silence, which wasn't that surprising.

"Well, D.J., I've talked to Selk, and he's agreed to drop the charges... under one condition," she took my hand.

I pulled away and cut her off, "NOPE! I don't want to hear it," shaking my head as I backed away from her. "Anything you and Selk agreed to, I'm not interested in," I waved my hands at her.

"D.J., come on. Lt. Keith is right. I know I can get the rest of the charges dropped, but that unauthorized contact with a minor charge is going to be a beast to beat. If Selk's willing to drop all the charges and make this go away, you've got to at least consider what it is he has to say," Mark pleaded.

"D.J., you know how I feel about him and what he's put you through, but little sis, I'm with them on this one," Joshua admitted. "You've got to at least hear what he has to offer," he hunched his shoulders as he motioned with his hands.

I dropped my head as I shook it from side to side. I knew better than to trust anything my mom had to say when it came to Selk. I still couldn't understand why she was so blinded by him, but deep in my heart, I knew that I was going to have to hear him out. Everyone waited for my response. "What? What does he want?" I slowly looked up at her.

She smiled and stepped forward to hold my hand again, "He just wants to sit down with you to talk. Just you and him," she assured me.

"Bullshit! Fucking Judas!" as I snatched away from her. "Momma as much as I'd like to believe that that's it, I can't," I shook my head. "There's no way that's ALL he wants, and you know it," I pointed at her.

"D.J.! I can't believe you!" she gasped. "I'm telling you, all he wants is to talk to you," she smiled.

"I still don't believe you, but set it up," as I turned to walk away.

"D.J. don't leave like that. Let me at least give you a ride home," she called out.

I turned to look at the group as I continued to walk backwards away from them, "I'm fine. I just want to be alone. Besides, I don't really have a home anymore...since home is where your heart is," I threw my arms up in surrender as I smiled then turned around, and continued down the street on my own.

"D.J. come back! You don't even have a coat!" Joshua yelled.

I just threw my hand up and continued to walk as the tears began to stream down my face. I already knew where this was going, and it was killing me to know my own mother was selling me down the river, again. I walked around until it got too cold and too dark to continue walking. When I finally got back to the condo, Mr. Charlie was near frantic and surprisingly, so was Selk.

As much as I wanted to feel bad about worrying Mr. Charlie, I really didn't have the energy to discuss my day or what I was thinking, staying out all day and night. And when I got upstairs, and Selk started in on me, I simply went to my room to take off my clothes and then into the bathroom where I sat in the shower crying until the water got too cold for me to stand it anymore. What was surprising is that Selk was still waiting for me in my bedroom.

"D.J., we've been out looking for you all damn day! How you gonna just disappear like that?" he stood there with his hands on his hips like he was my father, obviously waiting on me to respond but I didn't have anything to say, so I ignored him. I turned out the lights and crawled into my bed, pulling the covers over my head which completely infuriated Selk. He yanked the covers off of me and grabbed my shoulder to pull me towards him. "Don't ignore me! You hear me talking to you!" as I simply rolled back over as he pulled me back again. I just laid there with my eyes closed and never responded.

He used his fingers to open my eye, "You're playing a dangerous game D.J. You really don't wanna piss me off anymore!" he yelled. I just laid there with one eye open and didn't respond. What he didn't seem to understand is I didn't care anymore. There was nothing he could say or do to upset me anymore. The next thing I knew, I was up in the air and suddenly pinned up against the wall with my feet dangling. Still, I didn't respond. What he didn't realize is that I'd come to a simple conclusion on my walk...I didn't care what happened to me anymore, so there was nothing he could do or say to upset me.

Funny thing is, after a couple of seconds Selk realized something was dangerously different about me. I wasn't screaming, I wasn't struggling, I wasn't even trying to fight back. I was simply hanging there by my throat with a distant look on my face, so he let me go. I didn't say a word as my body fell to the ground with a thud. I slowly picked myself up enough to crawl back over to my bed, then pulled myself back up in it and pulled the covers back over me, as I turned my back to him once again. I laid there in the darkness praying for death, but a part of me was smiling on the inside. I could hear him on the phone with my mom, and he was scared. I could hear it in his voice as he paced back and forth doing a poor job of whispering to her as he'd occasionally stop and stare into my room.

It wasn't much later that she showed up, as she slid in the bed next to me softly rocking me as she called my name. "D.J., D.J.,... D.J. sweetie wake-up. We really need to talk." As I rolled over, I could see Selk standing in the doorway, biting his nails. I didn't feel like talking, so I simply laid there looking at her. "Now baby you're scaring us. Say something," as she pushed my hair out of my face.

I blinked a few times then began to turn back over without ever making a sound. In fact, the only reason they could tell I wasn't dead already was that I was blinking when she talked to me. I didn't feel the need to tell her what he'd done to me because I knew it would be a waste of time. She tucked me in and left the room to talk to Selk. I laid there in the darkness listening to them discuss me and what to do next. The really sad part is, any normal person would have probably called my therapist, but not these two. No, they simply decided to let me sleep and to try again tomorrow. Unfortunately for them tomorrow came and went without me ever leaving my bed, not even to go to the bathroom. I didn't leave my bed or my room for the next 3 days in fact. It wasn't until my mom brought the twins over that I would actually respond and even then my response was only to them.

We laughed and played for hours, but each time Selk or my mom would try to join us, I'd simply withdraw from the conversation. It was so bad at one point that even the social worker asked if I was alright.

"Sure, why do you ask?" as I tickled E.J.'s tummy.

"Well, you don't seem to be responding to anyone but the children," she responded.

I stopped what I was doing and gave her my full attention. "Oh, I didn't realize that would be a problem for you. See I thought you were here to judge my fitness as a mother and to protect my children from the crazy, violent woman they've made me out to be. So am I being violent?"

"Well no."

"Am I acting out in a way that would be detrimental to my boys?"

"Well no, no, you're not," she said as she began to back away.

"So I don't understand what the problem is. Is there a stipulation in what you're to watch for that says that I need to interact with anyone else but my sons?" I asked as E.J. jumped on my back, knocking me into J.T. "Do you feel that my kids are in any danger right now?" I asked as I pulled J.T. from under me as he squealed like a little piglet.

"No, I don't think they're in any danger, but it would be best to see you're interacting in a healthy manner as a family unit," she explained.

I hushed the boys as I stared at the social worker for a moment before I responded. "Interact in a healthy manner... as a family unit," as I turned my head slightly to the side as if I was trying to decide what that actually meant. "Is it healthy for me to be held captive in an apartment with someone who has done nothing but abuse me and torments me nearly every day, as he treats me like a dog, pretty much with the court's blessings?"

By the stunned look on her face, I could tell she wasn't expecting to hear what it was I had to say, so I continued.

"You want to see a 'healthy interaction as a family unit...' Well, isn't the interactions between me and my son's pretty damn healthy as a family unit? I mean you've been here damn near all day, and you've been able to observe me feed them, clean their behinds, play with them, and comfort them. Are you trying to tell me none of that has been healthy or activities of a family unit?" I stared at her waiting for an answer this time.

"Well, uhm..." she hesitated for a moment. "I have to admit, minus you withdrawing from the adults, I've seen nothing that would cause me to question your love or stability around your children," she sheepishly admitted.

"Well unless the court tells me that I have to play with the adults in this house, I think I'll save all my energy and emotion for my sons if that's okay with you." She knew it was a statement and not a question and went back to her seat in the corner. Just for show, when Selk came back in the room again, I got up and left and right on cue, the boys both laid out in the floor crying. I could hear him trying to settle them down, so I made sure to take my time coming back. As soon as they saw me standing in the doorway, they both made a beeline for me, holding on to my legs for dear life as they watched every move Selk made.

Just to be sure she was paying attention the next two times he came in to play with us, I got up and left, and each time the boys threw a hissy fit until I returned. He wised up and brought my mom in with him the last time which helped with the level of hysterics the boys went into, but they still fussed a lot until I returned, but this time I returned with my coat, purse, and a suitcase. And right on cue when they saw me, they stopped being cranky and made a mad dash for me. I picked them both up, gave them a tight hug and kiss before sitting them back down. I knelt down beside them as I began to explain, "I love you, but mommies going to go away for awhile."

"No mommy!" E.J. yelled as he grabbed me around my neck.

"Mommy stay! Mommy don't go!" J.T. yelled as he held on tight, making me fall backwards.

"Ouch!" I started laughing as everyone rushed over to help us up, but just as Selk touched me I snatched away and growled, "Don't you dare touch me. Don't even think about it," as I stared him down.

He was obviously embarrassed and quickly backed off, but still couldn't admit defeat. "And where do you think you're going?" Selk snapped at me.

They were all surprised that I actually answered him. "I'm going home," as I stood up and turned towards the door.

"Home? You are home!" he yelled before he realized it.

"No, I'm in prison. So until further notice, I will come here to play with my kids, but there's no reason for me to sleep here since I can't interact with my own children without supervision. They need to sleep in their own beds, and that can't happen if I'm here, so I'm leaving."

No one knew what to say to me as I turned to leave. Finally, Selk spoke up. "Wait, what am I supposed to do with them if you're not here?" he asked in a panic.

The social worker turned to look at him so fast that she almost broke her neck. I was just glad I got to see it. I gave him a cynical smile as I stepped closer to him, "This is what you wanted remember? To be in control. Well, now you are. Let's see what happens when I'm not here. How long will it take for you to send them to my mother's house?" as I looked over at the social worker. "You spent so much time hatching a plan to cripple me and make me do what you wanted, that you forgot one simple thing...." I waited, but he didn't respond. He knew he didn't have a response. "You have NEVER taken care of them on your own longer than a couple of hours.

You don't know what they like to eat or drink. You don't even know how to calm them down if they're upset or how to settle them down to get them to go to sleep. So how about we see what the social worker runs back to report tonight. She's already advised me that I'm not socializing properly with you and my mother, so let's see how she feels after watching you try to settle them down when I walk out this room let alone this house. Let's see if anyone ever figures out that *you* are the real unfit parent and that all this time that they've been investigating me was nothing but a waste, when you and I both know that I've never been any kind of threat to *you* or *MY* kids. That in fact the only thing I'm guilty of is trying to take care of my kids and stay away from YOU!"

Both Selk and my mom just stood there with their mouths hanging open. I kissed the boys goodbye and turned to leave but not before I said one more thing. I turned to the social worker and said, "I hope you don't leave too quickly. I'd hate for you to miss the real show. And just for kicks, how about you have her leave the house and really watch what happens next," I smiled. "Then you tell me…" as I took a step closer to her, "Who's the *real* danger to *my* kids," as I gave her a twisted grin and left. I hadn't taken 2 steps out of the boy's sights before they both began to scream bloody murder. It warmed my heart to hear my mother having a hard time calming them down as I walked out the front door without looking back.

I hadn't made it to the lobby before my phone started ringing off the hook. I knew it was either Selk or my mom so I chose to ignore it. I made it all the way out to the Ranch before a number worth answering came across the screen, it was my lawyer.

"Hello."

"D.J. what did you do?!" Mark said in a panic.

"What do you mean what did *I do*?" I asked, knowing full well what he was referring to.

"D.J., this isn't a game! Selk's lawyer called me, and she is furious. The social worker is talking about removing the twins from his care. There's an emergency hearing in the morning at 8:30."

"Fine, I'll be there. Is there anything else?" I asked void of any emotion in my voice.

"D.J. what's going on with you? This is serious business."

"I realize that, so I will see you in the morning," and hung up without saying bye, which was totally unlike me.

Maggie fixed me a cup of hot tea as I told her what had been going on for the last 6 days. As badly as I wanted a glass of wine I knew better than to have one, because one would have turned into two, and two would have turned into the whole bottle, and it would be my luck that they'd ask me for a urine sample or to blow in the breathalyzer in court in the morning. So I drank hot tea as I replayed the week's events to Maggie and Calliope, the Rottweiler, until they were both fully caught up to speed. By the end of the night, we had all shed a few tears before we called it a night.

The next morning, I was the first to arrive at the courthouse, which was probably best. I had time to go over what I wanted to say in my own defense. As we gathered in the courtroom, I realized that Lt. Keith was quietly sitting on the back row, in the corner. He gave me a quick smile and head nod as court was called to order.

We were in family court, so things were a little different than criminal court but to me, they were all becoming the same. Just this time, I was fighting to keep my boys out of foster care. I sat and listened to the social worker give her report, which was mostly based off of what she had witnessed yesterday, and to my surprise, she was actually on my side. When she finished giving her assessment of who was the actual caregiver and how the boys responded to both me and Selk, for the first time in a long time I was actually hopeful that Selk would be seen as the treacherous liar and fraud he really was, and that I'd get sole custody of my boys back.

Next, they spoke to my therapist and then the anger management counselor who all but told the Judge that I didn't have the typical anger management issues they dealt with. That I actually spent so much time and energy swallowing my feelings that my sadness and anger sometimes exploded in some not so constructive ways, but neither of them felt that I was a danger to my children or anyone else, only to myself, but not to the degree that the court had been made to believe. I wasn't suicidal, I was hurting and suffering from depression. And that hurt and depression manifested itself in some ways that had gone undiagnosed and treated until I'd hit rock bottom, but in no way was I the danger to society that I'd been made out to be.

I hadn't even realized that tears were running down my face until the Judge had the bailiff bring me some tissues and asked me if I needed a break. I quickly dried my face and said, "No ma'am. I'm okay to go on."

Next, Joshua spoke on my behalf and then Selk was called to the stand, and when I tell you the Judge lit into his tail, she lit into his tail. Finally, a Judge who wasn't falling for his spiel, big smile, or the fact he was a superstar athlete. The Judge took a huge chunk out of his butt and his ego. It made my heart warm to see him up there trying to sweet-talk the Judge to no avail. You could see the devastation set in the longer he had to answer questions and every time he tried to belittle me the Judge cut him off at the knees... it was great.

Once Selk was off the stand, the Judge did something none of us expected. "Let's take a short recess and reconvene in, let's say an hour, and I will render my decision then."

Mark stood up immediately, "But your honor, my client hasn't had a chance to testify," as he motioned towards me.

Slowly lowering her head and looking over her glasses at him with an awkward smile, "Well Mr. Adams, I'm a little surprised at your reaction." She paused for a split second, "I must say, I've never been accused of making a ruling without considering all of the testimony and facts presented to me. Nor have I seen an attorney so eager to have their client testify in a case when the Judge says that she or he will be able to make a ruling without it. But if you would like to roll the dice after witnessing what has already transpired here this morning, just let me know, and we can continue with Ms. Thomas taking the stand right now," she smiled as she waited for his response.

"Thomas? Who the fuck is that?" Selk said louder than he should have.

Again, the Judge lit into him. "Yes, her last name is legally Thomas Mr. Black," as she held up the court documents in front of her. "Is there a problem with that?" she glared at him.

"No your honor. He doesn't have a problem," his attorney quickly answered.

Mark looked down at me as I slowly shook my head no once, "No your honor. We trust your ability to make the proper decision," as he quickly took his seat.

"Well, in that case, this court is in recess," as she lowered her gavel, making a loud clanging sound.

We all went to our separate corners until time to be back in court. Lt. Keith agreed with Mark that it was very unusual for the main person in a case to not be allowed to take the stand, but from what he saw, she was going to rule in my favor. Eventually, my mother joined us in the little café in the lobby to add her two cents, but I was still giving her the silent treatment and didn't react to anything she had to say. I could tell the way I was treating her was hurting her feelings, but I really didn't care. Especially since I knew she'd gone to console Selk before she even attempted to comfort me.

The bailiff called us back in, and I soon learned my fate. I wish I could tell you that everything worked out in my favor….but I can't. Somethings just weren't in this Judge's control.

"I can't recall the last time I had a defendant in my courtroom who has been so obviously railroaded by the system. Not only do I find that Ms. Thomas has been the victim of the courts, but I also find that she has been a victim of Mr. Black and his malicious attempt to smear her good name and her character."

"We object your honor!" Selk's attorney yelled out as she jumped to her feet.

"Sit down Miss. Williamson or I'll hold you in contempt!" the Judge glared at her over her glasses. She quickly took her seat, and the Judge continued. "I've spent the last hour looking over all the case files going back to the very beginning, and I must say, I've never seen such a blatant misuse of power and state resources. Mr. Black, I don't know what motivated you to take the actions that you did to get this ball rolling, but from what I've seen and heard with my own eyes and ears, you should be ashamed of yourself for dragging Ms. Thomas, the mother of your children, through all this! And Ms. Thomas, let me say on behalf of the court, I apologize to you for what you've been put through over the last couple of years. And might I add that I'm so impressed with your perseverance and obvious love for your children to put up with it," as she moved the papers in front of her to the side.

I didn't dare speak and just gave her a head nod in thanks as I wiped a tear away.

"So back to the matter at hand," as she picked up a piece of paper. "This court finds that the minor children, J.T. Black and E.J. Black, will be returned to the sole custody of their mother, D.J. Thomas. This court also finds that there is no basis for supervised supervision now, nor was there ever a need for such an order, and hereby order that the state's case against Ms. Thomas is officially closed and permanently sealed. Also, Ms. Thomas will no longer be bound to this insane requirement for her to reside with Mr. Black and is released on her own fruition to live wherever she and her children should so choose. I also order Mr. Selkie Nathaniel Black, to reimburse all monies that Ms. Thomas had to pay out due to his maliciousness."

"That ain't fair!" Selk yelled as his lawyer grabbed his arm to keep him from standing up.

"Oh really? Let's discuss what is and ain't fair, as you so eloquently put it, Mr. Black," as the Judge leaned forward crossing her arms, staring at him over her glasses. "Fair would be me finding you in contempt of court and sentencing you to 90 days in the county jail for what you've put Ms. Thomas through. Fair, would be giving you another 90 days for what you've put your children through, and then another 90 days for what you've put this court through even though that still wouldn't add up to the number of days you've spent tormenting Ms. Thomas over the last year. Fair would be requiring you to have supervised visits with your children, the way you've caused Ms. Thomas to do since they obviously react very negatively to your presence in the first place. That would be fair Mr. Black, don't you agree Ms. Thomas?" as she looked over at me.

I just sat there like a bump on a log. I wasn't sure if I was supposed to actually respond or not, so I just nodded in agreement with half a huge grin on my face.

"But as badly as I'd like to, I just can't do that. I can't treat you that way, Mr. Black. At least not in accordance with state law. And since I believe in this system and what is right Mr. Black, what I've decided will be fair, according to the law is this..." as she sat up straight and began to read from a different piece of paper she was now holding. "Mr. Selkie Nathaniel Black, you are hereby ordered to pay all of Ms. D.J. Thomas's legal fees and reimburse her for any and all costs that she has encountered due to this ridiculous agreement requiring Ms. Thomas to reside with you. You will also reimburse her for all of these random drug tests that not so coincidentally had to be done every time she decided to travel. And you will also reimburse her for the cost of having to change her travel plans at the last minute to remain in compliance with this dumbass order," she shook her head glaring at Selk. "Also, she's to be reimbursed for the cost of any counseling beyond what she was already willingly participating in on her own accord. Mr. Black you are also ordered to reimburse the state and Ms. Thomas for the cost to have a social worker present for the time she was with her children. I also order you to participate in the following, in person, parenting courses..." she paused for a moment to look at him. "Online will not be acceptable Mr. Black, I'd hate to think you missed out on these experiences yourself and or hired someone to take the classes for you," she gave him a devilish grin. "A co-parenting class of at least 8 weeks, another course in parenting toddlers, and an additional single parenting course. All of which you must submit a certificate of completion of to this court within the next 7 months or I will find *you* in contempt of this court and sentence you to 6 months in the county jail," as she looked over her glasses at Selk daring him to say something.

"Ms. Thomas, I wish I could drop the criminal cases against you but unfortunately I can't. Those charges are completely out of my jurisdiction, but what I can do is provide the DA in your case my findings, with my strong recommendation to drop all of the charges against you. And should the DA choose NOT to heed my advice, Mr. Black I would strongly suggest that you drop these charges yourself," as she gave him a stern look. "I will continue to monitor the criminal court proceedings and should things take a turn for the worse for you Ms. Thomas, I will be revisiting who should maintain custody of the Black twins, until such a time that they can be reunited with their mother," as she went back to staring at Selk, burning a hole straight through him. And with a quick tap of her gavel, court was adjourned.

I just sat there for a moment in total shock, trying to fully process what had just happened. Mark all but picked me up out of my chair and gave me a tight congratulatory hug as the social worker reached over and patted me on the shoulder with her humble apologies. I was still reeling from the judges' verdict as Lt. Keith came over to hug me along with Joshua. But as happy as I was, I still felt a sadness that I did my best to conceal. Even now, my mom was, in essence, choosing Selk over me, her only living daughter. She gave me a quick hug then made haste over to Selk to console him and help calm him down. So like I said before, it was a good day for me, but deep down I knew Selk wouldn't give up so easily, especially now that he'd been embarrassed in open court.

One case down, too many more to go.

CHAPTER 31

L ife was good for awhile. The boys and I moved back out to the ranch and Selk spent the majority of his time with football and parenting classes. And when he did spend time with the boys, those visits were in essence supervised, since I sent a nanny with them each time he had them...a male nanny. I knew better than to trust any woman around Selk at this point, and even though Leo was gay, looking at him, you would have never guessed it. And even better, Selk wasn't his type, so he was the safest choice.

The only real worry I had was the pending felony charges against me that still hadn't been dropped or assigned a court date. But finally in early March, I got the call that I'd been dreading, the DA hadn't decided to drop the charges, and I had a court date. Mark and I met to discuss my case, and he informed me that Selk and his attorney wanted to meet with us, so he needed me to stay calm and hear them out.

Friday afternoon I dropped the boys off with Mama J and proceeded to my attorney's office for this unholy meeting, but before I got there, I received a call saying the meeting location had changed to a less formal spot, the restaurant in my old domicile, the bar at the condo. I thought to myself, 'how convenient for Selk,' but at least I'd have a familiar face on my side with Mr. Charlie being there.

I found a comfortable seat and waited for everyone else to show up. You would have thought that since he only had to take an elevator downstairs, Selk would be on time but of course, he was late. Once the niceties had dispensed, we finally got down to business and I found out how Selk was going to strong-arm his way back into my life. Selk was willing to tell the DA he wasn't going to testify to get him to drop all the charges against me if I was ready to accept his proposal and marry him. If I didn't agree to marry him, he'd help the DA put me behind bars for the next 10 – 20 years. I couldn't believe what I was hearing and all but told him so before I stormed out of the bar, running past Mr. Charlie with tears streaming down my face. The only reason Mr. Charlie caught up to me was because the valet had the keys to my car and didn't give them up quick enough.

"D.J. honey, what's wrong?" as he grabbed my arm.

"I can't! I just can't!"

"Wait a minute. Talk to me," as he hugged me. "Tell me what happened," as he walked me down the street away from the front doors.

"He will only tell the DA to drop the charges if I agree to marry him," I cried out as I buried my head in his chest.

"He what?! That son of a bitch!" as he held me tight. "Well, what did your lawyer say to that?"

"I didn't give him a chance. I cursed Selk out and ran out. If the DA doesn't drop the charges, I can be locked up for 10 to 20 years behind Selk's lies. If I go to court, I'm finished. And he knows that. No matter what we say, at the end of the day, I didn't have his permission to have the boys, and the social worker wasn't present. I can't deny that fact no matter what else comes out in court," I rambled off.

"D.J., D.J., first calm down and go talk things over with your lawyer. Have you all had a sit down with the DA yet? Ask him what he's willing to plead you down to before you go jumping off a bridge," Mr. Charlie advised.

Before I realized it, we had walked around the block and were coming up on the front of the building again, to a waiting crowd. The only person I acknowledged was Mark and asked him to meet me at his office, which he agreed to, of course. I hugged Mr. Charlie bye and proceeded to follow Mark to his office before I had another meltdown.

"D.J. calm down. First of all, let me reach out to the DA again and see what he's willing to offer before we jump to such an extreme. So please take a deep breath and try to stay calm and under control," he explained as he handed me a box of tissues.

"Mark, I'd rather go to jail then marry Selk. Please do something! He can't be my only option," I looked up at him through bloodshot eyes.

Mark asked his receptionist to bring me a cup of tea as he reached out to the DA in my case. Surprisingly enough, the DA was available and willing to talk to Mark about my case right then, over the phone. Mark told him that I was there and that he was putting him on speakerphone as he motioned for me to keep my mouth shut.

"I can reduce the other charges to misdemeanors but the contact with a minor charge the best I can do is a state felony and offer her 2 years with a $10,000 fine."

"NO! I can't go to jail! What about my boys? What would happen to them?" I cried as I gripped Mark's hand.

"Is that the best you can do? How about 2 years' probation and the fine?" Mark quickly asked.

"I'm sorry. You know we take child abuse very seriously, and I have people to answer to too. Besides, your client assaulted an officer in the process of being detained, and with her record, I won't have a hard time getting 10 years if she decides to take this thing to court, so I think I'm being very generous, don't you?"

"Come on now, her record? Just because she's been in court before doesn't make her some hardened criminal you need to throw the book at, and the only time she's ever been in court is behind Mr. Black's lies. And as far as child endangerment goes, didn't you get the family court's ruling?"

"Sure I did, but that's family court, not criminal court. We play by two totally different sets of rules, you know that. And the fact still remains that, she wasn't to have contact with her children without supervision or the custodial parent's permission and she had neither," he said so casually.

"Give me a moment to discuss this with my client."

"Sure, take your time. How about we talk again in the morning? I have a late arraignment I gotta get to anyway."

"Okay, 9AM then?"

"I'll be waiting for your call," as the line went dead.

I was already frantically pacing the room as he made his way around his desk towards me, "D.J. calm down. I can see it in your eyes. I'll take another run at him in the morning, but for now we need to have a serious talk," he explained as he gently squeezed my arm. I just stood there shaking my head at him as the tears began to well up in the corners of my eyes again. He quickly made his way over to his desk and started fiddling with his computer. He picked up the phone, "Marissa, please cancel my 2 o'clock meeting please."

Mark went into his mini-fridge and pulled out a bottle of water. "Would you like one?"

"Yes please," I sniffled.

"D.J. as your lawyer I have to tell you that we're probably not going to get a better deal than what was just offered," as he squeezed my hand. He could see the horror in my eyes at what he was saying. "But as a friend, I have to tell you. As bad as it may feel to you now, Selk's offer would be my recommendation. Agree to marry him and then he'll refuse to testify which would all but collapse the DA's case. Without a complainant, he has no case even if he tried to play hardball and take you to court. He can't compel a spouse to testify against the other," Mark sat there still holding my hand, waiting for me to respond.

You would have thought we were wax figures as still and quiet as we were. Finally, I slowly got up and walked over to the window and stared out into the distance. I didn't even try to stop the tears from rolling down my face as I thought to myself, *'How many times was I going to have to bend to Selkie? Why was this so important to him? It wasn't like he didn't have another child and baby mama already. Why was he so dead set on me being his wife? Why would you want to be married to someone who doesn't love you and can't stand to be in the same room as you?'* I stood there staring out into the blue sky trying to decide which prison I was willing to subject myself to. *'I can take the DA's offer and do the 2 years. They'll probably let me out early on good behavior...but then what's going to happen to the boys? Selk sure can't take care of them, and I'd die if he sent them to his mother, which he'd do just to spite me if he got custody. And then after that would I be able to get them back? '*

I finally wiped away my tears. I couldn't help but think it once again as I turned to face Mark, who was patiently waiting on me to respond to his comments. *'God hates me. That's all I can come up with. Why else would I be put through all of this drama? Why else would I be facing a prison cell or a prison marriage? What had I done to piss God off this bad? God had to hate me...that's what it was. God hates me,'* as I took a deep breath and sighed. "Make the call," I shook my head.

"Who am I calling?" Mark asked. I could tell by his tone he knew who I was talking about, but he wanted me to say it out loud.

"Selk I guess. Call Selk's attorney," as I collapsed in tears on his floor.

Mark rushed to my side and picked me up. He carried me over to the couch and yelled out, "Marissa! Come in here now!" as he sat me down and then sat down right beside me. Marissa was at his side before I realized it. "Get a cold, wet towel and bring it to me now," he told her as he moved my hair out my face. "D.J. it's going to be okay. I promise you, and it's a smart decision. It's not like you have to stay married to him. People get divorced every day."

I shook my head, "Not people in my family," I looked up at him with tears still streaming down my face as he put the cold towel on my forehead.

"Can I do anything else?" Marissa asked with a worried look on her face.

"If you don't mind, hand me that bottle of water and then that will be all. She just had a momentary freak-out is all," he explained as he dabbed my face. "And please clear my schedule for the rest of the day please."

"NO! You don't need to do that," I said as I squirmed to an upright position. "I've taken up enough of your day. You have other clients to tend to," as I scooted past him and took the water from Marissa. "Thank you," I said as I saluted her with the bottle before taking a sip.

"Nonsense D.J. I'm here for you as long as you need me. I know this isn't easy for you."

I tried blinking away the tears that were trying to form again. At that major fail, I quickly dashed over to my things, gathering them up, then rushing to the door. Problem is, Mark knew exactly what I was doing and stopped me as I reached for the doorknob.

"D.J., sit down for a minute. I can't let you leave in this state," he explained as he took my hand and led me back over to the couch.

Through my tears, "Mark, I don't want to talk. There's nothing to talk about. I can't go to jail, so I don't have a choice but to marry Selk. I just got my boys back. I can't lose them again," as I wiped my nose on the back of my hand before I caught myself. I stood there looking at the back of my hand, "Oh...that's nasty," I giggled as I picked up the towel and wiped my hands and my face again.

"Well, at least you're smiling," Mark said as he began to laugh. "And I completely understand," as he handed me the box of tissues from the end table.

I blew my nose, as I looked up at him, "I'm so embarrassed right now I don't know what to do," I shook my head. "You're assistant must think I'm a total freak," I giggled.

He chuckled for a moment, "Naw, she's used to it," he smiled.

"Oh, so you're in the habit of bringing your clients to tears in a crumpled heap on the floor," I said, trying not to laugh. We both laughed for a moment and then just quietly sat there. Finally, I asked, "Why is this happening to me? I just don't understand what I've done to deserve all of this," as I slumped into the couch shaking my head.

"D.J., like Judge Carruthers said, 'You haven't done anything but tried to stay strong.' This is all on him," he motioned. As he gently gripped my chin and lifted my head. "Unfortunately you've just gotten caught up in this mess, but I need you to stay strong and stay positive. Understand?" he said. "Besides, you must be some kind of woman for a man to fight this hard to keep you close," he continued as our eyes met.

I'd never realized how brown Mark's eyes were. I quickly shook off his gaze and moved to get up again. "Well, make the call. No point in waiting," as I walked over to the window again.

Mark joined me at the window, "D.J., are you sure about this," he asked as he rubbed my arm.

I looked up at him and smiled, "Yes, I'm sure," I nodded. But I was thinking to myself, *'Bitch, are you crazy! Of course you're not sure about this! Surely there's another way! Just take the boys and run!!!'* as I continued to smile at him for a few more seconds. I could tell by the way he was watching me that he was doing his best to read my mind. I turned my gaze back out the window, so Mark gave in to my wishes and pulled out his cell to make the call.

He hesitated for a second, "Are you sure about this?"

I took a deep breath, "Yes. I'm sure," I managed to say with a straight face. I watched a plane cross the sky, wishing I was on it, as I listened to Mark talk to Miss. Williamson. And no sooner than they'd hung up, my cell began ringing.

I ignored it at first and then Mark asked, "Aren't you going to get that?" as he leaned around me to make me look at him.

I smiled, "I already know who it is, and I'd prefer not to talk to her right now."

"How do you know it's a her?"

"Because Selk has my mom on speed dial and I guarantee you it's her," I smiled at him as he passed me my purse. "Thing is..." I frowned as a tear escaped my eye before I could blink it away, "I don't have it in me to hear her gloating right now," I shook my head as I dabbed my eye with a tissue. "I just don't have it in me," I said as I stared out the window without looking at my phone. Before he could respond, it rang again. I simply picked the phone up and handed it to him. "Here, if the ringing bothers you so much, you answer it," I said, barely looking at him.

I surprised him when I did that, but he took the phone and proceeded to answer it. The look of surprise on his face told me what I'd assumed was true. "Hello Mrs. Morgan....yes, yes she's right here," he admitted. I turned back to the window as I waved him off. "Mrs. Morgan, she's not ready to talk to anyone at the moment. Is there something I can tell her for you?"

It was sweet how caring he was, but he hadn't spent enough time around her to fully understand what he'd just stepped into. As he tried to handle my mother, I found myself missing Jeremiah more than I ever had before. My heart felt slower and was seriously aching, and before I realized it, I was talking out loud to him, "Zeke, why did you leave me? I can't do this without you. Damit man! I can't do this without you," as I dropped my head, and tears began to fall.

"What was that D.J.?" Mark asked.

Obviously startled, "Huh? Nothing," I shook my head like I was trying to clear my mind as I wiped my face clean.

"Your mom insists on talking to you," he held out the phone. I smirked at him as I kept shaking my head no. Still holding the phone out to me while he covered the mouthpiece, "Pleeese. She won't give up," he pleaded.

I started giggling. I couldn't help it. He looked so panicked. I finally took the phone from him as he collapsed in a nearby chair, "Stop being so dramatic," I laughed at him as I finally put the phone to my ear while I still shook my head at him. "Yes mother?" I rolled my eyes.

"D.J. I'm so glad you've finally come to your senses baby. You'll see... everything is going to be just fine."

I could feel her smiling through the phone, which irritated me to death, so I simply hung it up.

Mark's mouth fell open. "D... D.J., did you just hang-up on your mother?"

"Yep!" I smiled. "See how easy that was," as the phone began ringing again. This time I answered it with a serious attitude, "Look mother, I don't see anything to be happy about so I'm not going to celebrate this travesty with you. I'm marrying a man that I despise. A man that I wouldn't spit on if he was on fire. So NO, I'm not having this conversation with you right now," and hung up again.

Mark's mouth was dragging the ground at this point as I giggled and slowly walked over and closed his mouth. "You're lucky you're not outside, or you'd have a mouth full of bugs right now," I winked.

Mark simply scratched his head then finally said, "Your mom missed her calling."

I looked back at him as I washed my hands in his sink and then helped myself to a drink from his liquor cabinet. I held up a second glass, "Would you like one?"

"Yeah...yeah. I definitely would," as he loosened his tie and threw his leg over the arm of his chair.

"Light or dark?"

"Dark please."

I laughed as I finished making our glasses and handed him his. I sat down and took a long sip before I asked, "So...tell me. What was her true calling? Bitch personified..." I added before he had a chance to respond.

He started choking on his drink. "Damn it D.J.!" as he finally caught his breath. "I sure wasn't expecting that," as he shook his hand and wiped what he'd spilled off his lap. "No. I was thinking she should have been a trial attorney. She's relentless," he looked over at me with wide eyes.

I snorted at him as I took another slow sip of my drink. "I warned you not to answer the phone," I nodded at him. "Maybe next time you'll listen, counselor," I smiled.

Mark leaned forward and held his glass out to toast with me, "Point made Madame and fully noted," as our glasses made a high pitch *ting*.

We sat there sipping on our drinks silently watching my phone as it continued to ring back to back for the next 30 minutes. Finally, Mark got up, "Would you like another?"

"Sure. Why not?" as I handed him my glass as I turned my phone completely off.

Mark took his seat again and after a few sips of his glass, "Soooo, you know you're not going to be able to ignore her forever," he smiled.

I laid my head back, "Yeah, but I can for the rest of the night." I looked over at him and held up my glass to make an air toast. He simply laughed shaking his head and responded in like. Honestly, we could've probably stayed in his office the rest of the night, ignoring the world. It wasn't until Marissa came in to check on us and to see if it was okay for her to leave that we allowed the outside world to interrupt our quiet time.

While we had been ignoring our phones, Selk, his attorney, my mother, Lt. Keith, and the DA had all called more than once. The news was out now, so there was no way to put the genie back in the bottle at this point. What we didn't realize was that Selk had only bought me a continuance with the DA until after we were officially hitched.

The next morning Mark let the DA know that we were going to take our chance in court and by noon he'd received word from a source that the DA was going to try to fast track my case since they had already heard about my upcoming nuptials. We appeared in court the next week and found out that my trial date had been set. As we left the courthouse, Mark called Selk's attorney, and when they hung up, he broke their demands down to me. I wasn't as surprised as Mark, but in essence, that meant that I had exactly 3 months to get married before my case was headed to trial. As soon as I said *"I do,"* Selk would withdraw his complaint and refused to testify against me.

I didn't even bother to tear up at this news. I simply looked at Mark and said, "Would you like to join me for a drink?"

"Now?" as he looked at his watch.

I grinned and said, "It's 5 o'clock somewhere," as I hunched my shoulders at him as we reached his car.

"Sure, why not?" he shook his head. "I know if I could use a stiff one, you definitely can," he smiled as he opened the door for me to get in.

"Yep! I've heard of shotgun weddings, but I never dreamed I'd be the hostage at one," I patted his hand and started laughing as I took a seat.

We spent the next couple of hours drinking and cracking shotgun wedding jokes. As much as I hated the idea of letting people know what was going on, I finally got up the courage to let the Thomas family in on what I was about to do. So I thanked Mark for all he'd done and excused myself from the table to make a quick phone call.

My call took much longer than I expected even though I was just asking Joshua to get everyone together for me to meet with them to give them some news. Joshua wasn't trying to let me be so cryptic with the reason for my sudden meeting request, so I finally gave him a heads up as to what I was going to say which turned into a three-way call with Lt. Keith and him insisting that we all meet with Mark to come up with another plan. Being a lot tipsy and extra sarcastic, I told them that Mark and I were partaking in a liquid lunch and that they were more than welcome to join us. Who knew that 20 minutes later they would both be sitting at our table holding court. Poor Mark didn't know what hit him. And let me tell you, trying to sober up on a dime isn't a pretty sight.

They sat there arguing so long that I finally ordered something to eat to counteract the large amount of alcohol we'd consumed and to keep my mouth busy so not to offend either of my friends. I wasn't trying to argue with them. This was painful enough, without having to listen to them tell us all the reasons I shouldn't agree to this, when in the end neither of them could give me one good way to keep me out of jail. After nearly 2 hours of fussing, they both had to admit that marrying Selk was the only way to keep me from ending up behind bars and a felon forever.

We ended the night with one final toast. We held our glasses up as I said, "To marriage, the last legal form of imprisonment that will keep my black ass out of jail." You could tell by the way they all hesitated that they weren't expecting me to say that. I shrugged their shocked looks off, tapped each of their glasses, and downed my shot without them, then asked who was walking me upstairs? There was no point in me trying to drive home in my condition, and Mama J would have no problem keeping the boys for the night, so the best thing for me to do was to get a room and sleep it off. Besides, I needed a night to myself. I knew they were soon going to be few and far in between, come morning.

As I suspected all hell broke loose the next morning. My mother was calling non-stop, and so was Selk. Both of them already had lots of ideas and must-haves for this wedding so after the first couple of calls I decided to let them talk to my voicemail. Not that they cared or knew anything about it, but I had a meeting with the Thomas clan that was more important to me than this wedding and frankly the only thing on my radar at the moment.

Those who could meet with me on such short notice were already at Triple J's when I arrived. Joshua quickly locked the door and put up a sign that said closed for a private event as I made me a plate and took a seat. I was so glad Mama J had brought the twins in with her, they gave me something to hold onto as I began to explain why I wanted to meet with them. Once I finished my explanation, there was an eerie moment of silence before the eruption of questions and profanities began. I had Mattie, the young lady working the counter, take the boys back to the office until things calmed down.

Thank God for Joshua being here and already knowing what I was going to say. He was a major buffer and peacekeeper through the entire thing. When the commotion finally died down, Mama J was the one who offered up the final opinion and then the matter was officially closed to further discussion...at least in her presence.

"D.J. I consider you to be one of my own and I would never want anything bad to happen to you," as she took my hand. "That being said, I understand why you are doing what you're doing, especially after all you've been through. The Christian in me says to forgive and forget, but baby...there's a demon in me kicking up a fuss right now. So as much as I'm supporting you, I really hope that man drops dead sooner than later. If he's dead, the DA's case dies too, don't it?" she said so matter-of-factly. "So baby you do whatever you have to do to stay with them babies and keep them safe, you hear me..." as she squeezed my hand tightly.

I wasn't sure what to say after that, so I said the only thing I felt appropriate at the moment, "Yes ma'am," as a single tear ran down my face. No one else spoke for a long time, and when I had regained my composure, I felt like I needed to add one final thing. I cleared my throat a couple of times before I could get it out. "I need all of you to understand and believe that this is not easy for me. If there were another guaranteed way for me to stay out of jail and keep sole custody of the twins, I'd do it in a heartbeat, but the DA isn't budging on this case. So, unfortunately, this is my only option," as I dropped my head. As the tears began to free flow down my cheeks, "And if it is any consolation to any of you, with every fiber of my being I feel like I am dishonoring the memory of your brother, your son, and my true soulmate," as I broke down crying in Mama J's arms.

"Aww baby don't cry. Everything's going to be okay. God's got you in his hands," Mama J said as she rubbed my back.

"I don't know that I believe that anymore Mama," I sniffled. "What have I done to piss God off so badly that I'd have to go through all of this?" I asked. But before she could respond, "I will admit, I didn't understand why Jeremiah came into my life when he did, but I do believe that he was God's way of giving me hope when I was at my lowest point...being pregnant by a man I really didn't like," I shook my head. "But in the end, it all worked out in my favor, at least I thought it had. Who knew I was only living on borrowed time," I looked down at my feet.

"D.J. you were the best thing that ever happened to my little brother," Jessica said. "And as the attorney in the family let me just say, what you're doing is highly illegal and unethical, but so is the DA's lust for a win and their need for a pound of flesh. So don't cry another tear. If you decide that you want out of this marriage come to me, and I'll take care of you personally," she said as she gripped my shoulder.

"Thank you so much Jessica," as I stood up to hug her. "But divorce is not an option in my family, and that's what he and my mother are banking on. Nobody in our family has ever divorced, and I sure don't want to be the first," I shook my head. "But what I do need your help with is protecting what your brother left me. I don't want Selk to be able to touch one single dime, the property, or this business," I explained as I made eye contact with each of them. I could tell they were all much happier with what I was now telling them by the smiles and nods of approval I was now receiving. "Matter of fact I have an idea that I wanted to go over with you all anyway so now is as good a time as any," as I took my seat again.

"Sure, what's on your mind," John said as he leaned back in his chair like we were getting ready to discuss serious business.

"Well, how would you all feel about me turning the ranch into a retreat of sorts?" I could tell that this wasn't what they were expecting, so I continued before they had a chance to respond. "As you all know, there's a lady who's been living at the ranch taking care of the place in my absence. Well, the reason she's there is to escape from her abusive husband. He's very politically connected down here and it has been a serious struggle for her to disappear, so the ranch became her safe haven of sorts. Now what I'm proposing is to turn the property into a retreat to benefit abused women and children and make your family the controlling executors over it," as I waited for someone to respond, which took longer than I expected.

"Sooo, let me get this straight," Joshua said as he leaned forward on his knees. "You want to give up the house to strangers on a full-time bases? Well, where are you going to live? And how exactly would you go about maintaining the safety and secrecy of this place?"

"Exactly," Jessica jumped in. "Overly controlling men can be violent, and if you are going to allow these women and their children to stay on your property, you become responsible for maintaining their safety, and that could be a major legal headache if something bad were to happen to someone," she added.

"That's why I need your legal expertise, Mrs. Jessica. There have to be some grants that we can apply for to help fund this program beyond what I'm willing to invest. And Joshua, I'm going to be staying at the ranch, but we will eventually be living at the condo, with Selk. There's not a snowball's chance in hell I would ever allow Selk to live in Jeremiah's house. I'd sell it before that would ever happen," I gave him a stern look. "And besides, you and Jeremiah already have the house and the grounds wired like Fort Knox, so I figure we add a few more cameras and hire a couple of full-time and part-time security people, and that should cover us," I explained. "Also, the property next door to me is now for sale so if I was to buy that land as well, we could expand the living quarters and the stable area to accommodate single women living quarters and women with children living quarters. That way the main house would still remain more private, but it could be where the offices and main gathering rooms are, kinda like a welcoming center." I quickly added.

The room was quiet for a little while, as people simply looked at one another and stared off into space at times. After what felt like an eternity, Mama J smiled and said, "I think that would be a great way to honor Jeremiah's legacy," as she squeezed my hand.

"D.J., I can start looking into funding and the legal ramifications. I know that there will be special permits required to do what you're trying to do but to keep this place off the grid may take a little extra finessing," Jessica added, as she began furiously jotting down notes in her palm pilot.

I waited for the others to comment and finally asked, "Well guys...what are you all thinking?"

John cleared his throat, "D.J. I think that what you're trying to do is very admirable, but I'm still worried about this. Like Jessica already brought up, violent men are unpredictable, and I wouldn't want anyone to get hurt on our watch, but I also think Lt. Keith would be a great consultant to help us figure out the logistics of providing security."

"Even better, how about adding him to the Executive Board?" I suggested.

"Now that isn't a bad idea at all," Joshua added. "Having his expertise would be a great addition to the Board," as side conversations began to breakout.

For the first time, I was able to actually take a breath. I felt like there was something good going to come out of all of this even if I was going to be trapped in a marriage with the type of man I wanted to help protect other women and children from. As I settled into my own thoughts, Jordan touched me on the shoulder and said, "D.J., what's on your mind. You look worried?"

I reached up and smiled at her as I squeezed her hand, "I'm okay. Just trying to settle my spirit."

"Well, for what it's worth. I think you're being very brave under the circumstances."

"Well thank you for saying that," I smiled at her. "But I don't know how brave I am. I'm just trying to survive at this point," I hated to admit. But the honest truth was I was in survival mode, as I glanced down at my vibrating phone again. I took a deep breath as I finally answered it, moving away from the chatter of the group. "Hello."

"Where are you? We've been trying to reach you all day?" my mother insisted.

"I'm at Triple J's. Why? What's wrong now?" I asked impatiently.

"Don't take that tone with me young lady. And why are you there when we have a wedding to plan? Surely they can handle things at that place without you."

"Look, I have a business to help run, and that requires me to actually show up to work sometimes. And as far as this wedding is concerned, I give you my permission to do whatever you want, I really could care less what you plan," I admitted to her as I stared out the window watching cars go by.

"D.J. Morgan. I can't believe you said that."

What I couldn't believe is how surprised she sounded. I quickly made my way to the back office and told Mattie that she could go back out front for a while, closing the office door behind her. The boys were busy playing with their building blocks and cars and barely acknowledged my presence. "Mom, why do you sound so surprised? We both know I don't want to marry him so why on earth would you think I could give two damns about planning this wedding?"

"Watch your mouth young lady?"

"Yeah, yeah…I hear you, but why do you keep insisting on my participation in all of this when you know full well, I don't give a damn?" I asked louder than I intended. Both of the boys were now watching me instead of playing anymore. I quickly went over and sat with them, trying to reassure them that everything was okay as I held the phone to my ear with my shoulder.

"D.J., this is *your* wedding so you should give a damn and want to help plan it. Now I expect you to be here within the hour so that we can get going on this. Do you understand me?"

"I hear you mother, but I'm rather busy at the moment, and I'm not sure when I'll be able to meet you. How about you go plan til your heart's content and whatever you and Selk decide will be just fine with me. After all, this is the wedding of *your* dreams. Technically I already had mine," as I hung up the phone and really got into playing with the boys.

I had dozed off on the office couch with the boys when I came too, to Mama J gently rocking me.

"Oh, wow. What time is it?" I asked.

"It's a little past 2 sweetie. I hate to wake you, but your momma's here, and she don't look too happy."

"You're kidding," I said as I rolled my eyes and tried to slide from under the boys without waking them up.

"Here, let me take him for you," as she reached for E.J. barely disturbing him as she picked him up and placed him in the playpen.

"Man, this used to be so much easier," as I rolled J.T. off of me so I could finally get up. "She's not cutting up is she?" I asked as I put J.T. in the playpen next to his brother.

"Naw, she's just obviously irritated," Mama J. said. "You go deal with her. I will stay back here with them," as she shooed me to the door, trying not to giggle at me.

I stood at the double doors watching her talk with Joshua and John before I came out front. It was amazing to me how she could turn on the charm so easily and then take my head off in the next breath. Joshua noticed me at the door and slightly rolled his eyes, he already knew what was coming and didn't approve.

As I came through the doors, "There she is. We have some things to take care of young lady so get your things together and let's hop to it," she smiled.

"Hello mother. Why aren't you at work?" I asked sarcastically.

You could tell by her reaction I had embarrassed her with that one, as she cleared her throat. "Well, I took the next few days off to help you get a jump on your plans. There's not a lot of time before the big event you know."

"My plans?!" I hesitated, frowning up my face, but I knew better than to push her much further, so I decided to leave it at that. Joshua and John gave each other a look and quickly excused themselves. "Mom, I have a lot going on today, and the boys are in the back asleep, so I really don't have time for this today."

"That's fine, bring them with us. We need to get them fitted for their tuxes anyway."

"Wait... What tuxes?! What for?!" I asked louder than I should have, as I noticed the looks on a couple of customer's faces.

She grabbed my arm and pulled me closer with a smile on her face. Through clenched teeth, "Get the babies, and we can discuss this on our way."

I didn't feel like arguing with her and went to retrieve the boys. Joshua helped me get them in the car and kissed me on the cheek as he whispered in my ear, "Stay strong sis. What doesn't kill you only makes you stronger.

And just remember, you're not alone in this. We'll all get you through this okay?" as he gave me a hug.

I got choked up and couldn't say anything back. I knew if I tried that it would only end in tears so I stiffened up, and buried my feelings as far down inside me as I could. It was the beginning of my self-isolation from the things going on around me. I was learning to compartmentalize my emotions so as not to fall apart at the drop of a hat anymore. I gave Josh a weak smile and got in my car, with my mom on the passenger's side and drove off like everything was perfectly fine.

Immediately my mom lit into me about any and everything. Why was I ignoring her calls? Why did I have an attitude with Selk? Why wasn't I wearing any makeup? Why did my hair look terrible? What was I wearing? I needed to get a better attitude about this wedding...it went on and on until we arrived at our first stop and then picked up again in between the rest of many more stops she had planned for the day. When I was finally able to drop her back off at her car, the only thing I wanted was food and my bed. I quickly grabbed up the boys and ran in the restaurant to make us some to-go plates as my phone began to ring out of control again....it was Selk.

"Hello?"

"Hi baby! How's your day going?"

Baby? I thought, "My day is almost over, and that's a good thing. What's on your mind Selk?"

"I was just checking on my babies is all. I heard you got in a lot of wedding shopping today," he said.

I suddenly lost my appetite, but I went on and finished making our plates, as I tried to remain as pleasant'ish as I could, "Yeah, me and mom got out and looked at a bunch of stuff today," as I rolled my eyes at the boys. They both erupted into laughter, not really understanding why mommy was making a silly face at them, which made it even sweeter.

"Well, what are you up to tonight? I'd love to meet you guys for dinner."

"I'm actually making us to-go plates at the spot as we speak."

"Come on D.J.. You can eat that stuff any old time. I'm not far from there now, how about I swing by and pick y'all up and we can have dinner together...like a real family."

"Selk I know you mean well, but I'm exhausted, and I was looking forward to a quiet evening in, putting the boys down early and taking a long relaxing bubble bath to unwind."

"Well, that works too! Come by the condo, and I'll have chef fix us a nice meal, and then you can do all of that. We'll be married soon so you and the boys might as well get used to sleeping at the condo again."

What he was saying made total sense, but it wasn't like I was a willing participant with all of this. I was having a shotgun wedding, and the gun was definitely at my back. "Selk, I know you're trying to be nice, but I really just need to relax tonight."

"Before you go any further D.J., just come on out of there and let's talk on our way to the condo bar to eat. As soon as we're done, I'll either take you back to your car or you guys can come on up and spend the night, it's that simple."

I looked up to see him sitting in the middle of the parking lot watching me. I turned to Joy and asked her to keep an eye on the boys for a moment, which she quickly agreed to, of course. Everyone loved the boys, besides we were all like a family here. They watched intently as I went out the door to talk to Selk. "You know, it's really not a good idea for you to just pop up here," I motioned back towards the building as I glanced over my shoulder.

"Why not? It is a business open to the public isn't it," he smiled.

"You already know why Selk," I dropped my head shaking it. I really wasn't up for a sparring match with him tonight. "Let's just call this place off limits to you and yours, okay. I work with these people, and they are my family. Family that don't care for you, so please...to keep the peace don't come around here," I finally made eye contact with him.

I could see the anger in his eyes even though he had a slight smile on his face. "D.J. if that's what you want that's fine, I won't come by here again unless you ask me to, okay? But you know when we're married, I'll be a part of the business too," as he stroked the side of my face. I did all I could not to pull away or flinch, but it was apparent that I wasn't comfortable with him touching me. "You know D.J., we're going to be married soon, so you're going to have to get comfortable with me touching you again," as he lowered his hand and just stared at me.

I could feel myself starting to tear up, "yeah, I know. And Selk... please understand me when I say, no you won't have anything to do with this business or any other business me and the Thomas's are involved in together. Arrangements have already been made to make sure that if anything happens to me, all of my personal and business interests will be taken care of according to my wishes. Jessica has my power of attorney, and all of that will be handled by her law firm."

"What!? Who the hell is Jessica?"

"Jessica Thomas-White is Jeremiah's older sister. She's a lawyer and will be handling several things for me in the future."

Selk turned away from me and tightened his grip on the steering wheel before he responded, "Well, I can see this isn't a good time, so I won't keep you, but keep tomorrow evening open. I want to spend some time with you D.J., some real-time," he reached over and lifted my head to make eye contact with me.

I gave him an awkward look, "HUH! Wait...what exactly are you talking about?" I asked, already knowing what he was going to say.

"D.J., I want to make love to my fiancé. I want to hold you close and wake up with you next to me."

At that point, the tears began to slowly roll down my face. Blinking them away wasn't even an option anymore. The reality of the situation fully hit me. Selk was going to expect me to fulfill my wifely duties even though he knew I didn't want to marry him, nor did I want him to touch me. He knew he'd gotten my attention with that comment as he smirked and kissed the back of my hand.

"We'll talk later. You be careful getting home," he smiled as he slowly pulled away. I simply stood there crying in the middle of the parking lot until I could pull myself together and go back inside. I quickly went to the back to clean up my face then came back out front to thank Mavis and pack the boys up to go home.

When I arrived at the ranch, Maggie was walking up from the barn. She helped me get everything inside and volunteered to keep the boys occupied so that I could get myself settled. "Maggie, you are such a Godsend. I don't know what I would do without you here to help me out," I said as I gave her a big hug.

"D.J., where would I be if it weren't for you. You've given me and Calliope a beautiful house and all this land to lose ourselves on, and we're safe. Taking these two off your hands for a few minutes so you can catch your breath is the least I can do," as she hugged me back.

She took the boys to the playroom, and I went to the kitchen to get dinner ready. As I finished my second glass of wine, I heard them running up the hallway towards the kitchen with Calliope hot on their heels. To hear them giggle the way they were just made all the wrong in my world right. Amazingly enough, they were pretty easy to get down for the night as Maggie patiently waited for me out on the porch swing. Once I was sure they were sleeping, I joined her in the unseasonably warm air and cried as I told her about my day. The highlight to our evening was the excited look on her face when I explained my plan to turn this place into a retreat. She was already throwing ideas at me, more than I had it in me to deal with at the moment, so I told her to write it all down, and we'd discuss it at another time, which she was happy to do.

The night ended with a long and much needed bubble bath, listening to smooth jazz and thinking about all the times I spent doing this very thing with Jeremiah. It's funny how he was still my refuge from the storm.

CHAPTER 32

My life had quickly become a dreaded routine. Every morning I was either talking to my mom on the phone about the wedding, or I was with my mom shopping for the wedding. Things finally came to a head when we met with the wedding planner at the flower shop a month before the wedding. I was paying more attention to the twins than I was to any flower arrangements she had to show me. Both of my aunties were with us, more as a buffer between my mom and me than anything else. After an hour or so of looking at flowers, baby's breath, and a never-ending discussion concerning the colors of the wedding, which I finally settled on royal blue to make them leave me alone for a few seconds, the florist and the wedding planner both refused to do any more work on my wedding.

The question had been raised yet again, "what day" we were having this wedding on, and I blurted out, "June 6th at 6 o'clock PM." Everyone froze with looks of shock and horror on their faces, everyone but me that is. "What? You keep asking me to pick a date, so I did...6 - 6, at 6 sounds perfect to me, don't y'all think?" as I innocently looked up at them.

They were all standing there with their mouths hanging open looking mortified as I began laughing hysterically, rocking the boys. I laughed so hard that I had started crying. Now the wedding planner and the florist were the best in Houston, and they'd teamed up to work together on many of the biggest weddings in Texas, so they knew each other very well, when the florist blurted out, "It's obvious this child don't wanna get married! Why are you all making her?"

I immediately responded, "Finally! Someone is paying attention," as I dug around in the diaper bag for some Kleenex to blow my nose.

My mom shot me a look as she turned to her and said, "Well, that is your opinion, and frankly it's none of your business either way."

"And besides, we are paying you for your services, not your advice," Aunt Mayvis added with a huff. I notice Aunt Claudette slowly reach out and hold Aunt Mayvis's jacket to keep her from taking another step forward. My Aunt Mayvis was a pistol, and you never knew when she was going to explode on someone. That was my cue to start gathering up my things because I could tell this conversation was headed in the wrong direction.

The florist spoke up again, "Well ladies I've been at this for over 35 years, so I know when a bride just isn't interested in getting married, and in my humble opinion this young woman has absolutely no interest in this wedding, which tells me she doesn't want to get married."

"At least not to this fella," the wedding planner blurted out.

"With all due respect, I'll say it again…we are paying you for a service, not your advice," my mother said as she waved at the rest of us.

"Well, in that case, I think I can speak for both of us when I say, at this time, we are unable to help you with this wedding," the florets responded emphatically.

"Yes, you may speak for me as well," the wedding planner added.

"Well if that's how you want to be, I have no problem taking my business elsewhere!" my mother yelled, which was totally out of character for her. I'd never seen her act out in public before, that was usually Aunt Mayvis's m.o..

"Please leave my shop now!" as she walked over to the door and held it open for us.

I didn't ask any questions as I took the twins by a hand and did as I was asked. It was at that point that Aunt Mayvis did what she typically does, and the yelling and pushing began. I remember hearing someone yell, *'How dare you,'* and then glass breaking. It wasn't until the *'You people'* comment that Aunt Claudette had something to say as well. I was surprised that a police car never pulled up because 10 minutes later here came my mom and Aunt Claudette, dragging Aunt Mayvis out of the store swinging a hand full of roses. I sat in the back of the van with the twins just shaking my head. There were no words for what had just happened, and I knew better than to say anything to any of them, to keep them from turning their wrath on me. Sadly my plan didn't work.

"And *you* young lady! 6 6 6 huh?!" my mom twisted around to look at me before she pulled off. "You better fix that attitude quick fast and in a hurry! The next place we go you better put a smile on your face and at least *act* like you want to be there," as she gave me a long death stare before she turned back around so that she could drive.

Even back then me and the twins had an unbreakable connection. Without me saying a word, they both reached over to take my hand and squeezed it to comfort me. I simply smiled over at each of them fighting back my tears, knowing full well that this would not be the last time my mother's fury would be directed at me today or over the next few weeks. And just as I predicted the same yelling and shoving match happened at the next two flower shops, which led to me being yelled at once we made it back in the van, each time. Needless to say, after we were asked to leave by the third shop, that brought an end to trying to hire a florist or a wedding planner at the last minute and my Aunties, and my mom decided that they would do everything themselves.

We spent the rest of the day arguing over colors and searching for bridesmaid dresses and tuxedos for the twins. Since they wouldn't get off my back about it, I finally selected royal blue and black as the final wedding colors, which seemed to make them happy. It quickly became painfully obvious that it would be smarter to buy the twins suits rather than to trying to rent them suits, so I had the pleasure of fighting with them to try them on. Even though it was a battle, it was easier than getting them to hold still for the tailor with all those pins.

At the end of a very long week, we finally even managed to pick out a few accessories for me, including hundreds of beads to add to my debutante dress. I'm as bad as the twins when it comes to trying things on, so we decided to just recycle the wedding dress I already owned by adding a lot of beading to it, an excessively long train, and a veil. By the middle of May, everything was done except for a couple of the bridesmaid dresses that still needed to be properly fitted and the final beading on my dress. And yes, the date was still June 6th, just not at 6 pm. We split the difference and said 3 PM, but everything else was done. As much as I wasn't looking forward to my wedding day, I was happy that I was able to pass the time sewing all those beads on my dress to make my mom and aunties happy that I was participating, but it also kept me out of the major planning. It became my meditation time of sorts. When all was said and done, I have to admit the dress was absolutely beautiful.

Time seemed to fly by as I tried to stay busy and not think about my wedding, but whatever could go wrong, did go wrong as June 6th quickly approached. In hindsight, maybe I should have taken all the things that happened as a sign that maybe God was trying to keep me from getting married, but at the time, it never occurred to me. After the wedding though I secretly dubbed them the 7 signs of the wedding apocalypse.... They were a series of 7 events that took place to let me know that I had no business marrying this man.

We rode in silence for a couple of miles until I was ready to give her the story of my marriage. But before I began, I turned to Cyn and said, "Now listen very carefully little sister, because I'm not going to repeat myself and when I'm done, I want you to tell me…. Did God make a mistake and put me with that man, or did I make the mistake, and God had to save me from myself and that man?" I took a deep breath and said, "I present to you the 7 Signs from God, that I should not have gotten married to one Selkie Nathaniel Black…."

CHAPTER 33

1ˢᵗ Sɪɢɴ.....

Summer was supposed to fly in from New York the week before the wedding but got a nasty case of food poisoning, so she missed her flight. And because she missed her flight, she couldn't use her original ticket when she felt up to the trip 4 days before the wedding, except to fly out stand-by. I offered to buy her another ticket, but she insisted that she'd handle things herself, so she commenced to waiting at the airport for an open seat. After she spent the best part of 2 days camped out at the airport she finally got a seat only to be diverted to Miami for some insane reason. After an overnighter in sunny Florida, she finally made it to Houston, 5 hours before the wedding rehearsal.

I picked her up from the airport and took her directly to my Aunt Mayvis's house so that she could be properly fitted for her dress. Aunt Mayvis was a professional seamstress and had converted her garage into a sewing room years ago.

As we made our way through Houston traffic, the inquisition from my best friend began. "So, you're really going through with this?" Summer shook her head at me looking very disappointed.

"Yes. We've been through this a million times already. I'm getting married to Selk, tomorrow afternoon," I tried to smile.

"Don't give me that fake ass smile! I know you better than that," she waved me off as she turned to look out the window. "D.J., I just don't get why."

"Why what?"

"Why you choose NOW to allow your mother to push you into this unholy marriage. You're better than that. Stand up and grow a backbone and just tell her NO," she said as she shoved me.

I wasn't expecting that, causing me to swerve a little. "Are you crazy?! I know you don't want me to marry him, but do you have to kill us both?" I kept looking over at her as I gained control of the car. I shook my head for a moment as I let out a long sigh. "Summer, I know how you feel about Selk, and I've heard everything you've said over the past 3 months about this situation. And as much as I agree with you, nothing's changed," I glanced over at her for a second. "I have 2 choices….get married to Selk or go to jail, and for a very long time I might add."

"But there has to be another way!" she said, waving her hands around.

"Yeah, there should be, but there's not. So what else can I do?"

"You can always skip town and change your identity," she smiled. "People do it all the time and don't think I don't know you have the money to do it too," she gave me a wicked grin, as she crossed her arms across her chest and leaned up against the door watching me.

I kept glancing over at her, but I didn't confirm or deny that there was any truth to that statement for a few minutes. When she never said anything, I knew she was waiting for me to respond. As we pulled off the highway onto S. MacGregor Way, I finally acknowledged her last statement with a heartfelt laugh. As the light turned green, I said, "Summer, I can tell you're from Hollywood because that's some straight-up movie crap," as I continued to shake my head at her. "Who does that? Seriously, who does that?"

"What? People do it all the time. Like you don't hear about people disappearing then being found years later living in a completely new city and state under another name. Don't act like you don't," she hissed at me.

"Yeah, but I'm not a criminal or hiding from the mob. I'm a mother of twins just trying to survive the best way I know how. And having to disappear and never contact any of my friends or family, living on the lamb with not 1 baby but 2, is no way to live. For me or for them," I shook my head no.

"You make it sound so bad. Girl you and the boys can move to Cali and live it up in the sun and great weather year-round, and simply dis – a – ppear. And to top it off, you'd be closer to me," she smiled big.

We just stared at one another for a few seconds, and then both of us erupted in laughter. When we settled down, I looked at her as we pulled onto Aunt Mayvis's street. "So what are you trying to say? That you're moving back to California? When?"

"I was going to surprise you later, but I'm being transferred to San Francisco," she smiled.

"Well congratulations! But seriously, like no one would think to look for me in California…. where my best friend and old college roommate lives. Noooo, who would ever think such a silly thing?" as I pulled up in the driveway.

"You can be as sarcastic as you want but hiding out in LA versus your other 2 options... give me Cal-i-forn-i-a anytime," as she opened the door and got out before I could say anything else.

My mom met us at the front door, "Well it's about time! Where have you two been?" as she grabbed Summer's hand and dragged her through the door and straight back to the sewing room.

Before she had a chance to speak Aunt Mayvis was pulling at her clothes, "Take this stuff off so we can get this dress properly fitted. We don't have much time," as she pulled Summer's shirt up over her head in one swift motion.

The surprised look of horror on Summer's face was priceless as I plopped down at an empty sewing station giving her a *'Welcome to my world'* look. She quickly grabbed onto her pants as my mom was trying to pull them down. "Uhmmm, yeah. I can undress myself, ladies." As she shot me a *'Get these women!'* look, to which I simply shook my head *'No.'*

Summer figured out very quickly that the women in my family had no sense of personal space, nor did they hear anything you had to say when they were on a mission. They had her head spinning from how quickly they'd put the dress on her and take it off of her. She was getting an earful from Aunt Mayvis because she had lost so much weight since she'd had the tailor up in New York measure her for her dress. The dresses were form-fitting, and Summer's wasn't fitting anywhere, except for the length and even that needed to come up a bit since she wasn't wearing a heel as high as she had originally said she'd be.

They were on the third fitting I believe when a pin caught her as my mom was taking the dress off her again. And no, nobody but she and I even flinched when the pin caught her on the arm, and she screamed "OUCH!" grabbing at her arm.

What was said was, "Girl, you bet not even think about getting blood on this dress!" as Aunt Claudette pulled the 1st aid kit out and past her an alcohol pad and band-aide. I was helping her clean her wound and putting the band aid on the back of her arm as the 2nd sign reared its ugly head....

2ND SIGN.....

While my mom and aunties were all fiddling with Summer or finishing up other little details, the doorbell at the shop door began ringing nonstop, which never really happened. Everyone knew to come to the front door of the house and ring that bell, then someone would walk you out to the shop. Since they were all busy pinning and sewing, I was the lucky person to answer the door. As I opened it, I was met with a bridesmaid's dress being thrown in my face and an irate bridesmaid, J.R.'s twin's mother, Kimberly, screaming obscenities at me.

"Wait! What's going on?!" as I pulled Kim on in the shop, bringing all alterations to a screeching halt.

"Your brother's lost his damn mind! Is what's going on!" as she snatched away from me.

"What happened?" I asked, trying not to panic.

"I asked him if I caught the bouquet tomorrow, would we be making our own wedding plans and that motherfucker told me no!" as the tears began streaming down her face.

My mom rushed over, pushing me out of the way as she wrapped her arms around Kim and walked her over to a chair. "D.J. don't just stand there! Give her a tissue and go get her a glass of water!" she yelled at me.

I was like a deer in the headlights for a second as I grabbed the box of Kleenex and tossed them to Summer as I ran to the kitchen for the glass of water. I returned just in time to hear Kim say, "I'm sorry, but I can't be in the wedding."

I accidentally tipped the glass over too far spilling it all over the floor and splashing it on my dress as I said, "Huh? What did you just say?"

"D.J.! Watch what you're doing!" Aunt Mayvis yelled as she rushed over with a pin hanging out of the corner of her mouth, snatching the glass and throwing a towel at me, almost at the same time. "Now clean up that mess and be careful of your dress!" as she passed the glass to my mom, who handed it to Kim while giving me the death stare.

"Now, now baby. It's okay," she finally said, turning her attention back to Kim. "It's not the end of the world. Give him some time, you can still be in the wedding though," she said. Quickly adding, "There's no reason for you not to be, you're still family."

My mouth fell open as I dropped into a nearby chair. I couldn't believe this was happening. First of all, her lack of empathy for either of our feelings was utterly amazing. I didn't wanna get married and was being forced to because I got pregnant, and Kim wanted to get married to her silly son, the man who had gotten her pregnant no less, and she obviously wasn't going to make him marry her. I kind of zoned out with my own thoughts and missed the rest of the conversation at that point.

I snapped out of it as Kim stood up and said, "Mama Lisa, I just can't do it. I can't stand there with a smile on my face knowing that the father of my children isn't going to marry me. He's seeing another woman for God's sake!" as she turned and stormed out the room, slamming the door behind her.

We all just sat there with our mouths hanging wide open to that new revelation. Summer finally leaned over and whispered in my ear, "I take it none of you had any idea about that? I guess the wedding is off now," she softly giggled. I just stared at her as the tears began to well up in my eyes. She jumped up and grabbed a tissue and handed it to me, saying, "D.J. I was only kidding. Please don't cry," as she dabbed at the tears streaming down my face.

I looked at my mom and said, "Now what are we going to do? We can't have an uneven number of bridesmaids and Selk isn't going to get rid of any of his groomsmen," as my tears continued to flow.

"Stop all that crying before your face swells up!" she snapped at me as she picked up the phone.

Summer patted me on the hand as she whispered, "Who's she calling?"

I slowly turned to look at her and said, "Who do you think? J.R. of course," as I turned my gaze back to my mother.

My aunts went back to their sewing as my mother screamed at J.R. for 15 minutes and finally said, "Fine! Well, bring her over here right now! And damit! She better be able to fit into this dress!" as she slammed down the phone.

I don't know what I was thinking when I asked, "Who better fit what dress?"

All of her anger was immediately thrust upon me as she shot me a look and then stomped over and stood above me with her hands on her hips and began yelling at me. "Not another word out of you, young lady! Your brother is bringing this mystery woman over so she can take Kimberly's place! I swear if it ain't one of you, it's the other!"

Again, my mouth acted before I thought, "Wait? What did I do? This isn't my fault," as I pointed at myself with a bewildered look on my face.

"I blame you as much as I blame him. If you two could keep your damn legs closed none of this would be happening!" as she snatched the glass of water Summer had gone and got for me, out of my hand and began to drink it.

Finally, Aunt Claudette spoke up, "Now Lisa, that was uncalled for. D.J. is innocent in all this," as she waved her free hand back and forth.

"Oh no! She's not innocent at all! None of this would be happening if she'd married Selk before the babies arrived like I told her to. But nooooo... she had to marry some other man who up and died on her!" You could tell by her reaction, that she knew she was wrong for what she'd just said and the looks of horror on everyone's faces only made things worse. Who knew any of our eyes could get so wide.

She quickly took a seat next to me and grabbed my hands, "D.J. baby, I'm sorry. That came out all wrong," she said with a look of sorrow and remorse that would've swayed any jury.

I just stared at her as I slowly pulled my hands away as the tears began to really flow down my face. I just shook my head at her still not believing what she'd just said and finally said, "I...I can't believe you just said that. What kind of monster are *you*?!" as I jumped up, grabbing my keys off the table and ran from the room. I was in my car backing out of the driveway by the time any of them caught up to me. Poor Summer was stumbling out of the house with her shirt barely over her head and her pants barely on as I sped off without ever looking back.

My phone was ringing off the hook for hours. When I finally answered it, it was Joshua.

He sounded so panicked it was almost scary, "D.J., where are you? Everyone's going crazy out looking for you? Where are you?"

I softly said, "I'm with Miah," and simply hung up the phone.

A little while later I heard an engine rapidly approaching and the not so subtle sound of tires screeching in the distance, as a man began screaming my name. The sun was starting to set, so the glare made it hard for me to see who it was as I slowly opened my eyes, but I knew that voice anywhere. I squinted as my eyes tried to focus in the sunlight, as I watch the man rapidly approaching, still yelling my name. He got quiet and stopped moving when he finally saw my crumpled body laying on the ground. He didn't move for a few seconds as he stood there with his mouth hanging open, watching me as I quietly laid there, on top of Jeremiah's gravesite. Joshua was still out of breath as he slowly approached me and kneeled down beside me. "Are you hurt?"

I slowly shook my head, no. He let out a deep breath and didn't say anything as he simply took a seat across from me and began to slowly rub my back. He still didn't say anything as I slowly looked up at him with an extremely puffy face. We just sat there staring at each other for a while when he finally dropped his head and let out another slow, drawn-out breath.

"So what are you going to do?" is all he said as he quietly waited for a response.

My tears had stopped long ago, but with that simple question, the waterworks came rushing back like an avalanche. He rubbed my back as I cried and howled at the setting sun, screaming, "WHY?! WHY DID HE LEAVE

ME?!!!" over and over again. He never said a word. And after some time, the screaming stopped, and I finally stopped crying. I slowly sat up and curled up in a tight ball, as I leaned up against Jeremiah's headstone, gently rocking. I watched him as he watched me. It was nearly dark when I finally spoke. "How'd you figure out where I was?"

He gently pushed my hair out of my face and began picking the grass off my cheeks and out of my hair as he softly said, "Well, it wasn't hard when you said you were with J. The cemetery was the obvious place...especially since I'd already been to all the other places I figured you would be," he chuckled. "But what I wanna know, is how you got in here? I damn near had to get the governor on the phone to get them to unlock this place for me. And where's your car? I didn't see it out on the road."

"It's on the dirt road at the back of the property. I crawled through the bushes and jumped the fence," as our eyes met again.

He just stared at me for a second, and then we both broke out laughing as he scooted up next to me and wrapped me in his arms. I snuggled into his chest before I quickly pushed away.

"What's wrong?"

I looked up at him with a wild look on my face and began poking him in the chest. "Your...your heartbeat. It sounds just like his," I kept staring at him.

He smiled and began to laugh again as he pulled me in close again, "Well, I am his twin. I'm shocked you didn't think about that possibility before," as he rubbed my head.

"I guess that does make sense," as I began to relax to the familiar beat.

"So I'll ask you again D.J...." he paused for a second, "What are you going to do?"

"I don't know," as I closed my eyes and listened to the soothing sound of his heartbeat.

"Well, you're going to have to figure it out soon because we can't sit out here all night," as he slapped at his neck. "These damn mosquitoes are going to eat us alive," as he slapped his cheek.

I giggled as I said, "It must be all that sweet barbecue sauce running through your veins because they aren't biting me."

"Very funny little sis," as he rocked me from side to side, then tried to tickle me. I couldn't help but start laughing as I passively fought him off. We settled down again just as he said, "But seriously D.J., what are you gonna do? Are we going to get you and the twins on a plane, train, boat, or fast car out of here, or are you getting married tomorrow?"

Lightning bugs began to dance around us as I let out a slow exhale and said, "As much as I'd like to take you up on one of your first options, I can't run. So I guess I'm getting married tomorrow," as I began to sniffle, but I didn't start crying.

He pulled back from me and said, "Well then, I guess we need to get you up off the ground and see if we can catch the tail end of your wedding rehearsal, don'tcha think?" as he strained to see his watch, and then twisted his head to try to look into my eyes.

"Ahww man...do we have to?" as I moved so we could stand up.

"I know it's a hassle, but yeah...I think that would be best," he giggled as he jumped up and pulled me to my feet. We brushed ourselves off as he took my hand and guided me through the cemetery back to his truck, as he suggested that maybe it would be best if he drove me to my car instead of me jumping fences and crawling through bushes this late at night. I didn't fuss as I slapped my neck. "That's what you get. Little suckers are finally eating yo butt too," he cracked up laughing as we reached the truck.

"Ha ha ha. Very funny," as I slapped my arm. "Let's get out of here before they do eat us alive," as I jumped in the cab.

Just for good measure, Joshua followed me over to the church. He walked me up to the doors but refused to go in with me. As we stood there, he lowered his head, looking away from me and softly said, "D.J., you know how much I love you right?"

"Yes, I do." As I tried to make eye contact so I could try to read him to see where this was going.

"I just wanted you to hear me say that, since I won't be coming to your wedding tomorrow," as he slowly looked at me again.

"You...you what?" as the tears began to roll down my face. "What do you mean you're not coming? You've got to come! I can't do this without you!" as I buried my face in his chest, sobbing.

He squeezed me tight as he began to rub my back. "D.J. I can't. I just can't watch you say I do to him. Not without standing up and telling everyone in there all the reasons you shouldn't be marrying this clown."

"But maybe that's what needs to happen," I took a step back as I pleaded with him with my eyes.

"I'm sorry little sister," as he pushed me further away shaking his head. "I can't, I just can't do it."

I wrapped my arms around him, pulling him close and simply cried as I listened to his racing heartbeat. I finally let him go and wiped my face off with my shirttail and said, "I guess I understand. I don't want to watch me say I do either," as I gave him a half-hearted smile as I turned to go in the building.

He grabbed my hand, "Wait a second D.J.. I have something to give you," as he released my hand and sprinted back to the truck. He quickly returned and slowly showed me a jewelry box as he said, "I was out at the ranch last week getting most of the guns out of the house, and while I was in the office, I notice you and J's wedding rings in the safe. I know I didn't have any right to take them, but I did," as he slowly opened the lid on the box.

I took a deep breath and began digging at my chest as I stood there, staring at the necklace inside. I couldn't say anything as tears began to run down my face and I gently touched what I saw.

"I hope you're not mad, but when I saw them I felt like I had to take them and do this," he held his free hand up pointing at the necklace inside. I quickly wiped my face as I took the necklace from the box and held it up for him to put it on me. I twirled around and lifted my hair out of the way. "I take it from your excitement that you're not mad at me," as he closed the clasp and spun me around to see it.

I was still fingering the pendant that was now hanging around my neck, when I looked up at him with happy tears welling up in the corners of my eyes and said, "Joshua, it's perfect." I surprised him as I reached up and hugged him around the neck.

"Woah... I take it I done good then."

"You did great!" as I released his neck and took a step back. "It's absolutely beautiful," as a tear escaped my eye and Joshua brushed it away. "I never would have thought of doing this," I smiled. He had taken our rings and had the jeweler create a gorgeous 2 ring, floating pendant. They moved the sapphires from the top of Jeremiah's ring and placed them on the flat side and left holes in the top of the ring for the necklace to fit through. Then inside that somehow they attached my wedding band, and that held the beautiful floating Halo Knot from my engagement ring. "Now he will always be with me," I said as the door opened and my mother yelled my name.

"D.J. Morgan! Where on earth have you been? We've looked everywhere for you!" as she stared at me and Joshua. I slowly dropped the pendant down under my shirt so she wouldn't see it, but she never missed a thing.

"It's still Thomas mom," I said sarcastically.

Joshua bumped me as he said, "I told you that I would find her for you Mrs. Morgan and I did," with an impish grin on his face.

"Yes you did and thank you for that, but she's very late and needs to get inside now," as she reached up and pulled my new necklace out from under my shirt. I knew better than to snatch it out of her hands as her head tilted slightly to the side and a frown formed across her brow. She slowly looked up at me and Joshua and asked, "Is this the wedding ring Jeremiah gave you?"

I took the pendant out of her hands and put it back under my shirt. "Yes mother it is. These are Jeremiah and my wedding bands and the engagement ring. Joshua had it made for me," I said in a defiant town.

Her mouth was hanging slightly open when she obviously shook off her daze and softly said, "Well it's beautiful," as she swept away a tear that escaped from the corner of her eye. Joshua and I stood there with our mouths hanging open. Neither of us could believe what had just happened. But for once in my life, I chose to err on the side of caution and didn't ask any questions. As she blinked another tear away, "Well thank you again for finding her, but she needs to get inside. We're almost done," as she grabbed my wrist and began dragging me into the church.

I quickly turned to wave back at Joshua and said, "Thank you so much! It's beautiful, and I'll never take it off," as the heavy door closed behind me.

I wish I could tell you that Joshua changed his mind overnight and came to the wedding, but I can't. Joshua was a man of his word and not only did he not come, no one from the Thomas clan did either. Not that I was the least bit surprised.

"I found her!" she yelled down the aisle as she continued to drag me behind her. That was going to be a recurring theme at my wedding come to find out, but I digress.

Everyone began to talk at once as we reached the altar.

"Well thank you for joining us," Pastor Clive chuckled.

If looks could kill, I'd have been dead ten times over from the look Selk gave me as he stepped forward and took my hand from my mom, jerking down on my arm just enough to tell me how he was really feeling. He leaned down and kissed me on my cheek and quickly whispered in my ear, "How dare you embarrass me like this? I'll deal with you later," as he stood up straight with a huge smile on his face like nothing was wrong.

I just sighed and turned to the group and said, "I'm so sorry that I'm so late. Momentary freak out is all. I just needed a little time to myself," as I finally noticed two things. First, Summer was giving me a death stare as she slowly shook her head back and forth at me. I knew what that meant even before we had a chance to talk, and second, there was a bridesmaid standing there that I'd never seen before. I couldn't help it as I tilted my head to the side and gave her a questioning look.

"Hi D.J. I'm Jaleesa, J.R.'s girlfriend. It's my pleasure to meet you, and I'm so glad I could help you out," as she reached out to shake my hand.

I shot J.R. a quick frown as I turned back to her and smiled, reaching out my hand to shake hers. "Hi Jaleesa, nice to meet you. And it's I, who should be thanking you for being so willing to step in at the last minute to help us out. I hope the dress fit you okay." As I stepped back for a moment. I could see Summer rolling her eyes and mimicking what I was saying. I not so accidentally stepped on her foot as I backed away to show her my response.

"Ouch!" she yelled as she began hopping around on one foot. "That wasn't called for," she said just above her breath so I could hear her. I gave her a quick grin and took a seat behind them.

"Okay everyone. Now that the bride has arrived, let's run through this once again so she can see how the ceremony is going to flow," Aunt Mayvis explained. Everyone moaned as they did as they were instructed. I got to see everything from the processional to what songs were going to be sung throughout the ceremony, one of which I had not authorized. Apparently, Selk added a song during the first run-through, to be sung by his cousin. When everything was done Aunt Mayvis asked, "Does anyone have any questions about tomorrow?"

I thought to myself, *'I do...do we have to do this?'* but of course, I didn't say or do anything else to piss off the wrong people.

"Well, in that case, let's all get to the rehearsal dinner hosted by the groom," she smiled as she pointed over towards Selk. "It's a barbecue at D.J's parents' house. Do you all know how to get there?" A few of Selk's people didn't, but they would just follow someone who did know how to get out there.

Once that was worked out, Selk smiled and raised his hands above his head and said, "Well let's get this party started then!" to the cheers and clapping of everyone in attendance. Well everyone but me and Summer of course. As we all made our way into the parking lot, Selk slid up next to me, wrapping his arm around my waist and said, "Sweetie, why don't you ride with me," just loud enough for everyone to hear him as he gave me a not so gentle squeeze.

"Uhmm, I would, but I don't want to leave my car here overnight," I replied with a forced smile.

"Well, Summer can drive it for you," he pushed back.

Summer lifted her hand up to respond to him, but I jumped in before she had a chance to say anything. "Baby Summer doesn't drive a stick," I smiled, trying not to sound annoyed at him.

He frowned at me then slowly said, "Oh. Well okay then. I guess I'll see you out there," as he tightened his grip on my hand. Basically, another... *'You're pissing me off,'* squeeze.

Once Summer and I were safely in my car, she crossed her arms across her chest and said, "Liar, Liar, Pants on Fire!" I grinned at her and quickly backed out of the space and whipped around the car backing out in front of us because I didn't want prying ears to hear her as she went off on me. I quickly pulled out of the parking lot and took off like a shot, just in time.

"First, you know damn well I know how to drive a stick. Hell, I learned to drive on a fucking stick, and my damn car is a stick," she frowned at me. "Second, why in the fuck did you leave me behind? I nearly went bat shit crazy listening to them fuss at you, and about you, knowing I couldn't say anything to defend you without them turning on me! And third...Where in the HELL have you been!" she yelled as she finally took a breath.

I smiled at her as I checked my mirrors to make sure no one was following us too closely. When I felt we were far enough ahead of the pack, I took a deep breath and began to relax as I explained to her where I'd been and what I'd been doing. I also apologized profusely for leaving her behind, but I wasn't thinking straight when I left. I just had to get up and go.

Once I finished with my explanation, she simply looked at me sideways and said, "I get all of that, but what I don't understand for the life of me, is why in the HELL did you show up tonight?" as she sat there shaking her head at me. Before I could respond, "Do you know what kind of lead you would've had on the cops? I stood there with a smirk on my face, right up until you walked in at least, thinking to myself, *'Y'all might as well stop calling and driving around looking for her. My girl is so out of here,'*" as she fell out laughing. After a few seconds, I couldn't help but start laughing right along with her as she reached over and pulled my necklace out from under my shirt. She held the pendant in her hand as she smiled and slowly shook her head, "Well I'll tell you this much, Jeremiah sure must have loved you a lot to give you such an exquisite ring," as she gently laid it down, on top of my shirt of course. "And look at it this way, now we don't have to come up with your 'something blue,' because Jeremiah already provided it," she said with a huge Kool-Aid smile.

I began to tear up as I looked over at her and smiled for a moment. "Summer, he really was a special man, and we loved each other more than two people should probably ever love another person," as I reached over and squeezed her hand. She squeezed back as we rode in silence until we had almost reached my parents' house. As we waited for the light to change, I said, "Summer..."

"Yeah, what's up?"

"I really wish you had gotten to meet him," I quickly smiled at her as I held on to my pendant. "You would have loved him, just as much as I do," I finished, wiping a tear away just as the light changed.

She reached over and squeezed my shifting hand again as I turned the corner and said, "I wish I had too, but I already do," as the tears began to well up in her eyes.

"What the fuck is this?!" I said as I turned the corner and pulled up into the driveway.

She immediately started looking around, "What? What's wrong?"

3ᴿᴰ SIGN.....

"The van...that's the delivery van from Triple J's, I explained as I put the car in neutral and quickly got out say, "No, no, no, no, no he didn't!" as I ran in the house, with Summer hot on my heels.

"Wait up D.J.! What's wrong with that?" she quickly asked as I headed for the backyard, where the party was supposed to be.

As I flung the backdoor open, "Triple J's is the barbecue spot Jeremiah's family and I own," I gave her a leery look as I pushed the patio door open.

Her mouth instantly fell open as she looked down at the ground shaking her head and said, "That Son of a Bitch!" and slammed the door behind us.

Otis and Lexie were finishing up the set-up when I approached the tent. "What's going on?! Who ordered this?!" I yelled at them unintentionally, of course.

"Hay Ms. D.J.," Lexie said as she rushed over to me. "Now it all makes sense why Mr. Joshua refused to make this delivery and told me not to bother you with it," she explained as she passed me the catering invoice.

I quickly scanned the paper, steadily shaking my head. I finally passed Summer the paper so she could stop straining to read it over my shoulder. "So when did this order come in, because it damn sure wasn't there when I left the office yesterday?"

"Well, Tina took the order after you'd already left. But I confirmed it with Mr. Joshua before she got off the phone. He said it would be okay, but for Otis and me to deliver and set it up." You could tell she was nervous by the way she kept fidgeting.

We all just stood there for a few minutes, not having much to say as I finally reached over and squeezed Lexie's hand and gave her a smile. "Lexie, it's not your fault. And you did a wonderful job with the set-up. Thank you for all your hard work." Summer elbowed me as she pointed down at the tip line...it read $2. I frowned as I shook my head and took the invoice from Summer and added a couple of zeros making it a $2000 tip, initialed it, and then recalculated the total and signed the bottom. Summer grabbed her mouth, trying not to laugh out loud as she took the paper back to confirm what I'd just done and then gave it back to Lexie.

"Well thanks Ms. D.J.. I know how you are about catering orders, especially last-minute ones, but I think everyone will be happy with what we did," as she waved her arm like she was presenting a prize to someone.

Just about that time is when the door opened, and the real party started. Selk stepped out on the patio leading the group like he was the King or something. As I turned and headed straight for him, I heard Summer say, "Now this should be interesting," and started giggling.

I startled Selk when I grabbed his arm and began pulling him to the side, "We need to talk!" I growled.

As he regained his footing, he waved his free hand at the guests and said, "Hey, y'all go on in and get the party started while my soon to be wife and I sneak in a quickie," with a big smile on his face. I didn't acknowledge his comment as I continued to pull him back in the house as everyone else began to laugh and cheer. Once we were inside, I drug him through the house and out into the garage where we would definitely be alone. I slammed the door shut and the fight was on.

"What the fuck is this Selk?!" as I pointed towards the backyard. "This is pretty petty even for you!"

He stood there with a devilish smirk on his face, but he didn't immediately respond. He gave me a grunt as he turned his back and walked over to one of the cars and just leaned over it with his back to me. In hindsight, I should have known that things weren't going to go down the way I had thought. Or maybe I just wasn't thinking as I continued to hurl insults at him about how petty he was and completely out of order for this.

When he'd finally had enough, Selk slowly turned towards me and just like lightning, he backhanded me across my face, before I ever realized his hand was in motion. The force of his blow knocked me at least 15 feet back, as I fell over the lawnmower and into the bicycles sitting by the backdoor to the garage. I didn't even get a chance to recover from my fall when he snatched me up by my neck and threw me up against the wall, 2 feet off the ground. I held onto his wrist for dear life as I shook my head trying to regain my bearings.

"D.J., why are you making me do this? Why are you trying to do everything possible to piss me off today? This is supposed to be the happiest time of our lives, and yo bitch ass is ruining it for me," as he pulled me forward and slammed me back into the wall. It was scary how calm and soft-spoken he was right now, even though he still had me pinned to the wall, by my neck, 2 feet off the ground.

"Selk," I could barely choke out. "Let...me...go," as I flailed around trying to get loose.

And once again, as quickly as the attacked started, it ended. Only because the door opened and Dale peeked his head out, "Hey, we've been looking for you two. Come on, the party... has... already... started," his words slowed down, as he slowly stepped into the garage. "And the guests of honor... are nowhere to be seen."

Selk had pulled me in close to him with his arm around my shoulders and neck like we were all lovey-dovey. "Yeah man. We'll be right there," he chuckled. Trying not to let on to what was really going on.

But Dale could tell something was up as he stepped closer and touched me on my shoulder. My head was down and basically in Selk's armpit, so he pulled me as he gripped my shoulder, "Hey cuz, is everything okay out here?"

Selk tightened his grip on my arm as I swept my hair back out of my face and tried to put on a smile while keeping Dale from seeing the cheek Selk slapped. It was still on fire, so I knew it had to have a bruise. "Yeah... everything's okay."

"Are you sure," as he leaned down to try to make eye contact with me as he managed to give Selk a wayward look.

"She said she's fine man. Everything is good," as he stepped between us and turned Dale back towards the door. "Give us a minute to finish up our conversation, and we'll be right there," as he patted him on his shoulder and opened the door so he would hurry up and leave the garage.

"Yeah, well like I said." I could tell by the look on his face that Dale knew what was up, but he didn't say anything, since I didn't say anything. "You need to hurry up."

To be such a big guy, Selk could move so quickly and silently. Before I realized it, he was standing over me again, with a death grip on my shoulder. I immediately grabbed his wrist and began to cave under the pressure of the hold he had on me.

"Stop it Selk! You're hurting me!" as I pounded his wrist.

"Little girl, you have yet to understand what hurt is," as he slowly loosened his grip. He turned away again and walked over to the sink and wet a handful of paper towels from my dad's work station. I had collapsed on the bumper of the van when Selk began to wipe my busted lip off and gently wiped across the bruised area on my cheek. "D.J. my love...why do we have to play this game all the time?" as he continued to clean me up.

"Selk....I'm not playing a game," I said as I pushed his hand away and slid down to the floor and finally started crying into my hands. Through my tears, I finally said, "Selkie, I can't do this. I'd rather take my chance in court."

Selk slowly bent down beside me and ever so gently pushed my hair out of my face. "D.J., D.J., D.J...." as he gave me a gentle kiss on my forehead before he whispered in my ear, "No you're not, and you know why we both know you're not? Because you'd rather die than give me custody of the boys," as he giggled, then grabbed me by the chin, snatching my head up and passionately kissed me.

I pushed him back, "Get off me Selk!" not expecting him to fall, but in those slick shoes, he really didn't have a good grip on the cement floor of the garage as he fell back hitting his head on the wall.

Lucky for me, Summer opened the door just as he landed on his back or else he probably would have killed me when he recovered. She immediately jumped over him and rushed over to me, helping me to my feet. "D.J.! What happened?" as she began inspecting the damages.

"I'm okay. Nothing to worry about," as I winced when I touched my lip and she touched my cheek.

Summer immediately whirled around and went on the attack. "Look you overgrown ass hole! If you put another hand on her, I swear on my unborn children's heads that I'll kill you myself!" as she poked him in his chest.

Selk simply pushed her hand to the side as he brushed himself off with a giggle. "Look here," as he grabbed her wrist, scaring her and me.

I jumped to her side just as she began kicking and swinging with her free hand. "STOP IT SELK! LET HER GO!" as I pulled on his arm.

He just laughed at us both as he released her.

"Look mother fucker! You don't know me like that! And don't you EVER put your got damn hands on me again!" as she rushed him swinging.

I stepped in between them holding her back as best I could and yelled over my shoulder, "Get outta here Selk! Leave now!"

He tossed the wet paper towels at me and simply said, "Clean yourself up before you come outside to greet our guests," and turned toward the door, but not before he left us with one last word. "And D.J....be quick about it. Don't keep me waiting again." And just like that, he was gone.

"Are you okay," I asked her as I checked out her wrist.

"Am I alright? Are *you* alright? Look at your face D.J.! You *let* him do that to you?" as she touched my cheek.

I jerked my head away as I turned to look in the side mirror of the van to check the damages. I stretched my neck around to see exactly how much trauma I'd sustained as Summer pulled me around to look her in the face.

"D.J. you can't marry that animal. Look what he did to you...." as she stood there pleading with her water-filled eyes.

I took a deep breath as I simply pulled her in close and gave her a tight hug. We stood there hugging each other for a few minutes as we both cried on the others shoulder. Without warning, I pushed away from her and began wiping my face off as I stood up straight and said, "Summer, it's okay. I know what I've got to do and it's all going to be okay. I promise you that," as I gave her a smile. I kept nodding my head yes, as I gave her my little pep talk, but she kept shaking her head no.

"D.J., does your mom know about this? Does anyone know he's been beating you?"

"I wouldn't call it a beating," I smiled and hunched my shoulder at her as I turned to tend to my wounds in the side mirror again. "I'd call it more of an aggressive negotiation," I looked back at her. "He grabs me, and I push back. He shakes me, and I push back," as I ran my tongue over my lip with a slight grimace. "Needless to say, sometimes bruises happen," as I reached out and grabbed her hand. "It may look bad, but bruises heal," as I shook her hand.

She snatched away from me with a look of horror on her face, "Who are you and where is my best friend?" as she took several steps back shaking her head at me. "D.J. do you hear yourself? You've always been the one to fight back! That man can kill you! You can't win a fight against him...have you lost your mind?" she asked as the garage door swung open.

"What's going on out here? Selk has been at the party awhile now, what's taking you so long?" my mother asked with her hands on her hips, looking annoyed.

Summer never turned around to look at her as she crossed her arms and stared at me, "Yeah D.J....what's taking *you* so long?" with a slight tilt of her head.

I cleared my throat for a second, "Well I just needed to touch up my makeup first, then I'll be out there. Everything's fine," as I watched Summer's eyes widen to the size of saucers as her mouth fell open. I gave her a quick wide-eyed shake of my head as I turned back to the mirror to check out my face.

My mom hesitated for a second, "Well...hurry it up already. You're being very rude....again," as she turned and stormed out of the garage, slamming the door for good effect.

Summer dropped her head still shaking it back and forth, "D.J., I don't know what to say to you right now," as she slowly looked up at me. "Why on earth didn't you say something to her?"

"Because it wouldn't do any damn good! That's why," I snapped at her. "She is 100% team Selk, and I'm doing everything I can, NOT to lose my mind right now, so there's no way I can take having *my* mother tell me to stop doing, whatever the hell it is I'm doing to upset him!" as I pointed towards the backyard. "Do you have any idea what it's like to feel like the one person who should want to protect you is the one who is selling you to the devil? Do you?!" But before she could respond, "I can answer that for you....NO YOU DON'T! So no! There was no reason to tell her because if she was really on my side, I WOULDN'T BE GETTING MARRIED TO HIM TOMORROW! OR DID YOU CONVENIENTLY FORGET THAT HE ATTACKED ME WHEN I WAS STILL PREGNANT WITH THE TWINS? WHICH OBVIOUSLY MAKES NO GOT DAMN DIFFERENCE TO HER!!!" I screamed at her, pointing in the direction my mother had just gone, as the tears began to stream down my face. Summer immediately rushed me giving me a tight hug. We simply stood there hugging until I stopped crying. We never said another word about what happened. In fact, we never had this particular conversation ever again.

When we finally got me cleaned up enough, which meant that Summer and I had caked on enough makeup to cover-up my scrapes and bruises, we joined the party that was already in full swing. We actually walked into the tent just in time to see Selk's mom throw her back out trying to out dance my teenage cousins in a limbo contest. When I tell you it took everything in me not to fall out on the ground laughing, it took everything.

I took my seat next to Selk and did my best not to flinch or pull away when he leaned over to kiss me, as he whispered in my ear, "It's about damn time," giving me a tight squeeze.

"Well it took some time to cover up all of your fancy work dear," I smiled back so no one would be the wiser as to what was really going on. I turned away as he hissed in my ear and caught the steady gaze of my mother. We only locked eyes for a moment as I dropped my head and immediately turned away from her. So basically, for the rest of the night, whenever Selk tried to kiss or touch me, I acted my ass off to make everyone believe that we were as happy as could be. This became my new normal whenever we were in public or if we were around other people. I learned to be an academy award winning actress at my wedding rehearsal barbecue. Nobody ever had any idea of the abuse going on in our relationship until the very end.

Now the other very interesting thing that happened at that party was that my mother got skid row drunk that night. I can't remember ever seeing her drink more than a glass of wine, let alone half a case of it. At some point, she disappeared into the house, and Summer found her at the kitchen table, turning up a bottle of Champagne and came to get me. Dale overheard our conversation on our way out of the tent and followed us back into the house, where my mother was downing a bottle of Champagne all by herself. We all just stood there watching her as she literally held the bottle to her lips and drank from it.

She looked up at us and sarcastically asked, "What the funk are y'all staring at?" as she sat the bottle down on the table, and rather loudly I might add.

"Mom...are you okay? What's wrong?" I asked as I slowly took a seat beside her. Dale sat down on the other side of her and slowly moved the bottle away from her.

"Nothing...nothing at all," she slurred as she tried to make eye contact with each of us.

"Aunt Lisa, what's going on?" he asked, trying not to sound overly concerned.

"Am I not speaking English? I said nothing didn't I?" as she reached for the bottle, nearly knocking it off the table.

I looked at Dale and Summer with a surprised look on my face, as Summer began to giggle. "Momma I think maybe we need to help you to bed," as I stood up and took her by the arm to help her get up.

She slapped my hand, "Nonsense! It's a party, and I'm not going anywhere," she looked up at me, then took the bottle from Dale and turned it up again.

I looked at Dale and Summer and whispered, "What the hell? What are we gonna do?"

Summer was obviously not going to be any help as she took a couple steps back, crossed her arms across her chest, and leaned up against the wall shaking her head, then finally whispered, "Serves her right," with a devilish smirk on her face.

I moved over to her and whispered, "We can't let anyone else see her like this," as I pointed back and forth from the backyard to her.

"Hey, she's a grown-ass woman. Why are you so hell-bent on protecting her when *she*, should be protecting you?" she whispered as she took a step forward, obviously angry at me.

"You already know why. And because this isn't like her. I've never seen her drink more than a glass of wine in one sitting before."

"Again, serves her right. She's obviously guilty and damit, she should be," she stomped.

Dale still had a blank look on his face as he watched her and listened to Summer and me go back and forth.

"Come on Summer," as I stopped talking until the coast was clear. One of the guests had come in to go to the bathroom. When the door closed behind him, I quickly continued before he returned. "I get it, you're pissed at her, but you can't put this all on her."

She hesitated when we heard the bathroom door open again. Once the area was clear again, "Yes I can! So no I'm not gonna do a damn thing to protect her. And if I were you..."

"But you're not me," I cut her off. "And as my best friend and my Maid of Honor, you should be trying to help me and not working against me right now," I pointed at the floor.

"You know I can hear you both right?" she said as she took another long swig from the bottle, finishing it off. "Dale baby, get me another bottle out the fridge, would you love?" she said as she dropped the empty bottle, upside down in the case it came out of. We all looked down and noticed the other 3 bottles that were already in the box by her feet, also upside down.

"D.J., what's this about?" Dale finally asked.

I broke my staring contest with Summer and looked down at him, "It's about what's probably fueling my mother's sudden thirst," as I turned my attention back to Summer.

"Dale, what this is about is the fact that your dear, naive cousin thinks about everyone else's needs and wants over her own," she said without breaking eye contact with me.

"Stop it!" I snapped, as I grabbed her arm, yanking it down from her chest.

"Oh no you didn't! I'm not you!" as she snatched away from me. "And I'm not going to let anyone, including you Miss D.J. Morgan-Thomas, put their hands on me in a violent way. You may be okay with being Selk's punching bag, but don't get it twisted big sister, grab me like that again, and you're going to be picking yourself up off the ground for the second time tonight," she growled at me.

Dale immediately stood up and grabbed my arm, spinning me around towards him. "What's she talking about D.J.? Did he hit you? Is that what I walked in on in the garage?" as he tugged at my arm.

I grabbed my shoulder, "Please don't do that. My shoulder is hurting," as I rubbed it.

"Tell him *why* your shoulder hurts D.J.. Go on, I dare you," Summer said as she pulled me back around towards her.

As I started to say something, my mom's chair made a loud screeching sound as she suddenly pushed back from the table and stood up. "I'll get the funk'n bottle myself!" as she turned and stumbled to the refrigerator and opened the door, taking out 2 more bottles of Champagne before she stumbled back to her seat again. We all just stood there with our mouths hanging open, as she popped the cork and quickly put the bottle to her mouth so as not to spill anything as it rushed out.

I dropped my head as the first of many tears began to run down my face. "I can't believe this shit," I said as I snatched the bottle from her and took a long gulp myself.

"Hey! Get your own!" she yelled. "There's plenty more in the fridge," as she snatched the bottle from me. "Go help yourself," as she took another drink.

Dale grabbed my arm again and growled, "Don't you dare move," as he turned for the backdoor.

"What are you getting ready to do?" as I rushed over to block his exit.

"Move D.J." as he pushed me to the side and opened the door. "I'm going to get Selk," he said through clenched teeth as he marched out to the tent.

I quickly turned back to Summer, "Now look what you've done!" as I ran to the bathroom and began throwing up.

"What I've done?" she asked, as she gathered up my hair and pulled it out of my way.

"Yes…" as I heard Dale calling my name, causing me to start throwing up again.

"We're in here!" Summer yelled.

No sooner than she said it, there was Dale standing in the doorway with Selk in tow. Dale pushed their way in and closed the door behind them as he shoved Selk into the wall holding him there with one hand as he poked him in his chest with the other.

"What the fuck?!" Selk yelled as he grabbed Dale's wrist.

"Did you put your mother fucking hands on my cousin?" he growled as he leaned into Selk, poking him even harder.

Selk continued to try to break free as he began to explain, "Look man… she attacked me, and I defended myself," he pointed at me.

I looked up from the floor, "I what?" and started throwing up again.

Summer immediately lit into him, "You're a got damn liar punk! Dale, I walked in on him slamming her into the wall yelling at her, and her face was all red from where he'd hit her," as she picked me up off the floor with one hand and snatched the towel off the sink with the other, then wiped the heavy makeup off my face before I had a chance to stop her.

"Summer NO!" I yelled as I snatched the towel from her and turned my face away from Dale.

The bathroom got eerily silent for a minute. You could barely even hear any of us breathing as Dale slowly pulled my chin around so he could look at my face. He let Selk go as he took the towel away from me and slowly began to gently remove as much of the makeup as he could from my face. When he was done, he just stood there staring at me as his eyes began to water.

It was like Summer knew all hell was getting ready to break loose as she stepped back, slowly pulling me into the far corner with her. I never said a word as I watched a tear slowly run down the side of Dale's face as he just stared at me.

"Hold on man. Let, let me explain, okay?" Selk began to stutter as he grabbed Dale's arm and began waving his hand at him like he wanted him to hold on.

Dale finally dropped his head as he slowly shook it from side to side. He didn't say anything as he sniffled and wiped another tear away as he exploded. He grabbed Selk by his shoulder and with an upward swing caught him with a solid punch to his gut. "DON'T YOU EVER PUT YOUR MOTHER FUCKING HANDS ON MY COUSIN AGAIN!" As Selk crumpled to the floor like a ragdoll. "DO YOU UNDERSTAND ME? DO YOU UNDERSTAND ME?!" Dale kept yelling as he began to kick him in the side and then bent down and grabbed him by his collar, "DO YOU UNDERSTAND ME YOU PUSSY?!" He started pounding on Selk like he was a heavyweight boxer and Selk was a featherweight. "DO YOU HEAR ME MOTHER FUCKER! DO YOU HEAR ME!?" as blow after blow connected with Selk's jaw.

I didn't make a sound as I watched the energy to fight back slowly leave Selk's body, and the floor became a crimson mess. Finally, Summer pushed past me and grabbed Dale, pushing him up against the door yelling, "STOP! STOP! HE'S HAD ENOUGH!" as she looked back over her shoulder at Selk's battered body lying on the floor.

Dale stood there shaking his head and then suddenly threw a right jab, right past Summer's head, connecting with the wall, screaming, "AAAAAHHHHHHHHH!" as he turned around holding the back of his head and squatted. He was crying as he lowered his head between his knees, still shaking his head. "It wasn't supposed to be like this...it wasn't supposed to be like this," he whispered to nobody in particular.

Summer stood there with her hands in the air like she was surrendering, with her eyes wider than I'd ever seen before and her mouth hanging wide open, staring at me then at Dale. I stood there watching Dale as I began to smile at the sound of Selk's shallow moans. I slowly left my corner and knelt down beside Dale as I gently placed my hand on his back and picked up the towel from the floor, holding it up to Summer.

"Wet this for me, would you?" as I continued to hold the towel in the air, I laid my forehead on the side of Dale's head saying, "It's alright cousin. It's all going to be alright."

I could tell Summer was still shaken by the beat down that had just taken place as she nervously said, "Yeah, yeah...I got it," as the towel finally left my hand, and the water came on.

Summer gave me back the towel and I tossed it over onto Selk and said, "Clean yourself up," over my shoulder, as I pulled Dale up from the floor and washed his battered hands-off.

I heard Selk moan, "D.J., help me please," as I opened the door. I hesitated for a moment, but I never looked back or responded to his battered calls, as I walked Dale on out of the bathroom, pulling the door shut behind us. Needless to say, that was the last time Selk laid a finger on me like that, for a while anyway.

After that, Dale insisted on joining my mom at the kitchen table and commenced to turning up bottles right alongside her. When the party finally ended, the two of them had polished off a case of Champagne and a couple bottles of wine. Selk even managed to get himself up off the bathroom floor and get cleaned up for his bachelor party without too many people finding out about the ass whuppin he'd just sustained. Summer was convinced that the wedding was off, but yet again she would be wrong.

When we were finally able to walk my mom upstairs to her room, she looked up at me and said, "Baby, I know he's going to be the perfect husband to you now. He wouldn't dare put a hand on you after the conversation Dale just had with him," as she kissed the back of my hand and settled in for the night.

The surprised look on Summer's face was priceless. And as much as I nor Summer wanted to attend my bachelorette party, we both decided that it would be best. But that too turned out to be drama when Summer realized that none of the other bridesmaids, mainly Phaedra and Kimberly, who was no longer in the wedding, hadn't planned anything for me. So we decided to hit up a club. Unfortunately, that was where Selk's folks had taken him, so we ended up having a joint party until right before midnight when Summer and I left. After all, it is bad luck to see the bride after midnight before the wedding and all.

4ᵀᴴ SIGN.....

Summer and I had finally settled down at my parent's house for the night when all hell broke loose. It was just about 2AM when the smoke detectors started sounding off and my dad got to pounding on my bedroom door for us to get up. When we opened the door, the hallway was full of smoke and P.J. was yelling for us to get out of the house. I grabbed one baby, and Summer grabbed the other, and we ran down the stairs to the waiting arms of the firemen rushing into the house with axes and hoses.

From all the smoke you would have thought the entire house was going up in flames, but it turned out that the wires behind the kitchen stove had caught on fire. Luckily only the area around the stove was affected, but the thing is, that was a brand new stove and wiring. My parents had just remodeled the kitchen a couple of months ago, so everything in there was practically new and top of the line. On top of that, we'd been in this house for over 20 years, and we'd never had anything like this to happen. Not even a major grease fire.

Now mind you while all the excitement was going on downstairs, Summer has gone back upstairs to retrieve the wedding rings against the advice of the firemen. I didn't want to add to the mayhem, but as soon as she came back out of the house, I went back in the house with the boys. It was almost 3AM, and it was colder than the boys were used to, so I decided that it was time for us to go back inside and put them to bed since the majority of the smoke was gone, and the fire had long since been put out. Summer and the others finally came back in the house around 3:30 when they were given the all clear.

The problem was when Summer came to bed, she was not the least bit happy to find both of the twins asleep with me in the bed. When she didn't get the response she was looking for from me, she went and complained to my mom who understood her plight and quickly removed the two of them from the bed and took them to her room, where they got to sleep in the big bed with their grandparents. Once the bed switching was complete, Summer was able to comfortably crawl in bed with me, and we all finally got to get some rest before the big day ahead of us.

5ᵀᴴ SIGN.....

I'm not an early riser, and I'm sure not a cheerful early riser, so after the night we'd had no one including me would have ever guessed that I'd get up and out of the house on time that morning. I was due at the beauty salon to get my hair done for the wedding by 6:30AM so that my cousin Jaqué could get me in and out before her regular customers arrived that Saturday morning. Not only did I get up and showered without the alarm going off, I was at the salon by 6AM with a smile on my face. I actually woke Jaqué up.

It was around 8AM when Jaqué's first client showed up as she was straightening my hair, so she asked her client if she minded waiting until she finished with me. Of course, she said that she was fine with that, but I insisted on waiting instead. I had no problem moving to another chair while she washed, conditioned, and then got her set and under the dryer. The funny thing was, as we finally got my hair straight and began creating a style that would work well with my vail, she had 2 more clients show up as well, so again I waited until she could get back to me.

It was close to 11:45 when we were both finally satisfied with our fabulous creation and received the approval of her other clients, who by the way, had all stayed to see the finished product. We got to having so much fun laughing and cutting up that I honestly forgot all about my wedding, which was made painfully obvious when my mom called the shop looking for me.

"Hi Aunt Lisa…. yeah, she's right here," Jaqué said as she gave me a look that let me know I was in big trouble. "It's for you D.J.," as she passed me the phone.

I rolled my eyes as I noticed the time, it was nearly 1:15, and my wedding was supposed to start at 3 o'clock. I slowly took the phone from her, "Hello?" I said like I didn't know who it was.

"D.J., did you forget what today is?" she said in a much calmer voice than I expected.

"No ma'am."

"Well I'm trying to figure out why we're all here getting ready, but you're not. Especially since you left the house before 6 this morning."

"Well, I just kinda lost track of time as other people started showing up," I winced. I couldn't help but notice the looks Jaqué and her clients kept giving me, so I turned the chair away from them to keep me from laughing.

"I would advise you to get your happy self here immediately young lady. DO YOU UNDERSTAND ME?!" she finally yelled at me.

"Yes ma'am. I'm leaving now," I rolled my eyes as the line went dead. I slowly gathered myself as I turned to hang up the phone. I hadn't noticed how quiet the room had gotten until I actually stood up and turned around to face everyone. All eyes were definitely on me. I lowered my head as I quickly passed behind Jaqué to hang up the phone.

"Hey little cousin," Jaqué said as she gently patted my shoulder.

"Yeah," I said as I tried to blink the tears that were welling up in my eyes away.

"Chin up. It's going to be okay," as she hugged me and then sent me on my way.

I have to admit, I took my time getting to the church. My cousin's beauty shop was only about 15 - 20 minutes from the church, but it took me at least 30 minutes to get there. As I pulled in the parking lot about 1:45 PM, I was greeted by Aunt Mayvis and of course my mother, who was beyond fit to be tied.

"Glad you decided to grace us with your presence," Aunt Mayvis said as she opened my car door.

"I can't believe you have us waiting on you like a couple of doormen," my mother shouted.

I slowly gathered my things out of the passenger's seat, without responding to either of them, which was obviously taking too long as my mother snatched the headpiece and veil out of my hands and stomped off.

"D.J., my sweet, sweet niece. Why must you antagonize your mother on today of all days?"

"What did I do?" I asked as I looped my arm in hers.

"Well for starters, you are just showing up to a 3 o'clock wedding at 1:45," she gave me a sarcastic grin. I just dropped my head and silently followed her into the church. What could I say to that, that wouldn't make me look like a bigger ass than I already did? Aunt Mayvis opened a door to what was usually a Sunday school classroom and yelled, "SURPRISE!" as she shoved me through the door.

All of my bridesmaids were in there, putting on their dresses and finishing up their makeup. I smiled as everyone rushed me telling me how beautiful my hair was and how well rested I looked. They asked if I was ready for my big day, which I knew better than to respond to. As I helped them finish dressing Aunt Mayvis and Aunt Claudette came back in to check on us. The looks on their faces was priceless.

"Uhm, D.J..." Aunt Claudette started.

I turned to look at her as I helped Jaleesa get her hair pin in properly, "Yes ma'am?"

"I think you misunderstand how this is supposed to work dear."

"Huh?"

As she pointed to the group of women I was helping to get dressed and get their makeup on, "They are supposed to be getting you dressed and doing your makeup, not the other way around," she smiled.

Aunt Mayvis rushed me, "It's 2:15 D.J., and you haven't started getting dressed," as she twirled me around and yanked my shirt off in one move.

I covered my chest, "Hey wait a minute," I put my hand up to stop her.

"How about I go across the hall and get ready? There's more room over there anyway," I explained.

"Well, fine. But you need to hurry. We were going to try to get in a few pictures of the bridal party before the ceremony," she explained as she and Aunt Claudette began scooping up all the pieces to my wedding ensemble and taking them across the hall for me.

I don't know where my mom came from, but I heard her as soon as she stepped in the doorway. "Now what's going on? And why aren't you dressed yet?" Before anyone could respond, "I swear D.J. you're doing everything possible to ruin this event," she said with her hands on her hips.

Aunt Claudette intervened before I had a chance to respond. "Lisa, we've got this. You can go relax for a bit while we get her ready, okay." And just like that, my aunties rushed me across the hall and out of my mother's line of fire.

"Is it okay if Summer comes over here?"

"Sure it is, if that's what you want," Aunt Mayvis said as she laid my dress out and quickly went back across the hall to get Summer.

"And thank you for handling her for me, Aunt Claudette," I blushed.

"Well, we wouldn't need to handle her if you would just get with the program and stop acting out," she smiled as she swatted me on the top of my head.

"Yeaaah. About that..." I slowly shook my head as I stared at the ground.

"Enough said on the matter," she put her hand up to stop me. "I'm not getting in between you and your mother's spat. I've already said my piece about this wedding situation to your mom, and now I'm out of it," she explained as the door opened. "Do you need our help or can you and Summer get you ready..." as she looked at her watch. "In 40 minutes tops?"

"Sure we can," I tried to smile. But everything inside me was screaming, *'HELL NO!'* I'll say this if nothing else my family was great at acting like nothing was going on when someone walked in the room. That was the last time me and Aunt Claudette spoke about my wedding.

"Well okay then, you'd better hop to it," Aunt Mayvis smiled before they left us alone.

6ᵀᴴ Sign.....

As the door closed behind them, I collapsed on a chair crying. "I don't want to do this. I just don't want to do this...."

Summer tried her best to comfort me but very quickly called my attention to a small dilemma as she leaned over me, rubbing my back. "D.J. I would sit next to you right now, but this dress doesn't have much give, and I'm afraid if I sit down it's going to A: split or B: I'm not going to be able to stand up again." I slowly looked up at her and began to laugh. What she said was funny no matter what else was going on. "Here take this towel and dry your face while I get a washcloth."

I was still giggling when she returned with the wet cloth. As I looked up at her with bloodshot eyes, "What am I doing?"

"I've been asking myself that every day since you told me about this travesty D.J.. And every time I see a glimmer of the D.J. I once knew, I get my feelings hurt," she continued as she passed me the Visine from her makeup bag. "What's that look for?" she asked.

"You have a makeup bag?" I asked with a surprised look on my face.

We just stared at one another for a moment, then both of us broke out in laughter. "Yes, Miss smarty pants I have a makeup bag. I do occasionally wear the stuff," as she batted her eyes.

In all my tears, I hadn't even noticed. She was such a natural beauty that I never even thought about it. When we were done laughing, I finally stood up and said, "Let's get to it."

"If you're sure about this," she gave me a questioning look.

"Summer the only thing I'm sure about is that if I'm not ready in the next 30 minutes or so, it's going to take Jesus Himself to save us from my mother," as I pointed at the two of us.

She twisted up her face a little, "You're right. We better get to moving," as she snatched the washcloth and hurried back to the bathroom and wet it again. "Do you need to hit the hot spots or are you good?"

I took a quick sniff of my underarms, "I'm good, but just in case let me do a quick touch up anyway."

"I was thinking the same thing. Here you go."

I cleaned myself up and dried off as the first tap came at the door. "Who is it?" I did my best not to sound annoyed.

"Hay D.J. it's me, Phaedra. Do you need any help?"

"No thanks! We're good!" I yelled out.

"Well okay then, just call out if you need us."

I shook my head as Summer began putting on my makeup for me as I put on my hose and all the slips that went under my dress. "Who thought of all of this fluff," I asked as Aunt Mayvis came through the door without warning.

"D.J.! You still don't have your dress on!" she quickly closed the door and came on in.

"We're almost ready to put it on," I said in a panic.

"Here Summer, grab this side and let's get this thing on her before her mother comes in here and pitches a fit." I was surprised at how panicked she sounded as I held my arms up and allowed them to slide the dress over my head, covering up all the froufrou lace I was already wearing.

As Summer zipped up the back, I caught a glimpse of myself in a full-length mirror I'd never noticed before. "Is this thing puffy enough or what?" as I ran my hands down the front of the dress like I was smoothing it out.

"Oh, stop that now," Aunt Claudette said out of nowhere, startling all of us.

"Where'd you come from C?" Aunt Mayvis asked as she adjusted the veil she was trying to get pinned down properly.

Summer threw a drape around my neck as she began to put a few final touches on my makeup and pulled at the curls falling down to the side of my face. As they were all standing back admiring their work, my mom entered the room. She just stood there smiling at me as tears began to well up in her eyes.

"Don't you start Lisa," Aunt Mayvis said. "If you start crying, we're all going to end up crying, and I know you don't want her to get makeup all over this beautiful gown," as she handed my mom a tissue.

She dabbed at her eyes, but she still hadn't said a word. I turned around to get a better look at myself in the mirror as she came and stood beside me and wrapped her arm around my waist, and gave me a gentle squeeze. "You are absolutely breathtaking," I didn't know what to say immediately as a tear fell before I even realized it was there. "No, no, don't cry. I wasn't trying to make you cry baby," she said as she quickly dabbed my face dry.

"Well, thank you mom," I finally choked out.

"Well, in true bridal fashion, I have something for you for good luck," she smiled as she pulled out a small jewelry box. "Since your dress is technically your something old, even though we made some beautiful changes, this can be your something borrowed. It's your grandmother's favorite hairpin." as she clipped it on the side of my French roll. "I knew it would look perfect with all the beading you added to your dress," she smiled as she took a step back to admire her work.

I heard Aunt Mayvis whisper to Aunt Claudette, "I was wondering where that pin got to. I guess we know now, huh?"

"Shhhh, this isn't the time for that," as she bumped Aunt Mayvis.

"Wow mom! It's beautiful," as I turned my head to get a better look at it.

Aunt Claudette cleared her throat, "Well me and May got you something new," she smiled as Aunt Mayvis opened another jewelry box.

"D.J. after all the work you put into adding all those beads to your dress, when we saw these at the store, we just knew we had to get them for you," she smiled, slowly opening the box. It contained the most beautiful pair of diamond and pearl earrings I'd ever seen, let alone owned before.

"Oh my, these are absolutely gorgeous," I smiled as they each took one and put them on me.

The tears began to well up in my eyes again as Summer passed me a tissue. "Well, I guess I'm up," she smiled. "D.J. I love you like a sister, and I have your something blue." I knew something was up by the wicked grin she gave me.

"Yes," I gave her a questioning grin as I turned to face her.

"D.J. I felt like this would be the perfect something blue when I saw it," as she pulled out the necklace Joshua had given me last night. The necklace with me and Jeremiah's wedding rings as the charm.

My eyes got big as I just stood there in shock. I could hear my aunties' reactions as to how beautiful and unique it was, even though they sounded so far away, almost like they were in a tunnel. What I honed in on was my mother's face. Her expression was the one that frightened me so. Summer knew exactly what she was doing as she put the necklace on me and quickly whispered in my ear.

"I know he'd want to be with you today if nothing more than to give you strength," as she stepped around and gave me a kiss.

I knew better than to react as I continued to watch my mother's expression turn from shock to anger, to something I couldn't quite read. She slowly moved closer to me and stood directly in front of me, but didn't say anything or make another move. Meanwhile, Summer had eased herself in between us just in case my mother's reaction became a little more aggressive than expected. My mom finally reached for my necklace and instinctively I wrapped my hand around it to prevent her from snatching it off my neck, which startled both of my aunts.

My mom turned her head slightly as she said, "D.J., you don't have to worry. I was just going to adjust it a little. It really is a beautiful piece," as she smiled at me and gently removed my grip off the charm and carefully placed it on my chest. "There, now it's perfect," she smiled at me with tears welling up in the corners of her eyes again.

I chose not to smile and just gave her a tight hug that no one in the room was expecting, including her. Before I let her go, I whispered in her ear, "Mommy, I love you very much. And I forgive you for forcing me to do this.

Hopefully, this won't be the cause of death of your only living daughter," as I kissed her on her cheek and slowly rubbed away the lipstick that I'd left behind.

Her body had stiffened up, as I took a step back so that I could look her in the face. As our eyes met, she began to tremble causing my aunties to rush to her side, pretty much talking at the same time.

"Lisa, what's wrong?"

"Lisa, are you okay?"

"D.J....what did you say to her?" Aunt Claudette frantically asked.

I just shook my head at her as I turned away from what was happening in front of me. I didn't want to see my mother break down and honestly, that wasn't my intent when I told her what I did. My aunties rushed her from the room as she began to audibly sob. I dabbed at my nose in the mirror as I noticed Summer's expression as she stood behind me. "What's wrong with you?"

She hesitated for a moment as the first tear fell. "D.J....what did you say to your mom?"

"I told her that I loved her and that I forgive her for forcing me to do this. And that hopefully, this won't be the reason for the death of her only living daughter," as I turned to face her. What I wasn't expecting, was what she did next. Summer took my hand and slowly began to kneel down in a praying position. My mouth fell open as she began to pray.

"Heavenly Father, I humbly ask you to bless my sister and allow her to do what is in *her* heart. Father God, come down with your holy spirit and protect and keep her, let her know that you are with her and love her. Father God, we know that sometimes we do things out of our love for others when we should be loving ourselves, but even in that, you still have the final say. So Lord, I'm asking, I'm downright begging you, to give D.J. the strength to say no to this unholy union and fix all the legal wrongs that have pushed her to this point. Lord, we know that you can make a way out of no way and you can fix whatever we mess up. These things we do pray, in your sweet Son's holy name, Amen."

I was still standing there with my mouth hanging open and my eyes so wide you could have wrapped my eyelids over the top of my head. It took me a minute to recover as the tears began to stream down my face. Thank God for waterproof makeup, or I would have surely ruined my dress. Summer finally released the grip she had on my hand and slowly pushed herself up off the floor, without ripping her dress.

"Wha, wha...what was that?" I finally managed to get out.

"What was what?" she asked as if nothing had just happened, as she smoothed out her dress and began to fix her hair in the mirror.

450

"You prayed for me...to God," I said still in shock.

Summer smiled at me in the mirror before she went over and picked up my makeup foundation and began touching up my face. "D.J., D.J., I do know *how* to pray. Remember, I did graduate from a Catholic high school," she began to laugh as the door opened before we could continue.

"D.J., its time," Aunt Mayvis smiled.

"Oh...okay. Just a second please."

"You don't have a second young lady," as she rushed to my side and began to push me towards the door. "Technically, you're already late. We have 3 minutes to get this party started."

"But, but what about the pictures?"

"Too late for that," as she pushed me down the hall and out the door.

I kept trying to see Summer to talk to her about what had just happened, but she stayed just far enough away from me that I couldn't see her until they put her inline in front of me. At that point, I gave up on trying to talk to my friend. The thing was, Summer had been a devout, self-professed Atheist from the first time I met her back in college. She got a giggle out of telling everyone that she was a witch even though she had come to Spelman from a Catholic high school. So for her to get down on her knees in that tight ass dress and pray to God, had to be a major sign from the Lord.

The processional began almost on time, at least close enough for me. It was 15 after 3 when *Here Comes The Bride,* began to play, and everyone stood up as I made my grand entrance into the sanctuary. Other than the fact there was wall to wall people in there, I can't tell you who was there exactly. All I saw were bodies and blurred out faces as I looked down that center aisle that was growing longer and longer with every step we took, getting me closer to Selk.

I remember hearing people whisper as my dad leaned over to me and asked, "Would you like to pick-up your feet? Or do I need to keep dragging you down the aisle?"

I didn't realize that I was dragging my feet although I do recall feeling like my dad was pulling me, and my body wasn't really moving very fast. I dropped my head slightly as I began to blush and said, "No, I'll walk on my own."

Finally, I made it down the aisle to the extended version of *Here Comes The Bride*. You would think that that would be the final surprise in the ceremony, but sadly it wasn't. There would be a couple more surprises in-store and the last one....well that one was the doozy.

7ᵀᴴ Sign.....

We had successfully made it through the ceremony without too many hiccups, including all of the groomsmen standing there in shades when I made it down the aisle, to the God awful song Selk's cousin sang. When I say tone-deaf and off-key, I'm being very generous about how bad she really sounded, but I digress. Right before the vows my cousin Jaqué was supposed to sing *Here And Now,* by Luther Vandross. But to everyone's surprise, especially mine, she and Keith Richardson, a man from our church who I'd had a secret crush on since I was a little girl, stood up and sang a duet. They sang *A Whole New World,* the theme song from the movie *Aladdin*.

A couple of weeks before the wedding I had jokingly told Jaqué how much I loved that song and wished I could have it played during the wedding, but it just didn't fit the sentiments of this wedding. Besides doing my hair for free, singing at my wedding was part of her gift to me. Jaqué had secretly put the entire production together on her own, including the backup singers...her brother and two of his daughters. When they finished, all you could hear besides the clapping from the standing ovation they received, were the sniffles from people crying, including me.

Once we had regained our composure, it was time to recite the vows. Selk didn't have any problem with his, which he quickly said, "I do," too.

Me, on the other hand, ...well let's just say it didn't go so smoothly. When Pastor Clive asked me, "Do you D.J. Thomas, take Selkie Nathaniel Black, to be your lawfully wedded husband, to have and to hold, for better or for worse, for richer or for poorer, in sickness and in health, to love and to cherish, from this day forward, until death do you part?"

I froze like a deer in headlight, but you could also hear the whispers... "He said Thomas...when did her name change to Thomas?"

I started swaying from side to side and just never said a word, as Selk's grip on my hands got tighter and tighter. "Ouch!" I said bringing me back to reality. "I'm sorry, can you repeat that?" I blushed.

After Pastor Clive repeated the vows to me again, you could hear people beginning to whisper to one another, "She's getting ready to pass out," and "Oh no, she's going to say no."

I cleared my throat more than a few times, but my mouth had dried up like the Mojave Desert, and for the life of me, I couldn't form the words that I was supposed to say. As everyone impatiently waited for me to speak, my brain literally turned to mush, and it was taking everything in me not to bolt from the room as I told myself, *'Run nigga, run!'* over and over again.

I continued to stand there rocking back and forth when Summer stepped closer to me and whispered in my ear, "I have the keys to your car in my bra. We can make a run for it and take off if you want."

Lucky for me, no one else could really see my face, but I quickly glanced over at her pleading with my eyes, *'HELP ME!,'* without turning my head too much, as the tears began to stream down my face, she took a Kleenex and dabbed my eyes. The pain from Selk squeezing my hands so tightly is the only thing that finally shook me out of my trance. Without looking up at him, I softly said, "I do."

Summer looked so disappointed as she stepped back into her place, just as Pastor Clive said, "Can you repeat that? And a lot louder this time," with a chuckle.

"I do," as the tears stopped flowing, but Selk's grip didn't really loosen up.

Even though I made it through the wedding, things immediately began to take a turn for the worse after it was over. To begin, it took forever to get through the 101 pictures the photographer wanted to take, before we got to the reception, which was only next door. And when all was said and done, no one had thought to set me a plate of food aside in case all of the food was gone after the receiving line ended, and the cake was cut. I was starving after the reception, that's how we ended up back at my parent's house so that I could get something to eat.

After we opened the presents we'd received at the wedding is when everyone decided to watch the uncut version of the video of the ceremony. The look on Selk's face was priceless when his grandmother of all people, busted out laughing and said, "Poor D.J.... Baby, I just knew you were get'n ready to pass smooth out up there, but I sure didn't realize it took you that long to say 'I do,'" as they rewound the tape for the second time to check the exact amount of time again.

I knew better than to respond as I quickly excused myself from the room and hid in the kitchen for a little while. Summer soon joined me at the sink, where I was keeping myself occupied by hand washing the dishes, something that I'd never typically do...that's what dishwashers are for. Summer didn't say anything to me. She simply smiled at me as she began to dry what I'd washed and rinsed off. We never said a word to each other. We didn't really need to, there wasn't much left to say at that point. It felt like forever going through it but come to find out, it actually took me 5 minutes to say *'I do.'* Video doesn't lie, and neither did the 7 signs that I really shouldn't have married Selk, and that I should have run as fast as I could in the opposite direction.

CHAPTER 34

S elk and I finally said our goodbyes around 10 o'clock and made our way to our bridal room at the Marriott hotel, close to the airport. We were due to fly out at 8AM bound for Florida, to catch a boat for our 10-day honeymoon cruise through the Caribbean. My mom was keeping the twins, so all I needed to do was try to relax and try to enjoy the next 10 nights and 11 days onboard a ship with Selk. Marcus, Selk's best man and best friend from high school, was going to give us a lift to the airport in the morning since he was staying at our condo for the night and then driving back to Paris, Texas to visit his family in the morning. And since Summer was flying back to New York about the same time we were leaving, she stayed at the condo as well, so we didn't have to double back to pick her up from Cypress.

I changed into the lacy white outfit my mother had gotten me for my wedding night and joined Selk in the bed. It was painfully obvious by the grin on his face and the growing erection I could see under the covers, that he was more than pleased and ready for what he saw. Unfortunately for him, I suddenly developed a massive migraine, so all he got that night was a peck on the cheek and a heartfelt good-night.

The next morning while we were waiting for our flights, Summer and I discussed the wedding and the wedding night. When she learned of my headache, she quickly pulled me to the side so that we could talk in private.

"D.J., are you telling me that you didn't have sex with him last night?" she asked just a little too excited.

"Calm down," as I glanced around. "That would be a yes. I got changed for bed, and when I came out of the bathroom and saw his erection, my head started killing me. It was all I could do to make it to the bed." Summer just stood there, gripping my arm with a huge smile on her face. "What's with the cryptic grin?"

"Don't you get it?" as she started pulling on my arm getting more and more excited.

"Get what?" as I shewed her off of me.

"You didn't have sex last night."

"I'm fully aware of that. I was there you know," I giggled.

"D.J....it's not too late to get this thing annulled," she grinned as her eyes began to water.

"Summer, what are you talking about?"

"You didn't consummate your marriage last night which means you can still walk, or in this case, run away," she bounced up and down as she gave me a tight hug.

"Huh?"

"Don't you see? You didn't have sex with him, so legally your marriage hasn't been consummated which means you can seek to have this marriage annulled and treated as if it never happened," she said much louder than she should have. Selk and Marcus were now watching us along with several other people in the concourse.

As I squeezed her arm to quiet her down, "Summer," I said through clenched teeth and a smile. "Maybe you need to quiet down just a little bit," as I turned to smile in Selk's direction. "It's the weekend, and his attorney hasn't let the DA know that he won't be testifying against me yet, so that really isn't an option," I continued to smile.

"Well if you can hold him off a few days longer, you know I can get my dad's law firm to take your case pro bono, and we can easily get you out of this self-imposed prison you've created," as she waved at Selk and Marcus with a silly grin on her face.

Of course, that brought the two of them closer to us with lots of questions. "So, what's going on over here?" Marcus asked while making moon eyes at Summer.

"Nothing much. Just waiting to get on these planes," I smiled.

"Sure that's it? It looked like there was a lot more than meets the eye going on over here," Selk said as he watched me and Summer's faces.

"Nope. Just talking about how much fun that cruise you've booked is going to be," she gave a sheepish grin. "And how much more fun it would be if I was going with her?" she quickly added.

I nearly choked on my juice as I tried to regain my composure.

Her sense of humor was lost on Selk. "That would defeat the purpose of having a romantic honeymoon for two, don't ya think?"

"If I go and you stay, we could just call it a girl's trip," she gave him a sarcastic grin.

You could tell by the look on Marcus's face he had no idea what was going on, and I felt no need to fill him in on what was happening. Lucky for both of us, *'Now boarding Southwest flight 813 non-stop to New York City, LaGuardia Airport at gate B12,'* came over the intercom breaking up this barely civil conversation.

I jumped to my feet and gave Summer a tight hug. "Thank you for coming, and I love you."

"I love you too. And remember, if you need anything, and I do mean anything," she pulled back from me, "I'm just a phone call away," she said with a tear in her eye.

"I know," I sniffled. "Everything is going to be just fine, watch what I say," as I tapped her on the nose.

She turned to pick up her bag, "Bye Marcus. It was great to meet you," she smiled.

"Same here. I'll definitely look you up when I'm out in Cali in August," he smiled big.

"Yeah, you do that," she tapped him on the hand.

I stood there, trying not to cry as she turned and walked away. And of course, Selk couldn't just let it go. "Hey! No goodbyes for me?" he smiled with his hands up questioning her. And in true Summer fashion, she barely glanced over her shoulder as she threw up a peace sign and never said a word as she handed the ticket agent her boarding pass and quickly disappeared out of sight.

I continued to stare through the window at her plane as *'Now boarding American Airlines flight 1049 to Miami through gate B15. First-class and...,'* came over the intercom as the last few people walked through the doors my best friend had just disappeared through. Everything in me wanted to run down that jet bridge to her plane instead of going to our gate. "Hey, that's us. Let's go D.J." Selk called out as he grabbed his suitcase but left my bag behind. I just stood there watching him walk away when Marcus turned back and picked my carry-on bag up and looped his arm in mine as he walked me to gate B15.

"Thanks," I gave him a slight nudge. "It's amazing how different the two of you are," I admitted as I held onto his wrist for a second.

"He's a little rough around the edges, but he loves you D.J." he gently bumped me. "That I'm sure of," he smiled as he hugged me back.

I just shook my head as Selk talked to the ticket agent. "Yeah, if you say so," I softly replied as Selk approached.

"Alright man," giving Marcus the typical man hug and dap. "Thanks for giving us a ride today and I'll definitely catch up with you when we get back."

"Alright my brother," as they did some hand thing that ended with a finger snap. "And you two take care of each other out there in the deep blue sea," he winked at me.

I gave him a slight smile as I dropped my head a little. "Well thanks again for all you've done and be careful out there on the highway."

"Come on, I've got a surprise for you," as Selk took my hand to lead me down the jetway.

"So what's the big surprise Selk," as I adjusted my purse and overnight bag, trying to keep up with his long strides.

"Welcome aboard Mr. and Mrs. Black. Let me help you with your bags," the flight attendant offered as she took the bag off my shoulder.

I didn't say anything, but I was definitely thinking, *'What the hell is going on? I've never seen them be so friendly before,'* as she waved us to our seats. Then it became clear what was going on. We were sitting in first class.

"Ta-da!" Selk said with a huge grin on his face. "Are you surprised?" he asked as he all but shoved me into the window seat.

"Yeah, just a bit," I said as I put my seatbelt on. "When did you do this?" I asked.

"While you were lollygagging around with Marcus. I told the agent that we were going on our honeymoon, so she very kindly upgraded us when she realized who I was," he beamed with pride.

"Hmmm," I grinned as I turned to look out the window.

"That's it...that's all you've got to say?" he looked so disappointed.

"Uhmm, nice surprise Selk," I smirked as I turned back to the window. I watched a Southwest plane rise up in the air and found myself wondering if that was Summer's plane when the flight attendant asked if we'd like something to drink.

"No thank you. I'm fine for now," I smiled at her.

"What?" he said with a surprised look on his face. "Are you kidding me right now? Half the pleasure of first-class is getting served before the plane even leaves the ground," he said still obviously annoyed with me. "Yeah, I'll take a rum and coke, and she'll have a white wine."

"Uhhh, no I won't. I don't want anything right now thank you," I waved my hand as the attendant slowly backed away.

"Not a problem, I'll be back momentarily with your drink Sir," she finally smiled.

"Why are you being such a bitch D.J.? You're just not going to be happy until you ruin this for me, are you?" he said just above his breath as he grabbed my wrist.

I snatched away from him, "First of all, I'd advise you to check your tone and how you address me. Second, if I'm not thirsty right now, I'm not thirsty so get over yourself already." I wasn't yelling, but I wasn't whispering either as Selk quickly looked around in embarrassment. "And finally, if you don't mind, I'm going to take a nap. My headache seems to be coming back," as I fished around in my bag for my *footprints* blanket and my sleeping mask, quickly sliding it on as I covered up with my blanket and turned my face away from Selk. I heard him talking to the flight attendant again, but I actually did doze off before we even took off.

I woke up to the pilot giving us the temperature in sunny Miami. We quickly disembarked from the plane and collected our luggage only to figure out that we had flown into the wrong city. Mr. Hook-up man had accepted upgraded tickets to Miami, but our boat was sailing out of Orlando.

"Really Selk? You didn't think to make sure where we were sailing out of before you let one of your hook-ups switch our tickets?" I said disgustedly.

"Well, how was I supposed to know he'd switch the airports?"

"Because *you* are the one who planned this dumbass trip, REMEMBER!" I yelled at him as we made our way over to the ticket agent.

"Hola, ¿cómo Puedo ayudarte hoy?" the agent smiled.

"I'm sorry, No hablo español. Hablo English by chance?" I asked, obviously flustered.

"Lo Siento pero no hablo inglés," she shook her head at me.

I dropped my head for a second then gave Selk a look that could kill. "So, what are we going to do now genius?"

"How am I supposed to know? I don't speak Spanish either. At least nothing that's going to be any help to us right now," he said.

"Look, is there anybody here that can help us? We flew into the wrong airport. We need to get to Orlando," I tried to explain calmly.

"¿Qué estás diciendo no entiendo?" she said as she picked up the phone and began talking to someone on the other line.

I was so hoping she was calling someone to help us, but that would not be the case. A couple of minutes later, another young woman approached the desk, "Wah gwan ou may mi help?"

"I'm sorry, but I don't understand you. Do you speak English?" I slowly asked her.

"Mi speak ah litle English," she smiled.

"We flew into the wrong airport. We need to get to Orlando," I explained again.

She just stood there shaking her head at me, "Dis ah Miami nah Orlando."

I slapped the counter out of frustration, "What the hell are you saying?" as I looked around for someone else to talk to.

My outburst actually got the attention of a security guard that was passing by who decided to stop and find out what was going on. "¿Comó puedo ayudarle?"

"Awww HELL NO!" I turned away from him. "Is there anybody in this damn airport that speaks English?" I yelled, startling all three of them.

"Cálmate señora," the officer said as he tried to pat my shoulder.

I quickly snatched away from him yelling, "First of all, don't touch me! And secondly, get me somebody who understands fucking English!"

"D.J., all the yelling isn't called for," Selk nervously said looking around as the officer started talking into his walkie talkie.

"None of this would be called for if for once in your miserable life you could just stick with the plan and not try to get something for nothing!" I yelled at him. When they saw Selk back down, they refused to say anything else to me at that point. I continued on my rampage for another 15 to 20 minutes before a man that I never would have guessed was of any authority, by the way he was dressed, approached us.

"Hello Madame. How may I help you?" he asked with a heavy Spanish accent as he extended his hand. Selk could tell by the look on my face what was about to happen as he simply stepped out of the line of fire with his head down. I went off on that poor man purely out of frustration.

"Did I leave the got damn United States of America and nobody told me?! How in the hell can I be in a major U.S. International Airport and nobody up in this bitch speaks fucking English?! And who the hell are you and how the hell are you going to help me get the hell out of Miami and on to Orlando before I miss my got damn boat?" I railed off.

The beautifully tanned gentleman was nearly beet red as he handed me a business card and introduced himself as the Assistant Airport Director. He also apologized to me for the inconvenience of flying into the wrong airport and not having anyone readily available to assist us. Apparently, they were still running a skeleton crew due to the hurricane that had just come through a couple of days ago, so most of the airport staff was off, taking care of their families. He took our tickets from Selk as he stepped behind the counter and explained to the first young lady what we needed to be done.

"Volaron accidentalmente al aeropuerto equivocado. ¿Qué tenemos que los lleve a Orlando antes de la 1:00 PM? " All I could do is drop my head as I began to blush because it hit me how insensitive I had just been and how ignorant I must have sounded.

"Bien, ahora entiendo el problema," as she began clicking away on the keyboard. "No tenemos vuelo, pero Delta sí, que sale en 20 minutos. Asi que tendrán que darse prisa."

"Ma'am, American doesn't have a flight due to leave in the time frame that you need to get there, but Delta does, but it leaves in 20 minutes so you'll have to hurry," he explained.

"That's fine," I snorted. "How much?" I rolled my eyes at Selk, who still had the good sense not to say a word.

By the look on his face as he squinted at the screen, I already knew it was going to be steep. "I'm afraid it's going to be $536," he said with a slight wince.

"That's fine," as I dug in my purse for the envelope of money, my favorite uncle had just given me the night before as a wedding gift. Who would have thought this is what I would have to spend the $800 he gave me on the side, as I counted out 6 crisp $100 bills.

They all began to smile as they quickly issued our tickets, and the security guard ushered us onto the back of a golf cart and whisked us away, through the terminal to the Delta gate. We got there just as we heard, 'This is the final boarding call for all passengers on Delta Airlines flight 197 to Orlando.'

They had even radioed ahead to let them know that we would be checking all of our luggage at the gate to make sure it all made it on the plane with us. When I tell you that I was not only grateful to the entire airport staff for going above and beyond to get us to the correct destination on time, I felt as small as a pea. I continued to feel smaller and smaller for every insensitive, borderline racist thing that had come out of my mouth. And I really hoped to God that they really didn't understand a single, evil word that had come out of my mouth that morning.

As we settled into our seats, that surprisingly enough were together at this late booking time, I leaned over to Selk to throw in one more quick jab... "I know you're used to first class, but I figured coach is just as good when it gets us to the right airport on time." Selk didn't say anything in response, but by the way his body tightened up, that was all the confirmation I needed that my message had hit the target, as I sat back with a smile on my face and watched us rise up into the great blue yonder.

I'd managed to doze off on our short 48-minute hop from Miami to Orlando, but we definitely hit the ground running. Once we had collected all of our luggage again, we finally managed to hail a cab which took forever to do. Apparently, the storm that had affected Miami was just leaving Orlando, so this airport was running at a snail's pace as well. As we explained to the driver where we needed to be, it quickly occurred to me again that there was not only a language barrier, there was a cultural barrier going on as well.

Our driver was either Cuban or Dominican, but either way, he wasn't very inclined to take directions from a woman, at least not a black one. He kept directing his conversation and answers to Selk, which was pissing me off to the point of exploding, again.

"Excuse me Sir, we appreciate the tour and all, but we really need to get to our boat. Would you mind picking up the pace please?" I said as calmly as I possibly could. When he didn't acknowledge my request, I let out a long sigh as I leaned between the seats and tapped him on the shoulder, "Excuse me Sir, but did you understand what I said?"

"Sí, te entendí, jovencita…" he looked into the rearview mirror at me, "Relax señora… you have time. The boat, it not going to leave without you. Así que siéntate y relájate," he gave me a forced smile.

Selk pulled my shoulder to make me sit back again, "D.J. try to relax. We have time," as Selk looked at his watch.

I brushed his hand off my shoulder as I growled, "We're going to miss all the festivities *before* the boat leaves because of you and your so-called *hook-up*, so don't tell me to relax. This is all your fault! I don't know why I let you plan this trip! I told you what flights would be best and what did you tell me, *'I got this D.J.. I got this.'* You ain't got shit!" I rolled my eyes and stared out my window. Needless to say, we road in silence the rest of the way to the ship.

As we pulled up alongside a huge boat, I noticed a few porters pulling luggage up the gangway. I could tell we had missed all the pre-departure festivities with all the streamers hanging off the ship and confetti floating in the water. Selk knew not to say anything to me as he ran around to the other side of the cab and attempted to open my door, but the attendants beat him to it. It was about 10 minutes til 2 as a woman rushed out of a building asking for our boarding documents and what our names were. Selk barely had time to pay the cab driver as they whisked us away.

Security was a breeze compared to the airport, I'm not sure they even checked our luggage as someone grabbed our bags and threw them in a huge bin and rolled them away before we had our cabin key or anything else. As the young woman passed us two keys, a very young man approached and said, "Please follow me," in an accent I've never heard before.

We quickly followed him up the gangway and down multiple crowded hallways with overhead lights flashing and people rushing around holding life jacket's as someone gave instructions over the intercom, *'In case of an emergency you will hear this alarm and the following instructions. All passengers, please report to your assigned muster station with your life jacket and a photo ID or passport…. En caso de emergencia, oirá esta alarma y las siguientes instrucciones. Todos los pasajeros por favor Repórtense a su estación de reunir asignado con su chaleco salvavidas y una identificación con foto o pasaporte…. In case of an emergency you will hear this alarm and the following instructions. All passengers, please report to your assigned muster station with your life jacket and a photo ID or passport…. En cas d'urgence, vous entendrez cette alarme et les instructions suivantes. Tous les passagers doivent se présenter au poste de rassemblement assigné avec votre gilet de sauvetage et une photo d'identité ou passeport... In case of an emergency...'* They must have repeated those instructions in at least 4 other translations before we had made it to our cabin to retrieve our life vests.

The porter rushed us in our cabin, or should I say our closet, and pointed in the direction our vests should be as he handed me a card with the muster station directions. We scooped our life vests up and ran back out into the hallway trying to figure out exactly where we were supposed to be since the porter had disappeared on us. As we hurried along, I took a moment to tell Selk how I really felt about our cabin.

"I blame you for all of this!"

"What now?" he said over his shoulder as he ducked down just in time to avoid hitting his head on the Bridgeway.

"That looks NOTHING like the cabin you showed me in the brochure. That cabin isn't as big as my closet for Christ's sake!"

"D.J. can we *please* get through the next 20 minutes without you having a temper tantrum or a breakdown? I swear nothing is ever good enough for you."

"Good enough," I said as I barely had time to jump over some sort of buoy rope they were pulling across the deck, "Good enough? The room I agreed to was spacious and had enough room to turn around in if I wanted to. That room was barely big enough for both of us to squeeze by each other without hugging the wall."

We had finally reached our muster station, as the final instructions were being given. Apparently, they had already asked the group if they could understand American English. While aboard the ship, I came to learn there was a difference since they only translated the instructions in Spanish as well. There was a group of around 30 people standing there as the crew members took turns explaining how the lifeboat worked and how to board the lifeboat.

Amazingly enough, the lifeboat was bigger than many of the fishing boats I'd ever been on or even seen up close. Our group had a color and a number assigned to us, which indicated what lifeboat we were assigned to and in what order we would be allowed to get on the lifeboat. If anything happened while we were out to sea, we were to meet in this spot where our IDs would be checked, and we would be walked over to our assigned lifeboat when it was our time to board it. We were in group 2 of the 5 groups that were assigned to our lifeboat. The only items we would be allowed to bring with us is a photo ID or passport and our life vests, so there was no point in bringing any of our personal belongings because we would not be allowed to board the lifeboat with them.

I sarcastically whispered, "Well even the passengers on the Minnow got to take their clothes with them," which got a giggle out of a couple of people close by me, as Selk bumped me and gave me a scowling look.

"I hate to contradict such a pretty lady, but you're wrong Miss," a voice whispered out of nowhere catching me completely off guard.

"Huh?" I looked around with a half shocked, half-embarrassed look on my face.

"You're wrong. The passengers on the Minnow didn't get to take their luggage with them. The boat crashed on the beach, so actually their luggage landed with them," he smiled as the woman next to him shook her head and rolled her eyes.

I couldn't help but giggle as I shook my head and turned back to the instructions being given by the crew for a moment. I quickly leaned back towards him and said, "I stand corrected. But if we crash into an island, we won't need our life vest or this lifeboat, will we? So that means I can grab a bag of whatnots and run screaming for my life anyway. Right?"

He burst out laughing as the woman with him elbowed him, "SHHHHHH!" with her finger to her lips, giving both of us a stern look.

We both stood up straight and tried not to giggle as we were all dismissed. "I'm Eric Glazner. And who do I have the pleasure of clowning around with today?" he asked with an extended hand.

I smiled as I shook his hand, "Nice to make your acquaintance Eric Glazner. I'm D.J. Thomas."

"That would be Black," Selk said as he broke up our handshake and conversation with his own outstretched hand. You could tell he'd surprised both of us with his comment. Eric looked surprised, and I looked like I'd just forgot to take out the garbage as I rolled my eyes. "Her last name is Black, not Thomas. We were just married last night, and this is our honeymoon," he said with an arrogant smirk on his face.

"Well, it's nice to me both of you then," as he shook Selk's hand. "And this beautiful drink of chocolate milk is my partner in crime, Trinity Mooreland," he smiled.

"Hi. It's nice to meet you both and congratulations on your marriage," she smiled as she shook both of our hands. "And don't worry about that name thing, you'll get used to it...in time," she winked at me. "That's why I didn't bother changing mine. I'd been Mooreland for 38 years and 2 graduate-level degrees when this joker finally asked me to marry him. I wasn't trying to confuse everyone around me as well as myself," she laughed.

He moaned and rolled his eyes as I began to giggle. Selk just stood there watching us like a bump on a log. It wasn't often that he wasn't the center of attention, so I think the whole thing made him uncomfortable. That and the fact that he didn't care for any man who found me attractive or seemed to pay me the least bit of attention. When the laughing and greetings ended, we all walked back inside with a few more pleasantries until we went our separate ways.

As we made our way back to our cabin, I felt a sense of relief knowing there was at least one other couple that I liked, and silently prayed that we would run into again. As we turned the corner and finally located our cabin, the unmistakable mixed matched luggage we'd brought on board was waiting for us at our cabin door. I pushed past it to open the door and held it open so Selk could drag our bags in.

"Oh, your hands are too good to lift a couple of these bags?" he gave me a cynical look.

"Maybe I'd be more inclined to help you if I hadn't missed the part of this trip that I was most looking forward too. You know, the pre-departure party where we'd get to dance and eat hors d'oeuvres out on the deck, and get to throw confetti and streamers off the side of the ship with everyone else who seemed to make it here on time," I smiled as he drug my last bag inside the cabin.

Did I say how small this room was? When he finally had our bags inside, there was literally nowhere for us to stand. I was forced up onto the bed that was probably half an inch larger than a twin size bed while Selk moved the bags closer to the bathroom to free up some space. As he started unpacking his bag, I stretched out on the bed and continued to fuss at him.

"Soooo, what happened to the cabin you showed me?" as I looked at my nails and waited for a response, as I rested on my elbow.

"When I confirmed what you liked with the travel agent, there weren't any more cabins in that size available. So I told her to work it out best she could. When we finally connected again to confirm, the only rooms available with an ocean view was this size room," he hesitated for a second. "Now D.J. you know the one thing you said was non-negotiable was the view. You had to have an ocean view, remember?" he quickly asked as he finished unpacking his last bag.

"Yeah...I remember that, but I also specifically asked for space too I believe," I gave him a smug smile.

"Well they didn't have anything spacious with an ocean view, so I had to make a quick decision before even this was gone too," he explained as he closed the last drawer he'd had opened. As he turned to look at me again,

"So are you going to just lay there picking at your nails, or are you going to unpack your bags?"

I pursed my lips together and laid there staring at him for a moment, then finally said, "I think I've had enough excitement for a couple of hours. I'm going to take a nap," as I fluffed up my pillow and rolled my back to him.

"You're kidding, right? You slept on both the planes, and we just got here!"

I simply threw my arm up in the air, shewing him away. And with one last huff, I heard the door slam behind him. I waited a few minutes to make sure he wasn't coming back before I jumped up to inspect the rest of the closet we now called our cabin. I pushed past our bags and opened the sliding door at the end of our bed to see how much room Selk had left me in the closet to hang my clothes. I was a little surprised to see plenty of room left for my things as I turned to open the door neither of us had dared to go through yet. It had to be the bathroom, and I guess we both were scared to see how small it was. As small as our room was, it had to be tiny. I took a deep breath and slowly pushed the door open to my complete horror. I quickly peeked around the door that had abruptly stopped with a clanging noise. It had actually stopped when it hit the edge of the toilet.

"Awww HELL NAW!" as tears began to well up in the corners of my eyes. I believe they were more from anger than being sad but either way, I quickly brushed them away as I stepped into what little room there was and stood in front of the sink as I looked over the spacing of the bathroom in total disbelief. I slowly closed the bathroom door behind me as I gawked at the space that they had allotted for both the toilet and the shower, which was a cat's whisker away from taking up the same space. When I regained my composure, I turned to the side and slowly opened the door to try to convince myself that I wasn't seeing what I was seeing. The room was so small the door actually stopped on the front edge of the toilet which meant if either of us were using the toilet there was no way the door could be open nor would there be any showering while someone was using the commode either. The shower curtain was wrapped around the water spout, but when I moved it to the position it would be in if someone were in the shower, it literally laid on the toilet as well.

I instantly got a headache and turned to leave the claustrophobic space and turned into the door because I wasn't thinking as I pulled it open. When I finally managed to escape the small space with a cold washcloth, there came a knock at the door.

"Yes, may I help you?" I asked as I answered the door.

"Excuseer me mevrouw, wilt u dat ik uw bagage meeneem?" she shook her head as if she realized what she'd just done. "I'm sorry, would you like me to take your luggage Madame?"

I smiled at her to let her know that I now understood, "I'm sorry, I'm moving kinda slowly. I haven't finished unpacking it yet," as I stepped aside so she could see the filled-up space.

"Geen problem," looking up, realizing what she'd done. "No problem, Madame? Ik kom…" she rolled her eyes, then took in a deep sighing breath. "I'll check back later if that's okay."

"Yes, yes, that will be fine. Actually, if you give me 10 minutes, I can have them empty and stacked for you. If you like I can set them outside the door for you?" I smiled at her.

"Dank je. That would be fine," she smiled.

We both knew what she meant, even though it was in two languages. I closed the door, and despite my lingering headache I unpacked my bags and folded them into one another along with Selk's. What I wasn't expecting was the lack of space for all of my toiletries and Selk's in our bathroom, so I took it upon myself to leave the majority of his things out on the dresser instead of putting them in the bathroom alongside mine. As I scurried around the room trying to put everything I'd dumped on the bed away, I could hear the cabin stewardess talking to someone else in the hallway and quickly moved our emptied bags over to the door. I accidentally startled her and another young woman as I snatched the door open with a grin on my face.

"Here you go. I consolidated our bags into these two for the sake of space and time," as I pushed them into the hallway.

"Merci Madame," as she placed a couple of pre-prepared tags on them and handed them off to another steward. "Nous allons les retourner avant votre débarquement," as the other young woman gave her a slight shove letting her know what she'd just done. "Excusez-moi, excusez-moi… We will return them before your landing," she blushed.

I giggled as I waved at them, "Je vous remercie. C'est bon," in my best attempt at speaking French.

Both of them looked at me with wide, delighted eyes, "Merci beaucoup mademoiselle."

"Thank you missen," she smiled as they waved goodbye to me.

When I closed the door, my head was no longer hurting, but I still felt the need to take a nap. I really was tired, and I knew Selk would be back at any time, pushing me to join him in whatever shenanigans he'd thought up for the evening. As usual, I was right. I hadn't been asleep long when Selk came back to the cabin, smelling of alcohol and snuggled in behind me, rubbing on my body and kissing the back of my neck.

At first, I just tried wiggling away to no avail, and finally, I asked, "Selkie really?" I moaned. "I just fell asleep good."

"D.J. you've been in here for hours. It's almost time for dinner," as he continued to grind on me and lick my neck.

It took a second for what he'd just said to register, causing me to sit straight up in the bed. "It's dinner time? Stop playing!" as I tried to focus in on my watch.

He pulled me back down to him and slid on top of me. "Yeah," as he kissed down my neck to my chest. "They made the first seating all call about 30 minutes ago. And we are scheduled to eat during the first seating *Mrs. Black*," as he unbuttoned my top and flipped the snap on my bra, exposing my breast.

I thought to myself, *'Well that settles it. No more front closures for me.'* I tried to get up from under him, without causing an argument, but I couldn't move him as he allowed his full weight to hold me down. He began sucking my nipples as he caressed my breast. "Selk, we really need to get dressed for dinner. We probably only have another 30 minutes or so before they start seating people," I whimpered as I softly pleaded with him.

"I'm eating now," he chuckled.

I tried to squirm from under him again, "But I'm not. So let's postpone this until, after dinner, shall we."

Selk immediately stopped what he was doing and gave me a cold hard look. A cold shiver went up my spine as he lifted his body off of me just enough to look me in my eyes. "D.J. I respected your wishes when you said I couldn't make love to you on our wedding night because you had a headache. I even left you alone this morning when you refused to let me join you in the shower. But right here, right now...my generous nature isn't trying to hear any of your silly excuses as to why I can't make love to my wife. You need to get it through your head how this is going to go down..." he paused for a moment as he poked his finger into my chest, "You...wife," turning his finger back towards himself, "Me...husband." Wiggling his finger between us, "*We* are going to make love and *consummate* this union now, or you my dear will be facing a jury of your peers no matter what else goes down between us after this moment. Do I make myself clear?" he pulled my chin back around until we were face to face again. "Now, I realize that you had your reservations about marrying me, but we're married now. And as a married couple, there are a few benefits that come with that, like all the sex ones heart can handle with their spouse. And since we are now married, I don't think *we* will be needing any condoms anymore do you?" he said, obviously waiting for a response.

I tried clearing my throat a couple of times as I finally managed to say, "We need to use the condoms because I'm not on any birth control," as another tear ran down the side of my face.

He gave me a cryptic smile. "Oh really? So I have a question for you my love," as he moved off of me just enough so that he was able to undress me. "Were you on birth control when you were with the cop?"

I already knew where this conversation was going as I simply shook my head no, as the tears began to free flow down the sides of my face.

"Hmmm. So did *he* wear a condom when he made love to you?" as he removed my panties.

Again, I just shook my head no, as I began to stare at the ceiling.

"How about this one...," as he unbuttoned his shirt and dropped it to the floor. "Did you willingly *consummate* your marriage on your wedding night with him?" he stood up and looked down at me.

"I was still in the hospital Selk, we couldn't consummate our union," I quickly informed him, trying to stare a hole through his forehead.

"But you would have if you could have though," he calmly continued as he unzipped his pants and they fell to the floor with his boxers quickly following, exposing his very erect penis.

I didn't answer as I turned my head away from him again.

"I'll take your silence as a yes," as I felt the pressure of his body lower down on top of me again. I stiffened up as he began kissing on my neck. Without flinching, he quickly moved down to my breasts and began tugging on my nipples with his teeth. He slid a hand down my thigh as he began playing with my clit while he continued to suck on my nipples. Once he got the response from my body that he was searching for, he pulled back for a moment and moved my head to look him in the eyes, "D.J. understand me when I say, I'm not wearing a condom and you won't be taking any birth control." He lowered his head to my ear and whispered, "I plan on having lots of little linebackers with you," as he slowly ran his tongue down my earlobe as he spread my legs wide and slid his rock hard dick inside me.

The tears began to run down my face faster and faster with every thrust of his hips and flick of his tongue. I hated my body for responding to the things he was doing to me since I wasn't enjoying what was happening in the least little bit. And the more I denied him any expression of enjoyment the rougher and more aggressive he got. I had long since shut my eyes, but when he flipped me on my stomach, I suddenly realized that even with my eyes tightly shut, I was somehow still watching what Selk was doing to me. I watched from above as Selk interlaced his fingers in mine and forced my legs further apart using his knees and penetrated me again, forcing himself deeper and deeper inside of me with each pelvic thrust. I don't know how he stayed erect so long, but he didn't cum until I finally let out a series of long moans and grunts, over the course of several positions. Now that may sound like I was finally getting into it but my response was actually to the pain I was feeling from him ramming himself inside of me over and over again, harder and harder, as he began to squeeze and pulled on my nipples while he twisted my body into various, not so comfortable, sexual positions.

I don't know what was fueling him more. His jealousy of Jeremiah, his anger with me for not wanting him, the alcohol that was now seeping out of his pores as it dripped all over me, or a combination of all three. But Selkie was fucking me like he'd never fucked me before. As bad as it was, I saw no signs of him stopping until he flipped me back on to my back again and slowed down as he gently began making love to me. With each kiss and slow caress of my hair, his thrusts slowed down and became more drawn out as he gently began to stroke me, inside and out. He wrapped my legs around him and took his time moving inside and outside of my body, as he gazed into my eyes. It was at that moment that I realized that what I had thought was sweat dripping off him, down onto my face, was actually his tears. Selk was crying as he so lovingly stared into my eyes, as his body began to spasm, he finally came, collapsing on top of me.

I was too afraid to move at first, worried that he'd be able to begin again if he thought I was trying to get away from him, but after a few minutes of uncomfortable silence, I realized that he had fallen fast asleep. My body began to relax as the tears stopped flowing and the aerial show ended, with the unwanted view of his still, sweaty body on top of me from above, finally dissipated. As I gently squirmed my way from under him, I collapsed on the floor as the last of my body became completely free of Selk's weight. My legs were like jelly, and I couldn't immediately stand up. I sat there on the floor in a crumpled mess, holding on to the side of the bed trying to muffle the sounds of my cries, so not to wake Selk up. It hurt to cry just as much as it hurt to move as my tears and pain became one, but eventually, I managed to get to my feet and make my way into the bathroom. Through silent tears, I managed to wash Selk's sweat, secretions, and tears off of me but no matter how hard I scrubbed, I couldn't wash away the feeling of disgust and betrayal as I slid down the shower wall and cried until I couldn't cry anymore.

Even though Selk slept the rest of that night, I couldn't bring myself to lay down next to him as tired as I was, both emotionally and physically. Instead of going to bed, I wondered the ship watching all the happy couples that night. I eventually made my way out onto one of the decks and leaned over the railing as I stared out into the darkness and the deep black sea. As the salty air kissed my face I began to think about how I could end my pain if I accidentally, on purpose, fell over the railing into the dark waters, but just as quickly I began to worry that someone might get hurt trying to rescue me, so I finally settled onto a lounge chair instead. As I watched the stars and clouds pass us bye, I began to chastise myself for my weakness. For not having the strength to say no, for not having the guts to fight back, for not being brave enough to take my chances in court. My first night on that ship, I learned to despise my new husband and loathe myself, as my anger and hatred kept me warm out on that cold deck the entire night long.

I woke up to the gentle shaking of a vaguely familiar voice, "D.J., D.J., wake up."

I sat straight up in a panic when I realized where I was. "Oh my God! What time is it?" I asked quickly looking around.

"Calm down. Calm down. It's a little after 5AM," as Eric looked down at his watch. "I realized it was you as I passed by you on my morning run," now carefully watching me. "Why are you asleep out here on the deck anyway? What, your bed wasn't comfortable enough for you, Queen?" as he took a seat next to me and began to laugh.

"I've got to go. I must have fallen asleep out here after my walk last night," I tried to jump up.

Eric gently grabbed my wrist, holding me in place as he gave me a worried look, "Is everything okay D.J.?"

Out of nowhere, "Of course everything's okay. Isn't that right, my love?" as Selk bent down and kissed me on the forehead.

I snatched away from Eric and jumped to my feet instantly. "I'm just fine. I must have dozed off while I was enjoying the warm salt air and all the stars last night," I forced a smile. I could tell by the look on Eric's face he wasn't believing my story as he slowly stood up and began to stretch, almost like nothing out of the ordinary was going on.

Selk wrapped his arm around my waist and pulling me close, "I've been looking everywhere for you. How'd you two end up together?" as he gave me a look I'd come to know very well.

"Well, Eric was..."

Before I could finish, "I was taking my morning jog when I realized it was D.J. sleeping on the lounge chair, so I stopped to check on her," he paused. "It's not every day, you see someone who's not drunk, fast asleep on deck this early in the morning," he smiled back.

"Well, I guess I'm going to have to keep a better eye on her then, don't you?" Selk laughed. The sound of his voice startled me again as I felt his grip tightening on my waist, I began to laugh too, but I could tell Eric wasn't impressed.

"Well, I best be off if I want to finish my run before the decks start filling up with sunbathers and such," as he began to run in place. "Hopefully, I'll see you later," he smiled at me before locking eyes with Selk.

"That would be nice to see you and Trinity later," I said to break up the awkwardness.

Finally breaking his gaze with Selk, he smiled down at me and said, "D.J., I guess we'll have to make sure that happens," as he smiled then turned to continue his morning jog.

Once he was out of earshot, "So this is how you're going to do it?"

"Selk what on earth are you talking about," I pulled away from him as I walked towards the door.

Surprisingly enough he didn't grab my arm to stop me, but he did have to take a few quick steps to catch up and wrapped his arm around me again as he opened the door, "What am I talking about? I've been looking for you for hours, and when I find you, you're all cozy with him watching the sunrise. That's what I'm talking about," he growled at me.

"For once, just stop being paranoid, please. I fell asleep in the lounge chair. Apparently, he jogs early in the morning, and when he saw me there, he simply stopped and woke me up. No more no less," as we made our way down the corridors of the ship, heading back to our closet of a cabin. "So there wasn't some secret randevú going on. And neither of us had some secret plan to meet up behind you or Trinity's backs," I finished as we reached our cabin door.

Selk held onto the handle to keep me from opening the door, "D.J...." shaking his head, "You really don't want to push me," he gave me a stern look, as he slowly pushed the door open and allowed me to pass.

I almost responded but quickly changed my mind, knowing the door would soon be closing behind us and I didn't want a repeat of last night. I quickly dug around in a couple of drawers looking for something else to wear as the subtle click of the door, sent a shiver up my spine. I tried my best not to look uneasy as I closed the final drawer and made a beeline for the bathroom and closed the door behind me. As I quickly removed my close and climbed into the shower all I kept thinking was, *'Please don't come in here, please don't come in here, please don't come in here...'* But no sooner had I pulled the shower curtain closed, there he stood completely naked with a hard-on and a grin.

"I know you've got room for me," he smiled.

"As nice as that sounds, there's really not," I smiled as I backed into the corner, showing him that there was barely enough space for me.

Of course, he didn't listen as he squeezed in with me, "See, there's plenty of room," he smiled as I stood there penned to the wall.

"Selk, this shower isn't big enough for both of us," I replied, trying my best not to show how annoyed I was with him. "And now, I'm basically waterless."

"Well here, let's change positions," as he made just enough room for me to squeeze past him. "There, is that more to your liking?" as he took the washcloth from me and began to lather it up and wash my back.

"Sure it is," I managed to say without a hint of sarcasm, even though I was feeling so very sarcastic.

"See, this is nice don't cha think?" as he turned me around and began washing my front side as well. I didn't respond to his question because I was concentrating so hard on not tensing up to his touch as he began to wash lower and lower on my body. He snapped me back out of my trance when he barked at me, "D.J.! You're bleeding!" as he held the washcloth up for my inspection.

"HUH?" as I began to frown.

"Don't tell me your damn period is starting! Not this week! Not on our fucking honeymoon!" as he slammed the cloth in my hand and stormed out of the shower still mumbling under his breath.

Part of me was excited, but the other part of me was a little scared as I continued to stare at the bloody cloth I was holding. My period was last week, so there was no way this could be from that. "Selk?" I calmly asked as I peeked out of the shower.

"What?" he said obviously disgusted with me, as he brushed his teeth.

"I wasn't prepared for this. Would you mind going down to the gift shop and getting me some tampons or pads please?" I asked as sweetly as I possibly could.

"You've got to be shitting me?!" as he spit out his toothpaste in the sink. "I've never bought anything like that in my entire life!" he gave me a stupid look.

"Well sweetie," I smiled. "I guess this is one of those benefits of having a spouse you mentioned. So would you be a dream and go get those for me please," I smiled at him with an over-exaggerated grin. Part of me was telling myself, 'Don't push your luck,' while the other side was saying, 'Make him pay D.J., make him pay,' as I continued to smile at him.

His mouth fell open at my comment, as toothpaste dripped down his face. He began to shake his head as he finally turned back to the mirror in front of him and finished brushing his teeth. I stood there peeking out the shower, watching him as he gargled then slowly turned back towards me again, still with a half disgusted look on his face. "Yeah D.J.... I guess I will," he frowned as he slowly wiped his mouth off as he glanced back over at me.

"Thank you hon, the smallest box they have should do for now. I'll get more when we pull into port," as I disappeared behind the curtain again. Once I heard the door close behind him, I started checking myself out better. I quickly retrieved a douche from the closet and tried to determine what the cause of my sudden bleeding was from. As I squeezed the bottle and watched the liquid flow down my leg into the drain, I knew from the immediate burning sensation when the solution touched my insides that the pounding I'd received from Selk the night before had to have torn or bruised something inside of me and now it was bleeding. And although I was concerned about how much damage he might have done to me, I was instantly relieved too. I knew there was no way Selk was going to try to have sex with me again if he thought I was on my period. I was in the clear for at least six more days.

I finished my shower then patiently waited for Selk's return. To make things even more believable, as soon as I heard his key hit the lock, I sat on the toilet like I was waiting there for him to return with what I needed. "Selk, is that you?" I called out knowing full well it was him.

"Yeah, it's me," he said as he opened the bathroom door and passed me the box without really looking in the door.

"Thank you!" I quickly took the box from him. I had already put a panty liner in my underwear since the bleeding wasn't really that heavy anymore, but I opened up a tampon and threw the wrapper in the trashcan just for optics as I flushed the toilet, just to make everything sound legit. After enough time passed to make it seem like I had been waiting on him to finish up in the bathroom, I came out and immediately kissed him on the cheek. I actually startled him.

"What was that for?" he jumped away from me with a suspicious look on his face.

"Thanks for doing that for me," I smiled as I put a dab of cologne on my wrist. "I could tell how uncomfortable you were with doing that," I glanced over at him as I rubbed my wrist together.

"Yeah," he rubbed his head as he began to actually blush. "That was definitely an experience," as he stared at his feet.

"So," I quickly flopped down on the bed beside him. "You ready for some breakfast or what? I'm starving," I smiled.

He gave me a puzzled look for a second, before he responded, "You want to eat breakfast?"

Breakfast was never my thing, but for some reason, I suddenly had an appetite, "Yes," I quickly stood up, pulling him to his feet. "I don't know why but I'm famished, aren't you?" I asked, knowing he had to be since we had missed dinner last night.

"Well, now that you mention it, I am rather hungry," he rubbed his stomach. I grabbed my purse off the chair as he opened the door, "After you."

I smiled as I walked through the door thinking, *'Thank you, you prick,'* but I said, "Thanks hon," as I smiled and waited for him to follow me into the hallway.

We didn't say much as we made our way to the main dining room where they had a breakfast buffet set-up and open seating, which was a major relief. I was afraid we were going to be assigned to a table like we were for dinner. I was done fixing my plate well before Selk since I mainly selected items that were already prepared like the fresh fruit and a couple slices of bacon. Selk, on the other hand, was waiting on an omelet, so he was still at that station when I saw Eric and Trinity at a corner booth and decided to join them. Luckily they had already settled in at a table large enough for additional people.

"Hi you two! Mind if we join you?"

"No, not at all. The more, the merrier," Trinity replied as she scooted closer to Eric to make room.

"How are you doing this fine morning?" Eric smiled.

"I'm okay, just a little stiff is all," I grinned as I slid in beside Trinity.

"I bet," Trinity laughed. "Eric told me he found you asleep out on the deck this morning. What was that about?" she asked as she watched my every move as she slowly sipped on her coffee.

I bashfully smiled as I explained how I wondered out on the deck and simply got lost in the darkness and stars, and how I must have dozed off.

"Yeah, is that not something?" Selk added, startling us all.

"Hey, man! Nice to see you again this morning," as Eric stood up to shake Selk's hand.

"Same here," Selk laughed. "Just glad it's inside, out of the breeze," as he plopped down beside me. "And look at all this great food," as he held my hand and began to say grace.

I jerked my head around and gave him a surprised look, as I followed suit and bowed my head until he was done. I could tell by Trinity and Eric's reactions they could tell there was something wrong with this whole scenario. See the thing is, Selk was putting on a show and didn't bother to let me in on the details. He never initiated grace before a meal, that was always my thing or someone else's thing, but never since I'd known him was that his thing.

When he was done, he took over the conversation as always, "So where are you two from?"

"We're both from Chi-town. Born and raised," Eric smiled. "And you two?"

"We're from H-town," Selk replied. "Well, she is anyway. I'm originally from a little town in Northeast Texas about 15 miles south of the Texas, Oklahoma border called Paris, Texas."

"Nice," Eric smiled. "So is this your first cruise?"

"Yes, it is. How could you tell?" Selk smiled.

But before Eric could respond, "Well actually, this is my second cruise. I once took a 3-day cruise with my family when I was a kid," I smiled as I continued to nibble on my fruit. Selk was immediately embarrassed as he kicked me under the table. "Oww!" I said before I caught myself.

"You okay D.J.?" Trinity asked.

I quickly smiled, "Yeah, Mr. Clumsy accidentally stepped on my toes," I finally giggled as I stopped rubbing my leg.

"I'm sorry! I was just stretching my leg," Selk apologized.

Everyone at the table knew he was just trying to save face, so none of us responded. We all silently, picked at our plates for a little while longer after that, everyone but Selk that is. He continued to eat like nothing had ever happened. Finally, Trinity broke the silence with another question.

"So tell us, how did you two lovebirds meet?" she smiled as she played in her bowl of oatmeal with raisins. I could tell by the way she asked her question she wasn't really celebrating our union, she was actually trying to figure out 'why,' we were together.

Selk immediately began to regale them of stories on how we met and how he spent all those years pursuing me. I had long since lost my appetite, so I simply pushed my food around my plate until Selk finished his very well censured, watered-down version of how we finally made it down the aisle. He even managed to pull out a photo of the boys and a picture of all of us together, that I couldn't even remember taking. By the time Selk was finished with our story, minus the abuse and Jeremiah, nearly everyone in the dining room was gone, including most of the people who had been serving us on the buffet line.

I took a deep breath as I finally interrupted, "Selk," I smiled as I playfully tapped him on the arm. "I don't think they were expecting all of that," I giggled.

Naturally, he shot me a quick look that he played off even quicker with a bashful laugh as he began to rub his head, "yeah, your right babe." Turning his attention back to our table guests, "You have to forgive me, I can go on and on when it comes to our story," he smiled at them.

I could tell by the way they took turns watching me throughout Selk's story, that they were already putting two and two together and I doubt it was adding up to four. But they played it off masterfully, "No worries brother," Eric chuckled. "When you're in love, you're in love, and you get lost as you shout it from the rooftops," he glanced over at my expressionless face as he smiled at Selk. When Selk tapped my leg under the table, I finally gave everyone the smile that had been missing throughout Selk's story. The ship was already docked at our first port of call in Freeport, on Grand Bahama Island, so we finally said our goodbyes after deciding to venture out together around noon.

I have to admit it, I was so relieved that I wouldn't be on my own with Selk. So when we made it back to the cabin, I was happy to see the room had been cleaned, so I decided to crawl up in the bed for a much-needed nap when Selk disappeared into the bathroom. By the time he came out, I was fast asleep, and for once he chose not to bother me. I'd set the alarm before I'd dozed off which turned out to be a good thing since I woke up to an empty room when it went off. I quickly changed my clothes expecting Selk to come busting through the door fussing about me not being ready at any moment, but to my surprise, he never showed up. And at 12:30 I decided to go looking for him since we were late for our noon excursion.

I spent nearly an hour and a half searching the boat for Selk when I finally decided to check with the cruise director's office to see if he'd already left the ship, and wouldn't you know it, he had swiped out at 12:15. After calming down, I decided to venture into town myself even though I only had a few hours before I had to return to the ship. After asking what I needed to make sure to see in what little time there was left, I decided to go take a look at the Garden of the Groves. The director suggested that I visit the outdoor flea market instead, but I wasn't a big shopper so elected to take a cab to the gardens.

I immediately got lost in the lush greenery and waterfalls of the gardens. It took me back to when I was a child living on Guam. As I made my way along the path, all of my stress and anxiety disappeared. I truly could have spent the rest of my day there, but in the back of my mind, I knew eventually I'd have to return to reality and get back on that ship. As I rounded the bin to a magnificent waterfall, who of all people did I spot but Trinity and Eric taking pictures under the falls.

"Hay! Can't you two read? The sign says to stay on the path!" I yelled, startling them.

They started laughing when they realized who it was yelling at them. "What are you doing here? Selk said you were nursing a headache and decided to stay on board." Trinity explained as they made their way over to me.

I shook my head with a slight grin, "That figures," as I grabbed her hand to help her over the railing. "No, I took a nap expecting him to wake me, but he never came back to the cabin. So after looking for him for over an hour, I decided to venture out on my own."

Eric jumped the railing without either of our assistance. As he brushed himself off, he said, "Now that's a wonderful husband for you," as he glanced up at me for only a second. "Your honeymoon is definitely getting off to a bang," he chuckled as we began to follow the path again. "First night on the boat, you fall asleep out on the deck, and now you almost slept through the first port. If one didn't know better, I'd guess that you were either very stressed or pregnant," as he kissed the back of Trinity's hand.

"Well thank God it's not the latter of the two!" I said before I caught myself. I giggled as I gave them a sheepish grin, "What I meant to say is that I'm not pregnant. Just the stresses of a new marriage, I guess."

We walked in silence for a few minutes then Trinity grabbed my wrist as she stopped walking. "D.J., it's none of our business, but I've been at this for a long time, so I know the signs of domestic abuse," she smiled.

"It's not what you think," I pulled away and began to walk a little faster.

"D.J. stop!" Eric yelled after me bring me to a halt. I just stood there with my back to them as they caught up to me. They walked me over to a bench and sat on each side of me holding my hands.

"D.J., it's obvious to anyone paying attention that you don't want to be married...at least not to him. So why did you do it and how long has he been hurting you? I only ask because you don't seem like the type of woman I typically counsel?" Trinity said.

I sat there, trying to blink away my tears and figure out exactly what to say to them. "And what type of woman would that be?" is all I could come up with.

"A woman with low self-esteem, who's afraid to speak up for herself," she quickly responded.

I let out a quick huff as the tears began to roll down my face, "Yeaaah, that definitely isn't me," I grinned. I began to rock as they simply held my hands and gave me the time to gather my thoughts. I sat up straight and gave my head a slight shake as I began to look back and forth between the two of them. And with a final exhale, I began to explain to them why I was actually married to one Selkie Nathaniel Black. We had become so engrossed in my version of our unholy union that we completely lost track of time. We snapped back to reality when we heard the ships horn sound and took off running towards the garden entrance.

Luckily there were a couple of cabs there, so we were able to get back to the ship pretty quickly. As we ran up the gangplank and checked in, we all broke out laughing as the director explained that we had just made it back before they began the process to push off. Why we were laughing, I don't really know, but we all got a giggle out of that as we found a quiet, secluded spot to finish our conversation.

When we were sure that we were alone, Eric took my hand and said, "Now it all makes sense. I told Trinity my gut was telling me something wasn't right, but I didn't want to cause you any harm this morning by getting into it with Selk," he shook his head. "What can we do for you," he quickly turned to me, grabbing up both of my hands and squeezing.

I shook my head, "Nothing. There's nothing anyone can do at this point," I blinked away my tears.

"But D.J....nobody has to live this way," Trinity begged.

I smiled at her, "I have to live this way," I patted her hand. "It's this or jail, and I can't let him take my boys again," I blinked away a tear. "I've got to try to learn not to set him off and simply get through one day at a time," I began to squeeze their hands as I smiled back and forth, making eye contact with each of them. "This here is my new reality, and there's nothing you, or anyone else can do about it. I made this bed, and now I have to lie in it," I smiled.

"There you are! I've been looking for you for hours!" Selk's voice came out of nowhere from above us. He was standing on a landing looking down at us as he disappeared as quickly as he'd appeared.

I quickly squeezed Eric's hand as he jumped to his feet. He looked back at me with as much pain as I was feeling at the moment. I gave him a quick smile letting him know it was going to be okay as I quickly got to my feet, wiped my face, and turned to face Selk as he rounded the corner, making a beeline for us. I said under my breath, "I've got this," as I watched Selk approach.

"I came back looking for you and you were gone. Where've you been?" he said, trying to sound more worried than pissed off.

"I looked for you too. And when the cruise director told me you had already gone ashore, I decided to do the same," I smiled at him.

Selk was obviously not happy that I'd just called him out as he grabbed me and gave me a tight hug, whispering in my ear, "I'll deal with you later." He kissed me and said, "I was just so worried. I checked to see if you were back on board and when they said you were I was frantic because you never came back to the room."

I pulled away, "Selk, stop being so dramatic. We just got back a few minutes ago."

We all stood there in silence as Selk finally said, "D.J., it's been 3 hours since we left the port."

"What?" my mouth fell open as I grabbed Eric's wrist to look at his watch. "Oh my God. We had no idea. We were just talking and must have lost track of time," I looked at them with a wild look in my eyes.

Trinity gave me a look and quickly added, "We were just so engrossed in our conversation that we didn't realize how long we'd been talking."

I slowly turned back towards Selk, "I apologize. I didn't' realize what time it was," as I took his hand. I looked back at Trinity and Eric, "Well, I enjoyed our walk through the gardens. I guess I'll see you later on," I smiled.

Slowly Trinity said, "D.J. we're so glad we were able to enjoy the island with you, and we're even happier it was you who caught us being bad," she laughed.

"Ain't that the truth," Eric laughed as he kissed her on her forehead.

I laughed, "I bet you are. Well, we'll catch you two later," as I turned to leave with Selk. "So, did you enjoy the island?" I asked Selk as he led me away.

"It was okay, but it looks like you had a much better time than me," he quietly said as he squeezed my hand. He quickly glanced back over his shoulder at Eric and Trinity and gave them a quick head nod as we turned the corner. "But I can't wait to hear all about your adventure with them," he gave me a wicked smile as he kissed the side of my head. I knew it was going to be a long night, but I had no idea what drama was in store.

We talked about my day as we both showered and changed for dinner, which went pretty well since I did the majority of my explaining from the confines of the bathroom. Which basically means Selk couldn't see my facial expressions and that I was making it all up as I went along. Anyway, when I came out of the bathroom, he immediately went in, so there wasn't much time for a physical confrontation. Unfortunately, when we made it to the dining room, I found out that tonight was "Newlyweds night" so all the newly married couples were dining together and being celebrated. Once again, luck wasn't on my side because Selk and I were seated at a table for two, which meant we could continue his interrogation of my activities on the day without anyone really hearing us.

I survived dinner, but at the end of the evening, they brought each couple a small celebratory wedding cake and a bottle of Champagne. I, of course, turned down the waiters offer to pour me a glass which sent Selk into a verbal tizzy, surprising me and the waiter.

"Come on D.J. don't be a downer. Let's toast our wedding the right way. One glass isn't going to kill you! So stop being a big baby and drink up!" he yelled at me. He knew he was safe to get so animated since there was loud music and a group walking around serenading the tables. Our waiter was looking rather nervous, so I finally removed my hand from over my glass and allowed him to pour a small amount. Selk took the opportunity to stand to his feet and take the bottle from the waiter and fill my glass to the top. "There," as he sat down. "That's a real glass of Champagne," as he lifted his glass to toast with me.

I slowly shook my head as I lifted my glass along with everyone else. I sat the glass back on the table as the waiter sliced the cake and placed a piece in front of us and then quickly left our table. I went to take a bite, but Selk just couldn't let it go as he put his empty glass down. "What? You can't even take a sip with me?"

"Selk I haven't had a drink in a while, and I don't think drinking on a boat in the middle of the ocean is where I need to start that up again," as I pushed the glass further away from me.

"It's not like you're on a rowboat D.J.. It's a big ass ship, and you can barely tell when it's rocking," as he moved his chair next to me. I nervously looked around because I knew this wasn't going to end well. And right on cue he reached under the table and grabbed my thigh like it was the last piece of chicken at the 4th of July picnic. Through clenched teeth, he growled, "Now pick up your fucking glass and drink. Understand me?" he smiled and kissed me on the neck like he didn't have a death grip on my leg still.

"Selk stop it! You're hurting me!" I tried to remain calm.

"You don't know what hurt is. But I guarantee you, you will if you don't cooperate," he smiled as he kissed my cheek.

I knew exactly what he was referring to, but I took this moment to remind him of what happened in the bathroom during our rehearsal BBQ. The smile on his face quickly faded, but of course, it didn't take long for a brutal rebuttal. He gave me a devilish grin as he leaned in to kiss me, then he said as he softly stroked my neck, "D.J. you know there's a lot of open water between here and home and I'd hate for you to accidentally find yourself swimming for your life..." He paused, as he leaned in closer to whisper in my ear, "like your cop did that night, but this time, you won't be so lucky," he chuckled. "I don't see any cars or trees to cling to way out here."

I immediately stiffened up with this not so subtle threat that confirmed what I believed to be true long ago... Selk was responsible for our accident that night on the way to the hospital.

"Now that I have your complete attention my love. Pick up your fucking glass and drink with me," as he pushed the glass closer to me, continuing to smile for the room.

The tears began to well up in the corners of my eyes, but I managed to blink them away before anyone noticed. I knew Selk wasn't making an idle threat as I slowly picked up the glass and took a sip. "There are you happy?" I said as I sat the glass down, trying not to act like anything was out of order.

"Not yet my love," as he licked my neck stopping at my ear, "But by the time I get you back to Texas, I know I will be," he whispered as he began to nibble on my ear. I quickly dabbed at my eyes with my napkin just as the singers reached our table with their serenade. Selk was always playing to the crowd as he kissed my neck and then handed me my glass and then picked his up and wrapped his arm around mine for us to drink together like we were this happy couple drinking to a happy future together. I took a slow sip, but Selk wouldn't allow me to lower my arm again. The serenaders had long since moved on to the next table, but Selk wouldn't release my arm so I could move the glass away from my face until the glass was completely empty. No sooner than I had put it back on the table, he filled it back up again. I gave him a look that he completely ignored as he took a bite of my cake. "This is good. You ought to try some," as he cut off another piece and tried to feed it to me. I just sat there looking at him in total disgust. I finally opened my mouth to avoid a scene as Selk smiled and whispered, "See how easy that was," as he proceeded to finish off my slice of cake and his own. By the time we left the dining room, the alcohol had kicked in, and Selk was all but caring me. I heard him talking to familiar voices, but I couldn't really make out any faces as the boat began to spin more and more out of control.

"Selk," I slurred.

"Yes baby?"

"I think I'm about to be sick," as I began throwing up on him and me.

"Oh my God! What did you do to her?" a woman's voice yelled out.

"I didn't do anything," as he nearly dropped me. "She had a couple glasses of Champagne at dinner is all. I guess it went to her head."

I continued to throw up as someone held a bag under my chin, and Selk sprinted us towards our cabin.

"Here, give me your key?" she demanded.

"I got it!"

"You can't handle her, the bag, and the door, can you?" she insisted. I could finally focus as we entered the room...it was Trinity giving him what for.

I moaned as Selk swung me around and sidestepped into the bathroom with me, "Trinity," I slurred. "Yes, love it's me," as she squeezed in the bathroom with us.

"I got her from here! Weren't you going to dinner?" he asked as he pushed past the door and sat me in the shower.

"Uhhhh," I began fighting the water as it hit my face. "Stop it! Stop it!" as the water went off.

"Eric will understand something important came up. Matter of fact, why don't you go tell him what happened and that I'll be there as soon as I get her cleaned up and settled."

"I think I can take care of my own wife."

"Oh really? Well, from where I'm standing, I think you need a lot of help," she insisted. "Now step aside please as I finish cleaning her up." I can't tell you what Selk's face was saying, but all I remember is a loud huffing sound and water running at the sink, then quiet.

"D.J....what happened?" she finally asked me.

"He made me drink with him," I laid over and began to cry. "Then the room started spinning, and I felt sick," I explained. "Oh my God! I'm so embarrassed," I grabbed her wrist. "I'm a mess," as I began retching again and leaned out of the shower just in time to throw up in the toilet.

"Oh sweetie, it's going to be okay. And don't worry about being embarrassed. I guarantee you many a person has thrown up on a cruise ship," she began to laugh. I laid over the basin moaning and throwing up until I couldn't throw up anymore. "Will you be okay here by yourself while I get you something to put on?"

"Yeah, I should be fine," I laid over on my arm as she disappeared into the cabin area. I heard drawers opening and closing then she was back helping me to my feet.

"Here, let's get you dried off and into something comfortable," as she helped me off the floor and began removing the wet close I had on.

I was trying not to cry as the tears finally broke through again, "I'm so sorry about all of this, but thank you so much for all you're doing for me," as she helped me into an oversized t-shirt I'd brought to wear over my bathing suit. "I know this can't be how you imagined spending your cruise," I sniffled.

"No worries D.J.. I tend to help people in need no matter where I am and sweetie you need me and Eric more than you know," she smiled. I quickly brushed my teeth and stumbled to the bed. "There, now if you need anything and I do mean anything, I'm leaving our cabin number right here, you send an attendant or even Selk to come and get one of us, you hear?"

"Yes ma'am."

"I'm putting the trash can right here so if you feel the urge to throw-up again, just lean over the edge of the bed and do it here. Don't go trying to get to the bathroom as unsteady as you are. We don't need you falling and hitting your head in here. You're gonna need all your senses to deal with that new husband of yours," she said as she tucked me in.

"Ain't that the truth," as I snuggled in. Trinity turned to leave as I grabbed her wrist, "Trin…" I paused a moment, "Thank you again for everything," as I gave her hand a quick squeeze.

"D.J. my dear, you're more than welcome. Now get some rest, and I'll be back to check on you later," as she patted my hand. I fell asleep almost as fast as she had left the room.

I slept through the night with the occasional episode of dry heaves, but for the most part, I remained in bed for the next two days. Trinity stopped by multiple times each day to check on me and bring me something to eat, but every time I tried to get something down, it basically came right back up, which prolonged my cabin stay. I even missed going ashore on Tortola, in the British Virgin Islands, but I did manage to go ashore for a couple of hours on St. Thomas, in the US Virgin Islands.

Getting back on solid ground was probably the best medicine I could've received, because after a few hours on St. Thomas, I was able to keep my food down and the queasiness fully left me. What I wasn't expecting was Selk teasing and making fun of me the rest of our time on the boat. He didn't insist that I drink anything alcoholic again, but you could tell he took pleasure in trying to make me feel bad about getting sick and spending so much time in the cabin. The other interesting thing that happened is that he never let me out of his sight when I wasn't in the cabin. For the next six days, I did everything in my power not to throw myself overboard as Selk tormented me more and more. If it hadn't been for Trinity, Eric, and a black family celebrating their family reunion onboard, I probably would have given up leaving my cabin all together just to avoid the ever-watchful eyes of my new warden, I mean husband. At the end of the cruise, I exchanged information with Trinity and promised to keep in touch. It was an honest promise at the time, but unfortunately, my new life took immediate hold on me, and I wasn't able to keep up with that commitment.

CHAPTER 35

When we finally made it back to Texas Selk had to immediately report to training camp, so I had to go out to my parents' house to pick up the twins alone. As I gathered up all their things my mom's excitement finally spilled over as she asked, "How was it?" expecting me to be happy and so gung ho.

I simply replied, "The honeymoon is over," as I finished gathering up the twins and their stuff.

"Come on D.J.. You must have had a little fun," she said, with a concerned look on her face.

"Well let's see…" I paused for a second, staring off into space. "No, it was pretty much a continuation of the nightmare of the day before my wedding. But this time I got the added luxury of being humiliated and abused in front of a ship full of strangers," I smiled at her. "Mom, when I say the honeymoon is over, I mean, I survived it, to try to survive another day."

By the disappointed look on her face, I could tell that at that very moment my mom finally realized that her 'only living daughter' was doomed to a loveless marriage and that she had made the biggest mistake she could ever have made with me, forcing me to marry a man that I would never love, that would probably never stop abusing me.

Since Selk was at training camp for the next two weeks, I decided to take the boys and stay out on the ranch. The open-air would do us all some good, and it would give me a chance to meet our newest residents. While I'd been on my honeymoon, the two horses I'd purchased had been delivered to the property. Maggie could barely contain herself as we all went out to the barn to inspect our new additions. Magnolia was a 3-year-old Clydesdale that I had found at a silent auction, and Glory was a 6-year-old Thoroughbred like Beast. Glory had had an impressive racing career when she was younger but hadn't done so well the last two years. Her owners finally decided to sell her for basically nothing, after her second miscarriage.

Maggie let me know that both horses were transitioning well and were very easy to handle, which became very apparent as E.J. slipped into Glory's stall and she didn't make a sound. She simply sniffed him and went back to eating her hay as he rubbed her chest and front leg. As sweet as the sight was I still quickly shewed him out of the stall to avoid any type of accidents. We all had a great time getting to know the new horses, especially Beast, who was very happy to have new companions. Matter of fact, Glory and Beast hit it off so well that the following spring they gave us another new addition we named Raider, as in Tomb Raider. He was a big surprise to us all since Glory never showed any signs of being pregnant. Even the vet was surprised at how healthy the little guy was and how tiny Glory was to have been pregnant, especially through what turned out to be a really rough winter. Just goes to show you how a low-stress environment and love can make all the difference in the world.

Anyway, when Selk got home from camp to an empty condo, he immediately began blowing up my phone. I let him know that we would be back on Sunday if I'd received a call from my lawyer letting me know that the DA had, in fact, dropped my case. Of course he wasn't happy with what I said, but I made it perfectly clear to him that there was really no point in playing this "under one roof" game if I still had to go to trial. Needless to say, by Friday I'd received a call from my attorney letting me know that the DA had decided to drop my case in light of his star complainant's refusal to testify against me. I was finally able to breathe, knowing that I wouldn't have to worry about going to jail or being separated from my boys, but the harsh reality was that I was still drowning.

The twins and I returned to the condo after church on Sunday to a grumpy Selk and a staffless condo. Selk met me at the door, but instead of helping me bring the boys in and all of our things, he began asking 101 questions about why we were out at that house and what we were doing. Selk followed me around like I was going to steal something and when I finally had enough I plopped down on my old bed and just stared at him.

"What Selk? What do you want?"

"I'm hungry, so I was wondering when you were going to cook?"

"Cook? Where's Chef Chris at? He and Sonya should have been back yesterday."

"Well, I let them go."

I slowly turned up on my elbow to face him, "What do you mean by 'you let them go?'"

"We're married now so what do I need them for? I've got you now," he smiled.

I just laid there watching him for a moment then I finally sat up on the edge of the bed and fell out laughing. You could tell by the surprised look on Selk's face he didn't know exactly what to make of my reaction. When I could finally catch my breath, I crossed the room and patted him on the arm, "You've got jokes," as I passed him to go check on the boys.

"I'm not joking D.J., I let them go."

That stopped me in my tracks as I just stood there, allowing what he'd just said to me fully sink in. I slowly turned to face him, "Why on earth would you do something like that? And without consulting me first?" I glared at him.

"I didn't need to consult you, that's why. You're a housewife so you might as well be the one keeping the house and taking care of your husband."

"First of all, I'll never be your housewife. Second, I have more than one job and the boys to take care of. And third, in all the years you've known me, when have I ever cooked and clean for you?"

"Well, never, but we weren't married either. And as far as your 'jobs' go, quit. You don't need the money and your 'job' is to take care of your man," he said so smugly.

I stood there watching him until I heard a crash come from the boys' room. I shook my head at him as I let out a light hearted laugh and turned my attention back to the boys but calling out over my shoulder, "Just for the record, I'm not quitting my jobs, and I'm definitely not becoming your beckoned housewife. You chose to let the house staff go, so I guess you're going to learn how to cook for yourself now," as I turned the corner to the twin's room.

Selk's response was to go destroy the kitchen while fixing only himself something to eat, which I let him have it. I ordered something up from the club for me and the boys and left the kitchen just the way Selk left it. I also purposefully fell asleep on the daybed in the twin's room so that I didn't have to sleep next to Selk that night. Needless to say by morning Selk was fit to be tied and he knew that he was in a run for his money since he no longer had anything to threaten me with.

By the end of the week, the house was a complete mess, and Selk had started calling me out of my name. Lazy bitch was his favorite name to start off with and they gradually became more degrading over time. By the end of the second week I was out and out refusing to have sex with him and the wrestling matches began...sometimes I won and he left me alone, but sometimes he won and we had a repeat of our first night on the ship. Eventually, I stopped fighting so much to prevent Selk from getting so rough with me. My body couldn't take that kind of pounding then having to immediately function properly to care for the boys.

After a few months alone with Selk, I went back to work at the Medical

Examiner's office working nights to avoid sleeping with Selk altogether. Unfortunately even that stopped working when Selk got cut from the Oilers on the final day of team cuts. And this time he didn't even make the practice squad, so for the first time in his football career, Selk had no football in his life. All this idle time on his hands only made my life more miserable and Selk more unpredictable.

By the end of September, Selk was not only smoking weed in the house he was still spending money like crazy to impress friends, who were spending more and more time at the condo. They all knew I adamantly opposed any kind of smoking in the house but especially around the twins, which very quickly became a constant source of tension as they sprayed the place down with potpourri to try to cover-up the weed smell before I got home, like I didn't know what they were trying to do.

It was October 5th when Selk stopped taking no for an answer to sex altogether. It was my first night off in several weeks and my mom had agreed to keep the boys so that I could get some much-needed rest, but when Selk came in and found me there asleep and the house empty, no to sex wasn't even an option. I woke up to him positioning my body to make it easier for him to penetrate me, but before I could say a word, he covered my mouth with his hand to prevent me from speaking and began pumping harder and harder. I squirmed to get away from him which only made things worse as he applied all of his body weight on top of me while pinning my hands above my head with one hand and continuing to cover my mouth with the other. I cried and moaned even when he finally crawled off of me.

Before he fell asleep, he said, "You are going to start giving me what I need, when I need it...one way or the other."

I laid there terrified and in pain, fully awake for the rest of the night. I finally dozed off as the sun began to come up, but the need to throw up woke me again as I barely had time to make it to the bathroom. That was the first morning of many more to come that I spent with my head in a toilet bowl. In the beginning I thought I was constantly throwing up because I was so stressed but when a co-worker asked if there was any chance I might be pregnant my fears began to shift to that possibility. I waited until my birthday to find out for sure and wouldn't you know it, the test came back positive, I was definitely pregnant.

Before my birthday party, I called Selk into our bathroom and handed him a small, neatly wrapped box with a big red bow on it. He gave me a peculiar look as he shook it and asked, "What is this?"

I gave him a quick grin, "Open it."

He watched me for a moment then finally began ripping the bow and paper off like it was Christmas morning. "What's this?" he asked as he picked the pregnancy test up.

"It's a pregnancy test," I said sarcastically.

"I know it's a pregnancy test. Why are you giving it to me?" as he flipped it around.

"Because I thought you'd like to know, you're going to be a daddy again," I said expressionlessly.

"You've got to be kidding me! What the hell do we need with another kid?"

"My thoughts exactly Mr. No Condom and no birth control pills," as I turned and left him in the bathroom, all alone holding the pregnancy test.

Selk drank more that night then I'd seen him drink in a very long time. By the end of the night most of our guests had gone, not because of the time but due to Selk's not so subtle outbursts towards me and anyone else who dared to question his actions. I guess the idea of adding to our little family was unsettling to him for two main reasons. First, he wasn't working so he was having to become a "house husband" which was never his plan and second, I had already begun to pay the majority of our bills which was devastating to his ever-shrinking ego. Adding another mouth to feed was the last thing we needed in our lives.

After that night, things began to get worse day by day. The verbal and mental abuse drastically intensified along with more frequent ruff sex. Needless to say, by Christmas I had suffered a miscarriage, to Selk's delight. By New Years his friends were calling me out of my name, and they were always at the condo. I'd get off work and come home to his friends sleeping everywhere and the signs of weed smoking and alcohol all over the house. By mid-January I was pregnant again and actually attempted suicide. I took a bottle of sleeping pills and drank a bottle of rum as a chaser. Selk covered it up, and I lost the baby before anyone else even knew I was pregnant. Well one thing was for sure, we didn't have to argue about me being on birth control anymore after that.

Unfortunately, the arguing was still an everyday occurrence, but now they had begun to traffic cocaine through the condo, which only added to our daily fights. By Valentine's Day I'd had enough of Selk's friends sleeping over and their nastiness so when I came in from work I woke him up and let him know that I was setting the alarm and he had 30 minutes to get them and all the drugs and alcohol cleaned up or I was calling the police. Of course Selk had some very unkind words for me for waking him up and threatening to call the police, so to prove my point I set the alarm and proceeded to take a shower. As I was getting dressed someone made the mistake of opening the door and the alarm went off. Selk came bursting in the bathroom begging me to turn it off after he realized that I had changed the code. They had barely cleaned up their mess and made it to the back stairway before the police arrived. Selk charmed them of course as I crawled into bed for some much-needed rest. After that they were cautious about pissing me off, but they all still took advantage of me whenever they could. That became our routine. Arguing about his friends, arguing about them being at the condo all the time, arguing about all the drinking, smoking, and other drugs in the house. Arguing just because we woke up another day in the same space.

April would turn out to be a pivotal turning point in my life. Even on birth control, I still managed to get pregnant. I was a couple months along when I was in the grocery store with my mom and the boys and a man approached us and asks to speak to me alone. Now he looked vaguely familiar, but when he insisted that it was imperative that he talk to me in private, I asked my mom to take the boys so we could talk alone. Hesitantly she did as I asked and the young man explained to me that we went to high school together and reminded me that his name was Michael Jones. Again, I vaguely remembered him, so I indulged him a little longer.

"What can I do for you, Michael Jones?"

"Well, it's not really what you can do for me, it's what I'm going to do for you."

He was beginning to make me a little uneasy with his cryptic response, so I simply said, "I'm listening."

"D.J. I could get into serious trouble with what I'm getting ready to tell you so I need you to keep this information to yourself," as he looked around for anyone who might be listening.

"Okay, now you're worrying me," as I nervously rubbed my stomach.

"I'm an officer in the HPD Narcotics unit, and we've been doing surveillance on a couple of properties of interest. As part of the investigation we run the plates on all cars coming and going from these properties and to my surprise your name came back on the registration of a car that is frequenting one of these houses. I knew there couldn't be two D.J. Morgan's running around H-town so when I saw you today I had to find out what's going on with you?"

"I guarantee you it's not me driving the car, it has to be my husband you're seeing since I'm not allowed to drive," as I pulled my shirt tighter so he could see my baby bump. "I keep having contractions when I shift the gears, so my 'husband' drops me off at work at night, so anytime you've seen my car, I guarantee you I'm at work."

"I knew it had to be a good reason for this D.J.," he smiled at me. "I just knew that you couldn't have changed that much since high school. You were super smart and only hung out with the best crowd," he giggled.

"Well, I work nights in the Medical Examiner's Office. Give them a call, and as for Anita King, she's my supervisor."

"I know Mrs. King. Her dad was my Captain until he retired."

"That would be the one. She typically works 10 – 7 so that she can see everyone on both shifts." I patted him on the wrist.

"I'll do that and D.J.," he paused for a moment, "If there's anything I can do for you, give me a call okay?" as he handed me his business card.

I tried to smile at him, but it was hard since my mind was racing as I kept asking myself, *'What has Selk gotten me into now?'* I was finally able to muster somewhat of a smile, "Thank you Michael. And thank you for taking a chance on me. I promise you, you'll see it isn't me at that house." He simply nodded at me as he quickly turned and walked away.

I didn't say anything to Selk about what happened that afternoon when I got home. I still wasn't sure if I should. But I did let Anita know that someone from Houston PD would be calling about me, and I needed her to answer any questions they had about me and to keep this conversation between us. I didn't need anyone finding out, more for Michaels' sake than my own. When I came in for work the next night, I had a message waiting for me on my desk that Anita needed to see me. My stomach fell as I read it even though I already knew what it was about. Before I had a chance to go to her, she came to me.

"D.J., I need to speak to you in my office please."

"Yes ma'am," as I quickly stopped what I was doing and followed her to her office.

"D.J. a detective from the Narcotics unit called to find out if you were at work on several days and at what time. If you're under investigation, I'm not going to be able to allow you to continue to work down here. We can't have anything we do, be scrutinized by a defense lawyer or defendant. So if there's something you need to tell me, I'm here for you."

"Anita, I promise you this has nothing to do with me. Was I at work on the days you were asked about?"

"Well now that you mention it, yes. Every one of them."

I shook my head as I looked at the floor, "I knew it." I slowly looked up at her as I let out a long sigh, "It's Selk and who he's hanging out with."

She took a seat at her desk and seemed to relax more with my response. We sat in silence for a few minutes until she finally said, "D.J., are you safe?"

The question caught me off guard, "Huh? Why would you ask me that? But I'm okay."

"Well, we've all noticed some changes in you, and I hate to say it, but they're not all for the best. You seem distracted, and you're not your usual pleasant self."

I could feel my face heating up as my embarrassment grew. "Anita, I'm sorry, I have been distracted lately," I looked away for a moment. "I wasn't ready to say anything yet, but I'm pregnant. And I'd like to keep that to myself until I have to let people know if you don't mind."

"D.J., congratulations," she leaned forward on her desk smiling. "By your expression, I take it you're not happy about this though?"

I rubbed my legs as I began to rock, "No. I'm not happy about this, but it is what it is right now. I haven't even told Selk or my family."

That got her attention as she jumped to her feet and sat next to me. As she held my hand, "D.J., are you okay?"

I blinked away the first tears that began to well up in my eyes but couldn't keep them from falling when I turned to look her in the face. "No I'm not," I fell into her lap crying.

"Oh sweetie...what is it? What can I do?" she asked me as she rubbed my back.

"I don't know what to do for myself anymore. And now I have to figure out if I should tell my husband or not what's going on, not only with me being pregnant but with this investigation thing. And what if something happens while I'm at work and Selk has the twins with him? What do I do then? I can't trust the state, and with my history with them it might take an act from God to get my kids back."

"D.J. one thing at a time. You've got to tell him you're pregnant and then make other arrangements for the twins. I can always move you back to day shift if that will help? But you've got to get ahead of this situation before our men in blue are looking at you directly."

"I know. I just don't have it in me to keep fighting with Selk all the time, and this is only going to make things worse."

"That just may be, but you can't sit back and do nothing," as she got up and disappeared in her bathroom then quickly returned with a wet cloth.

I sat up and began wiping off my face, "How did God ever let me get into this mess?" I asked, not really wanting a response.

"Baby the one thing I've learned in all my years is God doesn't get us into messes, but He definitely gets us out of'em."

I just nodded my head and pulled myself together, then went back to my desk. I kept to myself the rest of the evening trying to decide what I should do next. When Selk finally showed up to pick me up that morning, I had a long heart to heart with him on the way home. I told him about the pregnancy and my conversation with Michael. Of course, he called me a crazy bitch more than once, but as we made our way into the condo I left him with this final warning.

"Selkie, you can call me every name in the book, but two undeniable things are true..."

"Oh yeah, and what's that?" he snapped at me before I could continue my thought.

"First, the police are getting ready to raid Bert's grandmother's house, and if you do or say anything to warn them about what's getting ready to happen, we are both going to jail for interfering in an ongoing investigation. And second, if you choose to ignore my warning and you're there when it happens, you're going to jail. And you Mr. Black, are on your own. The only thing I'm going to do is fight the state to get my car back, and God forbid you have the twins with you, to get my boys back. And you...well my advice to you is to make sure your momma has enough money to get your blackass out because I'm not going to lift a finger to help you." And with that I left him sitting in the car and went upstairs.

As much as he hated to admit that I might be telling the truth about what was about to go down at Bert's grandma's house, he knew for sure I wasn't playing with him about not bailing him out of jail or getting him a lawyer, so gradually Selk backed off from spending time over there when I was at work, and by the end of the next week he wasn't going over there at all. The week after that, the house was raided and everyone going and coming from the property was scooped up in the bust. And in Selkie style, when his boys asked how he got so lucky he blamed me, and I quote, *"The Bitch wouldn't let him use her car anymore."* And with that they dropped their questions, and it put a stop to their suspecting him of being a snitch.

You would think that things would calm down after that, but of course that wouldn't be the case. By June it was getting hard to see my feet again, and Selk was up to new tricks. My mom and I were in Walmart shopping with the twins, when a man approached us and wants to speak with me privately. My stoic reaction worried my mom as she demanded to know what was going on and insisted that I keep walking. My heart was beating in my ears, but I was finally able to calm her down and send her and the boys on ahead for what I suspected was going to be another inquisition into my whereabouts because of Selk.

"D.J. I don't know if you remember me, but we went to high school together, I was a freshman your senior year. My name is Gabriel Franklin," as he reached out his hand to shake mine.

I put on the best smile I could, "You're right Gabriel Franklin, I don't remember you but what can I do for you this afternoon?" as he guided me to a quiet corner in the back of the store.

"D.J. I could lose my job for what I'm about to do, but when I saw your name coming up on the caller ID of one of our phone taps, I couldn't believe my eyes. I mean how many D.J. Morgan's can there be in the Houston area?" he let out a light-hearted laugh. I simply smiled at him and waited for him to continue. "Anyway, I work for the FBI on a multijurisdictional drug trafficking task force, and we are monitoring the calls of a few inmates of interest, and one of the numbers that is frequently accepting collect calls from one of these prisoners came up as yours. Do you know Thaddeus Jones by chance?" as he gave me a questioning look.

I slowly shook my head, no.

"You might know him by King," he continued to watch my every move.

"No...I don't know anyone by the name Thaddeus Jones or King," as I let out a long exhale, "And if someone is accepting collect calls at my house it's not me, it's my husband or one of his crazy friends."

"Your husband? I didn't realize that you were married," as he scratched his head for a moment.

"I am, and it's him, not me. I guarantee you if collect calls are being accepted it's happening when I'm at work. I work in the Houston Medical Examiner's Office. Give them a call and as for Anita King, she's my supervisor. I promise you any day a call was accepted, I was at work."

"I knew it had to be a good reason for this D.J.," he smiled at me. "I just knew that you couldn't have changed that much since high school. You hung out with the smart kids and the athletes. For the life of me, I couldn't imagine you hanging out with drug dealers and gangbangers."

Why did I feel like I was having a déjà vu moment? Once again I found myself being reminded by an old schoolmate, that I didn't remember, how nice and straight-laced I used to be. As I listened to him talk, I thought to myself, *'how in the hell did I get here?'* Once he finished telling me what was going on, we finally said our goodbyes and I found my mom and the boys in the deli getting a snack.

"D.J. Morgan...what was that all about? That's the second time some man has wanted to talk to you privately. What in the Sam Hills is going on?"

"Mom, don't you mean D.J. Black? And I really don't want to get into it, okay."

For once in her life, my mom didn't press the issue. I guess she could tell by the exhausted look on my face that I really didn't have it in me to argue with her right now. It didn't help matters any when I requested to spend the rest of the day at her house instead of going home.

"D.J. baby, you're scaring me," as we pulled out of the Walmart parking lot.

"Momma, I'm scaring myself," as I leaned over on the window and closed my eyes.

I didn't bother giving Anita a heads up as to the call she would probably be receiving soon, but when I returned to work the next day, she was waiting for me at the front door. She immediately ushered me into her office and closed the door. "D.J. what is going on? I got a call from the FBI about you this morning," she said in a hushed voice as if the walls had ears.

"Did you answer his questions?" was all I said.

"Well, yes. Yes, I did, but what's this about?" she begged.

"It's Selk again," I shook my head as I stared at the floor. "That's all I can tell you. It's Selk," I sighed.

"What in the hell has he gotten you into D.J.? It's one thing for HPD to be asking about you, but this is serious...these are the Feds," she began pacing.

I just sat there shaking my head, "Don't you think I know that. And the only reason my name came up is because the damn house phone is in my name," as the first tears began to fall.

"Oh sweetie....I wasn't trying to upset you. But this is serious D.J.. You can't go on like this. *We* can't go on like this."

"Well, what would you have me do? I can't control him, and I'm never around when he's getting into the things he's getting into. The one saving grace is that I'm here when he's doing whatever the police and the Feds are worried about. So I don't care how many times they call please tell them whatever they want to know about me," I gripped her hand like she was my only lifeline.

"D.J. I can only let this go so far before the brass gets wind of this. I told you before, we can't afford any signs of impropriety in our office, and when the authorities keep making inquiries into one of our lab techs, well that just smells of misconduct."

"Trust me, I know," as I rubbed my stomach. "I just knew Selk was going to fly right after that last scare, but I guess he's moving on to bigger and badder troubles," I shook my head.

"Well, I think maybe you need to take some time off D.J." as she took her seat.

I struggled to my feet, "Are you firing me?"

"No, no D.J. I'm not firing you. I just think maybe you need a couple of days to get things at home straight is all." I couldn't help but look completely devastated by her words. I just stood there with my mouth hanging open all but begging her with my eyes not to send me home. She ignored me for a few minutes then finally said, "D.J., I know a great divorce lawyer if you decide you need one," and then she went back to working on her computer as if I wasn't even there.

I dropped my head and whispered, "Til death do us part," and turned for the door.

"What was that?" she asked.

"Nothing...nothing at all," I mumbled as I closed the door behind me. I called my dad to come back and get me, and then I called Selk to let him know I was coming home and that we needed to talk, privately. Of course he had several choice words for me, but he was at the condo when I got there, and the place was completely empty. I proceeded to tell him what had happened at the Walmart and right on cue, he began pacing and yelling at me.

"You stupid bitch! King is already serving time. They can't charge him with new stuff because of a phone call," he laughed as he began another rant at me.

I sat watching Selk pace and curse at me for longer than I should have, but when I decided that I'd heard enough, I slowly stood up, stretched my back and simply turned to him and said with a smirk on my face, "Selk... actually they can, and King is doing State time. We're now talking Federal time and maybe it hasn't fully sunk in yet so let me help you out. Anything Federal trumps the State so it doesn't matter that he's doing State time if the Feds pursue a case against him and that's what they're doing, so anyone connected to him is likely to go down as well." I could tell the full weight of what I'd just said was beginning to hit home as the sanctimonious look on Selk's face slowly faded, and he took a seat with a very worried look on his face. I turned to go to my old room because the idea of sleeping next to Selk was upsetting my stomach, but before I disappeared out of sight I turned back and said, "Selk..." pausing long enough for him to acknowledge the fact that I was talking to him.

"Yeah, what?" he gave me a disgusted look.

"Same rules apply as before. If you get caught up in whatever happens to King and you go to jail, you Mr. Black are on your own. Make sure your momma has enough money to get you an attorney because I'm not going to lift a finger to help you," as I smiled and began shaking my head at him as I turned and disappeared down the hall not waiting for a response. The next thing I knew I heard the master bedroom door slam. I could have cared less as I got undressed and took a shower.

I laid in bed wide awake for what felt like hours waiting on the call I knew was going to come since I should have been at work, and sure enough, around 8:30 the phone rang. I quickly answered it to a recording asking me if I would accept a collect call from Thaddeus Jones, an inmate at Kegan State Prison. My immediate answer, "No," and I hung up the phone. A few minutes later, the phone rang again, and Selk and I answered at the same time. I didn't say anything as I waited for the service to ask me if I accepted the charges and I quickly screamed "NO!" before Selk had a chance to respond. This time I waited to see what would happen. I heard a click and Selk yell, *'What the fuck?!'* almost simultaneously. Before I could put the receiver down Selk was bursting into my room screaming at me.

"ARE YOU CRAZY? WHY IN THE FUCK DID YOU DO THAT, YOU STUPID BITCH? And don't you ever say no to a call from him!"

I calmly said, "No, and because the phone is in my name, I have the right to say no if I don't want to accept a charge on 'MY' phone."

"Your phone? Since when did it become 'YOUR' phone?"

"Since the day I had to put it in my name because it kept getting cut-off in yours! Now get the hell out of my room so I can get some rest," as I boldly rolled over and turned my back to him. Even though he didn't say anything, I knew he was still there because I could hear him breathing. When I couldn't hear him anymore I waited a couple more minutes before I rolled over to make sure he was gone. I quickly locked my door before I went back to bed. Needless to say the phone didn't ring again that night and as soon as I woke up that morning, I called the phone company and put a block on the phone.

That afternoon the usual crew showed up and took over the den. I got tired of their noise pretty quickly and decided to go to the master bedroom to watch tv in peace, but before I could gather my things and leave the room, I overheard Selk trying to explain why King's calls were rejected the night before.

"Not only did the bitch refuse his calls last night, she put a mother fucking block on the phone this morning."

"Shut up man! You play'n," Bert replied.

"Man, King ain't gonna like that shit at all. You know how he is," Cliff hissed.

"You need to put that bitch in her place man. I'm tell'n you, you beat that ass one good time, and she'll start acting right," Kidd piped up. Kidd had been beating his girl ever since I met him, so I wasn't the least bit surprised he came up with that one.

"Yeah, that's what he needs to do...but we all know he ain't gonna do it," Bert laughed.

As I made my way up the stairs, I heard Selk finally say, "Y'all know her crazy ass is pregnant. It's easier to just ignore her for now."

His lame excuses brought a smile to my face as I said to myself, *"Yeah, he knows Dale will beat his ass if I tell him that he touched me again,"* as I giggled. I hadn't settled in good when Selk showed up insisting that I give him the keys to my car so that they could make a quick run. After a quick argument they all left, without my car, and didn't return for the rest of the night. In case I hadn't explained to you already why Selk was using my car so much, it was because all of the cars in his name had been repossessed, unbeknownst to his friends, and the only car at the condo was one of my cars, and it was there only so he could drive me around or in case of an emergency.

Since I wasn't going back to work for the rest of the week, I had my mom drop the twins off at the condo after she picked them up from the daycare. She had started keeping them in the evenings when I had to work. For once she didn't ask a million questions and just agreed to do it for me when I asked her to after I found out about Selk and the drug house. It didn't hurt that she couldn't stand smelling smoke on the boys, which only happened coincidently when I was at work as well.

That weekend a new face showed up among the regular crew, and it was pretty clear he was the one running things. I heard Raffi, whose real name was Raphael, and Selk call him KJon as they tried to explain to him that I wasn't a problem even though it was obvious that I wasn't a part of their group activities. I heard him say more than once that he didn't like the idea of me in the house while they discussed business, especially since King felt like there was something fishy going on already. That became our new routine for awhile, they called me names, and I ignored their presence for the most part. But as time passed I could tell that KJon didn't care for me at all. When he saw me he'd always get quiet and just glare at me.

I ignored his looks just like I ignored the rest of them, but it was something about him that always made me really uneasy. It was the last week of June when he and I finally came to blows, and things took a violent turn for me. That Tuesday I hadn't been feeling well and called in sick to work without telling Selk. Per the usual arrangement my mom was supposed to be keeping the boys, so Selk had no idea I was going to be home that night. I don't know how long they'd been there when I finally woke up, but you could've bought them all for a penny when I came down the stairs and interrupted their party.

KJon was the first to see me and startled Selk and everyone else when he pointed at me, as he exhaled a huge cloud of smoke and yelled, "What the fuck is she doing here?! Man, I told you I don't want that bitch around when we're talk'n bizness! You a hard-headed motherfucker, I see!"

"Man I'm tell'n you. She ain't gonna be no trouble," Bert said again as I made my way past them as I went to the kitchen.

"KJon man, her dumb ass is supposed to be at work! I had no idea she was even here." Selk explained. "But since you here, get me something to drink while you in there fat ass!" Selk yelled out.

As always, I ignored him and their chatter as I searched through the fridge for anything to make me a quick bite to eat. I glanced up for a moment to see KJon standing behind me with a crazy look on his face. A cold shiver went up my back as I closed the door and asked, "Can I help you," sarcastically trying not to show any fear.

But he could see right through me as he stepped even closer and smiled down at me and said, "Matter of fact you can," as he reached over and began rubbing my stomach.

Instinctively I slapped his hand away saying, "Don't touch me. Don't you ever touch me!"

He grabbed my wrist tight and pushed me back up against the refrigerator. "No! Don't you ever touch me BITCH!"

"Get the fuck out of my house!" I screamed as I pushed him away from me, catching him off-guard.

"What the fuck?!" as he stumbled back knocking the bowl of fruit I'd already made to the ground with a loud crash. That brought several of the guys rushing into the kitchen to see what was going on.

"What's going on?!" Selk yelled.

"I'm about to teach yo ho a lesson is what's going on," KJon replied as he grabbed me by the neck and pinned me to the wall.

I slapped and kicked at him as I yelled at Selk, "GET YO FRIEND! AND EVERYBODY ELSE GET THE FUCK OUT OF MY HOUSE! NOW!!" When KJon didn't let me go, and my cries went unanswered, I knew I was in serious trouble even though I tried not to let on.

They all just stood there watching as KJon stared them down like he was daring one of them to say something or move to intervene. He finally turned all of his attention back to me as he pressed his body up against mine and gave me a devilish smile and said, "Like I was saying before you so rudely interrupted me before. You can help me," as he gave Selk a quick glance. "Y'all know what the best piece of pussy you'll ever have is?" he smiled over his shoulder. Nobody said a word as they just stood there watching me continue to struggle to get away from him. "Pussy you don't have to worry about getting knocked up because it already is," as he slid his free hand up my leg, pushing my dress up, and snatching my panties down, as he began biting my neck and pressing his body even harder up against me.

I had long since begun to cry as I screamed at him to stop. Everything began to blur as I was finally able to push him off of me a little, scratching him across his face. That only added fuel to the fire as he slapped me knocking me to the floor. Finally I heard someone speak up on my behalf, even though it wasn't Selk.

"Hay man. Come on....that ain't right," Raffi stepped forward and grabbed KJon's arm.

KJon hesitated for only a second before he snatched away from Raffi and grabbed me by my hair and kicked me as he pulled me to my feet by my head. "Fuck this ho and anyone of you mother fuckers who got something to say! It's past time we teach this bitch who's boss, and I'm going to wear this pussy out," as he pushed past all of them as he drug me down the hallway to the guest bedroom and slammed the door behind him. He slapped me again and again as he threw me on the bed and sat on top of me. "You gon learn today bitch," as he slid off me and unfastened his pants allowing them to fall to the floor.

I heard someone yell, "Man, this ain't right! Do something!" I assumed they were saying it to Selk, but who really knows.

"Shut the fuck up before you get us all killed! You know that niggas crazy," someone else said. It was so close I could tell they were standing at the door, but it never opened.

I tried to push past him nearly tripping myself as my panties finally dropped to my ankles. But just as I reached for the doorknob, he grabbed me by my hair and pulled me back, slinging me across the room and back onto the bed. Before I could turn off my stomach he bent me over and climbed on top of humping like a crazy man. "Ahhh yeah," as he kept ramming himself harder and harder inside of me. The louder I screamed and clawed at the bed trying to get away the harder he pumped. I continued to beg him to stop as he held on tighter to the back of my head finally pulled my head back and whispering in my ear, "Just as I figured... This pussy is tight. Selk ain't hit this in a long time."

"Please stop," I sobbed as he pumped harder and harder until he finally collapsed on top of me. I laid there audibly crying as his body slowly became dead weight on top of mine, letting me know he had probably fallen asleep as still as he was. Just as I finally managed to wiggle out from under him, he came to, grabbing me by my hair again.

"Where the fuck you think you going? Bitch, I ain't done with you yet," as he climbed on top of me again as he pulled my dress up over my head and held me down with his body as he struggled to take off my bra. Once he got it off, he actually got off of me and just stared down at me for a moment. "You know for a pregnant chick you still have a pretty bang'n body," he chuckled as he began fingering me and pulling at my nipples with his teeth.

"Please stop," I cried, turning away from him. I tried to push his hand away and cover my breasts up which only irritated him as he snatched my arms away from my body pinning me to the bed.

"Oh come on baby. You know you like it," as he pulled his fingers up to show me the sticky residue from my body betraying me yet again. "Anyone this wet has to be enjoying this a little bit," as he forced his fingers in my mouth. I bit down as hard as I could making him pull back, yanking his fingers out of my mouth as he let out a blood-curdling scream.

The door flew open just as he slapped me again and again. I couldn't make out the faces, but I could see the wide eyes watching what was going on as the blood began to drip from his fingers. He stopped for a minute and looked back at the faces silently watching him, "This bitch bit me," as he slowly licked the open wounds on his hand.

"Somebody please help me," I whimpered as I reached towards the door.

"Nobody's gonna help you, stupid bitch!" as he pushed my hand away and shoved my head back down on the bed. "I'm the head nigga in charge... even in yo house bitch! You ain't figured that out yet?" as he reached down and forced his penis back inside me again and began pumping away. "When I'm done, who's got next?" he grunted as he pumped harder and harder looking back over his shoulder towards the ever watching audience in the doorway. Nobody said a word as they watched him have his way with me. I can't tell you where Selk was the entire time I was being raped and brutalized, but I can tell you that he didn't lift a finger to help me. I vaguely remember the bodies slowly disappearing from the doorway as KJon continued his onslaught. I cried so long that I was crying without any tears when he finally climbed off of me. He didn't say a word to me when he was finally done, he just put his clothes back on and left the room.

I laid there in a bloody, broken heap on the inside and out for hours. I must have passed out at some point because when I came to it was well after midnight, and the condo was completely still, not a sound to be heard. I reached for the phone to call for help, but to my horror there wasn't a dial tone. I fumbled around in the dark accidentally sending the bedside lamp crashing to the floor as I felt along the phone cord to find that the cord had been cut in two. I could feel the warmth of my tears running down my face, stinging every open area they touched as they finally dropped from my chin onto my bare chest. I was beginning to cramp as I stumbled down the hallway to the bathroom where I collapsed on the floor and started throwing up. I managed to crawl through my mess to the side of the toilet when I felt someone scoop me up off the floor. I squeezed my eyes shut as tight as I could, afraid to see who was about to attack me now, as I barely flailed my arms and legs around in a feeble attempt to fight back. I was so beaten down I didn't have it in me to scream as every hair on my body stood up and one voice inside me screamed at me, *'FIGHT BACK!'* as another voice humbly cried, *'God, please just take me now,'* as my head dropped down to my chest, and I simply cried as my body moved through the air.

"Shhh, shhhh….calm down D.J., I'm not going to hurt you," the voice softly whispered as he lowered me down into the tub and a sudden rush of warm water hit my face. You would have thought the water was acid the way I curled up in the fetal position and covered my head as I scooted to the back of the tub to get away from it, but I still didn't make a sound. "I'm so sorry this happened to you, but there wasn't nothin I could do."

I suddenly recognized the voice, and my body went limp. It was Raffi of all people who had finally come to my aide. As he explained to me what I couldn't do or say around KJon anymore, I laid there shivering under the stream of warm water, as he gently washed me from head to toe. My lips quivered more and more as he washed my battered body, but I didn't dare open my eyes. As he rinsed the soap from my hair I was finally able to open my eyes and said, "I can't believe it's you…"

He smiled down on me like he genuinely cared about me. We'd known each other for a while now and probably hadn't said two kind words to each other since I'd married Selk. As he gently wrapped a towel around my head he said, "D.J….I promise you on my life. As long as I'm around, nothing like this will ever happen to you again. And D.J….for all our sakes you can't tell the cops about this. I'm sorry, but you can never say a word about this to anyone, and I do mean anyone," as he wrapped me in a towel and carried me up to the master bedroom. He began to dry me off and dressed me as I closed my eyes and drifted in and out of consciousness. I came to again to Raffi gently shaking me as he pulled the blanket up over me. "D.J. wake up…" I blinked a couple of times letting him know I was awake. "D.J., I need you to hear me and hear me well," as he tucked the blanket tightly around me. "KJon is a hired gun out of Chicago, and he's now King's second in command while he's away. Understand me when I say that he's a stone-cold killer. And D.J., I swear to you that you don't have to worry about anyone ever telling anybody about what happened here tonight. He'd kill all of us if this ever got out, and that includes you and anyone you love D.J.. That's a fact."

As sad as he looked, you would have thought he had been the one raped and beaten. I didn't say anything as I just laid there watching him for a few seconds. Finally, I reached from underneath the blanket and gently squeezed his hand as the tears began to stream down the sides of my face. Barely above a whisper, I said, "Thank you Raphael," and rolled over, turning my back to him. He didn't say anything, but he didn't let go of my hand either. He sat there a few minutes still squeezing my hand and then quietly let go and left the room, closing the door behind him.

I laid there crying in the dark praying for death as the cramps got worse and worse. The pain finally got so intense that I got up, slid on some sweats, and walked downstairs to get the phone. Surprisingly Raffi was still here and jumped to his feet when he saw me.

"What's wrong D.J.?" he asked as he rushed to my side.

"Somethings wrong with the baby," as I held onto the wall and my stomach at the same time.

"My cars in the garage. I'll take you to the hospital," as he ran over to the couch and put his shoes on then helped me onto the elevator. We didn't say anything else until we pulled up in the ER drive. As Raffi opened the car door and helped me out of the car, he quickly picked me up and whispered in my ear as he carried me in the hospital, "Remember what I said. You can't tell anyone what really happened to you, okay?"

I simply looked at him and nodded yes, as they put me on a gurney and whisked me away. That was the last time I saw Raffi that night. I came to screaming and swinging at nothing but air. My mom had been asleep in the chair beside my bed when I scared the life out of her as she jumped to her feet calling my name. Suddenly there was a couple of nurses rushing through the door, one pushing buttons as the other joined my mom in trying to calm me down.

"D.J., D.J., you're okay," they were both saying at the same time as they tried to console me.

I realized where I was and immediately settled down and began to feel my stomach, "Is the baby okay?"

"Yes, but we need to watch you closely for a few days," she explained as she checked my IV site.

"I need to get out of here," I said as I moved to get out of the bed.

I stopped in my tracks as I heard, "Hold your horse's little lady," come through the door. My eyes got wide as I dropped my head and froze. It was Lt. Keith along with Dr. Cleveland coming in the door.

Never looking up from the floor, "What are you doing here?" I asked.

"When we get a report of a possible assault and rape from the hospital,

HPD tends to send a detective, but when the alleged victim is someone near and dear to my heart, I tend to show up myself," he explained as he gripped my hand.

When I heard assault and rape, my head snapped up, "That's not what happened. This has all been a big mistake," I tried to explain.

"D.J., I've been doing this for a very long time, and I know when I see someone who's been beaten and raped," Dr. Cleveland finally chimed in. "You've not only been in and out of consciousness since that man carried you in here, but you've been mumbling and crying since we got you stabilized."

Lt. Keith sat on the bed next to me, took out his notebook and asked, "Who is Ralph and KJ?"

I nervously shook my head, "I don't know who they are? I don't know any Ralph and KJ." Everyone in the room could tell I wasn't telling the truth as agitated as I'd gotten.

"D.J. honey we're trying to help you. Please tell them who they are," my mom begged me. The room was quiet for only a moment before she continued. "Are they the men that approached us insisting on speaking with you alone in Walmart and the grocery store a few weeks ago?"

I snapped my head around, "Mom shut-up! You don't have any idea what you're talking about! And I don't know any KJ or Ralph," I barked at her, startling even Lt. Keith. I grabbed my head as it started to explode, making me lay back in the bed.

"D.J., first of all, you need to stay still and remain calm." Turning to the nurse Dr. Cleveland said, "Please give her another 5 mg of Morphine along with 10 mg of Phenergan please."

"I'm fine. Nobody attacked me and what she's talking about has nothing to do with this," I said through a long exhale.

"I need to speak with D.J. alone please," Lt. Keith said as he stood up and looked at my mom, then over at Dr. Cleveland.

"I really don't want to leave her right now," my mom tried to explain as Dr. Cleveland took her by the shoulders and walked her out the room, just as the nurse came back with the meds Dr. Cleveland had asked her to give me.

When the room was finally empty, Lt. Keith closed the door behind her and then pulled up a seat next to my bed. "D.J., we've been through a lot together, and this is no time to bullshit me," he paused for a moment as we made eye contact. "Why is Narco and the Feds investigating you? And does this have anything to do with that?"

I tried my best not to flinch as I slowly responded, "I'm not under investigation, and no it doesn't."

He shook his head at me and gave a slight chuckle as he leaned back in his chair and closed his notebook. "I forgot about you and those half-truths J used to complain about," he mumbled.

I immediately snapped at him, "Keep Jeremiah out of this," as tears began to well up in the corners of my eyes.

Lt. Keith slowly leaned forward onto his knees, dragging his fingers through his hair, as he slowly said, "So let me get this straight…you being attacked has nothing to do with a drug raid that went down at 3422 Kelley Drive a week after your car stopped showing up there or the collect calls being accepted from Kegan State pen that suddenly stopped being accepted after the Feds spoke with Anita?" he cocked his head to the side and simply watched me.

I couldn't contain my surprise as I closed my eyes and simply laid there, finally staring at the ceiling trying to blink away my tears as I began to slowly shake my head from side to side. "No, this has nothing to do with any of that."

He suddenly jerked forward and began to squeeze my hand. "D.J. if you're in trouble we can protect you. We have programs for just this very thing," he slowly dropped his head before saying almost in a whisper, "And to think, we actually thought it was best to keep you and the twins out of WITSEC," as he slowly let my hand go. We sat in silence for just a moment as he seemed to get lost in his thoughts. Taking my hand again, "Now look here D.J., I know this has nothing to do with you and everything to do with that damn Selk, but if you don't cooperate with us, and tell us what you know, there's nothing I can do for you. You've got to trust me and tell me what's really going on."

I never even tried to deny he was wrong in thinking that something wasn't right, as I slowly shook my head and finally made eye contact with him, speaking in a low monotone voice, void of any real emotion. "No. You can't help me this time. They will kill me, my boys, everyone else who was there, and the people I care most about, just because, if I talk." I could see the surprise and pain on his face with the realization that everything he was thinking, was actually right. I gave his hand a quick squeeze as I finished with, "So if you would, please go now. I need to get some rest," as I pulled my hand away and turned my back to him.

He let out a long sigh as I felt his hand on my back, "D.J., you know how to reach me," as I heard the chair screech when he stood up to leave. From the distance of his voice, I could tell he was at the door when he said, "D.J., please call me day or night, at the office or at home if you change your mind. J will kill me if anything happens to you," as the door shut behind him.

I could no longer hold back my tears and said to myself, "If only you could help me. If only Jeremiah was here."

A few minutes later I heard the door opening, but I didn't bother turning to see who it was and played sleep hoping they'd just go away. As the door closed without my name being called, I got a feeling this wasn't a friendly visitor as they crept closer to my bed. The hairs on the back of my neck stood up as a body leaned down and whispered in my ear, "Good girl. You didn't tell the pig anything. Keep it that way if you wanna live." I immediately got a queasy feeling when he started talking, but I didn't dare move. It was KJon, himself. "And by the way," as he ran his tongue along my ear. "You were the best piece of pussy I've had in a long time. I can't wait to get another taste," as he kissed my cheek and backed away from the bed.

I held it together until I heard the door click behind him. Almost immediately, alarms started going off, and I leaned over the rail and began throwing up all over the floor. Within seconds my room was full of medical staff, my mom, and even Lt. Keith was back trying to figure out what had just happened. Once I stopped throwing up and hyperventilating, I loosened my grip on Dr. Cleveland's lab coat long enough to say, "I think my water just broke," as I went limp in the bed.

His eyes got as big as saucers as he snatched the covers back to reveal the fact that I was lying in a bloody pool of fluid. "Call the OR and let them know we're on our way up now!" as he unlocked the bed's wheels and the nurses started snatching cords. Someone shoved a bunch of towels between my legs as they rushed me out the door, toward the elevators.

I passed out just as the elevator door opened, but not before I saw my mom reaching for me as she let out a blood-curdling scream, "NOOOOOO!" suddenly collapsing into Lt. Keith's arms in the hallway as the doors closed separating the two of us.

When I came to, I could tell I wasn't pregnant anymore without even asking. When my mom realized I was awake, she began calling out my name. "D.J., D.J. baby," as she ran to the door and yelled out, "Help me! She's awake!" and was at my side again just as quickly.

I was still groggy as a bright light flashed in my eyes. I jerked my head away, "Again with that blinding light shit."

Dr. Cleveland laughed as he said, "Well she's definitely back with us," as he reached under the covers and began pushing on my abdomen. "How does that feel D.J.?" as he continued to press harder.

"It hurts like hell, and I'd really wish you'd stop," I moaned as I grimaced. I tried to pull myself up higher in the bed, and the pain stopped me immediately.

"Here, I have you connected to a PCA pump again," as he pushed the button then handed it to me. Within a couple of minutes I felt better as I began to focus on the faces in the room. I was still groggy as I slowly made eye contact with each one of them and gave them each a slight smile. As I scanned the room, Dr. Cleveland explained to me what happened when he took me to surgery. "D.J. I'm not going to lie to you. It was touch and go for a minute. We didn't realize it when you came in, but there was a small laceration on the backside of your uterus that must have ruptured when you began throwing up again. Once we got the bleeding under control I was able to repair it, so you didn't require a hysterectomy, but..." he hesitated. "We couldn't save the baby. She was just too small."

A single tear slowly ran down the side of my face, but I didn't give him any other response as I continued to scan the room.

"D.J., did you understand me? You lost the baby," he repeated again.

I started to clear my throat to speak, but a face in the back suddenly made me do a double-take and freeze with my mouth hanging open. The look of sheer horror on my face made everyone stop what they were doing and look to see who I was staring at. My eyes had locked onto Selk's sad face standing in the back, almost out of sight. The single tear quickly turned into a flood of tears that I couldn't blink away as the first alarm went off.

"D.J....what's wrong?" Lt. Keith begged stepping forward. He gripped my hand, as he looked back over at Selk again locking eyes with him, "Talk to me D.J.. What happened to you last night?" finally turning back to me. I could see the emotion in his eyes as he begged me, "Sweetheart I will protect you. I swear on my own children's lives...I will keep you and your children safe, but I need you to tell me what's going on," as tears began to well up in his eyes.

I finally shook the shock of seeing Selk's face off as I turned away from Lt. Keith's piercing glare and locked eyes with Selk again as I said, "Lt. Keith, thank you. But it's like I already told you, you can't help me this time," as I took in a deep breath a slowly closed my eyes.

"D.J. baby you've got to tell us what happened!" my mom begged me.

"Now you care?" I whispered as I pushed the PCA button again and again.

She gasped as she squeezed my hand, "Why would you say that? Of course I care what happens to you D.J."

I opened my eyes long enough to make eye contact with her as I said, "This is just one of the joys I get to endure being married to your favorite son-in-law," as the tears continued to stream down my face. I pulled my hand away from her as I slowly closed my eyes and turned my head away from her. "I'm really tired now. So if you all don't mind, I'd really like to try to get a little sleep while I'm not hurting so much if that would be okay?" I never opened my eyes again as the tears continued to stream down the sides of my face, as I heard her begin to cry.

After what seemed like an eternity, Dr. Cleveland finally cleared his throat and said, "Okay everyone. Let's give her some time to rest. She's had a long night and an even longer day. You can all come back and try to reason with her again in the morning."

No one really challenged him as each one of them, squeezed my hand, and kissed me on my cheek as they left my room. Everyone had said their goodbyes but Selk. He stayed in the back of the group so that he could be the last one to leave. He began to speak as he approached my bed causing the heart monitor to alarm when I started to panic a little, which caused the room to fill up again.

"What did you do to her you son of a bitch?!" Lt. Keith yelled at him as he grabbed him by his shirt.

Selk was so surprised he actually stuttered, "I, I didn't do anything?" he pleaded as he stumbled backwards. "I was about to tell her how sorry I am about not being there for her when that alarm went off." He looked so sad and sincere it was almost endearing, but I couldn't have given a damn right now even though I tried to smooth things over for him anyway.

"It's okay. I'm fine," I patted Lt. Keith's hand. "Can you all give us a minute please? It's okay, I promise," I tried to reassure them. I hesitated for only a moment when I saw the look on my mom's face. She actually looked concerned for my safety, almost like she was trying to protect me, as tears continued to run down her face. I hit the PCA button again as I explained, "A sharp pain hit me is all. It came out of nowhere and caught me off guard. I'm fine, I promise."

"Well, ...okay, if you say so. But I'll be right outside the door until *he* leaves," Lt. Keith pointed at Selk.

"That's fine. Thank you again for being so concerned," I smiled.

I tried to remain calm as the room emptied out, leaving me and Selk alone again. Neither of us said anything for a long time as we just stared at one another. Finally, Selk took a deep breath and cautiously approached the bed again, taking a seat this time. It surprised me, but I felt like he did it as much to calm his nerves as much as it was to calm my nerves. I mean, how dangerous could he be sitting lower than me with the police right outside my room.

"D.J.," he said as he slowly reached for my hand. I immediately moved out of his reach. He dropped his head and said, "I deserved that." I didn't say anything, there wasn't any point in responding since we both knew it was a true statement. "D.J. I just want you to know that I'm sorry this happened to you. I never expected you to..."

"Stop right there. I'm tired, so you need to go," I turned away from him. As mad as I was I didn't want him to see me cry.

"But D.J. let me explain," he stood up and grabbed my hand.

I growled, "Selk, let me go, or I'm going to scream to high heaven." He immediately dropped my hand. "Now get out." Not another word was said between us that night. Selk grabbed his jacket and left without as much as a goodbye. I closed my eyes as the tears started running down my cheeks again. I hit the PCA button again even though my body wasn't really hurting. My soul was broken. And I needed that pain to go away, so I kept hitting that button every few minutes until I was finally numb enough to fall asleep.

Three days later, I was released from the hospital, even though Dr. Cleveland wanted to keep me another couple of days for observation. I was ready to get out of that room and spend time with my babies out on the ranch. My mom actually agreed with me when I asked to be taken out to "my house" instead of going back to the condo. Mr. Charlie had already visited and called to check on me a couple of times while I was in the hospital, so he was very happy to know I wasn't coming back to the condo as well. The surprise was that Selk wanted me to come back to the condo when he found out that I'd been released from the hospital. He even drove out to the ranch to talk to me, which he quickly learned was a big mistake.

See, not only was Calliope protective of her momma, she was also very protective of me and the boys. On top of that, she wasn't that keen on men. Even though J.T. was usually happy to see his dad, E.J. was always standoffish for a few minutes which was all it took for Calliope to react negatively to Selks' presence. She took an immediate defensive post between him and the house even though J.T. was already in his arms. I stood on the porch waiting to see exactly what was about to happen.

"D.J., would you mind calling your dog off please," he said nervously.

"She's not my dog."

"Well then who's dog is she?" he asked louder than he should have. Calliope immediately stood up and began to growl at him.

"Calliope, heel girl," as I patted the side of my leg calling her over to me. She quietly did as she was asked and took a seat beside me.

"Well for a dog that doesn't belong to you, she sure minds you well," he smiled.

"Uh hmm," I rolled my eyes. "That's close enough Selk. She's pretty calm now, but I don't know what might happen if you come up on this porch uninvited," I gave him a quick smirk as I turned to go sit on the porch swing.

"Daddy, come see my new pony," J.T. pulled at him to follow him out to the stables.

"I really need to talk to mommy right now. Maybe in a minute."

"No, it's fine, let's go see the horses," as I slowly came down the steps, with Calliope fast on my heels. I got a giggle at how fast Selk got out of her way as she began to keep pace with him and the twins, as we began to walk towards the barn.

I really wasn't trying to hear his pleas for me to come back into town, so the horses were the perfect distraction. Beast still didn't take well to strange men so I knew that I'd have to pay close attention to him with Selk around. He was definitely Jeremiah's baby. And you could tell anytime a man he didn't already know well attempted to handle him, which is exactly, what Selk tried to do causing him to rear up on his back legs.

"Whoa, whoa....it's okay boy. It's okay," I calmly said as I stepped between Selk and Beast holding my hands up.

Selk jumped back, almost knocking the twins over, "What the fuck is wrong with the animals around this place?!" I gave Beast a treat as I gently rubbed his muzzle, not really flinching when E.J. slid the bottom of the stall door over and crawled under the bars. Selk wasn't fast enough to grab him, "Get back here! That horse is dangerous!"

I wasn't the least bit surprised when Beast didn't move as both boys began rubbing on his legs and pulling at his tail. It was just another day around the barn for him when the boys or any of the other kids were around, but the look on Selk's face was priceless. Beast didn't even get excited as Calliope stepped in the doorway of his stall growling. He did stop chewing on his hay for a moment to assess the situation but quickly went back to enjoying his rub down when he realized that she was keeping Selk from coming any closer to his stall.

"Now, as you were saying," as I moved over to see what had Raider acting up.

"I need you to come home."

I gave him a twisted look, "You *need* me to come to the condo? And why would I do that?" as I shook my head at him.

"Because KJon knows what happened and feels it would be better to keep an eye on you," he dropped his head.

I didn't know what to say as I dropped the hay I was holding, and my mouth fell open. I couldn't believe what I was hearing as I silently replayed his words over and over again in my head.

"D.J. I know this sounds crazy, but I think it will be safer for you at the condo. If you're there, KJon won't have any reason to worry about you talking to the police about what happened. Don't you see, he's not going to bother you, but he won't take the chance that you're telling anyone what we've been talking about either," as he reached for my arm.

I didn't have to say a word about him touching me as Calliope charged him, grabbing onto his outstretched arm. Selk got to kicking and screaming, causing the boys to start crying and the horses to panicking. It was all I could do not to fall to the ground crying in sheer laughter, but I maintained my outside composure and called Calliope off as I scooped the boys up and out of the way of the horses. "All you've done is manage to upset everyone today!" as I balanced the crying boys on each hip until I sat them on the bales of hay in the corner so that I could get the horses to calm down. And Ms. Calliope simply took a seat at the boy's feet and watched Selk as he continued to jump around like he was on fire, panting and holding onto his arm like it was about to fall off or something. Once I had the horses settled down, I scooped the boys up and began to make our way out of the barn with Selk hot on my heels.

"That damn dog needs to be put down!" as he continued to inspect his arm.

Maggie must have heard the commotion all the way up in the house because I looked up and there she was running full speed towards us, "What's going on? What happened? I heard someone screaming bloody murder," she said almost out of breath.

"Oh nothing. Calliope thought he was hurting me and intervened on my behalf," I said as I passed the boys to her, barely breaking stride as I continued on up to the house like nothing had even happened.

"That dog attacked me! And I'm pressing charges! She needs to be put down," Selk huffed as we reached the porch.

Maggie looked terrified at what he was saying, so I stopped long enough to calm things down. "Look Selk. I'd warned you already to watch your step, and you knew she was watching your every move. So basically you deserved what you got. Besides, she didn't even break the skin," as I pointed at his forearm.

"Well, that's not the point," he quickly added as he took a long look at his entire arm. Not finding one single scratch.

"No, that is the point. If a 95 pound Rottweiler was actually trying to hurt you, there would've been plenty of marks to prove it," I calmly took a seat on the porch swing and cleaned E.J.'s face-off with the tail of my shirt. "Besides, as soon as I called her off she let you go. So my advice to you would be that the next time someone warns you to watch your step around their dog, you do just that. Calliope is very protective of the women and children at this house. Never forget that," as I reached down and petted her head. "She's not gonna ask if we're okay before she acts," I shot him a look that obviously hit the mark as Calliope sat down in between us. "She's simply going to re-act, and then let the chips fall where they may. So no, you're not going to press charges, and there's no way on God's green earth she's going anywhere until it's her time. Calliope is a sweetheart and basically one of the kids around here," as E.J. climbed down from my lap and joined his brother who was already sitting on Calliope's back and riding her like she was a horse, as she calmly laid at Maggie and my feet.

Everything had finally calmed down, including Selk, when Maggie decided to take Calliope inside, just in case. Selk was finally brave enough to sit down now that the coast was clear. After a few more minutes of silence, I sent the boys inside to get cleaned up for a late lunch.

"D.J., like I tried to say in the hospital," he dropped his head and paused for a moment. "I'm so sorry I wasn't there for you, it never should have gotten that far. Everything got out of hand so fast, and I didn't know what to do."

"You didn't know what to do?" as I slid forward on the edge of the swing staring a hole through his forehead. "You...didn't....know....what....to....do," I repeated even slower. "Well even the damn dog knew what to do when she thought I was being hurt, but my *husband*...the one who swore to protect me, is telling me, that he didn't know what the fuck to do when I was being attacked! By one of his boys no less!" I had gradually started to yell.

"Shhh, shhh before what's her face hears you," Selk nervously looked around.

I immediately jumped to my feet, "GET THE HELL OFF MY PROPERTY!" as I stormed past him and into the house.

He jumped to his feet and chased after me, which again wasn't the brightest idea. I stormed through the kitchen with Selk following closely behind me and who did he manage to trip over, you guessed it, Calliope. He landed hard on his face as he hit the kitchen floor, finding himself nose to nose with her once she spun around on him. As I slammed my bedroom door I heard her growling and barking as Maggie screamed, "No Calliope! No!"

She could have eaten his face off for all I cared. The house had gotten eerily quiet as I laid in my bed crying, when there finally came a knock at my door. "D.J....it's Maggie. Can I come in?"

I sniffled, "Yhea," as I braced for little bodies to jump up on my back but was very surprised that the twins didn't follow her in. I quickly wiped my face off as I turned to her, "Where are the boys?" almost in a panic.

"They're still at the table eating with their dad. Don't worry, Calliope is keeping a close watch on them," she giggled as she shut the door. "Are you okay? What's going on?" she asked as she sat down next to me.

"I can't really talk about it," as I patted her hand. "But thanks for checking on me," I finally smiled at her.

"Well, you know I'm here for you if you need me," as she started to giggle again, "And obviously so is Calliope." At that, we both broke out in an uncontrollable laughter.

"I'll have to get her a big soup bone," I smiled as I shoulder bumped Maggie. We just sat there for a moment until I said, "Even the damn horses don't like him. Beast almost kicked his face-off," I shook my head.

"Like my momma always said, 'Animals will always tell you when a person is bad.' They have a sixth sense about it, ya know?"

"Yeah, well someone special once told me to always pay close attention to children and animals, they have a sense about people and their intentions. I guess he was spot on," I slowly dropped my head and stared at the floor.

"I wish I'd gotten to meet him," she squeezed my hand.

"Meet who?" I asked.

"Jeremiah," she smiled. "He must have really been a special man."

"He was," I nodded my head with a big smile. "He was beyond a dream," as I wiped away a tear. "I never knew I could love anyone so much, or anyone would ever love and protect me that much," I chuckled. "He was truly my everything," I drifted off.

"Well, when things get bad with mister," as she motioned towards the door, "Just think of Jeremiah and what he'd do or say. That's your kryptonite against Selk and all his bullshit...the love Jeremiah had for you and those boys, and the love you had in him. Nobody can ever take that away from you D.J.," as she gripped my hand even tighter.

I blinked away a tear as I gave her a sheepish grin and gripped her hand back, "You're so right. He was my strength then, and he definitely needs to be my strength now," and with that I got up, packed our bags and followed Selk back into town to the condo.

The first night wasn't bad, but right on cue, the house began filling up around noon on Saturday. But one of the main things that did change at the condo was that the boys now had beds in the master bedroom. Selk had gotten a daybed with a trundle for our room along with a microwave and mini-fridge, so once all of his people got there, me and the boys could stay in our bedroom behind a locked door. This new arrangement actually worked out well that weekend, but due to their illegal activity, even that became an issue in time.

CHAPTER 36

See, the 4th of July had always been a favorite holiday for me because I loved the fireworks. It had been a little over a week since I'd been attacked and lost my baby girl, so I was actually looking forward to the 4th of July so that my family and friends would stop focusing on me so much, and we could get back to some normalcy. Little did I realize that morning, that by the end of the day, that would be the farthest thing from the truth.

We spent the day at my Aunt Claudette's house in Woodland Heights until E.J. began to run a fever. Selk had long since disappeared, so I decided to go back to the condo rather than my parents' house in Cypress so that I could still see the fireworks from the balcony. It was rare for me to use the valets to park my car, but I knew Mr. Charlie was at work and would have no problem helping me get the boys and all our things up to the condo, so I did. As we made our way up the stairs to my room Mr. Charlie mentioned a large box being delivered earlier in the day from somewhere out of Florida. I didn't worry about it at the time, but as the night passed, something in me wouldn't stop thinking about it. I'd long since put the boys down when something inside me said, 'Check your closet.'

I began to hear voices coming from the living room, so I quickly closed the door and locked it before I went to inspect my closet. I moved things around finding nothing out of place, but something kept pushing me to dig around. Just as I had decided there was nothing to be found, I caught a glimpse of what looked like a box out of the corner of my eye. It was in the very back of the closet behind a bunch of clothes I hadn't touched all year. As I moved the clothes away I realized it had to have been the box that Mr. Charlie had told me about earlier in the day. It had a Florida postmark and everything. I drug it out into the open and proceeded to open it up to find it full of boxes of candy bars. At least that's what I thought until I dug a little deeper to find large brown cellophane-wrapped bricks a couple of inches beneath the chocolate boxes. I immediately knew what I'd found, and without thinking about it, I pushed the box towards the bathroom.

It was too big to fit through the bathroom doorway, so I began tossing the bricks out of it onto the bathroom floor until there was nothing left in the box. I found a protective mask in my work bag as I turned my attention back to the bricks now covering my bathroom floor. I grabbed a pair of scissors and slowly sliced the cellophane open and dumped the contents into the toilet, repeatedly flushing until the contents were no longer visible in the blue water. I can't tell you how long I was in there flushing package after package of cocaine down my toilet, but I can tell you my legs were numb from being on my knees so long by the time I got through. As I gave the toilet one final flush, wouldn't you know it, someone was banging on the bedroom door like they were the police. I ignored him at first, but when the one voice became multiple voices that wouldn't go away, I finally opened the door as the insults became more degrading and the threats of violence increased.

"Bitch why didn't you open the door when I knocked the first damn time?!" Kidd yelled as he pushed past me immediately noticing the box sitting outside the bathroom door. "And why you wearing a mask? You finally realize how drove you look," he grinned.

"First of all, you washed up, football reject. Who the hell do you think you are, barging in my room like you belong here?" I grabbed his arm as I removed the mask.

He snatched away and growled, "Bitch don't you ever put your hands on me! I ain't Selk, and I'll beat your ass," as he slowly turned his attention back to the box that the others had already begun to move towards.

I quickly jumped in his way as he reached for the box. "I wish you would raise your hand to me. I ain't your wife..." I glanced over at the boys as they began to stir around. "Kidd, don't get it twisted...what happened here last week won't ever happen again," as I turned and walked over to my nightstand.

"Oh yeah," he giggled. "And why is that?" he said so smugly with his back to me.

"This is why," I whipped around holding a gun at him, as I quickly crossed the room towards him, causing him to stumble and fall as the others quickly backtracked towards the bedroom door, trying to get away from me. "Any more questions?" as I began to wave the gun around the room.

"Crazy bitch!" he said from the floor of the bathroom. "Where the fuck did you get that?"

"That's none of your got damn business. Just know, if you ever think about putting your hands on me, your dentist is going to have to ID your body," as I pulled the hammer back with a quick flick of my thumb.

"D.J.....let's talk about this calmly...like adults," he immediately held his hands up and began scooting back until he was up against the wall.

"I am calm. Don't I look calm," as I dropped my head to the side with a smirk on my face.

"D.J.! What the hell?!" Raffi yelled as he lunged for the gun, snatching it out of my hand.

Kidd eased to a standing position as he noticed the mess around the toilet. He was still trembling as he pointed at me, but continued to look around the bathroom, "That bitch is crazy man!" As his eyes stopped on the trashcan containing the empty cellophane wrappers, his eyes got as big as saucers.

"Yeah, just remember that the next time you threaten me," I said over Raffi's shoulder as he pushed me back in the bedroom.

"She's fucking crazy! She just got us all killed!" as he pushed past us and ran down the stairs.

"D.J.," he quickly closed the door behind him, still not realizing what Kidd had just discovered. "What were you thinking?" he asked with a horrified look on his face. But before I had a chance to respond he asked, "And where did you get a gun?" as he cleared the chamber and removed the clip.

"The pawnshop," I said matter-of-factly as I rubbed E.J.'s back, trying to rock him back to sleep before he completely woke up.

"D.J. you can't go pulling guns on people. Are you trying to get yourself killed?" he asked, still sounding more worried than I cared to hear in his voice.

I slowly looked up at him, "Do you know what it feels like to be afraid in your own house? Do you know what it feels like to wonder, 'Is this the night my kids are going to lose their mother?'" He didn't respond as he slowly lowered his head. "No. I didn't think so," I continued. "What else was I supposed to do? I refuse to be y'all's victim anymore. If I'm going to go down, I'm going down fighting. And I plan on taking a few of you assholes with me."

"D.J., what happened to you was awful, and I'm sorry," he stood there shaking his head. "But when you pull a gun on someone you better be ready to pull the trigger," his head snapped up. "When you pull a gun on someone they have two options...back down or shoot back, and in this crowd," he pointed toward the door, "Some of them will shoot back without hesitation. You just got lucky tonight. Kidd ain't no true gangsta, but some of these niggas are. And one of them would have shot you without flinching," as he turned the safety off, then back on again with a smirk on his face, before he handed me my gun back.

I lowered my head as the tears began to stream down my face, "I wasn't going to shoot him. I just wanted to scare him. Besides, you saw it, the safety was on," I looked up almost begging for understanding with my eyes.

"A gun is no way to get your point across D.J.. This ain't a damn game."

About that time, Selk came bursting through the door screaming at me. "What the fuck is wrong with you?! You pulled a gun on that man?! And please tell me you didn't do what he's saying you did," as his eyes got wide when he saw the gun in my hand.

Raffi stepped in between us and held Selk back. "Hold up dog. I've taken care of it. She knows she was wrong, and it won't happen again."

"You damn right!" Selk yelled as he pushed Raffi out of the way and snatch the gun from me. "Who did you buy it from?" as he inspected it. "And when did you buy it?"

"It's legal. I bought it from a store after I got out of the hospital," I said proudly.

"Do you know what would have happened if KJon had been here? Do you?!" he yelled at me. Selk had already turned his attention to the empty box before I had a chance to respond. He hysterically came rushing out of the bathroom, "Where is it?" grabbing me up by my arms.

"It's with the tidy bowl man," I said proudly.

Selk let my arm go, as he slowly kneeled down beside me with his face in his hands. With an eerie calmness he said, "No you didn't. Please tell me you didn't do what I think you did…" never looking up at me.

"I did it. I warned you to quit running drugs through here, and today, you boldly had it delivered here…where our children live. Are you crazy?" I quickly added, "And after all the run-ins with the police already, you do this." Selk was still balled up in the floor as I fussed at him. I guess Raffi had finally caught on to what was happening as he went to inspect the bathroom.

Suddenly Raffi came running out of the bathroom and began shaking me like a ragdoll as he yelled at me, "What were you thinking D.J.?! What the hell were you thinking?!" finally letting me go as he walked over to the window and began to mumble under his breath.

I quietly sat there as the tears continued to stream down my cheeks. "I, I just wanted to protect myself," I finally said.

"Well, that's the last thing you did. You just put a fucking target on your back!" Raffi snapped at me. "A target I can't protect you from! What the fuck D.J.!?"

Before I had a chance to respond, Selk had snatched me off the bed by my hair and threw me across the room. I hit the wall with a hard thud as he began kicking me over and over again. I vaguely remember hearing voices as Raffi struggled to pull Selk off of me.

"Selk! Man stop it! She just got out of the hospital! You're gonna kill her man!"

"Who cares!? She just got me killed!" as he slammed me into the wall over and over again.

"SOMEBODY HELP ME! SOMEBODY HELP ME NOW!" Raffi screamed as the twins began to wail.

Suddenly the room was full of people trying to pull Selk off of me as someone grabbed the boys and ran from the room with them. I drifted in and out of consciousness to the sounds of their cries as they began to grow fainter the further they got from the room. I could feel the life leaving my body as Selk's grip on my throat loosened and I could suddenly breathe again, taking in a long breath of air, as they finally got Selk off of me. Once again, I found myself laying on the floor in a crumpled, bloody mess as I heard him repeat over and over again, "She just got us all killed man. She just got us all killed..." as he began to openly sob.

"Correction...she got you killed," Cliff said, as Raffi knelt down beside me.

Raffi gently lifted my head up by my chin, "D.J....can you hear me?" he asked as he pulled my hair out of my face.

I slowly whimpered, "Yes," as I recoiled from the taste of blood in my mouth. I started to slowly pull myself across the floor towards the bathroom, "Get out! Get out! And leave me alone."

"Come on man, we gotta go," Cliff said as he pulled Selk to his feet. "We gotta figure out what to do about this."

Selk and I locked eyes for a moment as he dropped his head and finally let out a long sigh, "Yeah man, there's gonna be hell to pay for this. In ways, you can't even imagine," as he turned away from the bathroom and laid my gun on the bed.

"Well what about her?" Bert asked.

"What about her?" Selk responded as he began to pack a bag.

Raffi helped me up to the sink where I started cleaning myself up as I heard a drawer slam, obviously startling me as high as I jumped. "FUCK THAT BITCH!" Selk screamed.

Bert hesitated for a moment before he continued, "You're going to leave her here...with a gun?" he asked, with a confused look on his face.

"Do you know what King is going to have KJon do to us...to me?" he grabbed him by the chest and then slowly let him go. "When he finds out that she flushed over $500,000 of his product down the fucking toilet what do you think he's going to say?! I don't give a fuck about her! How about what about fucking me?!" he yelled as he began to pound his chest.

Nobody else had anything to say as I crawled in the shower fully clothed. I sat there in a tight ball, crying and rocking, until I had enough energy to actually remove my clothes and wash myself off. When I finally turned the water off the room was quiet except for the faint sound of the tv. I was already stiffening up as I gently wrapped a towel around me and stepped to the door and poked my head out to find no signs of anyone but the twins. There they were, quietly laying in the middle of my bed with juice boxes, watching cartoons.

Once I had finished getting dressed, I packed them both a bag of clothes and toys, along with the photo albums I'd been putting together for them since I'd gotten back from my honeymoon. They were full of sonogram pictures, pictures of me as I became more pregnant with them, and then me and Jeremiah while I was still pregnant with them. There were pictures of them in the hospital after they were born, and several pictures of all of us together after Jeremiah's glorious return. I had even managed to put a picture or two with me and Selk in the album just so they could see us all together. I gathered the twins and their bags up and made my way down to my car and loaded us all up and quietly drove out to my parents' house in Cypress. The boys were good and sleep by the time we arrived, and so were my parents. I gently tucked them into bed and crept into my parents' room to let my mom know the boys were there.

"D.J., what's going on," she immediately sat up, rubbing her eyes, trying to focus. "It's nearly 1 o'clock in the morning," as she reached for the light beside her bed.

I quickly stopped her, knowing I'd never get away if she saw my face, "Momma everything is okay. I just need you to keep the boys tonight. I have something to do, and they can't be with me is all," I quickly turned to leave the room, but she grabbed my wrist and wouldn't let go.

She clicked on the light, but I refused to turn around to face her as she said, "D.J., talk to me baby. What is going on?" she begged.

I stood there with my back to her as the tears began to run down my face. "I can't talk about it right now, but you will understand everything in the morning, I promise," as I wiggled away from her and quickly left her room, closing the door behind me.

I was already in my car and pulling out of the driveway by the time she made it out onto the front porch as she began to yell my name, "D.J.! D.J.! Come back and talk to me!" she yelled, as I pulled around the corner and never looked back.

I can't tell you the exact moment that I decided to take my own life, but I do remember trying to figure out where I could crash my car without hurting anybody else. I drove around in the darkness until I remembered that there was a section of the Jackson Hill St. bridge that still hadn't been completely repaired after an 18 wheeler took out a large section of the guard railing that was to prevent cars from ending up in the Buffalo Bayou river. And with all the rain we'd had lately the river was higher than it typically was, which would be the perfect place to take a long watery nap without involving anyone else in my demise at this late, late hour.

Just to be sure there wasn't anyone watching and to make sure where the opening was, I passed over the bridge a couple of times, in a fog of total despair, to determine the exact course that would best serve my purpose. It was almost 3AM, so the streets were deserted as I expected. With a sudden rush of certainty, I slammed on the gas pedal, and the car lunged forward as I sped off towards the gap in the bridge railing. Through my tears and heaviness, I whispered, "God take care of my boys. Please keep them safe and forgive me...this is the only way out," as I jerked the wheel to veer off the bridge just as I reached the opening.

I'd managed to get my car up to almost 100 mph as the tip of my car passed through the opening of the railing, almost in slow motion as I saw the railing pass by my window, but with a sudden jerk, my car stopped in mid-air. I could hear the engine still revving as I pushed the gas pedal down harder as panic began to set in. I sat there crying hysterically, trying to figure out what was happening, when out of the darkness came a majestic sounding voice calling out my name.

"D.J. Morgan. What do you think you're doing?"

My eyes couldn't have gotten any wider as I wildly looked around, searching the darkness to figure out where the voice was coming from. In a panic, I finally managed to say, "Huh?"

Immediately the voice responded, *"What are you doing? Why have you stopped trusting in Me? I've never stopped believing in you..."*

And with a sudden fury, I began to scream and cry out, using all kinds of obscenities as I told the voice that God had given up on me a long time ago and all the things that I'd been through, and how tired I was. The louder I yelled, the louder the engine of my car was revving as I held the gas pedal to the floor and began to violently jerk on the steering wheel like I could make the car start moving again with my actions and my words. The night suddenly grew still. The trees were no longer swaying in the wind, and the sound of the water below disappeared like it wasn't even there.

"STOP and LISTEN!" was all I heard making me freeze instantly. *"D.J. I*

will take care of you. All you have to do is listen and believe in Me. Wait until I tell you what to do and when to do it D.J.. Believe in me and that I am with you at all times because I am always with you, and I will fix your problems. I promise you that I will get you out of this situation. All you need to do is trust and believe in me..."

A calmness instantly came over me as I took my foot completely of the gas pedal and began to wipe away my tears. It's like that cloak of sadness and pain that had engulfed my soul was no longer there. I quietly sat there as my car began to back up until all four of my tires were once again firmly on the ground. I glanced down and noticed that even though my car was still in drive, it wasn't moving forward. My head instantly fell forward onto the steering wheel, and I started crying and praying. When I was finally able to regain my composure, I put the still idling car into reverse, backed away from the opening, and calmly drove back out to my parents' home. I curled up alongside my babies and fell fast asleep.

In the morning we went home before anyone else was awake, like nothing had ever happened. I scared Selk out of his mind when we came through the door. In his mind, I was probably either long gone, leaving him to clean up this mess alone, and/or coming back to shoot him where he stood. He tiptoed around me the entire day until Cliff, Kidd, and Raffi showed up late that evening. You could've bought them all for a penny when I walked through the room to their complete surprise. No one said a word to me as their mouths all hung open watching my every move. I actually got a giggle as I purposefully made my presence known throughout the evening.

I'd just put the boys down when the phone began ringing off the hook. Even though Selk and his boys were there, I quickly answered it to avoid waking the twins up. Now usually when I heard voices on the line I'd immediately hang the phone up, but that voice from last night said, *'Be silent and listen.'* It was KJon yelling at Selk about the missing shipment and what was going to happen if he didn't figure out how to rectify the problem.

Apparently, the box of cocaine was on its way up to Chicago and was only being stashed at our place since the police and DEA, were once again sniffing around many of their stash houses. With a shipment this large they couldn't take a chance that the place would get raided while the drugs were still on the premises. And since Selk was no longer on the police's radar, our condo was the best place to store the drugs until the new transporter could get there since the old transporter and the distro got caught up in a drug sting out in Cali. KJon told Selk that gave him a month, maybe two, to either replace the product or pay for it himself. But either way, there would still be consequences for what happened. It was up to him as to how severe they would be once the heat was off.

The thing was, everyone believed that Selk was still rolling in dough, but the sad truth was that Selk was flat broke. With all his showing off and being the life of the party, he'd run through his money before the Oilers finally cut him. In fact, we'd been living off of my paycheck and reserves since before we got married. Deep-down, part of me felt like that is why Selk was so gung-ho about marrying me. He was broke and needed a cash cow so that he wouldn't have to face the fact that in all of his showboating and big timing, he had burned through his money like he had an orchard full of money trees. Selk was dirt broke and worse off than before he ever played pro-ball.

KJon ended the conversation with, "I'm headed your way, so make sure the bitch is out of the way when I get there. We've got serious business to discuss, and we don't need any wondering ears around." And with that he was gone. I waited until I was sure that Selk had hung up the phone before I did and waited for the devil to arrive.

A little before midnight, I was in the kitchen fixing me a snack when the doorbell rang. I immediately knew who it was, but if I had any doubt as to who it might be, I was completely sure when Raffi came running in the kitchen, ushering me upstairs and slammed the door behind me as he yelled at me to stay in there and lock the door. I initially did as I was instructed but again that voice inside me urged me again to *'Be silent and pay attention,'* so I turned the tv down so that when I crack the door open none of them would hear me and I could hear for myself what was so important for this late-night gathering.

I listened until I heard them start laughing and cutting up about how Selk was going to have to come out of pocket for the drugs I'd flushed. I didn't care to hear him blow smoke about how it wasn't going to be a problem and how it would be taken care of by the deadline. My stomach began to turn at his lies because not only did he not have the money to cover the loss, I wasn't giving it to him. At some point, I dozed off but woke to the sound of drawers opening and closing.

"Now what's going on?" I asked as I tried to focus on the clock by the bed.

"Nothing for you to worry about. I've got to go up to Dallas for a few days is all," he replied as he shoved what looked like an old workout hoodie he had in a bag.

"Well, could you keep it down before you wake the boys please," I said as I flopped back down on my pillow.

"Yeah, whatever," he mumbled as the drawer he was rifling through closed louder than necessary, waking E.J. up.

I jumped up to comfort him before he woke his brother up as I snapped at Selk, "You did that shit on purpose."

He smiled as he turned for the door and said, "Ya think," as he slammed the door behind him, waking J.T. up.

"I hate you Selk!" I yelled as I rocked both the boys, trying to settle them back down so that I could get a couple more hours of sleep.

Selk was gone almost a week, but something quite pivotal happened on the third evening he was gone. A breaking story came on about a quadruple homicide that had taken place in Oak Cliff, a little neighborhood in Dallas.

This is Steve Smith, and I'm Marlene McClinton, cutting into your evening programing with some breaking news out of Dallas, Texas.

Steve continued, *"A spokesman for the Dallas PD have confirmed that the bodies of the slain men looked like something out of an old gangster movie. The mafia-style killings had taken place earlier in the day according to police sources."*

Marlene jumped in with, *"The 4 men had all been beaten severely. They were all bound and gagged with their hands tied behind their backs, with a single gunshot to the back of each of their heads. The bodies have been identified as 20-year-old Marcus Davis and 25-year-old Adrian Cooper of the Oak Cliff Crips gang, and 20-year-old Alonzo Jones and 24-year-old Anthony Greer of the Oak Cliff Bloods gang."*

"Yes, Marlene…The police feel that this was probably a drug deal gone bad since they did find drugs at the scene. However, the number of assailants were unknown at this time, but two different caliber weapons were used to commit these horrible offenses."

I didn't give the report much attention until that little voice said, *'D.J., listen and pay attention,'* just as Marlene continued.

"Marcus Davis went by the street name of Skillet, Adrian Cooper went by the street name of Papa Smurf, Alonzo Jones went by the street name of Zo, and Anthony Greer went by the street name of Tony G or Lil Tony."

I nearly fell off the couch as my mouth fell open, as I began to recall the conversation that I had been eavesdropping on just 3 days before. KJon had said that they were going to handle some pressing business with Smurf and Lil Tony. My mind began racing back and forth as I tried to remember what else I'd overheard that night. I ran to the kitchen to grab a notepad so I could write down the details of the conversation while I could still remember them.

As I took a seat on the couch, I remember hearing Steve say, *"We're asking anyone who may have any information concerning this heinous crime to please call the Dallas PD Crime stoppers hotline, 24 hours a day at blah, blah, blah,"* was all I heard at that point.

I furiously wrote down everything I could remember even if I didn't feel like it meant that much at the time. By the time the late evening news came on they had even more details as to what happened in that warehouse in South Oak Cliff. As I got caught up in my own thoughts of what could've happened and who the shooters were, a thought suddenly hit me that sent me scrabbling upstairs to the lockbox in the back of my closet. As I frantically entered the combination and slung the top open, to my horror my gun was missing. The only signs of the gun ever being there were a few stray 9mm bullets left rolling around in the bottom.

I dropped the box and began tearing up my room in search of my pistol until that voice I was becoming more accustomed to hearing said, *'Stop looking. It's not here.'* At that moment, a wave of fear swept over me as I fell to the floor and began sobbing. But a funny thing happened as I lay there crying to high heaven, the voice asked me, *'Do you trust me?'*

I tried to get myself together as I finally lifted my head and said, "Yes. I trust you."

The voice said, *'Write down any and everything you can remember them talking about from the first time you met...dates, times, places, and the people involved.'*

I immediately asked, "Everybody?" with a look of panic on my face as my heart began to race.

It was like the voice knew exactly why I'd asked that question. *'Yes... everybody. Including Dale.'*

"But, but, Dale is my cousin," I explained. See the thing is, Dale was once involved with King and the crew for a little while after he lost his way. He had started using drugs and was drinking a lot after both of his parents died in a car accident one Sunday afternoon. They had not long left church when a drunk driver hit them in a head-on collision, killing his dad on impact and his mother died later that night at the hospital, from all of her injuries. Dale hated God for some time after that, and he became the perfect pawn in King's drug operation.

'Do you trust me?'

I sat there searching for what to say and finally lowered my head as I let out a long breath, "Yes, I trust you."

'Then do as I have told you, and when it's time, all of this shall be behind you. But you must act quickly and keep what you are doing to yourself. No one can know until I tell you. Do you understand?'

All I could say was, "Yes." Instantly a peace came over me, and I suddenly felt like everything was going to be okay. I picked myself up off the floor, cleaned up my mess, and put the lockbox back where it had been like nothing had ever happened. I made a few more notes on my pad then went to bed. The next day I drove out to the ranch and dug out a journal I'd long since forgotten about that Jeremiah had given me before he died. I spent hours writing down everything I could remember and then locked it away in the safe.

Things went on that way for the rest of July and into August. They tormented me and called me out my name, while I did my best to hold it together and take detailed notes on whatever I heard and lock them away in the safe at the ranch. It must have been around the 15th of August when I overheard Selk talking to Raffi and Bert about KJon telling him that things had settled down enough to get the transport back on track, so the clock was ticking. He had until the 30th to either pay King what he owed or show up with his product. If he hadn't made restitution by midnight on the 30th, and not a minute after, there would be a greenlight on his ass.

Like I said before, I already knew Selk couldn't come up with the money, especially since he'd already approached me about it multiple times and I'd told him no without hesitation each time. The fella's stayed calm as Selk finally manned up and explained to them his actual financial situation and of course adding that "the Bitch" has the money to cover but refuses to come off it.

Kidd startled me as he tapped me on the shoulder. "What are you doing Miss Nosey Body? Eavesdropping are we?" he smirked as he and Cliff stood there watching me.

I tried to act like nothing was going on, "That's a pretty big word for you, ain't it? And how did you get in without knocking first? Rude much," I added as I passed by them and walked towards the kitchen.

For whatever reason, Kidd chose to follow me into the kitchen. "The door was unlocked, and you forget Miss Priss...I do have a college degree, unlike the rest of them," as he looked me up and down, "Present company included," he smirked.

"Well not that it's any of your business, I do have an Associate's degree for now, but when it's all said and done, you and your raggedy crew will be calling me Doctor, thank you very much," I smiled back.

"Whatever..." as he rolled his eyes. "Stupid bitch," he said over his shoulder as he headed off in the direction of the den. I quickly tiptoed down the hall to find out if he was going to tell them I'd been listening at the door, but lucky for me he didn't. Apparently, they were already discussing more pressing matters.

"Man I hate to be the bearer of bad news, but I just had a meeting with KJon, and there is a bounty on your wife's head," Cliff announced.

The room got completely silent as they all sat there with their mouths hanging open. Finally, Selk asked, "Wha...what did you just say?"

Kidd popped a chip in his mouth as he flopped down in a chair. "You heard him... there's a $50,000 Dead or Alive bounty on D.J.'s head," as he leaned forward and picked the chip bowl up, sitting it down in his lap.

"Y'all...that shit ain't funny, stop playing," Raffi said as he slid forward, onto his knees staring a hole through Kidd's head. "What are you talking about? And who does that anyway? A bounty," he waved him off.

"This is Texas," Kidd laughed.

"What don't you understand? They just greenlit her ass," Cliff said so matter-of-factly.

"Seriously....a Dead or Alive bounty?" Bert dropped his head as he slowly made eye contact with Selk as he shook his head at him. "Do you know how many wannabes are going to come crawling out of the woodwork on this?" He paused for a second, "Kidd, this shit ain't funny man, so stop playing."

"Man, don't shoot the messenger. We just left a meeting with King and KJon, and that's what they decided... I didn't have shit to do with it," he huffed as he tossed another chip in the air and caught it in his mouth. With all that was being said I was now standing in the doorway, but everyone but Kidd's back was to me, so they didn't notice me. We made eye contact as he smiled and said, "And I'm not joking. Apparently King feels she's becoming more of a liability than she's worth and of course KJon is pushing for her to be taught a lesson and made an example of what happens when you cross them," he added, as he continued crunching on chips as if this was an everyday conversation and I wasn't there.

Raffi snatched the bowl away from him and slammed it back on the table as he slowly turned to Selk and said, "So what are we gonna do now? How do you want to handle this?" he asked as he looked back and forth between Selk and Bert.

"Mannnnn, this ain't my mess to clean up," Bert huffed as he threw his hands above his head and slid all the way back in his seat.

"That ain't cool, and you know it!" Raffi grabbed him by his collar.

"Let go of me!," he shoved him off. "Well it ain't! And we all knew what could happen when we signed up for all of this."

"We did....she didn't," Raffi replied.

"Well, she's a big girl who knows how the streets work..." Cliff jumped in, but before he could continue his thought, Raffi cut him off.

"Bullshit! And y'all know it! D.J. is a rich kid from the burbs, slumming.

She don't know the streets. She's seen only what we've exposed her too. No more, no less," he looked around the room. "And y'all know it!" he began pointing at all of them. "We exposed her to this shit, so WE, need to figure out how to get her out of it! Point blank period!" he shouted as he slapped the table, then began pacing the room, still not taking notice of my presence.

"NO! D.J. got herself in this mess when she decided to take what didn't belong to her!" Kidd jumped to his feet. "You've always been sweet on her, and we all fucking know it! That's why you keep trying to protect that bitch! Well not me mister," Kidd began pounding on his chest. "She ain't my problem and I ain't doing a mother-fucking thing to help her!" he started pointing at the door, making everyone aware of my presence. The looks on their faces were priceless. "I ain't gonna take her out, but I'm damn sure not gonna take a bullet for her ass either," he said plopping back down on the couch next to Bert, with his arms crossed.

"WELL FUCK ALL YOU SORRY BASTARDS!" I screamed, finally rushing in the room, scaring everybody. "Especially you Selk!" pushing Raffi out of my way. Everyone but Selk scrambled to their feet and moved out of my way.

Cliff surprised me when he grabbed my arm and quickly began to explain, "D.J., if it makes you feel any better, King just wants his money or his product. He's not the type to go after women or children unless absolutely necessary. It's really KJon who wants your head on a platter," he said with a stupid look on his face.

I looked him up and down, then stared at his hand on my arm, and then slowly back up at him. He quickly released me and took a couple steps away from me, as I turned my fury back on Selk. "You're the reason I'm in this fucking mess! If it hadn't been for you, none of this would have ever happened! I warned you to many times to count, to stop running drugs through my house!" I began to tear up but managed to blink them away as I bent over and poked him in the chest.

"ME!!!!! How the hell is this my fault?!" he finally jumped to his feet. "It's like Kidd said... you're the one who decided to flush King's caine down the toilet! You're the one who's been pissing KJon off every chance you get! And don't think we don't know that you've been creeping through her listening to our fucking conversations!" he yelled as he stood over me, squeezing my arm tighter and tighter.

Raffi quickly stepped in-between us, "Hey man, chill," as he loosened Selk's grip on my arm.

I snatched away from Selk, "Sorry excuse for a man...." as I looked around at each of them before shouting, "ALL OF YOU!" staring directly into Kidd's eyes before I turned and ran from the room. I knew I wasn't going to be able to hold back my tears much longer and I absolutely refused to let them see me cry. I wouldn't give them that satisfaction. I ran to my room and slammed the bedroom door just as the tears started flowing. I jumped up in my bed and began wailing into my pillow. What was I going to do? I could easily pay King off, but that wouldn't change the fact that KJon wanted me dead.

I laid there crying until I couldn't cry anymore, which happened around the same time the twins came bursting through the door. I had been in my room crying for hours and had lost track of time. Apparently Selk and Raffi picked them up from daycare and dropped them off at the condo before they went back out. I somehow managed to put a smile on my face and get the twins fed and ready for bed before Selk and crew returned later that night.

I had just gotten E.J. down when I overheard Selk say to someone, "I'll beat the shit out of her if I have to, but she's coming up off that damn money. I swear on my father's grave she is."

I quickly closed the door and miraculously lifted both the boys up at the same time and managed to situate them on top of me before the bedroom door slowly opened. I laid there trying not to tremble as I played like I was asleep. The only thing I was sure of at that moment was that Selk wouldn't hurt the boys, me on the other hand, he had nothing to lose.

"Selk man come on. Don't wake them up. Just talk to her in the morning," Raffi begged just above a whisper.

"Fuck that shit man. You heard KJon tonight. He wants my head on a silver platter if I don't pay back what she lost them, plus interest. And on top of that she's got a $50,000 Dead or Alive price on her head that we still don't know is going to be lifted even if I do pay him. Why should my kids lose both their parents because of her dumbass?" he asked.

"Because at some point in time, you loved her." The room got quiet again for a few moments. "Besides, she's your wife, and it's your duty to protect her. On top of that, she's the mother of your kid's man, that's why." Raffi sounded so convincing I wondered how Selk could ignore him at this point.

J.T. began to whimper nearly making me give away the fact that I wasn't really asleep, as I slightly adjusted how we were arranged in the bed. Selk still hadn't responded as I let out a long sigh as I rolled over towards the door, holding J.T. on my side with one arm as I pulled E.J. even closer to my chest with the other, cradling him in my elbow.

Finally, Selk said, "Whatever man. I won't touch her...not tonight anyway."

"Good man," Raffi said. I could hear him patting Selk on the back,

"You're a good man Selkie Black, don't let anybody tell you any different," he laughed as he turned and loudly went back down the stairs to the others. He trusted Selk a lot more than I did, leaving him in the room with me but Selk didn't touch me like he said he wouldn't, but he did stand there for a long time staring at me while calling me every name but a child of God. He repeated this routine multiple times over the next few hours until he finally left the house around midnight with the others.

I was so nervous and stressed out my entire body was aching worse than if he had beaten me up again. I began to cry as I heard the storm roll in but managed to fall asleep for a few hours. It was thundering and lightning when Selk woke me up.

"Look D.J.," as he snatched the covers off of me. "Get up! We're going to the bank."

"We're what?" I asked, obviously shook.

"We're going to the bank to get the money to pay King back. KJon is crazy! He ain't playing about this money!" he yelled, waking the boys up. They immediately began to cry as he turned on them, "SHUT THE FUCK UP BEFORE I GIVE YOU BOTH SOMETHING TO CRY ABOUT! Got damn crybabies! Crying all the fucking time," he shook his head at me. "This is your fault. Soft ass kids, crying at every fucking thing."

I jumped out of bed and scooped them both up in my arms, "Shhhh, hush now. It's okay," as I sat on the end of the bed and began to rock them. "Hush now...mommy's got you," I gently kissed them on their foreheads as I continued to rock them. When I finally had them calm I looked at Selk and said, "Wait here," as I carried the boys to the kitchen and quickly made them both a bowl of cereal and a cup of juice. I knelt down between them as I rubbed their heads, "Now stay here while mommy goes back to her room to talk to daddy. Okay?" I kissed them both on the forehead again as I took a moment to stare into their eyes again, almost as if this would be the last time that I would see them. They both smiled back at me and agreed in their own way, as I took one final breath and turned to go back upstairs to deal with Selk.

I closed the door behind me as dumb as that sounds, but I didn't want the twins to hear or see what Selk was about to do to me. And right on cue as I turned to face him, I found myself being snatched up by my neck and carried across the room until he slammed me into the wall and pinned me there by my throat. I flailed around trying to loosen Selk's grip on my neck to no avail as it became more and more difficult to breathe. The scariest part of it all was the fact that Selk had yet to say a single word to me, he just had this look of fury in his eyes. A look that I'd never seen on his face before. In a last-ditch effort, I kicked my foot up and made a perfect connection with his balls, causing him to instantly release me as we both fell to the floor. Me coughing and gasping for air and him moaning and rolling around holding his dick.

"D.J.," he coughed as I scrambled to my feet and he rolled up onto his knees, still breathing heavy as he grabbed my ankle.

I kicked at him with my free leg, "Let me go Selk."

He pulled me down to him and began shaking me like a ragdoll until my head hit the edge of the dresser. I could already feel the blood slowly running down my temple when Selk finally let me go. I was holding the side of my head when without warning, Selk grabbed Jeremiah's necklace from around my neck. I lunged for it as he held me at bay with one good stiff-arm.

"NO! GIVE IT BACK!" I wildly swung and grabbed at him.

"I'm going to get the money I need one way or the other D.J.," as he grabbed my wrist and took my wedding ring off as well.

"Take that! Just give me back my necklace!" as I struggled to my feet, but I couldn't do much more than scoot up against the wall. The room began to spin as I felt myself falling but couldn't stop myself. I must have hit my head a lot harder than I'd realized because when I finally came to, it was to the sound of rain beating against the window and both of the boys screaming to high heaven as they laid on my back calling for me to wake up.

I slowly regained my bearings as I tried to console them and stop my head from pounding all at the same time. "Mommy's okay guys. Mommy's okay," as I sat there with them still crying as they clung to my neck. It took some time, but eventually, they calmed down, and I was able to finally stand up. I don't know when they found me that way, but sadly we were all covered in my blood, along with a huge spot on the carpet. It took a while, but I managed to get all of us cleaned up when I finally noticed what Selk had actually done. I don't know if he did it before he attacked me or after, but all of my jewelry was gone. I frantically searched the closet where I kept my jewelry box containing more sentimental pieces that I'd collected over the years, and it was all gone too. I fell to the floor crying causing the boys to immediately join me at my sides again, but this time I didn't really care as I rocked back and forth on my knees hysterically crying, as I held the black satin box that Joshua used to present the necklace and pendant he'd had made for me, out of me and Jeremiah's wedding rings. I cried and cried as I gripped the box to my chest, and my heart broke into a thousand pieces, once again.

I was still in a daze as I somehow made it to my car with the boys following closely behind me. We were all still crying as I started up the engine and just sat there listening to it idle louder and louder. A loud clap of thunder is the only thing that shook me from my trance as I pulled out of my spot and slowly made my way out onto the deserted streets of Houston, Texas at 1 o'clock in the morning. It was pouring down rain like you couldn't believe, but I aimlessly drove around in the storm until I somehow ended up at my parents front door around 3 AM. I scared my mother to death as I stood there in a rainstorm, completely incoherent and half-dazed, talking to myself with two half-naked toddlers on my hips screaming bloody murder, and a bloody gash that had begun to bleed again, on the side of my head.

Apparently, my mom had rushed me in the house and planted us safely on the couch as she tended to my wound and attempted to dry us off, but when she and my dad couldn't get the twins away from me, they gave up, and my mom called Aunt Claudette. After my mom told her what was happening she advised them to leave me be until she got there. When Aunt Claudette got there, she checked under my bandage and then she and my mom talked. After that she tried talking to me, simply trying to reach me and figure out what had happened. When she couldn't get through to me, she made a quick phone call and then went back to trying to get the boys away from me. I continued to mumble and fight them until I finally loosened my death grip on them enough for my mom to whisk them away. The terrifying screams of the twins is actually what caused me to gradually come out of my trance. I was squeezing them so tight that I was actually hurting them and when their cries went from a usual upset cry to a cry of pain, something inside of me clicked, and I let them go.

Aunt Claudette and I talked for some time then she finally allowed me to lay down after she was convinced that I hadn't taken anything she needed to be worrying about. As I dozed off, I remember hearing her on the phone canceling the psych transport she'd ordered earlier and told my mom to keep a close eye on me. A couple hours later Aunt Claudette woke me up and helped me get dressed as she explained to me that I had an appointment with a therapist in a couple of hours. Basically, she put one of my brother's sweat suits on me so she could take me to a psychiatrist she frequently worked with and trusted.

After what felt like forever, I walked out of my newest therapist office with a new bandage covering the 5 stitches I'd received on my forehead and a swollen face from all the crying I'd done. Aunt Claudette left with a feeling of relief and satisfaction that I wasn't a danger to myself or my children, even though I had just had what they called a mild psychotic break. After hours of drawn-out discussions with Aunt Claudette as to what needed to happen with me next, we were finally able to convince my mom to allow me to leave her side and return home. We all eventually agreed that the twins would stay at my parents' house for the next few weeks so that I could get some much-needed rest and had a chance to get acclimated to my new normal. One of the conditions for me not to be held on a 72-hour inpatient psych hold was that I agree to meet with my new psychiatrist 3 times a week and attend different therapy groups every day for the next couple of weeks. Honestly, I'd have agreed to see the psychiatrist every day if it kept me out of a padded room again.

I kissed the boys goodbye and made my way back into Houston. As I pulled onto the parkway, the spirit I'd heard that night on the bridge began to speak to me again. I thought I was tripping and actually turned the radio off when I heard the voice softly call out my name.

'D.J.'

"Yes," as I slowly began to grip the steering wheel.

'Do you trust me?'

"Yes, I trust you," I calmly said.

'D.J., it's time.'

"Time for what?" I quickly asked as a sense of peace swept over me as the spirit instructed me on what I needed to do next.

'Just listen, and do everything exactly as I tell you to.' As much as I wanted to say something I didn't. I just sat there and listened. 'D.J. get the journal that you've been keeping all your notes in and write Thaddeus a letter. In this letter you are going to chronologize everything that you ever witnessed. List every date, time, place, and name, including Dale's involvement as well. You're going to list any and all transportation methods and schedules, the attempt on you and Jeremiah's lives, every murder, and where the bodies are buried. And D.J., as painful as it is, you even need to include your rape, along with what happened to you in the hospital leading up to the miscarriage and everything up to today.'

The tears were already streaming down my face, but I couldn't hold my peace any longer, "Are you serious? I can't tell him about that."

'You can, and you will D.J.. You have more strength in you than you believe. I know it's going to be difficult, but you must do it. And when you're done, here's what you're going to do next. You're going to make 4 copies of your letter, have each copy notarized and seal them each in an envelope. Place each copy of the letter in its own larger envelope along with a note with instructions on what needs to be done with the sealed envelope should anything and I do mean anything happens to you or someone you care about. Send 3 of them to different locations to people you can trust. The final letter you are to give to Thaddeus's attorney, and just like that, the voice was gone.

I didn't bother to argue, fuss, or fight. I simply dried my tears, turned the car around, and headed out to the ranch. After I called my mom and Aunt Claudette to let them know where I was and that I had arrived safely, I spent the rest of the night writing that letter to King. I included everything in it just as I had been told to do. I spoke on how they were flying product in on major airlines and having it delivered by UPS to Dale's empty houses. How they would pay some crackhead off the street to wait for the package to be delivered, sign for it, and then disappear before the DEA or anyone else even knew what was going on. I told him how I'd been approached by a Houston PD and a Federal agent in those stores, what they told me, and when I finally told Selk what I'd learned. I told him how KJon beat and raped me over and over again that night and how Raffi, took care of me and got me to the hospital, only for me to miscarry after KJon snuck into my room after I had kept quiet about what had really happened to me, and threaten me again. I even told him about the beating I took behind flushing his product down the toilet that night and every conversation that had taken place around me since, especially the latest beating that left me stripped of all my jewelry and passed out bleeding on the floor for my children to find me. I explained that I knew about the 4 murders in Dallas and several other murders in Tulsa, LA, St. Louis, Detroit, and Chicago after that. I even told him where the bodies were buried. By, the time all was said and done, I'd told King everything, including the part about realizing he was the gold-toothed man that saved me from the car that night, only to watch me slip into the water presumably dead.

I hate to admit it, but with every flick of my pen, all the weight I'd been carrying over the past three years was lifted. I cried as I concluded the letter explaining to Thaddeus that I had several notarized copies of the letter he was presently reading and how if ANYTHING happened to me or anyone I truly loved, that the other copies would be sent to the State police, the Feds, & the NY Times. Eventually, somebody would listen and start looking into the things I had claimed, since it would be fairly easy to trace the events I'd described and follow the crumbs for themselves.

As dangerous as it was for me to sit out on my porch, late at night with a bounty on my head, I did it anyway. I sipped on a few glasses of wine as I lost myself in the stars. The night sky was clearer than I'd seen it in weeks. As I made my way inside, I caught a glimpse of a shooting star and made a wish. I wished for the impossible, that I would be able to be with Jeremiah again, in this lifetime or the next. As I went into the house and locked up, I realized that I had a warm feeling in the space that I used to call my heart.

I didn't immediately get the letter notarized or send off the copies as I'd been told. I stayed at the ranch for several days, only leaving to attend my therapy sessions. To be exact, it was the afternoon of August 23rd, exactly 7 days before King's deadline, that I finally headed back into Houston with the sole purpose of carrying out my assigned mission. I had spent the entire morning typing up my letter to make sure that there could be no possible misunderstanding because of my fancy penmanship. I needed this letter to be black and white, cut and dry, 100% legible to the naked eye, and 1000% clear. Once I was happy with how it turned out, I printed off four copies, drove to my bank in Houston where I signed each one and had all 4 copies notarized with the branch notary republic. I had already addressed the 2 envelopes I intended to mail and placed 1 of the sealed notarized copies in each of them and stuck them in their outgoing mail. Each envelope contained very explicit instructions not to open the thick envelope and what to do with it should anything happen to me. The other 1 I took to a bank I had never used before and placed it in a safety deposit box and requested 2 keys. Next, I stopped by my attorney's office and added a codicil to my will, for his eyes only concerning the new safety deposit box, that I wanted to be attached to my Will, along with one of the keys and what to do with it should anything happen to me. Finally, I proceeded to King's attorney's office to deliver his letter personally. Once I gave him a quick overview of what the letter contained and that I needed him to get it to King, as a matter of life or death, he agreed to take care of its delivery, and I calmly left. As I made the drive back out to the ranch, I felt confident in the things that I'd just done. All I could do now is wait to see where the chips would fall next.

My cockiness was short-lived 3 days later when I received a frantic call from my mom. I stupidly had sent her one of the letters, thinking that she would follow my directions and not open the thick envelope. I should have known better. Mrs. Lisa Jean Morgan was not built to follow orders, especially from her fragile, "only living" daughter. As I raced to my mother's office to keep her from completely screwing up what I had so painstakingly set into motion, I talked myself through what to say to her. In the end, it was the fact that my mother is so selfish that I was able to win her over and convinced her to keep her mouth shut, and to lock the letter away in a very safe place until doomsday.

The overly honest, when it suited her, law-abiding Lisa Jean Morgan only agreed to keep her mouth shut because she could not bear the thought of her "only living daughter" and her grandchildren, being placed in the Federal Witness Protection Program, never to be heard from again for a few weeks, let alone for life. In the end, it was my mother's need to constantly be in her children's lives that kept her from running to the police station and ratting me out to Lt. Keith or only God knows who else. But also in this moment, I think my mom was beginning to truly see the strength in me. After that near disaster, I decided to call the other person that I'd sent a letter and explain what was going on, which turned out to be a very smart move on my part. It's funny how people do the opposite of what you tell them too, even when you've told them not to worry and give them explicit directions...and they call themselves highly educated and evolved.

Anyway, I spent the next couple of days trying not to worry every second of every day, which became more difficult as the 30th quickly approached and I still hadn't heard from King's attorney. The 30th had come and was almost gone when I finally received a call from King's lawyer asking me to come by his office as soon as possible, even though it was well after office hours. I quickly got myself together, and let my mom know where I was headed and that I'd call her as soon as I was through. We said our final, "I love you's" as I pulled into the parking garage of the lawyer's office. He met me at the elevator and walked me to his office without ever saying a word to me. Once we were behind closed doors, he simply passed me a note from his desk and stood there watching my every move. It simply said:

Your debt is forgiven. You won't be touched!

~ King

My heart skipped a beat as I began to tear up and just stood there staring at the note, rereading it over and over again. My thoughts were only interrupted by the lawyer clearing his throat as he held out a handkerchief for me to wipe away my tears. I looked up at him with bloodshot, happy eyes, and said, "Thank you." And I quickly turned my attention back to the note in my hand.

A few minutes later, he cleared his throat again as he handed me his business card and said, "My home number is on the back. If you ever need anything, please feel free to call me anytime, day or night."

I had no words as I nodded okay and turned for the door, still holding onto the note and his business card as if my life depended on them. I glanced back at him for a split second to see him nodding at me with a huge smile across his face. Once I was safely in my car and had pulled out onto the street, I called my mom to give her the good news, and then I called my other contact to let them know that all was well too. As we laughed and cried together that night, I still couldn't help but wonder if I would ever really be safe again, but in 3 days' time, I'd have my answer.

On September 2nd I decide to join a couple of my girlfriends, my brother

J.R., and my cousin Cedric at a club. While we were there, I ran into a guy from high school that I used to date. He'd been watching me the entire night which J.R. and Cedric felt the need to keep informing me of when he finally approached and asked if he could talk to me outside. The lights were about to come on anyway, so I agreed and told the others that I'd meet them outside. Besides that, I had valeted my car, so we didn't have far to walk once we got outside.

He nervously looked around then finally said, "How've you been D.J.? Long-time no see."

"I've been maintaining. Trying to stay out of trouble. What've you been do'n with yourself these days?" I asked, trying not to look worried.

"You know me," he smiled. "Getting my hustle on as always," as he brushed my hair outta my face as the wind began to blow. "Sure about that? I've been hear'n some interesting things about you in these streets."

I tried not to show my nervousness as I began to look around for the valet or J.R. and Cedric, as I smiled and asked, "Oh yeah? What have you heard?" as I continued to search for anybody with a friendly face as the crowd began to fill up the parking lot. Now what I hadn't told you is that Tyrone was a longtime drug dealer here in Houston, with well-known ties to some of the crews King controlled.

The valet pulled up with my car just as Ty, leaned in to whisper, not so quietly in my ear, "How'd you get the Golden Ticket?" just as J.R. and Cedric appeared out of nowhere.

"What about a Golden Ticket?" J.R. curiously asked as he and Cedric watched our every move.

"Nothing for you to worry about playa. Just chat'n it up with your big sis," he patted J.R. on the shoulder. "Holla at cha'll later. And D.J.," he paused, "Stay safe," he winked at me as he quickly walked away, disappearing into the crowd.

"What was that about Deeg?" J.R. asked, holding my arm so I couldn't get away.

"It was nothing. Just chat'n it up like he said," I smiled as I got in my car and closed the door.

Cedric tapped on the glass as I started rolling forward, "Yo D.J., we need to talk."

I smiled as I continued to pull away, waving goodbye to them. As I made my way back out to the ranch, I caught a flat and had to pull over on the side of the road. A shiver went up my spine as I realized that I'd just broken down only a few feet from where Jeremiah and I had been run off the road that night on the way to the hospital. It took me a second to clear my head as I got out to survey the damage. I popped the trunk and found what I needed to change the tire, the only problem was when I tried to loosen the lug nuts I couldn't get them to budge, any of them.

As I noticed the time, I decided that I better call my mom to let her know that I was okay and what was going on before J.R. went busting up in the house without me. I explained where I was and how dark the road was under the canopy of trees but reassured her that I was okay and not to worry. I'd figure something out. I tried to catch up with J.R. and Cedric, but neither of them picked up their phones. I sat there for 20 or 30 minutes hoping that someone would come along, but at this time of night, deep down I knew that the chances of that happening was slim to none at best.

My phone suddenly rang nearly giving me a heart attack. I fumbled to answer it to hear the panic-stricken voice of my mother on the other end half fussing at me for not coming to her house instead of going out to the ranch at that time of night, half trying to figure out what to do to help me.

"Momma calm down. I have an idea. Let me call you back in a few," I explained, hanging up before she had time to respond. I dug around in my purse to find my wallet and pulled out the business card I'd received from King's attorney. It was nearly 3 in the morning, but he was my last hope as I began to dial his home number, I said out loud, "He said anything, at any time."

On the third ring, a very groggy woman's voice answered the phone, "Hello?"

"I'm sorry for waking you, but is Mr. Goldberg available? Tell him it's D.J. Black, and I really need to speak with him." I could hear the frustration in her voice as she tried to wake him up, but within seconds he was on the phone with me and sounded more awake than I did.

"Yes, Mrs. Black. What can I do for you?"

"I'm really sorry for waking you at this hour, but I haven't been able to reach anyone else who can help me. See I caught a flat on my way home tonight, and I can't get the lug nuts off to change the tire myself. I called Triple-A and they can't get anyone out to me for at least 3 hours. Is there any way you can help me?" I quickly explained without taking a breath.

"Yes, yes, don't you worry. Where are you exactly?" I could tell he was scribbling down the information as I told him where I was. "Okay, I got it. Stay in your car and lock your doors. Someone will be there to help you in a few minutes."

"Okay. Thank you Mr. Goldberg, and again, I'm sorry for calling you so early in the morning."

"Don't you fret dear. Anytime means anytime," as the line went dead.

I called my mom to let her know what was going on and not 20 minutes later, I saw headlights approach. "Hey ma, I see lights approaching."

"Well stay in your car D.J.. There's no telling what drunk fool may be coming towards you."

"Well, they weren't coming for me. They just flew right past me," I sighed. Suddenly the car slammed on its breaks and came to a complete stop in the middle of the road. "Uhmm, momma, that car...it just stopped in the middle of the road, and now it's turning around coming back towards me." It slowly crept up past me then pulled another U-turn and pulled up right behind me.

"D.J.! D.J.! What's going on? Talk to me girl!" she yelled at me.

"Hold on ma, I'ma put you on speaker. Just be quiet," they're getting out of the car.

Two men slowly approached, but only one came up to my window while the other started checking out my tire. He gently tapped on my window, so I let it down part of the way.

"Hay Ms. Lady. We heard you were having some car troubles."

"Yeah, I caught a flat and couldn't get the lug nuts off to change the tire."

"Well, don't you worry about it. That's what we're here for. You just sit back and relax while we take care of this."

I nervously said, "Okay, well, thank you."

"Pop your trunk, and my man will get you back on your way in a few. Matter-of-fact, while you're waiting, how about you call whomever you need to, to let'em know you're okay so they don't get nervous and send up any red flairs," he chuckled as he patted the roof of my car, then went back to his partner and tended to the tire.

"What's happening D.J., talk to me," my mom whispered loudly.

"They're changing the tire," I smiled as I watched them in the side mirror.

"Seriously?"

"Seriously mom," I started to giggle.

Messing with her, I didn't notice the guy standing at my window again. I screamed when I looked over, and he was standing there with his face in my window.

"D.J. baby are you alright?!" my mom yelled.

Holding my chest, "yeah mommy, I'm okay," I tried to laugh to calm us both.

"Sorry bout that. Guess I should'a made some noise so you'd know I was here. We're all done, and everything is back in your trunk." He passed me a business card for a tire shop in the 8th ward, "Take that tire there and ask for Otis. Just tell him Slim sent you and he will hook you up, on me."

I looked at the card for a moment and said, "Thank you kindly, but you don't need to do that. You've done enough already," I smiled.

"With a beautiful smile like that, I have to," as he patted the roof of my car and simply walked away.

I quickly started my car up and got back on the road with my mom now buzzing in my ear the entire time with questions about who I called and was I being followed...blah, blah, blah. After I hadn't responded for a while, she got quiet and checked to make sure I was still there. I just started laughing, and she immediately snapped at me, "D.J. Morgan, I don't think this is the least bit funny young lady. You could've been killed out there in the middle of the night. And how do we know someone didn't cut your tire hoping you'd get on the highway and have a blowout and crash?"

"Momma, momma, don't you see?" I laughed.

"See what D.J.?" she asked, still obviously annoyed.

"King called off the dogs mom. King has really called off the dogs."

I could hear her gasp as she suddenly began to cry, "D.J. are you telling me, that you are really safe? I don't have to sit up worrying about you every second of the day anymore?"

"Yes momma. WE are all very safe," I smiled as I pulled into my driveway. "I'm pulling up to my door now mom. I'll call you back in the morning. Goodnight." Once again I hung up before she could respond. I called attorney Goldberg again just to let him know I'd made it home safely and that everything was okay.

He picked up on the first ring by the way. "Thank you for letting me know D.J.. And like I said before, call me anytime you need help. Day or night."

"Yes Sir, and thanks again," as I hung up and calmly entered my house without a care in the world.

CHAPTER 37

I was finally able to take a moment to breathe as Cyn talked to her ride on the phone. I pulled into a gas station while I waited to find out where they wanted to meet up, but I could tell by Cyn's tone, this was going to be an even longer night than I had expected. When she finally hung up, I could tell something wasn't quite right. "What's wrong?"

Cyn just stared at her phone for a few seconds before she answered. "I'm staying with my brother and sister-in-law here in Houston, but I forgot to call my brother to let him know my plans had changed. Apparently, he's left me a couple of messages, but my phone never rang," as she was looking through her call log.

"Yeah, and..." I impatiently asked.

"So they went to a party over in Galveston and haven't made it back to town yet."

"So what does that mean for you?"

"Well, they're on their way back, but they're at least 45 minutes away and didn't leave a door key behind," she slowly flinched.

I just stared at her for a moment, then let out a long moan as I glanced at the clock. It was already 1AM, and I still had another good hour and a half drive ahead of me. I laid my head back and shut my eyes. "Sooo, I guess we're going to wait then," I finally said with a forced smile on my face. I was dog tired and the idea of waiting around another hour then driving another 2 hours didn't sound that inviting to me. "Well I guess we can go wait inside that IHOP at least."

"D.J. I am so sorry about this. I never intended to be this much of a bother."

"It'll be okay. I just need to let Pam know that I'm going to be a little later than planned. Go on in and get us a table, and I'll be right in."

"Okay, can I get you anything to start?"

"Water is fine. Thank you." After I called Pam, I joined Cyn at the table, who was just about ready to order. The waitress quickly took our orders and left us alone, just in time for Cyn to refocus on my life.

"So that still doesn't tell me how you ended up divorced, but it does explain why you hate your ex so."

"Isn't that enough for one day? I'm tired of talking."

"Come on D.J. We've got time, and you gotta finish this story. Why did you get a divorce when everything should have calmed down?" she impatiently asked.

"Fine," I shook my head at her. "Let me run to the little girl's room first, and then I'll finish the story." You would have thought that I was in there for a year when I got back to the table the way she acted.

"Took you long enough," she huffed.

"Are you serious right now? I wasn't gone a good five minutes," I frowned at her.

"Anyway, back to what happened next," she wiggled around, then stared at me like I was finishing a bedtime story.

I took a long breath and picked up where we'd left off.....

—————————)((∘))(————————

It wasn't until the following Friday, August 8th to be exact, that I decided to go back to the condo to pick up a few more of our things. The boys had taken off down the hallway to play in their room as I packed up some of our stuff and of course no sooner than I had gotten in a rhythm, there they were begging for something to eat. So I broke away from packing my clothes and followed them into the kitchen. I got them settled down in the den watching cartoons while they ate and went back to the kitchen to straighten up the mess I'd made. As I finished cleaning the countertop, Selk appeared out of nowhere yelling at me.

"What the fuck did you do?!" as he grabbed my arm.

I snatched away from him, "What are you talking about now?!"

"Everybody's telling me that I'm a snitch and that I have no loyalty. And that you're blackmailing King! So what the fuck did you do?!" he growled.

"I did what I had to do to protect me and my kids. Besides you should be happy...aren't you still alive? I would think you'd be saying thank you," I finished with a smirk on my face.

"You stupid BITCH!" he yelled, as he grabbed me by my throat and slammed me into the fridge.

I kicked and screamed at him, "Let go Selk!" He responded by tightening his grip and dragging me across the kitchen and pinning me to the pantry wall. I kicked and screamed with everything in me as I struggled to reach the butcher knife I'd just used to slice the turkey for the boy's sandwiches. He continued to slam me into the wall as I got a glimpse of 2 little bodies, standing behind him. Selk slung me around into the kitchen island, and at that moment I saw my firstborn child, standing there with the butcher knife I'd been trying to reach in his tiny hand, while his brother stood there with tears streaming down his little face and his hands covering up his ears.

He quietly stood there holding the knife out in front of him, shaking his head at me and finally said, "No mommy....no mommy. No," and began to back away from us.

I instantly stopped struggling as I held on to Selk's wrists and looked him straight in his eyes, "Selk," I squeaked. "You need to either let me go or hit me now. And if you hit me, I'd advise you to kill me or put me in an irreversible coma because when I get free, I promise you this..." as his grip began to loosen. "You will either be looking down the barrel of a gun by nightfall or talking to my lawyer come morning. Either way, as of right now, we're officially over and done with."

Without warning, Selk released me and took a couple of steps back. "Crazy bitch! I didn't hit you, and you bet not tell anybody that I did."

"Technically you did when you slammed me into the walls and drug me around the kitchen by my neck," I responded as I held my throat and tried to slow my breathing down. "You've put your hands on me for the last time," I shot him a look of death as I slowly picked myself up off the floor. "I'd advise you to start running now Mr. Black," I continued to stare at him. I screamed, "BOYS! LET'S GO!" as I ran past Selk and grabbed my purse. I was standing at the elevator, waiting for it to arrive when the twins joined me at my side. All I had on my mind was finding a gun and putting a bullet between Selk's eyes.

Now the fact that they were both in tears didn't even register until we were flying up and down the streets of Houston looking for a gun. I went to everyone's house I could think of and wouldn't you know it, not one of them were home or answered their door if they were. Even my uncle who worked night shift was nowhere to be found. At some point J.R. saw me flying down the street like a deranged woman and managed to force me over so he could jump in my car. I was in such a rage by that time that, that what I was seeing was all a blur and I really couldn't hear anything going on besides my angry voice telling me to keep searching for a gun, and to empty it into his head, chest, and groin.

Eventually, J.R. was able to calm me down to the point of regaining somewhat of my sanity and convinced me to go out to my parent's house, even though I'd already been there looking for my mother's gun...but alas I couldn't find it either. As the sound of J.R.'s voice began to get through to me, the blood-red haze began to lift, and I was nearly in my right mind as we pulled up in my parent's driveway. I was shocked to see them both standing there waiting on us, since it was just a little after 2PM and both of them should've still been at work.

Luckily the boys had fallen asleep while I was driving around like a crazy person and they stayed that way for several more hours as I explained to my parents and J.R. what had happened at the condo. And to my amazement, both of my parents were on the same accord for once in my adult life when it came to me and my marriage. In a blanket of tears, my mom hugged me, and began rocking me, as she said, "D.J. my love, you are not going back there do you hear me?"

I was shocked. I couldn't believe my ears and nearly fainted when my dad added, "And you're staying here with us for a while. Right now you need to be close to family."

I could see J.R.'s expression out of the corner of my eye, and even he looked surprised. For the first time in a long time I chose to keep my mouth shut and not argue. After dinner, I gave Jessica a call and asked if she had time to meet with me tomorrow.

"D.J. are you okay? Is there anything wrong?" she asked.

"Everything will be just fine when I'm single again."

Without hesitation, she said, "Little Sis you come by whenever you want. I'll leave word with my receptionist to interrupt me and let me know that you're here, even if I am busy."

"Thank you Jess. I really appreciate it," as I blinked away my tears.

"I'm just glad you remembered what I said. I love you D.J.. See you tomorrow." And with that the line went silent.

Early the next morning, I drove into Houston to meet with Jessica and get the ball rolling on my divorce. To her surprise, there were only 3 things I asked for...sole custody of the boys, child support, and the location of the jewelry he'd taken, specifically my necklace and the earrings my aunts had given me on my wedding day. It only took a couple of hours to get everything together and properly formatted for me to sign. By 11AM my petition for divorce was on its way to the County Clerk's Office to be filed by one of Jessica's associates. It was like the weight of the world had begun to lift off my shoulders.

I'd love to tell you that once we'd filed the paperwork, everything was over quick and easy, but again, I can't. I guess Selk took my threat to heart and packed his belongings and left town that night. It took the process server nearly 6 months to locate him so we could have him served with the divorce papers. Then after that I still had to wait 90 days until I could go to divorce court.

On July 19ᵗʰ of all days, I finally had my day in court. Jessica and I watched as people went before the Judge hopeful and left in tears. Judge Veronica Harrison was one of the first black female Judges assigned to the bench in Texas, let alone Houston. And now that she was presiding over divorce court, she was known to be a hardass when it came to granting divorces, but today it seemed like she was in a particularly ungenerous mood. So far every couple she'd seen had to go to weekly marriage counseling for at least 3 months or longer. I was as nervous as a hooker in church by the time my case was called, and everybody in that courtroom could tell. Before Jessica could even get a word out, Judge Harrison lit into us.

"I'm not even sure why I'm hearing this case."

"Well, your Honor, my client…"

"Oh, I'm sorry. Did you think I was finished? Well, I wasn't," she glared down at Jessica and me over her glasses.

"I'm sorry your Honor," Jessica said, almost as if she were embarrassed.

"Now. Like I was saying… I'm not even sure why I'm hearing this case. Mrs. Black has barely been married for 2 years. That's not enough time to know if you like your spouse or not, let alone try to make it work," she continued.

As she continued to flip through the papers, I heard the voice say, *'Pray D.J.. Pray now.'*

"And furthermore, where is the defendant in this case? Did he not show up to protest this divorce because I'm…"

As she talked, I simply clasped my hands together, bowed my head and began to pray, "Dear Heavenly Father. I believe and trust in you. Thank you for bringing me this far, but Dear Lord, I still need you to carry me the rest of the way. I beg you to show yourself here today and undo this mess I've allowed others and my own pride to get me into, a marriage that's trying to kill me Lord. As I stand here today Lord please allow this Judge to just grant me my freedom and give me my life back without all this marriage counseling stuff. I've done my penitence. I've been to purgatory and made it out alive only through Your Heavenly Grace. Father God please just FIX IT in my favor. These things I do pray in Your most Holy Son, Jesus Christ's name. Amen."

When I opened my eyes, it hit me. The courtroom was so quiet you could've heard a mouse fart. I could feel Jessica's grip tightening on my forearm as I sheepishly looked up to see the horrified look on her face as she quietly hissed, "Shhhhh," at me.

———————

I quickly regained my composure and said, "I'm sorry for interrupting you your Honor," as I slowly lowered my head in shame.

No one said a word for an uncomfortable length of time when the Judge finally leaned over her podium and asked, "What did you just say, young lady?"

I stuttered, "I, I, I said I'm sorry..."

"No. No! No! Not that. What were you just whispering, while I was still talking?"

"I was just praying your Honor. I asked God to fix it. To undo a marriage, that I have allowed myself and others to get me into, before it kills me. I asked God to just let you sign those papers and set me free without sending me to marriage counseling. I've been to hell and back with this man, and I've barely survived the beatings, the miscarriages..." I paused for a moment, "...the attempts to take my own life," I dropped my head before I continued. "Til death do us part," I shook my head. I slowly looked up at her again, pleading with my eyes and my hands as I said, "Your honor, I've paid the piper more than once, trying to honor my vows to a demon your Honor and only God knows the full-lengths I've had to go through to find peace and safety in the deadly life I've been living. Your Honor, please just sign those papers and set me free. In Jesus name, set me free from this nightmare that we called a marriage," as the tears began to stream down my face. Jessica pulled me in tight to console me as the bailiff handed her a bunch of Kleenex.

"Your honor as you can see, this marriage has taken a significant toll on my client not only physically but emotionally. She's not asking for much your Honor, just sole custody of their minor children, child support, and the whereabouts to the jewelry that Mr. Black took without her permission."

Judge Harrison just sat there for a moment with her mouth hanging open. You could tell when she finally shook off the shock of what I'd just said to her, as she cleared her throat, took a sip of water, and then quickly dabbed at her eye. "In my 35 years on this bench, no one has ever prayed in the middle of a case let alone in the middle of me asking questions. You, Mrs. D.J. Black, must truly need to be divorced and in the worst kind of way. I'm signing this divorce decree as it is written, and hereby enter a judgment in favor of the plaintiff, Mrs. D.J. Black, and declare that this uncontested divorce is hereby dissolved on the bases of irreconcilable differences. Mrs. Black, will you be retaining your married name or your maiden name at this time?"

"Because of our children, I will be maintaining my married name your Honor," I said with a rush of joy and excitement that I could barely contain.

"As you wish Mrs. Black," as she scribbled her signature on the document. "But before I render this order into the records, let me say this to all of you still sitting here in this gallery today," as she leaned forward on her forearms and slowly pulled her glasses off, as she made eye contact with each person in her courtroom. "If any one of you, tries to come up here, and pray your way out of your marriage, I promise you that you'll be going to marriage counseling for a year. Do you all understand me?"

In unison, they all said, "Yes, your Honor."

"This motion is so ordered. This court is now in recess for 15 minutes," as she lowered her gavel with one loud bang.

I jumped into Jessica's arms and yelled, "THANK YOU, JESUS!" as we embraced one another and rocked for a few minutes. I was once again crying, but this time it was tears of sheer joy and happiness. I knew at that very moment that God loved me, and that Jeremiah was still with me. See July 19th was Jeremiah's birthday, and now it was also the day that I was officially set free.

That night I drove out to the ranch to be alone and to feel closer to Jeremiah. I took a long bubble bath listening to our favorite song over and over again as I drank half a bottle of Jeremiah's private reserve. It was the bottle we intended to open on our first anniversary. As I fell asleep that night, I could almost feel Jeremiah's arms wrapped around me. For the first time since his death I not only felt safe, I felt loved.

I quickly wiped away a tear that had escaped down my cheek and waited for Cyn to start bombarding me with questions. To my surprise, that moment never came as her phone began to ring. It was her brother letting her know he was pulling up outside. She quickly got off the phone and motioned for the waitress to come over with her check.

"Cyn, dinner is on me don't worry about it."

"D.J. you don't have to do that. If anyone should be getting treated, it should be you."

"No worries. Take the keys and get your things. I think I need a moment, and like I said, I got the check," I smiled as I placed my hand over both checks pulling them closer to me.

"Well thank you," she said as she went outside to meet her brother. She quickly returned with my keys and gave me a hug, reminding me that we needed to meet up after the game. I told her to give me a call. As she turned to leave, she stopped for a second and turned back to me and calmly said, "You know you need to write all that down. It would make a great book and an even better movie," as she gave me a huge smile and nod. "And thank you. I think I now understand what you were trying to say to me about trying to make something out of something that shouldn't be," as she rushed over and gave me an even longer hug.

"I'm glad you understand," as I hugged her back. "Hay Cyn…"

"Yeah D.J.?"

"Promise me I won't wake up one day, and you've written a book about this, okay."

She simply winked at me then turned and disappeared into the darkness.

As she drove away with her family, I thought to myself, *'I know I'm going to see this in print one day. She's a reporter for God sakes, she can't keep anything to herself.'*

I sat there for a few more minutes trying to gather my thoughts as the feelings I'd buried years ago for Jeremiah came flooding back. "Oh Miah, how different our lives could have been, if only…" I caught myself saying out loud, as I wiped a tear away, hoping nobody heard me talking to myself. I quickly made my way to the ladies room to get myself together, then made my way to the front to pay our checks.

The young lady at the register smiled and said, "The gentleman already took care of it ma'am."

"What gentleman?"

"Uhmm, him." as I stared out the window in the direction, she was pointing. "The man getting into the burgundy truck over there. And he also left this for you," as she slid a small box over to me.

"Okay, thank you," I said with a confused look on my face. I moved towards the door as I slowly opened the box to find my wedding ring necklace. I burst out the door to try to catch this stranger before he pulled off, but when he saw me coming he quickly sped off before I could stop him. I jumped in my car and began to follow him flashing my lights and honking the horn at him, trying to get his attention. We came to a red light, and I immediately dropped the top, waving my hands at him like a madwoman yelling, "Excuse me Sir! Excuse me!" I tried to make out his face through the dark tinted windows, but I couldn't. "May I talk to you for a moment?!" I nervously yelled.

The light changed, but instead of pulling away, he slowly pulled up and into the gas station up ahead, and I followed him in. Before I was able to put my car in park good, his driver side door opened and a tall, caramel-colored man with burn scars on his arm and hints of gray hair climbed from the cab of the truck and slowly turned to face me. I'd started to approach him with my hand out, but when he had completely turned around, he stopped me in my tracks.

"Hello Little Mama," the badly scarred man said with a voice that took my breath away. The lights began to dim as everything went black. I came to in the passenger's seat of my car with this man from my dreams, dabbing my brow with a damp towel and his big brown eyes peering down at me.

"What, what happened?" I asked as I focused in on his face once again. "Jeremiah?" I asked with a quiver in my voice not truly believing what I was seeing, as I reached for his face.

He simply smiled as he stroked my cheek, "It's been a long time D.J.. I never expected to see you again. You're more beautiful than I remembered," he smiled as he wiped away my tears.

I gazed into his eyes and finally managed to say, "This can't be happening," as I looked down at the necklace that we were both now holding onto for dear life. "I'm supposed to be getting married soon," as I collapsed into his arms crying tears of joy, while the rhythm I so longed to hear again brought a wave of peace over me as our heartbeats synced up again, making me feel as if I'd found the home I'd been longing for, for such a long time.

As I laid there crying in Jeremiah's arms, it hit me.... Once again, God had jokes and very questionable timing. But mostly I felt the joy from how God had come through for me again. In this lifetime instead of the next, just as I had requested....as I once wished upon a star.

The End!

REFERENCES

Chapter 18

1. Krauss, Alison. 1990. Ghost in This House. Comp. Hugh Prestwood.

Chapter 29

2. Rochelle, K.. 2005. "Blue Daze." Atlanta.

Chapter 30

3. Urban, Keith. 2000. *Your Everything.* Comp. Chris Lindsey and Bob Regan.

www.ingramcontent.com/pod-product-compliance
Lightning Source LLC
Chambersburg PA
CBHW022233020726
47496CB00004B/885